The Gifts of the Child Christ

AND OTHER STORIES AND FAIRY TALES

by
George MacDonald

edited by
Glenn Edward Sadler

WILLIAM B. EERDMANS PUBLISHING COMPANY
GRAND RAPIDS, MICHIGAN / CAMBRIDGE, U.K.

© 1973, 1996 Wm. B. Eerdmans Publishing Co.
255 Jefferson Ave. S.E., Grand Rapids, Michigan 49503 /
P.O. Box 163, Cambridge CB3 9PU U.K.

First edition published 1973
This revised edition published 1996

Printed in the United States of America

02 01 00 99   7 6 5 4 3 2

Library of Congress Cataloging-in-Publication Data

MacDonald, George, 1824-1905.
The gifts of the child Christ:
and other stories and fairy tales
edited by Glenn Edward Sadler.
p.   cm.
ISBN 0-8028-4165-1 (paper: alk. paper)
1. Fantastic fiction, Scottish. 2. Fairy
tales — Scotland. 3. Christian fiction.
I. Sadler, Glenn Edward. II. Title.
PR4966.S23   1996
823'.8 — dc20   96-11533
CIP

*The Gifts
of the
Child Christ*

George MacDonald
collection of Glenn Sadler

For my Mother
and Father

A word from George MacDonald's granddaughter —

"My love for my grandfather's Fairy Tales was started at an early age — about five, I think — because my father (Bernard MacDonald) read them to me at night as bedtime stories. As I grew older, the children's books, e.g., *A Rough Shaking, Ranald Bannerman's Boyhood, The Light Princess* (my favorite) and others became very familiar to me and my small friends. Nowadays I occasionally meet elderly people of my own age who have vivid memories of *The Princess and the Goblin* and *At the Back of the North Wind.*

"My recollections of my grandfather are of a very old man with a saintly face, lovable expression, beetling eyebrows and a shock of white hair."

Lilia Mary Mathers
May 7, 1972
Husbands Bosworth
Nr. Rugby, Warwicks
England

Contents

List of Illustrations

Introduction

As G. K. Chesterton predicted correctly in 1924, George MacDonald's reputation as a writer still depends on his works of fantasy fiction. His longer fairy tales — *The Princess and the Goblin* and its sequel *The Princess and Curdie* and *At the Back of the North Wind* (his classic) — are still read and enjoyed today by readers of all ages. Although MacDonald's shorter stories are less known, except perhaps for "The Light Princess" and "The Golden Key," they deserve a wider audience. For in his shorter fairy tales, MacDonald explores with extraordinary diversity his belief that the literary fairy tale can provide readers with something more than lively entertainment.

In this one volume are contained all the best shorter fairy tales and stories that George MacDonald wrote. The original two-volume edition of *The Gifts of the Child Christ* was published by Eerdmans in 1973. In this revised edition, all the stories have been retained, and the short story "Stephen Archer" has been added. Included also are all the illustrations of MacDonald's stories that are available by Arthur Hughes and other artists of the period.

More than any of his nineteenth-century contemporaries, George MacDonald experimented with the form and content of the traditional fairy tale. In his fairy tale–parables, or "double stories," as he liked to describe them, one discovers that MacDonald created his own kind of fairy tale. As he continued throughout his life to search for the proper form for his visions and dreams, MacDonald translated his ideas into three basic variations of the fairy tale, which he attempted to develop: the domestic story, the double story or parable, and the read-aloud tale. Into each type MacDonald incorporated his own reconstruction of themes and symbols drawn from his lifelong reading of his favorite fairy tales.

It is perhaps strange that George MacDonald never wrote a "pure fairy tale" of the sort that could be compared to those of Charles Perrault or the Brothers Grimm. The closest he ever came to writing a traditional fairy tale is — perhaps — "Little Daylight" or "The Light Princess." However, MacDonald reflects in his more carefree tales "Cross Purposes" and "The Carasoyn" ["The Fairy Fleet"] his close reading and understanding of fairy-tale lore. In these experimental tales one meets a curious mixture of mortal and fairy-tale beings who live on the "borders of Fairy-land" and who sport and play tricks on each other as if they all belonged to the same world. In contrast are MacDonald's more frightening stories "The Shadows," "The Castle: A Parable," "The Cruel Painter," and "The Gray Wolf," in which he explores the physical and spiritual distortions of human nature. These stories are modeled after the German *Märchen* and remind one of Hans Christian Andersen's darker tales. MacDonald admired Andersen, and, like him, he knew how to take the events and objects of the commonplace — births and deaths, castles and keys, fish and wolves — and transform them into symbols of life-experiences that went far beyond the ordinary dimensions of the fairy tale.

In his essay "The Fantastic Imagination" — here reprinted — MacDonald defines the fairy tale and expresses his intense fondness for its "mood-engendering" and "thought-provoking" power, which he experienced from his childhood. At an early age MacDonald discovered the fairy-tale craft of transformation as he disguised in his autobiographical novels the local scenes, people, and events that he knew as a child in Huntly, Aberdeenshire, in North East Scotland.

George MacDonald was born in 1824, the second of six children — all boys — the third of whom, John MacKay, died in infancy, in 1829, when MacDonald was only five years old. His mother's death followed three years later in 1832, when MacDonald was eight. MacDonald seems never to have forgotten the many family births and deaths that he knew as a young child and later as a father. Perhaps with the death of his own son and daughter in mind, MacDonald wrote in 1882, at age fifty-eight, the domestic tale "The Gifts of the Child Christ," in which the child Phosy reunites her father and stepmother in love through the death of her infant brother, whom she mistakenly thinks is the Christ child.

Presenting miniature portraits of human relationships, MacDonald pursues in each of his domestic tales — "The Gifts of the Child Christ," "Stephen Archer," "The Butcher's Bills," "The Broken Swords," and "The Wow o' Rivven" — his most intimate feelings about romance, courtship, marriage, and the restorative power of love. In "Stephen Archer," for example, a bookseller — "a good-looking fellow about thirty, with dark eyes, overhanging brows," but "no smile" — finds the love of his life through a chance act of kindness toward an undeserving truant who steals from his shop. MacDonald may have had in mind his brother John, who was in Russia, where there were signs of war, when he wrote in 1854, at age thirty, his first published story, "The Broken Swords," about a young soldier who rids himself of guilt and regains his sense of honor by caring for a helpless young girl and defending her honor to the death.

In "The Butcher's Bills," a domestic tale about married life, MacDonald states poetically at the beginning that "the one genuine and worthy interest a tale ought to have" is to present "a door through which we may walk into one region or another of the human heart, and there find ourselves not altogether unacquainted or from home."

Reflecting on his own childhood and youth, MacDonald claims that he was an early student of "the human soul." From his own father, who claimed that the family had the gift of second sight, MacDonald no doubt heard his first "ghost story" — and perhaps others like the werewolf tale "The Gray Wolf." His son Greville records that after the death of MacDonald's brother John Hill, his father, Charles Edward, saw his deceased son. Shortly after the burial, at dusk, MacDonald's father was going out a back gate at The Farm in Huntly that led up to the moor. He "saw a figure coming towards the gate. The figure passed on, but then turned," and the father saw it was his son "John, with plaid over his shoulder in his customary manner. The old man hastened after, but, because of his lameness, failed to overtake the wayfarer before he disappeared at a bend in the road."

Frequently when he was in search of plots for his stories, MacDonald would return, whenever he could, to Scotland. Such visits were, unfortunately, often related to illness or another death in the family. In July, 1891, when MacDonald was sixty-seven, he took his last visit to Huntly, where he stayed with his bachelor cousin James at The Farm. It was a memorable visit that gave him another story, as he wrote to his wife:

I have been out for a few miles drive — to the old church of Ruthven, of which only the gable and belfry remain, with a beautiful old bell, looking quite new, though I think the date on it is 250 years ago, with the legend in Latin "Every kingdom against itself shall be laid waste." Right at the foot of the belfry the fool of my story ["The Wow o' Rivven"] is buried, with a gravestone set up by the people of Huntly telling about him, and how he thought that bell now above his body always said: "Come hame, come hame."

For MacDonald the meaning of domestic activities and relationships went far beyond the daily struggles of life. He felt that even the simplest occurrences could have significance beyond the obvious. As a writer of fantasy fiction, MacDonald became fascinated by the spiritual changes that took place in the lives of the characters in his stories. For example, he describes with compassion and understanding in "The Gifts of the Child Christ" how the infant death of a child restores a marriage that lacks love and understanding. MacDonald had a special feeling for the less fortunate — the so-called fools of society like the village-child Feel Jock ("The Wow o' Rivven"), who grows up to be "almost an idiot." It is a curious fact that most of the children in MacDonald's stories are orphans or foundlings, like Mossy and Tangle in "The Golden Key," who must make life's greatest discoveries on their own, aided only by the all-knowing Wise Woman.

Having lost his position as a minister, George MacDonald began his formal career as a writer with the publication in 1858 of an Adult Faerie Romance, *Phantastes*, which he wrote as an experimental work. Next, he published another fantasy, "The Portent" (1860), about second sight, and then he turned to writing novels. His first collection of tales appeared in 1864 as a novel entitled *Adela Cathcart*, which, although it failed as a novel, presents an interesting treatment of MacDonald's theory of the curative and therapeutic power of storytelling. The stories in it are joined loosely by a frame narrative around the character of Adela Cathcart, daughter of Colonel Cathcart, who suffers from severe depression and is in need of physical restoration. Visitors arrive at the Colonel's house for Christmas dinner, and each in turn tells a story, hoping to raise Adela's spirits. She responds to each story, including "The Light Princess," "The Bell," "The Shadows," "The Broken Swords," "The Giant's Heart," and

"The Cruel Painter," and seems generally to show signs of gradual improvement.

It was in 1867, however, that MacDonald published his first major collection of fairy tales — still his best — entitled *Dealings with the Fairies,* "Where more is meant than meets the eye." In each of the five tales in the volume — "The Light Princess," "The Giant's Heart," "The Shadows," "Cross Purposes," and "The Golden Key" — MacDonald took a slightly different approach to transforming the fairy tale into a "double story." He described De La Motte Fouqué's "Undine" as his favorite fairy tale and the "most beautiful," and in *Dealings with the Fairies* he attempted to imitate its pattern of opposites and produce parables of nature, intermingling spiritual and natural beings. From Fouqué's enchanting tale of the water sprite Undine, who goes in search of a human soul and marries the noble knight Huldbrand of Ringstetten, MacDonald borrowed ideas for several of his fairy tale–parables — "Photogen and Nycteris," "The Light Princess," "Little Daylight," and "The Golden Key."

Critics of MacDonald's fantasy stories often focus on the meaning and symbolism in them. Many have suggested that MacDonald's special talent was his ability to create parallel or superimposed worlds of the real and ideal, of heights and depths, of reason and imagination — and even of significant gender differences — as symbolic representations for his dreams and visions. It is interesting, however, that on several occasions MacDonald denied that his stories had any single intention or allegorical meaning. In his essay "The Fantastic Imagination," MacDonald claims that the meaning of his stories exists only in the mind of the individual reader and not in any allegorical pattern imposed on them: "A fairytale is not an allegory. There may be allegory in it, but it is not an allegory." He went on to say that a fairy tale "cannot help having some meaning; if it have proportion and harmony it has vitality, and vitality is truth. The beauty may be plainer in it than the truth, but without the truth the beauty could not be, and the fairytale would give no delight. Everyone, however, who feels the story, will read its meaning after his own nature and development: one man will read one meaning in it, another will another." And he adds that "children are not likely to trouble you about the meaning. They find what they are capable of finding, and more would be too much."

For first-time readers of MacDonald's fairy tales and "double stories" it is possible, as he suggests, to enjoy the events of the stories without fully understanding their significance. After several rereadings of such parables as "The Golden Key" or "The Wise Woman," the symbolic richness and layers of meaning will begin to yield their meaning. Like Hans Christian Andersen's stories, which also contain soul-searching creatures, MacDonald's fairy tale–parables are best enjoyed as life adventures that depict the spiritual conflicts within the human soul.

One of MacDonald's best attempts at "double-story" writing is "The History of Photogen and Nycteris," or "The Day Boy and the Night Girl," which he subtitled "A Day and Night Märchen." As in so many of his parable-tales, in this one MacDonald creates a series of natural opposites: day-night, boy-girl, light-dark, sun-moon, garden-woods. And for each contrasting double, he provides a corresponding spiritual equivalent or mood — happiness and sorrow, desire and fulfillment. We meet a witch named Watho, "who desired to know everything," and who steals two newborn children, a boy and girl, from their mother and subjects them to opposite living conditions, placing the boy in constant light and the girl in continual darkness. Reminiscent of the two children in Grimms's "Hansel and Gretel," the boy and girl in MacDonald's story, Photogen and Nycteris, learn to depend on each other for their survival. Symbolically, each child must undergo a spiritual awakening and change before he/she can be fully liberated: "Embracing each the other, they stood in the midst of the wide grassy land, neither of them able to move a step, each supported only by the leaning weakness of the other, each ready to fall if the other should move." Although, like other of MacDonald's parables, this tale is symbolically inconsistent, there are hints that MacDonald is describing in fairy-tale language the relation of the body to the soul and suggesting that only through mutual dependence on each other can either survive and escape the witch's imprisonment of death.

A reader coming to MacDonald's stories for the first time may well wonder about their meaning. However, an experienced reader of MacDonald will recognize familiar patterns throughout his stories. Like MacDonald's children, who are always sent on a quest of self-discovery into the woods, the reader will also arrive, eventually, at the door of the Wise Woman's hut, there to experience the trials and rewards of life.

Unquestionably the most original fairy-tale creation in George MacDonald's fantasy fiction is the Wise Woman, otherwise known as Mistress North Wind. MacDonald's stories could hardly exist without her, and yet her full name and origin remain a mystery. She has been called great-great-grandmother, fairy godmother, Mother Nature, and has even been identified by some critics as Sophia, or divine wisdom. We know, however, that she had her biographical roots in MacDonald's grandmother Isabella Robertson, who lived in the house (with a connecting door) next to the one in which George MacDonald was born. Known for her religious fervor, demanding sense of justice, and strong will, she apparently made a lasting impression on MacDonald as a child. Although she appears as a real character in MacDonald's autobiographical novels, it is in his parable stories "The Wise Woman" and "The Golden Key" that most is revealed about her.

In "The Golden Key," we meet two (motherless) children, Mossy and Tangle, who go on a quest in search of the golden key that will unlock the meaning of life and the nature of desire itself. With earnestness Mossy asks, "Where was the lock to which the key belonged? It must be some-where, for how could anybody be so silly as make a key for which there was no lock?" As if in reply, MacDonald offers the reader a series of paradoxical opposites with corresponding images from which to choose — keys without locks, huts without doors, rainbows of colors with stairs to climb — "airfish, swimming into the thicket of branches" and into "a cottage-door."

It would be pointless to try to identify the exact symbolic meaning of such objects. For MacDonald such creations simply belonged to the imaginative world of the fairy tale; he hoped that each would carry its own special meaning and make an imprint on the consciousness of his reader. Taking a larger view, one discovers that in "The Golden Key" MacDonald is developing a parable of the passages of life — childhood, middle years, old age — and that he is searching in each period for the real values and meaning of life. Like Photogen and Nycteris, Mossy and Tangle must learn the importance of trusting one another and themselves to Nature's primordial myths of desire, fulfillment, and renewal.

As a writer of fantasy fiction, George MacDonald spent his life creating the character of the Wise Woman. It was through her teachings that he tried to communicate many of his most important messages to his readers about the nature and power of goodness. The Wise Woman became for him a symbol of God as both Father and Mother, as he explains in *Adela Cathcart* at the conclusion to the curate's parable-sermon: "Him who is Father and Mother both in one" — "father and mother and home." A model single parent, the Wise Woman represents the two sides of the divine nature: justice and compassionate love. She functions most significantly throughout MacDonald's stories as the instructive voice of the author himself in the tale. From her life lessons, MacDonald's children and adults alike learn that giving is better than getting, that longing is more meaningful than having.

Reading MacDonald's parable-stories for the first time is somewhat like looking into the mirror of appearances commonly found in fairy tales — but with a difference. The reader of MacDonald's stories will not necessarily be most impressed by the events of the story or even by the allegorical pattern of symbolism in them but rather by a sense of encounter with the inner world of the fairy tale — the untold parable of the soul itself.

MacDonald's fantasy stories have inspired many illustrators to try to capture their striking contrast of realism and otherworldiness. The stark black-and-white drawings of the sculptor A. G. Walker that illustrate MacDonald's longest and best-structured fairy tale–parable, "The Wise Woman" (which have not been reproduced since they appeared in 1895), are especially appropriate for a tale filled with practical advice about parenting and childhood development. It is, however, the dreamlike quality of otherworldliness in MacDonald's stories that has attracted most artists, including Arthur Hughes, to his fantasy fiction.

MacDonald and Hughes, who were introduced by their mutual friend the sculptor Alexander Munro, shared the same visionary sensitivity for the relation of the real to the ideal and the angelic. Both MacDonald and Hughes viewed life through the eyes of a child, finding wonder in ordinary events and the intermingling of human and spiritual beings in the natural world. An example of the artistic bond that existed between them is Hughes's captivating last painting of the nativity scene (here reproduced), which once belonged to George MacDonald and his son Greville. It depicts perfectly the delicate emotions that MacDonald explores in his story about the Christ child. That Hughes did so few illustrations for MacDonald's shorter stories is indeed regrettable. However, in his five woodcuts for "The Light Princess" and the remarkable ones for "Cross Purposes" ("The Odd Little Man and His Umbrellas"), one sees the imaginative genius that Hughes and MacDonald shared for sleight-of-hand transformations — turning umbrellas into geese — and for making the fantastic believable.

As a teller of tales, MacDonald had an exceptional talent. Some of his best fairy tales, like "The Light Princess" (one of his favorites), had their origin as read-aloud tales, which he told to his own family and friends during holiday gatherings. Such tales as "Little Daylight," "The Giant's Heart," and "Papa's Story" are still quite suitable as read-aloud bedtime stories. At the beginning of "Uncle Cornelius's Story," MacDonald sketches his own approach to the art of storytelling as Uncle Cornie cleverly incites the interest of his listeners by creating the necessary atmosphere for his ghostly yarn.

George MacDonald's shorter fantasy stories are perhaps best characterized by the title of the last story in this volume: "Birth, Dreaming, and Death," or "The Schoolmaster's Story." Disguised in the form of a parable, the story presents a moving vignette of the trials and rewards of MacDonald's own married life. A nameless young schoolmaster struggles with his calling in life while being concerned about providing for his wife and newborn child and then must face with his wife the death of that child. It is a story of loss turned into gain that George MacDonald experienced throughout his life.

During a stormy night, as the schoolmaster lies in his bed and dreams that he hears a knock at the door above the howling wintry wind, an orphan child appears, "his hair . . . filled with drifted snow, and his little hands and cheeks . . . blue with cold." Forgetting his own troubles, the schoolmaster takes pity on the child, carries him into the house, and places him by a blazing fire. Meanwhile, the schoolmaster's wife is also lost in dreams, facing "in the faintness and trembling joy of new motherhood" the death of her firstborn child. As in "The Gifts of the Child Christ," the Christ child appears to the schoolmaster and his wife, enabling both to find comfort and meaning in their loss.

In his autobiographical story "Birth, Dreaming, and Death," George MacDonald created, perhaps without knowing it, his most intimate domestic "double story" of all — the story of his own life of spiritual struggle and endurance, a living parable of the compassionate soul.

GLENN EDWARD SADLER
Howglen Farm
Catawissa, Pennsylvania

"Undine"

The Fantastic Imagination

That we have in English no word corresponding to the German *Mährchen*, drives us to use the word *Fairytale*, regardless of the fact that the tale may have nothing to do with any sort of fairy. The old use of the word *Fairy*, by Spenser at least, might, however, well be adduced, were justification or excuse necessary where *need must*.

Were I asked, what is a fairytale? I should reply, *Read* Undine: *that is a fairytale; then read this and that as well, and you will see what is a fairytale.* Were I further begged to describe the *fairytale*, or define what it is, I would make answer, that I should as soon think of describing the abstract human face, or stating what must go to constitute a human being. A fairytale is just a fairytale, as a face is just a face; and of all fairytales I know, I think *Undine* the most beautiful.

Many a man, however, who would not attempt to define *a man*, might venture to say something as to what a man ought to be: even so much I will not in this place venture with regard to the fairytale, for my long past work in that kind might but poorly instance or illustrate my now more matured judgment. I will but say some things helpful to the reading, in right-minded fashion, of such fairytales as I would wish to write, or care to read.

Some thinkers would feel sorely hampered if at liberty to use no forms but such as existed in nature, or to invent nothing save in accordance with the laws of the world of the senses; but it must not therefore be imagined that they desire escape from the region of law. Nothing lawless can show the least reason why it should exist, or could at best have more than an appearance of life.

The natural world has its laws, and no man must interfere with them in the way of presentment any more than in the way of use; but they themselves may suggest laws of other kinds, and man may, if he pleases, invent a little world of his own, with its own laws; for there is that in him which delights in calling up new forms — which is the nearest, perhaps, he can come to creation. When such forms are new embodiments of old truths, we call them products of the Imagination; when they are mere inventions, however lovely, I should call them the work of the Fancy: in either case, Law has been diligently at work.

His world once invented, the highest law that comes next into play is, that there shall be harmony between the laws by which the new world has begun to exist; and in the process of his creation, the inventor must hold by those laws. The moment he forgets one of them, he makes the story, by its own postulates, incredible. To be able to live a moment in an imagined world, we must see the laws of its existence obeyed. Those broken, we fall out of it. The imagination in us, whose exercise is essential to the most temporary submission to the imagination of another, immediately, with the disappearance of Law, ceases to act. Suppose the gracious creatures of some childlike region of Fairyland talking either cockney or Gascon! Would not the tale, however lovelily begun, sink at once to the level of the Burlesque — of all forms of literature the least worthy? A man's inventions may be stupid or clever, but if he do not hold by the laws of them, or if he make one law jar with another, he contradicts himself as an inventor, he is no artist. He does not rightly consort his instruments, or he tunes them in different keys. The mind of man is the product of live Law; it thinks by law, it dwells in the midst of law, it gathers from law its growth; with law, therefore, can it alone work to any result. Inharmonious, unconsorting ideas will come to a man, but if he try to use one of such, his work will grow dull, and he will drop it from mere lack of interest. Law is the soil in which alone beauty will grow; beauty is the only stuff in which Truth can be clothed; and you may, if you will, call Imagination the tailor that cuts her garments to fit her, and Fancy his journeyman that puts the pieces of them together, or perhaps at most embroiders their button-holes. Obeying law, the maker works like his creator; not obeying law, he is such a fool as heaps a pile of stones and calls it a church.

In the moral world it is different: there a man may clothe in new forms, and for this employ his imagination freely, but he must invent nothing. He may not, for any purpose, turn its laws upside down. He must not meddle with the relations of live souls. The laws of the spirit of man must hold, alike in this world and in any world he may invent. It were no offense to suppose a world in which everything repelled instead of attracted the things around it; it would be wicked to write a tale representing a man it called good as always doing bad things, or a man it called bad as always doing good things: the notion itself is absolutely lawless. In physical things a man may invent; in moral things he must obey — and take their laws with him into his invented world as well.

"You write as if a fairytale were a thing of importance: must it have a meaning?"

It cannot help having some meaning; if it have proportion and harmony it has vitality, and vitality is truth. The beauty may be plainer in it than the truth, but without the truth the beauty could not be, and the fairytale would give no delight. Everyone, however, who feels the story, will read its meaning after his own nature and development: one man will read one meaning in it, another will read another.

"If so, how am I to assure myself that I am not reading my own meaning into it, but yours out of it?"

Why should you be so assured? It may be better that you should read your meaning into it. That may be a higher operation of your intellect than the mere reading of mine out of it: your meaning may be superior to mine.

"Suppose my child ask me what the fairytale means, what am I to say?"

If you do not know what it means, what is easier than to say so? If you do see a meaning in it, there it is for you to give him. A genuine work of art must mean many things; the truer its art, the more things it will mean. If my drawing, on the other hand, is so far from being a work of art that it needs THIS IS A HORSE written under it, what can it matter that neither you nor your child should know what it means? It is there not so much to convey a meaning as to wake a meaning. If it do not even wake an interest, throw it aside. A meaning may be there, but it is not for you. If, again, you do not know a horse when you see it, the name written under it will not serve you much. At all events, the business of the painter is not to teach zoology.

But indeed your children are not likely to trouble you about the meaning. They find what they are capable of finding, and more would be too much. For my part, I do not write for children, but for the childlike, whether of five, or fifty, or seventy-five.

A fairytale is not an allegory. There may be allegory in it, but it is not an allegory. He must be an artist indeed who can, in any mode, produce a strict allegory that is not a weariness to the spirit. An allegory must be Mastery or Moorditch.

A fairytale, like a butterfly or a bee, helps itself on all sides, sips at every wholesome flower, and spoils not one. The true fairytale is, to my mind, very like the sonata. We all know that a sonata means something; and where there is the faculty of talking with suitable vagueness, and choosing metaphor sufficiently loose, mind may approach mind, in the interpretation of a sonata, with the result of a more or less contenting consciousness of sympathy. But if two or three men sat down to write each what the sonata meant to him, what approximation to definite idea would be the result? Little enough — and that little more than needful. We should find it had roused related, if not identical, feelings, but probably not one common thought. Has the sonata therefore failed? Had it undertaken to convey, or ought it to be expected to impart anything defined, anything notionally recognizable?

"But words are not music; words at least are meant and fitted to carry a precise meaning!"

It is very seldom indeed that they carry the exact meaning of any user of them! And if they can be so used as to convey definite meaning, it does not follow that they ought never to carry anything else. Words are live things that may be variously employed to various ends. They can convey a scientific fact, or throw a shadow of her child's dream on the heart of a mother. They are things to put together like the pieces of a dissected map, or to arrange like the notes on a stave. Is the music in them to go for nothing? It can hardly help the definiteness of a meaning: is it therefore to be disregarded? They have length, and breadth, and outline: have they nothing to do with depth? Have they only to describe, never to impress? Has nothing any claim to their use but the definite? The cause of a child's tears may be altogether undefinable: has the mother therefore no antidote for his vague misery? That may be strong in colour which has no evident outline. A fairytale, a sonata, a gathering storm, a limitless night, seizes you and sweeps you away: do you begin at once to wrestle with it and ask whence its power over you, whither it is carrying you? The law of each is in the mind of its composer; that law makes one man feel

THE FANTASTIC IMAGINATION

this way, another man feel that way. To one the sonata is a world of odour and beauty, to another of soothing only and sweetness. To one, the cloudy rendezvous is a wild dance, with a terror at its heart; to another, a majestic march of heavenly hosts, with Truth in their centre pointing their course, but as yet restraining her voice. The greatest forces lie in the region of the uncomprehended.

I will go farther. — The best thing you can do for your fellow, next to rousing his conscience, is — not to give him things to think about, but to wake things up that are in him; or say, to make him think things for himself. The best Nature does for us is to work in us such moods in which thoughts of high import arise. Does any aspect of Nature wake but one thought? Does she never suggest only one definite thing? Does she make any two men in the same place at the same moment think the same thing? Is she therefore a failure, because she is not definite? Is it nothing that she rouses the something deeper than the understanding — the power that underlies thoughts? Does she not set feeling, and so thinking at work? Would it be better that she did this after one fashion and not after many fashions? Nature is mood-engendering, thought-provoking: such ought the sonata, such ought the fairytale to be.

"But a man may then imagine in your work what he pleases, what you never meant!"

Not what he pleases, but what he can. If he be not a true man, he will draw evil out of the best; we need not mind how he treats any work of art! If he be a true man, he will imagine true things; what matter whether I meant them or not? They are there none the less that I cannot claim putting them there! One difference between God's work and man's is, that, while God's work cannot mean more than he meant, man's must mean more than he meant. For in everything that God has made, there is layer upon layer of ascending significance; also he expresses the same thought in higher and higher kinds of that thought: it is God's things, his embodied thoughts, which alone a man has to use, modified and adapted to his own purposes, for the expression of his thoughts; therefore he cannot help his words and figures falling into such combinations in the mind of another as he had himself not foreseen, so many are the thoughts allied to every other thought, so many are the relations involved in every figure, so many the facts hinted in every symbol. A man may well himself discover truth in what he wrote; for he was dealing all the time with things that came from thoughts beyond his own.

THE FANTASTIC IMAGINATION ❧ XXV

"But surely you would explain your idea to one who asked you?"

I say again, if I cannot draw a horse, I will not write *THIS IS A HORSE* under what I foolishly meant for one. Any key to a work of imagination would be nearly, if not quite, as absurd. The tale is there, not to hide, but to show: if it show nothing at your window, do not open your door to it; leave it out in the cold. To ask me to explain, is to say, "Roses! Boil them, or we won't have them!" My tales may not be roses, but I will not boil them.

So long as I think my dog can bark, I will not sit up to bark for him.

If a writer's aim be logical conviction, he must spare no logical pains, not merely to be understood, but to escape being misunderstood; where his object is to move by suggestion, to cause to imagine, then let him assail the soul of his reader as the wind assails an aeolian harp. If there be music in my reader, I would gladly wake it. Let fairytale of mine go for a firefly that now flashes, now is dark, but may flash again. Caught in a hand which does not love its kind, it will turn to an insignificant, ugly thing, that can neither flash nor fly.

The best way with music, I imagine, is not to bring the forces of our intellect to bear upon it, but to be still and let it work on that part of us for whose sake it exists. We spoil countless previous things by intellectual greed. He who will be a man, and will not be a child, must — he cannot help himself — become a little man, that is, a dwarf. He will, however, need no consolation, for he is sure to think himself a very large creature indeed.

If any strain of my "broken music" make a child's eyes flash, or his mother's grow for a moment dim, my labour will not have been in vain.

The Gifts of the Child Christ

CHAPTER I

"My hearers, we grow old," said the preacher. "Be it summer or be it spring with us now, autumn will soon settle down into winter, that winter whose snow melts only in the grave. The wind of the world sets for the tomb. Some of us rejoice to be swept along on its swift wings, and hear it bellowing in the hollows of earth and sky; but it will grow a terror to the man of trembling limb and withered brain, until at length he will long for the shelter of the tomb to escape its roaring and buffeting. Happy the man who shall then be able to believe that old age itself, with its pitiable decays and sad dreams of youth, is the chastening of the Lord, a sure sign of his love and his fatherhood."

It was the first Sunday in Advent; but "the chastening of the Lord" came into almost every sermon that man preached.

"Eloquent! But after all, *can* this kind of thing be true?" said to himself a man of about thirty, who sat decorously listening. For many years he had thought he believed this kind of thing — but of late he was not so sure.

Beside him sat his wife, in her new winter bonnet, her pretty face turned up toward the preacher; but her eyes — nothing else — revealed that she was not listening. She was much younger than her husband — hardly twenty, indeed.

In the upper corner of the pew sat a pale-faced child about five, sucking her thumb, and staring at the preacher.

The sermon over, they walked home in proximity. The husband looked gloomy, and his eyes sought the ground. The wife looked more smiling than cheerful, and her pretty eyes went hither and thither. Behind them walked the child — steadily, "with level-fronting eyelids."

It was a late-built region of large, commonplace houses, and at one of them they stopped and entered. The door of the dining-room was open, showing the table laid for their Sunday dinner. The gentleman passed on to the library behind it, the lady went up to her bedroom, and the child a stage higher to the nursery.

It wanted half an hour to dinner. Mr. Greatorex sat down, drummed with his fingers on the arm of his easy-chair, took up a book of arctic exploration, threw it again on the table, got up, and went to the smoking-room. He had built it for his wife's sake, but was often glad of it for his own. Again he seated himself, took a cigar, and smoked gloomily.

Having reached her bedroom, Mrs. Greatorex took off her bonnet, and stood for ten minutes turning it round and round. Earnestly she regarded it — now gave a twist to the wire-stem of a flower, then spread wider the loop of a bow. She was meditating what it lacked of perfection rather than brooding over its merits: she was keen in bonnets.

Little Sophy — or, as she called herself by a transposition of consonant sounds common with children, Phosy — found her nurse Alice in the nursery. But she was lost in the pages of a certain London weekly, which had found her in a mood open to its influences, and did not even look up when the child entered. With some effort Phosy drew off her gloves, and with more difficulty untied her hat. Then she took off her jacket, smoothed her hair, and retreated to a corner. There a large shabby doll lay upon her little chair: she took it up, disposed it gently upon the bed, seated herself in its place, got a little book from where she had left it under the chair, smoothed down her skirts, and began simultaneously to read and suck her thumb. The book was an unhealthy one, a cup filled to the brim with a poverty-stricken and selfish religion: such are always breaking out like an eruption here and there over the body of the Church, doing their part, doubtless, in carrying off the evil humours generated by poverty of blood, or the congestion of self-preservation. It is wonderful out of what spoiled fruit some children will suck sweetness.

But she did not read far: her thoughts went back to a phrase which had haunted her ever since first she went to church: "Whom the Lord loveth, he chasteneth."

❧

"I wish he would chasten me," she thought for the hundredth time.

The small Christian had no suspicion that her whole life had been a period of chastening — that few children indeed had to live in such a sunless atmosphere as hers.

Alice threw down the newspaper, gazed from the window into the back-yard of the next house, saw nothing but an elderly man-servant brushing a garment, and turned upon Sophy.

"Why don't you hang up your jacket, miss?" she said, sharply.

The little one rose, opened the wardrobe-door wide, carried a chair to it, fetched her jacket from the bed, clambered up on the chair, and, leaning far forward to reach a peg, tumbled right into the bottom of the wardrobe.

"You clumsy!" exclaimed the nurse angrily, and pulling her out by the arm, shook her.

Alice was not generally rough to her, but there were reasons to-day.

Phosy crept back to her seat, pale, frightened, and a little hurt. Alice hung up the jacket, closed the wardrobe, and, turning, contemplated her own pretty face and neat figure in the glass opposite. The dinner-bell rang.

"There, I declare!" she cried, and wheeled round on Phosy. "And your hair not brushed yet, miss! Will you ever learn to do a thing without being told it? Thank goodness, I shan't be plagued with you long! But I pity her as comes after me: I do!"

"If the Lord would but chasten me!" said the child to herself, as she rose and laid down her book with a sigh.

The maid seized her roughly by the arm, and brushed her hair with an angry haste that made the child's eyes water, and herself feel a little ashamed at the sight of them.

"How could anybody love such a troublesome chit?" she said, seeking the comfort of justification from the child herself.

Another sigh was the poor little damsel's only answer. She looked very white and solemn as she entered the dining-room.

Mr. Greatorex was a merchant in the City. But he was more of a man than a merchant, which all merchants are not. Also, he was more scrupulous in his dealings than some merchants in the same line of business, who yet stood as well with the world as he; but, on the other hand, he had the meanness to pride himself upon it as if it had been something he might have done without and yet held up his head.

Some six years before, he had married to please his parents; and a year before, he had married to please himself. His first wife had intellect, education, and heart, but little individuality — not enough to reflect the individuality of her husband. The consequence was, he found her uninteresting. He was kind and indulgent, however, and not even her best friend blamed him much for manifesting nothing beyond the average devotion of husbands. But in truth his wife had great capabilities, only they had never ripened, and when she died, a fortnight after giving birth to Sophy, her husband had not a suspicion of the large amount of undeveloped power that had passed away with her.

Her child was so like her both in countenance and manner that he was too constantly reminded of her unlamented mother; and he loved neither enough to discover that, in a sense as true as marvellous, the child was the very flower-bud of her mother's nature, in which her retarded blossom had yet a chance of being slowly carried to perfection. Love alone gives insight, and the father took her merely for a miniature edition of the volume which he seemed to have laid aside forever in the dust of the earth's lumber-room. Instead, therefore, of watering the roots of his little human slip from the well of his affections, he had scarcely as yet perceived more in relation to her than that he was legally accountable for her existence, and bound to give her shelter and food. If he had questioned himself on the matter, he would have replied that love was not wanting, only waiting upon her growth, and the development of something to interest him.

Little right as he had had to expect anything from his first marriage, he had yet cherished some hopes therein — tolerably vague, it is true, yet hardly faint enough, it would seem, for he was disappointed in them. When its bonds fell from him, however, he flattered himself that he had not worn them in vain, but had through them arrived at a knowledge of women as rare as profound. But whatever the reach of this knowledge, it was not sufficient to prevent him from harbouring the presumptuous hope of so choosing and so fashioning the heart and mind of a woman that they should be as concave mirrors to his own. I do not mean that he would have admitted the figure, but such was really the end he blindly sought. I wonder how many of those who have been disappointed in such an attempt have been thereby aroused to the perception of what a frightful failure their success would have been on both sides. It was bad enough that Augustus Greatorex's theories had cramped his own development; it would have been ten-fold worse had they been operative to the stunting of another soul.

Letty Merewether was the daughter of a bishop *in partibus.* She had been born tolerably innocent, had grown up more than tolerably pretty, and was, when she came to England at the age of sixteen, as nearly a genuine example of Locke's sheet of white paper as could well have fallen to the hand of such an experimenter as Greatorex would fain become.

In his suit he had prospered — perhaps too easily. He loved the girl, or at least loved the modified reflection of her in his own mind; while she, thoroughly admiring the dignity, good looks and accomplishments of the man whose attentions flattered her self-opinion, accorded him deference enough to encourage his vainest hopes. Although she knew little, fluttering over the merest surfaces of existence, she had sense enough to know that he talked sense to her, and foolishness enough to put it down to her own credit, while for the sense itself she cared little or nothing. And Greatorex, without even knowing what she was roughhewn for, would take upon him to shape her ends! — and ambition the Divinity never permits to succeed: he who fancies himself the carver finds himself but the chisel, or indeed perhaps only the mallet, in the hand of the true workman.

During the days of his courtship, then, Letty listened and smiled, or answered with what he took for a spiritual response, when it was merely a brain-echo. Looking down into the pond of her being, whose surface was not yet ruffled by any bubbling of springs from below, he saw the reflection of himself and was satisfied. An able man on his hobby looks a centaur of wisdom and folly; but if he be at all a wise man, the beast will one day or other show him the jade's favor of unseating him. Meantime Augustus Greatorex was fooled, not by poor little Letty, who was not capable of fooling him, but by himself. Letty had made no pretenses; had been interested, and had shown her interest; had understood, or seemed to understand, what he said to her, and forgotten it the next moment — had no pocket to put it in, did not know what to do with it, and let it drop into the Limbo of Vanity. They had not been married many days before the scouts of advancing disappointment were upon them. Augustus resisted manfully for a time. But the truth was each of the two had to become a great deal more than either was, before any approach to unity was possible. He tried to interest her in one subject after another — tried her first, I am ashamed to say, with political economy. In that instance, when he came home to dinner he found that she had not got beyond the first page of the book he had left with her. But she had the best of excuses, namely, that of that page she had not understood a sentence. He saw his mistake, and tried her with poetry. But Milton, with whom unfortunately he commenced his approaches, was to her, if not equally unintelligible, equally uninteresting. He tried her next with the elements of science, but with no better success. He returned to poetry, and read some of the *Faerie Queene* with her: she was, or seemed to be, interested in all his talk about it, and inclined to go on with it in his absence, but found the first stanza she tried more than enough without him to give life to it. She could give it none, and therefore it gave her none. I believe she read a chapter of the Bible every day, but the only books she read with any real interest were novels of a sort that Augustus despised. It never occurred to him that he ought at once to have made friends of this Momus of unrighteousness, for by them he might have found entrance to the sealed chamber. He ought to have read with her the books she did like, for by them only could he make her think, and from them alone could he lead her to better. It is but from the very step upon which one stands that one can move to the next. Besides those books, there was nothing in her scheme of the universe but fashion, dress, calls, the park, other-peopledom, concerts, plays, church-going — whatever could show itself on the frosted glass of her *camera obscura* — make an interest of motion and colour in her darkened chamber. Without these, her bosom's mistress would have found life unendurable, for not yet had she ascended her throne, but lay on the floor of her nursery, surrounded with toys that imitated life.

It was no wonder, therefore, that Augustus was at length compelled to allow himself disappointed. That it was the fault of his self-confidence made the thing no whit better. He was too much of a man not to cherish a certain tenderness for her, but he soon found to his dismay that it had begun to be mingled with a shadow of contempt. Against this he struggled, but with fluctuating success. He stopped later and later at business, and when he came home spent more and more of his time in the smoking-room, where by and by he had bookshelves put up. Occasionally he would accept an invitation to dinner and accompany his wife, but he detested evening parties, and when Letty, who never refused an invitation if she could help it, went to one, he remained at home with his books. But his power of reading began to diminish. He became restless and irritable. Something kept gnawing at his heart. There was a sore spot in it. The spot grew larger and larger, and by degrees the centre of his consciousness came to be a soreness: his cherished idea had been fooled; he had taken a silly girl for a woman of undeveloped wealth; — a bubble, a surface whereon fair colours chased each other, for a hearted crystal.

On her part, Letty too had her grief, which, unlike Augustus, she did not keep to herself, receiving in return from more than one of her friends the soothing assurance that Augustus was only like all other men; that women were but their toys, which they cast away when weary of them. Letty did not see that she was herself making a toy of her life, or that Augustus was right in refusing to play with such a costly and delicate thing. Neither did Augustus see that, having, by his own blunder, married a mere child, he was bound to deal with her as one, and not let the child suffer for his fault more than what could not be helped. It is not by pressing our insights upon them, but by bathing the sealed eyelids of the human kittens, that we can help them.

And all the time poor little Phosy was left to the care of Alice, a clever, careless, good-hearted, self-satisfied damsel, who, although seldom so rough in her behaviour as we have just seen her, abandoned the child almost entirely to her own resources. It was often she sat alone in the nursery, wishing the Lord would chasten her — because then he would love her.

The first course was nearly over ere Augustus had brought himself to ask —

"What did you think of the sermon today, Letty?"

"Not much," answered Letty. "I am not fond of finery. I prefer simplicity."

Augustus held his peace bitterly. For it was just finery in a sermon, without knowing it, that Letty was fond of: what seemed to him a flimsy syllabub of sacred things, beaten up with the whisk of composition, was charming to Letty; while, on the contrary, if a man such as they had been listening to was carried away by the thoughts that struggled in him for utterance, the result, to her judgment, was finery, and the object display. In excuse it must be remembered that she had been used to her father's style, which no one could have aspersed with lack of sobriety.

Presently she spoke again.

"Gus, dear, couldn't you make up your mind for once to go with me to Lady Ashdaile's to-morrow? I am getting quite ashamed of appearing so often without you."

"There is another way of avoiding that unpleasantness," remarked her husband drily.

"You cruel creature!" returned Letty playfully. "But I must go this once, for I promised Mrs. Holden."

"You know, Letty," said her husband, after a little pause, "it gets of more and more consequence that you should not fatigue yourself. By keeping such late hours in such stifling rooms you are endangering two lives — remember that, Letty. If you stay at home to-morrow, I will come home early, and read to you all the evening."

"Gussy, that *would* be charming. You *know* there is nothing in the world I should enjoy so much. But this time I really mustn't."

She launched into a list of all the great nobodies and small somebodies who were to be there, and whom she positively must see: it might be her only chance.

Those last words quenched a sarcasm on Augustus' lips. He was kinder than usual the rest of the evening, and read her to sleep with the *Pilgrim's Progress.*

Phosy sat in a corner, listened, and understood. Or where she misunderstood, it was an honest misunderstanding, which never does much hurt. Neither father nor mother spoke to her till they bade her good night. Neither saw the hungry heart under the mask of the still face. The father never imagined her already fit for the modelling she was better without, and the stepmother had to become a mother before she could value her.

Phosy went to bed to dream of the Valley of Humiliation.

CHAPTER II

The next morning Alice gave her mistress warning. It was quite unexpected, and she looked at her aghast.

"Alice," she said at length, "you're never going to leave me at such a time!"

"I'm sorry it don't suit you, ma'am, but I must."

"Why, Alice? What is the matter? Has Sophy been troublesome?"

"No, ma'am; there's no harm in that child."

"Then what can it be, Alice? Perhaps you are going to be married sooner than you expected?"

Alice gave her chin a little toss, pressed her lip together, and was silent.

"I have always been kind to you," resumed her mistress.

"I'm sure, ma'am, I never made no complaints!" returned Alice, but as she spoke she drew herself up straighter than before.

"Then what is it?" said her mistress.

"The fact is, ma'am," answered the girl, almost fiercely, "I cannot any longer endure a state of domestic slavery."

"I don't understand you a bit better," said Mrs. Greatorex, trying, but in vain, to smile, and therefore looking angrier than she was.

"I mean, ma'am — an' I see no reason as I shouldn't say it, for it's the truth — there's a worm at the root of society where one yuman bein's got to do the dirty work of another. I don't mind sweepin' up my own dust, but I won't sweep up nobody else's. I ain't a goin' to demean myself no longer! There!"

"Leave the room, Alice," said Mrs. Greatorex; and when, with a toss and a flounce, the young woman had vanished, she burst into tears of anger and annoyance.

The day passed. The evening came. She dressed without Alice's usual help, and went to Lady Ashdaile's with her friend. There a reaction took place, and her spirits rose unnaturally. She even danced — to the disgust of one or two quick-eyed matrons who sat by the wall.

When she came home she found her husband sitting up for her. He said next to nothing, and sat up an hour longer with his book.

In the night she was taken ill. Her husband called Alice, and ran himself to fetch the doctor. For some hours she seemed in danger, but by noon was much better. Only the greatest care was necessary.

As soon as she could speak, she told Augustus of Alice's warning, and he sent for her to the library.

She stood before him with flushed cheeks and flashing eyes.

"I understand, Alice, you have given your mistress warning," he said gently.

"Yes, sir."

"Your mistress is very ill, Alice."

"Yes, sir."

"Don't you think it would be ungrateful of you to leave her in her present condition? She's not likely to be strong for some time to come."

The use of the world "ungrateful" was an unfortunate one. Alice begged to know what she had to be grateful for. Was her work worth nothing? And her master, as every one must who claims that which can only be freely given, found himself in the wrong.

"Well, Alice," he said, "we won't dispute that point; and if you are really determined on going, you must do the best you can for your mistress for the rest of the month."

Alice's sense of injury was soothed by her master's forbearance. She had always rather approved of Mr. Greatorex, and she left the room more softly than she had entered it.

Letty had a fortnight in bed, during which she reflected a little.

The very next day on which she left her room, Alice sought an interview with her master, and declared she could not stay out her month; she must go home at once.

She had been very attentive to her mistress during the fortnight: there must be something to account for her strange behaviour.

"Come now, Alice," said her master, "what's at the back of all this? You have been a good, well-behaved, obliging girl till now, and I am certain you would never be like this if there weren't something wrong somewhere."

"Something wrong, sir! No, indeed, sir! Except you call it wrong to have an old uncle as dies and leaves ever so much money — thousands on thousands, the lawyers say."

"And does it come to you then, Alice?"

"I get my share, sir. He left it to be parted even between his nephews and nieces."

"Why, Alice, you are quite an heiress, then!" returned her master, scarcely, however, believing the thing so grand as Alice would have it. "But, don't you think now it would be rather hard that your fortune should be Mrs. Greatorex's misfortune?"

"Well, I don't see as how it shouldn't," replied Alice. "It's mis'ess's fortun' as 'as been my misfortun' — ain't it now, sir? An' why shouldn't it be the other way next?"

"I don't quite see how your mistress's fortune can be said to be your misfortune, Alice."

"Anybody would see that, sir, as wasn't blinded by class-prejudices."

"Class-prejudices!" exclaimed Mr. Greatorex, in surprise at the word.

"It's a term they use, I believe, sir! But it's plain enough that if mis'ess hadn't 'a' been better off than me, she wouldn't ha' been able to secure my services — as you calls it."

"That is certainly plain enough," returned Mr. Greatorex. "But suppose nobody had been able to secure your services, what would have become of you?"

"By that time the people'd have rose to assert their rights."

"To what? — To fortunes like yours?"

"To bread and cheese at least, sir," returned Alice, pertly.

"Well, but you've had something better than bread and cheese."

"I don't make no complaints as to the style of livin' in the house, sir, but that's all one, so long as it's on the vile condition of domestic slavery — which it's nothing can justify."

"Then of course, although you are now a woman of property, you will never dream of having any one to wait on you," said her master, amused with the volume of human nature thus opened to him.

"All I say, sir, is — it's my turn now; and I ain't goin' to be sit upon by no one. I know my dooty to myself."

"I didn't know there was such a duty, Alice," said her master.

Something in his tone displeased her.

"Then you know now, sir," she said, and bounced out of the room.

The next moment, however, ashamed of her rudeness, she re-entered, saying,

"I don't want to be unkind, sir, but I must go home. I've got a brother that's ill, too, and wants to see me. If you don't object to me goin' home for a month, I promise you to come back and see mis'ess through her trouble — as a friend, you know, sir."

"But just listen to me first, Alice," said Mr. Greatorex. "I've had something to do with wills in my time, and I can assure you it is not likely to be less than a year before you can touch the money. You had much better stay where you are till your uncle's affairs are settled. You don't know what may happen. There's many a slip between cup and lip, you know."

"Oh! it's all right. Everybody knows the money's left to his nephews and nieces, and me and my brother's as good as any."

"I don't doubt it: still, if you'll take my advice, you'll keep a sound roof over your head till another's ready for you."

Alice only threw her chin in the air, and said almost threateningly,

"Am I to go for the month, sir?"

"I'll talk to your mistress about it," answered Mr. Greatorex, not at all sure that such an arrangement would be for his wife's comfort.

But the next day Mrs. Greatorex had a long talk with Alice, and the result was that on the following Monday she was to go home for a month, and then return for two months more at least. What Mr. Greatorex had said about the legacy, had had its effect, and, besides, her mistress had spoken to her with pleasure in her good fortune. About Sophy no one felt any anxiety: she was no trouble to any one, and the housemaid would see to her.

CHAPTER III

On the Sunday evening, Alice's lover, having heard, not from herself, but by a side wind, that she was going home the next day, made his appearance in Wimborne Square, somewhat perplexed — both at the move, and at her leaving him in ignorance of the same. He was a cabinet-maker in an honest shop in the neighbourhood, and in education, faculty, and general worth, considerably Alice's superior — a fact which had hitherto rather pleased her, but now gave zest to the change which she imagined had subverted their former relation. Full of the sense of her new superiority, she met him draped in an indescribable strangeness. John Jephson felt, at the very first word, as if her voice came from the other side of the English Channel. He wondered what he had done, or rather what Alice could imagine he had done or said, to put her in such tantrums.

"Alice, my dear," he said — for John was a man to go straight at the enemy, "what's amiss? What's come over you? You ain't altogether like your own self to-night! And here I find you're goin' away, and ne'er a word to me about it! What have I done?"

Alice's chin alone made reply. She waited the fitting moment, with splendour to astonish, and with grandeur to subdue her lover. To tell the sad truth, she was no longer sure that it would be well to encourage him on the old footing; was she not standing on tiptoe, her skirts in her hand, on the brink of the brook that parted serfdom from gentility, on the point of stepping daintily across, and leaving domestic slavery, red hands, caps, and obedience behind her? How then was she to marry a man that had black nails, and smelt of glue? It was incumbent on her at least, for propriety's sake, to render him at once aware that it was in condescension ineffable she took any notice of him.

"Alice, my girl!" began John again, in expostulatory tone.

"Miss Cox, if you please, John Jephson," interposed Alice.

"What on 'arth's come over you?" exclaimed John, with the first throb of rousing indignation. "But if you ain't your own self no more,

THE GIFTS OF THE CHILD CHRIST

why, Miss Cox be it. 'T seems to me's if I warn't my own self no more —
's if I'd got into some un else, or't least hedn't got my own ears on m'own
head. — Never saw or heerd Alice like this afore!" he added, turning in
gloomy bewilderment to the housemaid for a word of human sympathy.

The movement did not altogether please Alice, and she felt she must
justify her behaviour.

"You see, John," she said, with dignity, keeping her back towards
him, and pretending to dust the globe of a lamp, "there's things as no
woman can help, and therefore as no man has no right to complain of
them. It's not as if I'd gone an' done it, or changed myself, no more 'n if
it 'ad took place in my cradle. What can I help it, if the world goes and
changes itself? Am *I* to blame? — tell me that. It's not that I make no
complaint, but I tell you it ain't me, it's circumstances as is gone and
changed theirselves, and bein' as circumstances is changed, things ain't the
same as they was, and Miss is the properer term from you to me, John
Jephson."

"Dang it if I know what you're a drivin' at, Alice! — Miss Cox! —
and I beg yer perdon, miss, I'm sure. — Dang me if I do!"

"Don't swear, John Jephson — leastways before a lady. It's now
proper."

"It seems to me, Miss Cox, as if the wind was a settin' from Bedlam,
or may be Colney Hatch," said John, who was considered a humourist
among his comrades. "I wouldn't take no liberties with a lady, Miss Cox;
but if I might be so bold as to arst the joke of the thing — "

"Joke, indeed!" cried Alice. "Do you call a dead uncle and ten
thousand pounds a joke?"

"God bless me!" said John. "You don't mean it, Alice?"

"I do mean it, and that you'll find, John Jephson. I'm goin' to bid
you good-bye tomorrer."

"Whoy, Alice!" exclaimed honest John, aghast.

"It's truth I tell ye," said Alice.

"And for how long?" gasped John, forefeeling illimitable misfortune.

"That depends," returned Alice, who did not care to lessen the effect
of her communication by mentioning her promised return for a season.
" — It ain't likely," she added, "as a heiress is a goin' to act the nuss-maid
much longer."

"But Alice," said John, "you don't mean to say — it's not in your
mind now — it can't be, Alice — you're only jokin' with me — "

"Indeed, and I'm not!" interjected Alice, with a sniff.

"I don't mean that way, you know. What I mean is, you don't mean as how this 'ere money — dang it all! — as how it's to be all over between you and me? — You *can't* mean that, Alice!" ended the poor fellow, with a choking in his throat.

It was very hard upon him! He must either look as if he wanted to share her money, or else as if he were ready to give her up.

"Arst yourself, John Jephson," answered Alice, "whether it's likely a young lady of fortun' would be keepin' company with a young man as didn't know how to take off his hat to her in the park?"

Alice did not above half mean what she said: she wished mainly to enhance her own importance. At the same time she did mean it half, and that would have been enough for Jephson. He rose, grievously wounded.

"Good-bye, Alice," he said, taking the hand she did not refuse. "Ye're throwin' from ye what all yer money won't buy."

She gave a scornful little laugh, and John walked out of the kitchen.

At the door he turned with one lingering look; but in Alice there was no sign of softening. She turned scornfully away, and no doubt enjoyed her triumph to the full.

The next morning she went away.

CHAPTER IV

Mr. Greatorex had ceased to regard the advent of Christmas with much interest. Naturally gifted with a strong religious tendency, he had, since his first marriage, taken, not to denial, but to the side of objection, spending much energy in contempt for the foolish opinions of others, a self-indulgence which does less than little to further the growth of one's own spirit in truth and righteousness. The only person who stands excused — I do not say justified — in so doing, is the man who, having been taught the same opinions, has found them a legion of adversaries barring his way to the truth. But having got rid of them for himself, it is, I suspect, worse than useless to attack them again, save as the ally of those who are fighting their way through the same ranks to the truth. Greatorex had been indulging his intellect at the expense of his heart. A man may have light in the brain and darkness in the heart. It were better to be an owl than a strong-eyed apteryx. He was on the path which naturally ends in blindness and unbelief. I fancy, if he had not been neglectful of his child, she would ere this time have relighted his Christmas-candles for him; but now his second disappointment in marriage had so dulled his heart that he had begun to regard life as a stupid affair, in which the most enviable fool was the man who could still expect to realize an ideal. He had set out on a false track altogether, but had not yet discovered that there had been an immoral element at work in his mistake.

For what right had he to desire the fashioning of any woman after his ideas? Did not the angel of her eternal Ideal for ever behold the face of her Father in heaven? The best that can be said for him is, that, notwithstanding his disappointment and her faults, yea, notwithstanding his own faults, which were, with all his cultivation and strength of character, yet more serious that hers, he was still kind to her; yes, I may say for him, notwithstanding even her silliness, which is a sickening fault, and one which no supremacy of beauty can overshadow, he still loved her a little. Hence the care he showed for her in respect of the coming sorrow was genuine; it did not all belong to this desire for a son to whom he might be a father indeed — after his own fancies, however. Letty, on her part, was as full of expectation as the girl who has been promised a doll that can shut and open its eyes, and cry when it is pinched; her carelessness of its safe arrival came of ignorance and not indifference.

It cannot but seem strange that such a man should have been so careless of the child he had. But from the first she had painfully reminded him of her mother, with whom in truth he had never quarreled, but with whom he had not found life the less irksome on that account. Add to this that he had been growing fonder of business, — a fact which indicated, in a man of his endowment and development, an inclination downwards of the plane of his life. It was some time since he had given up reading poetry. History had almost followed: he now read little except politics, travels, and popular expositions of scientific progress.

That year Christmas Eve fell upon a Monday. The day before, Letty not feeling very well, her husband thought it better not to leave her, and gave up going to church. Phosy was utterly forgotten, but she dressed herself, and at the usual hour appeared with her prayer-book in her hand ready for church. When her father told her that he was not going, she looked so blank that he took pity upon her, and accompanied her to the church-door, promising to meet her as she came out. Phosy sighed from relief as she entered, for she had a vague idea that by going to church to pray for it she might move the Lord to chasten her. At least he would see her there, and might think of it. She had never had such an attention from her father before, never such dignity conferred upon her as to be allowed to appear in church alone, sitting in the pew by herself like a grown damsel. But I doubt if there was any pride in her stately step, or any vanity in the smile — no, not smile, but illuminated mist, the vapour of smiles, which haunted her sweet little solemn church-window of a face, as she walked up the aisle.

The preacher was one of whom she had never heard her father speak slighting word, in whom her unbounded trust had never been shaken. Also he was one who believed with his whole soul in the things that make Christmas precious. To him the birth of the wonderful baby hinted at hundreds of strange things in the economy of the planet. That a man could so thoroughly persuade himself that he believed the old fable, was matter of marvel to some of his friends who held blind Nature the eternal mother, and Night the everlasting grandmother of all things. But the child Phosy, in her dreams or out of them, in church or nursery, with her book or her doll, was never out of the region of wonders, and would have believed, or tried to believe, anything that did not involve a moral impossibility.

What the preacher said I need not even partially repeat; it is enough to mention a certain metamorphosed deposit from the stream of his eloquence carried home in her mind by Phosy: from some of his sayings about the birth of Jesus into the world, into the family, into the individual human bosom, she had got it into her head that Christmas Day was not a birthday like that she had herself last year, but that, in some wonderful way, to her requiring no explanation, the baby Jesus was born every Christmas Day afresh. What became of him afterwards she did not know, and indeed she had never yet thought to ask how it was that he could come to every house in London as well as No. 1, Wimborne Square. Little of a home as another might think it, that house was yet to her the centre of all houses, and the wonder had not yet widened rippling beyond it: into the spot of the pool the eternal gift would fall.

Her father forgot the time over his book, but so entranced was her heart with the expectation of the promised visit, now so near — the day after to-morrow — that, if she did not altogether forget to look for him

THE GIFTS OF THE CHILD CHRIST

as she stepped down the stair from the church door to the street, his absence caused her no uneasiness; and when, just as she reached it, he opened the house-door in tardy haste to redeem his promise, she looked up at him with a solemn, smileless repose, born of spiritual tension and speechless anticipation, upon her face, and walking past him without change in the rhythm of her motion, marched stately up the stairs to the nursery. I believe the centre of her hope was that when the baby came she would beg him on her knees to ask the Lord to chasten her.

When dessert was over, her mother on the sofa in the drawing-room, and her father in an easy chair, with a bottle of his favourite wine by his side, she crept out of the room and away again to the nursery. There she reached up to her little bookshelf, and, full of the sermon as spongy mists are full of the sunlight, took thence a volume of stories from the German, the re-reading of one of which, narrating the visit of the Christ-child, laden with gifts, to a certain household, and what he gave to each and all therein, she had, although sorely tempted, saved up until now, and sat down with it by the fire, the only light she had. When the housemaid, suddenly remembering she must put her to bed, and at the same time discovering it was a whole hour past her usual time, hurried to the nursery, she found her fast asleep in her little arm-chair, her book on her lap, and the fire self-consumed into a dark cave with a somber glow in its deepest hollows. Dreams had doubtless come to deepen the impressions of sermon and *mährchen,* for as she slowly yielded to the hands of Polly putting her to bed, her lips, unconsciously moved of the slumbering but not sleeping spirit, more than once murmured the words *Lord loveth and chasteneth.* Right blessedly would I enter the dreams of such a child — revel in them, as a bee in the heavenly gulf of a cactus-flower.

CHAPTER V

On Christmas Eve the church bells were ringing through the murky air of London, whose streets lay flaring and steaming below. The brightest of their constellations were the butchers' shops, with their shows of prize beef; around them, the eddies of the human tides were most confused and knotted. But the toy-shops were brilliant also. To Phosy they would have been the treasure-caves of the Christ-child — all mysteries, all with insides to them — boxes, and desks, and windmills, and dove-cots, and hens with chickens, and who could tell what all? In every one of those shops her eyes would have searched for the Christ-child, the giver of all their wealth. For to her he was everywhere that night — ubiquitous as the luminous mist that brooded all over London — of which, however, she saw nothing but the glow above the mews. John Jephson was out in the middle of all the snow, drifting about in it: he saw nothing that had pleasure in it, his heart was so heavy. He never thought once of the Christ-child, or even of the Christ-man, as the giver of anything. Birth is the one standing promise-hope for the race, but for poor John this Christmas held no promise. With all his humour, he was one of those people, generally dull and slow — God grant me and mine such dulness and such sloth — who, having once loved, cannot cease. During the fortnight he had scarce had a moment's ease from the sting of his Alice's treatment. The honest fellow's feelings were no study to himself; he knew nothing but the pleasure and the pain of them; but I believe it was not mainly for himself that he was sorry. Like Othello, "the pity of it" haunted him: he had taken Alice for a downright girl, about whom there was and could be no mistake; and the first hot blast of prosperity had swept her away like a hectic leaf. What were all the shops dressed out in holly and mistletoe, what were all the rushing flaming gas-jets, what the fattest of prize-pigs to John, who could never more imagine a spare-rib on the table between Alice and him of a Sunday? His imagination ran on seeing her pass in her carriage, and drop him a nod of condescension as she swept noisily by him — trudging home weary from his work to his loveless fireside. *He* didn't want her money! Honestly, he would rather have her without than with money, for he now regarded it as an enemy, seeing what evil changes it could work. "There be some devil in it, sure!" he said to himself. True, he had never found any in his week's wages, but he did remember once finding the devil in a month's wages received in the lump.

As he was thus thinking with himself, a carriage came suddenly from a side street into the crowd, and while he stared at it, thinking Alice might be sitting inside it while he was tramping the pavement alone, she passed him on the other side on foot — was actually pushed against him: he looked round, and saw a young woman, carrying a small bag, disappearing in the crowd. "There's an air of Alice about *her*," said John to himself, seeing her back only. But of course it couldn't be Alice; for her he must look in the

THE GIFTS OF THE CHILD CHRIST

carriages now! And what a fool he was: every young woman reminded him of the one he had lost! Perhaps if he was to call the next day — Polly was a good-natured creature — he might hear some news of her.

It had been a troubled fortnight with Mrs. Greatorex. She wished much that she could have talked to her husband more freely, but she had not learned to feel at home with him. Yet he had been kinder and more attentive than usual all the time, so much so that Letty thought with herself — if she gave him a boy, he would certainly return to his first devotion. She said *boy,* because any one might see he cared little for Phosy. She had never discovered that he was disappointed in himself, but, since her disregard of his wishes had brought evil upon her, she had begun to suspect that he had some ground for being dissatisfied with her. She never dreamed of his kindness as the effort of a conscientious nature to make the best of what could not now be otherwise helped. Her own poverty of spirit and lack of worth achieved, she knew as little of it as she did of the riches of Michael the archangel. One must have begun to gather wisdom before he can see his own folly.

That evening she was seated alone in the drawing-room, her husband having left her to smoke his cigar, when the butler entered and informed her that Alice had returned, but was behaving so oddly that they did not know what to do with her. Asking wherein her oddness consisted, and learning that it was mostly in silence and tears, she was not sorry to gather that some disappointment had befallen her, and felt considerable curiosity to know what it was. She therefore told him to send her upstairs.

Meantime Polly, the housemaid, seeing plainly enough from her return in the middle of her holiday, and from her utter dejection, that Alice's expectations had been frustrated, and cherishing no little resentment against her because of her *uppishness* on the first news of her good fortune, had been ungenerous enough to take her revenge in a way as stinging in effect as bitter in intention; for she loudly protested that no amount of such luck as she pretended to suppose in Alice's possession, would have induced *her* to behave herself so that a handsome honest fellow like John Jephson should be driven to despise her, and take up with her betters. When her mistress's message came, Alice was only too glad to find refuge from the kitchen in the drawing-room.

The moment she entered, she fell on her knees at the foot of the couch on which her mistress lay, covered her face with her hands, and sobbed grievously.

Nor was the change more remarkable in her bearing than in her person. She was pale and worn, and had a hunted look — was in fact a mere shadow of what she had been. For a time her mistress found it impossible to quiet her so as to draw from her her story: tears and sobs combined with repugnance to hold her silent.

"Oh, ma'am!" she burst out at length, wringing her hands, "how ever *can* I tell you? You will never speak to me again. Little did I think such a disgrace was waiting me!"

"It was no fault of yours if you were misinformed," said her mistress, "or that your uncle was not the rich man you fancied."

"Oh, ma'am, there was no mistake there! He was more than twice as rich as I fancied. If he had only died a beggar, and left things as they was!"

"Then he didn't leave it to his nephews and nieces as they told you? — Well, there's no disgrace in that."

"Oh! but he did, ma'am: that was all right; no mistake there either, ma'am. — And to think o' me behavin' as I did — to you and master as was so good to me! Who'll ever take any more notice of me now, after what has come out — as I'm sure I no more dreamed on than the child unborn!"

An agonized burst of fresh weeping followed, and it was with prolonged difficulty, and by incessant questioning, that Mrs. Greatorex at length drew from her the following facts.

Before Alice and her brother could receive the legacy to which they laid claim, it was necessary to produce certain documents, the absence of which, as of any proof to take their place, led to the unavoidable publication of a fact previously known only to a living few — namely, that the father and mother of Alice Hopwood had never been married, which fact deprived them of the smallest claim on the legacy, and fell like a millstone upon Alice and her pride. From the height of her miserable arrogance she fell prone — not merely hurled back into the lowly condition from which she had raised her head only to despise it with base unrighteousness, and to adopt and reassert the principles she had abhorred when they affected herself — not merely this, but, in her own judgment at least, no longer the respectable member of society she had hitherto been justified in supposing herself. The relation of her father and mother she felt overshadow her with a disgrace unfathomable — the more overwhelming that it cast her from the gates of the Paradise she

THE GIFTS OF THE CHILD CHRIST

had seemed on the point of entering: her fall she measured by the height of the social ambition she had cherished, and had seemed on the point of attaining. But it is not an evil that the devil's money, which this legacy had from the first proved to Alice, should turn to a hot cinder in the hand. Rarely had a more haughty spirit than hers gone before a fall, and rarely has the fall been more sudden or more abject. And the consciousness of the behaviour into which her false riches had seduced her, changed the whip of her chastisement into scorpions. Worst of all, she had insulted her lover as beneath her notice, and the next moment had found herself too vile for his. Judging by herself, in the injustice of bitter humiliation she imagined him scoffing with his mates at the base-born menial who would set up for a fine lady. But had she been more worthy of honest John, she would have understood him better. As it was, no really good fortune could have befallen her but such as now seemed to her the depth of evil fortune. Without humiliation to prepare the way for humility, she must have become capable of more and more baseness, until she lost all that makes life worth having.

When Mrs. Greatorex had given her what consolation she found handy, and at length dismissed her, the girl, unable to endure her own company, sought the nursery, where she caught Phosy in her arms and embraced her with fervour. Never in her life having been the object of any such display of feeling, Phosy was much astonished: when Alice had set her down and she had resumed her seat by the fireside, she went on staring for a while — and then a strange sort of miming ensued.

It was Phosy's habit — one less rare with children than may by most be imagined — to do what she could to enter into any state of mind whose shows were sufficiently marked for her observation. She sought to lay hold of the feeling that produced the expression: less than the reproduction of a similar condition in her own imaginative sensorium, object to her leisurely examination, would in no case satisfy the little metaphysician. But what was indeed very odd was the means she took for arriving at the sympathetic knowledge she desired. As if she had been the most earnest student of dramatic expression through the facial muscles, she would sit watching the countenance of the object of her solicitude, all the time, with full consciousness, fashioning her own as nearly as she could into the lines and forms of the other: in proportion as she succeeded, the small psychologist imagined she felt in herself the condition that produced the phenomenon she observed — as if the shape of her face cast inward its shadow upon her mind, and so revealed to it, through the two faces, what was moving and shaping in the mind of the other.

In the present instance, having at length, after modelling and re-modelling her face like that of a gutta-percha doll for some time, composed it finally into the best correspondence she could effect, she sat brooding for a while, with Alice's expression as it were frozen upon it. Gradually the forms assumed melted away, and allowed her still, solemn face to look out from behind them. The moment this evanishment was complete, she rose and went to Alice, where she sat staring into the fire, unconscious of the scrutiny she had been undergoing, and, looking up in her face, took her thumb out of her mouth, and said,

"Is the Lord chastening Alice? I wish he would chasten Phosy."

Her face was calm as that of the Sphinx; there was no mist in the depth of her gray eyes, not a cloud on the wide heaven of her forehead.

Was the child crazed? What could the atom mean, with her big eyes looking right into her? Alice never had understood her: it were indeed strange if the less should comprehend the greater! She was not yet capable of recognizing the word of the Lord in the mouth of babes and sucklings. But there was a something in Phosy's face besides its calmness and unin-telligibility. What it was Alice could never have told — yet it did her good. She lifted the child on her lap. There she soon fell asleep. Alice undressed her, laid her in her crib, and went to bed herself.

But, weary as she was, she had to rise again before she got to sleep. Her mistress was again taken ill. Doctor and nurse were sent for in hot haste; hansom cabs came and went throughout the night, like nosiy moths to the one lighted house in the street; there were soft steps within, and doors were gently opened and shut. The waters of Mara had risen and filled the house.

Towards morning they were ebbing slowly away. Letty did not know that her husband was watching by their bedside. The street was quiet now. So was the house. Most of its people had been up throughout the night, but now they had all gone to bed except the strange nurse and Mr. Greatorex.

It was the morning of Christmas Day, and little Phosy knew it in every cranny of her soul. She was not of those who had been up all night, and now she was awake, early and wide, and the moment she awoke she was speculating: He was coming to-day — *how* would he come? Where should she find the baby Jesus? And when would he come? In the morning, or the afternoon, or in the evening? Could such a grief be in store for her as that he would not appear until night, when she would be again in bed? But she would not sleep till all hope was gone. Would everybody be gathered to meet him, or would he show himself to one after another, each alone? Then her turn would be last, and oh, if he would not come to the nursery! But perhaps he would not appear to her at all! — for was she not one whom the Lord did not care to chasten?

Expectation grew and wrought in her until she could lie in bed no longer. Alice was fast asleep. It must be early, but whether it was yet light or not she could not tell for the curtains. Anyhow she would get up and dress, and then she would be ready for Jesus whenever he should come. True, she was not able to dress herself very well, but he would know, and would not mind. She made all the haste she could, consistently with taking pains, and was soon attired after a fashion.

She crept out of the room and down the stair. The house was very still. What if Jesus should come and find nobody awake? Would he go again and give them no presents? She couldn't expect any herself — but might he not let her take theirs for the rest? Perhaps she ought to wake them all, but she dared not without being sure.

On the last landing above the first floor, she saw, by the low gaslight at the end of the corridor, an unknown figure pass the foot of the stair: could she have anything to do with the marvel of the day? The woman looked up, and Phosy dropped the question. Yet she might be a char-woman, whose assistance the expected advent rendered necessary. When she reached the bottom of the stair she saw her disappearing in her step-mother's room. That she did not like. It was the one room into which she could not go. But, as the house was so still, she would search everywhere else, and if she did not find him, would then sit down in the hall and wait for him.

The room next the foot of the stairs, and opposite her stepmother's, was the spare room, with which she associated ideas of state and grandeur: where better could she begin than at the guest-chamber? — There! — Could it be? Yes! — Through the chink of the scarce-closed door she saw light. Either he was already there or there they were expecting him. From that moment she felt as if lifted out of the body. Far exalted above all dread, she peeped modestly in, and then entered. Beyond the foot of the bed, a candle stood on a little low table, but nobody was to be seen. There was a stool near the table: she would sit on it by the candle, and wait for him. But ere she reached it, she caught sight of something upon the bed that drew her thither. She stood entranced. — *Could* it be. — It *might* be. Perhaps he had left it there while he went into her mamma's room with something for her. — The loveliest of dolls ever imagined! She drew nearer. The light was low, and the shadows were many: she could not be sure what it was. But when she had gone close up to it, she concluded with certainty that it was in very truth a doll — perhaps intended for her — but beyond doubt the most exquisite of dolls. She dragged a chair to the bed, got up, pushed her little arms softly under it, and drawing it gently to her, slid down with it. When she felt her feet firm on the floor, filled with the solemn composure of holy awe she carried the gift of the child Jesus to the candle, that she might the better admire its beauty and know its preciousness. But the light had no sooner fallen upon it than a strange undefinable doubt awoke within her. Whatever it was, it was the very essence of loveliness — the tiny darling with its alabaster face, and its delicately modelled hands and fingers! A long nightgown covered the rest. — Was it possible? — Could it be? — Yes, indeed! it must be — it could be nothing else than a real baby! What a goose she had been! Of course it was baby Jesus himself! — for was not this his very own Christmas day on which he was always born? — If she had felt awe of his gift before, what a grandeur of adoring love, what a divine dignity possessed her, holding in her arms the very child himself! One shudder of bliss passed through her, and in an agony of possession she clasped the baby to her great heart — then at once became still with the satisfaction of eternity, with the peace of God. She sat down on the stool, near the little table, with her back to the candle, that its rays should not fall on the eyes of the sleeping Jesus and wake him: there she sat, lost in the very majesty of bliss, at once the mother and the slave of the Lord Jesus.

She sat for a time still as marble waiting for marble to awake, heedful as tenderest woman not to rouse him before his time, though her heart was swelling with the eager petition that he would ask his Father to be as good as chasten her. And as she sat, she began, after her wont, to model her face to the likeness of his, that she might understand his stillness — the absolute peace that dwelt on his countenance. But as she did so, again a sudden doubt invaded her: Jesus lay so very still — never moved, never opened his pale eye-lids! And now set thinking, she noted that he did not breathe. She had seen babies asleep, and their breath came and went —

their little bosoms heaved up and down, and sometimes they would smile, and sometimes they would moan and sigh. But Jesus did none of all these things: was it not strange? And then he was cold — oh, so cold!

A blue silk coverlid lay on the bed: she half rose and dragged it off, and contrived to wind it around herself and the baby. Sad at heart, very sad, but undismayed, she sat and watched him on her lap.

CHAPTER VI

Meantime the morning of Christmas Day grew. The light came and filled the house. The sleepers slept late, but at length they stirred. Alice awoke last — from a troubled sleep, in which the events of the night mingled with her own lost condition and destiny. After all Polly had been kind, she thought, and got Sophy up without disturbing her.

She had been but a few minutes down, when a strange and appalling rumour made itself — I cannot say audible, but — somehow known through the house, and every one hurried up in horrible dismay.

The nurse had gone into the spare room, and missed the little dead thing she had laid there. The bed was between her and Phosy, and she never saw her. The doctor had been sharp with her about something the night before: she now took her revenge in suspicion of him, and after a hasty and fruitless visit of inquiry to the kitchen, hurried to Mr. Greatorex.

The servants crowded to the spare room, and when their master, incredulous indeed, yet shocked at the tidings brought him, hastened to the spot, he found them all in the room, gathered at the foot of the bed. A little sunlight filtered through the red window-curtains, and gave a strange pallid expression to the flame of the candle, which had now burned very low. At first he saw nothing but the group of servants, silent, motionless, with heads leaning forward, intently gazing: he had come just in time: another moment and they would have ruined the lovely sight. He stepped forward, and saw Phosy, half shrouded in blue, the candle behind illuminating the hair she had found too rebellious to brush, and making of it a faint aureole about her head and white face, whence cold and sorrow had driven all the flush, rendering it colourless as that upon her arm which had never seen the light. She had pored on the little face until she knew death, and now she sat a speechless mother of sorrow, bending in the dim light of the tomb over the body of her holy infant.

How it was I cannot tell, but the moment her father saw her she looked up, and the spell of her dumbness broke.

"Jesus is dead," she said, slowly and sadly, but with perfect calmness. "He is dead," she repeated. "He came too early, and there was no one up to take care of him, and he's dead — dead — dead!"

But as she spoke the last words, the frozen lump of agony gave way; the well of her heart suddenly filled, swelled, overflowed; the last word was half sob, half shriek of utter despair and loss.

Alice darted forward and took the dead baby tenderly from her. The same moment her father raised the little mother and clasped her to his bosom. Her arms went round his neck, her head sank on his shoulder, and sobbing in grievous misery, yet already a little comforted, he bore her from the room.

"No, no, Phosy!" they heard him say. "Jesus is not dead, thank God. It is only your little brother that hadn't life enough, and is gone back to God for more."

Weeping the women went down the stairs. Alice's tears were still flowing, when John Jephson entered. Her own troubles forgotten in the emotion of the scene she had just witnessed, she ran to his arms and wept on his bosom.

John stood as one astonied.

"O Lord! this *is* a Christmas!" he sighed at last.

"Oh John!" cried Alice, and tore herself from his embrace, "I forgot! You'll never speak to me again, John! Don't do it, John."

And with the words she gave a stifled cry, and fell a weeping again, behind her two shielding hands.

"Why, Alice! — you ain't married, are you?" gasped John, to whom that was the only possible evil.

"No, John, and never shall be: a respectable man like you would never think of looking twice at a poor girl like me!"

"Let's have one more look anyhow," said John, drawing her hands from her face. "Tell me what's the matter, and if there's anything can be done to right you, I'll work day and night to do it, Alice."

"There's nothing *can* be done, John," replied Alice, and would again have floated out on the ocean of her misery, but in spite of wind and tide, that is sobs and tears, she held on by the shore at his entreaty, and told

26   ❦   THE GIFTS OF THE CHILD CHRIST

her tale, not even omitting the fact that when she went to the eldest of the cousins, inheriting through the misfortune of her and her brother so much more than their expected share, and "demeaned herself" to beg a little help for her brother, who was dying of consumption, he had all but ordered her out of the house, swearing he had nothing to do with her and her brother, and saying she ought to be ashamed to show her face.

"And that when we used to make mud pies together!" concluded Alice with indignation. "There John! you have it all," she added. " — — And now?"

With the word she gave a deep, humbly questioning look into his honest eyes.

"Is that all, Alice?" he asked.

"Yes, John; ain't it enough?" she returned.

"More'n enough," answered John. "I swear to you, Alice, you're worth to me ten times what you would ha' been, even if you'd ha' had me, with ten thousand pounds in your ridicule. Why, my woman, I never saw you look one 'alf so 'an'some as you do now!"

"But the disgrace of it, John!" said Alice, hanging her head, and so hiding the pleasure that would dawn through all the mist of her misery.

"Let your father and mother settle that betwixt 'em, Alice. 'Tain't none o' my business. Please God, we'll do different. — When shall it be, my girl?"

"When you like, John," answered Alice, without raising her head, thoughtfully.

When she had withdrawn herself from the too rigorous embrace with which he received her consent, she remarked —

"I do believe, John, money ain't a good thing! Sure as I live, with the very wind o' that money, the devil entered into me. Didn't you hate me, John? Speak the truth now."

"No, Alice. I did cry a bit over you, though. You *was* possessed like."

"I *was* possessed. I do believe if that money hadn't been took from me, I'd never had had you, John. Ain't it awful to think on?"

"Well, no. O' coorse! How could ye?" said Jephson — with reluctance.

"Now, John, don't yet talk like that, for I won't stand it. Don't you go for to set me up again with excusin' of me. I'm a nasty conceited cat, I am — and all for nothing but mean pride."

"Mind ye, ye're mine now, Alice; an' what's mine's mine, an' I won't have it abused. I knows you twice the woman you was afore, and all the world couldn't gi' me such another Christmas-box — no, not if it was all gold watches and roast beef."

When Mr. Greatorex returned to his wife's room, and thought to find her asleep as he had left her, he was dismayed to hear sounds of soft weeping from the bed. Some tone or stray word, never intended to reach her ear, had been enough to reveal the truth concerning her baby.

"Hush! hush!" he said, with more love in his heart than had moved there for many months, and therefore more in his tone than she had heart for as many; — "if you cry you will be ill. Hush, my dear!"

In a moment, ere he could prevent her, she had flung her arms around his neck as he stooped over her.

"Husband! husband!" she cried, "is it my fault?"

"You behaved perfectly," he returned. "No woman could have been braver."

"Ah, but I wouldn't stay at home when you wanted me."

"Never mind that now, my child," he said.

At the word she pulled his face down to hers.

"I have *you,* and I don't care," he added.

"*Do* you care to have me?" she said, with a sob that ended in a loud cry. "Oh! I don't deserve it. But I *will* be good after this. I promise you I will."

"Then you must begin now, my darling. You must lie perfectly still, and not cry a bit, or you will go after the baby, and I shall be left alone."

She looked up at him with such a light in her face as he had never dreamed of there before. He had never seen her so lovely. Then she withdrew her arms, repressed her tears, smiled, and turned her face away. He put her hands under the clothes, and in a minute or two she was again fast asleep.

CHAPTER VII

That day, when Phosy and her father had sat down to their Christmas dinner, he rose again, and taking her up as she sat, chair and all, set her down close to him, on the other side of the corner of the table. It was the

❧

first of a new covenant between them. The father's eyes having been suddenly opened to her character and preciousness, as well as to his own neglected duty in regard to her, it was as if a well of life had burst forth at his feet. And every day, as he looked in her face and talked to her, it was with more and more respect for what he found in her, with growing tenderness for her predilections, and reverence for the divine idea enclosed in her ignorance, for her childish wisdom, and her calm seeking — until at length he would have been horrified at the thought of training her up in *his* way: had she not a way of her own to go — following — not the dead Jesus, but Him who liveth for evermore? In the endeavour to help her, he had to find his own position towards the truth; and the results were weighty. — Nor did the child's influence work forward merely. In his intercourse with her he was so often reminded of his first wife, and that with the gloss or comment of a childish reproduction, that his memories of her at length grew a little tender, and through the child he began to understand the nature and worth of the mother. In her child she had given him what she could not be herself. Unable to keep up with him, she had handed him her baby, and dropped on the path.

Nor was little Sophy his only comfort. Through their common loss and her husband's tenderness, Letty began to grow a woman. And her growth was the more rapid that, himself taught through Phosy, her husband no longer desired to make her adopt his tastes, and judge with his experiences, but, as became the elder and the tried, entered into her tastes and experiences — became, as it were, a child again with her, that, through the thing she was, he might help the thing she had to be.

As soon as she was able to bear it, he told her the story of the dead Jesus, and with the tale came to her heart love for Phosy. She had lost a son for a season, but she had gained a daughter for ever.

Such were the gifts of the Christ-child brought to one household that Christmas. And the days of the mourning of that household were ended.

Stephen Archer

Stephen Archer was a stationer, bookseller, and newsmonger in one of the suburbs of London. The newspapers hung in a sort of rack at his door, as if for the convenience of the public to help themselves in passing. On his counter lay penny weeklies and books coming out in parts, amongst which the *Family Herald* was in force, and the *London Journal* not to be found. I had occasion once to try the extent of his stock, for I required a good many copies of one of Shakespeare's plays — at a penny, if I could find such. He shook his head, and told me he could not encourage the sale of such productions. This pleased me; for, although it was of little consequence what he thought concerning Shakespeare, it was of the utmost import that he should prefer principle to pence. So I loitered in the shop, looking for something to buy; but there was nothing in the way of literature: his whole stock as far as I could see, consisted of little religious volumes of gay binding and inferior print: he had nothing even from the Halifax press. He was a good-looking fellow, about thirty, with dark eyes, overhanging brows that indicated thought, mouth of character, and no smile. I was interested in him.

I asked if he would mind getting the plays I wanted. He said he would rather not. I bade him good morning.

More than a year after, I saw him again. I had passed his shop many times, but this morning, I forget why, I went in. I could hardly recall the former appearance of the man, so was it swallowed up in a new expression. His face was alive, and his behavior courteous. A similar change had passed upon his stock. There was *Punch* and *Fun* amongst the papers, and tenpenny Shakespeares on the counter, printed on straw-paper, with ugly wood-cuts. The former class of publications had not vanished, but was mingled with cheap editions of some worthy of being called books.

"I see you have changed your mind since I saw you last," I said.

"You have the advantage of me, sir," he returned. "I did not know you were a customer."

"Not much of that," I replied; "only in intention. I wanted you to get me some penny Shakespeares, and you would not take the order."

"Oh! I think I remember," he answered, with just a trace of confusion; adding, with a smile, "I'm married now"; and I fancied I could read a sort of triumph over his former self.

I laughed, of course — the best expression of sympathy at hand — and, after a little talk, left the shop, resolved to look in again soon. Before a month was over, I had made the acquaintance of his wife too, and between them learned so much of their history as to be able to give the following particulars concerning it.

Stephen Archer was one of the deacons, rather a young one perhaps, of a dissenting congregation. The chapel was one of the oldest in the neighborhood, quite triumphant in ugliness, but possessed of a history which gave it high rank with those who frequented it. The sacred odour of the names of pastors who had occupied its pulpit, lingered about its walls — names unknown beyond its precincts, but starry in the eyes of those whose world lay within its tabernacle. People generally do not know what a power some of these small *conventicles* are in the education of the world. If only as an outlet for the energies of men of lowly education and position, who in connexion with most of the churches of the Establishment would find no employment, they are of inestimable value.

To Stephen Archer, for instance, when I saw him first, his chapel was the sole door out of the common world into the infinite. When he entered, as certainly did the awe and the hush of the sacred place overshadow his spirit as if it had been a gorgeous cathedral-house borne aloft upon the joined palms of its Gothic arches. The Master is truer than men think, and the power of His presence, as Browning has so well set forth in his "Christmas Eve," is where two or three are gathered in His name. And inasmuch as Stephen was not a man of imagination, he had the greater need of the undefined influences of the place.

He had been chief in establishing a small mission amongst the poor in the neighborhood, with the working of which he occupied the greater part of his spare time. I will not venture to assert that his mind was pure from the ambition of gathering from these to swell the flock at the little chapel; nay, I will not even assert that there never arose a suggestion of the enemy that the pence of these rescued brands might alleviate the burden upon the heads and shoulders of the poorly prosperous caryatids of his church; but I do say that Stephen was an honest man in the main, ever ready to grow honester: and who can demand more?

One evening, as he was putting up the shutters of his window, his attention was arrested by a shuffling behind him. Glancing round, he set down the shutter, and the next instant boxed a boy's ears, who ran away howling and mildly excavating his eyeballs, while a young, pale-faced woman, with the largest black eyes he had ever see, expostulated with him on the proceeding.

"Oh, sir!" she said, "he wasn't troubling you." There was a touch of indignation in the tone.

"I'm sorry I can't return the compliment," said Stephen, rather illogically. "If I'd ha' known you liked to have your shins kicked, I might ha' let the young rascal alone. But you see I didn't know it."

"He's my brother," said the young woman, conclusively.

"The more shame to him," returned Stephen. "If he'd been your husband, now, there might ha' been more harm than good in interferin', 'cause he'd only give it you the worse after; but brothers! Well, I'm sure it's a pity I interfered."

"I don't see the difference," she retorted, still with offense.

"I beg your pardon, then," said Stephen. "I promise you I won't interfere next time."

So saying, he turned, took up his shutter, and proceeded to close his shop. The young woman walked on.

Stephen gave an inward growl or two at the depravity of human nature, and set out to make his usual visits; but before he reached the place, he had begun to doubt whether the old Adam had not overcome him in the matter of boxing the boy's ears; and the following interviews appeared in consequence less satisfactory than usual. Disappointed with himself, he could not be so hopeful about others.

As he was descending a stair so narrow that it was only just possible for two people to pass, he met the same young woman ascending. Glad of the opportunity, he stepped aside with his best manners and said:

"His attention was arrested by a shuffling behind him"

"I am sorry I offended you this evening. I did not know that the boy was your brother."

"Oh, sir!" she returned — for to one in her position, Stephen Archer was a gentleman: had he not a shop of his own? — "you didn't hurt him much; only I'm so anxious to save him."

"To be sure," returned Stephen, "that is the one thing needful."

"Yes, sir," she rejoined. "I try hard, but boys will be boys."

"There is but one way, you know," said Stephen, following the words with a certain formula which I will not repeat.

The girl stared. "I don't know about that," she said. "What I want is to keep him out of prison. Sometimes I think I shan't be able long. Oh, sir! if you be the gentleman that goes about here, couldn't you help me? I can't get anything for him to do, and I can't be at home to look after him."

"What is he about all day, then?"

"The streets," she answered. "I don't know as he's ever done anything he oughtn't to, but he came home once in a fright, and that breathless with running, that I thought he'd ha' fainted. If I only could get him into a place!"

"Do you live here?" he asked.

"Yes, sir; I do."

At the moment a half-bestial sound below, accompanied by uncertain footsteps, announced the arrival of a drunken bricklayer.

"There's Joe Bradley," she said, in some alarm. "Come into my room, sir, till he's gone up; there's no harm in him when he's sober, but he ain't been sober for a week now."

Stephen obeyed; and she, taking a key from her pocket, and unlocking a door on the landing, led him into a room to which his back-parlour was a paradise. She offered him the only chair in the room, and took her place on the edge of the bed, which showed a clean but much-worn patchwork quilt. Charley slept on the bed, and she on a shake-down in the corner. The room was not untidy, though the walls and floor were not clean; indeed there were not in it articles enough to make it untidy withal.

"Where do you go on Sundays?" asked Stephen.

"Nowheres. I ain't got nobody," she added, with a smile, "to take me nowheres."

"What do you do then?"

"I've plenty to do mending of Charley's trousers. You see they're only shoddy, and as fast as I patch 'em in one place they're out in another."

"But you oughtn't to work Sundays."

"I have heard tell of people as say you oughtn't to work of a Sunday; but where's the differ when you've got a brother to look after? He ain't got no mother."

"But you're breaking the fourth commandment; and you know where people go that do that. You believe in hell, I suppose."

"I always thought that was a bad word."

"To be sure! But it's where you'll go if you break the Sabbath."

"Oh, sir!" she said, bursting into tears, "I don't care what become of me if I could only save that boy."

"What do you mean by *saving* him?"

"Keep him out of prison, to be sure. I shouldn't mind the workus myself, if I could get him into a place."

A place was her heaven, a prison her hell.

Stephen looked at her more attentively. No one who merely glanced at her could help seeing her eyes first, and no one who regarded them could help thinking her nice-looking at least, all in a shabby cotton dress and black shawl as she was. It was only the "penury and pine" that kept her from being beautiful. Her features were both regular and delicate, with an anxious mystery about the thin tremulous lips, and a beseeching look, like that of an animal, in her fine eyes, hazy with the trouble that haunted her mouth. Stephen had the good sense not to press the Sabbath question, and by degrees drew her story from her.

Her father had been a watchmaker, but, giving way to drink, had been, as far back as she could remember, entirely dependent on her mother, who by charing and jobbing managed to keep the family alive. Sara was then the only child, but, within a few months after her father's death, her mother died in giving birth to the boy. With her last breath she had commended him to his sister. Sara had brought him up — how she hardly knew. He had been everything to her. The child that her mother had given her was all her thought. Those who start with the idea "that people with nought are naughty," whose eyes are offended by rags, whose ears cannot distinguish between vulgarity and wickedness, and who think the first duty is care for self, must be excused from believing that Sara Coulter passed through all that had been *decreed* for her without losing her simplicity and purity. But God is in the back slums as certainly as — perhaps to some eyes more evidently than — in Belgravia. That which was the burden of her life — namely, the care of her brother — was her salvation. After hearing her story, which he had to draw from her, because she had no impulse to talk about herself, Stephen went home to turn the matter over in his mind.

The next Sunday, after he had had his dinner, he went out into the same region, and found himself at Sara's door. She was busy over a garment of Charley's, who was sitting on the bed with half a loaf in his hand. When he recognized Stephen he jumped down, and would have rushed from the room; but changing his mind, possibly because of the condition of his lower limbs, he turned, and springing into the bed, scrambled under the counterpane, and drew it over his head.

"I am sorry to see you working on Sunday," Stephen said, with an emphasis that referred to their previous conversation.

"You would not have the boy go naked?" she returned, with again a touch of indignation. She had been thinking how easily a man of Stephen's social position could get him a place if he would. Then recollecting her manners, she added, "I should get him better clothes if he had a place. Wouldn't you like to get a place now, Charley?"

"Yes," said Charley, from under the counterpane, and began to peep at the visitor.

He was not an ill-looking boy — only roguish to a degree. His eyes, as black as his sister's, but only half as big, danced and twinkled with mischief. Archer would have taken him off to his ragged class, but even of rags he had not at the moment the complement necessary for admittance. He left them, therefore, with a few commonplaces of religious phrase, falling utterly meaningless. But he was not one to confine his ministrations to words: he was an honest man. Before the next Sunday it was clear to him that he could do nothing for the soul of Sara until he had taken the weight of her brother off it.

When he called the next Sunday the same vision precisely met his view. She might have been sitting there ever since, with those wonderfully-patched trousers in her hands, and the boy beside her, gnawing at his lump of bread. But many a long seam had passed through her fingers since then, for she worked at a clothes-shop all the week with the sewing-machine, whence arose the possibility of patching Charley's clothes, for the overseer granted her a cutting or two now and then.

After a little chat, Stephen put the question:

"If I find a place for Charley, will you go to Providence Chapel next Sunday?"

"I will go *anywhere* you please, Mr. Archer," she answered, looking up quickly with a flushed face. She would have accompanied him to any casino in London just as readily: her sole thought was to keep Charley out of prison. Her father had been in prison once; to keep her mother's child out of prison was the grand object of her life.

"Well," he resumed, with some hesitation, for he had arrived at the resolution through difficulties, whose fogs yet lingered about him, "if he will be an honest, careful boy, I will take him myself."

"Charley! Charley!" cried Sara, utterly neglectful of the source of the benefaction; and rising, she went to the bed and hugged him.

"Don't, Sara!" said Charley, petulantly. "I don't want girls to squash me. Leave go, I say. You mend my trousers, and I'll take care of *myself.*"

"The little wretch!" thought Stephen.

Sara returned to her seat, and her needle went almost as fast as her sewing-machine. A glow had arisen now, and rested on her pale cheek: Stephen found himself staring at a kind of transfiguration, back from the ghostly to the human. His admiration extended itself to her deft and slender fingers and there brooded until his conscience informed him that he was actually admiring the breaking of the Sabbath; whereupon he rose. But all the time he was about amongst the rest of his people, his thoughts kept wandering back to the desolate room, the thankless boy, and the ministering woman. Before leaving, however, he had arranged with Sara that she should bring her brother to the shop the next day.

The awe with which she entered it was not shared by Charley, who was never ripe for anything but frolic. Had not Stephen been influenced by a desire to do good, and possibly by another feeling too embryonic for detection, he would never have dreamed of making an errand boy of a will-o'-the-wisp. As such, however, he was installed, and from that moment an anxiety unknown before took possession of Stephen's bosom. He was never at ease, for he never knew what the boy might be about. He would have parted with him the first fortnight, but the idea of the prison had passed from Sara's heart into his, and he saw that to turn the boy away from his first place would be to accelerate his gravitation thitherward. He had all the tricks of a newspaper boy indigenous in him. Repeated were the complaints brought to the shop. One time the paper was thrown down the area, and brought into the breakfast-room defiled with wet. At another it was found on the door-step, without the bell having been rung, which could hardly have been from forgetfulness, for Charley's delight was to set the bell ringing furiously, and then wait till the cook appeared, taking good care however to leave space between them for a start. Sometimes the paper was not delivered at all, and Stephen could not help suspecting that he had sold it in the street. Yet both for his sake and Sara's he endured, and did not even box his ears. The boy hardly seemed to be wicked: the spirit that possessed him was rather a *polter-geist,* as the Germans would call it, than a demon.

Meantime, the Sunday after Charley's appointment, Archer, seated in his pew, searched all the chapel for the fulfillment of Sara's part of the agreement, namely her presence. But he could see her nowhere. The fact was, her promise was so easy that she had scarcely thought of it after, not suspecting that Stephen laid any stress upon its fulfillment, and, indeed, not knowing where the chapel was. She had managed to buy a bit of something of the shoddy species, and while Stephen was looking for her in the chapel, she was making a jacket for Charley. Greatly disappointed, and chiefly, I do believe, that she had not kept her word, Stephen went in the afternoon to call upon her.

He found her working away as before, and saving time by taking her dinner while she worked, for a piece of bread lay on the table by her elbow, and beside it a little brown sugar to make the bread go down. The sight went to Stephen's heart, for he had just made his dinner off baked mutton and potatoes, washed down with his half-pint of stout.

"Sara!" he said solemnly, "you promised to come to our chapel, and you have not kept your word." He never thought that "our chapel" was not the landmark of the region.

"Oh, Mr. Archer," she answered, "I didn't know as you cared about it. But," she went on, rising and pushing her bread on one side to make room for her work, "I'll put on my bonnet directly." Then she checked herself, and added, "Oh! I beg your pardon, sir — I'm so shabby! You couldn't be seen with the likes of me."

It touched Stephen's chivalry — and something deeper than chivalry. He had had no intention of walking with her.

"There's no chapel in the afternoon," he said; "but I'll come and fetch you in the evening."

Thus it came about that Sara was seated in Stephen's pew, next to Stephen himself, and Stephen felt a strange pleasure unknown before, like that of the shepherd who having brought the stray back to the fold cares little that its wool is torn by the bushes, and it looks a ragged and disreputable sheep. It was only Sara's wool that might seem disreputable, for she was a very good-faced sheep. He found the hymns for her, and they shared the same book. He did not know then that Sara could not read a word of them.

The gathered people, the stillness, the gaslights, the solemn ascent of the minister into the pulpit, the hearty singing of the congregation, doubtless had their effect upon Sara, for she had never been to a chapel and hardly to any place of assembly before. From all amusements, the burden of Charley and her own retiring nature had kept her back.

But she could make nothing of the sermon. She confessed afterwards that she did not know she had anything to do with it. Like "the Northern Farmer," she took it all for the clergyman's business, which she amongst the rest had to see done. She did not even wonder why Stephen should have wanted to bring her there. She sat when other people sat, pretended to kneel when other people pretended to kneel, and stood up when other people stood up — still brooding upon Charley's jacket.

But Archer's feelings were not those he had expected. He had brought her, intending her to be done good to; but before the sermon was over he wished he had not brought her. He resisted the feeling for a long time, but at length yielded to it entirely; the object of his solicitude all the while conscious only of the lighted stillness and the new barrier between Charley and Newgate. The fact with regard to Stephen was that a certain hard *pan,* occasioned by continual ploughings to the same depth and no deeper, in the soil of his mind, began this night to be broken up from within, and that through the presence of a young woman who did not for herself put together two words of the whole discourse.

The pastor was preaching upon the saying of St. Paul, that he could wish himself accursed from Christ for his brethren. Great part of his sermon was an attempt to prove that he could not have meant what his words implied. For the preacher's mind was so filled with the supposed paramount duty of saving his own soul, that the enthusiasm of the Apostle was simply incredible. Listening with that woman by his side, Stephen for the first time grew doubtful of the wisdom of his pastor. Nor could he endure that such should be the first doctrine Sara heard from his lips. Thus was he already and grandly repaid for his kindness; for the presence of a woman who without any conscious religion was to herself a law of love, brought him so far into sympathy with the mighty soul of St. Paul, that from that moment the blessing of doubt was at work in his, undermining prison walls.

He walked home with Sara almost in silence, for he found it impossible to impress upon her those parts of the sermon with which he had no fault to find, lest she should retort upon that one point. The arrows which Sara escaped, however, could from her ignorance have struck her only with their feather end.

Things proceeded in much the same fashion for a while. Charley went home at night to his sister's lodging, generally more than two hours after leaving the shop, but gave her no new ground of complaint. Every Sunday evening Sara went to the chapel, taking Charley with her when she could persuade him to go; and, in obedience with the supposed wish of Stephen, sat in his pew. He did not go home with her any more for a while, and indeed visited her but seldom, anxious to avoid scandal, more especially as he was a deacon.

But now that Charley was so far safe, Sara's cheek began to generate a little of that celestial rosy red which is the blossom of the woman-plant, although after all it hardly equaled the heart of the blush rose. She grew a little rounder in form too, for she lived rather better now, — buying herself a rasher of bacon twice a week. Hence she began to be in more danger, as any one acquainted with her surroundings will easily comprehend. But what seemed at first the ruin of her hopes dissipated this danger.

One evening, when she returned from her work, she found Stephen in her room. She made him the submissive grateful salutation, half courtesy, half bow, with which she always greeted him, and awaited his will.

"I am very sorry to have to tell you, Sara, that your brother — "

She turned white as a shroud, and her great black eyes grew greater and blacker as she stared in agonized expectancy while Stephen hesitated in search of a better form of communication. Finding none, he blurted out the fact —

" — has robbed me, and run away."

"Don't send him to prison, Mr. Archer," shrieked Sara, and laid herself on the floor at his feet with a groveling motion, as if striving with her mother earth for comfort. There was not a film of art in this. She had never been to a theatre. The natural urging of life gave the truest shape to her entreaty. Her posture was the result of the same feeling which made the nations of old bring their sacrifices to the altar of a deity who, possibly benevolent in the main, had yet cause to be inimical to them. From the prostrate living sacrifice arose the one prayer, "Don't send him to prison; don't send him to prison!"

Stephen gazed at her in bewildered admiration, half divine and all human. A certain consciousness of power had, I confess, a part in his silence, but the only definite shape this consciousness took was of beneficence. Attributing his silence to unwillingness, Sara got half-way from the ground — that is, to her knees — and lifted a face of utter entreaty to the sight of Stephen. I will not say words fail me to describe the intensity of its prayer, for words fail me to describe the commonest phenomenon of nature: all I can is to say, that it made Stephen's heart too large for its confining walls. "Mr. Archer," she said, in a voice hollow with emotion, "I will do *anything* you like. I will be your slave. Don't send Charley to prison."

The words were spoken with a certain strange dignity of self-abnegation. It is not alone the country people of Cumberland or of Scotland, who in their highest moments are capable of poetic utterance.

An indescribable thrill of conscious delight shot through the frame of Stephen as the woman spoke the words. But the gentleman in him triumphed. I would have said *the Christian,* for whatever there was in Stephen of the *gentle* was there in virtue of the *Christian,* only he failed in one point: instead of saying at once, that he had no intention of prosecuting the boy, he pretended, I believe from the satanic delight in power that possesses every man of us, that he would turn it over in his mind. It might have been more dangerous, but it would have been more divine, if he had lifted the kneeling woman to his heart, and told her that not for the wealth of an imagination would he proceed against her brother. The divinity, however, was taking its course, both rough-hewing and shaping the ends of the two.

She rose from the ground, sat on the one chair, with her face to the wall, and wept helplessly, with the added sting, perhaps, of a faint personal disappointment. Stephen failed to attract her notice, and left the room. She started up when she heard the door close, and flew to open it, but was only in time to hear the outer door. She sat down and cried again.

Stephen had gone to find the boy if he might, and bring him to his sister. He ought to have said so, for to permit suffering for the sake of a joyful surprise is not good. Going home first, he was hardly seated in his room, to turn over not the matter but the means, when a knock came to the shop-door, the sole entrance, and there were two policemen bringing the deserter in a cab. He had been run over in the very act of decamping with the contents of the till, had lain all but insensible at the hospital while his broken leg was being set, but, as soon as he came to himself, had gone into such a fury of determination to return to his master, that the house-surgeon saw that the only chance for the ungovernable creature was to yield. Perhaps he had some dim idea of restoring the money ere his master should have discovered its loss. As he was very little, they made a couch for him in the cab, and so sent him.

It would appear that the suffering and the faintness had given his conscience a chance of being heard. The accident was to Charley what the sight of the mountain-peak was to the boy Wordsworth. He was delirious when he arrived, and instead of showing any contrition towards his master, only testified an extravagant joy at finding him again. Stephen had him taken into the back room, and laid upon his own bed. One of the policemen fetched the charwoman, and when she arrived, Stephen went to find Sara.

She was sitting almost as he had left her, with a dull, hopeless look.

"I am sorry to say Charley has had an accident," he said.

She started up and clasped her hands.

"He is not in prison?" she panted in a husky voice.

"No; he is at my house. Come and see him. I don't think he is in any danger, but his leg is broken."

A gleam of joy crossed Sara's countenance. She did not mind the broken leg, for he was safe from her terror. She put on her bonnet, tied the strings with trembling hands, and went with Stephen.

"You see God wants to keep him out of prison too," he said, as they walked along the street.

But to Sara this hardly conveyed an idea. She walked by his side in silence.

"Charley! Charley!" she cried, when she saw him white on the bed, rolling his head from side to side. Charley ordered her away with words awful to hear, but which from him meant no more than words of ordinary temper in the mouth of the well-nurtured man or woman. She had spoiled and indulged him all his life, and now for the first time she was nothing to him, while the master who had lectured and restrained him was everything. When the surgeon wanted to change his dressings, he would not let him touch them till his master came. Before he was able to leave his bed, he had developed for Stephen a terrier-like attachment. But, after the first feverishness was over, his sister waited upon him.

Stephen got a lodging, and abandoned his back room to the brother and sister. But he had to attend to his shop, and therefore saw much of both of them. Finding then to his astonishment that Sara could not read, he gave all his odd moments to her instruction, and her mind being at rest about Charley so long as she had him in bed, her spirit had leisure to think of other things.

She learned rapidly. The lesson-book was of course the New Testament; and Stephen soon discovered that Sara's questions, moving his pity at first because of the ignorance they displayed, always left him thinking about some point that had never occurred to him before; so that at length he regarded Sara as a being of superior intelligence way-laid and obstructed by unfriendly powers upon her path towards the threshold of the kingdom, while she looked up to him as to one supreme in knowledge as in goodness. But she never could understand the pastor. This would have been a great trouble to Stephen, had not his vanity been flattered by her understanding of himself. He did not consider that growing love had enlightened his eyes to see into her heart, and enabled him thus to use an ordinary human language for the embodiment of common-sense ideas; whereas the speech of the pastor contained such an admixture of technicalities as to be unintelligible to the neophyte.

Stephen was now distressed to find that whereas formerly he had received everything without question that his minister spoke, he now in general went home in a doubting, questioning mood, begotten of asking himself what Sara would say. He feared at first that the old Adam was beginning to get the upper hand of him, and that Satan was laying snares for his soul. But when he found at the same time that his conscience was growing more scrupulous concerning his business affairs, his hope sprouted afresh.

One day, after Charley had been out for the first time, Sara, with a little tremor of voice and manner, addressed Stephen thus: —

"I shall take Charley home to-morrow, if you please, Mr. Archer."

"You don't mean to say, Sara, you've been paying for those lodgings all this time?" half-asked, half-exclaimed Stephen.

"Yes, Mr. Archer. We must have somewhere to go to. It ain't easy to get a room at any moment, now them railways is everywheres."

"But I hope as how you're comfortable where you are, Sara?"

"Yes, Mr. Archer. But what am I to do for all your kindness?"

"You can pay me all in a lump, if you like, Sara. Only you don't owe me nothing."

Her colour came and went. She was not used to men. She could not tell what he would have her understand, and could not help trembling.

"What do you mean, Mr Archer?" she faltered out.

"I mean you can give me yourself, Sara, and that'll clear all scores."

"But, Mr. Archer — you've been a-teaching of me good things — You *don't* mean to marry me!" exclaimed Sara, bursting into tears.

"Of course I do, Sara. Don't cry about it. I won't if you don't like."

This is how Stephen came to change his mind about his stock in trade.

The Butcher's Bills

I

Husband and Wife

I am going to tell a story of married life. My title will prepare the reader for something hardly heroic; but I trust it will not be found lacking in the one genuine and worthy interest a tale ought to have — namely, that it presents a door through which we may walk into one region or another of the human heart, and there find ourselves not altogether unacquainted or from home.

There was a law among the Jews which forbade the yoking together of certain animals, either because, being unequal in size or strength, one of them must be oppressed, or for the sake of some lesson thus embodied to the Eastern mind — possibly for both reasons. Half the tragedy would be taken out of social life if this law could be applied to human beings in their various relations. I do not say that this would be well, or that we could afford to lose the result of the tragedy thus occasioned. Neither do I believe that there are so many instances of unequal yoking as the misprising judgments of men by men and women by women might lead us to imagine. Not every one declared by the wisdom of acquaintance to have thrown himself or herself away must therefore be set down as unequally yoked. Or it may even be that the inequality is there, but the loss on the other side. How some people could ever have come together must always be a puzzle until one knows the history of the affair; but not a few whom most of us would judge quite unsuited to each other do yet get on pretty well from the first, and better and better the longer they are together, and that with mutual advantage, improvement, and development. Essential humanity is deeper than the accidents of individuality; the common is more powerful than the peculiar; and the honest heart will always be learning to act more and more in accordance with the laws of its being. It must be of much more consequence to any lady that her husband should be a man on whose word she can depend than that he should be of a gracious presence. But if instead of coming nearer to a true understanding of each other, the two should from the first keep falling asunder, then something tragic may almost be looked for.

Duncan and Lucy Dempster were a couple the very mention of whose Christian names together would have seemed amusing to the friends who had long ceased to talk of their unfitness. Indeed, I doubt if in their innermost privacy they ever addressed each other except as Mr. and Mrs. Dempster. For the first time to see them together, no one could help wondering how the conjunction could have been effected. Dempster was of Scotch descent, but the hereditary high cheek-bone seemed to have got into his nose, which was too heavy a pendant for the low forehead from which it hung. About an inch from the end it took a swift and unexpected curve downwards, and was a curious and abnormal nose, which could not properly be assorted with any known class of noses. A long upper lip, a large, firm, and not quite ugly mouth, with a chin both long and square, completed a face which, with its low forehead, being yet longer than usual, had a particularly equine look. He was rather under the middle height, slender, and well enough made — altogether an ordinary mortal, known on 'Change as an able, keen, and laborious man of business. What his special business was I do not know. He went to the city by the eight o'clock omnibus every morning, dived into a court, entered a little square, rushed up two flights of stairs to a couple of rooms, and sat down in the back one before an office table on a hair-seated chair. It was a dingy place — not so dirty as it looked, I daresay. Even the windows, being of bad glass, did, I believe, look dirtier than they were. It was a place where, so far as the eye of an outsider could tell, much or nothing might be doing. Its occupant always wore his hat in it, and his hat always looked shabby. Some people said he was rich, others that he would be one day. Some said he was a responsible man, whatever the epithet may have been intended to mean. I believe he was quite as honest as the recognized laws of his trade demanded — and for how many could I say more? Nobody said he was avaricious — but then he moved amongst men whose very notion was first to make money, after that to be religious, or to enjoy themselves, as the case might be. And no one either ever said of him that he was a good man, or a generous. He was about forty years of age, looking somehow as if he had never been younger. He had had a fair education — better than is generally considered necessary for mercantile purposes — but it would have been hard to discover any signs of it in the spending of his leisure. On Sunday mornings he went with his wife to church, and when he came home had a good dinner, of which now and then a friend took his share. If no stranger was present he took his wine by himself, and went to sleep in his easy chair of marone-coloured leather, while his wife sat on the other side of the fire if it was winter, or a little way off by the open window if it was summer, gently yawned now and then, and looked at him with eyes a little troubled. Then he went off again by the eight o'clock omnibus on Monday morning, and not an idea more or less had he in his head, not a hair's-breadth of difference was there in his conduct or pursuits, that he had been to church and spent the day out of business. That may, however, for anything I know, have been as much the clergyman's fault as his. He was the sort of man you might call machine-made, one in whom humanity, if in no wise caricatured, was yet in no wise ennobled.

His wife was ten years younger than he — hardly less than beautiful — only that over her countenance seemed to have gathered a kind of haze of commonness. At first sight, notwithstanding, one could not help perceiving that she was china and he was delft. She was graceful as she sat, long-necked, slope-shouldered, and quite as tall as her husband, with a marked daintiness about her in the absence of the extremes of the fashion, in the quality of the lace she wore on her black silk dress, and in the wide white sleeves of fine cambric that covered her arms from the shoulder to the wrist. She had a morally delicate air, a look of scrupulous nicety and lavender-stored linen. She had long dark lashes; and when they rose, the eyelids revealed eyes of uncommon beauty. She had good features, good teeth, and a good complexion. The main feeling she produced and left was of ladyhood — little more.

Sunday afternoon came fifty-two times in the year. I mention this because then always, and nearly then only, could one calculate on seeing them together. It came to them in a suburb of London, and the look of it was dull. Doubtless Mr. Dempster's dinner and his repose after it were interesting to him, but I cannot help thinking his wife found it dreary. She had, however, got used to it. The house was a good old one, of red brick, much larger than they required, but not expensive, and had a general look of the refinement of its mistress. In the summer the windows of the dining-room would generally be open, for they looked into a really lovely garden behind the house, and the scent of the jasmine that crept all around them would come in plentifully. I wonder what the scent of jasmine did in Duncan Dempster's world. Perhaps it never got farther than the general ante-chamber of the sensorium. It often made his wife sad — she could not tell why. To him I daresay it smelt agreeable, but I can hardly believe it ever woke in him the dreamy sensation it gave her — of something she had not had enough of, she could not say what. When the heat was gone off a little he would walk out on the lawn, which was well kept and well watered, with many flowering shrubs about it. Why he did so, I cannot tell. He looked at nothing in particular, only walked about for a few minutes, no doubt derived some pleasure of a mild nature from something, and walked in again to tea. One might have expected he would have cultivated the acquaintance of his garden a little, if it were only for the pleasure the contrast would give him when he got back to his loved office, for a greater contrast could not well have been found than between his dingy dreary haunt on weekdays — a place which nothing but duty could have made other than repugnant to any free soul — and this nest of greenery and light and odour. Sweet scents floated in clouds invisible about the place; flower eyes and stars and bells and bunches shone and glowed and lurked all around; his very feet might have learned a lesson of that which is beyond the sense from the turf he trod; but all the time, if he were not exactly seeing in mind's eye the walls and tables of his office in the City square, his thoughts were not the less brooding over such business as he there transacted. For Mr. Dempster's was not a free soul. How could it be when all his energies were given to making money? This he counted his *calling* — and I believe actually contrived to associate some feeling of duty with the notion of leaving behind him a plump round sum of money, as if money in accumulation and following flood, instead of money in peaceful current, were the good thing for the world! Hence the whole realm of real life, the universe of thought and growth, was a high-hedged park to him, within which he never even tried to look — not even knowing that he was shut out from it, for the hedge was of his own growing. What shall ever wake such a man to a sense of indwelling poverty, or make him

THE BUTCHER'S BILLS

begin to hunger after any lowliest expansion? Does a reader retort, "The man was comfortable, and why should he be troubled?" If the end of being, I answer, is only comfort in self, I yield. But what if there should be at the heart of the universe a Thought to which the being of such men is distasteful? What if to that Thought they look blots in light, ugly things? May there not lie in that direction some possible reason why they should bethink themselves? Dempster, however, was not yet a clinker out of which all the life was burned, however much he looked like one. There was in him that which might yet burn — and give light and heat.

On Sunday evenings Mrs. Dempster would have gladly gone to church again, if only — though to herself she never allowed this for one of her reasons — to slip from under the weight of her husband's presence. He seldom spoke to her more than a sentence at a time, but he did like to have her near him, and I suppose held, through the bare presence, some kind of dull one-sided communication with her; what did a woman know about business? and what did he know about except business? It is true he had a rudimentary pleasure in music — and would sometimes ask her to play to him, when he would listen, and after his fashion enjoy. But although here was a gift that might be developed until his soul could echo the music of the spheres, the embodied souls of Handel or Mendelssohn were to him but clouds of sound wrapped about kernels — let me say of stock or bonds.

For a year or so after their marriage it had been the custom that, the first thing after breakfast on Monday morning, she should bring him her account-book, that they might together go over her week's expenses. She must cultivate the business habits in which, he said, he found her more than deficient. How could he endure in a wife what would have been preposterous in a clerk, and would have led to his immediate dismissal? It was in his eyes necessary that the same strict record of receipt and expenditure should be kept in the household as in the office; how else was one to know in what direction things were going? he said. He required of his wife, therefore, that every individual thing that cost money, even to what she spent upon her own person, should be entered in her book. She had no money of her own, neither did he allow her any special sum for her private needs; but he made her a tolerably liberal weekly allowance, from which she had to pay everything except house-rent and taxes, an arrangement which I cannot believe a good one, as it will inevitably lead some conscientious wives to self-denial severer than necessary, and on the other hand will tempt the vulgar nature to make a purse for herself by means of savings off everybody else. It was especially distasteful to Mrs. Dempster to have to set down every little article of personal requirement that she bought. It would probably have seemed to her but a trifle had they both been young when they married, and had there been that tenderness of love between them which so soon sets everything more than right; but as it was, she could never get over the feeling that the man was strange to her. As it was, she would have got over this. But there was in her a certain constitutional lack of precision, combined with a want of energy and a weakness of will, that rendered her more than careless where her liking was not interested. Hence, while she would have been horrified at playing a wrong note or singing out of tune, she not only had no anxiety, for the thing's own sake, to have her accounts correct, but shrunk from every effort in that direction. Now I can perfectly understand her recoil from the whole affair, with her added dislike to the smallness of the thing required of her; but seeing she did begin with doing it after a fashion, it is not so easy to understand why, doing it, she should not make a consolation of doing it with absolute exactness. Not even her dread of her husband's dissatisfaction — which was by no means small — could prevail to make her, instead of still trusting a memory that constantly placed her false, put down a thing at once, nor postpone it to a far less convenient season. Hence it came that her accounts, though never much out, never balanced; and the weekly audit, while it grew more and more irksome to the one, grew more and more unsatisfactory to the other. For to Mr. Dempster's dusty eyes exactitude wore the robe of rectitude, and before long, precisely and merely from the continued unsatisfactory condition of her accounts, he began, in a hidden corner of his righteous soul, to reflect on the moral condition of his wife herself as unsatisfactory. Now such it certainly was, but he was not the man to judge it correctly, or to perceive the true significance of her failing. In business, while scrupulous as to the requirements of custom and recognized right, he nevertheless did things from which her soul would have recoiled like "the tender horns of cockled snails"; yet it was to him not merely a strange and inexplicable fact that she should *never* be able to show to a penny, nay, often not to a shilling or eighteenpence, how the week's allowance went, but a painful one as indicating something beyond perversity. And truly it was no very hard task he required of her, for, seeing they had no children, only three servants, and saw little company, her housekeeping could not be a very heavy or involved affair. Perhaps if it had been more difficult she would have done it better, but anyhow she hated the whole thing, procrastinated, and setting down several things together, was *sure* to forget some article or mistake some price; yet not one atom more would she distrust her memory the next time she was tempted. But it was a small fault at worst, and if her husband had loved her enough to understand the bearings of it in relation to her mental and moral condition he would have tried to content himself that at least she did not exceed her allowance; and would of all things have avoided making such a matter of burden upon the consciousness of one so differently educated, if not constituted, from himself. It is but fair to add on the other side that, if she had loved him after anything like a wifely ideal, which I confess was not yet possible to her, it would not have been many weeks before she had a first correct account to show him. Convinced, at length, that accuracy was not to be had from her, and satisfying himself with dissatisfaction, he one morning threw from him the little ruled book, and declared, in a wrath which he sought to smother into dignified but hopeless rebuke, that he would trouble himself with her no further. She burst into tears, took up the book, left the room, cried a little, resolved to astonish him the next Monday, and never set down another item. When it came, and breakfast was over, he gave her the usual cheque, and left at once for town. Nor had the accounts ever again been alluded to between them.

Now this might have been very well, or at least not very ill, if both had done tolerably well thereafter — that is, if the one had continued to attend to her expenditure as well as before, and the other, when he threw away the account-book, had dismissed from his mind the whole matter. But Dempster was one of those dangerous men — more dangerous, however, to themselves than to others — who never forget, that is, get over, an offense or disappointment. They respect themselves so much, and, out of their respect for themselves, build so much upon success, set so much by never being defeated but always gaining their point, that when they are driven to confess themselves foiled, the confession is made from the "poor dumb mouth" of a wound that cannot be healed. It is there for ever — will be there at least until they find another God to worship than their own paltry selves. Hence it came that the bourn between the two spiritual estates yawned a little wider at one point, and a mist of dissatisfaction would not infrequently rise from a certain stagnant pool in its hollow. The cause was paltry in one sense, but nothing to which belongs the name of

Cause can fail to mingle the element of awfulness even with its paltriness. Its worst effect was that it hindered approximation in other parts of their marching natures.

And as to Mrs. Dempster, I am sorry for the apparent justification which what I have to confess concerning her must give to the severe whims of such husbands as hers: from that very Monday morning she began to grow a little careless about her expenditure — which she had never been before. By degrees bill after bill was allowed to filch from the provision of the following week, and when that was devoured, then from that of the week after. It was not that she was in the least more expensive upon herself, or that she consciously wasted anything; but, altogether averse to house-keeping, she ceased to exercise the same outlook upon the expenditure of the house, did not keep her horses together, left the management more and more to her cook; while the consciousness that she was not doing her duty made her more and more uncomfortable, and the knowledge that things were going farther and farther wrong, made her hate the idea of accounts worse and worse, until she came at length to regard them with such a loathing as might have fitted some extreme of moral evil. The bills which were supposed by her husband to be regularly settled every week were at last months behind, and the week's money spent in meeting the most pressing of its demands, while what it could no longer cover was cast upon the growing heap of evil for the time to come.

I must say this for her, however, that there was a small sum of money she expected on the death of a crazy aunt, which, if she could but lay hold of it without her husband's knowledge, she meant to devote to the clearing off of everything, when she vowed to herself to do better in the time to come.

The worst thing in it all was that her fear of her husband kept increasing, and that she felt more and more uncomfortable in his presence. Hence that troubled look in her eye, always more marked when her husband sat dozing in his chair on a Sunday afternoon.

It was natural, too, that, although they never quarrelled, their inter-course should not grow of a more tender character. Seldom was there a salient point in their few scattered sentences of conversation, except, indeed, it were some piece of news either had to communicate. Occasion-ally the wife read something from the newspaper, but never except at her husband's request. In general he enjoyed his newspaper over a chop at his office. Two or three times since their marriage — now eight years — he had made a transient resolve pointing at the improvement of her mind, and to that end had taken from his great glass-armoured bookcase some *standard* work — invariably, I believe, upon party-politics — from which he had made her read him a chapter. But, unhappily, she had always got to the end of it without gaining the slightest glimmer of true notion of what the author was driving at.

It almost moves me to pity to think of the vagueness of that rudimentary humanity in Mr. Dempster which made him dream of doing something to improve his wife's mind. What did he ever do to improve his own? It is hard to understand how horses find themselves so comfortable in their stables that, be the day ever so fine, the country ever so lovely, the air ever so exhilarating, they are always rejoiced to get back into their dull twilight: it is harder to me to understand how Mr. Dempster could be so comfortable in his own mind that he never wanted to get out of it, even at the risk of being beside himself; but no doubt the dimness of its twilight had a good deal to do with his content. And then there is that in every human mind which no man's neighbour, nay, no man himself, can understand. My neighbour may in his turn be regarding my mind as a gloomy place to live in, while I find it no undesirable residence — though chiefly because of the number of windows it affords me for looking out of it. Still, if Dempster's dingy office in the City was not altogether a sufficing type of the mind that used it, I consider it a very fairly good one.

But wherein was Mrs. Dempster so very different from her husband as I rudely fancy some of my readers imagining her? Whatever may have been her reasons for marrying him — one would suppose they must have been weighty — to do so she must have been in a very undeveloped condition, and in that condition she still remained. I do not mean that she was less developed than ninety-nine out of the hundred: most women affect me only as valuable crude material out of which precious things are making. How much they might be, just be, shall be! For now they stand like so many Lot's-wives — some many rough-hewn marble blocks, rather, of which a Divinity is having the ends. Mrs. Dempster had all the making of a lovely woman, but notwithstanding her grace, her beauty, her sweetness, her lark-like ballading too, she was a very ordinary woman in that region of her which knew what she meant when she said "I." Of this fact she had hardly a suspicion, however; for until aspiration brings humility, people are generally pretty well satisfied with themselves, having no idea what poor creatures they are. She saw in her mirror a superior woman, regarded herself as one of the finer works of creation. The worst was that from the first she had counted herself superior to her husband, and in marrying him had felt not merely that she was conferring a favour, which every husband would allow, but that she was lowering herself without elevating him. Now it is true that she was pleasanter to look at, that her manners were sweeter, and her notions of the becoming far less easily satisfied than his; also that she was a little less deficient in vague reverence for certain forms of the higher than he. But I know of nothing in her to determine her classification as of greater value than he, except indeed that she was on the whole rather more honest. She read novels and he did not; she passed shallow judgment, where he scorned to judge; she read all the middling poetry that came in her way, and copied books full of it; but she could no more have appreciated one of Milton's or Shakespeare's smallest powers than she could have laughed over a page of Chinese. She liked to hear that and that popular preacher, and when her husband called his sermons humbug, she heard it with a shocked countenance; but was she better or worse than her husband when, admiring them as she did, she permitted them to have no more influence upon her conduct than if they had been the merest humbug ever uttered by ambitious demagogue? In truth, I cannot see that in the matter of worth there was much as yet to choose between them.

It is hardly necessary, then, to say that there was little appreciable approximation of any kind going on between them. If only they would have read Dickens together! Who knows what might have come of it! But this dull close animal proximity, without the smallest conscious nearness of heart or mind or soul — and so little chance, from very lacking of wants, for showing each other kindnesses — surely it is a killing sort of thing! And yet, and yet, there is always a something — call it habit, or any poorest name you please — grows up between two who are much together, at least when they neither quarrel nor thwart each other's designs, which, tending with its roots towards the deeper human, blossoms into — a wretched little flower indeed, yet afar off partaking of the nature of love. The Something seldom reveals its existence until they are parted. I suspect that with not a few, Death is the love-messenger at the stroke of whose dart the stream of love first begins to flow in the selfish bosom.

It is now necessary to mention a little break in the monotony of Mrs. Dempster's life, which, but for what came afterwards, could claim no record. One morning her page announced Major Strong, and possibly she received the gentleman who entered with a brighter face than she had ever shown her husband. The major had just arrived from India. He had been much at her father's house while she was yet a mere girl, being then engaged to one of her sisters, who died after he went abroad, and before he could return to marry her. He was now a widower, a fine-looking, frank, manly fellow. The expression of his countenance was little altered, and the sight of him revived in the memory of Mrs. Dempster many recollections of a happy girlhood, when the prospect of such a life as she now led with tolerable content would have seemed simply unendurable. When her husband came home she told him as much as he cared to hear of the visitor she had had, and he made no objection to her asking him to dine the next Sunday. When he arrived Mr. Dempster saw a man of his own age, bronzed and big, with not much waist left, but a good carriage and pleasant face. He made himself agreeable at dinner, appreciated his host's wine, and told good stories that pleased the business man as showing that he knew "what was what." He accorded him his more particular approval, speaking to his wife, on the ground that he was a man of the world, with none of the army slang about him. Mr. Dempster was not aware that he had himself more business peculiarities than any officer in her majesty's service had military ones.

After this Major Strong frequently called upon Mrs. Dempster. They were good friends, and did each other no harm whatever, and the husband neither showed nor felt the least jealousy. They sang together, occasionally went out shopping, and three or four times went together to the play. Mr. Dempster, so long as he had his usual comforts, did not pine in his wife's absence, but did show a little more pleasure when she came home to him than usually when he came home to her. This lasted for a few months. Then the major went back to India, and for a time the lady missed him a good deal, which, considering the dulness of her life, was not very surprising or reprehensible.

II

An Astonishment

Now comes the strange part of my story.

One evening the housemaid opened the door to Mr. Dempster on his return from the city; and perhaps the fact that it was the maid, and not the page as usual, roused his observation, which, except in business matters, was not remarkably operative. He glanced at the young woman, when an eye far less keen than his could not have failed to remark a strangely excited expression on her countenance.

"Where is the boy?" he asked

"Just run to the doctor's, sir," she answered.

Then first he remembered that when he left in the morning his wife had been feeling altogether well, but he had never thought of her since.

"How is your mistress?" he said.

"She's rather poorly, sir, but — but — she's as well as could be expected."

"What does the fool mean?" said Dempster to himself, and very nearly said it aloud, for he was not over polite to any in his service. But he did not say it aloud. He advanced into the hall with deliberation, and made for the stair.

"Oh, please, sir," the maid cried in a tone of perturbation, when, turning from shutting the door, she saw his intention, "you can't go up to mis'ess's room just at this minute, sir. Please go in the dining-room, sir."

"What do you mean?" he asked, turning angrily upon the girl, for of all things he hated mystery.

Like every one else in the house, and office both, she stood in awe of him, and his look frightened her.

"Please go in the dining-room," she gasped entreatingly.

"What!" he said and did turn towards the dining-room, "is your mistress so ill she can't see me?"

"Oh, no, sir! — at least I don't know exactly. Cook's with her, sir. She's over the worst, anyhow."

"What on earth do you mean, girl? Speak out, will you? What is the matter with your mistress?"

As he spoke he stepped into the room, the maid following him. The same moment he spied a whitish bundle of something on the rug in front of the fire.

"What do you mean by leaving things like that in the dining-room?" he went on more angrily still.

"Please, sir," answered the girl, going and lifting the bundle carefully, "it's the baby!"

"The baby!" shouted Mr. Dempster, and looked at her from head to foot. "What baby?" Then bethinking himself that it must belong to some visitor in the drawing-room with his wife, he moderated his tone. "Make haste; take it away!" he said. "I don't want babies here! There's a time and a place for everything! — What *are* you about?"

For, instead of obeying her master and taking it away, the maid was carefully looking in the blanket for the baby. Having found it and turned aside the covering from its face, she came nearer, and holding up the little vision, about the size and colour of a roll of red wax taper, said: —

"Look at it, sir! It's your own, and worth looking at."

Never before had she dared speak to him so!

I will not venture to assert that Mr. Dempster turned white, but his countenance changed, and he dropped into the chair behind him, feeling less of a business man than had been his consciousness for the last twenty years. He was hit hard. The absolutely Incredible had hit him. Babies might be born in a day, but surely not without previous preparation on the part of Nature at least, if not on that of the mother; and in this case if the mother had prepared herself, certainly she had not prepared him for the event. It was as if the treasures of Nature's germens were tumbling all together. His head swam. He could not speak a word.

"Yes, sir," the maid went on, relieved of her trepidation in perceiving that her master too was mortal, and that her word had such power over him — proud also of knowing more of his concerns than he did himself, "she was took about an hour and a half ago. We've kep' sendin' an' sendin' after the doctor, but he ain't never been yet; only cook, she knows a deal an' she says she's been very bad, sir. But the young gentleman come at last, bless him! and now she's doing' as well as could be expected, sir — cook says."

"God bless me!" said the astonished father, and relapsed into the silence of bewilderment.

Eight years married with never a glimmer of offspring — and now, all at once, and without a whisper of warning, the father of a "young gentleman!" How could it be other than perplexing — discomposing, indeed! — yet it was right pleasant too. Only it would have been more pleasant if experience could have justified the affair! Nature — no, not Nature — or, if Nature, then Nature sure in some unnatural mood, had stolen a march upon him, had gone contrary to all that had ever been revealed of her doings before! and why had she pitched on him — just him, Duncan Dempster, to exercise one of her more grotesque and wayward moods upon? — to play at hide-and-seek with after this fashion? She had not treated him with exactly proper respect, he thought, or, rather vaguely felt.

"Business is business," he remarked, under his breath, "and this cannot be called proper business behaviour. What is there about me to make game of? Really, my wife ought — — "

What his wife ought or ought not to have done, however, had not yet made itself clear to him, and his endeavour to excogitate being in that direction broken off, gave way to the pleasure of knowing himself a father, or perhaps more truly of having an heir. In the strength of it he rose, went to the cellaret, and poured himself out a glass of his favourite port, which he sat down to drink in silence and meditation. He was rather a picture just then and there, though not a very lovely one, seated, with his hat still on his head, in the middle of the room, upon a chair half-way between the dining-table and the sideboard, with his glass of wine in his hand. He was pondering partly the pleasure, but still mainly the peculiarity of his position. A bishop once told me that, shortly after he had been raised to the episcopal dignity, a friend's horses, whose driver had tumbled off the box drunk, ran away with him and upset the carriage. He crept out of the window over his head, and the first thought that came to him as he sat perched on the side of the carriage, while it was jumbled along by the maddened horses, was, "What do bishops do in such circumstances?" Equally perplexing was the question Dempster had to ask himself: how husbands who, after being married eight years, suddenly and unexpectedly received the gift of a first-born, were in the habit of comporting themselves! He poured himself out another glass, and with it came the reflection, both amusing and consoling, that his brother, who was confidently expecting his tidy five figures to crown the earthly bliss of one or more of his large family some day, would be equally but less agreeably surprised. "Serve him right!" he said to himself. "What business have they to be looking out for my death?" And for a moment the heavens appeared a little more just than he was ordinarily in the habit of regarding them. He said to himself he would work harder than ever now. There would now be some good in making money! He had never given his mind to it yet, he said: now the world should see what he could do when he did give his mind to it!

Hitherto gathering had been his main pleasure, but with the thought of his money would now not seldom be mingled the thought of the little thing in the blanket! He began to find himself strangely happy. I use the wrong phrase — for the fact is, he had never yet found himself at all, he knew nothing of the person except a self-painted and immensely flattered portrait that hung in the innermost chamber of his heart — I mean the innermost chamber he knew anything of: there were many chambers there of which he did not even know the doors. Yet a few minutes as he sat there, and he was actually cherishing a little pride in the wife who had done so much better for him than he had at length come to expect. If not a good accountant, she was at least a good wife, and a very fair housekeeper: he had no doubt she would prove a good mother. He would gladly have gone to her at once, to let her know how much he was pleased with her behaviour. As for that little bit of red clay — "terra cotta," he called it to himself, as he looked round with a smile at the blanket, which the house-maid had replaced on the rug before the fire — who could imagine him a potentate upon 'Change — perhaps in time a director of European affairs! He was not in the way of joking — of all things about money; the very thought of business filled him from top to toe with seriousness; but he did make that small joke, and accompany it with a grim smile.

He was startled from his musing by the entrance of the doctor, who had in the meantime arrived and seen the lady, and now came to look at the baby. He congratulated Mr. Dempster on having at length a son and heir, but warned him that his wife was far from being beyond danger yet. The whole thing was entirely out of the common, he said, and she must be taken the greatest possible care of. The words woke a gentle pity in the heart of the man, for by nature all men have some tenderness for women in such circumstances, but they did not trouble him greatly — for such dangers belonged to their calling, their *business* in life, and, doubtless, if she had attended to that business earlier she would have found it easier.

"Did you ever know such a thing before, doctor?" he asked, with the importance of one honoured by a personal visit from the Marvellous.

"Never in my own practice," answered the doctor, whom the cook had instructed in the wonders of the case, "but I have read of such a thing." And Mr. Dempster swelled like a turkey-cock.

It was several days before he was allowed to see the mother. Perhaps had she expressed a strong desire to see him, it might have been risked sooner, but she had neither expressed nor manifested any. He kissed her, spoke a few stupid words in a kind tone, asking her how she did, but paying no heed to her answer, and turned aside to look at the baby.

Mrs. Dempster recovered but slowly, and not very satisfactorily. She did not seem to care much about the child. She tried to nurse him, but was not very successful. She took him when the nurse brought him, and yielded him again with the same indifference, showing neither pleasure to receive nor unwillingness to part with him. The nurse did not fail to observe it and remark upon it: *she* had never seen a mother care so little for her child! there was little of the mother in *her* any way! it was no wonder she was so long about it. It troubled the father a little that she should not care for his child: some slight fermentation had commenced in the seemingly dead mass of human affection that had lain so long neglected in his being, and it seemed strange to him that, while he was living for the child in the City, she should be so indifferent to him at home. For already he had begun to keep his vow, already his greater keenness in business was remarked in the City. But it boded little good for either that the gift of God should stir up in him the worship of Mammon. More sons are damned by their fathers' money than by anything else whatever outside of themselves.

There was the excuse to be made for Mrs. Dempster that she continued far from strong — and her husband made it: he would have made it more heartily if he had himself ever in his life known what it was to be ill. By degrees she grew stronger, however, until, to persons who had not known her before, she would have seemed in tolerable health. For a week or two after she was again going about the house, she continued to nurse the baby, but after that she became unable to do so, and therewith began to neglect him entirely. She never asked to see him, and when the nurse brought him would turn her head aside, and tell her to take it away. So far from his being a pleasure to her, the very sight of the child brought the hot dew upon her forehead. Her husband frowned and wondered, but, unaccustomed to open his mind either to her or to any one else, not unwisely sought to understand the thing before speaking of it, and in the meantime commenced a genuine attempt to make up to the baby for his

THE BUTCHER'S BILLS

mother's neglect. Almost without a notion how even to take him in his arms, he would now send for him the moment he had had his tea, and after a fashion, ludicrous in the eyes of the nurse, would dandle and caress him, and strut about with him before his wife, glancing up at her every now and then, to point the lesson that such was the manner in which a parent ought to behave to a child. In his presence she never made any active show of her dislike, but her look seemed all the time fixed on something far away, as if she had nothing to do with the affair.

III

Another Astonishment

But a second and very different astonishment awaited Mr. Dempster. Again one evening, on his return from the City, he saw a strange look on the face of the girl who opened the door — but this time it was a look of fear.

"Well?" he said, in a tone at once alarmed and peremptory.

She made no answer, but turned whiter than before.

"Where is your mistress?" he demanded.

"Nobody knows, sir," she answered.

"Nobody knows! What would you have me understand by such an answer?"

"It's the bare truth, sir. Nobody knows where she is."

"God bless me!" cried the husband. "What does it all mean?"

And again he sunk down upon a chair — this time in the hall, and stared at the girl as if waiting further enlightenment.

But there was little enough to be had. Only one point was clear: his wife was nowhere to be found. He sent for every one in the house, and cross-questioned each to discover the last occasion on which she had been seen. It was some time since she had been missed; how long before that she had been seen there was no certainty to be had. He ran to the doctor, then from one to another of her acquaintance, then to her mother, who lived on the opposite side of London. She, like the rest, could tell him nothing. In her anxiety she would have gone back with him, but he was surly, and would not allow her. It was getting towards morning before he reached home, but no relieving news awaited him. What to think was as much a perplexity to him as what to do. He was not in the agony in which a man would have been who thoroughly loved his wife, but he cared enough about her to feel uncomfortable; and the cries of the child, who was suffering from some ailment, made him miserable: in his perplexity and dull sense of helplessness he wondered whether she might not have given the baby poison before she went. Then the thing would make such a talk! and, of all things, Duncan Dempster hated being talked about. How busy people's brains would be with all his affairs! How many explanations of the mystery would be suggested on 'Change! Some would say, "What business had a man like him with a fine lady for a wife? one so much younger than himself too!" He could remember making some remark of another, before he was married. "Served him right!" they would say. And with that the first movement of suspicion awoke in him — purely and solely from his own mind's reflection of the imagined minds of others. While in his mind's ear he heard them talking, almost before he knew what they meant the words came to him: "There was that Major Strong, you know!"

"She's gone to him!" he cried aloud, and, springing from the bed on which he had thrown himself, he paced the chamber in a fury. He had no word for it but hers that he was now in India! They had only been waiting till — By heaven, that child was none of his! And therewith rushed into his mind the conviction that everything was thus explained. No man ever yet entertained an unhappy suspicion, but straightway an army of proofs positive came crowding to the service of the lie. It is astounding with what manifest probability everything will fall in to prove that a fact which has no foundation whatever! There is no end to the perfection with which a man may fool himself while taking absolute precautions against being fooled by others. Every fact, being a living fact, has endless sides and relations; but of all these, the man whose being hangs upon one thought, will see only those sides and relations which fall in with that thought. Dempster even recalled the words of the maid, "It's mis'ess's," as embodying the girl's belief that it was not master's. Where a man, whether by nature jealous or not, is in a jealous condition, there is no need of an Iago to parade before him the proofs of his wrong. It was because Shakespeare would neither have Desdemona less than perfect, nor Othello other than the most trusting and least suspicious of men, that he had to invent an all but incredible villain to effect the needful catastrophe.

But why should a man, who has cared so little for his wife, become instantly, upon the bare suspicion, so utter a prey to consuming misery? There was a character in his suffering which could not be attributed to any degree of anger, shame, or dread of ridicule. The truth was, there lay in his being a possibility of love to his wife far beyond anything his miserably stunted consciousness had an idea of; and the conviction of her faithlessness now wrought upon him in the office of Death, to let him know what he had lost. It magnified her beauty in his eyes, her gentleness, her grace; and he thought with a pang how little he had made of her or it.

But the next moment wrath at the idea of another man's child being imposed upon him as his, with the consequent loss of his precious money, swept every other feeling before it. For by law the child was his, whoever might be the father of it. During a whole minute he felt on the point of tying a stone about its neck, carrying it out, and throwing it into the river Lea. Then, with the laugh of a hyena, he set about arranging in his mind the proofs of her guilt. First came eight childless years with himself; next the concealment of her condition, and the absurd pretense that she had known nothing of it; then the trouble of mind into which she had fallen; then her strange unnatural aversion to her own child; and now, last of all, conclusive of a guilty conscience, her flight from his house. He would give himself no trouble to find her; why should he search after his own shame! He would neither attempt to conceal nor to explain the fact that she had left him — people might say what they pleased — try him for murder if they liked! As to the child she had so kindly left to console him for her absence, he would not drown him, neither would he bring him up in his house; he would give him an ordinary education, and apprentice him to a trade. For his money, he would leave it to a hospital — a rich one, able to defend his will if disputed. For what was the child? A monster — a creature that had no right to existence!

Not one of those who knew him best would have believed him capable of being so moved, nor did one of them now know it, for he hid his suffering with the success of a man not unaccustomed to make a mask of his face. There are not a few men who, except something of the nature of a catastrophe befall them, will pass through life without having or affording a suspicion of what is in them. Everything hitherto had tended to suppress the live elements of Duncan Dempster; but now, like the fire of a volcano in a land of ice, the vitality in him had begun to show itself.

Sheer weariness drove him, as the morning began to break, to lie down again; but he neither undressed nor slept, and rose at his usual hour. When he entered the dining-room, where breakfast was laid as usual — only for one instead of two — he found by his plate, among letters addressed to his wife, a packet directed to himself. It had not been through the post, and the address was in his wife's hand. He opened it. A sheet of paper was wrapped around a roll of unpaid butcher's bills, amounting to something like eighty pounds, and a note from the butcher craving immediate settlement. On the sheet of paper was written, also in his wife's hand, these words: "I am quite unworthy of being your wife any longer"; that was all.

Now here, to a man who had loved her enough to understand her, was a clue to the whole — to Dempster it was the strongest possible confirmation of what he had already concluded. To him it appeared as certain as anything he called truth, that for years, while keeping a fair face to her husband — a man who had never refused her anything — he did not recall the fact that almost never had she asked or he offered anything — she had been deceiving him, spending money she would not account for, pretending to pay everything when she had been ruining his credit with the neighbourhood, making him, a far richer man than any but himself knew, appear to be living beyond his means, when he was every month investing far more than he spent. It was injury upon injury! Then, as a last mark of her contempt, she had taken pains that these beggarly butcher's bills should reach him from her own hand! He would trouble himself about such a woman not a moment longer!

He went from breakfast to his omnibus as usual, walked straight to his office, and spent the day according to custom. I need hardly say that the first thing he did was to write a cheque for the butcher. He made no further inquiry after her whatever, nor was any made of him there, for scarcely one of the people with whom he did business had been to his house, or had even seen his wife.

In the suburb where he lived it was different; but he paid no heed to any inquiry, beyond saying he knew nothing about her. To her relatives he said that if they wanted her they might find her for themselves. She had gone to please herself, and he was not going to ruin himself by running about the world after her.

Night after night he came home to his desolate house; took no comfort from his child; made no confession that he stood in need of comfort. But he had a dull sensation as if the sun had forsaken the world, and an endless night had begun. The simile, of course, is mine — the sensation only was his; *he* could never have expressed anything that went on in the region wherein men suffer.

A few days made a marked difference in his appearance. He was a hard man; but not so hard as people had thought him; and besides, *no* man can rule his own spirit except he has the spirit of right on his side, neither is any man proof against the inroads of good. Even Lady Macbeth was defeated by the imagination she had braved. Add to this, that no man can, even by those who understand him best, be labelled as a box containing such and such elements, for the humanity in him is deeper than any individuality, and may manifest itself at some crisis in a way altogether beside expectation.

His feeling was not at first of an elevated kind. After the grinding wrath had abated, self-pity came largely to the surface — not by any means a grand emotion, though very dear to boys and girls in their first consciousness of self, and in them pardonable enough. On the same ground it must be pardoned in a man who, with all his experience of the world, was more ignorant of the region of emotion, and more undeveloped morally, than multitudes of children: in him it was an indication that the shell was beginning to break. He said to himself that he was old beside her, and that she had begun to weary of him, and despise him. Gradually upon this, however, supervened at intervals a faint shadow of pity for her who could not have been happy or she would not have left him.

Days and weeks passed, and there was no sign of Mrs. Dempster. The child was not sent out to nurse, and throve well enough. His father never took the least notice of him.

IV

What It Meant

Some of my readers, perhaps all of them, will have concluded that Mrs. Dempster was a little out of her mind. Such, indeed, was the fact, and one not greatly to be wondered at, after such a peculiar experience as she had had. Some small degree of congestion, and the consequent pressure on some portion of the brain, had sent certain faculties to sleep, and, perhaps, roused others into morbid activity. That it is impossible to tell where sanity ends and insanity begins, is a trite remark indeed; but like many things which it is useless to say, it has the more need to be thought of. If I yield to an impulse of which I know I shall be ashamed, is it not the act of a madman? And may not the act lead to a habit, and at length to a despised, perhaps feared and hated, old age, twisting at the ragged ends of a miserable life?

However certain it is that mental disorder had to do with Mrs. Dempster's departure from her home, it is almost as certain she would never have gone had it not been for the unpaid bills haunting her consciousness, a combination of demon and ghost. The misery had all the time been growing upon her, and must have had no small share in the subversion of her microcosm. When that was effected, the evil thing that lay at the root of it all rose and pounced upon her. Wrong is its own avenger. She had been doing wrong, and knowingly for years, and now the plant of evil was blossoming towards its fruit. If one say the evil was but a trifle, I take her judgment, not his, upon that. She had been lazy towards duty, had persistently turned aside from what she knew to be her business, until she dared not even look at it. And now that the crisis was at hand, as omened by that letter from the butcher, with the sense of her wrong-doing was mingled the terror of her husband. What would he think, say, and do? Not yet had she, after all these years, any deep insight into his character; else perhaps she might have read there that, much as he loved money, the pleasure of seeing signal failure follow the neglect of his instructions would quite compensate him for the loss. What the bills amounted to, she had not an idea. Not until she had made up her mind to leave her home could she muster the courage to get them together. Then she even counted up the total and set down the sum in her memory — which sum thereafter haunted her like the name of her devil.

As to the making up of her mind — she could remember very little of that process — or indeed of the turning of her resolve into action. She left the house in the plainest dress her wardrobe could afford her, and with just one half-crown in her pocket. Her design was to seek a situation, as a refuge from her husband and his wrath. It was a curious thing, that, while it gave her no trouble to leave her baby, whom indeed she had not that day seen, and to whom for some time she had ceased to be necessary, her only notion was to get a place as nurse.

At that time, I presume, there were few or no such offices for engaging servants as are now common; at all events, the plan Mrs. Dempster took, when she had reached a part of London she judged sufficiently distant for her purpose, was to go from shop to shop inquiring after a situation. But she met with no prospect of success, and at last, greatly in need of rest and refreshment, went into a small coffee shop. The woman who kept it was taken by her appearance, her manners, and her evident trouble, and, happening to have heard of a lady who wanted a nurse, gave her the address. She went at once, and applied for the place. The lady was much pleased with her, and agreed to take her, provided she received a satisfactory character of her. For such a demand Mrs. Dempster was unprepared; she had never thought what reference she could give, and, her resources for deception easily exhausted, gave, driven to extremity, the name and address of her mother. So met the extremes of loss and salvation! She returned to the coffee shop, and the lady wrote at once to the address of the young woman's late mistress, as she supposed.

The kindness of her new friend was not exhausted; she gave her a share of her own bed that night. Mrs. Dempster had now but two shillings, which she offered her, promising to pay her the rest out of the first wages she received. But the good woman would take no more than one of them, and that in full payment of what she owed her, and Mrs. Dempster left the shop in tears, to linger about the neighbourhood until the hour should arrive at which the lady had told her to call again. Apparently she must have cherished the hope that her mother, divining her extremity, would give her the character she could honestly claim. But as she drew near the door which she hoped would prove a refuge, her mother was approaching it also, and at the turning of a corner they ran into each other's arms. The elderly lady had a hackney coach waiting for her in the next street and Mrs. Dempster, too tired to resist, got into it at once at her mother's desire. Ere they reached the mother's house, which, as I have said, was a long way from Mr. Dempster's, the daughter told everything, and the mother had perceived more than the daughter could tell: her eyes had revealed that all was not right behind them. She soothed her as none but a mother can, easily persuading her she would make everything right, and undertaking herself to pay the money owing to the butcher. But it was soon evident that for the present there must be no suggestion of her going back to her husband; for, imagining from something, that her mother was taking her to him, she jumped up and had all but opened the door of the cab when her mother succeeded in mastering her. As soon as she was persuaded that such had never been the intention, she was quiet. Whey they reached the house she was easily induced to go to bed at once.

Her mother lived in a very humble way, with one servant, a trustworthy woman. To her she confided the whole story, and with her consulted as to what had better be done. Between them they resolved to keep her, for a while at least, in retirement and silence. To this conclusion they came on the following grounds: First, the daughter's terror and the mother's own fear of Mr. Dempster; next, it must be confessed, the resentment of both mistress and servant because of his rudeness when he came to inquire after her; third, the evident condition of the poor creature's mind; and last, the longing of the two women to have her to themselves, that they might nurse and cosset her to their hearts' content.

They were to have more of this indulgence, however, than, for her sake, they would have desired, for before morning she was very ill. She had brain fever, in fact, and they had their hands full, especially as they desired to take every precaution to prevent the neighbourhood from knowing there was any one but themselves in the house.

It was a severe attack, but she passed the crisis favourably, and began to recover. One morning, after a quieter night than usual, she called her mother, and told her she had had a strange dream — that she had a baby somewhere, but could not find him, and was wandering about looking for him.

"Wasn't it a curious dream, mamma?" she said. "I wish it were a true one. I knew exactly what my baby was like, and went into house after house full of children, sure that I could pick him out of thousands. I was just going up to the door of the Foundling Hospital to look for him there when I woke."

As she ceased, a strange trouble passed like a cloud over her forehead and eyes, and her hand, worn almost transparent by the fever, followed it over forehead and eyes. She seemed trying to recall something forgotten. But her mother thought it better to say nothing.

Each of the two nights following she had the same dream.

"Three times, mother," she said. "I am not superstitious, as you know, but I can't help feeling as if it must mean something. I don't know what to make of it else — except it be that I haven't got over the fever yet.

THE BUTCHER'S BILLS

And, indeed, I am afraid my head is not quite right, for I can't be sure sometimes, such a hold has my dream of me, that I haven't got a baby somewhere about the world. Give me your hand, mother, and sing to me."

Still her mother thought it more prudent to say nothing, and do what she could to divert her thoughts; for she judged it must be better to let her brain come right, as it were, of itself.

In the middle of the next night she woke her with a cry.

"O, mother, mother! I know it all now. I am not out of my mind any more. How I came here I cannot tell — but I know I have a husband and baby at Hackney — and — oh, such a horrible roll of butcher's bills!"

"Yes, yes, my dear! I know all about it," answered her mother. "But never mind; you can pay them all yourself now, for I heard only yesterday that your aunt Lucy is dead, and has left you the hundred pounds she promised you twenty years ago."

"Oh, bless her!" cried Mrs. Dempster, springing out of bed, much to the dismay of her mother, who boded a return of the fever. "I must go home to my baby at once. But tell me about it, mama. How did I come here? I seem to remember being in a carriage with you, and that is the last I know."

Then, upon condition that she got into bed at once, and promised not to move until she gave her leave, her mother consented to tell her all she knew. She listened in silence, with face flushed and eyes glowing, but drank a cooling draught, lay down again, and at daybreak was fast asleep. When she awoke she was herself again.

V

What Came of It

Meantime, things were going, as they should, in rather a dull fashion with Duncan Dempster. His chariot wheels were gone, and he drove heavily. The weather was good; he seldom failed of the box-seat on the omnibus; a ray of light, the first he had ever seen there, visited his table, reflected from a new window on the opposite side of a court into the heart of his dismal back office; and best of all, business was better than usual. Yet was

Dempster not cheerful. He was not, indeed, a man an acquaintance would ever have thought of calling cheerful; but in grays there are gradations; and however differently a man's barometer may be set from those of other people, it has its ups and downs, its fair weather and foul. But not yet had he an idea how much his mental equilibrium had been dependent upon the dim consciousness of having that quiet uninterested wife in the comfortable house at Hackney. It had been stronger than it seemed, the spidery, invisible line connecting that office and that house, along which had run twice a day the hard dumpling that dwelt in Mr. Dempster's bosom. Vaguely connected with that home after all must have been that endless careful gathering of treasure in the city; for now, though he could not more stop making money than he could stop breathing, it had not the same interest as formerly. Indeed, he had less interest than before in keeping his lungs themselves going. But he kept on doing everything as usual.

Not one of the men he met ever said a word to him about his wife. The general impression was that she had left him for preferable society, and no one wondered at her throwing aside such "a dry old stick," whom even the devoted slaves of business contemned as having nothing in him but business.

A further change was, however, in progress within him. The first sign of it was that he began to doubt whether his wife had indeed been false to him — had forsaken him in any other company than that of Death. But there was one great difficulty in the way of the conclusion. It was impossible for him to imagine suicide as proceeding from any cause but insanity, and what could have produced the disorder in one who had no cares or anxieties, everything she wanted, and nothing to trouble her, a devoted husband, and a happy home? Yet the mere idea made him think more pitifully, and so more tenderly of her than before. It had not yet occurred to him to consider whether he might not have had something to do with her conduct or condition. Blame was a thing he had never made acquaintance with — least of all in the form of self-blame. To himself he was simply all right — the poised centre of things capable of righteous judgment on everyone else. But it must not be forgotten how little he knew about his own affairs at all; his was a very different condition from that of one who had closed his eyes and hardened his heart to suspicions concerning himself. His eyes had never yet been opened to anything but the order of things in the money world — its laws, its penalties, its rewards

— those he did understand. But apparently he was worth troubling. A slow dissatisfaction was now preying upon him — a sense of want — of not having something he once had, a vague discomfort, growing restless. The feeling was no doubt the worse that the birth of the child had brought such a sudden rush of fresh interest into his occupation, which doubt concerning that birth had again so suddenly checked; but even if the child should prove after all his own, a supposition he was not willing to admit as possibly a true one, he could never without his mother feel any enthusiasm about him, even such enthusiasm as might be allowed to a man who knew money from moonshine, and common sense from hysterics. Yet once and again, about this time, the nurse coming into the room after a few minutes' absence, found him bending over the sleeping infant, and, as she described him, "looking as if he would have cried if he had only known how."

One frosty evening in the late autumn the forsaken husband came from London — I doubt if he would now have said "home" — as usual, on the top of the omnibus. His was a tough nature physically, as well as morally, and if he had found himself inside an omnibus he would have thought he was going to die. The sun was down. A green hue rose from the horizon half-way to the zenith, but a pale yellow lingered over the vanished sun, like the gold at the bottom of a chrysolite. The stars were twinkling small and sharp in the azure overhead. A cold wind blew in little gusts, now from this side, now from that, as they went steadily along. The horses' hoofs rang loud on the hard road. The night got hold of him: it was at this season, and on nights like these, that he had haunted the house of Lucy's father, doing his best to persuade her to make him, as he said, a happy man. It now seemed as if then, and then only, he had been a happy man. Certainly, of all his life, it was the time when he came nearest to having a peep out of the upper windows of the house of life. He had been a dweller in the lower regions, a hewer of wood to the god of the cellar; and after his marriage, he had gone straight down again to the temple of the earthy god — to a worship whose god and temple and treasure caves will one day drop suddenly from under the votary's feet, and leave him dangling in the air without even a pocket about him — without even his banker's book to show for his respectability.

The night, I say, recalled the lovely season of his courtship, and again, in the mirror of loss, he caught a glimpse of things beyond him. Ah, if only that time and its hopes had remained with him! How different things would have been now! If Lucy had proved what he thought her! — remained what she seemed — the gentle, complaisant, yielding lady he imagined her, promising him a life of bliss! Alas, she would not even keep account of five pounds a week to please him! He never thought whether he, on his part, might not have, in some measure, come short of her expectations in a husband; whether she, the more lovely in inward design and outward fashion, might not have indulged yet more exquisite dreams of bliss which, by devotion to his ideal of life, he had done his part in disappointing. He only thought what a foolishness it all was; that thus it would go on to the end of the book; that youth after youth would have his turn of such a wooing, and such a disappointment. Sunsets, indeed! The suns of man's happiness never did anything but set! Out of money even — and who could say there was any poetry in that? — there was not half the satisfaction to be got that one expected. It was all a mess of expectations and disappointments mashed up together — nothing more. That was the world — on a fair judgment.

Such were his reflections till the driver pulled up for him to get down at his own gate. As he got down the said driver glanced up curiously at the row of windows on the first floor, and as soon as Mr. Dempster's back was turned, pointed to them with the butt-end of his whip, and nodded queerly to the gentleman who sat on his other side.

"That's more'n I've seen this six weeks," he said. "There's something more'n common up this evenin', sir."

There was light in the drawing-room — that was all the wonder; but at those windows Mr. Dempster himself look so fixedly that he had nearly stumbled up his own door-steps.

He carried a latch-key now, for he did not care to stand at the door till the boy answered the bell; people's eyes, as they passed, seemed to burn holes in the back of his coat.

He opened the street door quietly, and went straight up the stair to the drawing-room. Perhaps he thought to detect some liberty taken by his servants. He was a little earlier than usual. He opened that door, took two steps into the room, and stood arrested, motionless. With his shabby hat on his head, his shabby greatcoat on his back — for he grudged every penny spent on his clothes — his arms hanging down by his sides, and his knees bent, ready to tremble, he looked not a little out of keeping in the soft-lighted, dainty, delicate-hued drawing-room. Could he believe his eyes? The light of a large lamp was centred upon a gracious figure in white

❧   THE BUTCHER'S BILLS

— his wife, just as he used to see her before he married her! That was the way her hair would break loose as she ran down the stair to meet him! — only then there was no baby in her lap for it to fall over like a torrent of unlighted water over a white stone! It was a lovely sight.

He had stood but a moment when she looked up and saw him. She started, but gave no cry louder than a little moan. Instantly she rose. Turning, she laid the baby on the sofa, and flitted to him like a wraith. Arrived where he stood yet motionless, she fell upon her knees and clasped his. He was far too bewildered now to ask himself what husbands did in such circumstances, and stood like a block.

"Husband! husband!" she cried, "Forgive me." With one hand she hid her face, although it was bent to the ground, and with the other held up to him a bit of paper. He took it from the thin white fingers; it might explain something — help him out of this bewilderment, half nightmare, half heavenly vision. He opened it. Nothing but a hundred-pound note! The familiar sight of bank paper, however, seemed to restore his speech.

"What does this mean, Lucy? Upon my word! Permit me to say — —"

He was growing angry.

"It is to pay the butcher," she said, with a faltering voice.

"Damn the butcher!" he cried. "I hope you've got something else to say to me! Where have you been all this time?"

"At my mother's. I've had a brain fever, and been out of my mind. It was all about the butcher's bill."

Dempster stared. Perhaps he could not understand how a woman who would not keep accounts should be to such a degree troubled at the result of her neglect.

"Look at me, if you don't believe me," she cried, and as she spoke she rose and lifted her face to his.

He gazed at it for a moment — pale, thin, and worn; and out of it shone the beautiful eyes, larger than before, but shimmering uncertain like the stars of a humid night, although they looked straight into his.

Something queer was suddenly the matter with his throat — something he had never felt before — a constriction such as, had he been superstitious, he might have taken for the prologue to a rope. Then the thought came — what a brute he must be that his wife should have been afraid to tell him her trouble! Thereupon he tried to speak, but his throat was irresponsive to his will. Eve's apple kept sliding up and down in it, and would not let the words out. He had never been so served by members

"Husband! Husband!" she cried, "Forgive me."

of his own body in his life before! It was positive rebellion, and would get him into trouble with his wife. There it was! Didn't he say so?

"Can't you forgive me, Mr. Dempster?" she said, and the voice was so sweet and so sad! "It is my own money. Aunt Lucy is dead, and left it me. I think it will be enough to pay all my debts; and I promise you — I do promise you that I will set down every halfpenny after this. Do try me once again — for baby's sake."

This last was a sudden thought. She turned and ran to the sofa. Dempster stood where he was, fighting the strange uncomfortable feeling in his throat. It would not yield a jot. Was he going to die suddenly of choking? Was it a judgment upon him? Diphtheria, perhaps! It was much about in the City!

She was back, and holding up to him their sleeping child.

The poor fellow was not half the brute he looked — only he could *not* tell what to do with that confounded lump in his throat! He dared not try to speak, for it only choked him the more. He put his arms round them both, and pressed them to his bosom. Then the lump in his throat melted and ran out of his eyes, and all doubt vanished like a mist before the sun. But he never knew that he had wept. His wife did, and that was enough.

The next morning, for the first time in his life, he lost the eight o'clock omnibus.

The following Monday morning she brought her week's account to him. He turned from it testily, but she insisted on his going over it. There was not the mistake of a halfpenny. He went to town with a smile in his heart, and that night brought her home a cheque for ten pounds instead of five.

One day, in the middle of the same week, he came upon her sitting over the little blue-red-ruled book with a troubled countenance. She took no notice of his entrance.

"Do leave those accounts," he said, "and attend to me."

She shook her head impatiently, and made him no other answer. One moment more, however, and she started up, threw her arms about his neck, and cried triumphantly,

"It's buttons! — fourpence-halfpenny I paid for buttons!"

The Broken Swords

The eyes of three, two sisters and a brother, gazed for the last time on a great pale-golden star, that followed the sun down the steep west. It went down to arise again; and the brother about to depart might return, but more than the usual doubt hung upon his future. For between the white dresses of the sisters, shone his scarlet coat and golden swordknot, which he had put on for the first time, more to gratify their pride than his own vanity. The brightening moon, as if prophetic of a future memory, had already begun to dim the scarlet and the gold, and to give them a pale, ghostly hue. In her thoughtful light the whole group seemed more like a meeting in the land of shadows, than a parting in the substantial earth. — But which should be called the land of realities? — the region where appearance, and space, and time drive between, and stop the flowing currents of the soul's speech? or that region where heart meets heart, and appearance has become the slave to utterance, and space and time are forgotten?

Through the quiet air came the far-off rush of water, and the near cry of the land-rail. Now and then a chilly wind blew unheeded through the startled and jostling leaves that shaded the ivy-seat. Else, there was calm everywhere, rendered yet deeper and more intense by the dusky sorrow that filled their hearts. For, far away, hundreds of miles beyond the hearing of their ears, roared the great war-guns; next week their brother must sail with his regiment to join the army; and to-morrow he must leave his home.

The sisters looked on him tenderly, with vague fears about his fate.

Yet little they divined it. That the face they loved might lie pale and bloody, in a heap of slain, was the worst image of it that arose before them; but this, had they seen the future, they would, in ignorance of the further future, have infinitely preferred to that which awaited him. And even while they looked on him, a dim feeling of the unsuitableness of his lot filled their minds. For, indeed, to all judgments it must have seemed unsuitable that the home-boy, the loved of his mother, the pet of his sisters, who was happy, womanlike (as Coleridge says), if he possessed the signs of love, having never yet sought for its proofs — that he should be sent amongst soldiers, to command and be commanded; to kill, or perhaps to be himself crushed out of the fair earth in the uproar that brings back for the moment the reign of Night and Chaos. No wonder that to his sisters it seemed strange and sad. Yet such was their own position in the battle of life, in which their father had died with doubtful conquest, that when their old military uncle sent the boy an ensign's commission, they did not dream of refusing the only path open, as they thought, to an honourable profession, even though it might lead to the trench-grave. They heard it as the voice of destiny, wept, and yielded.

If they had possessed a deeper insight into his character, they would have discovered yet further reason to doubt the fitness of the profession chosen for him; and if they had ever seen him at school, it is possible the doubt of fitness might have strengthened into a certainty of incongruity. His comparative inactivity amongst his school fellows, though occasioned by no dulness of intellect, might have suggested the necessity of a quiet life, if inclination and liking had been the arbiters in the choice. Nor was this inactivity the result of defective animal spirits either, for sometimes his mirth and boyish frolic were unbounded; but it seemed to proceed from an over-activity of the inward life, absorbing, and in some measure checking, the outward manifestation. He had so much to do in his own hidden kingdom, that he had not time to take his place in the polity and strife of the commonwealth around him. Hence, while other boys were acting, he was thinking. In this point of difference, he felt keenly the superiority of many of his companions; for another boy would have the obstacle overcome, or the adversary subdued, while he was meditating on the propriety, or on the means, of effecting the desired end. He envied their promptitude, while they never saw reason to envy his wisdom; for his conscience, tender and not strong, frequently transformed slowness of determination into irresolution: while a delicacy of the sympathetic nerves

THE BROKEN SWORDS

tended to distract him from any predetermined course, by the diversity of their vibrations, responsive to influences from all quarters, and destructive to unity of purpose.

Of such a one, the *a priori* judgment would be, that he ought to be left to meditate and grow for some time, before being called upon to produce the fruits of action. But add to these mental conditions a vivid imagination, and a high sense of honour, nourished in childhood by the reading of the old knightly romances, and then put the youth in a position in which action is imperative, and you have elements of strife sufficient to reduce that fair kingdom of his to utter anarchy and madness. Yet so little do we know ourselves, and so different are the symbols with which the imagination works its algebra, from the realities which those symbols represent, that as yet the youth felt no uneasiness, but contemplated his new calling with a glad enthusiasm and some vanity; for all his prospect lay in the glow of the scarlet and the gold. Nor did this excitement receive any check till the day before his departure, on which day I have introduced him to my readers, when, accidentally taking up a newspaper of a week old, his eye fell on these words — *"Already crying women are to be met in the streets."* With this cloud afar on his horizon, which, though no bigger than a man's hand, yet cast a perceptible shadow over his mind, he departed next morning. The coach carried him beyond the consecrated circle of home laws and impulses, out into the great tumult, above which rises ever and anon the cry of Cain, "Am I my brother's keeper?"

Every tragedy of higher order, constructed in Christian times, will correspond more or less to the grand drama of the Bible; wherein the first act opens with a brilliant sunset vision of Paradise, in which childish sense and need are served with all the profusion of the indulgent nurse. But the glory fades off into grey and black, and night settles down upon the heart which, rightly uncontent with the childish, and not having yet learned the childlike, seeks knowledge and manhood as a thing denied by the Maker, and yet to be gained by the creature; so sets forth alone to climb the heavens, and instead of climbing, falls into the abyss. Then follows the long dismal night of feverish efforts and delirious vision, or, it may be, helpless despair; till at length a deeper stratum of the soul is heaved to the surface; and amid the first dawn of morning, the youth says within him, "I have sinned against my *Maker* — I will arise and go to my *Father.*" More or less, I say, will Christian tragedy correspond to this — a fall and a rising again; not a rising only, but a victory; not a victory merely, but a triumph. Such, in its way and degree, is my story. I have shown, in one passing scene, the home paradise; now I have to show a scene of a far differing nature.

The young ensign was lying in his tent, weary, but wakeful. All day long the cannon had been bellowing against the walls of the city, which now lay with wide, gaping breach, ready for the morrow's storm, but covered yet with the friendly darkness. His regiment was ordered to be ready with the earliest dawn to march up to the breach. That day, for the first time, there had been blood on his sword — there the sword lay, a spot on the chased hilt still. He had cut down one of the enemy in a skirmish with a sally party of the besieged, and the look of the man as he fell, haunted him. He felt, for the time, that he dared not pray to the Father, for the blood of a brother had rushed forth at the stroke of his arm, and there was one fewer of living souls on the earth because he lived thereon. And to-morrow he must lead a troop of men up to that poor disabled town, and turn them loose upon it, not knowing what might follow in the triumph of enraged and victorious foes, who for weeks had been subjected, by the constancy of the place, to the greatest privations. It was true the general had issued his commands against all disorder and pillage; but if the soldiers once yielded to temptation, what might not be done before the officers could reclaim them! All the wretched tales he had read of the sack of cities rushed back on his memory. He shuddered as he lay. Then his conscience began to speak, and to ask what right he had to be there. — Was the war a just one? — He could not tell; for this was a bad time for settling nice questions. But there he was, right or wrong, fighting and shedding blood on God's earth, beneath God's heaven.

Over and over he turned the question in his mind; again and again the spouting blood of his foe, and the death-look in his eye, rose before him; and the youth who at school could never fight with a companion because he was not sure that he was in the right, was alone in the midst of undoubting men of war, amongst whom he was driven helplessly along, upon the waves of a terrible necessity. What wonder that in the midst of these perplexities his courage should fail him! What wonder that the consciousness of fainting should increase the faintness! or that the dread of fear and its consequences should hasten and invigorate its attacks! To crown all, when he dropped into a troubled slumber at length, he found himself hurried, as on a storm of fire, through the streets of the captured town, from all the windows of which looked forth familiar faces, old and young, but distorted from the memory of his boyhood by fear and wild despair. On one spot lay the body of his father, with his face to the earth; and he woke at the cry of horror and rage that burst from his own lips, as he saw the rough, bloody hand of a soldier twisted in the loose hair of his elder sister, and the younger fainting in the arms of a scoundrel belonging to his own regiment.

He slept no more. As the grey morning broke, the troops appointed for the attack assembled without sound of trumpet or drum, and were silently formed in fitting order. The young ensign was in his place, weary and wretched after his miserable night. Before him he saw a great, broad-shouldered lieutenant, whose brawny hand seemed almost too large for his sword-hilt, and in any one of whose limbs played more animal life than in the whole body of the pale youth. The firm-set lips of this officer, and the fire of his eye, showed a concentrated resolution, which, by the contrast, increased the misery of the ensign, and seemed, as if the stronger absorbed the weaker, to draw out from him the last fibers of self-possession: the sight of unattainable determination, while it increased the feeling of the arduousness of that which required such determination, threw him into the great gulf which lay between him and it. In this disorder of his nervous and mental condition, with a doubting conscience and a shrinking heart, is it any wonder that the terrors which lay before him at the gap in those bristling walls, should draw near, and, making sudden inroad upon his soul, overwhelm the government of a will worn out by the tortures of an unassured spirit? What share fear contributed to unman him, it was impossible for him, in the dark, confused conflict of differing emotions, to determine; but doubtless a natural shrinking from danger, there being no excitement to deaden its influence, and no hope of victory to encourage to the struggle, seeing victory was dreadful to him as defeat, had its part in the sad result. Many men who have courage, are dependent on ignorance and a low state of the moral feeling for that courage; and a further progress towards the development of the higher nature would, for a time at least, entirely overthrow it. Nor could such loss of courage be rightly designated by the name of cowardice.

But, alas! the colonel happened to fix his eyes upon him as he passed along the file; and this completed his confusion. He betrayed such evident symptoms of perturbation, that that officer ordered him under arrest; and the result was, that chiefly for the sake of example to the army, he was, upon trial by court-martial, expelled from the service, and had his sword broken over his head. Alas for the delicate-minded youth! Alas for the home-darling!

Long after, he found at the bottom of his chest the pieces of the broken sword, and remembered that, at the time, he had lifted them from the ground and carried them away. But he could not recall under what impulse he had done so. Perhaps the agony he suffered, passing the bounds of mortal endurance, had opened for him a vista into the eternal, and had shown him, if not the injustice of the sentence passed upon him, yet his freedom from blame, or, endowing him with dim prophetic vision, had given him the assurance that some day the stain would be wiped from his soul, and leave him standing clear before the tribunal of his own honour. Some feeling like this, I say, may have caused him, with a passing gleam of indignant protest, to lift the fragments from the earth, and carry them away; even as the friends of a so-called traitor may bear away his mutilated body from the wheel. But if such was the case, the vision was soon overwhelmed and forgotten in the succeeding anguish. He could not see that, in mercy to his doubting spirit, the question which had agitated his mind almost to madness, and which no results of the impending conflict could have settled for him, was thus quietly set aside for the time; nor that, painful as was the dark, dreadful existence that he was now to pass in self-torment and moaning, it would go by, and leave his spirit clearer far, than if, in his apprehension, it had been stained with further blood-guiltiness, instead of the loss of honour. Years after, when he accidentally learned that on that very morning the whole of his company, with parts of several more, had, or ever they began to mount the breach, been blown to pieces by the explosion of a mine, he cried aloud in bitterness, "Would God that my fear had not been discovered before I reached that spot!" But surely it is better to pass into the next region of life having reaped some assurance, some firmness of character, determination of effort, and consciousness of the worth of life, in the present world; so approaching the future steadily and faithfully, and if in much darkness and ignorance, yet not in the oscillations of moral uncertainty.

Close upon the catastrophe followed a torpor, which lasted he did not know how long, and which wrapped in a thick fog all the succeeding events. For some time he can hardly be said to have had any conscious history. He awoke to life and torture when half-way across the sea towards his native country, where was no home any longer for him. To this point, and no farther, could his thoughts return in after years. But the misery which he then endured is hardly to be understood, save by those of like delicate temperament with himself. All day long he sat silent in his cabin; nor could any effort of the captain, or others on board, induce him to go on deck till night came on, when under the starlight, he ventured into the open air. The sky soothed him then, he knew not how. For the face of nature is the face of God, and must bear expressions that can influence, though unconsciously to them, the most ignorant and hopeless of His children. Often did he watch the clouds in hope of a storm, his spirit rising and falling as the sky darkened or cleared; he longed, in the necessary selfishness of such suffering, for a tumult of waters to swallow the vessel; and only the recollection of how many lives were involved in its safety besides his own, prevented him from praying to God for lightning and tempest, borne on which he might dash into the haven of the other world. One night, following a sultry calm day, he thought that Mercy had heard his unuttered prayer. The air and sea were intense darkness, till a light as intense for one moment annihilated it, and the succeeding darkness seemed shattered with the sharp reports of the thunder that cracked without reverberation. He who had shrunk from battle with his fellowmen, rushed to the mainmast, threw himself on his knees, and stretched forth his arms in speechless energy of supplication: but the storm passed away overhead, and left him kneeling still by the uninjured mast. At length the vessel reached her port. He hurried on shore to bury himself in the most secret place he could find. *Out of sight* was his first, his only thought. Return to his mother he would not, he could not; and, indeed, his friends never learned his fate, until it had carried him far beyond their reach.

For several weeks he lurked about like a malefactor, in low lodging-houses in narrow streets of the seaport to which the vessel had borne him, heeding no one, and but little shocked at the strange society and conver-sation with which, though only in bodily presence, he had to mingle. These formed the subjects of reflection in after times; and he came to the conclusion that, though much evil and much misery exist, sufficient to move prayers and tears in those who love their kind, yet there is less of both than those looking down from a more elevated social position upon the weltering heap of humanity, are ready to imagine; especially if they regard it likewise from the pedestal of self-congratulation on which a meager type of religion has elevated them. But at length his little stock of money was nearly expended, and there was nothing that he could do, or learn to do, in this seaport. He felt impelled to seek manual labour, partly because he thought it more likely he could obtain that sort of employment, without a request for reference as to his character, which would lead to inquiry about his previous history; and partly, perhaps, from an instinctive feeling that hard bodily labour would tend to lessen his inward suffering.

He left the town, therefore, at nightfall of a July day, carrying a little bundle of linen, and the remains of his money, somewhat augmented by the sale of various articles of clothing and convenience, which his change of life rendered superfluous and unsuitable. He directed his course northwards, travelling principally by night — so painfully did he shrink from the gaze even of footfarers like himself; and sleeping during the day in some hidden nook of wood or thicket, or under the shadow of a great tree in a solitary field. So fine was the season, that for three successive weeks he was able to travel thus without inconvenience, lying down when the sun grew hot in the forenoon, and generally waking when the first faint stars were hesitating in the great darkening heavens that covered and shielded him. For above every cloud, above every storm, rise up, calm, clear, divine, the deep infinite skies; they embrace the tempest even as the sunshine; by their permission it exists within their boundless peace: therefore it cannot hurt, and must pass away, while there they stand as ever, domed up eternally, lasting, strong, and pure.

Several times he attempted to get agricultural employment; but the whiteness of his hands and the tone of his voice not merely suggested unfitness for labour, but generated suspicion as the character of one who had evidently dropped from a rank so much higher, and was seeking admittance within the natural masonic boundaries and secrets and privileges of another. Disheartened somewhat, but hopeful, he journeyed on. I say hopeful; for the blessed power of life in the universe, in fresh air and sunshine absorbed by active exercise, in winds, yea in rain, though it fell but seldom, had begun to work its natural healing, soothing effect upon his perturbed spirit. And there was room for hope in his new endeavour. As his bodily strength increased, and his health, considerably impaired by inward suffering, improved, the trouble of his soul became more endurable — and in some measure to endure is to conquer and destroy. In proportion as the mind grows in the strength of patience, the disturber of its peace sickens and fades away. At length, one day, a widow lady in a village through which his road led him, gave him a day's work in her garden. He

THE BROKEN SWORDS

laboured hard and well, notwithstanding his soon-blistered hands, received his wages thankfully, and found a resting-place for the night on the low part of a hay-stack from which the upper portion had been cut away. Here he ate his supper of bread and cheese, pleased to have found such comfortable quarters, and soon fell fast asleep.

When he awoke, the whole heavens and earth seemed to give a full denial to sin and sorrow. The sun was just mounting over the horizon, looking up the clear cloud-mottled sky. From millions of water-drops hanging on the bending stalks of grass, sparkled his rays in varied refraction, transformed here to a gorgeous burning ruby, there to an emerald, green as the grass, and yonder to a flashing, sunny topaz. The chanting priest-lark had gone up from the low earth, as soon as the heavenly light had begun to enwrap and illumine the folds of its tabernacle; and had entered the high heavens with his offering, whence, unseen, he now dropped on the earth the sprinkled sounds of his overflowing blessedness. The poor youth rose but to kneel, and cry, from a bursting heart, "Hast Thou not, O Father, some care for me? Canst Thou not restore my lost honour? Can anything befall Thy children for which Thou hast no help? Surely, if the face of Thy world lie not, joy and not grief is at the heart of the universe. Is there none for me?"

The highest poetic feeling of which we are now conscious, springs not from the beholding of perfected beauty, but from the mute sympathy which the creation with all its children manifests with us in the groaning and travailing which look for the sonship. Because of our need and aspiration, the snowdrop gives birth in our hearts to a loftier spiritual and poetic feeling, than the rose most complete in form, colour, and odour. The rose is of Paradise — the snowdrop is of the striving, hoping, longing Earth. Perhaps our highest poetry is the expression of our aspirations in the sympathetic forms of visible nature. Nor is this merely a longing for a restored paradise; for even in the ordinary history of men, no man or woman that has fallen, can be restored to the position formerly held. Such must rise to a yet higher place, whence they can behold their former standing far beneath their feet. They must be restored by the attainment of something better than they ever possessed before, or not at all. If the law be a weariness, we must escape it by taking refuge with the spirit, for not otherwise can we fulfil the law than by being above the law. To escape the overhanging rocks of Sinai, we must climb to its secret top.

"Is thy strait horizon dreary?
Is thy foolish fancy chill?
Change the feet that have grown weary
For the wings that never will."

Thus, like one of the wandering knights searching the wide earth for the Sangreal, did he wander on, searching for his lost honour, or rather (for that he counted gone for ever) seeking unconsciously for the peace of mind which had departed from him, and taken with it, not the joy merely, but almost the possibility, of existence.

At last, when his little store was all but exhausted, he was employed by a market gardener, in the neighbourhood of a large country town, to work in his garden, and sometimes take his vegetables to market. With him he continued for a few weeks, and wished for no change; until, one day driving his cart through the town, he saw approaching him an elderly gentleman, whom he knew at once, by his gait and carriage, to be a military man. Now he had never seen his uncle the retired officer, but it struck him that this might be he; and under the tyranny of his passion for concealment, he fancied that, if it were he, he might recognise him by some family likeness — not considering the improbability of his looking at him. This fancy, with the painful effect which the sight of an officer, even in plain clothes, had upon him, recalling the torture of that frightful day, so overcame him, that he found himself at the other end of an alley before he recollected that he had the horse and cart in charge. This increased his difficulty; for now he dared not return, lest his inquiries after the vehicle, if the horse had strayed from the direct line, should attract attention, and cause interrogations which he would be unable to answer. The fatal want of self-possession seemed again to ruin him. He forsook the town by the nearest way, struck across the country to another line of road, and before he was missed, was miles away, still in a northerly direction.

But although he thus shunned the face of man, especially of any one who reminded him of the past, the loss of his reputation in their eyes was not the cause of his inward grief. That would have been comparatively powerless to disturb him, had he not lost his own respect. He quailed before his own thoughts; he was dishonoured in his own eyes. His perplexity had not yet sufficiently cleared away to allow him to see the extenuating circumstances of the case; not to say the fact that the peculiar mental condition in which he was at the time, removed the case quite out of the class of ordinary instances of cowardice. He condemned himself more severely than any of his judges would have dared; remembering that portion of his mental sensations which had savoured of fear, and forgetting the causes which had produced it. He judged himself a man stained with the foulest blot that could cleave to a soldier's name, a blot which nothing but death, not even death, could efface. But, inwardly condemned and outwardly degraded, his dread of recognition was intense; and feeling that he was in more danger of being discovered where the population was sparser, he resolved to hide himself once more in the midst of poverty; and, with this view, found his way to one of the largest of the manufacturing towns.

He reached it during the strike of a great part of the workmen; so that, though he found some difficulty in procuring employment, as might be expected from his ignorance of machine-labour, he yet was sooner successful than he would otherwise have been. Possessed of a natural aptitude for mechanical operations, he soon became a tolerable workman; and he found that his previous education assisted to the fitting execution of those operations even which were most purely mechanical.

He found also, at first, that the unrelaxing attention requisite for the mastering of the many niceties of his work, of necessity drew his mind somewhat from its brooding over his misfortune, hitherto almost ceaseless. Every now and then, however, a pang would shoot suddenly to his heart, and turn his face pale, even before his consciousness had time to inquire what was the matter. So by degrees, as attention became less necessary, and the nervo-mechanical action of his system increased with use, his thoughts again returned to their old misery. He would wake at night in his poor room, with the feeling that a ghostly nightmare sat on his soul; that a want — a loss — miserable, fearful — was present; that something of his heart was gone from him; and through the darkness he would hear the snap of the breaking sword, and lie for a moment overwhelmed beneath the assurance of the incredible fact. Could it be true that *he* was a coward? that *his* honour was gone, and in its place a stain? that *he* was a thing for men — and worse, for women — to point the finger at, laughing bitter laughter? Never lover or husband could have mourned with the same desolation over the departure of the loved; the girl alone, weeping scorching tears over *her* degradation, could resemble him in his agony, as he lay on his bed, and wept and moaned.

His sufferings had returned with the greater weight, that he was no longer upheld by the "divine air" and the open heavens, whose sunlight now only reached him late in an afternoon, as he stood at his loom, through windows so coated with dust that they looked like frosted glass; showing, as it passed through the air to fall on the dirty floor, how the breath of life was thick with dust of iron and wood, and films of cotton; amidst which his senses were now too much dulled by custom to detect the exhalations from greasy wheels and overtasked human-kind. Nor could he find comfort in the society of his fellow-labourers. True, it was a kind of comfort to have those near him who could not know of his grief; but there was so little in common between them, that any interchange of thought was impossible. At least, so it seemed to him. Yet sometimes his longing for human companionship would drive him out of his dreary room at night, and send him wandering through the lower part of the town, where he would gaze wistfully on the miserable faces that passed him, as if looking for some one — some angel, even there — to speak goodwill to his hungry heart.

Once he entered one of those gin-palaces, which, like the golden gates of hell, entice the miserable to worse misery, and seated himself close to a half-tipsy, good-natured wretch, who made room for him on a bench by the wall. He was comforted even by this proximity to one who would not repel him. But soon the paintings of warlike action — of knights, and horses, and mighty deeds done with battle-axe, and broad-sword, which adorned the panels all around, drove him forth even from this heaven of the damned; yet not before the impious thought had arisen in his heart, that the brilliantly painted and sculptural roof, with the gilded vine-leaves and bunches of grapes trained up the windows, all lighted with the great shining chandeliers, was only a microcosmic repetition of the bright heavens and the glowing earth, that overhung and surrounded the misery of man. But the memory of how kindly they had comforted and elevated him, at one period of his painful history, not only banished the wicked thought, but brought him more quiet, in the resurrection of a past blessing, than he had known for some time. The period, however, was now at hand when a new grief, followed by a new and more elevated activity, was to do its part towards the closing up of the fountain of bitterness.

Amongst his fellow-labourers, he had for a short time taken some interest in observing a young woman, who had lately joined them. There was nothing remarkable about her, except what at first sight seemed a

❧   THE BROKEN SWORDS

remarkable plainness. A slight scar over one of her rather prominent eyebrows, increased this impression of plainness. But the first day had not passed, before he began to see that there was something not altogether common in those deep eyes; and the plain look vanished before a closer observation, which also discovered, in the forehead and the lines of the mouth, traces of sorrow or other suffering. There was an expression, too, in the whole face, of fixedness of purpose, without any hardness of determination. Her countenance altogether seemed the index to an interesting mental history. Signs of mental trouble were always an attraction to him; in this case so great, that he overcame his shyness, and spoke to her one evening as they left the works. He often walked home with her after that; as, indeed, was natural, seeing that she occupied an attic in the same poor lodging-house in which he lived himself. The street did not bear the best character; nor, indeed, would the occupations of all the inmates of the house have stood investigation; but so retiring and quiet was this girl, and so seldom did she go abroad after work hours, that he had not discovered till then that she lived in the same street, not to say the same house, with himself.

He soon learned her history — a very common one as outward events, but not surely insignificant because common. Her father and mother were both dead, and hence she had to find her livelihood alone, and amidst associations which were always disagreeable, and sometimes painful. Her quick womanly instinct must have discovered that he too had a history; for though, his mental prostration favouring the operation of outward influences, he had greatly approximated in appearance to those amongst whom he laboured, there were yet signs, besides the educated accent of his speech, which would have distinguished him to an observer; but she put no questions to him, nor made any approach towards seeking a return of the confidence she reposed in him. It was a sensible alleviation to his sufferings to hear her kind voice, and look in her gentle face, as they walked home together; and at length the expectation of this pleasure began to present itself, in the midst of the busy, dreary work-hours, as the shadow of a heaven to close up the dismal, uninteresting day.

But one morning he missed her from her place, and a keener pain passed through him than he had felt of late; for he knew that the Plague was abroad, feeding in the low stagnant places of human abode; and he had but too much reason to dread that she might be now struggling in its grasp. He seized the first opportunity of slipping out and hurrying home. He sprang upstairs to her room. He found the door locked, but heard a faint moaning within. To avoid disturbing her, while determined to gain an entrance, he went down for the key of his own door, with which he succeeded in unlocking hers, and so crossed her threshold for the first time. There she lay on her bed, tossing in pain, and beginning to be delirious. Careless of his own life, and feeling that he could not die better than in helping the only friend he had; certain, likewise, of the difficulty of finding a nurse for one in this disease and of her station in life; and sure, likewise, that there could be no question of propriety, either in the circumstances with which they were surrounded, nor in this case of terrible fever almost as hopeless for her as dangerous to him, he instantly began the duties of a nurse, and returned no more to his employment. He had a little money in his possession, for he could not, in the way in which he lived, spend all his wages; so he proceeded to make her as comfortable as he could, with all the pent-up tenderness of a loving heart finding an outlet at length. When a boy at home, he had often taken the place of nurse, and he felt quite capable of performing its duties. Nor was his boyhood far behind yet, although the trials he had come through made it appear an age since he had lost his light heart. So he never left her bedside, except to procure what was necessary for her. She was too ill to oppose any of his measures, or to seek to prohibit his presence. Indeed, by the time he had returned with the first medicine, she was insensible; and she continued so through the whole of the following week, during which time he was constantly with her.

That action produces feeling is as often true as its converse; and it is not surprising that, while he smoothed the pillow for her head, he should have made a nest in his heart for the helpless girl. Slowly and unconsciously he learned to love her. The chasm between his early associations and the circumstances in which he found her, vanished as he drew near to the simple, essential womanhood. His heart saw hers and loved it; and he knew that, the centre once gained, he could, as from the fountain of life, as from the innermost secret of the holy place, the hidden germ of power and possibility, transform the outer intellect and outermost manners as he pleased. With what a thrill of joy, a feeling for a long time unknown to him, and till now never known in this form or with this intensity, the thought arose in his heart that here lay one who some day would love him; that he should have a place of refuge and rest; one to lie in his bosom and not despise him! "For," said he to himself, "I will call forth her soul from where it sleeps, like an unawakened echo, in an unknown cave; and like a child, of whom I once dreamed, that was mine, and to my delight turned in fear from all besides, and clung to me, this soul of hers will run with bewildered, half-sleeping eyes, and tottering steps, but with a cry of joy on its lips, to me as the life-giver. She will cling to me and worship me. Then will I tell her, for she must know all, that I am low and contemptible; that I am an outcast from the world, and that if she receive me, she will be to me as God. And I will fall down at her feet and pray her for comfort, for life, for restoration to myself; and she will throw herself beside me, and weep and love me, I know. And we will go through life together, working hard, but for each other; and when we die, she shall lead me into paradise as the prize her angel-hand found cast on a desert shore, from the storm of winds and waves which I was too weak to resist — and raised, and tended, and saved." Often did such thoughts as these pass through his mind while watching her bed; alternated, checked, and sometimes destroyed, by the fears which attended her precarious condition, but returning with every apparent betterment or hopeful symptom.

I will not stop to decide the nice question, how far the intention was right, of causing her to love him before she knew his story. If in the whole matter there was too much thought of self, my only apology is the sequel. One day, the ninth from the commencement of her illness, a letter arrived, addressed to her; which he, thinking he might prevent some inconvenience thereby, opened and read, in the confidence of that love which already made her and all belonging to her appear his own. It was from a soldier — *her lover*. It was plain that they had been betrothed before he left for the continent a year ago; but this was the first letter which he had written to her. It breathed changeless love, and hope, and confidence in her. He was so fascinated that he read it through without pause.

Laying it down, he sat pale, motionless, almost inanimate. From the hard-won sunny heights, he was once more cast down into the shadow of death. The second storm of life began, howling and raging, with yet more awful lulls between. "Is she not *mine?*" he said, in agony. "Do I not feel that she is mine? Who will watch over her as I? Who will kiss her soul to life as I? Shall she be torn away from me, when my soul seems to have dwelt with hers for ever in an eternal house? But have I not a right to her? Have I not given my life for hers? Is he not a soldier, and are there not many chances that he may never return? And it may be that, although they were engaged in word, soul has never touched soul with them; their love has never reached that point where it passes from the mortal to the immortal, the indissoluble: and so, in a sense, she may be yet free. Will he do for her what I will do? Shall this precious heart of hers, in which I see the buds of so many beauties, be left to wither and die?

But here the voice within him cried out, "Art thou the disposer of destinies? Wilt thou, in a universe where the visible God hath died for the Truth's sake, do evil that a good, which He might neglect or overlook, may be gained? Leave thou her to Him, and do thou right." And he said within himself, "Now is the real trial for my life! Shall I conquer or no?" And his heart awoke and cried, "I will. God forgive me for wronging the poor soldier! A brave man, brave at least, is better for her than I."

A great strength arose within him, and lifted him up to depart. "Surely I may kiss her once," he said. For the crisis was over, and she slept. He stooped towards her face, but before he had reached her lips he saw her eyelids tremble; and he who had longed for the opening of those eyes, as the gates of heaven, that she might love him, stricken now with fear lest she should love him, fled from her, before the eyelids that hid such strife and such victory from the unconscious maiden had time to unclose. But it was agony — quietly to pack up his bundle of linen in the room below, when he knew she was lying awake above, with her dear, pale face, and living eyes! What remained of his money, except a few shillings, he put up in a scrap of paper, and went out with his bundle in his hand, first to seek a nurse for his friend, and then to go he knew not whither. He met the factory people with whom he had worked, going to dinner, and amongst them a girl who had herself but lately recovered from the fever, and was yet hardly able for work. She was the only friend the sick girl had seemed to have amongst the women at the factory, and she was easily persuaded to go and take charge of her. He put the money in her hand, begging her to use it for the invalid, and promising to send the equivalent of her wages for the time he thought she would have to wait on her. This he easily did by the sale of a ring, which, besides his mother's watch, was the only article of value he had retained. He begged her likewise not to mention his name in the matter; and was foolish enough to expect that she would entirely keep the promise she had made him.

Wandering along the street, purposeless now and bereft, he spied a recruiting party at the door of a public-house; and on coming nearer, found, by one of those strange coincidences which do occur in life, and which have possibly their root in a hidden and wondrous law, that it was

THE BROKEN SWORDS

a party, perhaps a remnant, of the very regiment in which he had himself served, and in which his misfortune had befallen him. Almost simultaneously with the shock which the sight of the well-known number on the soldiers' knapsacks gave him, arose in his mind the romantic, ideal thought, of enlisting in the ranks of this same regiment, and recovering, as a private soldier and unknown, that honour which as officer he had lost. To this determination, the new necessity in which he now stood for action and change of life, doubtless contributed, though unconsciously. He offered himself to the sergeant; and, notwithstanding that his dress indicated a mode of life unsuitable as the antecedent to a soldier's, his appearance, and the necessity for recruits combined, led to his easy acceptance.

The English armies were employed in expelling the enemy from an invaded and helpless country. Whatever might be the political motives which had induced the Government to this measure, the young man was now able to feel that he could go and fight, individually and for his part, in the cause of liberty. He was free to possess his own motives for joining in the execution of the schemes of those who commanded his commanders.

With a heavy heart, but with more of inward hope and strength than he had ever known before, he marched with his comrades to the seaport and embarked. It seemed to him that because he had done right in his last trial, here was a new glorious chance held out to his hand. True, it was a terrible change to pass from a woman in whom he had hoped to find healing, into the society of rough men, to march with them, *"mi gleichem Tritt und Schritt,"* up to the bristling bayonets or the horrid vacancy of the cannon mouth. But it was the only cure for the evil that consumed his life.

He reached the army in safety, and gave himself, with religious assiduity, to the smaller duties of new position. No one had a brighter polish on his arms, or whiter belts than he. In the necessary movements, he soon became precise to a degree that attracted the attention of his officers; while his character was remarkable for all the virtues belonging to a perfect soldier.

One day, as he stood sentry, he saw the eyes of his colonel intently fixed on him. He felt his lip quiver, but he compressed and stilled it, and tried to look as unconscious as he could; which effort was assisted by the formal bearing required by his position. Now the colonel, such had been the losses of the regiment, had been promoted from a lieutenancy in the same, and had belonged to it at the time of the ensign's degradation. Indeed, had not the changes in the regiment been so great, he could hardly have escaped so long without discovery. But the poor fellow would have felt that his name was already free of reproach, if he had seen what followed on the close inspection which had awakened his apprehensions, and which, in fact, had convinced the colonel of his identity with the disgraced ensign. With a hasty and less soldierly step than usual, the colonel entered his tent, threw himself on his bend, and wept like a child. When he rose he was overheard to say these words — and these only escaped his lips: "He is nobler than I."

But this officer showed himself worthy of commanding such men as this private; for right nobly did he understand and meet his feelings. He uttered no word of the discovery he had made, till years afterwards; but it soon began to be remarked that whenever anything arduous, or in any manner distinguished, had to be done, this man was sure to be of the party appointed. In short, as often as he could, the colonel "set him in the forefront of the battle." Passing through all with wonderful escape, he was soon as much noted for his reckless bravery, as hitherto of his precision in the discharge of duties, bringing only commendation and no honour. But his final lustration was at hand.

A great part of the army was hastening, by forced marches, to raise the siege of a town which was already on the point of falling into the hands of the enemy. Forming one of a reconnoitering party, which preceded the main body at some considerable distance, he and his companions came suddenly upon one of the enemy's outposts, occupying a high, and on one side precipitous rock, a short way from the town, which it commanded. Retreat was impossible, for they were already discovered, and the bullets were falling amongst them like the first of a hail-storm. The only possibility of escape remaining for them was a nearly hopeless improbability. It lay in forcing the post on this steep rock; which if they could do before assistance came to the enemy, they might, perhaps, be able to hold out, by means of its defences, till the arrival of the army. Their position was at once understood by all; and, by a sudden, simultaneous impulse, they found themselves half-way up the steep ascent, and in the struggle of a close conflict, without being aware of any order to that effect from their officer. But their courage was of no avail; the advantages of the place were too great; and in a few minutes the whole party was cut to pieces, or stretched helpless on the rock. Our youth had fallen amongst the foremost; for a musket ball had grazed his skull, and laid him insensible.

But consciousness slowly returned, and he succeeded at last in raising himself and looking around him. The place was deserted. A few of his friends, alive, but grievously wounded, lay near him. The rest were dead. It appeared that, learning the proximity of the English forces from this rencontre with part of their advanced guard, and dreading lest the town, which was on the point of surrendering, should after all be snatched from their grasp, the commander of the enemy's forces had ordered an immediate and general assault; and had for this purpose recalled from their outposts the whole of his troops thus stationed, that he might make the attempt with the utmost strength he could accumulate.

As the youth's power of vision returned, he perceived, from the height where he lay, that the town was already in the hands of the enemy. But looking down into the level space immediately below him, he started to his feet at once; for a girl, bare-headed, was fleeing towards the rock, pursued by several soldiers. "Aha!" said he, divining her purpose — the soldiers behind and the rock before her — "I will help you to die!" And he stooped and wrenched from the dead fingers of a sergeant the sword which they clenched by the bloody hilt. A new throb of life pulsed through him to his very finger-tips; and on the brink of the unseen world he stood, with the blood rushing through his veins in a wild dance of excitement. One who lay near him wounded, but recovered afterwards, said that he looked like one inspired. With a keen eye he watched the chase. The girl drew nigh; and rushed up the path near which he was standing. Close on her footsteps came the soldiers, the distance gradually lessening between them.

Not many paces higher up, was a narrower part of the ascent, where the path was confined by great stones, or pieces of rock. Here had been the chief defence in the preceding assault, and in it lay many bodies of his friends. Thither he went and took his stand.

On the girl came, over the dead, with rigid hands and flying feet, the bloodless skin drawn tight on her features, and her eyes awfully large and wild. She did not see him though she bounded past so near that her hair flew in his eyes. "Never mind!" said he, "we shall meet soon." And he stepped into the narrow path just in time to face her pursuers — between her and them. Like the red lightning the bloody sword fell, and a man beneath it. Cling! clang! went the echoes in the rocks — and another man was down; for, in his excitement, he was a destroying angel to the breathless pursuers. His stature rose, his chest dilated; and as the third foe fell dead, the girl was safe; for her body lay a broken, empty, but undesecrated temple, at the foot of the rock. That moment his sword flew in shivers from his grasp. The next instant he fell, pierced to the heart; and his spirit rose triumphant, free, strong, and calm, above the stormy world, which at length lay vanquished beneath him.

The Wow O' Rivven

[The Bell]

Elsie Scott had let her work fall on her knees, and her hands on her work, and was looking out of the wide, low window of her room, which was on one of the ground floors of the village street. Through a gap in the household shrubbery of fuchsias and myrtles filling the window-sill, one passing on the foot-pavement might get a momentary glimpse of her pale face, lighted up with two blue eyes, over which some inward trouble had spread a faint, gauze-like haziness. But almost before her thoughts had had time to wander back to this trouble, a shout of children's voices, at the other end of the street, reached her ear. She listened a moment. A shadow of displeasure and pain crossed her countenance; and rising hastily, she betook herself to an inner apartment, and closed the door behind her.

Meantime the sounds drew nearer; and by and by an old man, whose strange appearance and dress showed that he had little capacity either for good or evil, passed the window. His clothes were comfortable enough in quality and condition, for they were the annual gift of a benevolent lady in the neighbourhood; but, being made to accommodate his taste, both known and traditional, they were somewhat peculiar in cut and adornment. Both coat and trousers were of a dark grey cloth; but the former, which, in its shape, partook of the military, had a straight collar of yellow, and narrow cuffs of the same; while upon both sleeves, about the place where a corporal wears his stripes, was expressed, in the same yellow cloth, a somewhat singular device. It was as close an imitation of a bell, with its tongue hanging out of its mouth, as the tailor's skill could produce from a single piece of cloth. The origin of the military cut of his coat was well known. His preference for it arose in the time of the wars of the first Napoleon, when the threatened invasion of the country caused the organization of many volunteer regiments. The martial show and exercises captivated the poor man's fancy; and from that time forward nothing pleased his vanity, and consequently conciliated his good-will more, than to style him by his favourite title — the *Colonel*. But the badge on his arm had a deeper origin, which will be partially manifest in the course of the story — if story it can be called. It was, indeed, the baptism of the fool, the outward and visible sign of his relation to the infinite and unseen. His countenance, however, although the features were not of any peculiarly low or animal type, showed no corresponding sign of the consciousness of such a relation, being as vacant as human countenance could well be.

The cause of Elsie's annoyance was that the fool was annoyed; he was followed by a troop of boys, who turned his rank into scorn, and assailed him with epithets hateful to him. Although the most harmless of creatures when let alone, he was dangerous when roused; and now he stooped repeatedly to pick up stones and hurl them at his tormentors, who took care, while abusing him, to keep at a considerable distance, lest he should get hold of them. Amidst the sounds of derision that followed him, might be heard the words frequently repeated — *"Come hame, come hame."* But in a few minutes the noise ceased, either from the interference of some friendly inhabitant, or that the boys grew weary, and departed in search of other amusement. By and by, Elsie might be seen again at her work in the window; but the cloud over her eyes was deeper, and her whole face more sad.

Indeed, so much did the persecution of this poor man affect her, that an onlooker would have been compelled to seek the cause in some yet deeper sympathy than that commonly felt for the oppressed, even by women. And such a sympathy existed, strange as it may seem, between the beautiful girl (for many called her a *bonnie lassie*) and this "tatter of humanity." Nothing would have been further from the thoughts of those that knew them, than the supposition of any correspondence or connexion between them; yet this sympathy sprang in part from a real similarity in their history and present condition.

All the facts that were known about *Feel Jock's* origin were these: that seventy years ago, a man who had gone with his horse and cart some miles from the village, to fetch home a load of peat from a desolate *moss*, had heard, while toiling along as rough a road on as lonely a hill-side as any

Jock

in Scotland, the cry of a child; and, searching about, had found the infant, hardly wrapt in rags, and untended, as if the earth herself had just given him birth, — that desert moor, wide and dismal, broken and watery, the only bosom for him to lie upon, and the cold, clear night-heaven his only covering. The man had brought him home, and the parish had taken parish-care of him. He had grown up, and proved what he now was — almost an idiot. Many of the townspeople were kind to him, and employed him in fetching water for them from the river or wells in the neighbour-hood, paying him for his trouble in victuals, or whisky, of which he was very fond. He seldom spoke; and the sentences he could utter were few; yet the tone, and even the words of his limited vocabulary, were sufficient to express gratitude and some measure of love towards those who were kind to him, and hatred of those who teased and insulted him. He lived a life without aim, and apparently to no purpose; in this resembling most of his more gifted fellow-men, who, with all the tools and materials necessary for building a noble mansion, are yet content with a clay hut.

Elsie, on the contrary, had been born in a comfortable farm-house, amidst homeliness and abundance. But at a very early age, she had lost both father and mother; not so early, however, but that she had faint memories of warm soft times on her mother's bosom, and of refuge in her mother's arms from the attacks of geese, and the pursuit of pigs. Therefore, in after-times, when she looked forward to heaven, it was as much a reverting to the old heavenly times of childhood and mother's love, as an anticipation of something yet to be revealed. Indeed, without some such memory, how should we ever picture to ourselves a perfect rest? But sometimes it would seem as if the more a heart was made capable of loving, the less it had to love; and poor Elsie, in passing from a mother's to a brother's guardianship, felt a change of spiritual temperature too keen. He was not a bad man, or incapable of benevolence when touched by the sight of want in anything of which he would himself have felt the privation; but he was so coarsely made, that only the purest animal necessities affected him; and a hard word, or unfeeling speech, could never have reached the quick of his nature through the hide that enclosed it. Elsie, on the contrary, was excessively and painfully sensitive, as if her nature constantly por-tended an invisible multitude of half-spiritual, half-nervous antennae, which shrank and trembled in every current of air at all below their own temperature. The effect of this upon her behaviour was such, that she was called odd; and the poor girl felt she was not like other people, yet could

THE WOW O' RIVVEN

not help it. Her brother, too, laughed at her without the slightest idea of the pain he occasioned, or the remotest feeling of curiosity as to what the inward and consistent causes of the outward abnormal condition might be. Tenderness was the divine comforting she needed; and it was altogether absent from her brother's character and behaviour.

Her neighbours looked on her with some interest, but they rather shunned than courted her acquaintance; especially after the return of certain nervous attacks, to which she had been subject in childhood, and which were again brought on by the events I must relate. It is curious how certain diseases repel, by a kind of awe, the sympathies of the neighbours: as if, by the fact of being subject to them, the patient were removed into another realm of existence, from which, like the dead with the living, she can hold communion with those around her only partially, and with a mixture of dread pervading the intercourse. Thus some of the deepest, purest wells of spiritual life, are, like those in old castles, choked up by the decay of the outer walls. But what tended more than anything, perhaps, to keep up the painful unrest of her soul (for the beauty of her character was evident in the fact that the irritation seldom reached her *mind*), was a circumstance at which, in its present connexion, some of my readers will smile, and others feel a shudder corresponding in kind to that of Elsie.

Her brother was very fond of a rather small, but ferocious-looking bull-dog, which followed close at his heels, wherever he went, with hanging head and slouching gait, never leaping or racing about like other dogs. When in the house, he always lay under his master's chair. He seemed to dislike Elsie, and she felt an unspeakable repugnance to him. Though she never mentioned her aversion, her brother easily saw it by the way in which she avoided the animal; and attributing it entirely to fear — which indeed had a great share in the matter — he would cruelly aggravate it, by telling her stories of the fierce hardihood and relentless persistency of this kind of animal. He dared not yet further increase her terror by offering to set the creature upon her, because it was doubtful whether he might be able to restrain him; but the mental suffering which he occasioned by this heartless conduct, and for which he had no sympathy, was as severe as many bodily sufferings to which he would have been sorry to subject her. Whenever the poor girl happened inadvertently to pass near the dog, which was seldom, a low growl made her aware of his proximity, and drove her to a quick retreat. He was, in fact, the animal impersonation of the animal opposition which she had continually to endure. Like chooses like; and the bull-dog *in* her brother made choice of the bull-dog *out of* him for his companion. So her day was one of shrinking fear and multiform discomfort.

But a nature capable of so much distress, must of necessity be *capable* of a corresponding amount of pleasure; and in her case this was manifest in the fact, that sleep and the quiet of her own room restored her wonderfully. If she was only let alone, a calm mood, filled with images of pleasure, soon took possession of her mind.

Her acquaintance with the fool had commenced some ten years previous to the time I write of, when she was quite a little girl, and had come from the country with her brother, who, having taken a small farm close to the town, preferred residing in the town to occupying the farmhouse, which was not comfortable. She looked at first with some terror on his uncouth appearance, and with much wonderment on his strange dress. This wonder was heightened by a conversation she overheard one day in the street, between the fool and a little pale-faced boy, who, approaching him respectfully, said, "Weel, cornel!" "Weel, laddie!" was the reply. "Fat dis the wow say, cornel?" "Come hame, come hame!" answered the *colonel*, with both accent and quantity heaped on the word *hame*. What the *wow* could be, she had no idea; only, as the years passed on, the strange word became in her mind indescribably associated with the strange shape in yellow cloth on his sleeves. Had she been a native of the town, she could not have failed to know its import, so familiar was every one with it, although it did not belong to the local vocabulary; but, as it was, years passed away before she discovered its meaning. And when, again and again, the fool, attempting to convey his gratitude for some kindness she had shown him, mumbled over the words — *"The wow o' Rivven — the wow o' Rivven,"* the wonder would return as to what could be the idea associated with them in his mind, but she made no advance towards their explanation.

That, however, which most attracted her to the old man, was his persecution by the children. They were to him what the bull-dog was to her — the constant source of irritation and annoyance. They could hardly hurt him, nor did he appear to dread other injury from them than insult, to which, fool though he was, he was keenly alive. Human gad-flies that they were! they sometimes stung him beyond endurance, and he would curse them in the impotence of his anger. Once or twice Elsie had been so far carried beyond her constitutional timidity, by sympathy for the distress of her friend, that she had gone out and talked to the boys, —

even scolded them, so that they slunk away ashamed, and began to stand as much in dread of her as of the clutches of their prey. So she, gentle and timid to excess, acquired among them the reputation of a termagant.* Popular opinion among children, as among men, is often just, but as often very unjust; for the same manifestations may proceed from opposite principles; and, therefore, as indices to character, may mislead as often as enlighten.

Next door to the house in which Elsie resided, dwelt a tradesman and his wife, who kept an indefinite sort of shop, in which various kinds of goods were exposed for sale. Their youngest son was about the same age as Elsie; and while they were rather more than children, and less than young people, he spent many of his evenings with her, somewhat to the loss of position in his classes at the parish school. They were, indeed, much attached to each other; and, peculiarly constituted as Elsie was, one may imagine what kind of heavenly messenger a companion stronger than herself must have been to her. In fact, if she could have framed the undefinable need of her child-like nature into an articulate prayer, it would have been — "Give me some one to love me stronger than I." Any love was helpful, yes, in its degree, saving to her poor troubled soul; but the hope, as they grew older together, that the powerful, yet tender-hearted youth, really loved her, and would one day make her his wife, was like the opening of heavenly eyes of life and love in the hitherto blank and death-like face of her existence. But nothing had been said of love, although they met and parted like lovers.

Doubtless, if the circles of their thought and feeling had continued as now to intersect each other, there would have been no interruption to their affection; but the time at length arrived when the old couple, seeing the rest of their family comfortably settled in life, resolved to make a gentleman of the youngest; and so sent him from school to college. The facilities existing in Scotland for providing a professional training enabled them to educate him as a surgeon. He parted from Elsie with some regret; but, far less dependent on her than she was on him, and full of the prospects of the future, he felt none of that sinking at the heart which seemed to lay her whole nature open to a fresh inroad of all the terrors and sorrows of her peculiar existence. No correspondence took place between them. New pursuits and relations, and the development of his

*A turbulent girl

tastes and judgments, entirely altered the position of poor Elsie in his memory. Having been, during their intercourse, far less of a man than she of a woman, he had no definite idea of the place he had occupied in her regard; and in his mind she receded into the background of the past, without his having any idea that she would suffer thereby, or that he was unjust towards her; while, in her thoughts, his image stood in the highest and clearest relief. It was the centre-point from which and towards which all lines radiated and converged; and although she could not but be doubtful about the future, yet there was much hope mingled with her doubts.

But when, at the close of two years, he visited his native village, and she saw before her, instead of the homely youth who had left her that winter evening, one who, to her inexperienced eyes, appeared a finished gentleman, her heart sank within her, as if she had found Nature herself false in her ripening processes, destroying the beautiful promise of a former year by changing instead of developing her creations. He spoke kindly to her, but not cordially. To her ear the voice seemed to come from a great distance out of the past; and while she looked upon him, that optical change passed over her vision, which all have experienced after gazing abstractedly on any object for a time: his form grew very small, and receded to an immeasurable distance; till, her imagination mingled with the twilight haze of her senses, she seemed to see him standing far off on a hill, with the bright horizon of sunset for a background to his clearly defined figure.

She knew no more till she found herself in bed in the dark; and the first message that reached her from the outer world, was the infernal growl of the bull-dog from the room below. Next day she saw her lover walking with two ladies, who would have thought it some degree of condescension to speak to her; and he passed the house without once looking towards it.

One who is sufficiently possessed by the demon of nervousness to be glad of the magnetic influences of a friend's company in a public promenade, or of a horse beneath him in passing through a churchyard, will have some faint idea of how utterly exposed and defenseless poor Elsie now felt on the crowded thoroughfare of life. And so the insensibility which had overtaken her, was not the ordinary swoon with which Nature relieves the overstrained nerves, but the return of the epileptic fits of her early childhood; and if the condition of the poor girl had been pitiable before, it was tenfold more so now. Yet she did not complain, but bore

THE WOW O' RIVVEN

all in silence, though it was evident that her health was giving way. But now, help came to her from a strange quarter, though many might not be willing to accord the name of help to that which rather hastened than retarded the progress of her decline.

She had gone to spend a few of the summer days with a relative in the country, some miles from her home, if home it could be called. One evening, towards sunset, she went out for a solitary walk. Passing from the little garden-gate, she went along a bare country road for some distance, and then turning aside by a footpath through a thicket of low trees, she came out in a lonely little churchyard on the hill-side. Hardly knowing whether or not she had intended to go there, she seated herself on a mound covered with long grass, one of many. Before her stood the ruins of an old church which was taking centuries to crumble. Little remained but the gable-wall, immensely thick, and covered with ancient ivy. The rays of the setting sun fell on a mound at its foot, not green like the rest, but of a rich, red-brown in the rosy sunset, and evidently but newly heaped up. Her eyes, too, rested upon it. Slowly the sun sank below the near horizon.

As the last brilliant point disappeared, the ivy darkened, and a wind arose and shook all its leaves, making them look cold and troubled; and to Elsie's ear came a low faint sound, as from a far-off bell. But close beside her — and she started and shivered at the sound — rose a deep, monotonous, almost sepulchral voice, *"Come Hame, come Hame! The wow, the wow!"*

At once she understood the whole. She sat in the churchyard of the ancient parish church of Ruthven; and when she lifted up her eyes, there she saw, in the half-ruined belfry, the old bell, all but hidden with ivy, which the passing wind had roused to utter one sleepy tone; and there, beside her, stood the fool with the bell on his arm; and to him and to her the *wow o' Rivven* said, *"Come hame, come hame!"* Ah, what did she want in the whole universe of God but a home? And though the ground beneath was hard, and the sky overhead far and boundless, and the hill-side lonely and companionless, yet somewhere within the visible, and beyond these the outer surfaces of creation, there might be a home for her; as round the wintry house the snows lie heaped up cold and white and dreary all the long *forenight,* while within, beyond the closed shutters, and giving no glimmer through the thick stone walls, the fires are blazing joyously, and the voices and laughter of young unfrozen children are heard, and nothing belongs to winter but the grey hairs on the heads of the parents, within whose warm hearts child-like voices are heard, and child-like thoughts move to and fro. The kernel of winter itself is spring, or a sleeping summer.

It was no wonder that the fool, cast out of the earth on a far more desolate spot than this, should seek to return within her bosom at this place of open doors, and should call it *home*. For surely the surface of the earth had no home for him. The mound at the foot of the gable contained the body of one who had shown him kindness. He had followed the funeral that afternoon from the town, and had remained behind the bell. Indeed, it was his custom, though Elsie had not known it, to follow every funeral going to this, his favourite churchyard of Ruthven; and, possibly in imitation of its booming, for it was still tolled at the funerals, he had given the old bell the name of *the wow*, and had translated its monotonous clangour into the articulate sounds — *come hame, come hame*. What precise meaning he attached to the words, it is impossible to say; but it was evident that the place possessed a strange attraction for him, drawing him towards it by the cords of some spiritual magnetism. It is possible that in the mind of the idiot there may have been some feeling about this churchyard and bell, which, in the mind of another, would have become a grand poetic thought; a feeling as if the ghostly old bell hung at the church-door of the invisible world, and ever and anon rang out joyous notes (though they sounded sad in the ears of the living), calling to the children of the unseen to *come home, come home*. She sat for some time in silence; for the bell did not ring again, and the fool spoke no more; till the dews began to fall, when she rose and went home, followed by her companion, who passed the night in the barn.

From that hour Elsie was furnished with a visual image of the rest she sought; an image which, mingling with deeper and holier thoughts, became, like the bow set in the cloud, the earthly pledge and sign of the fulfilment of heavenly hopes. Often when the wintry fog of cold discomfort and homelessness filled her soul, all at once the picture of the little churchyard — with the old gable and belfry, and the slanting sunlight steeping down to the very roots of the long grass on the graves — arose in the darkened chamber *(camera obscura)* of her soul; and again she heard the faint Aeolian sound of the bell, and the voice of the prophet-fool who interpreted the oracle, and the inward weariness was soothed by the promise of a long sleep. Who can tell how many have been counted fools simply because they were prophets; or how much of the madness in the world may be the utterance of thoughts true and just, but belonging to a region differing from ours in its nature and scenery!

But to Elsie looking out of her window came the mocking tones of the idle boys who had chosen as the vehicle of their scorn the very words which showed the relation of the fool to the eternal, and revealed in him an element higher far than any yet developed in them. They turned his glory into shame, like the enemies of David when they mocked the would-be king. And the best in a man is often that which is most condemned by those who have not attained to his goodness. The words, however, even as repeated by the boys, had not solely awakened indignation at the persecution of the old man: they had likewise comforted her with the thought of the refuge that awaited both him and her.

But the same evening a worse trial was in store for her. Again she sat near the window, oppressed by the consciousness that her brother had come in. He had gone up-stairs, and his dog had remained at the door, exchanging surly compliments with some of his own kind, when the fool came strolling past, and, I do not know from what cause, the dog flew at him. Elsie heard his cry and looked up. Her fear of the brute vanished in a moment before her sympathy for her friend. She darted from the house, and rushed towards the dog to drag him off the defenceless idiot, calling him by his name in a tone of anger and dislike. He left the fool, and, springing at Elsie, seized her by the arm above the elbow with such a grip that, in the midst of her agony, she fancied she heard the bone crack. But she uttered no cry, for the most apprehensive are sometimes the most courageous. Just then, however, her former lover was coming along the street, and, catching a glimpse of what had happened, was on the spot in an instant, took the dog by the throat with a grip not inferior to his own, and having thus compelled him to relax his hold, dashed him on the ground with a force that almost stunned him, and then with a superadded kick sent him away limping and howling; whereupon the fool, attacking him furiously with a stick, would certainly have finished him, had not his master descried his plight and come to his rescue.

Meantime the young surgeon had carried Elsie into the house; for, as soon as she was rescued from the dog, she had fallen down in one of her fits, which were becoming more and more frequent of themselves, and little needed such a shock as this to increase their violence. He was dressing her arm when she began to recover; and when she opened her eyes, in a state of half-consciousness, the first object she beheld, was his face bending over her. Recalling nothing of what had occurred, it seemed to her, in the dreamy condition in which the fit had left her, the same face, unchanged, which had once shone in upon her tardy spring-time, and promised to ripen it into summer. She forgot it had departed and left her in the wintry cold. And so she uttered wild words of love and trust; and the youth, while stung with remorse at his own neglect, was astonished to perceive the poetic forms of beauty in which the soul of the uneducated maiden burst into flower. But as her senses recovered themselves, the face gradually changed to her, as if the slow alteration of two years had been phatasma-gorically compressed into a few moments; and the glow departed from the maiden's thoughts and words, and her soul found itself at the narrow window of the present, from which she could behold but a drear country. — From the street came the iambic cry of the fool, *"Come hame, come hame."*

Tycho Brahe, I think, is said to have kept a fool, who frequently sat at his feet in his study, and to whose mutterings he used to listen in the pauses of his own thought. The shining soul of the astronomer drew forth the rainbow of harmony from the misty spray of words ascending ever from the dark gulf into which the thoughts of the idiot were ever falling. He beheld curious concurrences of words therein, and could read strange meanings from them — sometimes even received wondrous hints for the direction of celestial inquiry, from what, to any other, and it may be to the fool himself, was but a ceaseless and aimless babble. Such power lieth in words. It is not then to be wondered at, that the sounds I have mentioned should fall on the ears of Elsie, at such a moment, as a message from God himself. This then — all this dreariness — was but a passing show like the rest, and there lay somewhere for her a reality — a home. The tears burst up from her oppressed heart. She received the message, and prepared to go home. From that time her strength gradually sank, but her spirits as steadily rose.

The strength of the fool, too, began to fail, for he was old. He bore all the signs of age, even to the grey hairs, which betokened no wisdom. But one cannot say what wisdom might be in him, or how far he had not fought his own battle, and been victorious. Whether any notion of a continuance of life and thought dwelt in his brain, it is impossible to tell; but he seemed to have the idea that this was not his home; and those who saw him gradually approaching his end, might well anticipate for him a higher life in the world to come. He had passed through this world without

❧

ever awaking to such a consciousness of being as is common to mankind. He had spent his years like a weary dream though a long night, — a strange, dismal, unkindly dream; and now the morning was at hand. Often in his dream had he listened with sleepy senses to the ringing of the bell, but that bell would awake him at last. He was like a seed buried too deep in the soil, to which the light has never penetrated, and which, therefore, has never forced its way upwards to the open air, never experienced the resurrection of the dead. But seeds will grow ages after they have fallen into the earth; and, indeed, with many kinds, and within some limits, the older the seed before it germinate, the more plentiful the fruit. And may it not be believed of many human beings, that, the great Husbandman having sown them like seeds in the soil of human affairs, there they lie buried a life long; and only after the upturning of the soil by death, reach a position in which the awakening of their aspiration and the consequent growth become possible. Surely he had made nothing in vain.

A violent cold and cough brought him at last near to his end, and hearing that he was ill, Elsie ventured one bright spring day to go to see him. When she entered the miserable room where he lay, he held out his hand to her with something like a smile, and muttered feebly and painfully, "I'm gaein' to the wow, nae to come back again." Elsie could not restrain her tears; while the old man, looking fixedly at her, though with meaningless eyes, muttered, for the last time, *"Come hame! come hame!"* and sank into a lethargy, from which nothing could rouse him, till, next morning, he was waked by friendly death from the long sleep of this world's night. They bore him to his favourite churchyard, and buried him within the site of the old church, below his loved bell, which had ever been to him as the cuckoo-note of a coming spring. Thus he at length obeyed its summons, and went home.

Elsie lingered till the first summer days lay warm on the land. Several kind hearts in the village, hearing of her illness, visited her and ministered to her. Wondering at her sweetness and patience, they regretted they had not known her before. How much consolation might not their kindness have imparted, and how much might not their sympathy have strengthened her on her painful road! But they could not long have delayed her going home. Nor, mentally constituted as she was, would this have been at all to be desired. Indeed it was chiefly the expectation of departure that quieted and soothed her tremulous nature. It is true that a deep spring of hope and faith kept singing on in her heart, but this alone, without the anticipation of speedy release, could only have kept her mind at peace. It could not have reached, at least for a long time, the border land between body and mind, in which her disease lay.

One still night of summer, the nurse who watched by her bed-side heard her murmur through her sleep, "I hear it: *come hame — come hame.* I'm comin', I'm comin' — I'm gaein' hame to the wow, nae to come back." She awoke at the sound of her own words, and begged the nurse to convey to her brother her last request, that she might be buried by the side of the fool, within the old church of Ruthven. Then she turned her face to the wall, and in the morning was found quiet and cold. She must have died within a few minutes after her last words. She was buried according to her request; and thus she too went home.

Side by side rest the aged fool and the young maiden; for the bell called them and they obeyed; and surely they found the fire burning bright, and heard friendly voices, and felt sweet lips on theirs in the home to which they went. Surely both intellect and love were waiting them there.

Still the old bell hangs in the old gable; and whenever another is borne to the old churchyard, it keeps calling to those who are left behind, with the same sad, but friendly and unchanging voice — *"Come hame! come hame! come hame!"*

"Thy sun shall no more go down; neither shall thy moon withdraw itself: for the LORD shall be thine everlasting light, and the days of thy mourning shall be ended."

Isaiah lx. 20.

✺

The Light Princess

I

What! No Children?

Once upon a time, so long ago that I have quite forgotten the date, there lived a king and queen who had no children.

And the king said to himself, "All the queens of my acquaintance have children, some three, some seven, and some as many as twelve; and my queen has not one. I feel ill-used." So he made up his mind to be cross with his wife about it. But she bore it all like a good patient queen as she was. Then the king grew very cross indeed. But the queen pretended to take it all as a joke, and a very good one too.

"Why don't you have any daughters, at least?" said he. "I don't say *sons;* that might be too much to expect."

"I am sure, dear king, I am very sorry," said the queen.

"So you ought to be," retorted the king; "you are not going to make a virtue of *that,* surely."

But he was not an ill-tempered king, and in any matter of less moment would have let the queen have her own way with all his heart. This, however, was an affair of state.

The queen smiled.

"You must have patience with a lady, you know, dear king," said she.

She was, indeed, a very nice queen, and heartily sorry that she could not oblige the king immediately.

The king tried to have patience, but he succeeded very badly. It was more than he deserved, therefore, when, at last, the queen gave him a daughter — as lovely a little princess as ever cried.

II

Won't I, Just?

The day grew near when the infant must be christened. The king wrote all the invitations with his own hand. Of course somebody was forgotten.

Now it does not generally matter if somebody *is* forgotten, only you must mind who. Unfortunately, the king forgot without intending to forget; and so the chance fell upon the Princess Makemnoit, which was awkward. For the princess was the king's own sister; and he ought not to have forgotten her. But she had made herself so disagreeable to the old king, their father, that he had forgotten her in making his will; and so it was no wonder that her brother forgot her in writing his invitations. But poor relations don't do anything to keep you in mind of them. Why don't they? The king could not see into the garret she lived in, could he?

She was a sour, spiteful creature. The wrinkles of contempt crossed the wrinkles of peevishness, and made her face as full of wrinkles as a pat of butter. If ever a king could be justified in forgetting anybody, this king was justified in forgetting his sister, even at a christening. She looked very odd, too. Her forehead was as large as all the rest of her face, and projected over it like a precipice. When she was angry, her little eyes flashed blue. When she hated anybody, they shone yellow and green. What they looked like when she loved anybody, I do not know; for I never heard of her loving anybody but herself, and I do not think she could have managed that if she had not somehow got used to herself. But what made it highly imprudent in the king to forget her was — that she was awfully clever. In fact, she was a witch; and when she bewitched anybody, he very soon had enough of it; for she beat all the wicked fairies in wickedness, and all the clever ones in cleverness. She despised all the modes we read of in history, in which offended fairies and witches have taken their revenges; and

"The Christening"

therefore, after waiting and waiting in vain for an invitation, she made up her mind at last to go without one, and make the whole family miserable, like a princess as she was.

So she put on her best gown, went to the palace, was kindly received by the happy monarch, who forgot that he had forgotten her, and took her place in the procession to the royal chapel. When they were all gathered about the font, she contrived to get next to it, and throw something into the water; after which she maintained a very respectful demeanour till the water was applied to the child's face. But at that moment she turned round in her place three times, and muttered the following words, loud enough for those beside her to hear: —

"Light of spirit, by my charms,
  Light of body every part,
Never weary human arms —
  Only crush thy parents' heart!"

They all thought she had lost her wits, and was repeating some foolish nursery rhyme; but a shudder went through the whole of them notwithstanding. The baby, on the contrary, began to laugh and crow; while the nurse gave a start and a smothered cry, for she thought she was struck with paralysis: she could not feel the baby in her arms. But she clasped it tight and said nothing.

The mischief was done.

III

She Can't Be Ours

Her atrocious aunt had deprived the child of all her gravity. If you ask me how this was effected, I answer, "In the easiest way in the world. She had only to destroy gravitation." For the princess was a philosopher, and knew all the *ins* and *outs* of the laws of gravitation as well as the *ins* and *outs* of her boot-lace. And being a witch as well, she could abrogate those laws in a moment; or at least so clog their wheels and rust their bearings, that they would not work at all. But we have more to do with what followed than with how it was done.

The first awkwardness that resulted from this unhappy privation was, that the moment the nurse began to float the baby up and down, she flew from her arms towards the ceiling. Happily, the resistance of the air brought her ascending career to a close within a foot of it. There she remained, horizontal as when she left her nurse's arms, kicking and laughing amazingly. The nurse in terror flew to the bell, and begged the footman, who answered it, to bring up the house-steps directly. Trembling in every limb, she climbed upon the steps, and had to stand upon the very top, and reach up, before she could catch the floating tail of the baby's long clothes.

When the strange fact came to be known, there was a terrible commotion in the palace. The occasion of its discovery by the king was naturally a repetition of the nurse's experience. Astonished that he felt no weight when the child was laid in his arms, he began to wave her up and — not down; for she slowly ascended to the ceiling as before, and there remained floating in perfect comfort and satisfaction, as was testified by her peals of tiny laughter. The king stood staring up in speechless amazement, and trembled so that his beard shook like grass in the wind. At last, turning to the queen, who was just as horror-struck as himself, he said, gasping, staring, and stammering, —

"She can't be ours, queen!"

Now the queen was much cleverer than the king, and had begun already to suspect that "this effect defective came by cause."

"I am sure she is ours," answered she. "But we ought to have taken better care of her at the christening. People who were never invited ought not to have been present."

"Oh, ho!" said the king, tapping his forehead with his forefinger, "I have it all. I've found her out. Don't you see it, queen? Princess Makemnoit has bewitched her."

"That's just what I say," answered the queen.

"I beg your pardon, my love; I did not hear you. — John! bring the steps I get on my throne with."

For he was a little king with a great throne, like many other kings.

The throne-steps were brought, and set upon the dining-table, and John got upon the top of them. But he could not reach the little princess, who lay like a baby-laughter-cloud in the air, exploding continuously.

"Take the tongs, John," said his Majesty; and getting up on the table, he handed them to him.

John could reach the baby now, and the little princess was handed down by the tongs.

IV

Where Is She?

One fine summer day, a month after these her first adventures, during which time she had been very carefully watched, the princess was lying on the bed in the queen's own chamber, fast asleep. One of the windows was open, for it was noon, and the day was so sultry that the little girl was wrapped in nothing less ethereal than slumber itself. The queen came into the room, and not observing that the baby was on the bed, opened another window. A frolicsome fairy wind, which had been watching for a chance of mischief, rushed in at the one window, and taking its way over the bed where the child was lying, caught her up, and rolling and floating her along like a piece of flue, or a dandelion seed, carried her with it through the opposite window, and away. The queen went down-stairs, quite ignorant of the loss she had herself occasioned.

When the nurse returned, she supposed that her Majesty had carried her off, and, dreading a scolding, delayed making inquiry about her. But hearing nothing, she grew uneasy, and went at length to the queen's boudoir, where she found her Majesty.

"Please, your Majesty, shall I take the baby?" said she.

"Where is she?" asked the queen.

"Please forgive me. I know it was wrong."

"What do you mean?" said the queen, looking grave.

"Oh! don't frighten me, your Majesty!" exclaimed the nurse, clasping her hands.

The queen saw that something was amiss, and fell down in a faint. The nurse rushed about the palace, screaming, "My baby! my baby!"

Every one ran to the queen's room. But the queen could give no orders. They soon found out, however, that the princess was missing, and in a moment the palace was like a beehive in a garden; and in one minute more the queen was brought to herself by a great shout and a clapping of hands. They had found the princess fast asleep under a rose-bush, to which the elvish little wind-puff had carried her, finishing its mischief by shaking a shower of red rose-leaves all over the little white sleeper. Startled by the noise the servants made, she woke, and, furious with glee, scattered the rose-leaves in all directions, like a shower of spray in the sunset.

She was watched more carefully after this, no doubt; yet it would be endless to relate all the odd incidents resulting from this peculiarity of the young princess. But there never was a baby in a house, not to say a palace, that kept the household in such constant good humour, at least below-stairs. If it was not easy for her nurses to hold her, at least she made neither their arms nor their hearts ache. And she was so nice to play at ball with! There was positively no danger of letting her fall. They might throw her down, or knock her down, or push her down, but couldn't *let* her down. It is true, they might let her fly into the fire or the coal-hole, or through the window; but none of these accidents had happened as yet. If you heard peals of laughter resounding from some unknown region, you might be sure enough of the cause. Going down into the kitchen, or *the room,* you would find Jane and Thomas, and Robert and Susan, all and sum, playing at ball with the little princess. She was the ball herself, and did not enjoy it the less for that. Away she went, flying from one to another, screeching with laughter. And the servants loved the ball itself better even than the game. But they had to take some care how they threw her, for if she received an upward direction, she would never come down again without being fetched.

V

What Is to Be Done?

But above-stairs it was different. One day, for instance, after breakfast, the king went into his counting-house, and counted out his money.

The operation gave him no pleasure.

"To think," said he to himself, "that every one of these gold

"Playing at Ball"

sovereigns weighs a quarter of an ounce, and my real, live, flesh-and-blood princess weighs nothing at all!"

And he hated his gold sovereigns, as they lay with a broad smile of self-satisfaction all over their yellow faces.

The queen was in the parlour, eating bread and honey. But at the second mouthful she burst out crying, and could not swallow it. The king heard her sobbing. Glad of anybody, but especially of his queen, to quarrel with, he clashed his gold sovereigns into his money-box, clapped his crown on his head, and rushed into the parlour.

"What is all this about?" exclaimed he. "What are you crying for, queen?"

"I can't eat it," said the queen, looking ruefully at the honey-pot.

"No wonder!" retorted the king. "You've just eaten your breakfast — two turkey eggs, and three anchovies."

"Oh, that's not it!" sobbed her Majesty. "It's my child, my child!"

"Well, what's the matter with your child? She's neither up the chimney nor down the draw-well. Just hear her laughing."

Yet the king could not help a sigh, which he tried to turn into a cough, saying, —

"It is a good thing to be light-hearted, I am sure, whether she be ours or not."

"It is a bad thing to be light-headed," answered the queen, looking with prophetic soul far into the future.

"'Tis a good thing to be light-handed," said the king.

"'Tis a bad thing to be light-fingered," answered the queen.

"'Tis a good thing to be light-footed," said the king.

"'Tis a bad thing — " began the queen; but the king interrupted her.

"In fact," said he, with the tone of one who concludes an argument in which he has had only imaginary opponents, and in which, therefore, he has come off triumphant — "in fact, it is a good thing altogether to be light-bodied."

"But it is a bad thing altogether to be light-minded," retorted the queen, who was beginning to lose her temper.

This last answer quite discomfited his Majesty, who turned on his heel, and betook himself to his counting-house again. But he was not half-way towards it, when the voice of his queen overtook him.

"And it's a bad thing to be light-haired," screamed she, determined to have more last words, now that her spirit was roused.

The queen's hair was black as night; and the king's had been, and his daughter's was, golden as morning. But it was not this reflection on his hair that arrested him; it was the double use of the word *light*. For the king hated all witticisms, and punning especially. And besides, he could not tell whether the queen meant light-*haired* or light-*heired*; for why might she not aspirate her vowels when she was ex-asperated herself?

He turned upon his other heel, and rejoined her. She looked angry still, because she knew that she was guilty, or, what was much the same, knew that he thought so.

"My dear queen," said he, "duplicity of any sort is exceedingly objectionable between married people of any rank, not to say kings and queens; and the most objectionable form duplicity can assume is that of punning."

"There!" said the queen, "I never made a jest, but I broke it in the making. I am the most unfortunate woman in the world!"

She looked so rueful, that the king took her in his arms; and they sat down to consult.

"Can you bear this?" said the king.

"No, I can't," said the queen.

"Well, what's to be done?" said the king.

"I'm sure I don't know," said the queen. "But might you not try an apology?"

"To my older sister, I suppose you mean?" said the king.

"Yes," said the queen.

"Well, I don't mind," said the king.

So he went the next morning to the house of the princess, and, making a very humble apology, begged her to undo the spell. But the princess declared, with a grave face, that she knew nothing at all about it. Her eyes, however, shone pink, which was a sign that she was happy. She advised the king and queen to have patience, and to mend their ways. The king returned disconsolate. The queen tried to comfort him.

"We will wait till she is older. She may then be able to suggest something herself. She will know at least how she feels, and explain things to us."

"But what if she should marry?" exclaimed the king, in sudden consternation at the idea.

"Well, what of that?" rejoined the queen.

"Just think! If she were to have children! In the course of a hundred years the air might be as full of floating children as of gossamers in autumn."

"That is no business of ours," replied the queen. "Besides, by that time they will have learned to take care of themselves."

A sigh was the king's only answer.

He would have consulted the court physicians; but he was afraid they would try experiments upon her.

VI

She Laughs Too Much

Meantime, notwithstanding awkward occurrences, and griefs that she brought upon her parents, the little princess laughed and grew — not fat, but plump and tall. She reached the age of seventeen, without having fallen into any worse scrape than a chimney; by rescuing her from which, a little bird-nesting urchin got fame and a black face. Nor, thoughtless as she was, had she committed anything worse than laughter at everybody and everything that came in her way. When she was told, for the sake of experiment, that General Clanrunfort was cut to pieces with all his troops, she laughed; when she heard that the enemy was on his way to besiege her papa's capital, she laughed hugely; but when she was told that the city would certainly be abandoned to the mercy of the enemy's soldiery — why, then she laughed immoderately. She never could be brought to see the serious side of anything. When her mother cried, she said, —

"What queer faces mamma makes! And she squeezes water out of her cheeks! Funny mamma!"

And when her papa stormed at her, she laughed, and danced round and round him, clapping her hands, and crying —

"Do it again, papa. Do it again! It's such fun! Dear, funny papa!"

And if he tried to catch her, she glided from him in an instant, not in the least afraid of him, but thinking it part of the game not to be caught. With one push of her foot, she would be floating in the air above his head; or she would go dancing backwards and forwards and sideways, like a great butterfly. It happened several times, when her father and mother were holding a consultation about her in private, that they were interrupted by vainly repressed outbursts of laughter over their heads; and looking up with indignation, saw her floating at full length in the air above them, whence she regarded them with the most comical appreciation of the position.

One day an awkward accident happened. The princess had come out upon the lawn with one of her attendants, who held her by the hand. Spying her father at the other side of the lawn, she snatched her hand from the maid's, and sped across to him. Now when she wanted to run alone, her custom was to catch up a stone in each hand, so that she might come down again after a bound. Whatever she wore as part of her attire had no effect in this way: even gold, when it thus became as it were a part of herself, lost all its weight for the time. But whatever she only held in her hands retained its downward tendency. On this occasion she could see nothing to catch up but a huge toad, that was walking across the lawn as if he had a hundred years to do it in. Not knowing what disgust meant, for this was one of her peculiarities, she snatched up the toad and bounded away. She had almost reached her father, and he was holding out his arms to receive her, and take from her lips the kiss which hovered on them like a butterfly on a rosebud, when a puff of wind blew her aside into the arms of a young page, who had just been receiving a message from his Majesty. Now it was no great peculiarity in the princess that, once she was set agoing, it always cost her time and trouble to check herself. On this occasion there was no time. She *must* kiss — and she kissed the page. She did not mind it much; for she had no shyness in her composition; and she knew, besides, that she could not help it. So she only laughed, like a musical box. The poor page fared the worst. For the princess, trying to correct the unfortunate tendency of the kiss, put out her hands to keep her off the page; so that, along with the kiss, he received, on the other cheek, a slap with a huge black toad, which she poked right into his eye. He tried to laugh, too, but the attempt resulted in such an odd contortion of countenance, as showed that there was no danger of his pluming himself on the kiss. As for the king, his dignity was greatly hurt, and he did not speak to the page for a whole month.

I may here remark that it was very amusing to see her run, if her mode of progression would properly be called running. For first she would make a bound; then, having alighted, she would run a few steps, and make another bound. Sometimes she would fancy she had reached the ground before she actually had, and her feet would go backwards and forwards, running upon nothing at all, like those of a chicken on its back. Then she would laugh like the very spirit of fun; only in her laugh there was something missing. What it was, I find myself unable to describe. I think it was a certain tone, depending upon the possibility of sorrow — *morbidezza*, perhaps. She never smiled.

VII

Try Metaphysics

After a long avoidance of the painful subject, the king and queen resolved to hold a council of three upon it; and so they sent for the princess. In she came, sliding and flitting and gliding from one piece of furniture to another, and put herself at last in an arm-chair, in a sitting posture. Whether she could be said to *sit*, seeing she received no support from the seat of the chair, I do not pretend to determine.

"My dear child," said the king, "you must be aware by this time that you are not exactly like other people."

"Oh, you dear funny papa! I have got a nose, and two eyes, and all the rest. So have you. So has mamma."

"Now be serious, my dear, for once," said the queen.

"No, thank you, mamma; I had rather not."

"Would you not like to be able to walk like other people?" said the king.

"No indeed, I should think not. You only crawl. You are such slow coaches!"

"How do you feel, my child?" he resumed, after a pause of discomfiture.

"Quite well, thank you."

"I mean, what do you feel like?"

"Like nothing at all, that I know of."

"You must feel like something."

"I feel like a princess with such a funny papa, and such a dear pet of a queen-mamma!"

"Now really!" began the queen; but the princess interrupted her.

"Oh yes," she added, "I remember. I have a curious feeling sometimes, as if I were the only person that had any sense in the whole world."

She had been trying to behave herself with dignity; but now she burst into a violent fit of laughter, threw herself backwards over the chair, and went rolling about the floor in an ecstasy of enjoyment. The king picked her up easier than one does a down quilt, and replaced her in her former relation to the chair. The exact preposition expressing this relation I do not happen to know.

"Is there nothing you wish for?" resumed the king, who had learned by this time that it was useless to be angry with her.

"Oh, you dear papa! — yes," answered she.

"What is it, my darling?"

"I have been longing for it — oh, such a time! — ever since last night."

"Tell me what it is."

"Will you promise to let me have it?"

The king was on the point of saying *Yes,* but the wiser queen checked him with a single motion of her head.

"Tell me what it is first," said he.

"No, no. Promise first."

"I dare not. What is it?"

"Mind, I hold you to your promise. — It is — to be tied to the end of a string — a very long string indeed, and be flown like a kite. Oh such fun! I would rain rose-water, and hail sugar-plums, and snow whipped-cream, and — and — and — "

A fit of laughing checked her; and she would have been off again over the floor, had not the king started up and caught her just in time. Seeing that nothing but talk could be got out of her, he rang the bell, and sent her away with two of her ladies-in-waiting.

"Now, queen," he said, turning to her Majesty, "what *is* to be done?"

"There is but one thing left," answered she. "Let us consult the college of Metaphysicians."

"Bravo!" cried the king; "we will."

Now at the head of this college were two very wise Chinese philosophers — by name Hum-Drum, and Kopy-Keck. For them the king sent; and straightway they came. In a long speech he communicated to them what they knew very well already — as who did not? — namely, the peculiar condition of his daughter in relation to the globe on which she dwelt; and requested them to consult together as to what might be the cause and probable cure of her *infirmity.* The king laid stress upon the word, but failed to discover his own pun. The queen laughed; but Hum-Drum and Kopy-Keck heard with humility and retired in silence.

Their consultation consisted chiefly in propounding and supporting, for the thousandth time, each his favourite theories. For the condition of the princess afforded delightful scope for the discussion of every question arising from the division of thought — in fact, of all the Metaphysics of the Chinese Empire. But it is only justice to say that they did not altogether neglect the discussion of the practical question, *what was to be done.*

Hum-Drum was a Materialist, and Kopy-Keck was a Spiritualist. The former was slow and sententious; the latter was quick and flighty: the latter had generally the first word; the former the last.

"I reassert my former assertion," began Kopy-Keck, with a plunge. "There is not a fault in the princess, body or soul; only they are wrong put together. Listen to me now, Hum-Drum, and I will tell you in brief what I think. Don't speak. Don't answer me. I *won't* hear you till I have done." — At that decisive moment, when souls seek their appointed habitations, two eager souls met, struck, rebounded, lost their way, and arrived each at the wrong place. The soul of the princess was one of those, and she went far astray. She does not belong by rights to this world at all, but to some other planet, probably Mercury. Her proclivity to her true sphere destroys all the natural influence which this orb would otherwise possess over her corporeal frame. She cares for nothing here. There is no relation between her and this world.

"She must therefore be taught, by the sternest compulsion, to take an interest in the earth as the earth. She must study every department of its history — its animal history; its vegetable history; its mineral history; its social history; its moral history; its political history; its scientific history; its literary history; its musical history; its artistical history; above all, its metaphysical history. She must begin with the Chinese dynasty and end with Japan. But first of all she must study geology, and especially the history of the extinct races of animals — their natures, their habits, their loves, their hates, their revenges. She must — "

"Hold, h-o-o-old!" roared Hum-Drum. "It is certainly my turn now. My rooted and insubvertible conviction is, that the causes of the anomalies evident in the princess's condition are strictly and solely physical. But that is only tantamount to acknowledging that they exist. Hear my opinion. — From some cause or other, of no importance to our inquiry, the motion of her heart has been reversed. That remarkable combination of the suction and the force-pump works the wrong way — I mean in the case of the unfortunate princess: it draws in where it should force out, and forces out where it should draw in. The offices of the auricles and the ventricles are subverted. The blood is sent forth by the veins, and returns by the arteries. Consequently it is running the wrong way through all her corporeal organism — lungs and all. Is it then at all mysterious, seeing that such is the case, that on the other particular of gravitation as well, she should differ from normal humanity? My proposal for the cure is this: —

"Phlebotomize until she is reduced to the last point of safety. Let it be effected, if necessary, in a warm bath. When she is reduced to a state of perfect asphyxy, apply a ligature to the left ankle, drawing it as tight as the bone will bear. Apply, at the same moment, another of equal tension around the right wrist. By means of plates constructed for the purpose, place the other foot and hand under the receivers of two air-pumps. Exhaust the receivers. Exhibit a pint of French brandy, and await the result.

"Which would presently arrive in the form of grim Death," said Kopy-Keck.

"If it should, she would yet die in doing our duty," retorted Hum-Drum.

But their Majesties had too much tenderness for their volatile off-spring to subject her to either of the schemes of the equally unscrupulous philosophers. Indeed, the most complete knowledge of the laws of nature would have been unserviceable in her case; for it was impossible to classify her. She was a fifth imponderable body, sharing all the other properties of the ponderable.

VII

Try a Drop of Water

Perhaps the best thing for the princess would have been to fall in love. But how a princess who had no gravity could fall into anything is a difficulty — perhaps *the* difficulty. As for her own feelings on the subject, she did not even know that there was such a beehive of honey and stings to be fallen into. But now I come to mention another curious fact about her.

The palace was built on the shores of the loveliest lake in the world; and the princess loved this lake more than father or mother. The root of this preference no doubt, although the princess did not recognise it as such, was, that the moment she got into it, she recovered the natural right of which she had been so wickedly deprived — namely, gravity.

Whether this was owing to the fact that water had been employed as the means of conveying the injury, I do not know. But it is certain that she could swim and dive like the duck that her old nurse said she was. The manner in which this alleviation of her misfortune was discovered was as follows.

One summer evening, during the carnival of the country, she had been taken upon the lake by the king and queen, in the royal barge. They were accompanied by many of the courtiers in a fleet of little boats. In the middle of the lake she wanted to get into the lord chancellor's barge, for his daughter, who was a great favourite with her, was in it with her father. Now though the old king rarely condescended to make light of his misfortune, yet, happening on this occasion to be in a particularly good humour, as the barges approached each other, he caught up the princess to throw her into the chancellor's barge. He lost his balance, however, and, dropping into the bottom of the barge, lost his hold of his daughter; not, however, before imparting to her the downward tendency of his own person, though in a somewhat different direction; for, as the king fell into the boat, she fell into the water. With a burst of delighted laughter she disappeared in the lake. A cry of horror ascended from the boats. They had never seen the Princess go down before. Half the men were under water in a moment; but they had all, one after another, come up to the surface again for breath, when — tinkle, tinkle, babble, and gush! came the princess's laugh over the water from far away. There she was, swimming like a swan. Nor would she come out for king or queen, chancellor or daughter. She was perfectly obstinate.

But at the same time she seemed more sedate than usual. Perhaps that was because a great pleasure spoils laughing. At all events, after this, the passion of her life was to get into the water, and she was always the better behaved and the more beautiful the more she had of it. Summer and winter it was quite the same; only she could not stay so long in the water when they had to break the ice to let her in. Any day, from morning till evening in summer, she might be descried — a streak of white in the blue water — lying as still as the shadow of a cloud, or shooting along like a dolphin; disappearing, and coming up again far off, just where one did not expect her. She would have been in the lake of a night too, if she could have had her way; for the balcony of her window overhung a deep pool in it; and through a shallow reedy passage she could have swum out into the wide wet water, and no one would have been any wiser. Indeed, when she happened to wake in the moonlight, she could hardly resist the temptation. But there was the sad difficulty of getting into it. She had as great a dread of the air as some children have of the water. For the slightest gust of wind would blow her away; and a gust might arise in the stillest moment. And if she gave herself a push towards the water and just failed of reaching it, her situation would be dreadfully awkward, irrespective of the wind; for at best there she would have to remain, suspended in her night-gown, till she was seen and angled for by somebody from the window.

"Oh! if I had my gravity," thought she, contemplating the water, "I would flash off this balcony like a long white sea-bird, headlong into the darling wetness. Heigh-ho!"

This was the only consideration that made her wish to be like other people.

Another reason for her being fond of the water was that in it alone she enjoyed any freedom. For she could not walk out without a *cortège*, consisting in part of a troop of light-horse, for fear of the liberties which the wind might take with her. And the king grew more apprehensive with increasing years, till at last he would not allow her to walk abroad at all without some twenty silken cords fastened to as many parts of her dress, and held by twenty noblemen. Of course horseback was out of the question. But she bade good-by to all this ceremony when she got into the water.

And so remarkable were its effects upon her, especially in restoring her for the time to the ordinary human gravity, that Hum-Drum and Kopy-Keck agreed in recommending the king to bury her alive for three years; in the hope that, as the water did her so much good, the earth would do her yet more. But the king had some vulgar prejudices against the experiment, and would not give his consent. Foiled in this, they yet agreed

"The Princess Swimming"

in another recommendation; which, seeing that one imported his opinions from China and the other from Tibet, was very remarkable indeed. They argued that, if water of external origin and application could be so efficacious, water from a deeper source might work a perfect cure; in short, that if the poor afflicted princess could by any means be made to cry, she might recover her lost gravity.

But how was this to be brought about? Therein lay all the difficulty — to meet which the philosophers were not wise enough. To make the princess cry was as impossible as to make her weigh. They sent for a professional beggar; commanded him to prepare his most touching oracle of woe; helped him out of the court charade-box, to whatever he wanted for dressing up, and promised great rewards in the event of his success. But it was all in vain. She listened to the mendicant artist's story, and gazed at his marvellous make-up, till she could contain herself no longer, and went into the most undignified contortions for relief, shrieking, positively screeching with laughter.

When she had a little recovered herself, she ordered her attendants to drive him away, and not give him a single copper; whereupon his look of mortified discomfiture wrought her punishment and his revenge, for it sent her into violent hysterics, from which she was with difficulty recovered.

But so anxious was the king that the suggestion should have a fair trial, that he put himself in a rage one day, and, rushing up to her room, gave her an awful whipping. Yet not a tear would flow. She looked grave, and her laughing sounded uncommonly like screaming — that was all. The good old tyrant, though he put on his best gold spectacles to look, could not discover the smallest cloud in the serene blue of her eyes.

IX

Put Me in Again

It must have been about this time that the son of a king, who lived a thousand miles from Lagobel, set out to look for the daughter of a queen. He travelled far and wide, but as sure as he found a princess, he found some fault in her. Of course he could not marry a mere woman, however beautiful; and there was no princess to be found worthy of him. Whether the prince was so near perfection that he had a right to demand perfection itself, I cannot pretend to say. All I know is, that he was a fine, handsome, brave, generous, well-bred, and well-behaved youth, as all princes are.

In his wanderings he had come across some reports about our princess; but as everybody said she was bewitched, he never dreamed that she could bewitch him. For what indeed could a prince do with a princess that had lost her gravity? Who could tell what she might not lose next? She might lose her visibility, or her tangibility; or, in short, the power of making impressions upon the radical sensorium; so that he should never be able to tell whether she was dead or alive. Of course he made no further inquiries about her.

One day he lost sight of his retinue in a great forest. These forests are very useful in delivering princes from their courtiers, like a sieve that keeps back the bran. Then the princes get away to follow their fortunes. In this they have the advantage of the princesses, who are forced to marry before they have had a bit of fun. I wish our princesses got lost in a forest sometimes.

One lovely evening, after wandering about for many days, he found that he was approaching the outskirts of this forest; for the trees had got so thin that he could see the sunset though them; and he soon came upon a kind of heath. Next he came upon signs of human neighbourhood; but by this time it was getting late, and there was nobody in the fields to direct him.

After travelling for another hour, his horse, quite worn out with long labour and lack of food, fell, and was unable to rise again. So he continued his journey on foot. At length he entered another wood — not a wild forest, but a civilized wood, through which a footpath led him to the side of a lake. Along this path the prince pursued his way through the gathering darkness. Suddenly he paused, and listened. Strange sounds came across the water. It was, in fact, the princess laughing. Now there was something odd in her laugh, as I have already hinted; for the hatching of a real hearty laugh requires the incubation of gravity; and perhaps this was how the prince mistook the laughter for screaming. Looking over the lake, he saw something white in the water; and, in an instant, he had torn off his tunic, kicked off his sandals, and plunged in. He soon reached the white object, and found that it was a woman. There was not light enough to show that

"The Prince Lost in the Forest"

she was a princess, but quite enough to show that she was a lady, for it does not want much light to see that.

Now I cannot tell how it came about, — whether she pretended to be drowning, or whether he frightened her, or caught her so as to embarrass her, — but certainly he brought her to shore in a fashion ignominious to a swimmer, and more nearly drowned than she had ever expected to be; for the water had got into her throat as often as she had tried to speak.

At the place to which he bore her, the bank was only a foot or two above the water; so he gave her a strong lift out of the water, to lay her on the bank. But, her gravitation ceasing the moment she left the water, away she went up into the air, scolding and screaming.

"You naughty, *naughty,* NAUGHTY, *NAUGHTY* man!" she cried.

No one had ever succeeded in putting her into a passion before. — When the prince saw her ascend, he thought he must have been bewitched, and have mistaken a great swan for a lady. But the princess caught hold of the topmost cone upon a lofty fir. This came off; but she caught at another; and, in fact, stopped herself by gathering cones, dropping them as the stalks gave way. The prince, meantime, stood in the water, staring, and forgetting to get out. But the princess disappearing, he scrambled on shore, and went in the direction of the tree. There he found her climbing down one of the branches towards the stem. But in the darkness of the wood, the prince continued in some bewilderment as to what the phenomenon could be; until, reaching the ground, and seeing him standing there, she caught hold of him, and said, —

"I'll tell papa."

"Oh no, your won't!" returned the prince.

"Yes, I will," she persisted. "What business had you to pull me down out of the water, and throw me to the bottom of the air? I never did you any harm."

"Pardon me. I did not mean to hurt you."

"I don't believe you have any brains; and that is a worse loss than your wretched gravity. I pity you."

The prince now saw that he had come upon the bewitched princess, and had already offended her. But before he could think what to say next, she burst out angrily, giving a stamp with her foot that would have sent her aloft again but for the hold she had of his arm, —

"Put me up directly."

"Put you up where, you beauty?" asked the prince.

He had fallen in love with her almost, already; for her anger made her more charming than any one else had ever beheld her; and, as far as he could see, which certainly was not far, she had not a single fault about her, except, of course, that she had not any gravity. No prince, however, would judge of a princess by weight. The loveliness of her foot he would hardly estimate by the depth of the impression it could make in mud.

"Put you up where, you beauty?" asked the prince.

"In the water, you stupid!" answered the princess.

"Come, then," said the prince.

The condition of her dress, increasing her usual difficulty in walking, compelled her to cling to him; and he could hardly persuade himself that he was not in a delightful dream, notwithstanding the torrent of musical abuse with which she overwhelmed him. The prince being therefore in no hurry, they came upon the lake at quite another part, where the bank was twenty-five feet high at least; and when they had reached the edge, he turned towards the princess, and said, —

"How am I to put you in?"

"That is your business," she answered, quite snappishly. "You took me out — put me in again."

"Very well," said the prince; and, catching her up in his arms, he sprang with her from the rock. The princess had just time to give one delighted shriek of laughter before the water closed over them. When they came to the surface, she found that, for a moment or two, she could not even laugh, for she had gone down with such a rush, that it was with difficulty she recovered her breath. The instant they reached the surface —

"How do you like falling in?" said the prince.

After some effort the princess panted out, —

"Is that what you call *falling in?*"

"Yes," answered the prince, "I should think it a very tolerable specimen."

"It seemed to me like going up," rejoined she.

"My feeling was certainly one of elevation too," the prince conceded.

The princess did not appear to understand him, for she retorted his question: —

"How do *you* like falling in?" said the princess.

"Beyond everything," answered he; "for I have fallen in with the only perfect creature I ever saw."

"No more of that: I am tired of it," said the princess.

Perhaps she shared her father's aversion to punning.

"Don't you like falling in, then?" said the prince.

"It is the most delightful fun I ever had in my life," answered she. "I never fell before. I wish I could learn. To think I am the only person in my father's kingdom that can't fall!"

Here the poor princess looked almost sad.

"I shall be most happy to fall in with you any time you like," said the prince, devotedly.

"Thank you. I don't know. Perhaps it would not be proper. But I don't care. At all events, as we have fallen in, let us have a swim together."

"With all my heart," responded the prince.

And away they went, swimming, and diving, and floating, until at last they heard cries along the shore, and saw lights glancing in all directions. It was now quite late, and there was no moon.

"I must go home," said the princess. "I am very sorry, for this is delightful."

"So am I," returned the prince. "But I am glad I haven't a home to go to — at least, I don't exactly know where it is."

"I wish I hadn't one either," rejoined the princess; "it is so stupid! I have a great mind," she continued, "to play them all a trick. Why couldn't they leave me alone? They won't trust me in the lake for a single night! — You see where that green light is burning? That is the window of my room. Now if you would just swim there with me very quietly, and when we are all but under the balcony, give me such a push — *up* you call it — as you did a little while ago, I should be able to catch hold of the balcony, and get in at the window; and then they may look for me till tomorrow morning!"

"With more obedience than pleasure," said the prince, gallantly; and away they swam, very gently.

"Will you be in the lake to-morrow night?" the prince ventured to ask.

"To be sure I will. I don't think so. Perhaps," was the princess's somewhat strange answer.

But the prince was intelligent enough not to press her further; and merely whispered, as he gave her the parting lift, "Don't tell." The only answer the princess returned was a roguish look. She was already a yard above his head. The look seemed to say, "Never fear. It is too good fun to spoil that way."

So perfectly like other people had she been in the water, that even yet the prince could scarcely believe his eyes when he saw her ascend slowly, grasp the balcony, and disappear through the window. He turned, almost expecting to see her still by his side. But he was alone in the water. So he swam away quietly, and watched the lights roving about the shore for hours after the princess was safe in her chamber. As soon as they disappeared, he landed in search of his tunic and sword, and, after some trouble, found them again. Then he made the best of his way round the lake to the other side. There the wood was wilder, and the shore steeper — rising more immediately towards the mountains which surrounded the lake on all sides, and kept sending it messages of silvery streams from morning to night, and all night long. He soon found a spot whence he could see the green light in the princess's room, and where, even in the broad daylight, he would be in no danger of being discovered from the opposite shore. It was a sort of cave in the rock, where he provided himself a bed of withered leaves, and lay down too tired for hunger to keep him awake. All night long he dreamed that he was swimming with the princess.

X

Look at the Moon

Early the next morning the prince set out to look for something to eat, which he soon found at a forester's hut, where for many following days he was supplied with all that a brave prince could consider necessary. And having plenty to keep him alive for the present, he would not think of wants not yet in existence. Whenever Care intruded, this prince always bowed him out in the most princely manner.

When he returned from his breakfast to his watch-cave, he saw the princess already floating about in the lake, attended by the king and queen — whom he knew by their crowns — and a great company in lovely little boats, with canopies of all the colours of the rainbow, and flags and streamers of a great many more. It was a very bright day, and soon the prince, burned up with the heat, began to long for the cold

THE LIGHT PRINCESS

water and the cool princess. But he had to endure till twilight; for the boats had provisions on board, and it was not till the sun went down that the gay party began to vanish. Boat after boat drew away to the shore, following that of the king and queen, till only one, apparently the princess's own boat, remained. But she did not want to go home even yet, and the prince thought he saw her order the boat to the shore without her. At all events, it rowed away; and now, of all the radiant company, only one white speck remained. Then the prince began to sing.

And this is what he sang: —

> "Lady fair,
> Swan-white,
> Lift thine eyes,
> Banish night
> By the might
> Of thine eyes.

> "Snowy arms,
> Oars of snow,
> Oar her hither,
> Plashing low.
> Soft and slow,
> Oar her hither.

> "Stream behind her
> O'er the lake,
> Radiant whiteness!
> In her wake
> Following, following for her sake,
> Radiant whiteness!

> "Cling about her,
> Waters blue;
> Part not from her,
> But renew
> Cold and true
> Kisses round her.

THE LIGHT PRINCESS

"Lap me round,
Waters sad
That have left her;
Make me glad,
For ye had
Kissed her ere ye left her."

Before he had finished his song, the princess was just under the place where he sat, and looking up to find him. Her ears had led her truly.

"Would you like a fall, princess?" said the prince, looking down.

"Ah! there you are! Yes, if you please, prince," said the princess, looking up.

"How do you know I am a prince, princess?" said the prince.

"Because you are a very nice young man, prince," said the princess.

"Come up then, princess."

"Fetch me, prince."

The prince took off his scarf, then his sword-belt, then his tunic, and tied them all together, and let them down. But the line was far too short. He unwound his turban, and added it to the rest, when it was all but long enough; and his purse completed it. The princess just managed to lay hold of the knot of money, and was beside him in a moment. This rock was much higher than the other, and the splash and the dive were tremendous. The princess was in ecstasies of delight, and their swim was delicious.

Night after night they met, and swam about in the dark, clear lake; where such was the prince's gladness, that (whether the princess's way of looking at things infected him, or he was actually getting light-headed) he often fancied that he was swimming in the sky instead of the lake. But when he talked about being in heaven, the princess laughed at him dreadfully.

When the moon came, she brought them fresh pleasure. Everything looked strange and new in her light, with an old withered, yet unfading newness. When the moon was nearly full, one of their great delights was to dive deep in the water, and then, turning round, look up through it at the great blot of light close above them, shimmering and trembling and wavering, spreading and contracting, seeming to melt away, and again grow solid. Then they would shoot up through the blot; and lo! there was the moon, far off, clear and steady and cold, and very

THE LIGHT PRINCESS

lovely, at the bottom of a deeper and bluer lake than theirs, as the princess said.

The prince soon found out that while in the water the princess was very like other people. And besides this, she was not so forward in her questions or pert in her replies at sea as on shore. Neither did she laugh so much; and when she did laugh, it was more gently. She seemed altogether more modest and maidenly in the water than out of it. But when the prince, who had really fallen in love when he fell in the lake, began to talk to her about love, she always turned her head towards him and laughed. After a while she began to look puzzled, as if she were trying to understand what he meant, but could not — revealing a notion that he meant something. But as soon as ever she left the lake, she was so altered, that the prince said to himself, "If I marry her, I see no help for it: we must turn merman and mermaid, and go out to sea at once."

XI

Hiss!

The princess's pleasure in the lake had grown to a passion, and she could scarcely bear to be out of it for an hour. Imagine then her consternation, when, diving with the prince one night, a sudden suspicion seized her that the lake was not so deep as it used to be. The prince could not imagine what had happened. She shot to the surface, and, without a word, swam at full speed towards the higher side of the lake. He followed, begging to know if she was ill, or what was the matter. She never turned her head, or took the smallest notice of his question. Arrived at the shore, she coasted the rocks with minute inspection. But she was not able to come to a conclusion, for the moon was very small, and so she could not see well. She turned therefore and swam home, without saying a word to explain her conduct to the prince, of whose presence she seemed no longer conscious. He withdrew to his cave, in great perplexity and distress.

Next day she made many observations, which, alas! strengthened her fears. She saw that the banks were too dry; and that the grass on the shore, and the trailing plants on the rocks, were withering away. She caused marks to be made along the borders, and examined them, day after day, in all directions of the wind; till at last the horrible idea became a certain fact — that the surface of the lake was slowly sinking.

The poor princess nearly went out of the little mind she had. It was awful to her to see the lake, which she loved more than any living thing, lie dying before her eyes. It sank away, slowly vanishing. The tops of rocks that had never been seen till now, began to appear far down in the clear water. Before long they were dry in the sun. It was fearful to think of the mud that would soon lie there baking and festering, full of lovely creatures dying, and ugly creatures coming to life, like the unmaking of a world. And how hot the sun would be without any lake! She could not bear to swim in it any more, and began to pine away. Her life seemed bound up with it; and ever as the lake sank, she pined. People said she would not live an hour after the lake was gone.

But she never cried.

Proclamation was made to all the kingdom, that whosoever should discover the cause of the lake's decrease, would be rewarded after a princely fashion. Hum-Drum and Kopy-Keck applied themselves to their physics and metaphysics; but in vain. Not even they could suggest a cause.

Now the fact was that the old princess was at the root of the mischief. When she heard that her niece found more pleasure in the water than any one else had out of it, she went into a rage, and cursed herself for her want of foresight.

"But," said she, "I will soon set all right. The king and the people shall die of thirst; their brains shall boil and frizzle in their skulls before I will lose my revenge."

And she laughed a ferocious laugh, that made the hairs on the back of her black cat stand erect with terror.

Then she went to an old chest in the room, and opening it, took out what looked like a piece of dried seaweed. This she threw into a tub of water. Then she threw some powder into the water, and stirred it with her bare arm, muttering over it words of hideous sound, and yet more hideous import. Then she set the tub aside, and took from the chest a huge bunch of a hundred rusty keys, that clattered in her shaking hands. Then she sat down and proceeded to oil them all. Before she had finished, out from the tub, the water of which had kept on a slow motion ever since she had ceased stirring it, came the head and half the body of a

❧

huge gray snake. But the witch did not look round. It grew out of the tub, waving itself backwards and forwards with a slow horizontal motion, till it reached the princess, when it laid its head upon her shoulder, and gave a low hiss in her ear. She started — but with joy; and seeing the head resting on her shoulder, drew it towards her and kissed it. Then she drew it all out of the tub, and wound it round her body. It was one of those dreadful creatures which few have ever beheld — the White Snakes of Darkness.

Then she took the keys and went down to her cellar; and as she unlocked the door she said to herself, —

"This is worth living for!"

Locking the door behind her, she descended a few steps into the cellar, and crossing it, unlocked another door into a dark, narrow passage. She locked this also behind her, and descended a few more steps. If any one had followed the witch-princess, he would have heard her unlock exactly one hundred doors, and descend a few steps after unlocking each. When she had unlocked the last, she entered a vast cave, the roof of which was supported by huge natural pillars of rock. Now this room was the under side of the bottom of the lake.

She then untwined the snake from her body, and held it by the tail high above her. The hideous creature stretched up its head towards the roof of the cavern, which was just able to reach. It then began to move its head backwards and forwards, with a slow, oscillating motion, as if looking for something. At the same moment the witch began to walk round and round the cavern, coming nearer to the centre every circuit; while the head of the snake described the same path over the roof that she did over the floor, for she kept holding it up. And still it kept slowly oscillating. Round and round the cavern they went, ever lessening the circuit, till at last the snake made a sudden dart, and clung to the roof with its mouth.

"That's right, my beauty!" cried the princess; "drain it dry."

She let it go, left it hanging, and sat down on a great stone, with her black cat, which had followed her all round the cave, by her side. Then she began to knit and mutter awful words. The snake hung like a huge leech, sucking at the stone; the cat stood with his back arched, and his tail like a piece of cable, looking up at the snake; and the old woman sat and knitted and muttered. Seven days and seven nights they remained thus; when suddenly the serpent dropped from the roof as if exhausted, and shrivelled up till it was again like a piece of dried seaweed. The witch started to her feet, picked it up, put it in her pocket, and looked up at the roof. One drop of water was trembling on the spot where the snake had been sucking. As soon as she saw that, she turned and fled, followed by her cat. Shutting the door in a terrible hurry, she locked it, and having muttered some frightful words, sped to the next, which also she locked and muttered over; and so with all the hundred doors, till she arrived in her own cellar. There she sat down on the floor ready to faint, but listening with malicious delight to the rushing of the water, which she could hear distinctly through all the hundred doors.

But this was not enough. Now that she had tasted revenge, she lost her patience. Without further measures, the lake would be too long in disappearing. So the next night, with the last shred of the dying old moon rising, she took some of the water in which she had revived the snake, put it in a bottle, and set out, accompanied by her cat. Before morning she had made the entire circuit of the lake, muttering fearful words as she crossed every stream, and casting into it some of the water out of her bottle. When she had finished the circuit she muttered yet again, and flung a handful of water towards the moon. Thereupon every spring in the country ceased to throb and bubble, dying away like the pulse of a dying man. The next day there was no sound of falling water to be heard along the borders of the lake. The very courses were dry; and the mountains showed no silvery streaks down their dark sides. And not alone had the fountains of mother Earth ceased to flow; for all the babies throughout the country were crying dreadfully — only without tears.

XII

Where Is the Prince?

Never since the night when the princess left him so abruptly had the prince had a single interview with her. He had seen her once or twice in the lake; but as far as he could discover, she had not been in it any more at night. He had sat and sung, and looked in vain for his Nereid; while she, like a true Nereid, was wasting away with her lake, sinking as it sank, withering as it dried. When at length he discovered the change that was taking place in the level of the water, he was in great alarm and perplexity. He could not tell whether the lake was dying because the lady had forsaken it; or whether the lady would not come because the lake had begun to sink. But he resolved to know so much at least.

He disguised himself, and, going to the palace, requested to see the lord chamberlain. His appearance at once gained his request; and the lord chamberlain, being a man of some insight, perceived that there was more in the prince's solicitation than met the ear. He felt likewise that no one could tell whence a solution of the present difficulties might arise. So he granted the prince's prayer to be made shoe-black to the princess. It was rather cunning in the prince to request such an easy post, for the princess could not possibly soil as many shoes as other princesses.

He soon learned all that could be told about the princess. He went nearly distracted; but after roaming about the lake for days, and diving in every depth that remained, all that he could do was to put an extra polish on the dainty pair of boots that was never called for.

For the princess kept her room, with the curtains drawn to shut out the dying lake. But she could not shut it out of her mind for a moment. It haunted her imagination so that she felt as if the lake were her soul, drying up within her, first to mud, then to madness and death. She thus brooded over the change, with all its dreadful accompaniments, till she was nearly distracted. As for the prince, she had forgotten him. However much she had enjoyed his company in the water, she did not care for him without it. But she seemed to have forgotten her father and mother too.

The lake went on sinking. Small slimy spots began to appear, which glittered steadily amidst the changeful shine of the water. These grew to broad patches of mud, which widened and spread, with rocks here and there, and floundering fishes and crawling eels swarming. The people went everywhere catching these, and looking for anything that might have dropped from the royal boats.

At length the lake was all but gone, only a few of the deepest pools remaining unexhausted.

It happened one day that a party of youngsters found themselves on the brink of one of these pools in the very centre of the lake. It was a rocky basin of considerable depth. Looking in, they saw at the bottom something that shone yellow in the sun. A little boy jumped in and dived for it. It was a plate of gold covered with writing. They carried it to the king.

On one side of it stood these words: —

"Death alone from death can save.
Love is death, and so is brave.
Love can fill the deepest grave.
Love loves on beneath the wave."

Now this was enigmatical enough to the king and courtiers. But the reverse of the plate explained it a little. Its writing amounted to this: —
"If the lake should disappear, they must find the hole through which the water ran. But it would be useless to try to stop it by any ordinary means. There was but one effectual mode. — The body of a living man should alone stanch the flow. The man must give himself of his own will; and the lake must take his life as it filled. Otherwise the offering would be of no avail. If the nation could not provide one hero, it was time it should perish."

XIII

Here I Am

This was a very disheartening revelation to the king — not that he was unwilling to sacrifice a subject, but that he was hopeless of finding a man willing to sacrifice himself. No time was to be lost, however, for the princess was lying motionless on her bed, and taking no nourishment but lake-water, which was now none of the best. Therefore the king caused the contents of the wonderful plate of gold to be published throughout the country.

No one, however, came forward.

The prince, having gone several days' journey into the forest, to consult a hermit whom he had met there on his way to Lagobel, knew nothing of the oracle till his return.

When he had acquainted himself with all the particulars, he sat down and thought, —

❧   THE LIGHT PRINCESS

"She will die if I don't do it, and life would be nothing to me without her; so I shall lose nothing by doing it. And life will be as pleasant to her as ever, for she will soon forget me. And there will be so much more beauty and happiness in the world! — To be sure, I shall not see it." (Here the poor prince gave a sigh.) "How lovely the lake will be in the moonlight, with that glorious creature sporting in it like a wild goddess! — It is rather hard to be drowned by inches, though. Let me see — that will be seventy inches of me to drown." (Here he tried to laugh, but could not.) "The longer the better, however," he resumed; "for can I not bargain that the princess shall be beside me all the time? So I shall see her once more, kiss her perhaps, — who knows? and die looking in her eyes. It will be no death. At least, I shall not feel it. And to see the lake filling for the beauty again! — All right! I am ready."

He kissed the princess's boot, laid it down, and hurried to the king's apartment. But feeling, as he went, that anything sentimental would be disagreeable, he resolved to carry off the whole affair with nonchalance. So he knocked at the door of the king's counting-house, where it was all but a capital crime to disturb him.

When the king heard the knock he started up, and opened the door in a rage. Seeing only the shoeblack, he drew his sword. This, I am sorry to say, was his usual mode of asserting his regality when he thought his dignity was in danger. But the prince was not in the least alarmed.

"Please your majesty, I'm your butler," said he.

"My butler! you lying rascal! What do you mean?"

"I mean, I will cork your big bottle."

"Is the fellow mad?" bawled the king, raising the point of his sword.

"I will put a stopper — plug — what you call it, in your leaky lake, grand monarch," said the prince.

The king was in such a rage that before he could speak he had time to cool, and to reflect that it would be great waste to kill the only man who was willing to be useful in the present emergency, seeing that in the end the insolent fellow would be as dead as if he had died by his majesty's own hand.

"Oh!" said he at last, putting up his sword with difficulty, it was so long; "I am obliged to you, you young fool! Take a glass of wine?"

"No, thank you," replied the prince.

"Very well," said the king. "Would you like to run and see your parents before you make your experiment?"

"No, thank you," said the prince.

"Then we will go and look for the hole at once," said his majesty, and proceeded to call some attendants.

"Stop, please your majesty; I have a condition to make," interposed the prince.

"What!" exclaimed the king, "a condition! and with me! How dare you?"

"As you please," returned the prince, coolly. "I wish your majesty a good morning."

"You wretch! I will have you put in a sack, and stuck in the hole."

"Very well, your majesty," replied the prince, becoming a little more respectful, lest the wrath of the king should deprive him of the pleasure of dying for the princess. "But what good will that do your majesty? Please to remember that the oracle says the victim must offer himself."

"Well, you *have* offered yourself," retorted the king.

"Yes, upon one condition."

"Condition again!" roared the king, once more drawing his sword. "Begone! Somebody else will be glad enough to take the honour off your shoulders."

"Your majesty knows it will not be easy to get another to take my place."

"Well, what is your condition?" growled the king, feeling that the prince was right.

"Only this," replied the prince: "that, as I must on no account die before I am fairly drowned, and the waiting will be rather wearisome, the princess, your daughter, shall go with me, feed me with her own hands, and look at me now and then to comfort me; for you must confess it *is* rather hard. As soon as the water is up to my eyes, she may go and be happy, and forget her poor shoeblack."

Here the prince's voice faltered, and he very nearly grew sentimental, in spite of his resolution.

"Why didn't you tell me before what your condition was? Such a fuss about nothing!" exclaimed the king.

"Do you grant it?" persisted the prince.

"Of course I do," replied the king.

"Very well. I am ready."

"Go and have some dinner, then, while I set my people to find the place."

❧   THE LIGHT PRINCESS

The king ordered out his guards, and gave directions to the officers to find the hole in the lake at once. So the bed of the lake was marked out in divisions and thoroughly examined, and in an hour or so the hole was discovered. It was in the middle of a stone, near the centre of the lake, in the very pool where the golden plate had been found. It was a three-cornered hole of no great size. There was water all round the stone, but very little was flowing through the hole.

XIV

This Is Very Kind of You

The prince went to dress for the occasion, for he was resolved to die like a prince.

When the princess heard that a man had offered to die for her, she was so transported that she jumped off the bed, feeble as she was, and danced about the room for joy. She did not care who the man was; that was nothing to her. The hole wanted stopping; and if only a man would do, why, take one. In an hour or two more everything was ready. Her maid dressed her in haste, and they carried her to the side of the lake. When she saw it she shrieked, and covered her face with her hands. They bore her across to the stone, where they had already placed a little boat for her. The water was not deep enough to float it, but they hoped it would be, before long. They laid her on cushions, placed in the boat wines and fruits and other nice things, and stretched a canopy over all.

In a few minutes the prince appeared. The princess recognized him at once, but did not think it worthwhile to acknowledge him.

"Here I am," said the prince. "Put me in."

"They told me it was a shoeblack," said the princess.

"So I am," said the prince. "I blacked your little boots three times a day, because they were all I could get of you. Put me in."

The courtiers did not resent his bluntness, except by saying to each other that he was taking it out in impudence.

But how was he to be put in? The golden plate contained no instructions on this point. The prince looked at the hole, and saw but one way. He put both his legs into it, sitting on the stone, and, stooping forward, covered the corner that remained open with his two hands. In this uncomfortable position he resolved to abide his fate, and turning to the people, said, —

"Now you can go."

The king had already gone home to dinner.

"Now you can go," repeated the princess after him, like a parrot.

The people obeyed her and went.

Presently a little wave flowed over the stone, and wetted one of the prince's knees. But he did not mind it much. He began to sing, and the song he sang was this: —

"As a world that has no well,
Darkly bright in forest dell;
As a world without the gleam
Of the downward-going stream;
As a world without the glance
Of the ocean's fair expanse;
As a world where never rain
Glittered on the sunny plain; —
Such, my heart, thy world would be,
If no love did flow in thee.

"As a world without the sound
Of the rivulets underground;
Or the bubbling of the spring
Out of darkness wandering;
Or the mighty rush and flowing
Of the river's downward going;
Or the music-showers that drop
On the outspread beech's top;
Or the ocean's mighty voice,
When his lifted waves rejoice; —
Such, my soul, thy world would be,
If no love did sing in thee.

"Lady, keep thy world's delight;
Keep the waters in thy sight.

THE LIGHT PRINCESS

Love hath made me strong to go,
For thy sake, to realms below,
Where the water's shine and hum
Through the darkness never come:
Let, I pray, one thought of me
Spring, a little well, in thee;
Lest thy loveless soul be found
Like a dry and thirsty ground."

"Sing again, prince. It makes it less tedious," said the princess.

But the prince was too much overcome to sing any more, and a long pause followed.

"This is very kind of you, prince," said the princess at last, quite coolly, as she lay in the boat with her eyes shut.

"I am sorry I can't return the compliment," thought the prince; "but you are worth dying for, after all."

Again a wavelet, and another, and another flowed over the stone, and wetted both the prince's knees; but he did not speak or move.

Two — three — four hours passed in this way, the princess apparently asleep, and the prince very patient. But he was much disappointed in his position, for he had none of the consolation he had hoped for.

At last he could bear it no longer.

"Princess!" said he.

But at the moment up started the princess, crying, —

"I'm afloat! I'm afloat!"

And the little boat bumped against the stone.

"Princess!" repeated the prince, encouraged by seeing her wide awake and looking eagerly at the water.

"Well?" said she, without looking round.

"Your papa promised that you should look at me, and you haven't looked at me once."

"Did he?" "Then I suppose I must. But I am so sleepy!"

"Sleep then, darling, and don't mind me," said the poor prince.

"Really, you are very good," replied the princess. "I think I will go to sleep again."

"Just give me a glass of wine and a biscuit first," said the prince, very humbly.

"With all my heart," said the princess, and gaped as she said it.

She got the wine and the biscuit, however, and leaning over the side of the boat towards him, was compelled to look at him.

"Why, prince," she said, "you don't look well! Are you sure you don't mind it?"

"Not a bit," answered he, feeling very faint indeed. "Only I shall die before it is of any use to you, unless I have something to eat."

"There, then," said she, holding out the wine to him.

"Ah! you must feed me. I dare not move my hands. The water would run away directly."

"Good gracious!" said the princess; and she began at once to feed him with bits of biscuit and sips of wine.

As she fed him, he contrived to kiss the tips of her fingers now and then. She did not seem to mind it, one way or the other. But the prince felt better.

"Now, for your own sake, princess," said he, "I cannot let you go to sleep. You must sit and look at me, else I shall not be able to keep up."

"Well, I will do anything I can to oblige you," answered she, with condescension; and, sitting down, she did look at him, and kept looking at him with wonderful steadiness, considering all things.

The sun went down, and the moon rose, and, gush after gush, the waters were rising up the prince's body. They were up to his waist now.

"Why can't we go and have a swim?" said the princess. "There seems to be water enough just about here."

"I shall never swim more," said the prince.

"Oh, I forgot," said the princess, and was silent.

So the water grew and grew, and rose up and up on the prince. And the princess sat and looked at him. She fed him now and then. The night wore on. The waters rose and rose. The moon rose likewise higher and higher, and shone full on the face of the dying prince. The water was up to his neck.

"Will you kiss me, princess?" said he, feebly. The nonchalance was all gone now.

"Yes, I will," answered the princess, and kissed him with a long, sweet, cold kiss.

"Now," said he, with a sigh of content, "I die happy."

He did not speak again. The princess gave him some wine for the last time: he was past eating. Then she sat down again, and looked at him. The water rose and rose. It touched his chin. It touched his lower lip. It touched between his lips. He shut them hard to keep it out. The princess

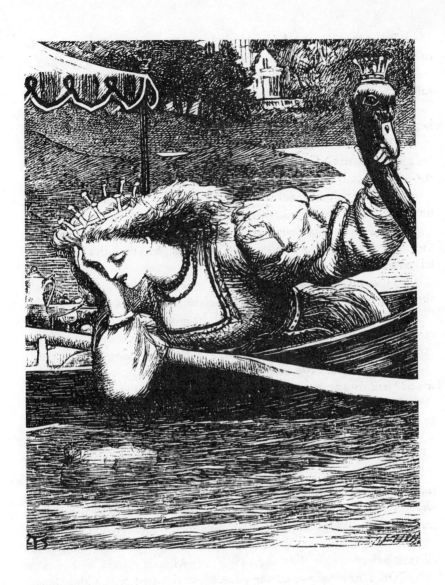

"On the Water"

began to feel strange. It touched his upper lip. He breathed through his nostrils. The princess looked wild. It covered his nostrils. Her eyes looked scared, and shone strange in the moonlight. His head fell back; the water closed over it, and the bubbles of his last breath bubbled up through the water. The princess gave a shriek, and sprang into the lake.

She laid hold first of one leg, and then of the other, and pulled and tugged, but she could not move either. She stopped to take breath, and that made her think that he could not get any breath. She was frantic. She got hold of him, and held his head above the water, which was possible now his hands were no longer on the hole. But it was of no use, for he was past breathing.

Love and water brought back all her strength. She got under the water, and pulled and pulled with her whole might, till at last she got one leg out. The other easily followed. How she got him into the boat she never could tell; but when she did, she fainted away. Coming to herself, she seized the oars, kept herself steady as best she could, and rowed and rowed, though she had never rowed before. Round rocks, and over shallows, and through mud she rowed, till she got to the landing-stairs of the palace. By this time her people were on the shore, for they had heard her shriek. She made them carry the prince to her own room, and lay him in her bed, and light a fire, and send for the doctors.

"But the lake, your highness!" said the chamberlain, who, roused by the noise, came in, in his nightcap.

"Go and drown yourself in it!" she said.

This was the last rudeness of which the princess was ever guilty; and one must allow that she had good cause to feel provoked with the lord chamberlain.

Had it been the king himself, he would have fared no better. But both he and the queen were fast asleep. And the chamberlain went back to his bed. Somehow, the doctors never came. So the princess and her old nurse were left with the prince. But the old nurse was a wise woman, and knew what to do.

They tried everything for a long time without success. The princess was nearly distracted between hope and fear, but she tried on and on, one thing after another, and everything over and over again.

At last, when they had all but given it up, just as the sun rose, the prince opened his eyes.

XV

Look at the Rain!

The princess burst into a passion of tears, and *fell* on the floor. There she lay for an hour, and her tears never ceased. All the pent-up crying of her life was spent now. And a rain came on, such as had never been seen in that country. The sun shone all the time, and the great drops, which fell straight to the earth, shone likewise. The palace was in the heart of a rainbow. It was a rain of rubies, and sapphires, and emeralds, and topazes. The torrents poured from the mountains like molten gold; and if it had not been for its subterraneous outlet, the lake would have overflowed and inundated the country. It was full from shore to shore.

But the princess did not heed the lake. She lay on the floor and wept. And this rain within doors was far more wonderful than the rain out of doors. For when it abated a little, and she proceeded to rise, she found, to her astonishment, that she could not. At length, after many efforts, she succeeded in getting upon her feet. But she tumbled down again directly. Hearing her fall, her old nurse uttered a yell of delight, and ran to her screaming, —

"My darling child! she's found her gravity!"

"Oh, that's it! is it?" said the princess, rubbing her shoulder and her knee alternately. "I consider it very unpleasant. I feel as if I should be crushed to pieces."

"Hurrah!" cried the prince from the bed. "If you've come round, princess, so have I. How's the lake?"

"Brimful," answered the nurse.

"Then we're all happy."

"That we are indeed!" answered the princess, sobbing.

And there was rejoicing all over the country that rainy day. Even the babies forgot their past troubles, and danced and crowed amazingly. And the king told stories, and the queen listened to them. And he divided the money in his box, and she the honey in her pot, among all the children. And there was such jubilation as was never heard of before.

Of course the prince and princess were betrothed at once. But the princess had to learn to walk, before they could be married with any propriety. And this was not so easy at her time of life, for she could walk no more than a baby. She was always falling down and hurting herself.

"Is this the gravity you used to make so much of?" said she one day to the prince, as he raised her from the floor. "For my part, I was a great deal more comfortable without it."

"No, no, that's not it. This is it," replied the prince, as he took her up, and carried her about like a baby, kissing her all the time. "This is gravity."

"That's better," said she. "I don't mind that so much."

And she smiled the sweetest, loveliest smile in the prince's face. And she gave him one little kiss in return for all his; and he thought them overpaid, for he was beside himself with delight. I fear she complained of her gravity more than once after this, notwithstanding.

It was a long time before she got reconciled to walking. But the pain of learning it was quite counterbalanced by two things, either of which would have been sufficient consolation. The first was, that the prince himself was her teacher; and the second, that she could tumble into the lake as often as she pleased. Still, she preferred to have the prince jump in with her; and the splash they made before was nothing to the splash they made now.

The lake never sank again. In process of time, it wore the roof of the cavern quite through, and was twice as deep as before.

The only revenge the princess took upon her aunt was to tread pretty hard on her gouty toe the next time she saw her. But she was sorry for it the very next day, when she heard that the water had undermined her house, and that it had fallen in the night, burying her in its ruins; whence no one ever ventured to dig up her body. There she lies to this day.

So the prince and princess lived and were happy; and had crowns of gold, and clothes of cloth, and shoes of leather, and children of boys and girls, not one of whom was ever known, on the most critical occasion, to lose the smallest atom of his or her due proportion of gravity.

The Shadows

Old Ralph Rinkelmann made his living by comic sketches, and all but lost it again by tragic poems. So he was just the man to be chosen king of the fairies, for in Fairy-land the sovereignty is elective.

It is no doubt very strange that fairies should desire to have a mortal king; but the fact is, that with all their knowledge and power, they cannot get rid of the feeling that some men are greater than they are, though they can neither fly nor play tricks. So at such times as there happen to be twice the usual number of sensible electors, such a man as Ralph Rinkelmann gets to be chosen.

They did not mean to insist on his residence; for they needed his presence only on special occasions. But they must get hold of him somehow, first of all, in order to make him king. Once he was crowned, they could get him as often as they pleased; but before this ceremony, there was a difficulty. For it is only between life and death that the fairies have power over grown-up mortals, and can carry them off to their country. So they had to watch for an opportunity.

Nor had they to wait long. For old Ralph was taken dreadfully ill; and while hovering between life and death, they carried him off, and crowned him King of Fairy-land. But after he was crowned, it was no wonder, considering the state of his health, that he should not be able to sit quite upright on the throne of Fairy-land; or that, in consequence, all the gnomes and goblins, and ugly, cruel things that live in the holes and corners of the kingdom, should take advantage of his condition, and run quite wild, playing him, king as he was, all sorts of tricks; crowding about his throne, climbing up the steps, and actually scrambling and quarreling like mice about his ears and eyes, so that he could see and think of nothing else. But I am not going to tell anything more about this part of his adventures just at present. By strong and sustained efforts, he succeeded, after much trouble and suffering, in reducing his rebellious subjects to order. They all vanished to their respective holes and corners; and King Ralph, coming to himself, found himself in his bed, half propped up with pillows.

But the room was full of dark creatures, which gambolled about in the firelight in such a strange, huge, though noiseless fashion, that he thought at first that some of his rebellious goblins had not been subdued with the rest, but had followed him beyond the bounds of Fairy-land into his own private house in London. How else could these mad, grotesque hippopotamus-calves make their ugly appearance in Ralph Rinkelmann's bedroom? But he soon found out that although they were like the underground goblins, they were very different as well, and would require quite different treatment. He felt convinced that they were his subjects too, but that he must have overlooked them somehow at his late coronation — if indeed they had been present; for he could not recollect that he had seen anything just like them before. He resolved, therefore, to pay particular attention to their habits, ways, and characters; else he saw plainly that they would soon be too much for him; as indeed this intrusion into his chamber, where Mrs. Rinkelmann, who must be queen if he was king, sat taking some tea by the fireside, evidently foreshadowed. But she, perceiving that he was looking about him with a more composed expression than his face had worn for many days, started up, and came quickly and quietly to his side, and her face was bright with gladness. Whereupon the fire burned up more cheerily; and the figures became more composed and respectful in their behaviour, retreating towards the wall like well-trained attendants. Then the king of Fairy-land had some tea and dry toast, and leaning back on his pillows, nearly fell asleep; but not quite, for he still watched the intruders.

Presently the queen left the room to give some of the young princes and princesses their tea; and the fire burned lower, and behold, the figures grew as black and as mad in their gambols as ever! Their favourite games seemed to be *Hide and Seek; Touch and Go; Grin and Vanish,* and many other such; and all in the king's bedchamber, too; so that it was quite alarming. It was almost as bad as if the house had been haunted by certain creatures which shall be nameless in a fairy story, because with them fairyland will not willingly have much to do.

"But it is a mercy that they have their slippers on!" said the king to himself; for his head ached.

As he lay back, with his eyes half shut and half open, too tired to pay longer attention to their games, but, on the whole, considerably more amused than offended with the liberties they took, for they seemed good-natured creatures, and more frolicsome than positively ill-mannered, he became suddenly aware that two of them had stepped forward from the walls, upon which, after the manner of great spiders, most of them preferred sprawling, and now stood in the middle of the floor at the foot of his majesty's bed, becking and bowing and ducking in the most grotesquely obsequious manner; while every now and then they turned solemnly round upon one heel, evidently considering that motion the highest token of homage they could show.

"What do you want?" said the king.

"That it may please your majesty to be better acquainted with us," answered they. "We are your majesty's subjects."

"I know you are. I shall be most happy," answered the king.

"We are not what your majesty takes us for, though. We are not so foolish as your majesty thinks us."

"It is impossible to take you for anything that I know of," rejoined the king, who wished to make them talk, and said whatever came uppermost; — "for soldiers, sailors, or anything: you will not stand still long enough. I suppose you really belong to the fire brigade; at least, you keep putting its light out."

"Don't jest, please your majesty." And as they said the words — for they both spoke at once throughout the interview — they performed a grave somerset towards the king.

"Not jest!" retorted he; "and with you? Why, you do nothing but jest. What are you?"

"The Shadows, sire. And when we do jest, sire, we always jest in earnest. But perhaps your majesty does not see us distinctly."

"I see you perfectly well," returned the king.

"Permit me, however," rejoined one of the Shadows; and as he spoke he approached the king; and lifting a dark forefinger, he drew it lightly but carefully across the ridge of his forehead, from temple to temple. The king felt the soft gliding touch go, like water, into every hollow, and over the top of every height of that mountain-chain of thought. He had involuntarily closed his eyes during the operation, and when he unclosed them again, as soon as the finger was withdrawn, he found that they were opened in more senses than one. The room appeared to have extended itself on all sides, till he could not exactly see where the walls were; and all about it stood the Shadows motionless. They were tall and solemn; rather awful, indeed, in their appearance, notwithstanding many remarkable traits of grotesqueness, for they looked just like the pictures of Puritans drawn by Cavaliers, with long arms, and very long, thin legs, from which hung large, loose feet, while in their countenances length of chin and nose predominated. The solemnity of their mien, however, overcame all the oddity of their form, so that they were very *eerie* indeed to look at, dressed as they all were in funereal black. But a single glance was all that the king was allowed to have; for the former operator waved his dusky palm across his vision, and once more the king saw only the fire-lighted walls, and dark shapes flickering about upon them. The two who had spoken for the rest seemed likewise to have vanished. But at last the king discovered them, standing one on each side of the fireplace. They kept close to the chimney-wall, and talked to each other across the length of the chimney-piece; thus avoiding the direct rays of the fire, which, though light is necessary to their appearing to human eyes, do not agree with them at all — much less give birth to them, as the king was soon to learn. After a few minutes they again approached the bed, and spoke thus: —

"It is now getting dark, please your majesty. We mean, out of doors in the snow. Your majesty may see, from where he is lying, the cold light of its great winding-sheet — a famous carpet for the Shadows to dance upon, your majesty. All our brothers and sisters will be at church now, before going to their night's work."

"Do they always go to church before they go to work?"

"They always go to church first."

"Where is the church?"

"In Iceland. Would your majesty like to see it?"

"How can I go and see it, when, as you know very well, I am ill in bed? Besides, I should be sure to take cold in a frosty night like this, even if I put on the blankets, and took the feather-bed for a muff."

A sort of quivering passed over their faces, which seemed to be their mode of laughing. The whole shape of the face shook and fluctuated as if it had been some dark fluid; till, by slow degrees of gathering calm, it settled into its former rest. Then one of them drew aside the curtains of the bed, and the window-curtains not having been yet drawn, the king beheld the white glimmering night outside, struggling with the heaps of darkness that tried to quench it; and the heavens full of stars, flashing and sparkling like live jewels. The other Shadow went towards the fire and vanished in it.

Scores of Shadows immediately began an insane dance all about the room; disappearing, one after the other, through the uncovered window, and gliding darkly away over the face of the white snow; for the window looked at once on a field of snow. In a few moments the room was quite cleared of them; but instead of being relieved by their absence, the king felt immediately as if he were in a dead-house, and could hardly breathe for the sense of emptiness and desolation that fell upon him. But as he lay looking out on the snow, which stretched blank and wide before him, he spied in the distance a long dark line which drew nearer and nearer, and showed itself at last to be all the Shadows, walking in a double row, and carrying in the midst of them something like a bier. They vanished under the window, but soon reappeared, having somehow climbed up the wall of the house; for they entered in perfect order by the window, as if melting through the transparency of the glass.

They still carried the bier or litter. It was covered with richest furs, and skins of gorgeous wild beasts, whose eyes were replaced by sapphires and emeralds, that glittered and gleamed in the fire and snow light. The outermost skin sparkled with frost, but the inside ones were soft and warm and dry as the down under a swan's wing. The Shadows approached the bed, and set the litter upon it. Then a number of them brought a huge fur robe, and wrapping it round the king, laid him on the litter in the midst of the furs. Nothing could be more gentle and respectful than the way in which they moved him; and he never thought of refusing to go. Then they put something on his head, and, lifting the litter, carried him once round the room, to fall into order. As he passed the mirror he saw that he was covered with royal ermine, and that his head wore a wonderful crown of gold, set with none but red stones: rubies and carbuncles and garnets, and others whose names he could not tell, glowed gloriously around his head, like the salamandrine essence of all the Christmas fires over the world. A sceptre lay beside him — a rod of ebony, surmounted by a cone-shaped diamond, which, cut in a hundred facets, flashed all the hues of the rainbow, and threw coloured gleams on every side, that looked like Shadows too, but more ethereal than those that bore him. Then the Shadows rose gently to the window, passed through it, and sinking slowly upon the field of outstretched snow, commenced an orderly gliding rather than march along the frozen surface. They took it by turns to bear the king, as they sped with the swiftness of thought, in a straight line towards the north. The pole-star rose above their heads with visible rapidity; for indeed they moved quite as fast as sad thoughts, though not with all the speed of happy desires. England and Scotland slid past the litter of the king of the Shadows. Over rivers and lakes they skimmed and glided. They climbed the high mountains, and crossed the valleys with a fearless bound; till they came to John-o'-Groat's house and the Northern Sea. The sea was not frozen; for all the stars shone as clear out of the deeps below as they shone out of the deeps above; and as the bearers slid along the blue-gray surface, with never a furrow in their track, so pure was the water beneath, that the king saw neither surface, bottom, nor substance to it, and seemed to be gliding only through the blue sphere of heaven, with the stars above him, and the stars below him, and between the stars and him nothing but an emptiness, where, for the first time in his life, his soul felt that it had room enough.

At length they reached the rocky shores of Iceland. There they landed, still pursuing their journey. All this time the king felt no cold; for the red stones in his crown kept him warm, and the emerald and sapphire eyes of the wild beasts kept the frosts from settling upon his litter.

Oftentimes upon their way they had to pass through forests, caverns, and rock-shadowed paths, where it was so dark that at first the king feared he should lose his Shadows altogether. But as soon as they entered such places, the diamond in his sceptre began to shine, and glow, and flash, sending out streams of light of all the colours that painter's soul could dream of; in which light the Shadows grew livelier and stronger than ever, speeding through the dark ways with an all but blinding swiftness. In the light of the diamond, too, some of their forms became more simple and human, while others seemed only to break out into a yet more untamable absurdity. Once, as they passed through a cave, the king actually saw some of their eyes — strange shadow-eyes: he had never seen any of their eyes before. But at the same moment when he saw their eyes, he knew their faces too, for they turned them full upon him for an instant; and the other Shadows, catching sight of these, shrank and shivered, and nearly vanished. Lovely faces they were; but the king was very thoughtful after he saw them,

"The Shadowy Funeral"

and continued rather troubled all the rest of the journey. He could not account for those faces being there, and the faces of Shadows, too, with living eyes.

But he soon found that amongst the Shadows a man must learn never to be surprised at anything; for if he does not, he will soon grow quite stupid, in consequence of the endless recurrence of surprises.

At last they climbed up the bed of a little stream, and then, passing through a narrow, rocky defile, came out suddenly upon the side of a mountain, overlooking a blue frozen lake in the very heart of mighty hills. Overhead, the *aurora borealis* was shivering and flashing like a battle of ten thousand spears. Underneath, its beams passed faintly over the blue ice and the sides of the snow-clad mountains, whose tops shot up like huge icicles all about, with here and there a star sparkling on the very tip of one. But as the northern lights in the sky above, so wavered and quivered, and shot hither and thither, the Shadows on the surface of the lake below; now gathering in groups, and now shivering asunder; now covering the whole surface of the lake, and anon condensed into one dark knot in the centre. Every here and there on the white mountains might be seen two or three shooting away towards the tops, to vanish beyond them, so that their number was gradually, though not visibly, diminishing.

"Please your majesty," said the Shadows, "this is our church — the Church of the Shadows."

And so saying, the king's body-guard set down the litter upon a rock, and plunged into the multitudes below. They soon returned, however, and bore the king down into the middle of the lake. All the Shadows came crowding round him, respectfully but fearlessly; and sure never such a grotesque assembly revealed itself before to mortal eyes. The king had seen all kinds of gnomes, goblins, and kobolds at his coronation; but they were quite rectilinear figures compared with the insane lawlessness of form in which the Shadows rejoiced; and the wildest gambols of the former were orderly dances of ceremony beside the apparently aimless and willful contortions of figure, and metamorphoses of shape, in which the latter indulged. They retained, however, all the time, to the surprise of the king, an identity, each of his own type, inexplicably perceptible through every change. Indeed, this preservation of the primary idea of each form was more wonderful than the bewildering and ridiculous alterations to which the form itself was every moment subjected.

"What are you?" said the king, leaning on his elbow, and looking around him.

"The Shadows, your majesty," answered several voices at once.

"What Shadows?"

"The human Shadows. The Shadows of men, women, and their children."

"Are you not the shadows of chairs and tables, and pokers and tongs, just as well?"

At this question a strange jarring commotion went through the assembly with a shock. Several of the figures shot up as high as the aurora, but instantly settled down again to human size, as if over-mastering their feelings, out of respect to him who had roused them. One who had bounded to the highest visible icy peak, and as suddenly returned, now elbowed his way through the rest, and made himself spokesman for them during the remaining part of the dialogue.

"Excuse our agitation, your majesty," said he. "I see your majesty has not yet thought proper to make himself acquainted with our nature and habits."

"I wish to do so now," replied the king.

"We are the Shadows," repeated the Shadow, solemnly.

"Well?" said the king.

"We do not often appear to men."

"Ha!" said the king.

"We do not belong to the sunshine at all. We go through it unseen, and only by a passing chill do men recognise an unknown presence."

"Ha!" said the king again.

"It is only in the twilight of the fire, or when one man or woman is alone with a single candle, or when any number of people are all feeling the same thing at once, making them one, that we show ourselves, and the truth of things."

"Can that be true that loves the night?" said the king.

"The darkness is the nurse of light," answered the Shadow.

"Can that be true which mocks at forms?" said the king.

"Truth rides abroad in shapeless storms," answered the Shadow.

"Ha! ha!" thought Ralph Rinkelmann, "it rhymes. The Shadow caps my questions with his answers. Very strange!" And he grew thoughtful again.

The Shadow was the first to resume.

"Please your majesty, may we present our petition?"

"By all means," replied the king. "I am not well enough to receive it in proper state."

"Never mind, your majesty. We do not care for much ceremony; and indeed none of us are quite well at present. The subject of our petition weighs upon us."

"Go on," said the king.

"Sire," began the Shadow, "our very existence is in danger. The various sorts of artificial light, both in houses and in men, women, and children, threaten to end our being. The use and the disposition of gaslights, especially high in the centres, blind the eyes by which alone we can be perceived. We are all but banished from towns. We are driven into villages and lonely houses, chiefly old farm-houses, out of which, even, our friends the fairies are fast disappearing. We therefore petition our king, by the power of his art, to restore us to our rights in the house itself, and in the hearts of its inhabitants."

"But," said the king, "you frighten the children."

"Very seldom, your majesty; and then only for their good. We seldom seek to frighten anybody. We mostly want to make people silent and thoughtful; to awe them a little, your majesty."

"You are much more likely to make them laugh," said the king.

"Are we?" said the Shadow.

And approaching the king one step, he stood quite still for a moment. The diamond of the king's sceptre shot out a vivid flame of violet light, and the king stared at the Shadow in silence, and his lip quivered. He never told what he saw then; but he would say:

"Just fancy what it might be if *some* flitting thoughts were to persist in staying to be looked at."

"It is only," resumed the Shadow, "when our thoughts are not fixed upon any particular object, that our bodies are subject to all the vagaries of elemental influences. Generally, amongst worldly men and frivolous women, we only attach ourselves to some article of furniture or of dress; and they never doubt that we are mere foolish and vague results of the dashing of the waves of the light against the solid forms of which their houses are full. We do not care to tell them the truth, for they would never see it. But let the worldly man — or the frivolous woman — and then — "

At each of the pauses indicated, the mass of Shadows throbbed and heaved with emotion; but they soon settled again into comparative still-

❧

ness. Once more the Shadow addressed himself to speak. But suddenly they all looked up, and the king, following their gaze, saw that the aurora had begun to pale.

"The moon is rising," said the Shadow. "As soon as she looks over the mountains into the valley, we must be gone, for we have plenty to do by the moon: we are powerful in her light. But if your majesty will come here to-morrow night, your majesty may learn a great deal more about us, and judge for himself whether it be fit to accord our petition; for then will be our grand annual assembly, in which we report to our chiefs the things we have attempted, and the good or bad success we have had."

"If you send for me," returned the king, "I will come."

Ere the Shadow could reply, the tip of the moon's crescent horn peeped up from behind an icy pinnacle, and one slender ray fell on the lake. It shone upon no Shadows. Ere the eye of the king could again seek the earth after beholding the first brightness of the moon's resurrection, they had vanished; and the surface of the lake glittered cold and blue in the pale moonlight.

There the king lay, alone in the midst of the frozen lake, with the moon staring at him. But at length he heard from somewhere a voice that he knew.

"Will you take another cup of tea, dear?" said Mrs. Rinkelmann.

And Ralph, coming slowly to himself, found that he was lying in his own bed.

"Yes, I will," he answered; "and rather a large piece of toast, if you please; for I have been a long journey since I saw you last."

"He has not come to himself quite," said Mrs. Rinkelmann, between her and herself.

"You would be rather surprised," continued Ralph, "if I told you where I had been."

"I dare say I should," responded his wife.

"Then I will tell you," rejoined Ralph.

But at that moment, a great Shadow bounced out of the fire with a single huge leap, and covered the whole room. Then it settled in one corner, and Ralph saw it shaking its fist at him from the end of a preposterous arm. So he took the hint, and held his peace. And it was as well for him. For I happen to know something about the Shadows too; and I know that if he had told his wife all about it just then, they would not have sent for him the following evening.

THE SHADOWS   �</br>

But as the king, after finishing his tea and toast, lay and looked about him, the shadows dancing in his room seemed to him odder and more inexplicable than ever. The whole chamber was full of mystery. So it generally was, but now it was more mysterious than ever. After all that he had seen in the Shadow-church, his own room and its shadows were yet more wonderful and unintelligible than those.

This made it the more likely that he had seen a true vision; for instead of making common things look commonplace, as a false vision would have done, it had made common things disclose the wonderful that was in them.

"The same applies to all art as well," thought Ralph Rinkelmann.

The next afternoon, as the twilight was growing dusky, the king lay wondering whether or not the Shadows would fetch him again. He wanted very much to go, for he had enjoyed the journey exceedingly, and he longed, besides, to hear some of the Shadows tell their stories. But the darkness grew deeper and deeper, and the Shadows did not come. The cause was, that Mrs. Rinkelmann sat by the fire in the gloaming; and they could not carry off the king while she was there. Some of them tried to frighten her away by playing the oddest pranks on the walls, and floor, and ceiling; but altogether without effect: the queen only smiled, for she had a good conscience. Suddenly, however, a dreadful scream was heard from the nursery, and Mrs. Rinkelmann rushed up-stairs to see what was the matter. No sooner had she gone than the two warders of the chimney-corners stepped out into the middle of the room, and said, in a low voice, —

"Is your majesty ready?"

"Have you no hearts?" said the king; "or are they as black as your faces? Did you not hear the child scream? I must know what is the matter with her before I go."

"Your majesty may keep his mind easy on that point," replied the warders. "We had tried everything we could think of to get rid of her majesty the queen, but without effect. So a young madcap Shadow, half against the will of the older ones of us, slipped up-stairs into the nursery; and has, no doubt, succeeded in appalling the baby, for he is very lithe and long-legged. — Now, your majesty."

"I will have no such tricks played in my nursery," said the king, rather angrily. "You might put the child beside itself."

"Then there would be twins, your majesty. And we rather like twins."

"None of your miserable jesting! You might put the child out of her wits."

"Impossible, sire; for she has not got into them yet."

"Go away," said the king.

"Forgive us, your majesty. Really, it will do the child good; for that Shadow will, all her life, be to her a symbol of what is ugly and bad. When she feels in danger of hating or envying any one, that Shadow will come back to her mind and make her shudder."

"Very well," said the king. "I like that. Let us go."

The Shadows went through the same ceremonies and preparations as before; during which, the young Shadow before-mentioned contrived to make such grimaces as kept the baby in terror, and the queen in the nursery, till all was ready. Then with a bound that doubled him up against the ceiling, and a kick of his legs six feet out behind him, he vanished through the nursery door, and reached the king's bed-chamber just in time to take his place with the last who were melting through the window in the rear of the litter, and settling down upon the snow beneath. Away they went as before, a gliding blackness over the white carpet. And it was Christmas-eve.

When they came in sight of the mountain-lake, the king saw that it was crowded over its whole surface with a changeful intermingling of Shadows. They were all talking and listening alternately, in pairs, trios, and groups of every size. Here and there, large companies were absorbed in attention to one elevated above the rest, not in a pulpit, or on a platform, but on the stilts of his own legs, elongated for the nonce. The aurora, right overhead, lighted up the lake and the sides of the mountains, by sending down from the zenith, nearly to the surface of the lake, great folded vapours, luminous with all the colours of a faint rainbow.

Many, however, as the words were that passed on all sides, not a shadow of a sound reached the ears of the king: the shadow-speech could not enter his corporeal organs. One of his guides, however, seeing that the king wanted to hear and could not, went through a strange manipulation of his head and ears; after which he could hear perfectly, though still only the voice to which, for the time, he directed his attention. This, however, was a great advantage, and one which the king longed to carry back with him to the world of men.

The king now discovered that this was not merely the church of the Shadows, but their news-exchange at the same time. For, as the Shadows have no writing or printing, the only way in which they can make each other acquainted with their doings and thinkings, is to meet and talk at this word-mart and parliament of shades. And as, in the world, people read their favourite authors, and listen to their favourite speakers, so here the Shadows seek their favourite Shadows, listen to their adventures, and hear generally what they have to say.

Feeling quite strong, the king rose and walked about amongst them, wrapped in his ermine robe, with his red crown on his head, and his diamond scepter in his hand. Every group of Shadows to which he drew near, ceased talking as soon as they saw him approach: but at a nod they went on again directly, conversing and relating and commenting, as if no one was there of other kind or of higher rank than themselves. So the king heard a good many stories. At some of them he laughed, and at some of them he cried. But if the stories that the Shadows told were printed, they would make a book that no publisher could produce fast enough to satisfy the buyers. I will record some of the things that the king heard, for he told them to me soon after. In fact, I was for some time his private secretary.

"I made him confess before a week was over," said a gloomy old Shadow.

"But what was the good of that?" rejoined a pert young one. "That could not undo what was done."

"Yes, it could."

"What! bring the dead to life?"

"No; but comfort the murderer. I could not bear to see the pitiable misery he was in. He was far happier with the rope round his neck, than he was with the purse in his pocket. I saved him from killing himself too."

"How did you make him confess?"

"Only by wallowing on the wall a little."

"How could that make him tell?"

"*He* knows."

The Shadow was silent; and the king turned to another, who was preparing to speak.

"I made a fashionable mother repent."

"How?" broke from several voices, in whose sound was mingled a touch of incredulity.

"Only by making a little coffin on the wall," was the reply.

"Did the fashionable mother confess too?"

"She had nothing more to confess than everybody knew."

"What did everybody know then?"

"That she might have been kissing a living child, when she followed a dead one to the grave. — The next will fare better."

"I put a stop to a wedding," said another.

"Horrid shade!" remarked a poetic imp.

"How?" said others. "Tell us how."

"Only by throwing a darkness, as if from the branch of a sconce, over the forehead of a fair girl. — They are not married yet, and I do not think they will be. But I loved the youth who loved her. How he started! It was a revelation to him."

"But did it not deceive him?"

"Quite the contrary."

"But it was only a shadow from the outside, not a shadow coming through from the soul of the girl."

"Yes. You may say so. But it was all that was wanted to make the meaning of her forehead manifest — yes, of her whole face, which had now and then, in the pauses of his passion, perplexed the youth. All of it, curled nostrils, pouting lips, projecting chin, instantly fell into harmony with that darkness between her eyebrows. The youth understood it in a moment, and went home miserable. And they're not married *yet*."

"I caught a toper alone, over his magnum of port," said a very dark Shadow; "and didn't I give it him! I made *delirium tremens* first; and then I settled into a funeral, passing slowly along the length of the opposite wall. I gave him plenty of plumes and mourning coaches. And then I gave him a funeral service, but I could not manage to make the surplice white, which was all the better for such a sinner. The wretch stared till his face passed from purple to gray, and actually left his fifth glass only, unfinished, and took refuge with his wife and children in the drawing-room, much to their surprise. I believe he actually drank a cup of tea; and although I have often looked in since, I have never caught him again, drinking alone at least."

"But does he drink less? Have you done him any good?"

"I hope so; but I am sorry to say I can't feel sure about it."

"Humph! Humph! Humph!" grunted various shadow throats.

"I had such fun once!" cried another. "I made such game of a young clergyman!"

"You have no right to make game of any one."

"Oh yes, I have — when it is for his good. He used to study his sermons — where do you think?"

"In his study, of course. Where else should it be?"

"Yes and no. Guess again."

"Out amongst the faces in the streets?"

"Guess again."

"In still green places in the country?"

"Guess again."

"In old books?"

"Guess again."

"No, no. Tell us."

"In the looking-glass. Ha! ha! ha!"

"He was fair game; fair shadow game."

"I thought so. And I made such fun of him one night on the wall! He had sense enough to see that it was himself, and very like an ape. So he got ashamed, turned the mirror with its face to the wall, and thought a little more about his people, and a little less about himself. I was very glad; for, please your majesty," — and here the speaker turned towards the king — "we don't like the creatures that live in the mirrors. You call them ghosts, don't you?"

Before the king could reply, another had commenced. But the story about the clergyman had made the king wish to hear one of the shadow-sermons. So he turned him towards a long Shadow, who was preaching to a very quiet and listening crowd. He was just concluding his sermon.

"Therefore, dear Shadows, it is the more needful that we love one another as much as we can, because that is not much. We have no such excuse for not loving as mortals have, for we do not die like them. I suppose it is the thought of that death that makes them hate so much. Then again, we go to sleep all day, most of us, and not in the night, as men do. And you know that we forget everything that happened the night before; therefore, we ought to love well, for the love is short. Ah! dear Shadow, whom I love now with all my shadowy soul, I shall not love thee to-morrow eve, I shall not know thee; I shall pass thee in the crowd and never dream that the Shadow whom I now love is near me then. Happy Shades! for we only remember our tales until we have told them here, and then they vanish in the shadow-churchyard, where we bury only our dead selves. Ah! brethren, who would be a man and remember? Who would be a man and weep? We ought indeed to love one another, for we alone inherit oblivion; we alone are renewed with eternal birth; we alone have no gathered weight of years. I will tell you the awful fate of one Shadow who rebelled against his nature, and sought to remember the past. He said, 'I *will* remember this eve.' He fought with the genial influences of kindly sleep when the sun rose on the awful dead day of light; and although he could not keep quite awake, he dreamed of the foregone eve, and he never forgot his dream. Then he tried again the next night, and the next, and the next; and he tempted another Shadow to try it with him. But at last their awful fate overtook them; for, instead of continuing to be Shadows, they began to cast shadows, as foolish men say; and so they thickened and thickened till they vanished out of our world. They are now condemned to walk the earth a man and a woman, with death behind them, and memories within them. Ah, brother Shades! let us love one another, for we shall soon forget. We are not men, but Shadows."

The king turned away, and pitied the poor Shadows far more than they pitied men.

"Oh! how we played with a musician one night," exclaimed a Shadow in another group, to which the king had first directed a passing thought, and then had stopped to listen. — "Up and down we went, like the hammers and dampers on his piano. But he took his revenge on us. For after he had watched us for half an hour in the twilight, he rose and went to his instrument and played a shadow-dance that fixed us all in sound for ever. Each could tell the very notes meant for him; and as long as he played we could not stop, but went on dancing and dancing after the music, just as the magician — I mean the musician — pleased. And he punished us well; for he nearly danced us all off our legs and out of shape into tired heaps of collapsed and palpitating darkness. We won't go near him for some time again, if we can only remember it. He had been very miserable all day, he was so poor; and we could not think of any way of comforting him except making him laugh. We did not succeed, with our wildest efforts; but it turned out better than we had expected, after all; for his shadow-dance got him into notice, and he is quite popular now, and making money fast. — If he does not take care, we shall have other work to do with him by-and-by, poor fellow!"

"I and some others did the same for a poor play-writer once. He had a Christmas piece to write, and being an original genius, it was not so easy for him to find a subject as it is for most of his class. I saw the trouble he was in, and collecting a few stray Shadows, we acted, in dumb show of course, the funniest bit of nonsense we could think of; and it was quite successful. The poor fellow watched every motion, roaring with laughter at us, and delight at the ideas we put into his head. He turned it all into words, and scenes, and actions; and the piece came off with a splendid success."

"But how long we have to look for a chance of doing anything worth doing!" said a long, thin, especially lugubrious Shadow. "I have only done one thing worth telling ever since we met last. But I am proud of that."

"What was it? What was it?" rose from twenty voices.

"I crept into a dining room, one twilight, soon after Christmas day. I had been drawn thither by the glow of a bright fire shining through red window-curtains. At first I thought there was no one there, and was on the point of leaving the room and going out again into the snowy street, when I suddenly caught the sparkle of eyes. I found that they belonged to a little boy who lay very still on a sofa. I crept into a dark corner by the side board, and watched him. He seemed very sad, and did nothing but stare into the fire. At last he sighed out, — 'I wish mamma would come home.' 'Poor boy!' thought I, 'there is no help for that but mamma.' Yet I would try to while away the time for him. So out of my corner I stretched a long shadow arm, reaching all across the ceiling, and pretended to make a grab at him. He was rather frightened at first; but he was a brave boy, and soon saw that it was all a joke. So when I did it again, he made a clutch at me; and then we had such fun! For though he often sighed and wished mamma would come home, he always began again with me; and on we went with the wildest game. At last his mother's knock came to the door, and, starting up in delight, he rushed into the hall to meet her, and forgot all about poor black me. But I did not mind that in the least; for when I glided out after him into the hall, I was well repaid for my trouble by hearing his mother say to him, — 'Why, Charlie, my dear, you look ever so much better since I left you!' At that moment I slipped through the closing door, and as I ran across the snow, I heard the mother say, — 'What Shadow can that be passing so quickly?' And Charlie answered with a merry laugh, — 'Oh! mamma, I suppose it must be the funny shadow that has been playing such games with me all the time you were out.' As soon as the door was shut, I crept along the wall and looked in at the dining-room window. And I heard his mamma say, as she led him into the room, — 'What an imagination the boy has!' Ha! ha! ha! Then she looked at him, and the tears came in her eyes; and she stooped down over him, and I heard the sounds of a mingling kiss and sob."

"I always look for nurseries full of children," said another; "and this winter I have been very fortunate. I am sure children belong especially to

❧

us. One evening, looking about in a great city, I saw through the window
into a large nursery, where the odious gas had not yet been lighted. Round
the fire sat a company of the most delightful children I had ever seen.
They were waiting patiently for their tea. It was too good an opportunity
to be lost. I hurried away, and gathering together twenty of the best
Shadows I could find, returned in a few moments; and entering the
nursery, we danced on the walls one of our best dances. To be sure it was
mostly extemporized; but I managed to keep it in harmony by singing
this song, which I made as we went on. Of course the children could not
hear it: they only saw the motions that answered to it; but with them they
seemed to be very much delighted indeed, as I shall presently prove to
you. This was the song: —

> 'Swing, swang, swingle, swuff!
> Flicker, flacker, fling, fluff!
> Thus we go,
> To and fro;
> Here and there,
> Everywhere,
> Born and bred;
> Never dead,
> Only gone.
>
> 'On! Come on.
> Looming, glooming,
> Spreading, fuming,
> Shattering, scattering,
> Parting, darting,
> Settling, starting,
> All our life
> Is a strife,
> And a wearying for rest
> On the darkness' friendly breast.
>
> 'Joining, splitting,
> Rising, sitting,
> Laughing, shaking,
> Sides all aching,

Grumbling, grim, and gruff.
Swingle, swangle, swuff!

'Now a knot of darkness;
   Now dissolved gloom;
Now a pall of blackness
   Hiding all the room.
Flicker, flacker, fluff!
Black, and black enough!
'Dancing now like demons;
   Lying like the dead;
Gladly would we stop it,
   And go down to bed!
But our work we still must do,
Shadow men, as well as you.

'Rooting, rising, shooting,
   Heaving, sinking, creeping;
Hid in corners crooning;
   Splitting, poking, leaping,
Gathering, towering, swooning.
   When we're lurking,
   Yet we're working,
For our labour we must do,
Shadow men, as well as you.
   Flicker, flacker, fling, fluff!
   Swing, swang, swingle, swuff!'

"'How thick the Shadows are!' said one of the children — a thought-ful little girl.

"'I wonder where they come from,' said a dreamy little boy.

"'I think they grow out of the wall,' answered the little girl; 'for I have been watching them come; first one, and then another, and then a whole lot of them. I am sure they grow out of the walls.'

"'Perhaps they have papas and mammas,' said an older boy, with a smile.

"'Yes, yes; and the doctor brings them in his pocket,' said another, a consequential little maiden.

❧   THE SHADOWS

" 'No; I'll tell you,' said the older boy, 'they're ghosts.'

" 'But ghosts are white.'

" 'Oh! but these have got black coming down the chimney.'

" 'No,' said a curious-looking, white-faced boy of fourteen, who had been reading by the firelight, and had stopped to hear the little ones talk; 'they're body ghosts; they're not soul ghosts.'

" 'A silence followed, broken by the first, the dreamy-eyed boy, who said, —

" 'I hope they didn't make me'; at which they all burst out laughing.

"Just then the nurse brought in their tea, and when she proceeded to light the gas we vanished."

"I stopped a murder," cried another.

"How? How? How?"

"I will tell you. I had been lurking about a sick room for some time, where a miser lay, apparently dying. I did not like the place at all, but felt as if I should be wanted there. There were plenty of lurking-places about, for the room was full of all sorts of old furniture, especially cabinets, chests, and presses. I believe he had in that room every bit of the property he had spent a long life in gathering. I found that he had gold and gold in those places; for one night, when his nurse was away, he crept out of bed, mumbling and shaking, and managed to open one of the chests, though he nearly fell down with the effort. I was peeping over his shoulder, and such a gleam of gold fell upon me, that it nearly killed me. But hearing his nurse coming, he slammed the lid down, and I recovered.

"I tried very hard, but I could not do him any good. For although I made all sorts of shapes on the walls and ceiling, representing evil deeds that he had done, of which there were plenty to choose from, I could make no shapes on his brain or conscience. He had no eyes for anything but gold. And it so happened that his nurse had neither eyes nor heart for anything else either.

"One day, as she was seated beside his bed, but where he could not see her, stirring some gruel in a basin, to cool it for him, I saw her take a little phial from her bosom, and I knew by the expression of her face both what it was and what she was going to do with it. Fortunately the cork was a little hard to get out, and this gave me one moment to think.

"The room was so crowded with all sorts of things, that although there were no curtains on the four-post bed to hide from the miser the sight of his precious treasures, there was yet but one small part of the

"The Miser and His Nurse"

ceiling suitable for casting myself upon in the shape I wished to assume. And this spot was hard to reach. But having discovered that upon this very place lay a dull gleam of firelight thrown from a strange old dusty mirror that stood away in some corner, I got in front of the fire, spied where the mirror was, threw myself upon it, and bounded from its face upon the oval pool of dim light on the ceiling, assuming, as I passed, the shape of an old stooping hag, who poured something from a phial into a basin. I made the handle of the spoon with my own nose, ha! ha!"

And the shadow-hand caressed the shadow-tip of the shadow-nose, before the shadow-tongue resumed.

"The old miser saw me: he would not taste the gruel that night, although his nurse coaxed and scolded till they were both weary. She pretended to taste it herself, and to think it very good; but at last retired into a corner, and after making as if she were eating it, took care to pour it all out into the ashes."

"But she must either succeed, or starve him, at last," interposed a Shadow.

"I will tell you."

"And," interposed another, "he was not worth saving."

"He might repent," suggested a third, who was more benevolent.

"No chance of that," returned the former. "Misers never do. The love of money has less in it to cure itself than any other wickedness into which wretched men can fall. What a mercy it is to be born a Shadow! Wickedness does not stick to us. What do we care for gold! — Rubbish!"

"Amen! Amen! Amen!" came from a hundred shadow-voices.

"You should have let her murder him, and so you would have been quit of him."

"And besides, how was he to escape at last? He could never get rid of her, you know."

"I was going to tell you," resumed the narrator, "only you had so many shadow-remarks to make, that you would not let me."

"Go on; go on."

"There was a little grandchild who used to come and see him sometimes — the only creature the miser cared for. Her mother was his daughter; but the old man would never see her, because she had married against his will. Her husband was now dead, but he had not forgiven her yet. After the shadow he had seen, however, he said to himself, as he lay awake that night — I saw the words on his face — 'How shall I get rid of that old devil? If I don't eat I shall die; and if I do eat I shall be poisoned. I wish little Mary would come. Ah! her mother would never have served me so.' He lay awake, thinking such things over and over again, all night long, and I stood watching him from a dark corner, till the dayspring came and shook me out. When I came back next night, the room was tidy and clean. His own daughter, a sad-faced but beautiful woman, sat by his bedside; and little Mary was curled up on the floor by the fire, imitating us, by making queer shadows on the ceiling with her twisted hands. But she could not think however they got there. And no wonder, for I helped her to some very unaccountable ones."

"I have a story about a granddaughter, too," said another, the moment that speaker ceased.

"Tell it. Tell it."

"Last Christmas-day," he began, "I and a troop of us set out in the twilight to find some house where we could all have something to do; for we had made up our minds to act together. We tried several, but found objections to them all. At last we espied a large lonely country-house, and hastening to it, we found great preparations making for the Christmas dinner. We rushed into it, scampered all over it, and made up our minds in a moment that it would do. We amused ourselves in the nursery first, where there were several children being dressed for dinner. We generally do go to the nursery first, your majesty. This time we were especially charmed with a little girl about five years old, who clapped her hands and danced about with delight at the antics we performed; and we said we would do something for her if we had a chance. The company began to arrive; and at every arrival, we rushed to the hall, and cut wonderful capers of welcome. Between times, we scudded away to see how the dressing went on. One girl about eighteen was delightful. She dressed herself as if she did not care much about it, but could not help doing it prettily. When she took her last look at the phantom in the glass, she half smiled to it. — But *we* do not like those creatures that come into the mirrors at all, your majesty. We don't understand them. They are dreadful to us. — She looked rather sad and pale, but very sweet and hopeful. So we wanted to know all about her, and soon found out that she was a distant relation and a great favourite of the gentleman of the house, an old man, in whose face benevolence was mingled with obstinacy and a deep shade of the tyrannical. We could not admire him much; but we would not make up our minds all at once: Shadows never do.

"The dinner-bell rang, and down we hurried. The children all looked happy, and we were merry. But there was one cross fellow among the servants, and didn't we plague him! and didn't we get fun out of him! When he was bringing up dishes, we lay in wait for him at every corner, and sprang upon him from the floor, and from over the banisters, and down from the cornices. He started and stumbled and blundered so in consequence, that his fellow-servants thought he was tipsy. Once he dropped a plate, and had to pick up the pieces, and hurry away with them; and didn't we pursue him as he went! It was lucky for him his master did not see how he went on; but we took care not to let him get into any real scrape, though he was quite dazed with the dodging of the unaccountable shadows. Sometimes he thought the walls were coming down upon him, sometimes that the floor was gaping to swallow him; sometimes that he would be knocked to pieces by the hurrying to and fro, or be smothered in the black crowd.

"When the blazing plum-pudding was carried in, we made a perfect shadow-carnival about it, dancing and mumming in the blue flames, like mad demons. And how the children screamed with delight!

"The old gentleman, who was very fond of children, was laughing his heartiest laugh, when a loud knock came to the hall-door. The fair maiden started, turned paler, and then red as the Christmas fire. I saw it, and flung my hands across her face. She was very glad, and I know she said in her heart, 'You kind Shadow!' which paid me well. Then I followed the rest into the hall, and found there a jolly, handsome, brown-faced sailor, evidently a son of the house. The old man received him with tears in his eyes, and the children with shouts of joy. The maiden escaped in the confusion, just in time to save herself from fainting. We crowded about the lamp to hide her retreat, and nearly put it out; and the butler could not get it to burn up before she had glided into her place again, relieved to find the room so dark. The sailor only had seen her go, and now he sat down beside her, and, without a word, got hold of her hand in the gloom. When we all scattered to the walls and the corners, and the lamp blazed up again, he let her hand go.

"During the rest of the dinner the old man watched the two, and saw that there was something between them, and was very angry. For he was an important man in his own estimation, and they had never consulted him. The fact was, they had never known their own minds till the sailor had gone upon his last voyage, and had learned each other's only this moment. — We found out all this by watching them, and then talking together about it afterwards. — The old gentleman saw, too, that his favourite, who was under such obligation to him for loving her so much, loved his son better than him; and he grew by degrees so jealous that he overshadowed the whole table with his morose looks and short answers. That kind of shadowing is very different from ours; and the Christmas dessert grew so gloomy that we Shadows could not bear it, and were delighted when the ladies rose to go to the drawing-room. The gentlemen would not stay behind the ladies, even for the sake of the well-known wine. So the moody host, notwithstanding his hospitality, was left alone at the table in the great silent room. We followed the company up-stairs to the drawing-room, and thence to the nursery for snap-dragon; but while they were busy with this most shadowy of games, nearly all the Shadows crept downstairs again to the dining-room, where the old man still sat, gnawing the bone of his own selfishness. They crowded into the room, and by using every kind of expansion — blowing themselves out like soap bubbles — they succeeded in heaping up the whole room with shade upon shade. They clustered thickest about the fire and the lamp, till at last they almost drowned them in hills of darkness.

"Before they had accomplished so much, the children, tired with fun and frolic, had been put to bed. But the little girl of five years old, with whom we had been so pleased when first we arrived, could not go to sleep. She had a little room of her own; and I had watched her to bed, and now kept her awake by gambolling in the rays of the night-light. When her eyes were fixed upon me, I took the shape of her grandfather, representing him on the wall as he sat in his chair, with his head bent down and his arms hanging listlessly by his sides. And the child remembered that that was just as she had seen him last; for she had happened to peep in at the dining-room door after all the rest had gone up-stairs. 'What if he should be sitting there still,' thought she, 'all alone in the dark!' She scrambled out of bed and crept down.

"Meantime the others had made the room below so dark, that only the face and white hair of the old man could be dimly discerned in the shadowy crowd. For he had filled his own mind with shadows, which we Shadows wanted to draw out of him. Those shadows are very different from us, your majesty knows. He was thinking of all the disappointments he had had in life, and of all the ingratitude he had met with. And he thought far more of the good he had done, than the good others had got.

'After all I have done for them,' said he, with a sigh of bitterness, 'not one of them cares a straw for me. My own children will be glad when I am gone!' — At that instant he lifted up his eyes and saw, standing close by the door, a tiny figure in a long nightgown. The door behind her was shut. It was my little friend, who had crept in noiselessly. A pang of icy fear shot to the old man's heart, but it melted away as fast, for we made a lane through us for a single ray from the fire to fall on the face of the little sprite; and he thought it was a child of his own that had died when just the age of her child-niece, who now stood looking for her grandfather among the Shadows. He thought she had come out of her grave in the cold darkness to ask why her father was sitting alone on Christmas-day. And he felt he had no answer to give his little ghost, but one he would be ashamed for her to hear. But his grandchild saw him now, and walked up to him with a childish stateliness, stumbling once or twice on what seemed her long shroud. Pushing through the crowded shadows, she reached him, climbed upon his knee, laid her little long-haired head on his shoulders, and said, — 'Ganpa! you goomy? Isn't it your Kissy-Day too, ganpa?'

"A new fount of love seemed to burst from the clay of the old man's heart. He clasped the child to his bosom, and wept. Then, without a word, he rose with her in his arms, carried her up to her room, and laying her down in her bed, covered her up, kissed her sweet little mouth unconscious of reproof, and then went to the drawing-room.

"As soon as he entered, he saw the culprits in a quiet corner alone. He went up to them, took a hand of each, and joining them in both his, said, 'God bless you!' Then he turned to the rest of the company, and 'Now,' said he, 'let's have a Christmas carol.' — And well he might; for though I have paid many visits to the house, I have never seen him cross since; and I am sure that must cost him a good deal of trouble."

"We have just come from a great palace," said another, "where we knew there were many children, and where we thought to hear glad voices, and see royally merry looks. But as soon as we entered, we became aware that one mighty Shadow shrouded the whole; and that Shadow deepened and deepened, till it gathered in darkness about the reposing form of a wise prince. Then we saw him, we could move no more, but clung heavily to the walls, and by our stillness added to the sorrow of the hour. And when we saw the mother of her people weeping with bowed head for the loss of him in whom she had trusted, we were seized with such a longing to be Shadows no more, but winged angels, which are the white shadows cast in heaven from the Light of Light, so as to gather around her, and hover over her with comforting, that we vanished from the walls, and found ourselves floating high above the towers of the palace, where we met the angels on their way, and knew that our service was not needed."

By this time there was a glimmer of approaching moonlight, and the king began to see several of those stranger Shadows, with human faces and eyes, moving about amongst the crowd. He knew at once that they did not belong to his dominion. They looked at him, and came near him, and passed slowly, but they never made any obeisance, or gave sign of homage. And what their eyes said to him, the king only could tell. And he did not tell.

"What are those other Shadows that move through the crowd?" said he to one of his subjects near him.

The Shadow started, looked round, shivered slightly, and laid his finger on his lips. Then leading the king a little aside, and looking carefully about him once more, —

"I do not know," said he, in a low tone, "what they are. I have heard of them often, but only once did I ever see any of them before. That was when some of us one night paid a visit to a man who sat much alone, and was said to think a great deal. We saw two of those sitting in the room with him, and he was as pale as they were. We could not cross the threshold, but shivered and shook, and felt ready to melt away. Is not your majesty afraid of them too?"

But the king made no answer; and before he could speak again, the moon had climbed above the mighty pillars of the church of the Shadows, and looked in at the great window of the sky.

The shapes had all vanished; and the king, again lifting up his eyes, saw but the wall of his own chamber, on which flickered the Shadow of a Little Child. He looked down, and there, sitting on a stool by the fire, he saw one of his own little ones, waiting to say good night to his father, and go to bed early, that he might rise early too, and be very good and happy all Christmas-day.

And Ralph Rinkelmann rejoiced that he was a man, and not a Shadow.

But as the Shadows vanished they left the sense of song in the king's brain. And the words of their song must have been something like these: —

"Shadows, Shadows, Shadows all!
Shadow birth and funeral!
Shadow moons gleam overhead;
Over shadow-graves we tread.
Shadow-hope lives, grows, and dies.
Shadow-love from shadow-eyes
Shadow-ward entices on
To shadow-words on shadow-stone,
Closing up the shadow-tale
With a shadow-shadow-wail.

"Shadow-man, thou art a gloom
Cast upon a shadow-tomb
Through the endless shadow air,
From the Shadow sitting there,
On a moveless shadow-throne,
Glooming through the ages gone;
North and south, and in and out,
East and west, and all about,
Flinging Shadows everywhere
On the Shadow-painted air.
Shadow-man, thou hast no story;
Nothing but a shadow-glory."

But Ralph Rinkelmann said to himself, —
     "They are but Shadows that sing thus; for a Shadow can see but
Shadows. A man sees a man where a Shadow sees only a Shadow."
     And he was comforted in himself.

The Castle: A Parable

On the top of a high cliff, forming part of the base of a great mountain, stood a lofty castle. When or how it was built, no man knew; nor could any one pretend to understand its architecture. Every one who looked upon it felt that it was lordly and noble; and where one part seemed not to agree with another, the wise and modest dared not to call them incongruous, but presumed that the whole might be constructed on some higher principle of architecture than they yet understood. What helped them to this conclusion was, that no one had ever seen the whole of the edifice; that, even of the portion best known, some part or other was always wrapt in thick folds of mist from the mountain; and that, when the sun shone upon this mist, the parts of the building that appeared through the vaporous veil, were strangely glorified in their indistinctness, so that they seemed to belong to some aerial abode in the land of the sunset; and the beholders could hardly tell whether they had ever seen them before, or whether they were now for the first time partially revealed.

Nor, although it was inhabited, could certain information be procured as to its internal construction. Those who dwelt in it often discovered rooms they had never entered before; yea, once or twice, whole suites of apartments, of which only dim legends had been handed down from former times. Some of them expected to find, one day, secret places, filled with treasures of wondrous jewels, amongst which they hoped to light upon Solomon's ring, which had for ages disappeared from the earth, but which had controlled the spirits, and the possession of which made a man simply what a man should be, the king of the world. Now and then, a narrow, winding stair, hitherto untrodden, would bring them forth on a new turret, whence new prospects of the circumjacent country were spread out before them. How many more of these there might be, or how much loftier, no one could tell. Nor could the foundations of the castle in the rock on which it was built be determined with the smallest approach to precision. Those of the family who had given themselves to exploring in that direction, found such a labyrinth of vaults and passages, and endless successions of down-going stairs, out of one underground space into a yet lower, that they came to the conclusion that at least the whole mountain was perforated and honeycombed in this fashion. They had a dim consciousness, too, of the presence, in those awful regions, of beings whom they could not comprehend. Once, they came upon the brink of a great black gulf, in which the eye could see nothing but darkness: they recoiled in horror; for the conviction flashed upon them that that gulf went down into the very central spaces of the earth, of which they had hitherto been wandering only in the upper crust; nay, that the seething blackness before them had relations mysterious, and beyond human comprehension, with the far-off voids of space, into which the stars dare not enter.

At the foot of the cliff whereon the castle stood, lay a deep lake, inaccessible save by a few avenues, being surrounded on all sides with precipices, which made the water look very black, although it was as pure as the night-sky. From a door in the castle, which was not to be otherwise entered, a broad flight of steps, cut in the rock, went down to the lake, and disappeared below its surface. Some thought the steps went to the very bottom of the water.

Now in this castle there dwelt a large family of brothers and sisters. They had never seen their father or mother. The younger had been educated by the elder, and these by an unseen care and ministration, about the sources of which they had, somehow or other, troubled themselves very little, for what people are accustomed to, they regard as coming from nobody; as if help and progress and joy and love were the natural crops of Chaos or old Night. But Tradition said that one day — it was utterly uncertain *when* — their father would come, and leave them no more; for he was still alive, though where he lived nobody knew. In the meantime all the rest had to obey their eldest brother, and listen to his counsels.

But almost all the family was very fond of liberty, as they called it; and liked to run up and down, hither and thither, roving about, with neither law nor order, just as they pleased. So they could not endure their brother's tyranny, as they called it. At one time they said that he was only one of themselves, and therefore they would not obey him at another, that he was not like them, and could not understand them, and *therefore* they would not obey him. Yet, sometimes, when he came and looked them full in the face, they were terrified, and dared not disobey, for he was stately, and stern and strong. Not one of them loved him heartily, except the eldest sister, who was very beautiful and silent, and whose eyes shone as if light lay somewhere deep behind them. Even she, although she loved him, thought him very hard sometimes; for when he had once said a thing plainly, he could not be persuaded to think it over again. So even she forgot him sometimes, and went her own ways, and enjoyed herself without him. Most of them regarded him as a sort of watchman, whose business it was to keep them in order; and so they were indignant and disliked him. Yet they all had a secret feeling that they ought to be subject to him; and after any particular act of disregard, none of them could think, with any peace, of the old story about the return of their father to his house. But indeed they never thought much about it, or about their father at all; for how could those who cared so little for their brother, whom they saw every day, care for their father whom they had never seen? — One chief cause of complaint against him was, that he interfered with their favourite studies and pursuits; whereas he only sought to make them give up trifling with earnest things, and seek for truth, and not for amusement, from the many wonders around them. He did not want them to turn to other studies, or to eschew pleasures; but, in those studies, to seek the highest things most, and other things in proportion to their true worth and nobleness. This could not fail to be distasteful to those who did not care for what was higher than they. And so matters went on for a time. They thought they could do better without their brother; and their brother knew they could not do at all without him, and tried to fulfill the charge committed into his hands.

At length, one day, for the thought seemed to strike them simultaneously, they conferred together about giving a great entertainment in their grandest rooms to any of their neighbours who chose to come, or indeed to any inhabitants of the earth or air who would visit them. They were too proud to reflect that some company might defile even the dwellers in what was undoubtedly the finest palace on the face of the earth. But what made the thing worse, was, that the old tradition said that these rooms were to be kept entirely for the use of the owner of the castle. And, indeed, whenever they entered them, such was the effect of their loftiness and grandeur upon their minds, that they always thought of the old story, and could not help believing it. Nor would the brother permit them to forget it now; but, appearing suddenly amongst them, when they had no expectation of being interrupted by him, he rebuked them, both for the indiscriminate nature of their invitation, and for the intention of introducing any one, not to speak of some who would doubtless make their appearance on the evening in question, into the rooms kept sacred for the use of the unknown father. But by this time their talk with each other had so excited their expectations of enjoyment, which had previously been strong enough, that anger sprung up within them at the thought of being deprived of their hopes, and they looked each other in the eyes; and the look said: "We are many, and he is one — let us get rid of him, for he is always finding fault, and thwarting us in the most innocent pleasures; — as if we would wish to do anything wrong!" So without a word spoken, they rushed upon him; and although he was stronger than any of them, and struggled hard at first, yet they overcame him at last. Indeed some of them thought he yielded to their violence long before they had the mastery of him; and this very submission terrified the more tender-hearted among them. However, they bound him; carried him down many stairs, and, having remembered an iron staple in the wall of a certain vault, with a thick rusty chain attached to it, they bore him thither, and made the chain fast around him. There they left him, shutting the great gnarring brazen door of the vault, as they departed for the upper regions of the castle.

Now all was in a tumult of preparation. Every one was talking of the coming festivity; but no one spoke of the deed they had done. A sudden paleness overspread the face, now of one, and now of another; but it passed away, and no one took any notice of it; they only plied the task of the moment the more energetically. Messengers were sent far and near, not to individuals or families, but publishing in all places of concourse a general invitation to any who chose to come on a certain day, and partake for certain succeeding days, of the hospitality of the dwellers in the castle. Many were the preparations immediately begun for complying with the invitation. But the noblest of their neighbours refused to appear; not from pride, but because of the unsuitableness and carelessness of such a mode. With some of them it was an old condition in the tenure of their estates, that they should go to no one's dwelling except visited in person, and expressly solicited. Others, knowing what sorts of persons would be there,

☙   THE CASTLE: A PARABLE

and that, from a certain physical antipathy, they could scarcely breathe in their company, made up their minds at once not to go. Yet multitudes, many of them beautiful and innocent as well as gay, resolved to appear.

Meanwhile the great rooms of the castle were got in readiness — that is, they proceeded to deface them with decorations; for there was a solemnity and stateliness about them in their ordinary condition, which was at once felt to be unsuitable for the light-hearted company so soon to move about in them with the self-same carelessness with which men walk abroad within the great heavens and hills and clouds. One day, while the workmen were busy, the eldest sister, of whom I have already spoken, happened to enter, she knew not why. Suddenly the great idea of the mighty halls dawned upon her, and filled her soul. The so-called decorations vanished from her view, and she felt as if she stood in her father's presence. She was at once elevated and humbled. As suddenly the idea faded and fled, and she beheld but the gaudy festoons and draperies and paintings which disfigured the grandeur. She wept and sped away. Now it was too late to interfere, and things must take their course. She would have been but a Cassandra-prophetess to those who saw but the pleasure before them. She had not been present when her brother was imprisoned; and indeed for some days had been so wrapt in her own business, that she had taken but little heed of anything that was going on. But they all expected her to show herself when the company was gathered; and they had applied to her for advice at various times during their operations.

At length the expected hour arrived, and the company began to assemble. It was a warm summer evening. The dark lake reflected the rose-coloured clouds in the west, and through the flush rowed many gaily-painted boats, with various coloured flags, towards the massy rock on which the castle stood. The trees and flowers seemed already asleep, and breathing forth their sweet dream-breath. Laughter and low voices rose from the breast of the lake to the ears of the youths and maidens looking forth expectant from the lofty windows. They went down to the broad platform at the top of the stairs in front of the door to receive their visitors. By degrees the festivities of the evening commenced. The same smiles flew forth both at eyes and lips, darting like beams through the gathering crowd. Music, from unseen sources, now rolled in billows, now crept in ripples through the sea of air that filled the lofty rooms. And in the dancing halls, when hand took hand, and form and motion were moulded and swayed by the indwelling music, it governed not these alone, but, as the ruling spirit of the place, every new burst of music for a new dance swept before it a new and accordant odour, and dyed the flames that glowed in the lofty lamps with a new and accordant stain. The floors bent beneath the feet of the time-keeping dancers. But twice in the evening some of the inmates started, and the pallor occasionally common to the household overspread their faces, for they felt underneath them a counter-motion to the dance, as if the floor rose slightly to answer their feet. And all the time their brother lay below in the dungeon, like John the Baptist in the castle of Herod, when the lords and captains sat around, and the daughter of Herodias danced before them. Outside, all around the castle, brooded the dark night unheeded; for the clouds had come up from all sides, and were crowding together overhead. In the infrequent pauses of the music, they might have heard, now and then, the gutsy rush of a lonely wind, coming and going no one could know whence or whither, born and dying unexpected and unregarded.

But when the festivities were at their height, when the external and passing confidence which is produced between superficial natures by a common pleasure, was at the full, a sudden crash of thunder quelled the music, as the thunder quells the noise of the uplifted sea. The windows were driven in, and torrents of rain, carried in the folds of a rushing wind, poured into the halls. The lights were swept away; and the great rooms, now dark within, were darkened yet more by the dazzling shoots of flame from the vault of blackness overhead. Those that ventured to look out of the windows saw, in the blue brilliancy of the quick-following jets of lightning, the lake at the foot of the rock, ordinarily so still and so dark, lighted up, not on the surface only, but down to half its depth; so that, as it tossed in the wind, like a tortured sea of writhing flames, or incandescent half-molten serpents of brass, they could not tell whether a strong phosphorescence did not issue from the transparent body of the waters, as if earth and sky lightened together, one consenting source of flaming utterance.

Sad was the condition of the late plastic mass of living form that had flowed into shape at the will and law of the music. Broken into individuals, the common transfusing spirit withdrawn, they stood drenched, cold, and benumbed, with clinging garments; light, order, harmony, purpose departed, and chaos restored; the issuings of life turned back on their sources, chilly and dead. And in every heart reigned that falsest of despairing convictions, that this was the only reality, and that was but a dream. The eldest sister stood with clasped hands and down-bent head, shivering and speechless, as if waiting for something to follow. Nor did she wait long. A terrible flash and thunder-peal made the castle rock; and in the pausing silence that followed, her quick sense heard the rattling of a chain far off, deep down; and soon the sound of heavy footsteps, accompanied with the clanking of iron, reached her ear. She felt that her brother was at hand. Even in the darkness, and amidst the bellowing of another deep-bosomed cloud-monster, she knew that he had entered the room. A moment after, a continuous pulsation of angry blue light began, which, lasting for some moments, revealed him standing amidst them, gaunt, haggard, and motionless; his hair and beard untrimmed, his face ghastly, his eyes large and hollow. The light seemed to gather around him as a centre. Indeed some believed that it throbbed and radiated from his person, and not from the stormy heavens above them. The lightning had rent the wall of his prison, and released the iron staple of his chain, which he had wound about him like a girdle. In his hand he carried an iron fetter-bar, which he had found on the floor of the vault. More terrified at his aspect than at all the violence of the storm, the visitors, with many a shriek and cry, rushed out into the tempestuous night. By degrees, the storm died away. Its last flash revealed the forms of the brothers and sisters lying prostrate, with their faces on the floor, and that fearful shape standing motionless amidst them still.

Morning dawned, and there they lay, and there he stood. But at a word from him, they arose and went about their various duties, though listlessly enough. The eldest sister was the last to rise; and when she did, it was only by a terrible effort that she was able to reach her room, where she fell again on the floor. There she remained lying for days. The brother caused the doors of the great suite of rooms to be closed, leaving them just as they were, with all the childish adornment scattered about, and the rain still falling in through the shattered windows. "Thus let them lie," said he, "till the rain and frost have cleansed them of paint and drapery: no storm can hurt the pillars and arches of these halls."

The hours of this day went heavily. The storm was gone, but the rain was left; the passion had departed, but the tears remained behind. Dull and dark the low misty clouds brooded over the castle and the lake, and shut out all the neighbourhood. Even if they had climbed to the loftiest known turret, they would have found it swathed in a garment of clinging vapor, affording no refreshment to the eye, and no hope to the heart. There was one lofty tower that rose sheer a hundred feet above the rest, and from which the fog could have been seen lying in a grey mass beneath; but that tower they had not yet discovered, nor another close beside it, the top of which was never seen, nor could be, for the highest clouds of heaven clustered continually around it. The rain fell continuously, though not heavily, without; and within, too, there were clouds from which dropped the tears which are the rain of the spirit. All the good of life seemed for the time departed, and their souls lived but as leafless trees that had forgotten the joy of the summer, and whom no wind prophetic of spring had yet visited. They moved about mechanically, and had not strength enough left to wish to die.

The next day the clouds were higher, and a little wind blew through such loopholes in the turrets as the false improvements of the inmates had not yet filled with glass, shutting out, as the storm, so the serene visitings of the heavens. Throughout the day, the brother took various opportunities of addressing a gentle command, now to one and now to another of his family. It was obeyed in silence. The wind blew fresher through the loopholes and the shattered windows of the great rooms, and found its way, by unknown passages, to faces and eyes hot with weeping. It cooled and blessed them. — When the sun arose the next day, it was in a clear sky.

By degrees, everything fell into the regularity of subordination. With the subordination came increase of freedom. The steps of the more youthful of the family were heard on the stairs and in the corridors more light and quick than ever before. Their brother had lost the terrors of aspect produced by his confinement, and his commands were issued more gently, and oftener with a smile, than in all their previous history. By degrees his presence was universally felt through the house. It was no surprise to any one at his studies, to see him by his side when he lifted up his eyes, though he had not before known that he was in the room. And although some dread still remained, it was rapidly vanishing before the advances of a firm friendship. Without immediately ordering their labours, he always influenced them, and often altered their direction and objects. The change soon evident in the household was remarkable. A simpler, nobler expression was visible on all the countenances. The voices of the men were deeper, and yet seemed by their very depth more feminine than before; while the voices of the women were softer and sweeter, and at the same time more full and decided. Now the eyes had often an expression as if their sight was absorbed

THE CASTLE: A PARABLE

in the gaze of the inward eyes; and when the eyes of two met, there passed between those eyes the utterance of a conviction that both meant the same thing. But the change was, of course, to be seen more clearly, though not more evidently, in individuals.

One of the brothers, for instance, was very fond of astronomy. He had his observatory on a lofty tower, which stood pretty clear of the others, towards the north and east. But hitherto, his astronomy, as he had called it, had been more of the character of astrology. Often, too, he might have been seen directing a heaven-searching telescope to catch the rapid transit of a fiery shooting-star, belonging altogether to the earthly atmosphere, and not to the serene heavens. He had to learn that the signs of the air are not the signs of the skies. Nay, once, his brother surprised him in the act of examining through his longest tube a patch of burning heath upon a distant hill. But now he was diligent from morning till night in the study of the laws of the truth that has to do with stars; and when the curtain of the sun-light was about to rise from before the heavenly worlds which it had hidden all day long, he might be seen preparing his instruments with that solemn countenance with which it becometh one to look into the mysterious harmonies of Nature. Now he learned what law and order and truth are, what consent and harmony mean; how the individual may find his own end in a higher end, where law and freedom mean the same thing, and the purest certainty exists without the slightest constraint. Thus he stood on the earth, and looked to the heavens.

Another, who had been much given to searching out the hollow places and recesses in the foundations of the castle, and who was often to be found with compass and ruler working away at a chart of the same which he had been in process of constructing, now came to the conclusion, that only by ascending the upper regions of his abode, could he become capable of understanding what lay beneath; and that, in all probability, one clear prospect, from the top of the highest attainable turret, over the castle as it lay below, would reveal more of the idea of its internal construction, than a year spent in wandering through its subterranean vaults. But the fact was, that the desire to ascend wakening within him had made him forget what was beneath; and having laid aside his chart for a time at least, he was now to be met in every quarter of the upper parts, searching and striving upward, now in one direction, now in another; and seeking, as he went, the best outlooks into the clear air of outer realities.

And they began to discover that they were all meditating different aspects of the same thing; and they brought together their various discoveries, and recognized the likeness between them; and the one thing often explained the other, and combining with it helped to a third. They grew in consequence more and more friendly and loving; so that every now and then, one turned to another and said, as in surprise, "Why, you are my brother!" — "Why, you are my sister!" And yet they had always known it.

The change reached to all. One, who lived on the air of sweet sounds, and who was almost always to be found seated by her harp or some other instrument, had, till the late storm, been generally merry and playful, though sometimes sad. But for a long time after that, she was often found weeping, and playing little simple airs which she had heard in childhood — backward longings, followed by fresh tears. Before long, however, a new element manifested itself in her music. It became yet more wild, and sometimes retained all its sadness, but it was mingled with anticipation and hope. The past and the future merged in one; and while memory yet brought the rain-cloud, expectation threw the rainbow across its bosom — and all was uttered in her music, which rose and swelled, now to defiance, now to victory; then died in a torrent of weeping.

As to the eldest sister, it was many days before she recovered from the shock. At length, one day, her brother came to her, took her by the hand, led her to an open window, and told her to seat herself by it, and look out. She did so; but at first saw nothing more than an unsympathizing blaze of sunlight. But as she looked, the horizon widened out, and the dome of the sky ascended, till the grandeur seized upon her soul, and she fell on her knees and wept. Now the heavens seemed to bend lovingly over her, and to stretch out wide cloud-arms to embrace her; the earth lay like the bosom of an infinite love beneath her, and the wind kissed her cheek with an odour of roses. She sprang to her feet, and turned, in an agony of hope, expecting to behold the face of the father, but there stood only her brother, looking calmly though lovingly on her emotion. She turned again to the window. On the hill-tops rested the sky: Heaven and Earth were one; and the prophecy awoke in her soul, that from betwixt them would the steps of the father approach.

Hitherto she had seen but Beauty; now she beheld truth. Often had she looked on such clouds as these, and loved the strange ethereal curves into which the winds moulded them; and had smiled as her little pet sister told her what curious animals she saw in them, and tried to point them

THE CASTLE: A PARABLE

out to her. Now they were as troops of angels, jubilant over her new birth, for they sang, in her soul, of beauty, and truth, and love. She looked down, and her little sister knelt beside her.

She was a curious child, with black, glittering eyes, and dark hair; at the mercy of every wandering wind; a frolicsome, daring girl, who laughed more than she smiled. She was generally in attendance on her sister, and was always finding and bringing her strange things. She never pulled a primrose, but she knew the haunts of all the orchis tribe, and brought from them bees and butterflies innumerable, as offerings to her sister. Curious moths and glow-worms were her greatest delight; and she loved the stars, because they were like the glow-worms. But the change had affected her too; for her sister saw that her eyes had lost their glittering look, and had become more liquid and transparent. And from that time she often observed that her gaiety was more gentle, her smile more frequent, her laugh less bell-like; and although she was as wild as ever, there was more elegance in her motions, and more music in her voice. And she clung to her sister with far greater fondness than before.

The land reposed in the embrace of the warm summer days. The clouds of heaven nestled around the towers of the castle; and the hearts of its inmates became conscious of a warm atmosphere — of a presence of love. They began to feel like the children of a household, when the mother is at home. Their faces and forms grew daily more and more beautiful, till they wondered as they gazed on each other. As they walked in the gardens of the castle, or in the country around, they were often visited, especially the eldest sister, by sounds that no one heard but themselves; issuing from woods and waters; and by forms of love that lightened out of flowers, and grass, and great rocks. Now and then the young children would come in with a slow, stately step, and, with great eyes that looked as if they would devour all the creation, say that they had met the father amongst the trees, and that he had kissed them; "And," added one of them once, "I grew so big!" But when others went out to look, they could see no one. And some said it must have been the brother, who grew more and more beautiful, and loving, and reverend, and who had lost all traces of hardness, so that they wondered they could ever have thought him stern and harsh. But the eldest sister held her peace, and looked up, and her eyes filled with tears. "Who can tell," thought she, "but the little children know more about it than we?"

Often, at sunrise, might be heard their hum of praise to their unseen father, whom they felt to be near, though they saw him not. Some words thereof once reached my ear through the folds of the music in which they floated, as in an upward snow-storm of sweet sounds. And these are some of the words I heard — but there was much I seemed to hear, which I could not understand, and some things which I understood but cannot utter again.

"We thank thee that we have a father, and not a maker; that thou hast begotten us, and not moulded us as images of clay; that we have come forth of thy heart, and have not been fashioned by thy hands. It *must* be so. Only the heart of a father is able to create. We rejoice in it, and bless thee that we know it. We thank thee for thyself. Be what thou art — our root and life, our beginning and end, our all in all. Come home to us. Thou livest; therefore we live. In thy light we see. Thou art — that is all our song."

Thus they worship, and love, and wait. Their hope and expectation grow ever stronger and brighter, that one day, ere long, the Father will show himself amongst them, and thenceforth dwell in his own house for evermore. What was once but an old legend has become the one desire of their hearts.

And the loftiest hope is the surest of being fulfilled.

The Carasoyn

[The Fairy Fleet]

I

The Mountain Stream

Once upon a time, there lived in a valley in Scotland, a boy about twelve years of age, the son of a shepherd. His mother was dead, and he had no sister or brother. His father was out all day on the hills with his sheep; but when he came home at night, he was as sure of finding the cottage neat and clean, the floor swept, a bright fire, and his supper waiting for him, as if he had had wife and daughter to look after his household, instead of only a boy. Therefore, although Colin could only read and write, and knew nothing of figures, he was ten times wiser, and more capable of learning anything, than if he had been at school all his days. He was never at a loss when anything had to be done. Somehow, he always blundered into the straight road to his end, while another would be putting on his shoes to look for it. And yet all the time that he was busiest working, he was busiest building castles in the air. I think the two ought always to go together.

And so Colin was never over-worked, but had plenty of time to himself. In winter he spent it in reading by the fireside, or carving pieces of wood with his pocket knife; and in summer he always went out for a ramble. His great delight was in a little stream which ran down the valley from the mountains above. Up this *burn* he would wander every afternoon, with his hands in his pockets. He never got far, however — he was so absorbed in watching its antics. Sometimes he would sit on a rock, staring at the water as it hurried through the stones, scolding, expostulating, muttering, and always having its own way. Sometimes he would stop by a deep pool, and watch the crimson-spotted trout, darting about as if their thoughts and not their tails sent them where they wanted to go. And when he stopped at the little cascade, tumbling smooth and shining over a hollowed rock, he seldom got beyond it.

But there was one thing which always troubled him. It was, that when the stream came near the cottage, it could find no other way than through the little yard where stood the cowhouse and the pigsty; and there, not finding a suitable channel, spread abroad in a disconsolate manner, becoming rather a puddle than a brook, all defiled with the treading of the cloven feet of the cow and the pigs. In fact, it looked quite lost and ruined; so that even after it had, with much labour, got out of the yard again, it took a long time to gather itself together, and not quite succeeding, slipped away as if ashamed, with spent forces and poverty-stricken speed; till at length, meeting the friendly help of a rivulet coming straight from the hills, it gathered heart and bounded on afresh.

"It can't be all that the cow drinks that makes the difference," said Colin to himself. "The pigs don't care about it. I do believe it's affronted at being dashed about. The cow isn't dirty, but she's rather stupid and inconsiderate. The pigs are dirty. Something must be done. Let me see."

He reconnoitered the whole ground. Upon the other side of the house all was rock, through which he could not cut; and he was forced to the conclusion that the only other course for the stream to take lay right through the cottage.

To most engineers this would have appeared the one course to be avoided; but Colin's heart danced at the thought of having his dear *burn* running right through the house. How cool it would be all the summer! How convenient for cooking; and how handy at meals! And then the music of it! How it would tell him stories, and sing him to sleep at night! What a companion it would be when his father was away! And then he could bathe in it when he liked. In winter — ah! — to be sure! But winter was a long way off.

The very next day his father went to the fair. So Colin set to work at once.

THE CARASOYN

It was not such a very difficult undertaking; for the walls of the cottage, and the floor as well, were of clay — the former nearly sun-dried into a brick, and the latter trampled hard; but still both assailable by pickaxe and spade. He cut through the walls, and dug a channel along the floor, letting in stones in the bottom and sides. After it got out of the cottage and through the small garden in front, it should find its own way to the channel below, for here the hill was very steep.

The same evening his father came home.

"What have you been about, Colin?" he asked, in great surprise, when he saw the trench in the floor.

"Wait a minute, father," said Colin, "till I have got your supper, and then I'll tell you."

So when his father was seated at the table, Colin darted out, and hurrying up to the stream, broke through the bank just in the place whence a natural hollow led straight to the cottage. The stream dashed out like a wild creature from a cage, faster than he could follow, and shot through the wall of the cottage. His father gave a shout; and when Colin went in, he found him sitting with his spoon half-way to his mouth, and his eyes fixed on the muddy water which rushed foaming through his floor.

"It will soon be clean, father," said Colin, "and then it will be so nice!"

His father made no answer, but continued staring. Colin went on with a long list of the advantages of having a brook running through your house. At length his father smiled and said: —

"You are a curious creature, Colin. But why shouldn't you have your fancies as well as older people? We'll try it awhile, and then we'll see about it."

The fact was, Colin's father had often thought what a lonely life the boy's was. And it seemed hard to take from him any pleasure he could have. So out rushed Colin at the front, to see how the brook would take the shortest way headlong down the hill to its old channel. And to see it go tumbling down that hill was a sight worth living for.

"It is a mercy," said Colin, "it has no neck to break, or it would break twenty times in a minute. It flings itself from rock to rock right down, just as I should like to do, if it weren't for my neck."

All that evening he was out and in without a moment's rest; now up to the beginning of the cut, now following the stream down to the cottage;

then through the cottage, and out again at the front door to see it dart across the garden, and dash itself down the hill.

At length his father told him he must go to bed. He took one more peep at the water, which was running quite clear now, and obeyed. His father followed him presently.

II

The Fairy Fleet

The bed was about a couple of yards from the edge of the brook. And as Colin was always first up in the morning, he slept at the front of the bed. So he lay for some time gazing at the faint glimmer of the water in the dull red light from the sod-covered fire, and listening to its sweet music as it hurried through to the night again, till its murmur changed into a lullaby, and sung him fast asleep.

Soon he found that he was coming awake again. He was lying listening to the sound of the busy stream. But it had gathered more sounds since he went to sleep — amongst the rest one of boards knocking together, and a tiny chattering and sweet laughter, like the tinkling of heather-bells. He opened his eyes. The moon was shining along the brook, lighting the smoky rafters above with its reflection from the water, which had been dammed back at its outlet from the cottage, so that it lay bank-full and level with the floor. But its surface was hardly to be seen, save by an occasional glimmer, for the crowded boats of a fairy fleet which had just arrived. The sailors were as busy as sailors could be, mooring along the banks, or running their boats high and dry on the shore. Some had little sails which glimmered white in the moonshine — half-lowered, or blowing out in the light breeze that crept down the course of the stream. Some were pulling about through the rest, oars flashing, tiny voices calling, tiny feet running, tiny hands hauling at ropes that ran through blocks of shining ivory. On the shore stood groups of fairy ladies in all colours of the rainbow, green predominating, waited upon by gentlemen all in green, but with red and yellow feathers in their caps. The queen had landed on the side next to Colin, and in a few minutes more twenty dances were going at once along the shores of the fairy river. And there lay great Colin's face, just above the bed-clothes, *glowering* at them like an ogre.

At last, after a few dances, he heard a clear, sweet, ringing voice say,

"I've had enough of this. I'm tired of doing like the big people. Let's have a game of Hey Cockolorum Jig!"

That instant every group sprang asunder, and every fairy began a frolic on his own account. They scattered all over the cottage, and Colin lost sight of most of them.

While he lay watching the antics of two of those near him, who behaved more like clowns at a fair than the gentlemen they had been a little while before, he heard a voice close to his ear; but though he looked everywhere about his pillow, he could see nothing. The voice stopped the moment he began to look, but began again as soon as he gave it up.

"You can't see me. I'm talking to you through a hole in the head of your bed."

"Don't look," said the voice. "If the queen sees me I shall be pinched. Oh, please don't."

The voice sounded as if its owner would cry presently. So Colin took good care not to look. It went on:

"Please, I am a little girl, not a fairy. The queen stole me the minute I was born, seven years ago, and I can't get away. I don't like the fairies. They are so silly. And they never grow any wiser. I grow wiser every year. I want to get back to my own people. They won't let me. They make me play at being somebody else all night long, and sleep all day. That's what they do themselves. And I should so like to be myself. The queen says that's not the way to be happy at all; but I do want very much to be a little girl. Do take me."

"How am I to get you?" asked Colin in a whisper, which sounded, after the sweet voice of the changeling, like the wind in a field of dry beans.

"The queen is so pleased with you that she is sure to offer you something. Choose me. Here she comes."

Immediately he heard another voice, shriller and stronger, in front of him; and, looking about, saw standing on the edge of the bed a lovely little creature, with a crown glittering with jewels, and a rush for a scepter in her hand, the blossom of which shone like a bunch of garnets.

"You great staring creature!" she said. "Your eyes are much too big to see with. What clumsy hobgoblins you thick folk are!"

So saying, she laid her wand across Colin's eyes.

"Now, then, stupid!" she said; and that instant Colin saw the room like a huge barn, full of creatures about two feet high. The beams overhead were crowded with fairies, playing all imaginable tricks, scrambling everywhere, knocking each other over, throwing dust and soot in each other's faces, grinning from behind corners, dropping on each other's necks, and tripping up each other's heels. Two had got hold of an empty egg-shell, and coming behind one sitting on the edge of the table, and laughing at some one on the floor, tumbled it right over him, so that he was lost in the cavernous hollow. But the lady-fairies mingled in none of these rough pranks. Their tricks were always graceful, and they had more to say than to do.

But the moment the queen had laid her wand across his eyes, she went on:

"Know, son of a human mortal, that thou hast pleased a queen of the fairies. Lady as I am over the elements, I cannot have everything I desire. One thing thou hast given me. Years have I longed for a path down this rivulet to the ocean below. Your horrid farm-yard, ever since your great-grandfather built this cottage, was the one obstacle. For we fairies hate dirt, not only in houses, but in fields and woods as well, and above all in running streams. But I can't talk like this any longer. I tell you what, you are a dear good boy, and you shall have what you please. Ask me for anything you like."

"May it please your majesty," said Colin, very deliberately, "I want a little girl that you carried away some seven years ago the moment she was born. May it please your majesty, I want her."

"It does not please my majesty," cried the queen, whose face had been growing very black. "Ask for something else."

"Then, whether it pleases your majesty or not," said Colin, bravely, "I hold your majesty to your word. I want that little girl, and that little girl I *will* have, and nothing else."

"You dare to talk so to me, you thick!"

"Yes, your majesty."

"Then you sha'n't have her."

"Then I'll turn the brook right through the dunghill," said Colin. "Do you think I'll let you come into my cottage to play at high jinks when you please, if you behave to me like this?"

And Colin sat up in bed, and looked the queen in the face. And as

THE CARASOYN

he did so he caught sight of the loveliest little creature peeping round the corner at the foot of the bed. And he knew she was the little girl, because she was quiet, and looked frightened, and was sucking her thumb.

Then the queen, seeing with whom she had to deal, and knowing that queens in Fairyland are bound by their word, began to try another plan with him. She put on her sweetest manner and looks; and as she did so, the little face at the foot of the bed grew more troubled, and the little head shook itself, and the little thumb dropped out of the little mouth.

"Dear Colin," said the queen, "you shall have the girl. But you must do something for me first."

The little girl shook her head as fast as ever she could, but Colin was taken up with the queen.

"To be sure I will. What is it?" he said.

And so he was bound by a new bargain, and was in the queen's power.

"You must fetch me a bottle of Carasoyn," said she.

"What is that?" asked Colin.

"A kind of wine that makes people happy."

"Why, are you not happy already?"

"No, Colin," answered the queen, with a sigh.

"You have everything you want."

"Except the Carasoyn," returned the queen.

"You do whatever you like, and go wherever you please."

"That's just it. I want something that I neither like nor please — that I don't know anything about. I want a bottle of Carasoyn."

And here she cried like a spoilt child, not like a sorrowful woman.

"But how am I to get it?"

"I don't know. You must find out."

"Oh! that's not fair," cried Colin.

But the queen burst into a fit of laughter that sounded like the bells of a hundred frolicking sheep, and bounding away to the side of the river, jumped on board of her boat. And like a swarm of bees gathered the courtiers and sailors; two creeping out of the bellows, one at the nozzle and the other at the valve; three out of the basket-hilt of the broadsword on the wall; six all white out of the meal-tub; and so from all parts of the cottage to the river-side. And amongst them Colin spied the little girl creeping on board the queen's boat, with her pinafore to her eyes; and the queen was shaking her fist at her. In five minutes more they had all scrambled into the boats, and the whole fleet was in motion down the stream. In another moment the cottage was empty, and everything had returned to its usual size.

"They'll be all dashed to pieces on the rocks," cried Colin, jumping up, and running into the garden. When he reached the fall, there was nothing to be seen but the swift plunge and rush of the broken water in the moonlight. He thought he heard cries and shouts coming up from below, and fancied he could distinguish the sobs of the little maiden whom he had so foolishly lost. But the sounds might be only those of the water, for to the different voices of a running stream there is no end. He followed its course all the way to its old channel, but saw nothing to indicate any disaster. Then he crept back to his bed, where he lay thinking what a fool he had been, till he cried himself to sleep over the little girl who would never grow into a woman.

III

The Old Woman and Her Hen

In the morning, however, his courage had returned; for the word Carasoyn was always saying itself in his brain.

"People in fairy stories," he said, "always find what they want. Why should not I find this Carasoyn? It does not seem likely. But the world doesn't go round by *likely*. So I will try."

But how was he to begin?

When Colin did not know what to do, he always did something. So as soon as his father was gone to the hill, he wandered up the stream down which the fairies had come.

"But I needn't go on so," he said, "for if the Carasoyn grew in the fairies' country, the queen would know how to get it."

All at once he remembered how he had lost himself on the moor when he was a little boy; and had gone into a hut and found there an old woman spinning. And she had told him such stories! and shown him the way home. So he thought she might be able to help him now; for he remembered that she was very old then, and must be older and still wiser

❧

now. And he resolved to go and look for the hut, and ask the old woman what he was to do.

So he left the stream, and climbed the hill, and soon came upon a desolate moor. The sun was clouded and the wind was cold, and everything looked dreary. And there was no sign of a hut anywhere. He wandered on, looking for it; and all at once found that he had forgotten the way back. At the same instant he saw the hut right before him. And then he remembered it was when he had lost himself that he saw it the former time.

"It seems the way to find some things is to lose yourself," said he to himself.

He went up to the cottage, which was like a large beehive built of turf, and knocked at the door.

"Come in, Colin," said a voice; and he entered, stooping low.

The old woman sat by a little fire, spinning, after the old fashion, with a distaff and spindle. She stopped the moment he went in.

"Come and sit down by the fire," she said, "and tell me what you want."

The Colin saw that she had no eyes.

"I am very sorry you are blind," he said.

"Never you mind that, my dear. I see more than you do for all my blindness. Tell me what you want, and I shall see at least what I can do for you."

"How do you know I want anything?" asked Colin.

"Now that's what I don't like," said the old woman. "Why do you waste words? Words should not be wasted any more than crumbs."

"I beg your pardon," returned Colin. "I will tell you all about it." And so he told her the whole story.

"Oh those children! those children!" said the old woman. "They are always doing some mischief. They never know how to enjoy themselves without hurting somebody or other. I really must give that queen a bit of my mind. Well, my dear, I like you; and I will tell you what must be done. You shall carry the silly queen her bottle of Carasoyn. But she won't like it when she gets it, I can tell her. That's my business, however. — First of all, Colin, you must dream three days without sleeping. Next, you must work three days without dreaming. And last, you must work and dream three days together."

"How am I to do all that?"

"I will help you all I can, but a great deal will depend on yourself. In the meantime you must have something to eat."

So saying, she rose, and going to a corner behind her bed, returned with a large golden-coloured egg in her hand. This she laid on the hearth, and covered over with hot ashes. She then chatted away to Colin about his father, and the sheep, and the cow, and the housework, and showed that she knew all about him. At length she drew the ashes off the egg, and put it on a plate.

"It shines like silver now," said Colin.

"That is a sign it is quite done," said she, and set it before him.

Colin had never tasted anything half so nice. And he had never seen such a quantity of meat in an egg. Before he had finished it he had made a hearty meal. But, in the meantime, the old woman said, —

"Shall I tell you a story while you have your dinner?"

"Oh, yes, please do," answered Colin. "You told me such stories before!"

"Jenny," said the old woman, "my wool is all done. Get me some more."

And from behind the bed out came a sober-coloured, but large and beautifully-shaped hen. She walked sedately across the floor, putting down her feet daintily, like a prim matron as she was, and stopping by the door, gave a *cluck, cluck.*

"Oh, the door is shut, is it?" said the old woman.

"Let me open it," said Colin.

"Do, my dear."

"What are all those white things?" he asked, for the cottage stood in the middle of a great bed of grass with white tops.

"Those are my sheep," said the old woman. "You will see."

Into the grass Jenny walked, and stretching up her neck, gathered the white woolly stuff in her beak. When she had as much as she could hold, she came back and dropped it on the floor; then picked the seeds out and swallowed them, and went back for more, The old woman took the wool, and fastening it on her distaff, began to spin, giving the spindle a twirl, and then dropping it and drawing out the thread from the distaff. But as soon as the spindle began to twirl, it began to sparkle all the colours of the rainbow, and it was a delight to see. And the hands of the woman, instead of being old and wrinkled, were young and long-fingered and fair, and they drew out the wool, and the spindle spun and flashed, and the hen kept going out and in, bringing wool and swallowing the seeds, and the old woman kept telling Colin one story after another, till he thought he could sit there all his life and listen. Sometimes it seemed the spindle that was flashing them, sometimes the long fingers that were spinning them, and sometimes the hen that was gathering them off the heads of the long dry grass and bringing them in her beak and laying them down on the floor.

All at once the spindle grew slower, and gradually ceased turning; the fingers stopped drawing out the thread, the hen retreated behind the bed, and the voice of the blind woman was silent.

"I suppose it is time for me to go," said Colin.

"Yes, it is," answered his hostess.

"Please tell me, then, how I am to dream three days without sleeping."

"That's over," said the old woman. "You've just finished that part. I told you I would help you all I could."

"Have I been here three days, then?" asked Colin, in astonishment.

"And nights too. And I and Jenny and the spindle are quite tired and want to sleep. Jenny has got three eggs to lay besides. Make haste, my boy."

"Please, then, tell me what I am to do next."

"Jenny will put you in the way. When you come where you are going, you will tell them that the old woman with the spindle desires them to lift Cumberbone Crag a yard higher, and to send a flue under Stonestarvit Moss. Jenny, show Colin the way."

Jenny came out with a surly *cluck* and led him a good way across the heath by a path only a hen could have found. But she turned suddenly and walked home again.

IV

The Goblin Blacksmith

Colin could just perceive something suggestive of a track, which he followed till the sun went down. Then he saw a dim light before him, keeping his eye upon which, he came at last to a smithy, where, looking in at the open door, he saw a huge, humpbacked smith working a forehammer in each hand.

He grinned out of the middle of his breast when he saw Colin, and said, "Come in; come in: my youngsters will be glad of you."

He was an awful looking creature, with a great hare lip, and a red ball for a nose. Whatever he did — speak, or laugh, or sneeze — he did not stop working one moment. As often as the sparks flew in his face, he snapped at them with his eyes (which were the colour of a half-dead coal), now with this one, now with that; and the more sparks they got into them the brighter his eyes grew. The moment Colin entered, he took a huge bar of iron from the furnace, and began laying on it so with his two foreham-mers that he disappeared in a cloud of sparks, and Colin had to shut his eyes and be glad to escape with a few burns on his face and hands. When he had beaten the iron till it was nearly black, the smith put it in the fire again, and called out a hundred odd names:

"Here Gob, Shag, Latchit, Licker, Freestone, Greywhackit, Mouse-trap, Potatoe-pot, Blob, Blotch, Blunker — "

And ever as he called, one dwarf after another came tumbling out of the chimney in the corner of which the fire was roaring. They crowded about Colin and began to make hideous faces and spit fire at him. But he kept a bold countenance. At length one pinched him, and he could not stand that, but struck him hard on the head. He thought he had knocked his own hand to pieces, it gave him such a jar; and the head rung like an iron pot.

"Come, come, young man?" cried the smith; "you keep your hand off my children."

"Tell them to keep their hands off me, then," said Colin.

And calling to mind his message, just as they began to crowd about him again with yet more spiteful looks, he added —

"Here, you imps! I won't stand it longer. Get to your work directly. The old woman with the spindle says you're to lift Cumberbone Crag a yard higher, and to send a flue under Stonestarvit Moss."

In a moment they had vanished in the chimney. In a moment more the smithy rocked to its foundations. But the smith took no notice, only worked more furiously than ever. Then came a great crack and a shock that threw Colin on the floor. The smith reeled, but never lost hold of his hammers or missed a blow on the anvil.

"Those boys will do themselves a mischief," he said; then turning to Colin, "Here, you sir, take that hammer. This is no safe place for idle people. If you don't work you'll be knocked to pieces in no time."

The same moment there came a wind from the chimney that blew all the fire into the middle of the smithy. The smith dashed up upon the forge, and rushed out of sight. Presently he returned with one of the goblins under his arm kicking and screaming, laid his ugly head down on the anvil, where he held him by the neck, and hit him a great blow with his hammer above the ear. The hammer rebounded, the goblin gave a shriek, and the smith flung him into the chimney, saying —

"That's the only way to *serve* him. You'll be more careful for one while, I guess, Slobberkin."

And thereupon he took up his other hammer and began to work again, saying to Colin,

"Now, young man, as long as you get a blow with your hammer in for every one of mine, you'll be quite safe; but if you stop, or lose the beat, I won't be answerable to the old woman with the spindle for the consequences."

Colin took up the hammer and did his best. But he soon found that he had never known what it was to work. The smith worked a hammer in each hand, and it was all Colin could do to work his little hammer with both his hands; so it was a terrible exertion to put in blow for blow with the smith. Once, when he lost the time, the smith's forehammer came down on the head of his, beat it flat on the anvil, and flung the handle to the other end of the smithy, where it struck the wall like the report of a cannon.

"I told you," said the smith. "There's another. Make haste, for the boys will be in want of you and me too before they get Cumberbone Crag half a foot higher."

Presently in came the biggest-headed of the family, out of the chimney.

"Six-foot wedges, and a three-yard crowbar!" he said; "or Cumberbone will cumber our bones presently."

The smith rushed behind the bellows, brought out a bar of iron three inches thick or so, cut off three yards, put the end in the fire, blew with might and main, and brought it out as white as paper. He and Colin then laid upon it till the end was flattened to an edge, which the smith turned up a little. He then handed the tool to the imp.

"Here, Gob," he said; "run with it, and the wedges will be ready by the time you come back."

Then to the wedges they set. And Colin worked like three. He never knew how he could work before. Not a moment's pause, except when the smith was at the forge for another glowing mass! And yet, to Colin's amazement, the more he worked, the stronger he seemed to grow. Instead of being worn out, the moment he had got his breath he wanted to be at it again; and he felt as if he had grown twice the size since he took hammer in hand. And the goblins kept running in and out all the time, now for one thing, now for another. Colin thought if they made use of all the tools they fetched, they must be working very hard indeed. And the convulsions felt in the smithy bore witness to their exertions somewhere in the neighbourhood.

And the longer they worked together, the more friendly grew the smith. At length he said — his words always adding energy to his blows —

"What does the old woman want to improve Stonestarvit Moss for?"

"I didn't know she did want to improve it," returned Colin.

"Why, anybody may see that. First, she wants Cumberbone Crag a yard higher — just enough to send the north-east blast over the Moss without touching it. Then she wants a hot flue passed under it. Plain as a fore-hammer! — What did you ask her to do for you? She's always doing things for people and making my bones ache."

"You don't seem to mind it much, though, sir," said Colin.

"No more I do," answered the smith, with a blow that drove the anvil half-way into the earth, from which it took him some trouble to drag it out again. "But I want to know what she is after now."

So Colin told him all he knew about it, which was merely his own story.

"I see, I see," said the smith. "It's all moonshine; but we must do as she says notwithstanding. And now it is my turn to give you a lift, for you have worked well. — As soon as you leave the smithy, go straight to Stonestarvit Moss. Get on the highest part of it; make a circle three yards across, and dig a trench round it. I will give you a spade. At the end of the first day you will see a vine break the earth. By the end of the second, it will be creeping all over the circle. And by the end of the third day, the grapes will be ripe. Squeeze them one by one into a bottle — I will give you a bottle — till it is full. Cork it up tight, and by the time the queen comes for it, it will be Carasoyn."

"Oh, thank you, thank you," cried Colin. "When am I to go?"

"As soon as the boys have lifted Cumberbone Crag, and bored the flue under the Moss. It is of no use till then."

"Well, I'll go on with my work," said Colin, and struck away at the anvil.

In a minute or two in came the same goblin whose head his father had hammered, and said, respectfully,

"It's all right, sir. The boys are gathering their tools, and will be home to supper directly."

"Are you sure you have lifted the Crag a yard?" said the smith.

"Slumkin says it's a half inch over the yard. Grungle says it's three-quarters. But that won't matter — will it?"

"No, I dare say not. But it is much better to be accurate. Is the flue done?"

"Yes, we managed that partly in lifting the crag."

"Very well. How's your head?"

"It rings a little."

"Let it ring you a lesson, then, Slobberkin, in future."

"Yes, sir."

"Now, master, you may go when you like," said the smith to Colin. "We've nothing here you can eat, I am sorry to say."

"Oh, I don't mind that. I'm not very hungry. But the old woman with the spindle said I was to work three days without dreaming."

"Well, you haven't been dreaming — have you?"

And the smith looked quite furious as he put the question, lifting his forehammer as if he would serve Colin like Slobberkin.

"No, that I haven't," answered Colin. "You took good care of that, sir."

The smith actually smiled.

"Then go along," he said. "It is all right."

"But I've only worked — "

"Three whole days and nights," interrupted the smith. "Get along with you. The boys will bother you if you don't. Here's your spade and here's your bottle."

V

The Moss Vineyard

Colin did not need a hint more, but was out of the smithy in a moment. He turned, however, to ask the way: there was nothing in sight but a great heap of peats which had been dug out of the moss, and was standing there to dry. Could he be on Stonestarvit Moss already? The sun was just setting. He would look out for the highest point at once. So he kept climbing, and at last reached a spot whence he could see all round him for a long way. Surely that must be Cumberbone Crag looking down on him! And there at his feet lay one of Jenny's eggs, as bright as silver. And there was a little path trodden and scratched by Jenny's feet, inclosing a circle just the size the smith told him to make. He set to work at once, ate Jenny's egg, and then dug the trench.

Those three days were the happiest he had ever known. For he understood everything he did himself, and all that everything was doing round about him. He saw what the rushes were, and why the blossom came out at the side, and why it was russet-coloured, and why the pith was white, and the skin green. And he said to himself, "If I were a rush now, that's just how I should make a point of growing." And he knew how the heather felt with its cold roots, and its head of purple bells; and the wise-looking cotton-grass, which the old woman called her sheep, and the white beard of which she spun into thread. And he knew what she spun it for: namely, to weave it into lovely white cloth of which to make nightgowns for all the good people that were like to die; for one with one of these nightgowns upon him never died, but was laid in a beautiful white bed, and the door was closed upon him, and no noise came near him, and he lay there, dreaming lovely cool dreams, till the world had turned round, and was ready for him to get up again and do something.

He felt the wind playing with every blade of grass in his charmed circle. He felt the rays of heat shooting up from the hot flue beneath the moss. He knew the moment when the vine was going to break from the earth, and he felt the juices gathering and flowing from the roots into the grapes. And all the time he seemed at home, tending the cow, or making his father's supper, or reading a fairy tale as he sat waiting for him to come home.

At length the evening of the third day arrived. Colin squeezed the rich red grapes into his bottle, corked it, shouldered his spade, and turned homewards, guided by a peak which he knew in the distance. After walking all night in the moonlight, he came at length upon a place which he recognized, and so down upon the brook, which he followed home.

He met his father going out with his sheep. Great was his delight to see Colin again, for he had been dreadfully anxious about him. Colin told him the whole story; and as at that time marvels were much easier to believe than they are now, Colin's father did not laugh at him, but went away to the hills thinking, while Colin went on to the cottage, where he found plenty to do, having been nine days gone. He laid the bottle carefully away with his Sunday clothes, and set about everything just as usual.

But though the fairy brook was running merrily as ever through the cottage, and although Colin watched late every night, and latest when the moon shone, no fairy fleet came glimmering and dancing in along the stream. Autumn was there at length, and cold fogs began to rise in the cottage, and so Colin turned the brook into its old course, and filled up the breaches in the walls and the channel along the floor, making all close against the blasts of winter. But he had never known such a weary winter before. He could not help constantly thinking how cold the little girl must be, and how she would be saying to herself, "I wish Colin hadn't been so silly and lost me."

VI

The Consequences

But at last the spring came, and after the spring the summer. And the very first warm day, Colin took his spade and pickaxe, and down rushed the stream once more, singing and bounding into the cottage. Colin was even more delighted than he had been the first time. And he watched late into the night, but there came neither moon nor fairy fleet. And more than a week passed thus.

At length, on the ninth night, Colin, who had just fallen asleep, opened his eyes with sudden wakefulness, and behold! the room was all in a glimmer with moonshine and fairy glitter. The boats were rocking on the water, and the queen and her court had landed, and were dancing merrily on the earthen floor. He lost no time.

"Queen! queen!" he said, "I've got your bottle of Carasoyn."

The dance ceased in a moment, and the queen bounded upon the edge of his bed.

"I can't bear the look of your great, glaring, ugly eyes," she said. "I must make you less before I can talk to you."

So once more she laid her rush wand across his eyes, whereupon Colin saw them all six times the size they were before, and queen went; on:

"Where is the Carasoyn?" "Give it to me."

"It is in my box under the bed. If your majesty will stand out of the way, I will get it for you."

The queen jumped on the floor, and Colin, leaning from the bed, pulled out his little box, and got out the bottle.

"There it is, your majesty," he said, but not offering it to her.

"Give it me directly," said the queen, holding out her hand.

"First give me my little girl," returned Colin, boldly.

"Do you dare to bargain with me?" said the queen, angrily.

"Your majesty deigned to bargain with me first," said Colin.

"But since then you tried to break all our necks. You made a wicked cataract out there on the other side of the garden. Our boats were all dashed to pieces, and we had to wait till our horses were fetched. If I had been killed, you couldn't have held me to my bargain, and I won't hold to it now."

"If you chose to go down my cataract — " began Colin.

"*Your* cataract!" cried the queen. "All the waters that run from Loch Lonely are mine, I can tell you — all the way to the sea."

"Except where they run through farmyards, your majesty."

"I'll rout you out of the country," said the queen.

"Meantime I'll put the bottle in the chest again," returned Colin.

The queen bit her lips with vexation.

"Come here, Changeling," she cried at length, in a flattering tone.

And the little girl came slowly up to her, and stood staring at Colin, with the tears in her eyes.

"Give me your hand, little girl," said he, holding out his.

She did so. It was cold as ice.

"Let go her hand," said the queen.

."I won't," said Colin. "She's mine."

"Give me the bottle then," said the queen.

"Don't," said the child.

But it was too late. The queen had it.

"Keep your girl," she cried, with an ugly laugh.

"Yes, keep me," cried the child.

The cry ended in a hiss.

Colin felt something slimy wriggling in his grasp, and looking down, saw that instead of a little girl he was holding a great writhing worm. He had almost flung it from him, but recovering himself, he grasped it tighter.

"If it's a snake, I'll choke it," he said. "If it's a girl, I'll keep her."

The same instant it changed to a little white rabbit, which looked him piteously in the face, and pulled to get its little forefoot out of his hand. But, though he tried not to hurt it, Colin would not let it go. Then the rabbit changed to a great black cat, with eyes that flashed green fire. She sputtered and spit and swelled her tail, but all to no purpose. Colin held fast. Then it was a wood pigeon, struggling and fluttering in terror to get its wing out of his hold. But Colin still held fast.

All this time the queen had been getting the cork out. The moment it yielded she gave a scream and dropped the bottle. The Carasoyn ran out, and a strange odour filled the cottage. The queen stood shivering and sobbing beside the bottle, and all her court came about her and shivered and sobbed too, and their faces grew ancient and wrinkled. Then the queen, bending and tottering like an old woman, led the way to the boats, and her courtiers followed her, limping and creeping and distorted. Colin stared in amazement. He saw them all go aboard, and he heard the sound of them like a far-off company of men and women crying bitterly. And away they floated down the stream, the rowers dipping no oar, but bending weeping over them, and letting the boats drift along the stream. They vanished from his sight, and the rush of the cataract came up on the night-wind louder than he had ever heard it before. — But alas! when he came to himself, he found his hand relaxed, and the dove flown. Once more there was nothing left but to cry himself asleep, as he well might.

In the morning he rose very wretched. But the moment he entered the cowhouse, there, beside the cow, on the milking stool, sat a lovely little girl, with just one white garment on her, crying bitterly.

"I am so cold," she said, sobbing.

He caught her up, ran with her into the house, put her into the bed, and ran back to the cow for a bowl of warm milk. This she drank eagerly, laid her head down, and fell fast asleep. Then Colin saw that though she must be eight years old by her own account, her face was scarcely older than that of a baby of as many months.

When his father came home you may be sure he stared to see the child in the bed. Colin told him what had happened. But his father said he had met a troop of gipsies on the hill that morning.

"And you were always a dreamer, Colin, even before you could speak."

"But don't you smell the Carasoyn still?" said Colin.

"I do smell something very pleasant, to be sure," returned his father; "but I think it is the wallflower on the top of the garden-wall. What a blossom there is of it this year! I am sure there is nothing sweeter in all Fairyland, Colin."

Colin allowed that.

The little girl slept for three whole days. And for three days more she never said another word than "I am so cold!" But after that she began to revive a little, and to take notice of things about her. For three weeks she would taste nothing but milk from the cow, and would not move from the chimney-corner. By degrees, however, she began to help Colin a little with his house-work, and as she did so, her face gathered more and more expression; and she made such progress, that by the end of three months she could do everything as well as Colin himself, and certainly more neatly. Whereupon he gave up his duties to her, and went out with his father to learn the calling of a shepherd.

Thus things went on for three years. And Fairy, as they called her, grew lovelier every day, and looked up to Colin more and more every day.

At the end of the three years, his father sent him to an old friend of his, a schoolmaster. Before he left, he made Fairy promise never to go near the brook after sundown. He had turned it into its old channel the very day she came to them. And he begged his father especially to look after her when the moon was high, for then she grew very restless and strange, and her eyes looked as if she saw things other people could not see.

When the end of the other three years had come, the schoolmaster would not let Colin go home, but insisted on sending him to college. And there he remained for three years more.

When he returned at the end of that time, he found Fairy so beautiful and so wise, that he fell dreadfully in love with her. And Fairy found out that she had been in love with him since ever so long — she did not know how long. And Colin's father agreed that they should be married as soon as Colin should have a house to take her to. So Colin went away to London, and worked very hard, till at last he managed to get a little cottage in Devonshire to live in. Then he went back to Scotland and married Fairy. And he was very glad to get her away from the neighbourhood of a queen who was not to be depended upon.

VII

The Banished Fairies

Those fairies had for a long time been doing wicked things. They had played many ill-natured pranks upon the human mortals; had stolen children upon whom they had no claim; had refused to deliver them up when they were demanded of them; had even terrified infants in their cradles; and, final proof of moral declension in fairies, had attempted to get rid of the obligations of their word, by all kinds of trickery and false logic.

It was not till they had sunk thus low that their queen began to long for the Carasoyn. She, no more than if she had been a daughter of Adam, could be happy while going on in that way; and, therefore, having heard of its marvellous virtues, and thinking it would stop her growing misery, she tried hard to procure it. For a hundred years she had tried in vain. Not till Colin arose did she succeed. But the Carasoyn was only for really good people, and therefore when the iron bottle which contained it was uncorked, she, and all her attendants, were, by the vapours thereof, suddenly changed into old men and women fairies. They crowded away weeping and lamenting, and Colin had as yet seen them no more.

For when the wickedness of any fairy tribe reaches its climax, the punishment that falls upon them is, that they are compelled to leave that part of the country where they and their ancestors have lived for more years than they can count, and wander away, driven by an inward restlessness, ever longing after the country they have left, but never able to turn round and go back to it, always thinking they will do so to-morrow, but when to-morrow comes, saying *to-morrow* again, till at last they find, not their old home, but the place of their doom — that is, a place where their restlessness leaves them, and they find they can remain. This partial repose, however, springs from no satisfaction with the place; it is only that their inward doom ceases to drive them further. They sit down to weep, and to long after the country they have left.

This is not because the country to which they have been driven is ugly and inclement — it may or may not be such: it is simply because it is not *their* country. If it would be, and it must be, torture to the fairy of a harebell to go and live in a hyacinth — a torture quite analogous to which many human beings undergo from their birth to their death, and some of them longer, for anything I can tell — think what it must be for a tribe of fairies to have to go and live in a country quite different from that in and for which they were born. To the whole tribe the country is what the flower is to the individual; and when a fairy is born to whom the whole country is what the individual flower is to the individual fairy, then the fairy is king or queen of the fairies, and always makes a new nursery rhyme for the young fairies, which is never forgotten. When, therefore, a tribe is banished, it is long before they can settle themselves into their new quarters. Their clothes do not fit them, as it were. They are constantly wriggling themselves into harmony with their new circumstances — which is only another word for clothes — and never quite succeeding. It is their punishment — and something more. Consequently their temper is not always of the evenest; indeed, and in a word, they are as like human mortals as may well be, considering the differences between them.

In the present case, you would say it was surely no great hardship to be banished from the heathy hills, the bare rocks, the wee trotting burnies of Scotland, to the rich valleys, the wooded shores, the great rivers, the grand ocean of the south of Devon. You may say they could not have been very wicked when this was all their punishment. If you do, you must have studied the human mortals to no great purpose. You do not believe that a man may be punished by being made very rich? I do. Anyhow, these fairies were not of your opinion, *for they were in it.* In the splendour of their Devon banishment, they sighed for their bare Scotland. Under the leafy foliage of the Devonshire valleys, with the purple and green ocean before them, that had seen ships of a thousand builds, or on the shore rich with shells and many-coloured creatures, they longed for the clear, cold, pensive, open sides of the far-stretching heathy sweeps, to which a gray, wild, torn sea, with memories only of Norsemen, whales, and mermaids, cried aloud. For the big rivers, on which reposed great old hulks scarred with battle, they longed after the rocks and stones and rowan and birch-trees of the solitary burns. The country they had left might be an ill-favoured thing, but it was their own.

Now that which happens to the aspect of a country when the fairies leave it, is that a kind of deadness falls over the landscape. The traveller feels the wind as before, but it does not seem to refresh him. The child sighs over his daisy chain, and cannot find a red-tipped one amongst all that he has gathered. The cowslips have not half the honey in them. The wasps outnumber the bees. The horses come from the plough more tired at night, hanging their heads to their very hoofs as they plod homewards. The youth and the maiden, though perfectly happy when they meet, find the road to and from the trysting-place unaccountably long and dreary. The hawthorn-blossom is neither so white nor so red as it used to be, and the dark rough bark looks through and makes it ragged. The day is neither so warm nor the night so friendly as before. In a word, that something which no one can describe or be content to go without is missing. Everything is common-place. Everything falls short of one's expectations.

But it does not follow that the country to which the fairies are banished is so much richer and more beautiful for their presence. If that country has its own fairies, it needs no more, and Devon in especial has been rich in fairies from the time of the Phoenicians, and ever so long before that. But supposing there were no aborigines left to quarrel with, it takes centuries before the new immigration can fit itself into its new home. Until this comes about, the queerest things are constantly happening. For however could a convolvulus grow right with the soul of a Canterbury-bell inside it, for instance? The banished fairies are forced to do the best they can, and take the flowers the nearest they can find.

VIII

Their Revenge

When Colin and his wife settled then in their farm-house, the same
tribe of fairies was already in the neighbourhood, and was not long in
discovering who had come after them. An assembly was immediately
called. Something must be done; but what, was disputed. Most of them
thought only of revenge — to be taken upon the children. But the queen
hesitated. Perhaps her sufferings had done her good. She suggested that
before coming to any conclusion they should wait and watch the household.

In consequence of this resolution they began to frequent the house
constantly, and sometimes in great numbers. But for a long time they
could do the children no mischief. Whatever they tried turned out to their
amusement. They were three, two girls and a boy; the girls nine and eight,
and the boy three years old.

When they succeeded in enticing them beyond the home-bound-
aries, they would at one time be seized with an unaccountable panic, and
turn and scurry home without knowing why; at another, a great butterfly
or dragon fly, or some other winged and lovely creature, would dart past
them, and away towards the house, and they after it, scampering; or the
voice of their mother would be heard calling from the door. But at last
their opportunity arrived.

One day the children were having such a game! The sisters had
blindfolded their little brother, and were carrying him now on their backs,
now in their arms, all about the place; now up stairs, talking about the
rugged mountain paths they were climbing; now down again, filling him
with the fancy that they were descending into a narrow valley; then they
would set the tap of a rain-water barrel running, and represent that they
were travelling along the bank of a rivulet. Now they were threading the
depths of a great forest: and when the low of a cow reached them from a
nigh field, that was the roaring of a lion or a tiger. At length they reached
a lake into which the rivulet ran, and then it was necessary to take off his
shoes and socks, that he might skim over the water on his bare feet, which
they dipped and dabbled now in this tub, now in that, standing for farm
and household purposes by the water-butt. The sisters kept their own
imaginations alive by carrying him through all the strange places inside

and outside of the house. When they told him they were ascending a precipice, they were, in fact, climbing a rather difficult ladder up to the door of the hayloft; when they told him they were traversing a pathless desert, they were, in fact, in a waste, empty place, a wide floor, used sometimes as a granary, with the rafters of the roof coming down to it on both sides, a place abundantly potent in their feelings to the generation of the desert in his; when they were wandering through a trackless forest, they were, in fact, winding about amongst the trees of a large orchard, which, in the moonlight, was vast enough for the fancy of any child. Had they uncovered his eyes at any moment, he would only have been seized with a wonder and awe of another sort, more overwhelming because more real, and more strange because not even in part bodied forth from his own brain.

In the course of the story, and while they bore the bare-footed child through the orchard, telling him they saw the fairies gliding about everywhere through the trees, not thinking that he believed every word they told him, they set him down, and the child suddenly opened his eyes. His sisters were gone. The moon was staring at him out of the sky, through the mossy branches of the apple-trees, which he thought looked like old women all about him, they were so thin and bony.

When the sisters, who had only for a moment run behind some of the trees, that they might cause him additional amazement, returned, he was gone. There was terrible lamentation in the house; but his father and mother, who were experienced in such matters, knew that the fairies must be in it, and cherished a hope that their son would yet be restored to them, though all their endeavours to find him were unavailing.

IX

The Fairy Fiddler

The father thought over many plans, but never came upon the right one. He did not know that they were the same tribe which had before carried away his wife when she was an infant. If he had, they might have done something sooner.

At length, one night, towards the close of seven years, about twelve o'clock, Colin suddenly opened his eyes, for he had been fast asleep and dreaming, and saw a few grotesque figures which he thought he must have seen before, dancing on the floor between him and the nearly extinguished fire. One of them had a violin, but when Colin first saw him he was not playing. Another of them was singing, and thus keeping the dance in time. This was what he sang, evidently addressed to the fiddler, who stood in the centre of the dance: —

> "Peterkin, Peterkin, tall and thin,
> What have you done with his cheek and his chin?
> What have you done with his ear and his eye?
> Hearken, hearken, and hear him cry."

Here Peterkin put his fiddle to his neck, and drew from it a wail just like the cry of a child, at which the dancers danced more furiously. Then he went on playing the tune the other had just sung, in accompaniment to his own reply: —

> "Silversnout, Silversnout, short and stout,
> I have cut them off and plucked them out,
> And salted them down in the Kelpie's Pool
> Because papa Colin is such a fool."

Then the fiddle cried like a child again, and they danced more wildly than ever.

Colin, filled with horror, although he did not more than half believe what they were saying, sat up in bed and stared at them with fierce eyes, waiting to hear what they would say next. Silversnout now resumed his part: —

> "Ho, ho! Ho! ho! and if he don't know,
> And fish them out of the pool, so — so," —

here they all pretended to be hauling in a net as they danced.

> "Before the end of the seven long years,
> Sweet babe will be left without eyes or ears."

Then Peterkin replied: —

> "Sweet babe will be left without cheek or chin,
> Only a hole to put porridge in;
> Porridge and milk, and haggis, and cakes:
> Sweet babe will gobble till his stomach aches."

From this last verse, Colin knew that they must be Scotch fairies, and all at once recollected their figures as belonging to the multitude he had once seen frolicking in his father's cottage. It was now Silversnout's turn. He began: —

> "But never more shall Colin see
> Sweet babe again upon his knee,
> With or without his cheek or chin,
> Except — — "

Here Silversnout caught sight of Colin's face staring at him from the bed, and with a shriek of laughter they all vanished, the tones of Peterkin's fiddle trailing after them through the darkness like the train of a shooting star.

X

The Old Woman and Her Hen

Now Colin had got the better of these fairies once, not by his own skill, but by the help that other powers had afforded him. What were those powers? First the old woman on the heath. Indeed, he might attribute it all to her. He would go back to Scotland and look for her and find her. But the old woman was never found except by the seeker losing himself. It could not be done otherwise. She would cease to be the old woman, and become her own hen, if ever the moment arrived when any one found her without losing himself. And Colin since that time had wandered so much all over the moor, wide as it was, that lay above his father's cottage, that he did not believe he was able to lose himself there any more. He had yet to learn that it did not so much matter where he lost himself, provided only he was lost.

Just at this time Colin's purse was nearly empty, and he set out to borrow the money of a friend who lived on the other side of Dartmoor. When he got there, he found that he had gone from home. Unable to rest, he set out again to return.

It was almost night when he started, and before he had got many miles into the moor, it was dark, for there was no moon, and it was so cloudy that he could not see the stars. He thought he knew the way quite well, but as the track even in daylight was in certain places very indistinct, it was no wonder that he strayed from it, and found that he had lost himself. The same moment that he became aware of this, he saw a light away to the left. He turned towards it and found it proceeded from a little hive-like hut, the door of which stood open. When he was within a yard or two of it, he heard a voice say —

"Come in, Colin; I'm waiting for you."

Colin obeyed at once, and found the old woman seated with her spindle and distaff, just as he had seen her when he was a boy on the moor above his father's cottage.

"How do you do, mother?" he said.

"I am always quite well. Never ask me that question."

"Well, then, I won't any more," returned Colin. "But I thought you lived in Scotland?"

"I don't live anywhere; but those that will do as I tell them, will always find me when they want me."

"Do you see yet, mother?"

"See! I always see so well that it is not worth while to burn eyelight. So I let them go out. They were expensive."

Where her eyes should have been, there was nothing but wrinkles.

"What do you want?" she resumed.

"I want my child. The fairies have got him."

"I know that."

"And they have taken out his eyes."

"I can make him see without them."

"And they've cut off his ears," said Colin.

"He can hear without them."

"And they've salted down his cheek and his chin."

"Now I don't believe that," said the old woman.

"I heard them say so myself," returned Colin.

"Those fairies are worse liars than any I know. But something must be done. Sit down and I'll tell you a story."

"There's only nine days of the seven years left," said Colin, in a tone of expostulation.

"I know that as well as you," answered the old woman. "Therefore, I say, there is no time to be lost. Sit down and listen to my story. Here, Jenny."

The hen came pacing solemnly out from under the bed.

"Off to the sheep-shearing, Jenny, and make haste, for I must spin faster than usual. There are but nine days left."

Jenny ran out at the door with her head on a level with her tail, as if the kite had been after her. In a few moments she returned with a bunch of wool, as they called it, though it was only cotton from the cotton-grass that grew all about the cottage, nearly as big as herself, in her bill, and then darted away for more. The old woman fastened it on her distaff, drew out a thread to her spindle, and then began to spin. And as she spun she told her story — fast, fast; and Jenny kept scampering out and in; and by the time Colin thought it must be midnight, the story was told, and seven of the nine days were over.

"Colin," said the old woman, "now that you know all about it, you must set off at once."

"I am ready," answered Colin, rising.

"Keep on the road Jenny will show you till you come to the cobbler's. Tell him the old woman with the distaff requests him to give you a lump of his wax."

"And what am I to do with it?"

"The cobbler always knows what his wax is for."

And with this answer, the old woman turned her face towards the fire, for, although it was summer, it was cold at night on the moor. Colin, moved by sudden curiosity, instead of walking out of the hut after Jenny, as he ought to have done, crept round by the wall, and peeped in the old woman's face. There, instead of wrinkled blindness, he saw a pair of flashing orbs of light, which were rather reflected on the fire than had the fire reflected in them. But the same instant the hut and all that was in it vanished, he felt the cold fog of the moor blowing upon him, and fell heavily to the earth.

XI

The Goblin Cobbler

When he came to himself he lay on the moor still. He got up and gazed around. The moon was up, but there was no hut to be seen. He was sorry enough now that he had been so foolish. He called, "Jenny, Jenny," but in vain. What was he to do? To-morrow was the eighth of the nine days left, and if before twelve at night the following day he had not rescued his boy, nothing could be done, at least for seven years more. True, the year was not quite out till about seven the following evening, but the fairies, instead of giving days of grace, always take them. He could do nothing but begin to walk, simply because that gave him a shadow more of a chance of finding the cobbler's than if he sat still, but there was no possibility of choosing one direction rather than another.

He wandered the rest of that night and the next day. He could not go home before the hour when the cobbler could no longer help him. Such was his anxiety, that although he neither ate nor drank, he never thought of the cause of his gathering weakness.

As it grew dark, however, he became painfully aware of it, and was just on the point of sitting down exhausted upon a great white stone that looked inviting, when he saw a faint glimmering in front of him. He was erect in a moment, and making towards the place. As he drew near he became aware of a noise made up of many smaller noises, such as might have proceeded from some kind of factory. Not till he was close to the place could he see that it was a long low hut, with one door, and no windows. The light shone from the door, which stood wide upen. He approached, and peeped in. There sat a multitude of cobblers, each on his stool, with his candle stuck in the hole in the seat, cobbling away. They looked rather little men, though not at all of fairy-size. The most remarkable thing about them was, that at any given moment they were all doing precisely the same thing, as if they had been a piece of machinery. When one drew the threads in stitching, they all did the same. If Colin saw one wax his thread, and looked up, he saw that they were all waxing their thread. If one took to hammering on his lapstone, they did not follow his example, but all together with him they caught up their lapstones and fell to hammering away, as if nothing but hammering could ever be demanded of them. And when he came to look at them more closely, he saw that

❧   THE CARASOYN every one was blind of an eye, and had a nose turned up like an awl. Every one of them, however, looked different from the rest, notwithstanding a very close resemblance in their features.

The moment they caught sight of him, they rose as one man, pointed their awls at him, and advanced towards him like a closing bush of aloes, glittering with spikes.

"Fine upper-leathers," said one and all, with a variety of accordant grimaces.

"Top of his head — good paste-bowl," was the next general remark.

"Coarse hair — good ends," followed.

"Sinews — good thread."

"Bones and blood — good paste for seven-leaguers."

"Ears — good loops to pull 'em on with. Pair short now."

"Soles — same for queen's slippers."

And so on they went, portioning out his body in the most irreverent fashion for the uses of their trade, till having come to his teeth, and said —

"Teeth — good brads," — they all gave a shriek like the whisk of the waxed threads through the leather, and sprung upon him with their awls drawn back like daggers. There was no time to lose.

"The old woman with the spindle — — " said Colin.

"Don't know her," shrieked the cobblers.

"The old woman with the distaff," said Colin, and they all scurried back to their seats and fell to hammering vigorously.

"She desired me," continued Colin, "to ask the cobbler for a lump of his wax."

Every one of them caught up his lump of wrought rosin, and held it out to Colin. He took the one offered by the nearest, and found that all their lumps were gone; after which they sat motionless and stared at him.

"But what am I to do with it?" asked Colin.

"I will walk a little way with you," said the one nearest, "and tell you all about it. The old woman is my grandmother, and a very worthy old soul she is."

Colin stepped out at the door of the workshop, and the cobbler followed him. Looking round, Colin saw all the stools vacant, and the place as still as an old churchyard. The cobbler, who now in his talk, gestures, and general demeanour appeared a very respectable, not to say conventional, little man, proceeded to give him all the information he required, accompanying it with the present of one of his favourite awls.

They walked a long way, till Colin was amazed to find that his strength stood out so well. But at length the cobbler said —

"I see, sir, that the sun is at hand. I must return to my vocation. When the sun is once up you will know where you are."

He turned aside a few yards from the path, and entered the open door of a cottage. In a moment the place resounded with the soft hammering of three hundred and thirteen cobblers, each with his candle stuck in a hole in the stool on which he sat. While Colin stood gazing in wonderment, the rim of the sun crept up above the horizon; and there the cottage stood white and sleeping, while the cobblers, their lights, their stools, and their tools had all vanished. Only there was still the sound of the hammers ringing in his head, where it seemed to shape itself into words something like these: a good deal had to give way to the rhyme, for they were more particular about their rhymes than their etymology:

> "Dub-a-dub, dub-a-dub,
> Cobbler's man
> Hammer it, stitch it,
> As fast as you can.
> The week-day ogre
> Is wanting his boots;
> The trip-a-trap fairy
> Is going bare-foots.
> Dream-daughter has worn out
> Her heels and her toeses,
> For want of cork slippers
> To walk over noses.
> Spark-eye, the smith,
> May shoe the nightmare,
> The kelpie and pookie,
> The nine-footed bear:
> We shoe the mermaids —
> The tips of their tails —
> Stitching the leather
> On to their scales.
> We shoe the brownie,

Clumsy and toeless,
And then he goes quiet
As a mole or a moless.
There is but one creature
That we cannot shoe,
And that is the Boneless,
All made of glue."

A great deal of nonsense of this sort went through Colin's head before the sounds died away. Then he found himself standing in the field outside his own orchard.

XII

The Wax and the Awl

The evening arrived. The sun was going down over the sea, cloudless, casting gold from him lavishly, when Colin arrived on the shore at some distance from his home. The tide was falling, and a good space of sand was uncovered, and lay glittering in the setting sun. This sand lay between some rocks and the sea; and from the rocks innumerable runnels of water that had been left behind in their hollows were hurrying back to their mother. These occasionally spread into little shallow lakes, resting in hollows in the sand. These lakes were in a constant ripple from the flow of the little streams through them; and the sun shining on these multitudinous ripples, the sand at the bottom shone like brown silk watered with gold, only that the golden lines were flitting about like living things, never for a moment in one place.

Now Colin had no need of fairy ointment to anoint his eyes and make him able to see fairies. Most people need this; but Colin was naturally gifted. Therefore, as he drew near a certain high rock, which he knew very well, and from which many streams were flowing back into the sea, he saw that the little lakes about it were crowded with fairies, playing all kinds of pranks in the water. It was a lovely sight to see them thus frolicking in the light of the setting sun, in their gay dresses, sparkling with jewels, or what looked like jewels, flashing all colours as they moved. But Colin had not much time to see them; for the moment they saw him, knowing that this was the man whom they had wronged by stealing his child, and knowing too that he saw them, they fled at once up the high rock and vanished. This was just what Colin wanted. He went all round and round the rock, looked in every direction in which there might be a pool, found more fairies, here and there, who fled like the first up the rock and disappeared. When he had thus driven them all from the sands, he approached the rock, taking the lump of cobbler's wax from his pocket as he went. He scrambled up the rock, and, without showing his face, put his hand on the uppermost edge of it, and began drawing a line with the wax all along. He went creeping round the rock, still drawing the wax along the edge, till he had completed the circuit. Then he peeped over.

Now in the heart of this rock, which was nearly covered at high-water, there was a big basin, known as the Kelpie's Pool, filled with sea-water and the loveliest sea-weed and many little sea-animals; and this was a favourite resort of the fairies. It was now, of course, crowded. When they saw his big head come peeping over, they burst into a loud fit of laughter, and began mocking him and making game of him in a hundred ways. Some made the ugliest faces they could, some queer gestures of contempt; others sung bits of songs, and so on; while the queen sat by herself on a projecting corner of the rock, with her feet in the water, and looked at him sulkily. Many of them kept on plunging and swimming and diving and floating, while they mocked him; and Colin would have enjoyed the sight much if they had not spoiled their beauty and their motions by their grimaces and their gestures.

"I want my child," said Colin.

"Give him his child," cried one.

Thereupon a dozen of them dived, and brought up a huge sea-slug — a horrid creature, like a lump of blubber — and held it up to him, saying —

"There he is; come down and fetch him."

Others offered him a blue lobster, struggling in their grasp; others, a spider-crab; others, a whelk; while some of them sung mocking verses, each capping the line the other gave. At length they lifted a dreadful object from the bottom. It was like a baby with his face half eaten away by the fishes, only that he had a huge nose, like the big toe of a lobster. But Colin was not to be taken in.

"Very well, good people," he said, "I will try something else."

He crept down the rock again, took out the little cobbler's awl, and began boring a hole. It went through the rock as if it had been butter, and as he drew it out the water followed in a far-reaching spout. He bored another, and went on boring till there were three hundred and thirteen spouts gushing from the rock, and running away in a strong little stream towards the sea. He then sat down on a ledge at the foot of the rock and waited.

By-and-by he heard a clamour of little voices from the basin. They had found that the water was getting very low. But when they discovered the holes by which it was escaping, "He's got Dottlecob's awl! He's got Dottlecob's awl!" they cried with one voice of horror.

When he heard this, Colin climbed the rock again to enjoy their confusion. But here I must explain a little.

In the former part of this history I showed how fond these fairies were of water. But the fact was, they were far too fond of it. It had grown a thorough dissipation with them. Their business had been chiefly to tend and help the flowers in which they lived, and to do good offices for every thing that had any kind of life about them. Hence their name of Good People. But from finding the good the water did to the flowers, and from sharing in the refreshment it brought, flowing up to them in tiny runnels through the veins of the plants, they had fallen in love with the water itself, for its own sake, or rather for the pleasure it gave to them, irrespective of the good it was to the flowers which lived upon it. So they neglected their business, and took to sailing on the streams, and plunging into every pool they could find. Hence the rapidity of their decline and fall.

Again, on coming to the sea-coast, they had found that the salt water did much to restore the beauty they had lost by partaking of the Carasoyn. Therefore they were constantly on the shore, bathing for ever in the water, especially that left in this pool by the ebbing tide, which was particularly to their taste; till at last they had grown entirely dependent for comfort on the sea-water, and, they thought, entirely dependent on it for existence also, at least such existence as was in the least worth possessing.

Therefore when they saw the big face of Colin peering once more over the ledge, they rushed at him in a rage, scrambling up the side of the rock like so many mad beetles. Colin drew back and let them come on. The moment the foremost put his foot on the line that Colin had drawn around the rock, he slipped and tumbled backwards head over heels into the pool, shrieking —

"He's got Dottlecob's wax!"

"He's got Dottlecob's wax!" screamed the next, as he fell backwards after his companion, and this took place till no one would approach the line. In fact no fairy could keep his footing on the wax, and the line was so broad — for as Colin rubbed it, it had melted and spread — that not one of them could spring over it. The queen now rose.

"What do you want, Colin?" she said.

"I want my child, as you know very well," answered Colin.

"Come and take him," returned the queen, and sat down again, not now with her feet in the water, for it was much too low for that.

But Colin knew better. He sat down on the edge of the basin. Unfortunately, the tail of his coat crossed the line. In a moment half-a-dozen of the fairies were out of the circle. Colin rose instantly, and there was not much harm done, for the multitude was still in prison. The water was nearly gone, beginning to leave the very roots of the long tangles uncovered. At length the queen could bear it no longer.

"Look here, Colin," she said; "I wish you well."

And as she spoke she rose and descended the side of the rock towards the water now far below her. She had to be very cautious too, the stones were so slippery, though there was none of Dottlecob's wax there. About half-way below where the surface of the pool had been, she stopped, and pushed a stone aside. Colin saw what seemed the entrance to a cave inside the rock. The queen went in. A few moments after she came out wringing her hands.

"Oh dear! oh dear! What shall I do?" she cried. "You horrid thick people will grow so. He's grown to such a size that I can't get him out."

"Will you let him go if I get him out?" asked Colin.

"I will, I will. We shall all be starved to death for want of sea-water if I don't," she answered.

"Swear by the cobbler's awl and the cobbler's wax," said Colin.

"I swear," said the queen.

"By the cobbler's awl and the cobbler's wax," insisted Colin.

"I swear by the cobbler's awl and the cobbler's wax," returned the queen.

"In the name of your people?"

"In the name of my people," said the queen, "that none of us here present will ever annoy you or your family hereafter."

"Then I'll come down," said Colin, and jumped into the basin. With the cobbler's awl he soon cleared a big opening into the rock, for it bored and cut it like butter. Then out crept a beautiful boy of about ten years old, into his father's arms, with eyes, and ears, and chin, and cheek all safe and sound. And he carried him home to his mother.

It was a disappointment to find him so much of a baby at his age; but that fault soon began to mend. And the house was full of jubilation. And little Colin told them the whole story of his sojourn among the fairies. And it did not take so long as you would think, for he fancied he had been there only about a week.

Cross Purposes

CHAPTER I

Once upon a time, the Queen of Fairyland, finding her own subjects far too well-behaved to be amusing, took a sudden longing to have a mortal or two at her Court. So, after looking about her for some time, she fixed upon two to bring to Fairyland.

But how were they to be brought?

"Please your majesty," said at last the daughter of the prime minister, "I will bring the girl."

The speaker, whose name was Peaseblossom, after her great-great-grandmother, looked so graceful, and hung her head so apologetically, that the Queen said at once, —

"How will you manage it, Peaseblossom?"

"I will open the road before her, and close it behind her."

"I have heard that you have pretty ways of doing things; so you may try."

The court happened to be held in an open forest glade of smooth turf, upon which there was just one mole-heap. As soon as the Queen had given her permission to Peaseblossom, up through the mole-heap came the head of a goblin, which cried out, —

"Please your majesty, I will bring the boy."

"You!" exclaimed the Queen. "How will you do it?"

The goblin began to wriggle himself out of the earth, as if he had been a snake, and the whole world his skin, till the court was convulsed with laughter. As soon as he got free, he began to roll over and over, in every possible manner, rotatory and cylindrical, all at once, until he reached the wood. The courtiers followed, holding their sides, so that the Queen was left sitting upon her throne in solitary state. When they reached the wood, the goblin, whose name was Toadstool, was nowhere to be seen. While they were looking for him, out popped his head from the mole-heap again, with the words, —

"So, your majesty."

"You have taken your own time to answer," said the Queen, laughing.

"And my own way too, eh! your majesty?" rejoined Toadstool, grinning.

"No doubt. Well, you may try."

And the goblin, making as much of a bow as he could with only half his neck above-ground, disappeared under it.

CHAPTER II

No mortal, or fairy either, can tell where Fairy-land begins and where it ends. But somewhere on the borders of Fairy-land there was a nice country village, in which lived some nice country people.

Alice was the daughter of the squire, a pretty, good-natured girl, whom her friends called fairylike, and others called silly. — One rosy summer evening, when the wall opposite her window was flaked all over with rosiness, she threw herself on her bed, and lay gazing at the wall. The rose-colour sank through her eyes and eyed her brain, and she began to feel as if she were reading a story-book. She thought she was looking at a western sea, with the waves all red with sunset. But when the colour died out, Alice gave a sigh to see how commonplace the wall grew. "I wish it was always sunset!" she said, half aloud. "I don't like gray things."

"I will take you where the sun is always setting, if you like, Alice," said a sweet, tiny voice near her. She looked down on the coverlet of the bed, and there, looking up at her, stood a lovely little creature. It seemed quite natural that the little lady should be there; for many things we never could believe, have only to happen, and then there is nothing strange about them. She was dressed in white, with a cloak of sunset-red — the colours of the sweetest of sweet-peas. On her head was a crown of twisted tendrils, with a little gold beetle in front.

"Are you a fairy?" asked Alice.

"Yes. Will you go with me to the sunset?"

"Yes, I will."

When Alice proceeded to rise, she found that she was no bigger than the fairy; and when she stood up on the counterpane, the bed looked like a great hall with a painted ceiling. As she walked towards Peaseblossom, she stumbled several times over the tufts that made the pattern. But the fairy took her by the hand and led her towards the foot of the bed. Long before they reached it, however, Alice saw that the fairy was a tall, slender lady, and that she herself was quite her own size. What she had taken for tufts on the counterpane were really bushes of furze, and broom, and heather, on the side of a slope.

"Where are we?" asked Alice.

"Going on," answered the fairy.

Alice, not liking the reply, said, —

"I want to go home."

"Good-bye, then," answered the fairy.

Alice looked round. A wide, hilly country lay all about them. She could not even tell from what quarter they had come.

"I must go with you, I see," she said.

Before they reached the bottom, they were walking over the loveliest meadow-grass. A little stream went cantering down beside them, without channel or bank, sometimes running between the blades, sometimes sweeping the grass all one way under it. And it made a great babbling for such a little stream and such a smooth course.

Gradually the slope grew gentler, and the stream flowed more softly and spread out wider. At length they came to a wood of long, straight poplars, growing out of the water, for the stream ran into the wood, and there stretched out into a lake. Alice thought they could go no farther; but Peaseblossom led her straight on, and they walked through.

It was now dark; but everything under the water gave out a pale, quiet light. There were deep pools here and there, but there was no mud, or frogs, or water-lizards, or eels. All the bottom was pure, lovely grass, brilliantly green. Down the banks of the pools she saw, all under water, primroses and violets and pimpernels. Any flower she wished to see she had only to look for, and she was sure to find it. When a pool came in their way, the fairy swam, and Alice swam by her; and when they got out they were quite dry, though the water was as delightfully wet as water should be. Besides the trees, tall, splendid lilies grew out of it, and holly-hocks and irises and sword-plants, and many other long-stemmed flowers. From every leaf and petal of these, from every branch-tip and tendril, dropped bright water. It gathered slowly at each point, but the points were so many that there was a constant musical plashing of diamond rain upon the still surface of the lake. As they went on, the moon rose and threw a pale mist of light over the whole, and the diamond drops turned to half-liquid pearls, and round every tree-top was a halo of moonlight, and the water went to sleep, and the flowers began to dream.

"Look," said the fairy; "those lilies are just dreaming themselves into a child's sleep. I can see them smiling. This is the place out of which go the things that appear to children every night."

"Is this dreamland, then?" asked Alice.

"If you like," answered the fairy.

"How far am I from home?"

"The farther you go, the nearer home you are."

Then the fairy lady gathered a bundle of poppies and gave it to Alice. The next deep pool that they came to, she told her to throw it in. Alice did so, and following it, laid her head upon it. That moment she began to sink. Down and down she went, till at last she felt herself lying on the long, thick grass at the bottom of the pool, with the poppies under her head and the clear water high over it. Up through it she saw the moon, whose bright face looked sleepy too, disturbed only by the little ripples of the rain from the tall flowers on the edges of the pool.

She fell fast asleep, and all night dreamed about home.

CHAPTER III

Richard — which is name enough for a fairy story — was the son of a widow in Alice's village. He was so poor that he did not find himself generally welcome; so he hardly went anywhere, but read books at home, and waited upon his mother. His manners, therefore, were shy, and suffi-ciently awkward to give an unfavourable impression to those who looked at outsides. Alice would have despised him; but he never came near enough for that.

Now Richard had been saving up his few pence in order to buy an umbrella for his mother; for the winter would come, and the one she had was almost torn to ribands. One bright summer evening, when he thought umbrellas must be cheap, he was walking across the market-place to buy one; there, in the middle of it, stood an odd-looking little man, actually selling umbrellas. Here was a chance for him! When he drew nearer, he found that the little man, while vaunting his umbrellas to the skies, was asking such absurdly small prices for them, that no one would venture to buy one. He had opened and laid them all out at full stretch on the market-place — about five-and-twenty of them, stick downwards, like little tents — and he stood beside, haranguing the people. But he would not allow one of the crowd to touch his umbrellas. As soon as his eye fell upon Richard, he changed his tone, and said, "Well, as nobody seems inclined to buy, I think, my dear umbrellas, we had better be going home." Whereupon the umbrellas got up, with some difficulty, and began hobbling away. The people stared at each other with open mouths, for they saw that what they had taken for a lot of umbrellas, was in reality a flock of black geese. A great turkey-cock went gobbling behind them, driving them all down a lane towards the forest. Richard thought with himself, "There is more in this than I can account for. But an umbrella that could lay eggs would be a very jolly umbrella." So by the time the people were beginning to laugh at each other, Richard was half-way down the lane at the heels of the geese. There he stooped and caught one of them, but instead of a goose he had a huge hedgehog in his hands, which he dropped in dismay; whereupon it waddled away a goose as before, and the whole of them began cackling and hissing in a way that he could not mistake. For the turkey cock, he gobbled and gabbled and choked himself and got right again in the most ridiculous manner. In fact, he seemed sometimes to forget that he was a turkey, and laughed like a fool. All at once, with a simultaneous long-necked hiss, they flew into the wood, and the turkey after them. But Richard soon got up with them again, and found them all hanging by their feet from the trees, in two rows, one on each side of the path, while the turkey was walking on. Him Richard followed; but the moment he reached the middle of the suspended geese, from every side arose the most frightful hisses, and their necks grew longer and longer, till there were nearly thirty broad bills close to his head, blowing in his

"The Odd Little Man and His Umbrellas"

face, in his ears, and at the back of his neck. But the turkey, looking round and seeing what was going on, turned and walked back. When he reached the place, he looked up at the first and gobbled at him in the wildest manner. That goose grew silent and dropped from the tree. Then he went to the next, and the next, and so on, till he had gobbled them all off the trees, one after another. But when Richard expected to see them go after the turkey, there was nothing there but a flock of huge mushrooms and puff-balls.

"I have had enough of this," thought Richard. "I will go home again."

"Go home, Richard," said a voice close to him.

Looking down, he saw, instead of the turkey, the most comical-looking little man he had ever seen.

"Go home, Master Richard," repeated he, grinning.

"Not for your bidding," answered Richard.

"Come on then, Master Richard."

"Nor that either, without a good reason."

"I will give you *such* an umbrella for your mother."

"I don't take presents from strangers."

"Bless you, I'm no stranger here! Oh no! not at all." And he set off in the manner usual with him, rolling every way at once.

Richard could not help laughing and following. At length Toadstool plumped into a great hole full of water. "Served him right!" thought Richard. "Served him right!" bawled the goblin, crawling out again, and shaking the water from him like a spaniel. "This is the very place I wanted, only I rolled too fast." However, he went on rolling again faster than before, though it was now up hill, till he came to the top of a considerable height, on which grew a number of palm trees.

"Have you a knife, Richard?" said the goblin, stopping all at once, as if he had been walking quietly along, just like other people.

Richard pulled out a pocket-knife and gave it to the creature, who instantly cut a deep gash in one of the trees. Then he bounded to another and did the same, and so on, till he had gashed them all. Richard, following him, saw that a little stream, clearer than the clearest water, began to flow from each, increasing in size the longer it flowed. Before he had reached the last there was quite a tinkling and rustling of little rills that ran down the stems of the palms. This grew and grew, till Richard saw that a full rivulet was flowing down the side of the hill.

"Here is your knife, Richard," said the goblin; but by the time he had put it in his pocket, the rivulet had grown to a small torrent.

"Now, Richard, come along," said Toadstool, and threw himself into the torrent.

"I would rather have a boat," returned Richard.

"Oh, you stupid!" cried toadstool, crawling up the side of the hill, down which the stream had already carried him some distance.

With every contortion that labour and difficulty could suggest, yet with incredible rapidity, he crawled to the very top of one of the trees, and tore down a huge leaf, which he threw on the ground, and himself after it, rebounding like a ball. He then laid the leaf on the water, held it by the stem, and told Richard to get upon it. He did so. It went down deep in the middle with his weight. Toadstool let it go, and it shot down the stream like an arrow. Thus began the strangest and most delightful voyage. The stream rushed careering and curveting down the hill-side, bright as a diamond, and soon reached a meadow plain. The goblin rolled alongside of the boat like a bundle of weeds; but Richard rode in triumph through the low grassy country upon the back of his watery steed. It went straight as an arrow, and, strange to tell, was heaped up on the ground, like a ridge of water or a wave, only rushing on endways. It needed no channel, and turned aside for no opposition. It flowed over everything that crossed its path, like a great serpent of water, with folds fitting into all the ups and downs of the way. If a wall came in its course it flowed against it, heaping itself up on itself till it reached the top, whence it plunged to the foot on the other side, and flowed on. Soon he found that it was running gently up a grassy hill. The waves kept curling back as if the wind blew them, or as if they could hardly keep from running down again. But still the stream mounted and flowed, and the waves with it. It found it difficult, but it could do it. When they reached the top, it bore them across a heathy country, rolling over purple heather, and blue hare-bells, and delicate ferns, and tall foxgloves crowded with bells purple and white. All the time, the palm-leaf curled its edges away from the water, and made a delightful boat for Richard, while Toadstool tumbled along in the stream like a porpoise. At length the water began to run very fast, and went faster and faster, till suddenly it plunged them into a deep lake, with a great splash, and stopped there. Toadstool went out of sight, and came up gasping and grinning, while Richard's boat tossed and heaved like a vessel in a storm at sea; but not a drop of water came in. Then the goblin began to swim, and pushed and tugged the boat along. But the lake was so still, and the motion so pleasant, that Richard fell fast asleep.

CHAPTER IV

When he woke, he found himself still afloat upon the broad palm-leaf. He was alone in the middle of a lake, with flowers and trees growing in and out of it everywhere. The sun was just over the tree-tops. A drip of water from the flowers greeted him with music; the mists were dissolving away; and where the sunlight fell on the lake the water was clear as glass. Casting his eyes downward, he saw, just beneath him, far down at the bottom, Alice — drowned, as he thought. He was in the act of plunging in, when he saw her open her eyes, and at the same moment begin to float up. He held out his hand, but she repelled it with disdain; and swimming to a tree, sat down on a low branch, wondering how ever the poor widow's son could have found his way into Fairyland. She did not like it. It was an invasion of privilege.

"How did you come here, young Richard?" she asked, from six yards off.

"A goblin brought me."

"Ah, I thought so. A fairy brought me."

"Where is your fairy?"

"Here I am," said Peaseblossom, rising slowly to the surface, just by the tree on which Alice was seated.

"Where is your goblin?" retorted Alice.

"Here I am," bawled Toadstool, rushing out of the water like a salmon, and casting a somersault in the air before he fell in again with a tremendous splash. His head rose again close beside Peaseblossom, who being used to such creatures only laughed.

"Isn't he handsome?" he grinned.

"Yes, very. He wants polishing though."

"You could do that for yourself, you know. Shall we change?"

"I don't mind. You'll find her rather silly."

"That's nothing. The boy's too sensible for me."

He dived, and rose at Alice's feet. She shrieked with terror. The fairy floated away like a water-lily towards Richard. "What a lovely creature!" thought he; but hearing Alice shriek again, he said,

"Don't leave Alice; she's frightened at that queer creature. — I don't think there's any harm in him, though, Alice."

"Oh, no. He won't hurt her," said Peaseblossom, "I'm tired of her. He's going to take her to the court, and I will take you."

"I don't want to go."

"But you must. You can't go home again. You don't know the way."

"Richard! Richard!" cried Alice, in an agony.

Richard sprang from his boat, and was by her side in a moment.

"He pinched me," cried Alice.

Richard hit the goblin a terrible blow on the head; but it took no more effect upon him than if his head had been a round ball of India-rubber. He gave Richard a furious look, however, and bawling out, "You'll repent that, Dick!" vanished under the water.

"Come along, Richard; make haste; he will murder you," cried the fairy.

"It is all your fault," said Richard. "I won't leave Alice."

Then the fairy saw it was all over with her and Toadstool; for they can do nothing with mortals against their will. So she floated away across the water in Richard's boat, holding her robe for a sail, and vanished, leaving the two alone in the lake.

"You have driven away my fairy!" cried Alice. "I shall never get home now. It is all your fault, you naughty young man."

"I drove away the goblin," remonstrated Richard.

"Will you please to sit on the other side of the tree. I wonder what my papa would say if he saw me talking to you!"

"Will you come to the next tree, Alice?" said Richard, after a pause.

Alice, who had been crying all the time that Richard was thinking, said, "I won't." Richard, therefore, plunged into the water without her, and swam for the tree. Before he had got half-way, however, he heard Alice crying, "Richard! Richard!" This was just what he wanted. So he turned back, and Alice threw herself into the water. With Richard's help she swam pretty well, and they reached the tree. "Now for the next!" said Richard; and they swam to the next, and then to the third. Every tree they reached was larger than the last, and every tree before them was larger still. So they swam from tree to tree, till they came to one that was so large that they could not see round it. What was to be done? Clearly, to climb this tree.

It was a dreadful prospect for Alice, but Richard proceeded to climb; and by putting her feet where he put his, and now and then getting hold of his ankle, she managed to make her way up. There were a great many stumps where branches had withered off, and the bark was nearly as rough as a hill-side, so there was plenty of foothold for them. When they had climbed a long time, and were getting very tired indeed, Alice cried out, "Richard, I shall drop — I shall. Why did you come this way?" And she began once more to cry. But at that moment Richard caught hold of a branch above his head, and reaching down his other hand got hold of Alice, and held her till she had recovered a little. In a few moments they reached the fork of the tree, and there they sat and rested. "This is capital!" said Richard, cheerily.

"What is?" asked Alice, sulkily.

"Why, we have room to rest, and there's no hurry for a minute or two. I'm tired."

"You selfish creature!" said Alice. "If you are tired, what must I be?"

"Tired too," answered Richard. "But we've got on bravely. And look! what's that?"

By this time the day was gone, and the night so near, that in the shadows of the tree all was dusky and dim. But there was still light enough to discover that in a niche of the tree sat a huge horned owl, with green spectacles on his beak, and a book in one foot. He took no heed of the intruders, but kept muttering to himself. And what do you think the owl was saying? I will tell you. He was talking about the book that he held upside down in his foot.

"Stupid book this-s-s-s! Nothing in it at all! Everything upside down! Stupid ass-s-s-s! Says owls can't read! *I* can read backwards!"

"I think that is the goblin again," said Richard, in a whisper. "However, if you ask a plain question, he must give you a plain answer, for they are not allowed to tell downright lies in Fairyland."

"Don't ask him, Richard; you know you gave him a dreadful blow."

"I gave him what he deserved, and he owes me the same. — Hallo! which is the way out?"

He wouldn't say *if you please*, because then it would not have been a plain question.

"Down stairs," hissed the owl, without ever lifting his eyes from the book, which all the time he read upside down, so learned was he.

"On your honor, as a respectable old owl?" asked Richard.

"No," hissed the owl; and Richard was almost sure that he was not really an owl. So he stood staring at him for a few moments, when all at once, without lifting his eyes from the book, the owl said, "I will sing a song," and began: —

> "Nobody knows the world but me.
> When they're all in bed, I sit up to see.
> I'm a better student than students all,
> For I never read till the darkness fall;
> And I never read without my glasses,
> And that is how my wisdom passes,
> Howlowlwhoolhoolwoolool.

> "I can see the wind. Now who can do that?
> I see the dreams that he has in his hat;
> I see him snorting them out as he goes —
> Out at his stupid old trumpet-nose.
> Ten thousand things that you couldn't think
> I write them down with pen and ink.
> Howlowlwhooloolwhitit that's wit.

> "You may call it learning — 'tis mother-wit.
> No one else sees the lady-moon sit
> On the sea, her nest, all night, but the owl,
> Hatching the boats and the long-legged fowl.
> When the oysters gape to sing by rote,
> She crams a pearl down each stupid throat.
> Howlowlwhitit that's wit, there's a fowl!"

And so singing, he threw the book in Richard's face, spread out his great, silent, soft wings, and sped away into the depths of the tree. When the book struck Richard, he found that it was only a lump of wet moss.

While talking to the owl he had spied a hollow behind one of the branches. Judging this to be the way the owl meant, he went to see, and found a rude, ill-defined staircase going down into the very heart of the trunk. But so large was the tree that this could not have hurt it in the least. Down this stair, then, Richard scrambled as best he could, followed by Alice — not of her own will, she gave him clearly to understand, but because she could do no better. Down, down they went, slipping and falling sometimes, but never very far, because the stair went round and round. It caught Richard when he slipped, and he caught Alice when she did. They had begun to fear that there was no end to the stair, it went round and round so steadily, when, creeping through a crack, they found themselves in a great hall, supported by thousands of pillars of gray stone. Where the little light came from they could not tell. This hall they began to cross in a straight line, hoping to reach one side, and intending to walk along it till they came to some opening. They kept straight by going from pillar to pillar, as they had done before by the trees. Any honest plan will do in Fairyland, if you only stick to it. And no plan will do if you do not stick to it.

It was very silent, and Alice disliked the silence more than the dimness, — so much, indeed, that she longed to hear Richard's voice. But she had always been so cross to him when he had spoken, that he thought it better to let her speak first; and she was too proud to do that. She would not even let him walk alongside of her, but always went slower when he wanted to wait for her; so that at last he strode on alone. And Alice followed. But by degrees the horror of silence grew upon her, and she felt at last as if there was no one in the universe but herself. The hall went on widening around her; their footsteps made no noise; the silence grew so intense that it seemed on the point of taking shape. At last she could bear it no longer. She ran after Richard, got up with him, and laid hold of his arm.

He had been thinking for some time what an obstinate, disagreeable girl Alice was, and wishing he had her safe home to be rid of her, when, feeling a hand, and looking round, he saw that it was the disagreeable girl. She soon began to be companionable after a fashion, for she began to think, putting everything together, that Richard must have been several times in Fairyland before now. "It is very strange," she said to herself; "for he is quite a poor boy, I am sure of that. His arms stick out beyond his jacket like the ribs of his mother's umbrella. And to think of me wandering about Fairyland with *him!*"

The moment she touched his arm, they saw an arch of blackness before them. They had walked straight to a door — not a very inviting one, for it opened upon an utterly dark passage. Where there was only one door, however, there was no difficulty about choosing. Richard walked straight through it; and from the greater fear of being left behind, Alice faced the lesser fear of going on. In a moment they were in total darkness. Alice clung to Richard's arm, and murmured, almost against her will, "Dear Richard!" It was strange that fear should speak like love; but it was in Fairyland. It was strange, too, that as soon as she spoke thus, Richard should fall in love with her all at once. But what was more curious still was, that, at the same moment, Richard saw her face. In spite of her fear, which had made her pale, she looked very lovely.

"Dear Alice!" said Richard, "how pale you look!"

"How can you tell that, Richard, when all is as black as pitch?"

"I can see your face. It gives out light. Now I see your hands. Now I can see your feet. Yes, I can see every spot where you are going to — No, don't put your foot there. There is an ugly toad just there."

The fact was, that the moment he began to love Alice, his eyes began to send forth light. What he thought came from Alice's face, really came from his eyes. All about her and her path he could see, and every minute saw better; but to his own path he was blind. He could not see his hand when he held it straight before his face, so dark was it. But he could see Alice, and that was better than seeing the way — ever so much.

At length Alice too began to see a face dawning through the darkness. It was Richard's face: but it was far handsomer than when she saw it last. Her eyes had begun to give light too. And she said to herself — "Can it be that I love the poor widow's son? — I suppose that must be it," she answered herself, with a smile; for she was not disgusted with herself at all. Richard saw the smile, and was glad. Her paleness had gone, and a sweet rosiness had taken its place. And now she saw Richard's path as he saw hers, and between the two sights they got on well.

They were now walking on a path betwixt two deep waters, which never moved, shining as black as ebony where the eyelight fell. But they saw ere long that this path kept growing narrower and narrower. At last, to Alice's dismay, the black waters met in front of them.

"What is to be done now, Richard?" she said.

When they fixed their eyes on the water before them, they saw that it was swarming with lizards, and frogs, and black snakes, and all kinds of strange and ugly creatures, especially some that had neither heads, nor tails, nor legs, nor fins, nor feelers, being, in fact, only living lumps. These kept jumping out and in, and sprawling upon the path. Richard thought for a few moments before replying to Alice's question, as, indeed, well he might. But he came to the conclusion that the path could not have gone on for the sake of stopping there; and that it must be a kind of finger that pointed on where it was not allowed to go itself. So he caught up Alice in his strong arms, and jumped into the middle of the horrid swarm. And just as minnows vanish if you throw anything amongst them, just so these wretched creatures vanished, right and left and every way.

He found the water broader than he had expected; and before he got over, he found Alice heavier than he could have believed; but upon a firm, rocky bottom, Richard waded through in safety. When he reached the other side, he found that the bank was a lofty, smooth, perpendicular rock, with some rough steps cut in it. By-and-by the steps led them right into the rock, and they were in a narrow passage once more, but, this time, leading up. It wound round and round, like the thread of a great screw. At last, Richard knocked his head against something, and could go no farther. The place was close and hot. He put up his hands, and pushed what felt like a warm stone: it moved a little.

"Go down, you brutes!" growled a voice above, quivering with anger, "You'll upset my pot and my cat, and my temper, too, if you push that way. Go down!"

Richard knocked very gently, and said: "Please let us out."

"O yes, I dare say! Very fine and soft-spoken! Go down, you goblin brutes! I've had enough of you. I'll scald the hair off your ugly heads if you do that again. Go down, I say!"

Seeing fair speech was of no avail, Richard told Alice to go down a little, out of the way; and, setting his shoulders to one end of the stone, heaved it up; whereupon down came the other end, with a pot, and a fire, and a cat which had been asleep beside it. She frightened Alice dreadfully as she rushed past her, showing nothing but her green lamping eyes.

Richard, peeping up, found that he had turned a hearthstone upside down. On the edge of the hole stood a little crooked old man, brandishing a mop-stick in a tremendous rage, and hesitating only where to strike him. But Richard put him out of his difficulty by springing up and taking the stick from him. Then, having lifted Alice out, he returned it with a bow, and heedless of the maledictions of the old man, proceeded to get the stone and the pot up again. For puss, she got out of herself.

Then the old man became a little more friendly, and said: "I beg your pardon, I thought you were goblins. They never will let me alone. But you must allow, it was rather an unusual way of paying a morning call." And the creature bowed conciliatingly.

"Richard and Alice in Trouble"

"It was, indeed," answered Richard. "I wish you had turned the door to us instead of the hearthstone." For he did not trust the old man. "But," he added, "I hope you will forgive us."

"Oh, certainly, certainly, my dear young people. Use your freedom. But such young people have no business to be out alone. It is against the rules."

"But what is one to do — I mean two to do — when they can't help it?"

"Yes, yes, of course; but now, you know, I must take charge of you. So you sit there, young gentleman; and you sit there, young lady."

He put a chair for one at one side of the hearth, and for the other at the other side, and then drew his chair between them. The cat got upon his hump, and then set up her own. So here was a wall that would let through no moonshine. But although both Richard and Alice were very much amused, they did not like to be parted in this peremptory manner. Still they thought it better not to anger the old man any more — in his own house, too.

But he had been once angered, and that was once too often, for he had made it a rule never to forgive without taking it out in humiliation.

It was so disagreeable to have him sitting there between them, that they felt as if they were far asunder. In order to get the better of the fancy, they wanted to hold each other's hand behind the dwarf's back. But the moment their hands began to approach, the back of the cat began to grow long, and its hump to grow high; and, in a moment more, Richard found himself crawling wearily up a steep hill, whose ridge rose against the stars, while a cold wind blew drearily over it. Not a habitation was in sight; and Alice had vanished from his eyes. He felt, however, that she must be somewhere on the other side, and so climbed and climbed, to get over the brow of the hill, and down to where he thought she must be. But the longer he climbed, the farther off the top of the hill seemed; till at last he sank quite exhausted, and — must I confess it? — very nearly began to cry. To think of being separated from Alice, all at once, and in such a disagreeable way! But he fell a-thinking instead, and soon said to himself: "This must be some trick of that wretched old man. Either this mountain is a cat or it is not. If it is a mountain, this won't hurt it; if it is a cat, I hope it will." With that, he pulled out his pocket-knife, and feeling for a soft place, drove it at one blow up to the handle in the side of the mountain.

A terrific shriek was the first result; and the second, that Alice and he sat looking at each other across the old man's hump, from which the cat-a-mountain had vanished. Their host sat staring at the blank fireplace, without ever turning round, pretending to know nothing of what had taken place.

"Come along, Alice," said Richard, rising. "This won't do. We won't stop here."

Alice rose at once, and put her hand in his. They walked towards the door. The old man took no notice of them. The moon was shining brightly through the window; but instead of stepping out into the moonlight when they opened the door, they stepped into a great beautiful hall, through the high gothic windows of which the same moon was shining. Out of this hall they could find no way, except by a staircase of stone which led upwards. They ascended it together. At the top Alice let go Richard's hand to peep into a little room, which looked all the colours of the rainbow, just like the inside of a diamond. Richard went a step or two along a corridor, but finding she had left him, turned and looked into the chamber. He could see her nowhere. The room was full of doors; and she must have mistaken the door. He heard her voice calling him, and hurried in the direction of the sound. But he could see nothing of her. "More tricks," he said to himself. "It is of no use to stab this one. I must wait till I see what can be done." Still he heard Alice calling him, and still he followed, as well as he could. At length he came to a doorway, open to the air, through which the moonlight fell. But when he reached it, he found that it was high up in the side of a tower, the wall of which went straight down from his feet, without stair or descent of any kind. Again he heard Alice call him, and lifting his eyes, saw her, across a wide castle-court, standing at another door just like the one he was at, with the moon shining full upon her.

"All right, Alice!" he cried. "Can you hear me?"

"Yes," answered she.

"Then listen. This is all a trick. It is all a lie of that old wretch in the kitchen. Just reach out your hand, Alice dear."

Alice did as Richard asked her; and, although they saw each other many yards off across the court, their hands met.

"There! I thought so!" exclaimed Richard, triumphantly. "Now, Alice, I don't believe it is more than a foot or two down to the court below, though it looks like a hundred feet. Keep fast hold of my hand, and jump when I count three." But Alice drew her hand from him in sudden dismay;

whereupon Richard said, "Well, I will try first," and jumped. The same moment, his cheery laugh came to Alice's ears, and she saw him standing safe on the ground, far below.

"Jump, dear Alice, and I will catch you," said he.

"I can't; I am afraid," answered she.

"The old man is somewhere near you. You had better jump," said Richard.

Alice jumped from the wall in terror, and only fell a foot or two into Richard's arms. The moment she touched the ground, they found themselves outside the door of a little cottage which they knew very well, for it was only just within the wood that bordered on their village. Hand in hand they ran home as fast as they could. When they reached a little gate that led into her father's grounds, Richard bade Alice good-bye. The tears came in her eyes. Richard and she seemed to have grown quite man and woman in Fairyland, and they did not want to part now. But they felt that they must. So Alice ran in the back way, and reached her own room before any one had missed her. Indeed, the last of the red had not quite faded from the west.

As Richard crossed the market-place on his way home, he saw an umbrella-man just selling the last of his umbrellas. He thought the man gave him a queer look as he passed, and felt very much inclined to punch his head. But remembering how useless it had been to punch the goblin's head, he thought it better not.

In reward of their courage, the Fairy Queen sent them permission to visit Fairyland as often as they pleased; and no goblin or fairy was allowed to interfere with them.

For Peaseblossom and Toadstool, they were both banished from court, and compelled to live together, for seven years, in an old tree that had just one green leaf upon it.

Toadstool did not mind it much, but Peaseblossom did.

The Golden Key

There was a boy who used to sit in the twilight and listen to his great-aunt's stories.

She told him that if he could reach the place where the end of the rainbow stands he would find there a golden key.

"And what is the key for?" the boy would ask. "What is it the key of? What will it open?"

"That nobody knows," his aunt would reply. "He has to find that out."

"I suppose, being gold," the boy once said, thoughtfully, "that I could get a good deal of money for it if I sold it."

"Better never find it than sell it," returned his aunt.

And then the boy went to bed and dreamed about the golden key.

Now all that his great-aunt told the boy about the golden key would have been nonsense, had it not been that their little house stood on the borders of Fairyland. For it is perfectly well known that out of Fairyland nobody ever can find where the rainbow stands. The creature takes such good care of its golden key, always flitting from place to place, lest any one should find it! But in Fairyland it is quite different. Things that look real in this country look very thin indeed in Fairyland, while some of the things that here cannot stand still for a moment, will not move there. So it was not in the least absurd of the old lady to tell her nephew such things about the golden key.

"Did you ever know anybody find it?" he asked, one evening.

"Yes. Your father, I believe, found it."

"And what did he do with it, can you tell me?"

"He never told me."

"What was it like?"

"He never showed it to me."

"How does a new key come there always?"

"I don't know. There it is."

"Perhaps it is the rainbow's egg."

"Perhaps it is. You will be a happy boy if you find the nest."

"Perhaps it comes tumbling down the rainbow from the sky."

"Perhaps it does."

One evening, in summer, he went into his own room, and stood at the lattice-window, and gazed into the forest which fringed the out-skirts of Fairyland. It came close up to his great-aunt's garden, and, indeed, sent some straggling trees into it. The forest lay to the east, and the sun, which was setting behind the cottage, looked straight into the dark wood with his level red eye. The trees were all old, and had few branches below, so that the sun could see a great way into the forest; and the boy, being keen-sighted, could see almost as far as the sun. The trunks stood like rows of red columns in the shine of the red sun, and he could see down aisle after aisle in the vanishing distance. And as he gazed into the forest he began to feel as if the trees were all waiting for him, and had something they could not go on with till he came to them. But he was hungry, and wanted his supper. So he lingered.

Suddenly, far among the trees, as far as the sun could shine, he saw a glorious thing. It was the end of a rainbow, large and brilliant. He could count all the seven colours, and could see shade after shade beyond the violet; while before the red stood a colour more gorgeous and mysterious still. It was a colour he had never seen before. Only the spring of the rainbow-arch was visible. He could see nothing of it above the trees.

"The golden key!" he said to himself, and darted out of the house, and into the wood.

He had not gone far before the sun set. But the rainbow only glowed the brighter. For the rainbow of Fairyland is not dependent upon the sun as ours is. The trees welcomed him. The bushes made way for him. The rainbow grew larger and brighter; and at length he found himself within two trees of it.

It was a grand sight, burning away there in silence, with its gorgeous, its lovely, its delicate colours, each distinct, all combining. He could now

THE GOLDEN KEY

see a great deal more of it. It rose high into the blue heavens, but bent so little that he could not tell how high the crown of the arch must reach. It was still only a small portion of a huge bow.

He stood gazing at it till he forgot himself with delight — even forgot the key which he had come to seek. And as he stood it grew more wonderful still. For in each of the colors, which was as large as the column of a church, he could faintly see beautiful forms slowly ascending as if by the steps of a winding stair. The forms appeared irregularly — now one, now many, now several, now none — men and women and children — all different, all beautiful.

He drew nearer to the rainbow. It vanished. He started back a step in dismay. It was there again, as beautiful as ever. So he contented himself with standing as near it as he might, and watching the forms that ascended the glorious colours towards the unknown height of the arch, which did not end abruptly, but faded away in the blue air, so gradually that he could not say where it ceased.

When the thought of the golden key returned, the boy very wisely proceeded to mark out in his mind the space covered by the foundation of the rainbow, in order that he might know where to search, should the rainbow disappear. It was based chiefly upon a bed of moss.

Meantime it had grown quite dark in the wood. The rainbow alone was visible by its own light. But the moment the moon rose the rainbow vanished. Nor could any change of place restore the vision to the boy's eyes. So he threw himself down upon the mossy bed, to wait till the sunlight would give him a chance of finding the key. There he fell fast asleep.

When he woke in the morning the sun was looking straight into his eyes. He turned away from it, and the same moment saw a brilliant little thing lying on the moss within a foot of his face. It was the golden key. The pipe of it was of plain gold, as bright as gold could be. The handle was curiously wrought and set with sapphires. In a terror of delight he put out his hand and took it, and had it.

He lay for a while, turning it over, and feeding his eyes upon its beauty. Then he jumped to his feet, remembering that the pretty thing was of no use to him yet. Where was the lock to which the key belonged? It must be somewhere, for how could anybody be so silly as make a key for which there was no lock? Where should he go to look for it? He gazed about him, up into the air, down to the earth, but saw no keyhole in the clouds, in the grass, or in the trees.

Just as he began to grow disconsolate, however, he saw something glimmering in the wood. It was a mere glimmer that he saw, but he took it for a glimmer of rainbow, and went towards it. — And now I will go back to the borders of the forest.

Not far from the house where the boy had lived, there was another house, the owner of which was a merchant, who was much away from home. He had lost his wife some years before, and had only one child, a little girl, whom he left to the charge of two servants, who were very idle and careless. So she was neglected and left untidy, and was sometimes ill-used besides.

Now it is well known that the little creatures commonly called fairies, though there are many different kinds of fairies in Fairyland, have an exceeding dislike to untidiness. Indeed, they are quite spiteful to slovenly people. Being used to all the lovely ways of the trees and flowers, and to the neatness of the birds and all woodland creatures, it makes them feel miserable, even in their deep woods and on their grassy carpets, to think that within the same moonlight lies a dirty, uncomfortable, slovenly house. And this makes them angry with the people that live in it, and they would gladly drive them out of the world if they could. They want the whole earth nice and clean. So they pinch the maids black and blue, and play them all manner of uncomfortable tricks.

But this house was quite a shame, and the fairies in the forest could not endure it. They tried everything on the maids without effect, and at last resolved upon making a clean riddance, beginning with the child. They ought to have known that it was not her fault, but they have little principle and much mischief in them, and they thought that if they got rid of her the maids would be sure to be turned away.

So one evening, the poor little girl having been put to bed early, before the sun was down, the servants went off to the village, locking the door behind them. The child did not know she was alone, and lay contentedly looking out of her window towards the forest, of which, however, she could not see much, because of the ivy and other creeping plants which had straggled across her window. All at once she saw an ape making faces at her out of the mirror, and the heads carved upon a great old wardrobe grinning fearfully. Then two old spider-legged chairs came forward into the middle of the room, and began to dance a queer, old-fashioned dance. This set her laughing, and she forgot the ape and the grinning heads. So the fairies saw they had made a mistake, and sent the chairs back to their places. But they knew that she had been reading the story of Silverhair all day. So the next moment she heard the voices of the three bears upon the stair, big voice, middle voice, and little voice, and she heard their soft, heavy tread, as if they had had stockings over their boots, coming nearer and nearer to the door of her room, till she could bear it no longer. She did just as Silverhair did, and as the fairies wanted her to do: she darted to the window, pulled it open, got upon the ivy, and so scrambled to the ground. She then fled to the forest as fast as she could run.

Now, although she did not know it, this was the very best way she could have gone; for nothing is ever so mischievous in its own place as it is out of it; and, besides, these mischievous creatures were only the children of Fairyland, as it were, and there are many other beings there as well; and if a wanderer gets in among them, the good ones will always help him more than the evil ones will be able to hurt him.

The sun was now set, and the darkness coming on, but the child thought of no danger but the bears behind her. If she had looked round, however, she would have seen that she was followed by a very different creature from a bear. It was a curious creature, made like a fish, but covered, instead of scales, with feathers of all colours, sparkling like those of a humming-bird. It had fins, not wings, and swam through the air as a fish does through the water. Its head was like the head of a small owl.

After running a long way, and as the last of the light was disappearing, she passed under a tree with drooping branches. It dropped its branches to the ground all about her, and caught her as in a trap. She struggled to get out, but the branches pressed her closer and closer to the trunk. She was in great terror and distress, when the air-fish, swimming into the thicket of branches, began tearing them with its beak. They loosened their hold at once, and the creature went on attacking them, till at length they let the child go. Then the air-fish came from behind her, and swam on in front, glittering and sparkling all lovely colours; and she followed.

It led her gently along till all at once it swam in at a cottage-door. The child followed still. There was a bright fire in the middle of the floor, upon which stood a pot without a lid, full of water that boiled and bubbled furiously. The air-fish swam straight to the pot and into the boiling water, where it lay quiet. A beautiful woman rose from the opposite side of the fire and came to meet the girl. She took her up in her arms, and said, —

"Ah, you are come at last! I have been looking for you a long time."

THE GOLDEN KEY

She sat down with her on her lap, and there the girl sat staring at her. She had never seen anything so beautiful. She was tall and strong, with white arms and neck, and a delicate flush on her face. The child could not tell what was the colour of her hair, but could not help thinking it had a tinge of dark green. She had not one ornament upon her, but she looked as if she had just put off quantities of diamonds and emeralds. Yet here she was in the simplest, poorest little cottage, where she was evidently at home. She was dressed in shining green.

The girl looked at the lady, and the lady looked at the girl.

"What is your name?" asked the lady.

"The servants always called me Tangle."

"Ah, that was because your hair was so untidy. But that was their fault, the naughty women! Still it is a pretty name, and I will call you Tangle too. You must not mind me asking you questions, for you may ask me the same questions, every one of them, and any others that you like. How old are you?"

"Ten," answered Tangle.

"You don't look like it," said the lady.

"How old are you, please?" returned Tangle.

"Thousands of years old," answered the lady.

"You don't look like it," said tangle.

"Don't I? I think I do. Don't you see how beautiful I am?"

And her great blue eyes looked down on the little Tangle, as if all the stars in the sky were melted in them to make their brightness.

"Ah! but," said Tangle, "when people live long they grow old. At least I always thought so."

"I have no time to grow old," said the lady, "I am too busy for that. It is very idle to grow old. — But I cannot have my little girl so untidy. Do you know I can't find a clean spot on your face to kiss?"

"Perhaps," suggested Tangle, feeling ashamed, but not too much so to say a word for herself — "perhaps that is because the tree made me cry so."

"My poor darling!" said the lady, looking now as if the moon were melted in her eyes, and kissing her little face, dirty as it was, "the naughty tree must suffer for making a girl cry."

"And what is your name, please?" asked Tangle.

"Grandmother," answered the lady.

"Is it really?"

"Yes, indeed. I never tell stories, even in fun."

"How good of you!"

"I couldn't if I tried. It would come true if I said it, and then I should be punished enough."

And she smiled like the sun through a summer-shower.

"But now," she went on, "I must get you washed and dressed, and then we shall have some supper."

"Oh! I had supper long ago," said Tangle.

"Yes, indeed you had," answered the lady — "three years ago. You don't know that it is three years since you ran away from the bears. You are thirteen and more now."

Tangle could only stare. She felt quite sure it was true.

"You will not be afraid of anything I do with you — will you?" said the lady.

"I will try very hard not to be; but I can't be certain, you know." replied Tangle.

"I like your saying so, and I shall be quite satisfied," answered the lady.

She took off the girl's night-gown, rose with her in her arms, and going to the wall of the cottage, opened a door. Then Tangle saw a deep tank, the sides of which were filled with green plants, which had flowers of all colours. There was a roof over it like the roof of the cottage. It was filled with beautiful clear water, in which swam a multitude of such fishes as the one that had led her to the cottage. It was the light their colours gave that showed the place in which they were.

The lady spoke some words Tangle could not understand, and threw her into the tank.

The fishes came crowding about her. Two or three of them got under her head and kept it up. The rest of them rubbed themselves all over her, and with their wet feathers washed her quite clean. Then the lady, who had been looking on all the time, spoke again; whereupon some thirty or forty of the fishes rose out of the water underneath Tangle, and so bore her up to the arms the lady held out to her. She carried her back to the fire, and, having dried her well, opened a chest, and taking out the finest linen garments, smelling of grass and lavender, put them upon her, and over all a green dress, just like her own, shining like hers, and soft like hers, and going into just such lovely folds from the waist, where it was tied with a brown cord, to her bare feet.

"Won't you give me a pair of shoes too, Grandmother?" said Tangle.

"No, my dear; no shoes. Look here. I wear no shoes."

So saying, she lifted her dress a little, and there were the loveliest white feet, but no shoes. Then Tangle was content to go without shoes too. And the lady sat down with her again, and combed her hair, and brushed it, and then left it to dry while she got the supper.

First she got bread out of one hole in the wall; then milk out of another, then several kinds of fruit out of a third; and then she went to the pot on the fire, and took out the fish, now nicely cooked, and, as soon as she had pulled off its feathered skin, ready to be eaten.

"But," exclaimed Tangle. And she stared at the fish, and could say no more.

"I know what you mean," returned the lady. "You do not like to eat the messenger that brought you home. But it is the kindest return you can make. The creature was afraid to go until it saw me put the pot on, and heard me promise it should be boiled the moment it returned with you. Then it darted out of the door at once. You saw it go into the pot of itself the moment it entered, did you not?"

"I did," answered Tangle, "and I thought it very strange; but then I saw you, and forgot all about the fish."

"In Fairyland," resumed the lady, as they sat down to the table, "the ambition of the animals is to be eaten by the people; for that is their highest end in that condition. But they are not therefore destroyed. Out of that pot comes something more than the dead fish, you will see."

Tangle now remarked that the lid was on the pot. But the lady took no further notice of it till they had eaten the fish, which Tangle found nicer than any fish she had ever tasted before. It was as white as snow, and as delicate as cream. And the moment she had swallowed a mouthful of it, a change she could not describe began to take place in her. She heard a murmuring all about her, which became more and more articulate, and at length, as she went on eating, grew intelligible. By the time she had finished her share, the sounds of all the animals in the forest came crowding through the door to her ears; for the door still stood wide open, though it was pitch dark outside; and they were no longer sounds only; they were speech, and speech that she could understand. She could tell what the insects in the cottage were saying to each other too. She had even a suspicion that the trees and flowers all about the cottage were holding midnight communications with each other; but what they said she could not hear.

⚹

As soon as the fish was eaten, the lady went to the fire and took the lid off the pot. A lovely little creature in human shape, with large white wings, rose out of it, and flew round and round the roof of the cottage; then dropped, fluttering, and nestled in the lap of the lady. She spoke to it some strange words, carried it to the door, and threw it out into the darkness. Tangle heard the flapping of its wings die away in the distance.

"Now have we done the fish any harm?" she said, returning.

"No," answered Tangle, "I do not think we have. I should not mind eating one every day."

"They must wait their time, like you and me too, my little Tangle." And she smiled a smile which the sadness in it made more lovely.

"But," she continued, "I think we may have one for supper tomorrow."

So saying she went to the door of the tank, and spoke; and now Tangle understood her perfectly.

"I want one of you," she said, — "the wisest."

Thereupon the fishes got together in the middle of the tank, with their heads forming a circle above the water, and their tails a larger circle beneath it. They were holding a council, in which their relative wisdom should be determined. At length one of them flew up into the lady's hand, looking lively and ready.

"You know where the rainbow stands?" she asked.

"Yes, Mother, quite well," answered the fish.

"Bring home a young man you will find there, who does not know where to go."

The fish was out of the door in a moment. Then the lady told Tangle it was time to go to bed; and, opening another door in the side of the cottage, showed her a little arbour, cool and green, with a bed of purple heath growing in it, upon which she threw a large wrapper made of the feathered skins of the wise fishes, shining gorgeous in the firelight. Tangle was soon lost in the strangest, loveliest dreams. And the beautiful lady was in every one of her dreams.

In the morning she awoke to the rustling of leaves over her head, and the sound of running water. But, to her surprise, she could find no door — nothing but the moss-grown wall of the cottage. So she crept through an opening in the arbour, and stood in the forest. Then she bathed in a stream that ran merrily through the trees, and felt happier; for having once been in her grandmother's pond, she must be clean and tidy ever after; and having put on her green dress, felt like a lady.

She spent that day in the wood, listening to the birds and beasts and creeping things. She understood all that they said, though she could not repeat a word of it; and every kind had a different language, while there was a common though more limited understanding between all the inhabitants of the forest. She saw nothing of the beautiful lady, but she felt that she was near her all the time; and she took care not to go out of sight of the cottage. It was round, like a snow-hut or a wigwam; and she could see neither door nor window in it. The fact was, it had no windows; and though it was full of doors, they all opened from the inside, and could not even be seen from the outside.

She was standing at the foot of a tree in the twilight, listening to a quarrel between a mole and a squirrel, in which the mole told the squirrel that the tail was the best of him, and the squirrel called the mole Spade-fists, when, the darkness having deepened around her, she became aware of something shining in her face, and looking round, saw that the door of the cottage was open, and the red light of the fire flowing from it like a river through the darkness. She left Mole and Squirrel to settle matters as they might, and darted off to the cottage. Entering, she found the pot boiling on the fire, and the grand, lovely lady sitting on the other side of it.

"I've been watching you all day," said the lady. "You shall have something to eat by-and-by, but we must wait till our supper comes home."

She took Tangle on her knee, and began to sing to her — such songs as made her wish she could listen to them for ever. But at length in rushed the shining fish, and snuggled down in the pot. It was followed by a youth who had outgrown his worn garments. His face was ruddy with health, and in his hand he carried a little jewel, which sparkled in the firelight.

The first words the lady said were, —

"What is that in your hand, Mossy?"

Now Mossy was the name his companions had given him, because he had a favourite stone covered with moss, on which he used to sit whole days reading; and they said the moss had begun to grow upon him too.

Mossy held out his hand. The moment the lady saw that it was the golden key, she rose from her chair, kissed Mossy on the forehead, made him sit down on her seat, and stood before him like a servant. Mossy could not bear this, and rose at once. But the lady begged him, with tears in her beautiful eyes, to sit, and let her wait on him.

THE GOLDEN KEY

"She took Tangle on her knee and began to sing to her"

"But you are great, splendid, beautiful lady," said Mossy.

"Yes, I am. But I work all day long — that is my pleasure; and you will have to leave me so soon!"

"How do you know that, if you please, madam?" asked Mossy.

"Because you have got the golden key."

"But I don't know what it is for. I can't find the key-hole. Will you tell me what to do?"

"You must look for the key-hole. That is your work. I cannot help you. I can only tell you that if you look for it you will find it."

"What kind of box will it open? What is there inside?"

"I do not know. I dream about it, but I know nothing."

"Must I go at once?"

"You may stop here to-night, and have some of my supper. But you must go in the morning. All I can do for you is to give you clothes. Here is a girl called Tangle, whom you must take with you."

"That *will* be nice," said Mossy.

"No, no!" said Tangle. "I don't want to leave you, please, Grandmother."

"You must go with him, Tangle. I am sorry to lose you, but it will be the best thing for you. Even the fishes, you see, have to go into the pot, and then out into the dark. If you fall in with the Old Man of the Sea, mind you ask him whether he has not got some more fishes ready for me. My tank is getting thin."

So saying, she took the fish from the pot, and put the lid on as before. They sat down and ate the fish, and then the winged creature rose from the pot, circled the roof, and settled on the lady's lap. She talked to it, carried it to the door, and threw it out into the dark. They heard the flap of its wings die away in the distance.

The lady then showed Mossy into just such another chamber as that of Tangle; and in the morning he found a suit of clothes laid beside him. He looked very handsome in them. But the wearer of Grandmother's clothes never thinks about how he or she looks, but thinks always how handsome other people are.

Tangle was very unwilling to go.

"Why should I leave you? I don't know the young man," she said to the lady.

"I am never allowed to keep my children long. You need not go with him except you please, but you must go some day; and I should like you to go with him, for he has the golden key. No girl need be afraid to go with a youth that has the golden key. You will take care of her, Mossy, will you not?"

"That I will," said Mossy.

And Tangle cast a glance at him, and thought she should like to go with him.

"And," said the lady, "if you should lose each other as you go through the — the — I never can remember the name of that country, — do not be afraid, but go on and on."

She kissed Tangle on the mouth and Mossy on the forehead, led them to the door, and waved her hand eastward. Mossy and Tangle took each other's hand and walked away into the depth of the forest. In his right hand Mossy held the golden key.

They wandered thus a long way, with endless amusement from the talk of the animals. They soon learned enough of their language to ask them necessary questions. The squirrels were always friendly, and gave them nuts out of their own hoards; but the bees were selfish and rude, justifying themselves on the ground that Tangle and Mossy were not subjects of their queen, and charity must begin at home, though indeed they had not one drone in their poorhouse at the time. Even the blinking moles would fetch them an earth-nut or a truffle now and then, talking as if their mouths, as well as their eyes and ears, were full of cotton wool, or their own velvety fur. By the time they got out of the forest they were very fond of each other, and Tangle was not in the least sorry that her grandmother had sent her away with Mossy.

At length the trees grew smaller, and stood farther apart, and the ground began to rise, and it got more and more steep, till the trees were all left behind, and the two were climbing a narrow path with rocks on each side. Suddenly they came upon a rude doorway, by which they entered a narrow gallery cut in the rock. It grew darker and darker, till it was pitch-dark, and they had to feel their way. At length the light began to return, and at last they came out upon a narrow path on the face of a lofty precipice. This path went winding down the rock to a wide plain, circular in shape, and surrounded on all sides by mountains. Those opposite to them were a great way off, and towered to an awful height, shooting up sharp, blue, ice-enamelled pinnacles. An utter silence reigned where they stood. Not even the sound of water reached them.

Looking down, they could not tell whether the valley below was a

"Mossy and Tangle in the Wood"

grassy plain or a great still lake. They had never seen any space look like it. The way to it was difficult and dangerous, but down the narrow path they went, and reached the bottom in safety. They found it composed of smooth, light-coloured sandstone, undulating in parts, but mostly level. It was no wonder to them now that they had not been able to tell what it was, for this surface was everywhere crowded with shadows. It was a sea of shadows. The mass was chiefly made up of the shadows of leaves innumerable, of all lovely and imaginative forms, waving to and fro, floating and quivering in the breath of a breeze whose motion was unfelt, whose sound was unheard. No forests clothed the mountain-sides, no trees were anywhere to be seen, and yet the shadows of the leaves, branches, and stems of all various trees covered the valley as far as their eyes could reach. They soon spied the shadows of flowers mingled with those of the leaves, and now and then the shadow of a bird with open beak, and throat distended with song. At times would appear the forms of strange, graceful creatures, running up and down the shadow-boles and along the branches, to disappear in the wind-tossed foliage. As they walked they waded knee-deep in the lovely lake. For the shadows were not merely lying on the surface of the ground, but heaped up above it like substantial forms of darkness, as if they had been cast upon a thousand different planes of the air. Tangle and Mossy often lifted their heads and gazed upwards to descry whence the shadows came; but they could see nothing more than a bright mist spread above them, higher than the tops of the mountains, which stood clear against it. No forests, no leaves, no birds were visible.

After a while, they reached more open spaces, where the shadows were thinner; and came even to portions over which shadows only flitted, leaving them clear for such as might follow. Now a wonderful form, half bird-like half human, would float across on outspread sailing pinions. Anon an exquisite shadow group of gambolling children would be followed by the loveliest female form, and that again by the grand stride of a Titanic shape, each disappearing in the surrounding press of shadowy foliage. Sometimes a profile of unspeakable beauty or grandeur would appear for a moment and vanish. Sometimes they seemed lovers that passed linked arm in arm, sometimes father and son, sometimes brothers in loving contest, sometimes sisters entwined in gracefullest community of complex form. Sometimes wild horses would tear across, free, or bestrode by noble shadows of ruling men. But some of the things which pleased them most they never knew how to describe.

About the middle of the plain they sat down to rest in the heart of a heap of shadows. After sitting for a while, each, looking up, saw the other in tears: they were each longing after the country whence the shadows fell.

"We *must* find the country from which the shadows come," said Mossy.

"We must, dear Mossy," responded Tangle. "What if your golden key should be the key to *it?*"

"Ah! that would be grand," returned Mossy. — "But we must rest here for a little, and then we shall be able to cross the plain before night."

So he lay down on the ground, and about him on every side, and over his head, was the constant play of the wonderful shadows. He could look through them, and see the one behind the other, till they mixed in a mass of darkness. Tangle, too, lay admiring, and wondering, and longing after the country whence the shadows came. When they were rested they rose and pursued their journey.

How long they were in crossing this plain I cannot tell; but before night Mossy's hair was streaked with grey, and Tangle had got wrinkles on her forehead.

As evening drew on, the shadows fell deeper and rose higher. At length they reached a place where they rose above their heads, and made all dark around them. Then they took hold of each other's hand, and walked on in silence and in some dismay. They felt the gathering darkness, and something strangely solemn besides, and the beauty of the shadows ceased to delight them. All at once Tangle found that she had not a hold of Mossy's hand, though when she lost it she could not tell.

"Mossy, Mossy!" she cried aloud in terror.

But no Mossy replied.

A moment after, the shadows sank to her feet, and down under her feet, and the mountains rose before her. She turned towards the gloomy region she had left, and called once more upon Mossy. There the gloom lay tossing and heaving, a dark, stormy, foamless sea of shadows, but no Mossy rose out of it, or came climbing up the hill on which she stood. She threw herself down and wept in despair.

Suddenly she remembered that the beautiful lady had told them, if they lost each other in a country of which she could not remember the name, they were not to be afraid, but to go straight on.

"And besides," she said to herself, "Mossy has the golden key, and so no harm will come to him, I do believe."

><

She rose from the ground, and went on.

Before long she arrived at a precipice, in the face of which a stair was cut. When she had ascended half-way, the stair ceased, and the path led straight into the mountain. She was afraid to enter, and turning again towards the stair, grew giddy at the sight of the depth beneath her, and was forced to throw herself down in the mouth of the cave.

When she opened her eyes, she saw a beautiful little creature with wings standing beside her, waiting.

"I know you," said Tangle. "You are my fish."

"Yes. But I am a fish no longer. I am an aëranth now."

"What is that?" asked Tangle.

"What you see I am," answered the shape. "And I am come to lead you through the mountain."

"Oh! thank you, dear fish — aëranth, I mean," returned Tangle, rising.

Thereupon the aëranth took to his wings, and flew on through the long, narrow passage, reminding Tangle very much of the way he had swum on before when he was a fish. And the moment his white wings moved, they began to throw off a continuous shower of sparks of all colors, which lighted up the passage before them. — All at once he vanished, and Tangle heard a low, sweet sound, quite different from the rush and crackle of his wings. Before her was an open arch, and through it came light, mixed with the sound of sea-waves.

She hurried out, and fell, tired and happy, upon the yellow sand of the shore. There she lay, half asleep with weariness and rest, listening to the low splash and retreat of the tiny waves, which seemed ever enticing the land to leave off being land, and become sea. And as she lay, her eyes were fixed upon the foot of a great rainbow standing far away against the sky on the other side of the sea. At length she fell fast asleep.

When she awoke, she saw an old man with long white hair down to his shoulders, leaning upon a stick covered with green buds, and so bending over her.

"What do you want here, beautiful woman?" he said.

"Am I beautiful? I am so glad!" answered Tangle, rising. "My grandmother is beautiful."

"Yes. But what do you want?" he repeated, kindly.

"I think I want you. Are not you the Old Man of the Sea?"

"I am."

"Then Grandmother says, have you any more fishes ready for her?"

"We will go and see, my dear," answered the old man, speaking yet more kindly than before. "And I can do something for you, can I not?"

"Yes — show me the way up to the country from which the shadows fall," said Tangle.

For there she hoped to find Mossy again.

"Ah! indeed, that would be worth doing," said the old man. "But I cannot, for I do not know the way myself. But I will send you to the Old Man of the Earth. Perhaps he can tell you. He is much older than I am."

Leaning on his staff, he conducted her along the shore to a steep rock, that looked like a petrified ship turned upside down. The door of it was the rudder of a great vessel, ages ago at the bottom of the sea. Immediately within the door was a stair in the rock, down which the old man went, and Tangle followed. At the bottom the old man had his house, and there he lived.

As soon as she entered it, Tangle heard a strange noise, unlike anything she had ever heard before. She soon found that it was the fishes talking. She tried to understand what they said; but their speech was so old-fashioned, and rude, and undefined, that she could not make much of it.

"I will go and see about those fishes for my daughter," said the Old Man of the Sea.

And moving a slide in the wall of his house, he first looked out, and then tapped upon a thick piece of crystal that filled the round opening. Tangle came up behind him, and peeping through the window into the heart of the great deep green ocean, saw the most curious creatures, some very ugly, all very odd, and with especially queer mouths, swimming about everywhere, above and below, but all coming towards the window in answer to the tap of the Old Man of the Sea. Only a few could get their mouths against the glass; but those who were floating miles away yet turned their heads towards it. The Old Man looked through the whole flock carefully for some minutes, and then turning to Tangle, said, —

"I am sorry I have not got one ready yet. I want more time than she does. But I will send some as soon as I can."

He then shut the slide.

Presently a great noise arose in the sea. The Old Man opened the slide again, and tapped on the glass, whereupon the fishes were all as still as sleep.

THE GOLDEN KEY

"They were only talking about you," he said. "And they do speak such nonsense! — To-morrow," he continued, "I must show you the way to the Old Man of the Earth. He lives a long way from here."

"Do let me go at once," said Tangle.

"No. That is not possible. You must come this way first."

He led her to a hole in the wall, which she had not observed before. It was covered with the green leaves and white blossoms of a creeping plant.

"Only white-blossoming plants can grow under the sea," said the Old Man. "In there you will find a bath, in which you must lie till I call you."

Tangle went in, and found a smaller room or cave, in the further corner of which was a great basin hollowed out of rock, and half-full of the clearest sea-water. Little streams were constantly running into it from cracks in the wall of the cavern. It was polished quite smooth inside, and had a carpet of yellow sand in the bottom of it. Large green leaves and white flowers of various plants crowded up and over it, draping and covering it almost entirely.

No sooner was she undressed and lying in the bath, than she began to feel as if the water were sinking into her, and she were receiving all the good of sleep without undergoing its forgetfulness. She felt the good coming all the time. And she grew happier and more hopeful than she had been since she lost Mossy. But she could not help thinking how very sad it was for a poor old man to live there all alone, and have to take care of a whole seaful of stupid and riotous fishes.

After about an hour, as she thought, she heard his voice calling her, and rose out of the bath. All the fatigue and aching of her long journey had vanished. She was as whole, and strong, and well as if she had slept for seven days.

Returning to the opening that led into the other part of the house, she started back with amazement, for through it she saw the form of a grand man, with a majestic and beautiful face, waiting for her.

"Come," he said; "I see you are ready."

She entered with reverence.

"Where is the Old Man of the Sea?" she asked, humbly.

"There is no one here but me," he answered, smiling. "Some people call me the Old Man of the Sea. Others have another name for me, and are terribly frightened when they meet me taking a walk by the shore.

Therefore I avoid being seen by them, for they are so afraid, that they never see what I really am. You see me now. — But I must show you the way to the Old Man of the Earth."

He led her into the cave where the bath was, and there she saw, in the opposite corner, a second opening in the rock.

"Go down that stair, and it will bring you to him," said the Old Man of the Sea.

With humble thanks Tangle took her leave. She went down the winding-stair, till she began to fear there was no end to it. Still down and down it went, rough and broken, with springs of water bursting out of the rocks and running down the steps beside her. It was quite dark about her, and yet she could see. For after being in that bath, people's eyes always give out a light they can see by. There were no creeping things in the way. All was safe and pleasant, though so dark and damp and deep.

At last there was not one step more, and she found herself in a glimmering cave. On a stone in the middle of it sat a figure with its back towards her — the figure of an old man bent double with age. From behind she could see his white beard spread out on the rocky floor in front of him. He did not move as she entered, so she passed round that she might stand before him and speak to him.

The moment she looked in his face, she saw that he was a youth of marvelous beauty. He sat entranced with the delight of what he beheld in a mirror of something like silver, which lay on the floor at his feet, and which from behind she had taken for his white beard. He sat on, heedless of her presence, pale with the joy of his vision. She stood and watched him. At length, all trembling, she spoke. But her voice made no sound. Yet the youth lifted up his head. He showed no surprise, however, at seeing her — only smiled a welcome.

"Are you the Old Man of the Earth?" Tangle had said.

And the youth answered, and Tangle heard him, though not with her ears: —

"I am. What can I do for you?"

"Tell me the way to the country whence the shadows fall."

"Ah! that I do not know. I only dream about it myself. I see its shadows sometimes in my mirror: the way to it I do not know. But I think the Old Man of the Fire must know. He is much older than I am. He is the oldest man of all."

"Where does he live?"

"I will show you the way to his place. I never saw him myself."

So saying, the young man rose, and then stood for a while gazing at Tangle.

"I wish I could see that country too." he said. "But I must mind my work."

He led her to the side of the cave, and told her to lay her ear against the wall.

"What do you hear?" he asked.

"I hear," answered Tangle, "the sound of a great water running inside the rock."

"That river runs down to the dwelling of the oldest man of all — the Old Man of the Fire. I wish I could go to see him. But I must mind my work. That river is the only way to him."

Then the Old Man of the Earth stooped over the floor of the cave, raised a huge stone from it, and left it leaning. It disclosed a great hole that went plumb-down.

"That is the way," he said.

"But there are no stairs."

"You must throw yourself in. There is no other way."

She turned and looked him full in the face — stood so for a whole minute, as she thought: it was a whole year — then threw herself head-long into the hole.

When she came to herself, she found herself gliding down fast and deep. Her head was under water, but that did not signify, for, when she thought about it, she could not remember that she had breathed once since her bath in the cave of the Old Man of the Sea. When she lifted up her head a sudden and fierce heat struck her, and she sank it again instantly, and went sweeping on.

Gradually the stream grew shallower. At length she could hardly keep her head under. Then the water could carry her no farther. She rose from the channel, and went step for step down the burning descent. The water ceased altogether. The heat was terrible. She felt scorched to the bone, but it did not touch her strength. It grew hotter and hotter. She said, "I can bear it no longer." Yet she went on.

At the long last, the stair ended at a rude archway in an all but glowing rock. Through this archway Tangle fell exhausted into a cool mossy cave. The floor and walls were covered with moss — green, soft,

THE GOLDEN KEY   277

and damp. A little stream spouted from a rent in the rock and fell into a basin of moss. She plunged her face into it and drank. Then she lifted her head and looked around. Then she rose and looked again. She saw no one in the cave. But the moment she stood upright she had a marvelous sense that she was in the secret of the earth and all its ways. Everything she had seen, or learned from books; all that her grandmother had said or sung to her; all the talk of the beasts, birds, and fishes; all that happened to her on her journey with Mossy, and since then in the heart of the earth with the Old man and the Older man — all was plain: she understood it all, and saw that everything meant the same thing, though she could not have put it into words again.

The next moment she descried, in a corner of the cave, a little naked child, sitting on the moss. He was playing with balls of various colours and sizes, which he disposed in strange figures upon the floor beside him. And now Tangle felt that there was something in her knowledge which was not in her understanding. For she knew there must be an infinite meaning in the change and sequence and individual forms of the figures into which the child arranged the balls, as well as in the varied harmonies of their colours, but what it all meant she could not tell.* He went on busily, tirelessly, playing his solitary game, without looking up, or seeming to know that there was a stranger in his deep-withdrawn cell. Diligently as a lace-maker shifts her bobbins, he shifted and arranged his balls. Flashes of meaning would now pass from them to Tangle, and now again all would be not merely obscure, but utterly dark. She stood looking for a long time, for there was fascination in the sight; and the longer she looked the more an indescribable vague intelligence went on rousing itself in her mind. For seven years she had stood there watching the naked child with his coloured balls, and it seemed to her like seven hours, when all at once the shape the balls took, she knew not why, reminded her of the Valley of Shadows, and she spoke: —

"Where is the Old Man of the Fire?" she said.

"Here I am," answered the child, rising and leaving his balls on the moss. "What can I do for you?"

There was such an awfulness of absolute repose on the face of the child that Tangle stood dumb before him. He had no smile, but the love in his large gray eyes was deep as the centre. And with the repose there

*I think I must be indebted to Novalis for these geometrical figures.

lay on his face a shimmer as of moonlight, which seemed as if any moment it might break into such a ravishing smile as would cause the beholder to weep himself to death. But the smile never came, and the moonlight lay there unbroken. For the heart of the child was too deep for any smile to reach from it to his face.

"Are you the oldest man of all?" Tangle at length, although filled with awe, ventured to ask.

"Yes, I am. I am very, very old. I am able to help you, I know. I can help everybody."

And the child drew near and looked up in her face so that she burst into tears.

"Can you tell me the way to the country the shadows fall from?" she sobbed.

"Yes. I know the way quite well. I go there myself sometimes. But you could not go my way; you are not old enough. I will show you how you can go."

"Do not send me out into the great heat again," prayed Tangle.

"I will not," answered the child.

And he reached up, and put his little cool hand on her heart.

"Now," he said, "you can go. The fire will not burn you. Come."

He led her from the cave, and following him through another archway, she found herself in a vast desert of sand and rock. The sky of it was of rock, lowering over them like solid thunderclouds; and the whole place was so hot that she saw, in bright rivulets, the yellow gold and white silver and red copper trickling molten from the rocks. But the heat never came near her.

When they had gone some distance, the child turned up a great stone, and took something like an egg from under it. He next drew a long curved line in the sand with his finger, and laid the egg in it. He then spoke something Tangle could not understand. The egg broke, a small snake came out, and, lying in the line in the sand, grew and grew till he filled it. The moment he was thus full-grown, he began to glide away, undulating like a sea-wave.

"Follow that serpent," said the child. "He will lead you the right way."

Tangle followed the serpent. But she could not go far without looking back at the marvellous Child. He stood alone in the midst of the glowing desert, beside a fountain of red flame that had burst forth at his feet, his naked whiteness glimmering a pale rosy red in the torrid fire. There he stood, looking after her, till, from the lengthening distance, she could see him no more. The serpent went straight on, turning neither to the right nor left.

Meantime Mossy had got out of the lake of shadows, and, following his mournful, lonely way, had reached the sea-shore. It was a dark, stormy evening. The sun had set. The wind was blowing from the sea. The waves had surrounded the rock within which lay the Old Man's house. A deep water rolled between it and the shore, upon which a majestic figure was walking alone.

Mossy went up to him and said, —

"Will you tell me where to find the Old Man of the Sea?"

"I am the Old Man of the Sea," the figure answered.

"I see a strong kingly man of middle age," returned Mossy.

Then the Old Man looked at him more intently, and said, —

"Your sight, young man, is better than that of most who take this way. The night is stormy: come to my house and tell me what I can do for you."

Mossy followed him. The waves flew from before the footsteps of the Old Man of the Sea, and Mossy followed upon dry sand.

When they had reached the cave, they sat down and gazed at each other.

Now Mossy was an old man by this time. He looked much older than the Old Man of the Sea, and his feet were very weary.

After looking at him for a moment, the Old Man took him by the hand and led him into his inner cave. There he helped him to undress, and laid him in the bath. And he saw that one of his hands Mossy did not open.

"What have you in that hand?" he asked.

Mossy opened his hand, and there lay the golden key.

"Ah!" said the Old Man, "that accounts for your knowing me. And I know the way you have to go."

"I want to find the country whence the shadows fall," said Mossy.

"I dare say you do. So do I. But meantime, one thing is certain. — What is the key for, do you think?"

"For a keyhole somewhere. But I don't know why I keep it. I never could find the keyhole. And I have lived a good while, I believe," said Mossy, sadly. "I'm not sure that I'm not old. I know my feet ache."

"Do they?" said the Old Man, as if he really meant to ask the question; and Mossy, who was still lying in the bath, watched his feet for a moment before he replied.

"No, they do not," he answered. "Perhaps I am not old either."

"Get up and look at yourself in the water."

He rose and looked at himself in the water, and there was not a gray hair on his head or a wrinkle on his skin.

"You have tasted of death now," said the Old Man. "Is it good?"

"It is good," said Mossy. "It is better than life."

"No," said the Old Man; "it is only more life. — Your feet will make no holes in the water now."

"What do you mean?"

"I will show you that presently."

They returned to the outer cave, and sat and talked together for a long time. At length the Old Man of the Sea rose, and said to Mossy, —

"Follow me."

He led him up the stair again, and opened another door. They stood on the level of the raging sea, looking towards the east. Across the waste of waters, against the bosom of a fierce black cloud, stood the foot of a rainbow, glowing in the dark.

"This indeed is my way," said Mossy, as soon as he saw the rainbow, and stepped out upon the sea. His feet made no holes in the water. He fought the wind, and clomb the waves, and went on towards the rainbow.

The storm died away. A lovely day and a lovelier night followed. A cool wind blew over the wide plain of the quiet ocean. And still Mossy journeyed eastward. But the rainbow had vanished with the storm.

Day after day he held on, and he thought he had no guide. He did not see how a shining fish under the waters directed his steps. He crossed the sea, and came to a great precipice of rock, up which he could discover but one path. Nor did this lead him farther than half-way up the rock, where it ended on a platform. Here he stood and pondered. — It could not be that the way stopped here, else what was the path for? It was a rough path, not very plain, yet certainly a path. — He examined the face of the rock. It was smooth as glass. But as his eyes kept roving hopelessly over it, something glittered, and he caught sight of a row of small sapphires. They bordered a little hole in the rock.

"The keyhole!" he cried.

He tried the key. It fitted. It turned. A great clang and clash, as of iron bolts on huge brazen caldrons, echoed thunderously within. He drew out the key. The rock in front of him began to fall. He retreated from it as far as the breadth of the platform would allow. A great slab fell at his feet. In front was still the solid rock, with this one slab fallen forward out of it. But the moment he stepped upon it, a second fell, just short of the edge of the first, making the next step of a stair, which thus kept dropping itself before him as he ascended into the heart of the precipice. It led him into a hall fit for such an approach — irregular and rude in formation, but floor, sides, pillars, and vaulted roof, all one mass of shining stones of every colour that light can show. In the centre stood seven columns, ranged from red to violet. And on the pedestal of one of them sat a woman, motionless, with her face bowed upon her knees. Seven years had she sat there waiting. She lifted her head as Mossy drew near. It was Tangle. Her hair had grown to her feet, and was rippled like the windless sea on broad sands. Her face was beautiful, like her grandmother's, and as still and peaceful as that of the Old Man of the Fire. Her form was tall and noble. Yet Mossy knew her at once.

"How beautiful you are, Tangle!" he said, in delight and astonishment.

"Am I?" she returned. "Oh, I have waited for you so long! But you, you are like the Old Man of the Sea. No. You are like the Old Man of the Earth. No, no. You are like the oldest man of all. You are like them all. And yet you are my own old Mossy! How did you come here? What did you do after I lost you? Did you find the keyhole? Have you got the key still?"

She had a hundred questions to ask him, and he a hundred more to ask her. They told each other all their adventures, and were as happy as man and woman could be. For they were younger and better, and stronger and wiser, than they had ever been before.

It began to grow dark. And they wanted more than ever to reach the country whence the shadows fall. So they looked about them for a way out of the cave. The door by which Mossy entered had closed again, and there was half a mile of rock between them and the sea. Neither could Tangle find the opening in the floor by which the serpent had led her thither. They searched till it grew so dark that they could see nothing, and gave it up.

After a while, however, the cave began to glimmer again. The light came from the moon, but it did not look like moonlight, for it gleamed through those seven pillars in the middle, and filled the place with all colours. And now Mossy saw that there was a pillar beside the red one, which he had not observed before. And it was of the same new colour that he had seen in the rainbow when he saw it first in the fairy forest. And on it he saw a sparkle of blue. It was the sapphires round the keyhole.

He took his key. It turned in the lock to the sounds of Aeolian music. A door opened upon slow hinges, and disclosed a winding stair within. The key vanished from his fingers. Tangle went up. Mossy followed. The door closed behind them. They climbed out of the earth; and, still climbing, rose above it. They were in the rainbow. Far abroad, over ocean and land, they could see through its transparent walls the earth beneath their feet. Stairs beside stairs wound up together, and beautiful beings of all ages climbed along with them.

They knew that they were going up to the country whence the shadows fall.

And by this time I think they must have got there.

The Wise Woman,
or the Lost Princess:
A Double Story

CHAPTER I

There was a certain country where things used to go rather oddly. For instance, you could never tell whether it was going to rain or hail, or whether or not the milk was going to turn sour. It was impossible to say whether the next baby would be a boy, or a girl, or even, after he was a week old, whether he would wake sweet-tempered or cross.

In strict accordance with the peculiar nature of this country of uncertainties, it came to pass one day, that in the midst of a shower of rain that might well be called golden, seeing the sun, shining as it fell, turned all its drops into molten topazes, and every drop was good for a grain of golden corn, or a yellow cowslip, or a buttercup, or a dandelion at least; — while this splendid rain was falling, I say, with a musical patter upon the great leaves of the horse-chestnuts, which hung like Vandyke collars about the necks of the creamy, red-spotted blossoms, and on the leaves of the sycamores, looking as if they had blood in their veins, and on a multitude of flowers, of which some stood up and boldly held out their cups to catch their share, while others cowered down, laughing, under the soft, patting blows of the heavy warm drops; — while this lovely rain was washing all the air clean from the motes, and the bad odors, and the poison-seeds that had escaped from their prisons during the long drought; — while it fell, splashing and sparkling, with a hum, and a rush, and a soft clashing — but stop! I am stealing, I find, and not that only, but with clumsy hands spoiling what I steal: —

> "O Rain! with your dull twofold sound,
> The clash hard by, and the murmur all round":

— there! take it, Mr. Coleridge; — while, as I was saying, the lovely little rivers whose fountains are the clouds, and which cut their own channels through the air, and make sweet noises rubbing against their banks as they hurry down and down, until at length they are pulled up on a sudden, with a musical plash, in the very heart of an odorous flower, that first gasps and then sighs up a blissful scent, or on the bald head of a stone that never says, Thank you; — while the very sheep felt it blessing them, though it could never reach their skins through the depth of their long wool, and the veriest hedgehog — I mean the one with the longest spikes — came and spiked himself out to impale as many of the drops as he could; — while the rain was thus falling, and the leaves, and the flowers, and the sheep, and the cattle, and the hedgehog, were all busily receiving the golden rain, something happened. It was not a great battle, nor an earthquake, nor a coronation, but something more important than all those put together. *A baby-girl was born;* and her father was a king; and her mother was a queen; and her uncles and aunts were princes and princesses; and her first-cousins were dukes and duchesses; and not one of her second-cousins was less than a marquis or marchioness, or of their third-cousins less than an earl or countess: and below a countess they did not care to count. So the little girl was Somebody; and yet for all that, strange to say, the first thing she did was to cry. I told you it was a strange country.

As she grew up, everybody about her did his best to convince her that she was Somebody; and the girl herself was so easily persuaded of it that she quite forgot that anybody had ever told her so, and took it for a fundamental, innate, primary, first-born, self-evident, necessary, and in-controvertible idea and principle that *she was Somebody.* And far be it from me to deny it. I will even go so far as to assert that in this odd country there was a huge number of Somebodies. Indeed, it was one of its oddities that every boy and girl in it was rather too ready to think he or she was

⁊₹   THE WISE WOMAN, OR THE LOST PRINCESS

Somebody; and the worst of it was that the princess never thought of there being more than one Somebody — and that was herself.

Far away to the north in the same country, on the side of a bleak hill, where a horse chestnut or a sycamore was never seen, where were no meadows rich with buttercups, only steep, rough, breezy slopes, covered with dry prickly furze and its flowers of red gold, or moister, softer broom with its flowers of yellow gold, and great sweeps of purple heather, mixed with bilberries, and crowberries, and cranberries — no, I am all wrong: there was nothing out yet but a few furze-blossoms; the rest were all waiting behind their doors till they were called; and no full, slow-gliding river with meadow-sweet along its oozy banks, only a little brook here and there, that dashed past without a moment to say, "How do you do?" — there (would you believe it?) while the same cloud that was dropping down golden rain all about the queen's new baby was dashing huge fierce handfuls of hail upon the hills, with such force that they flew spinning off the rocks and stones, went burrowing in the sheep's wool, stung the cheeks and chin of the shepherd with their sharp spiteful little blows, and made his dog wink and whine as they bounded off his hard wise head, and long sagacious nose; only, when they dropped plump down the chimney, and fell hissing in the fire, they caught it then, for the clever little fire soon sent them up the chimney again, a good deal swollen, and harmless enough for a while, there (what do you think?) among the hailstones, and the heather, and the cold mountain air, another little girl was born, whom the shepherd her father, and the shepherdess her mother, and a good many of her kindred too, thought Somebody. She had not an uncle or an aunt that was less than a shepherd or dairymaid, not a cousin that was less than a farm-labourer, not a second-cousin that was less than a grocer, and they did not count farther. And yet (would you believe it?) she too cried the very first thing. It *was* an odd country! And, what is still more surprising, the shepherd and shepherdess and the dairymaids and the labourers were not a bit wiser than the king and the queen and the dukes and the marquises and the earls; for they too, one and all, so constantly taught the little woman that she was Somebody, that she also forgot that there were a great many more Somebodies besides herself in the world.

It was, indeed, a peculiar country, very different from ours — so different, that my reader must not be too much surprised when I add the amazing fact, that most of its inhabitants, instead of enjoying the things they had, were always wanting the things they had not, often even the things it was least likely they ever could have. The grown men and women being like this, there is no reason to be further astonished that the Princess Rosamond — the name her parents gave her because it means *Rose of the World* — should grow up like them, wanting every thing she could and every thing she couldn't have. The things she could have were a great many too many, for her foolish parents always gave her what they could; but still there remained a few things they couldn't give her, for they were only a common king and queen. They could and did give her a lighted candle when she cried for it, and managed by much care that she should not burn her fingers or set her frock on fire; but when she cried for the moon, that they could not give her. They did the worst thing possible, instead, however; for they pretended to do what they could not. They got her a thin disc of brilliantly polished silver, as near the size of the moon as they could agree upon; and, for a time, she was delighted.

But, unfortunately, one evening she made the discovery that her moon was a little peculiar, inasmuch as she could not shine in the dark. Her nurse happened to snuff out the candles as she was playing with it; and instantly came a shriek of rage, for her moon had vanished. Presently, through the opening of the curtains, she caught sight of the real moon, far away in the sky, and shining quite calmly, as if she had been there all the time; and her rage increased to such a degree that if it had not passed off in a fit, I do not know what might have come of it.

As she grew up it was still the same, with this difference, that not only must she have everything, but she got tired of every thing almost as soon as she had it. There was an accumulation of things in her nursery and schoolroom and bedroom that was perfectly appalling. Her mother's wardrobes were almost useless to her, so packed were they with things of which she never took any notice. When she was five years old, they gave her a splendid gold repeater, so close set with diamonds and rubies, that the back was just one crust of gems. In one of her little tempers, as they called her hideously ugly rages, she dashed it against the back of the chimney, after which it never gave a single tick; and some of the diamonds went to the ash-pit. As she grew older still, she became fond of animals, not in a way that brought them much pleasure, or herself much satisfaction. When angry, she would beat them, and try to pull them to pieces, and as soon as she became a little used to them, would neglect them altogether. Then, if they could, they would run away, and she was furious. Some white mice, which she had ceased feeding altogether, did so; and

❧ THE WISE WOMAN, OR THE LOST PRINCESS

soon the palace was swarming with white mice. Their red eyes might be seen glowing, and their white skins gleaming, in every dark corner; but when it came to the king's finding a nest of them in his second-best crown, he was angry and ordered them to be drowned. The princess heard of it, however, and raised such a clamor, that there they were left until they should run away of themselves; and the poor king had to wear his best crown every day till then. Nothing that was the princess's property, whether she cared for it or not, was to be meddled with.

Of course, as she grew, she grew worse; for she never tried to grow better. She became more and more peevish and fretful every day — dissatisfied not only with what she had, but with all that was around her, and constantly wishing things in general to be different. She found fault with every thing and everybody, and all that happened, and grew more and more disagreeable to every one who had to do with her. At last, when she had nearly killed her nurse, and had all but succeeded in hanging herself, and was miserable from morning to night, her parents thought it time to do something.

A long way from the palace, in the heart of a deep wood of pine-trees, lived a wise woman. In some countries she would have been called a witch; but that would have been a mistake, for she never did any thing wicked, and had more power than any witch could have. As her fame was spread through all the country, the king heard of her; and thinking she might perhaps be able to suggest something, sent for her. In the dead of the night, lest the princess should know it, the king's messenger brought into the palace a tall woman, muffled from head to foot in a cloak of black cloth. In the presence of both their Majesties, the king, to do her honor, requested her to sit; but she declined, and stood waiting to hear what they had to say. Nor had she to wait long, for almost instantly they began to tell her the dreadful trouble they were in with their only child; first the king talking, then the queen interposing with some yet more dreadful fact, and at times both letting out a torrent of words together, so anxious were they to show the wise woman that their perplexity was real, and their daughter a very terrible one. For a long while there appeared no sign of approaching pause. But the wise woman stood patiently folded in her black cloak, and listened without word or motion. At length silence fell; for they had talked themselves tired, and could not think of any thing more to add to the list of their child's enormities.

After a minute, the wise woman unfolded her arms; and her cloak dropping open in front, disclosed a garment made of a strange stuff, which an old poet who knew her well has thus described: —

> "All lily white, withoutten spot or pride,
> That seemed like silke and silver woven neare;
> But neither silke nor silver therein did appeare."

"How very badly you have treated her!" said the wise woman. "Poor child!"

"Treated her badly?" gasped the king.

"She is a very wicked child," said the queen; and both glared with indignation.

"Yes, indeed!" returned the wise woman. "She is very naughty indeed, and that she must be made to feel; but it is half your fault too."

"What!" stammered the king. Haven't we given her every mortal thing she wanted?"

"Surely," said the wise woman; "what else could have all but killed her? You should have given her a few things of the other sort. But you are far too dull to understand me."

"You are very polite," remarked the king, with royal sarcasm on his thin, straight lips.

The wise woman made no answer beyond a deep sigh; and the king and queen sat silent also in their anger, glaring at the wise woman. The silence lasted again for a minute, and then the wise woman folded her cloak around her, and her shining garment vanished like the moon when a great cloud comes over her. Yet another minute passed and the silence endured, for the smouldering wrath of the king and queen choked the channels of their speech. Then the wise woman turned her back on them, and so stood. At this, the rage of the king broke forth; and he cried to the queen, stammering in his fierceness, —

"How should such an old hag as that teach Rosamond good manners? She knows nothing of them herself! Look how she stands! — actually with her back to us."

At the word the wise woman walked from the room. The great folding doors fell together behind her; and the same moment the king and queen were quarrelling like apes as to which of them was to blame for her departure. Before their altercation was over, for it lasted till the early morning, in rushed Rosamond, clutching in her hand a poor little white rabbit, of which she was very fond, and from which, only because

THE WISE WOMAN, OR THE LOST PRINCESS

"In rushed Rosamond"

it would not come to her when she called it, she was pulling handfuls of fur in the attempt to tear the squealing, pink-eared, red-eyed thing to pieces.

"Rosa, Rosa*mond!*" cried the queen; whereupon Rosamond threw the rabbit in her mother's face. The king started up in a fury, and ran to seize her. She darted shrieking from the room. The king rushed after her; but, to his amazement, she was nowhere to be seen: the huge hall was empty. — No: just outside the door, close to the threshold, with her back to it, sat the figure of the wise woman, muffled in her dark cloak, with her head bowed over her knees. As the king stood looking at her, she rose slowly, crossed the hall, and walked away down the marble staircase. The king called to her; but she never turned her head, or gave the least sign that she heard him. So quietly did she pass down the wide marble stair, that the king was all but persuaded he had seen only a shadow gliding across the white steps.

For the princess, she was nowhere to be found. The queen went into hysterics; and the rabbit ran away. The king sent out messengers in every direction, but in vain.

In a short time the palace was quiet — as quiet as it used to be before the princess was born. The king and queen cried a little now and then, for the hearts of parents were in that country strangely fashioned: and yet I am afraid the first movement of those very hearts would have been a jump of terror if the ears above them had heard the voice of Rosamond in one of the corridors. As for the rest of the household, they could not have made up a single tear amongst them. They thought, whatever it might be for the princess, it was, for every one else, the best thing that could have happened; and as to what had become of her, if their heads were puzzled, their hearts took no interest in the question. The lord-chancellor alone had an idea about it, but he was far too wise to utter it.

CHAPTER II

The fact, as is plain, was, that the princess had disappeared in the folds of the wise woman's cloak. When she rushed from the room, the wise woman caught her to her bosom and flung the black garment around her. The princess struggled wildly, for she was in fierce terror, and screamed as loud as choking fright would permit her; but her father, standing in the door, and looking down upon the wise women, saw never a movement of the cloak, so tight was she held by her captor. He was indeed aware of a most angry crying, which reminded him of his daughter; but it sounded to him so far away, that he took it for the passion of some child in the street, outside the palace-gates. Hence, unchallenged, the wise woman carried the princess down the marble stairs, out at the palace-door, down a great flight of steps outside, across a paved court, through the brazen gates, along half-roused streets where people were opening their shops, through the huge gates of the city, and out into the wide road, vanishing northwards; the princess struggling and screaming all the time, and the wise woman holding her tight. When at length she was too tired to struggle or scream any more, the wise woman unfolded her cloak, and set her down; and the princess saw the light and opened her swollen eyelids. There was nothing in sight that she had ever seen before. City and palace had disappeared. They were upon a wide road going straight on, with a ditch on each side of it, that behind them widened into the great moat surrounding the city. She cast up a terrified look into the wise woman's face, that gazed down upon her gravely and kindly. Now the princess did not in the least understand kindness. She always took it for a sign either of partiality or fear. So when the wise woman looked kindly upon her, she rushed at her, butting with her head like a ram: but the folds of the cloak had closed around the wise woman; and, when the princess ran against it, she found it hard as the cloak of a bronze statue, and fell back upon the road with a great bruise on her head. The wise woman lifted her again, and put her once more under the cloak, where she fell asleep, and where she awoke again only to find that she was still being carried on and on.

When at length the wise woman again stopped and set her down, she saw around her a bright moonlit night, on a wide heath, solitary and houseless. Here she felt more frightened than before; nor was her terror assuaged when, looking up, she saw a stern, immovable countenance, with cold eyes fixedly regarding her. All she knew of the world being derived from nursery-tales, she concluded that the wise woman was an ogress, carrying her home to eat her.

I have already said that the princess was, at this time of her life, such a low-minded creature, that severity had greater influence over her than kindness. She understood terror better far than tenderness. When the wise woman looked at her thus, she fell on her knees, and held up her hands to her, crying, —

"Oh, don't eat me! don't eat me!"

Now this being the best *she* could do, it was a sign she was a low creature. Think of it — to kick at kindness, and kneel from terror. But the sternness on the face of the wise woman came from the same heart and the same feeling as the kindness that had shone from it before. The only thing that could save the princess from her hatefulness, was that she should be made to mind somebody else than her own miserable Somebody.

Without saying a word, the wise woman reached down her hand, took one of Rosamond's, and, lifting her to her feet, led her along through the moonlight. Every now and then a gush of obstinacy would well up in the heart of the princess, and she would give a great, ill-tempered tug, and pull her hand away; but then the wise woman would gaze down upon her with such a look, that she instantly sought again the hand she had rejected, in pure terror lest she should be eaten upon the spot. And so they would walk on again; and when the wind blew the folds of the cloak against the princess, she found them soft as her mother's camel-hair shawl.

After a little while the wise woman began to sing to her, and the princess could not help listening; for the soft wind amongst the low dry bushes of the heath, the rustle of their own steps, and the trailing of the wise woman's cloak, were the only sounds beside.

And this is the song she sang: —

> Out in the cold,
> With a thin-worn fold
> Of withered gold
> Around her rolled,
> Hangs in the air the weary moon.
> She is old, old, old;
> And her bones all cold,
> And her tales all told,
> And her things all sold,
> And she has no breath to croon.

> Like a castaway clout,
> She is quite shut out!
> She might call and shout,
> But no one about
> Would ever call back, "Who's there?"
> There is never a hut,
> Not a door to shut,
> Not a footpath or rut,
> Long road or short cut,
> Leading to anywhere!

She is all alone
Like a dog-picked bone,
The poor old crone!
She fain would groan,
But she cannot find the breath.
She once had a fire;
But she built it no higher,
And only sat nigher
Till she saw it expire;
And now she is cold as death.

She never will smile
All the lonesome while
Oh the mile after mile,
And never a stile!
And never a tree or a stone!
She has not a tear:
Afar and anear
It is all so drear,
But she does not care,
Her heart is as dry as a bone.

None to come near her!
No one to cheer her!
No one to jeer her!
No one to hear her!
Not a thing to lift and hold!
She is always awake,
But her heart will not break;
She can only quake,
Shiver, and shake:
The old woman is very cold.

As strange as the song, was the crooning wailing tune that the wise woman sung. At the first note almost, you would have thought she wanted to frighten the princess; and so indeed she did. For when people *will* be naughty, they have to be frightened, and they are not expected to like it. The princess grew angry, pulled her hand away, and cried, —

"*You* are the ugly old woman. I hate you!"

Therewith she stood still, expecting the wise woman to stop also, perhaps coax her to go on: if she did, she was determined not to move a step. But the wise woman never even looked about: she kept walking on steadily, the same pace as before. Little Obstinate thought for certain she would turn; for she regarded herself as much too precious to be left behind. But on and on the wise woman went, until she had vanished away in the dim moonlight. Then all at once the princess perceived that she was left alone with the moon, looking down on her from the height of her loneliness. She was horribly frightened, and began to run after the wise woman, calling aloud. But the song she had just heard came back to the sound of her own running feet, —

> All all alone,
> Like a dog-picked bone!

and again, —

> She might call and shout,
> And no one about
> Would ever call back, "Who's there?"

and she screamed as she ran. How she wished she knew the old woman's name, that she might call it after her through the moonlight!

But the wise woman had, in truth, heard the first sound of her running feet, and stopped and turned, waiting. What with running and crying, however, and a fall or two as she ran, the princess never saw her until she fell right into her arms — and the same moment into a fresh rage; for as soon as any trouble was over the princess was always ready to begin another. The wise woman therefore pushed her away, and walked on; while the princess ran scolding and storming after her. She had to run till, from every fatigue, her rudeness ceased. Her heart gave way; she burst into tears, and ran on silently weeping.

A minute more and the wise woman stooped, and lifting her in her arms, folded her cloak around her. Instantly she fell asleep, and slept as soft and as soundly as if she had been in her own bed. She slept till the moon went down; she slept till the sun rose up; she slept till he climbed the topmost sky; she slept till he went down again, and the poor old moon came peaking and peering out once more: and all that time the wise woman went walking on and on very fast. And now they had reached a spot where a few fir-trees came to meet them through the moonlight.

At the same time the princess awaked, and popping her head out between the folds of the wise woman's cloak — a very ugly little owlet she looked — saw that they were entering the wood. Now there is something awful about every wood, especially in the moonlight; and perhaps a fir-wood is more awful than other woods. For one thing, it lets a little more light through, rendering the darkness a little more visible, as it were; and then the trees go stretching away up towards the moon, and look as if they cared nothing about the creatures below them — not like the broad trees with soft wide leaves that, in the darkness even, look sheltering. So the princess is not to be blamed that she was very much frightened. She is hardly to be blamed either that, assured the wise woman was an ogress carrying her to her castle to eat her up, she began again to kick and scream violently as those of my readers who are of the same sort as herself will consider the right and natural thing to do. The wrong in her was this — that she had led such a bad life, that she did not know a good woman when she saw her; took her for one like herself, even after she had slept in her arms.

Immediately the wise woman set her down, and, walking on, within a few paces vanished among the trees. Then the cries of the princess rent the air, but the fir-trees never heeded her; not one of their hard little needles gave a single shiver for all the noise she made. But there were creatures in the forest who were soon quite as much interested in her cries as the fir-trees were indifferent to them. They began to hearken and howl and snuff about, and run hither and thither, and grin with their white teeth, and light up the green lamps in their eyes. In a minute or two a whole army of wolves and hyenas were rushing from all quarters through the pillar-like stems of the fir-trees, to the place where she stood calling them, without knowing it. The noise she made herself, however, prevented her from hearing either their howls or the soft pattering of their many trampling feet as they bounded over the fallen fir needles and cones.

One huge old wolf had outsped the rest — not that he could run faster, but that from experience he could more exactly judge whence the cries came, and as he shot through the wood, she caught sight at last of his lamping eyes coming swiftly nearer and nearer. Terror silenced her. She

"One huge wolf outsped the rest"

stood with her mouth open, as if she were going to eat the wolf, but she had no breath to scream with, and her tongue curled up in her mouth like a withered and frozen leaf. She could do nothing but stare at the coming monster. And now he was taking a few shorter bounds, measuring the distance for the one final leap that should bring him upon her, when out stepped the wise woman from behind the very tree by which she had set the princess down, caught the wolf by the throat half-way in his spring, shook him once, and threw him from her dead. Then she turned towards the princess, who flung herself into her arms, and was instantly lapped in the folds of her cloak.

But now the huge army of wolves and hyenas had rushed like a sea around them, whose waves leaped with hoarse roar and hollow yell up against the wise woman. But she, like a strong stately vessel, moved unhurt through the midst of them. Even as they leaped against her cloak, they dropped and slunk away back through the crowd. Others ever succeeded, and ever in their turn fell, and drew back confounded. For some time she walked on attended and assailed on all sides by the howling

❧ THE WISE WOMAN, OR THE LOST PRINCESS

"The princess was instantly lapped into the folds of her cloak"

pack. Suddenly they turned and swept away, vanishing in the depths of the forest. She neither slackened nor hastened her step, but went walking on as before.

In a little while she unfolded her cloak, and let the princess look out. The firs had ceased; and they were on a lofty height of moorland, stony and bare and dry, with tufts of heather and a few small plants here and there. About the heath, on every side, lay the forest, looking in the moonlight like a cloud; and above the forest, like the shaven crown of a monk, rose the bare moor over which they were walking. Presently, a little way in front of them, the princess espied a white-washed cottage, gleaming in the moon. As they came nearer, she saw that the roof was covered with thatch, over which the moss had grown green. It was a very simple, humble place, not in the least terrible to look at, and yet, as soon as she saw it, her fear again awoke, and always, as soon as her fear awoke, the trust of the princess fell into a dead sleep. Foolish and useless as she might by this time have known it, she once more began kicking and screaming, whereupon, yet once more, the wise woman set her down on the heath, a few yards from the back of the cottage, and saying only, "No one ever gets into my house who does not knock at the door, and ask to come in," disappeared round the corner of the cottage, leaving the princess alone with the moon — two white faces in the cone of the night.

CHAPTER III

The moon stared at the princess, and the princess stared at the moon; but the moon had the best of it, and the princess began to cry. And now the question was between the moon and the cottage. The princess thought she knew the worst of the moon, and she knew nothing at all about the cottage, therefore she would stay with the moon. Strange, was it not, that she should have been so long with the wise woman, and yet know *nothing* about that cottage? As for the moon, she did not by any means know the worst of her, or even, that, if she were to fall asleep where she could find her, the old witch would certainly do her best to twist her face.

But she had scarcely sat a moment longer before she was assailed by all sorts of fresh fears. First of all, the soft wind blowing gently through

❧   THE WISE WOMAN, OR THE LOST PRINCESS

the dry stalks of the heather and its thousands of little bells raised a sweet rustling, which the princess took for the hissing of serpents, for you know she had been naughty for so long that she could not in a great many things tell the good from the bad. Then nobody could deny that there, all round about the heath, like a ring of darkness, lay the gloomy fir-wood, and the princess knew what it was full of, and every now and then she thought she heard the howling of its wolves and hyenas. And who could tell but some of them might break from their covert and sweep like a shadow across the heath? Indeed, it was not once nor twice that for a moment she was fully persuaded she saw a great beast coming leaping and bounding through the moonlight to have her all to himself. She did not know that not a single evil creature dared set foot on that heath, or that, if one should do so, it would that instant wither up and cease. If an army of them had rushed to invade it, it would have melted away on the edge of it, and ceased like a dying wave. — She even imagined that the moon was slowly coming nearer and nearer down the sky to take her and freeze her to death in her arms. The wise woman, too, she felt sure, although her cottage looked asleep, was watching her at some little window. In this, however, she would have been quite right, if she had only imagined enough — namely, that the wise woman was watching *over* her from the little window. But after all, somehow, the thought of the wise woman was less frightful than that of any of her other terrors, and at length she began to wonder whether it might not turn out that she was no ogress, but only a rude, ill-bred, tyrannical, yet on the whole not altogether ill-meaning person. Hardly had the possibility arisen in her mind, before she was on her feet: if the woman was any thing short of an ogress, her cottage must be better than that horrible loneliness, with nothing in all the world but a stare; and even an ogress had at least the shape and look of a human being.

She darted round the end of the cottage to find the front. But, to her surprise, she came only to another back, for no door was to be seen. She tried the farther end, but still no door. She must have passed it as she ran — but no — neither in gable nor in side was any to be found.

A cottage without a door! — she rushed at it in a rage and kicked at the wall with her feet. But the wall was hard as iron, and hurt her sadly through her gay silken slippers. She threw herself on the heath, which came up to the walls of the cottage on every side, and roared and screamed with rage. Suddenly, however, she remembered how her screaming had brought the horde of wolves and hyenas about her in the forest, and,

"In the palace at home"

ceasing at once, lay still, gazing yet again at the moon. And then came the thought of her parents in the palace at home. In her mind's eye she saw her mother sitting at her embroidery with the tears dropping upon it, and her father staring into the fire as if he were looking for her in its glowing caverns. It is true that if they had both been in tears by her side because of her naughtiness, she would not have cared a straw; but now her own forlorn condition somehow helped her to understand their grief at having lost her, and not only a great longing to be back in her comfortable home, but a feeble flutter of genuine love for her parents awoke in her heart as well, and she burst into real tears — soft mournful tears — very different from those of rage and disappointment to which she was so much used. And another very remarkable thing was that the moment she began to love her father and mother, she began to wish to see the wise woman again. The idea of her being an ogress vanished utterly, and she thought of her only as one to take her in from the moon, and the loneliness, and the terrors of the forest-haunted heath, and hide her in a cottage with not even a door for the horrid wolves to howl against.

But the old woman — as the princess called her, not knowing that her real name was the Wise Woman — had told her that she must knock

❧   THE WISE WOMAN, OR THE LOST PRINCESS

at the door: how was she to do that when there was no door? But again she bethought herself — that, if she could not do all she was told, she could, at least, do a part of it: if she could not knock at the door, she could at least knock — say on the wall, for there was nothing else to knock upon — and perhaps the old woman would hear her, and lift her in by some window. Thereupon, she rose at once to her feet, and picking up a stone, began to knock on the wall with it. A loud noise was the result, and she found she was knocking on the very door itself. For a moment she feared the old woman would be offended, but the next, there came a voice, saying.

"Who is there?"

The princess answered,

"Please, old woman, I did not mean to knock so loud."

To this there came no reply.

Then the princess knocked again, this time with her knuckles, and the voice came again, saying,

"Who is there?"

And the princess answered,

"Rosamond."

Then a second time there was silence. But the princess soon ventured to knock a third time.

"What do you want?" said the voice.

"Oh, please, let me in!" said the princess. "The moon will keep staring at me; and I hear the wolves in the wood."

Then the door opened, and the princess entered. She looked all around, but saw nothing of the wise woman.

It was a single bare little room, with a white deal table, and a few old wooden chairs, a fire of fir-wood on the hearth, the smoke of which smelt sweet, and a patch of thick-growing heath in one corner. Poor as it was, compared to the grand place Rosamond had left, she felt no little satisfaction as she shut the door, and looked around her. And what with the sufferings and terrors she had left outside, the new kind of tears she had shed, the love she had begun to feel for her parents, and the trust she had begun to place in the wise woman, it seemed to her as if her soul had grown larger of a sudden, and she had left the days of her childishness and naughtiness far behind her. People are so ready to think themselves changed when it is only their mood that is changed! Those who are good-tempered because it is a fine day, will be ill-tempered when it rains:

their selves are just the same both days; only in the one case, the fine weather has got into them, in the other the rainy. Rosamond, as she sat warming herself by the glow of the peat-fire, turning over in her mind all that had passed, and feeling how pleasant the change in her feelings was, began by degrees to think how very good she had grown, and how very good she was to have grown good, and how extremely good she must always have been that she was able to grow so very good as she now felt she had grown; and she became so absorbed in her self-admiration as never to notice either that the fire was dying, or that a heap of fir-cones lay in a corner near it. Suddenly, a great wind came roaring down the chimney, and scattered the ashes about the floor; a tremendous rain followed, and fell hissing on the embers; the moon was swallowed up, and there was darkness all about her. Then a flash of lightning, followed by a peal of thunder, so terrified the princess, that she cried aloud for the old woman, but there came no answer to her cry.

Then in her terror the princess grew angry, and saying to herself, "She must be somewhere in the place, else who was there to open the door to me?" began to shout and yell, and call the wise woman all the bad names she had been in the habit of throwing at her nurses. But there came not a single sound in reply.

Strange to say, the princess never thought of telling herself now how naughty she was, though that would surely have been reasonable. On the contrary, she thought she had a perfect right to be angry, for was she not most desperately ill used — and a princess too? But the wind howled on, and the rain kept pouring down the chimney, and every now and then the lightning burst out, and the thunder rushed after it, as if the great lumbering sound could ever think to catch up with the swift light!

At length the princess had again grown so angry, frightened, and miserable, all together, that she jumped up and hurried about the cottage with outstretched arms, trying to find the wise woman. But being in a bad temper always makes people stupid, and presently she struck her forehead such a blow against something — she thought herself it felt like the old woman's cloak — that she fell back — not on the floor, though, but on the patch of heather, which felt as soft and pleasant as any bed in the palace. There, worn out with weeping and rage, she soon fell fast asleep.

She dreamed that she was the old cold woman up in the sky, with no home and no friends, and no nothing at all, not even a pocket; wandering, wandering forever, over a desert of blue sand, never to get to

THE WISE WOMAN, OR THE LOST PRINCESS

anywhere, and never to lie down or die. It was no use stopping to look about her, for what had she to do but forever look about her as she went on and on and on — never seeing any thing, and never expecting to see any thing! The only shadow of a hope she had was, that she might by slow degrees grow thinner and thinner, until at last she wore away to nothing at all; only alas! she could not detect the least sign that she had yet begun to grow thinner. The hopelessness grew at length so unendurable that she woke with a start. Seeing the face of the wise woman bending over her, she threw her arms around her neck and held up her mouth to be kissed. And the kiss of the wise woman was like the rose-gardens of Damascus.

CHAPTER IV

The wise woman lifted her tenderly, and washed and dressed her far more carefully than even her nurse. Then she set her down by the fire, and prepared her breakfast. The princess was very hungry, and the bread and milk as good as it could be, so that she thought she had never in her life eaten any thing nicer. Nevertheless, as soon as she began to have enough, she said to herself —

"Ha! I see how it is! The old woman wants to fatten me! That is why she gives me such nice creamy milk. She doesn't kill me now because she's going to kill me then! She *is* an ogress, after all!"

Thereupon she laid down her spoon, and would not eat another mouthful — only followed the basin with longing looks, as the wise woman carried it away.

When she stopped eating, her hostess knew exactly what she was thinking; but it was one thing to understand the princess, and quite another to make the princess understand her: that would require time. For the present she took no notice, but went about the affairs of the house, sweeping the floor, brushing down the cobwebs, cleaning the hearth, dusting the table and chairs, and watering the bed to keep it fresh and alive — for she never had more than one guest at a time, and never would allow that guest to go to sleep upon any thing that had no life in it. All the time she was thus busied, she spoke not a word to the princess, which, with the princess, went to

"The kiss of the wise woman"

confirm her notion of her purposes. But whatever she might have said would have been only perverted by the princess into yet stronger proof of her evil designs, for a fancy in her own head would outweigh any multitude of facts in another's. She kept staring at the fire, and never looked round to see what the wise woman might be doing.

By and by she came close up to the back of her chair, and said, "Rosamond!"

But the princess had fallen into one of her sulky moods, and shut herself up with her own ugly Somebody; so she never looked round or even answered the wise woman.

"Rosamond," she repeated, "I am going out. If you are a good girl, that is, if you do as I tell you, I will carry you back to your father and mother the moment I return."

The princess did not take the least notice.

"Look at me, Rosamond," said the wise woman.

But Rosamond never moved — never even shrugged her shoulders — perhaps because they were already up to her ears, and could go no farther.

"I want to help you to do what I tell you," said the wise woman. "Look at me."

Still Rosamond was motionless and silent, saying only to herself,

"I know what she's after! She wants to show me her horrid teeth.

THE WISE WOMAN, OR THE LOST PRINCESS

But I won't look. I'm not going to be frightened out of my senses to please her."

"You had better look, Rosamond. Have you forgotten how you kissed me this morning?"

But Rosamond now regarded that little throb of affection as a momentary weakness into which the deceitful ogress had betrayed her, and almost despised herself for it. She was one of those who the more they are coaxed are the more disagreeable. For such, the wise woman had an awful punishment, but she remembered that the princess had been very ill brought up, and therefore wished to try her with all gentleness first.

She stood silent for a moment, to see what effect her words might have. But Rosamond only said to herself, —

"She wants to fatten and eat me."

And it was such a little while since she had looked into the wise woman's loving eyes, thrown her arms round her neck, and kissed her!

"Well," said the wise woman gently, after pausing as long as it seemed possible she might bethink herself, "I must tell you then without; only whoever listens with her back turned, listens but half, and gets but half the help."

"She wants to fatten me," said the princess.

"You must keep the cottage tidy while I am out. When I come back, I must see the fire bright, the hearth swept, and the kettle boiling; no dust on the table or chairs, the windows clear, the floor clean, and the heather in blossom — which last comes of sprinkling it with water three times a day. When you are hungry, put your hand into that hole in the wall, and you will find a meal."

"She wants to fatten me," said the princess.

"But on no account leave the house till I come back," continued the wise woman, "or you will grievously repent it. Remember what you have already gone through to reach it. Dangers lie all around this cottage of mine; but inside, it is the safest place — in fact the only quite safe place in all the country."

"She means to eat me," said the princess, "and therefore wants to frighten me from running away."

She heard the voice no more. Then, suddenly startled at the thought of being alone, she looked hastily over her shoulder. The cottage was indeed empty of all visible life. It was soundless, too: there was not even a ticking

"Noise of claws scratching"

clock or a flapping flame. The fire burned still and smouldering-wise; but it was all the company she had, and she turned again to stare into it.

Soon she began to grow weary of having nothing to do. Then she remembered that the old woman, as she called her, had told her to keep the house tidy.

"The miserable little pig-sty!" she said. "Where's the use of keeping such a hovel clean!"

But in truth she would have been glad of the employment, only just because she had been told to do it, she was unwilling; for there *are* people — however unlikely it may seem — who object to doing a thing for no other reason than that it is required of them.

"I am a princess," she said, "and it is very improper to ask me to do such a thing."

She might have judged it quite as suitable for a princess to sweep away the dust as to sit in the center of a world of dirt. But just because she ought, she wouldn't. Perhaps she feared that if she gave in to doing her duty once, she might have to do it always — which was true enough — for that was the very thing for which she had been specially born.

Unable, however, to feel quite comfortable in the resolve to neglect it, she said to herself, "I'm sure there's time enough for such a nasty job as that!" and sat on, watching the fire as it burned away, the glowing red casting off white flakes, and sinking lower and lower on the hearth.

By and by, merely for want of something to do, she would see what the old woman had left for her in the hole of the wall. But when she put in her hand she found nothing there, except the dust which she ought by this time to have wiped away. Never reflecting that the wise woman had told her she would find food there *when she was hungry,* she flew into one of her furies, calling her a cheat, and a thief, and a liar, and an ugly old witch, and an ogress, and I do not know how many wicked names besides. She raged until she was quite exhausted, and then fell fast asleep on her chair. When she awoke the fire was out.

By this time she was hungry; but without looking in the hole, she began again to storm at the wise woman, in which labour she would no doubt have once more exhausted herself, had not something white caught her eye: it was the corner of a napkin hanging from the hole in the wall. She bounded to it, and there was a dinner for her of something strangely good — one of her favourite dishes, only better than she had ever tasted it before. This might surely have at least changed her mood towards the wise woman; but she only grumbled to herself that it was as it ought to be, ate up the food, and lay down on the bed, never thinking of fire, or dust, or water for the heather.

The wind began to moan about the cottage, and grew louder and louder, till a great gust came down the chimney, and again scattered the white ashes all over the place. But the princess was by this time fast asleep, and never woke till the wind had sunk to silence. One of the consequences, however, of sleeping when one ought to be awake is waking when one ought to be asleep; and the princess awoke in the black midnight, and found enough to keep her awake. For although the wind had fallen, there was a far more terrible howling than that of the wildest wind all about the cottage. Nor was the howling all; the air was full of strange cries; and everywhere she heard the noise of claws scratching against the house, which seemed all doors and windows, so crowded were the sounds, and from so many directions. All the night long she lay half swooning, yet listening to the hideous noises. But with the first glimmer of morning they ceased.

Then she said to herself, "How fortunate it was that I woke! They would have eaten me up if I had been asleep." The miserable little wretch actually talked as if she had kept them out! If she had done her work in the day, she would have slept through the terrors of the darkness, and awaked fearless; whereas now, she had in the storehouse of her heart a whole harvest of agonies, reaped from the dun fields of the night!

They were neither wolves nor hyenas which had caused her such dismay, but creatures of the air, more frightful still, which, as soon as the smoke of the burning fir-wood ceased to spread itself abroad, and the sun was a sufficient distance down the sky, and the lone cold woman was out, came flying and howling about the cottage, trying to get in at every door and window. Down the chimney they would have got, but that at the heart of the fire there always lay a certain fir-cone, which looked like solid gold red-hot, and which, although it might easily get covered up with ashes, so as to be quite invisible, was continually in a glow fit to kindle all the fir-cones in the world; this it was which had kept the horrible birds — some say they have a claw at the tip of every wing-feather — from tearing the poor naughty princess to pieces, and gobbling her up.

When she rose and looked about her, she was dismayed to see what a state the cottage was in. The fire was out, and the windows were all dim with the wings and claws of the dirty birds, while the bed from which she had just risen was brown and withered, and half its purple bells had fallen. But she consoled herself that she could set all to rights in a few minutes — only she must breakfast first. And, sure enough, there was a basin of the delicious bread and milk ready for her in the hole of the wall!

After she had eaten it, she felt comfortable, and sat for a long time building castles in the air — till she was actually hungry again, without having done an atom of work. She ate again, and was idle again, and ate again. Then it grew dark, and she went trembling to bed, for now she remembered the horrors of the last night. This time she never slept at all, but spent the long hours in grievous terror, for the noises were worse than before. She vowed she would not pass another night in such a hateful haunted old shed for all the ugly women, witches, and ogresses in the wide world. In the morning, however, she fell asleep, and slept late.

Breakfast was of course her first thought, after which she could not avoid that of work. It made her very miserable, but she feared the consequences of being found with it undone. A few minutes before noon, she actually got up, took her pinafore for a duster, and proceeded to dust the table. But the wood-ashes flew about so, that it seemed useless to attempt getting rid of them, and she sat down again to think what was to be done. But there is very little indeed to be done when we will not do that which we have to do.

Her first thought now was to run away at once while the sun was high, and get through the forest before night came on. She fancied she could easily go back the way she had come, and get home to her father's

THE WISE WOMAN, OR THE LOST PRINCESS

palace. But not the most experienced traveller in the world can ever go back the way the wise woman has brought him.

She got up and went to the door. It was locked! What could the old woman have meant by telling her not to leave the cottage? She was indignant.

The wise woman had meant to make it difficult, but not impossible. Before the princess, however, could find the way out, she heard a hand at the door, and darted in terror behind it. The wise woman opened it, and, leaving it open, walked straight to the hearth. Rosamond immediately slid out, ran a little way, and then laid herself down in the long heather.

CHAPTER V

The wise woman walked straight up to the hearth, looked at the fire, looked at the bed, glanced round the room, and went up to the table. When she saw the one streak in the thick dust which the princess had left there, a smile, half sad, half pleased, like the sun peeping through a cloud on a rainy day in spring, gleamed over her face. She went at once to the door, and called in a loud voice.

"Rosamond, come to me."

All the wolves and hyenas, fast asleep in the wood, heard her voice, and shivered in their dreams. No wonder then that the princess trembled, and found herself compelled, she could not understand how, to obey the summons. She rose, like the guilty thing she felt, forsook of herself the hiding-place she had chosen, and walked slowly back to the cottage she had left full of the signs of her shame. When she entered, she saw the wise woman on her knees, building up the fire with fir-cones. Already the flame was climbing through the heap in all directions, crackling gently, and sending a sweet aromatic odor through the dusty cottage.

"That is my part of the work," she said, rising. "Now you do yours. But first let me remind you that if you had not put it off, you would have found it not only far easier, but by and by quite pleasant work, much more pleasant than you can imagine now; nor would you have found the time go wearily: you would neither have slept in the day and let the fire out, nor waked at night and heard the howling of the beast-birds. More than all, you would have been glad to see me when I came back; and would have leaped into my arms instead of standing there, looking so ugly and foolish."

As she spoke, suddenly she held up before the princess a tiny mirror, so clear that nobody looking into it could tell what it was made of, or even see it at all — only the thing reflected in it. Rosamond saw a child with dirty fat cheeks, greedy mouth, cowardly eyes — which, not daring to look forward, seemed trying to hide behind an impertinent nose — stooping shoulders, tangled hair, tattered clothes, and smears and stains everywhere. That was what she had made herself. And to tell the truth, she was shocked at the sight, and immediately began, in her dirty heart, to lay the blame on the wise woman, because she had taken her away from her nurses and her fine clothes; while all the time she knew well enough that, close by the heather-bed, was the loveliest little well, just big enough to wash in, the water of which was always springing fresh from the ground and running away through the wall. Beside it lay the whitest of linen towels, with a comb made of mother-of-pearl, and a brush of fir-needles, any one of which she had been far too lazy to use. She dashed the glass out of the wise woman's hand, and there it lay, broken into a thousand pieces!

Without a word, the wise woman stooped, and gathered the fragments — did not leave searching until she had gathered the last atom, and she laid them all carefully, one by one, in the fire, now blazing high on the hearth. Then she stood up and looked at the princess, who had been watching her sulkily.

"Rosamond," she said, with a countenance awful in its sternness, "until you have cleansed this room — "

"She calls it a room!" sneered the princess to herself.

"You shall have no morsel to eat. You may drink of the well, but nothing else you shall have. When the work I set you is done, you will find food in the same place as before. I am going from home again; and again I warn you not to leave the house."

"She calls it a house! — It's a good thing she's going out of it anyhow!" said the princess, turning her back for mere rudeness, for she was one who, even if she liked a thing before, would dislike it the moment any person in authority over her desired her to do it.

When she looked again, the wise woman had vanished.

Thereupon the princess ran at once to the door, and tried to open it; but open it would not. She searched on all sides, but could discover no way of getting out. The windows would not open — at least she could not open them; and the only outlet seemed the chimney, which she was afraid to try because of the fire, which looked angry, she thought, and shot out green flames when she went near it. So she sat down to consider. One may well wonder what room for consideration there was — with all her work lying undone behind her. She sat thus, however, considering, as she called it, until hunger began to sting her, when she jumped up and put her hand as usual in the hole of the wall: there was nothing there. She fell straight into one of her stupid rages; but neither her hunger nor the hole in the wall heeded her rage. Then, in a burst of self-pity, she fell a-weeping, but neither the hunger nor the hole cared for her tears. The darkness began to come on, and her hunger grew and grew, and the terror of the wild noises of the last night invaded her. Then she began to feel cold, and saw that the fire was dying. She darted to the heap of cones, and fed it. It blazed up cheerily, and she was comforted a little. Then she thought with herself it would surely be better to give in so far, and do a little work, than die of hunger. So catching up a duster, she began upon the table. The dust flew about and nearly choked her. She ran to the well to drink, and was refreshed and encouraged. Perceiving now that it was a tedious plan to wipe the dust from the table on to the floor, whence it would have all to be swept up again, she got a wooden platter, wiped the dust into that, carried it to the fire, and threw it in. But all the time she was getting more and more hungry and, although she tried the hole again and again, it was only to become more and more certain that work she must if she would eat.

At length all the furniture was dusted, and she began to sweep the floor, which, happily, she thought of sprinkling with water, as from the window she had seen them do to the marble court of the palace. That swept, she rushed again to the hole — but still no food! She was on the verge of another rage, when the thought came that she might have forgotten something. To her dismay she found that table and chairs and every thing was again covered with dust — not so badly as before, however. Again she set to work, driven by hunger, and drawn by the hope of eating, and yet again, after a second careful wiping, sought the hole. But no! nothing was there for her! What could it mean?

Her asking this question was a sign of progress: it showed that she expected the wise woman to keep her word. Then she bethought her that she had forgotten the household utensils, and the dishes and plates, some of which wanted to be washed as well as dusted.

Faint with hunger, she set to work yet again. One thing made her think of another, until at length she had cleaned every thing she could think of. Now surely she must find some food in the hole!

When this time also there was nothing, she began once more to abuse the wise woman as false and treacherous; — but ah! there was the bed unwatered! That was soon amended. — Still no supper! Ah! there was the hearth unswept, and the fire wanted making up! — Still no supper! What else could there be? She was at her wits' end, and in very weariness, not laziness this time, sat down and gazed into the fire. There, as she gazed, she spied something brilliant, — shining even, in the midst of the fire: it was the little mirror all whole again; but little she knew that the dust which she had thrown into the fire had helped to heal it. She drew it out carefully, and, looking into it, saw, not indeed the ugly creature she had seen there before, but still a very dirty little animal; whereupon she hurried to the well, took off her clothes, plunged into it, and washed herself clean. Then she brushed and combed her hair, made her clothes as tidy as might be, and ran to the hole in the wall: there was a huge basin of bread and milk!

Never had she eaten any thing with half the relish! Alas! however, when she had finished, she did not wash the basin, but left it as it was, revealing how entirely all the rest had been done only from hunger. Then she threw herself on the heather, and was fast asleep in a moment. Never an evil bird came near her all that night, nor had she so much as one troubled dream.

In the morning as she lay awake before getting up, she spied what seemed a door behind the tall eight-day clock that stood silent in the corner.

"Ah!" she thought, "that must be the way out!" and got up instantly. The first thing she did, however, was to go to the hole in the wall. Nothing was there.

"Well, I am hardly used!" she cried aloud. "All that cleaning for the cross old woman yesterday, and this for my trouble, — nothing for breakfast! Not even a crust of bread! Does Mistress Ogress fancy a princess will bear that?"

The poor foolish creature seemed to think that the work of one day ought to serve for the next day too! But that is nowhere the way in the whole universe. How could there be a universe in that case? And even she never dreamed of applying the same rule to her breakfast.

THE WISE WOMAN, OR THE LOST PRINCESS

"Gazed into the fire"

"How good I was all yesterday!" she said, "and how hungry and ill used I am to-day!"

But she would *not* be a slave, and do over again to-day what she had done only last night! *She* didn't care about her breakfast! She might have it no doubt if she dusted all the wretched place again, but she was not going to do that — at least, without seeing first what lay behind the clock!

Off she darted, and putting her hand behind the clock found the latch of a door. It lifted, and the door opened a little way. By squeezing hard, she managed to get behind the clock, and so through the door. But how she stared, when instead of the open heath, she found herself on the marble floor of a large and stately room, lighted only from above. Its walls were strengthened by pilasters, and in every space between was a large picture, from cornice to floor. She did not know what to make of it. Surely she had run all round the cottage, and certainly had seen nothing of this size near it! She forgot that she had also run round what she took for a hay-mow, a peat-stack, and several other things which looked of no consequence in the moonlight.

"So, then," she cried, "the old woman *is* a cheat! I believe she's an ogress, after all, and lives in a palace — though she pretends it's only a cottage, to keep people from suspecting that she eats good little children like me!"

Had the princess been tolerably tractable, she would, by this time, have known a good deal about the wise woman's beautiful house, whereas she had never till now got farther than the porch. Neither was she at all in its innermost places now.

But, king's daughter as she was, she was not a little daunted when, stepping forward from the recess of the door, she saw what a great lordly hall it was. She dared hardly look to the other end, it seemed so far off: so she began to gaze at the things near her, and the pictures first of all, for she had a great liking for pictures. One in particular attracted her attention. She came back to it several times, and at length stood absorbed in it.

A blue summer sky, with white fleecy clouds floating beneath it, hung over a hill green to the very top, and alive with streams darting down its sides toward the valley below. On the face of the hill strayed a flock of sheep feeding, attended by a shepherd and two dogs. A little way apart, a girl stood with bare feet in a brook, building across it a bridge of rough stones. The wind was blowing her hair back from her rosy face. A lamb was feeding close beside her; and a sheepdog was trying to reach her hand to lick it.

"Oh, how I wish I were that little girl!" said the princess aloud. "I wonder how it is that some people are made to be so much happier than others! If I were that little girl, no one would ever call me naughty."

She gazed and gazed at the picture. "It is the real country, with a real hill, and a real little girl upon it. I shall soon see whether this isn't another of the old witch's cheats!"

She went close up to the picture, lifted her foot, and stepped over the frame.

"I am free, I am free!" she exclaimed; and she felt the wind upon her cheek.

The sound of a closing door struck on her ear. She turned — and there was a blank wall, without door or window, behind her. The hill with the sheep was before her, and she set out at once to reach it.

Now, if I am asked how this could be, I can only answer, that it was a result of the interaction of things outside and things inside, of the wise woman's skill, and the silly child's folly. If this does not satisfy my questioner, I can only add, that the wise woman was able to do far more wonderful things than this.

✿   THE WISE WOMAN, OR THE LOST PRINCESS

CHAPTER VI

Meantime the wise woman was busy as she always was; and her business now was with the child of the shepherd and shepherdess, away in the north. Her name was Agnes.

Her father and mother were poor, and could not give her many things. Rosamond would have utterly despised the rude, simple playthings she had. Yet in one respect they were of more value far than hers; the king bought Rosamond's with his money; Agnes's father made hers with his hands.

And while Agnes had but few things — not seeing many things about her, and not even knowing that there were many things anywhere, she did not wish for many things, and was therefore neither covetous nor avaricious.

She played with the toys her father made her, and thought them the most wonderful things in the world — windmills, and little crooks, and water-wheels, and sometimes lambs made all of wool, and dolls made out of the leg-bones of sheep, which her mother dressed for her; and of such playthings she was never tired. Sometimes, however, she preferred playing with stones, which were plentiful, and flowers, which were few, or the brooks that ran down the hill, of which, although they were many, she could only play with one at a time, and that, indeed, troubled her a little — or live lambs that were not all wool, or the sheep-dogs, which were very friendly with her, and the best of playfellows, as she thought, for she had no human ones to compare them with. Neither was she greedy after nice things, but content, as well she might be, with the homely food provided for her. Nor was she by nature particularly self-willed or disobedient; she generally did what her father and mother wished, and believed what they told her. But by degrees they had spoiled her; and this was the way: they were so proud of her that they always repeated every thing she said, and told every thing she did, even when she was present; and so full of admiration of their child were they, that they wondered and laughed at and praised things in her which in another child would never have struck them as the least remarkable, and some things even which would in another have disgusted them altogether. Impertinent and rude things done by *their* child they thought *so* clever! laughing at them as something quite marvellous; her commonplace speeches were said over again as if they had been the finest poetry; and the pretty ways which every moderately good child has were extolled as if the result of her excellent taste, and the choice of her judgment and will. They would even say sometimes that she ought not to hear her own praises for fear it should make her vain, and then whisper them behind their hands, but so loud that she could not fail to hear every word. The consequence was that she soon came to believe — so soon, that she could not recall the time when she did not believe, as the most absolute fact in the universe, that she was *Somebody;* that is, she became most immoderately conceited.

Now as the least atom of conceit is a thing to be ashamed of, you may fancy what she was like with such a quantity of it inside her! At first it did not show itself outside in any very active form; but the wise woman had been to the cottage, and had seen her sitting alone, with such a smile of self-satisfaction upon her face as would have been quite startling to her, if she had ever been startled at any thing; for through that smile she could see lying at the root of it the worm that made it. For some smiles are like the ruddiness of certain apples, which is owing to a centipede, or other creeping thing, coiled up at the heart of them. Only her worm had a face and shape the very image of her own; and she looked so simpering, and mawkish, and self-conscious, and silly, that she made the wise woman feel rather sick.

Not that the child was a fool. Had she been, the wise woman would have only pitied and loved her, instead of feeling sick when she looked at her. She had very fair abilities, and were she once but made humble, would be capable not only of doing a good deal in time, but of beginning at once to grow to no end. But, if she were not made humble, her growing would be to a mass of distorted shapes all huddled together; so that, although the body she now showed might grow up straight and well-shaped and comely to behold, the new body that was growing inside of it, and would come out of it when she died, would be ugly, and crooked this way and that, like an aged hawthorn that has lived hundreds of years exposed upon all sides to salt sea-winds.

As time went on, this disease of self-conceit went on too, gradually devouring the good that was in her. For there is no fault that does not bring it brothers and sisters and cousins to live with it. By degrees, from thinking herself so clever, she came to fancy that whatever seemed to her, must of course be the correct judgment, and whatever she wished, the right thing; and grew so obstinate, that at length her parents feared to thwart her in any thing, knowing well that she would never give in. But there are victories far worse than defeats; and to overcome an angel too gentle to put out all his strength, and ride away in triumph on the back of a devil, is one of the poorest.

So long as she was left to take her own way and do as she would, she gave her parents little trouble. She would play about by herself in the little garden with its few hardy flowers, or amongst the heather where the bees were busy; or she would wander away amongst the hills, and be nobody knew where, sometimes from morning to night; nor did her parents venture to find fault with her.

She never went into rages like the princess, and would have thought Rosamond — oh, so ugly and vile! if she had seen her in one of her passions. But she was no better, for all that, and was quite as ugly in the eyes of the wise woman, who could not only see but read her face. What is there to choose between a face distorted to hideousness by anger, and one distorted to silliness by self-complacency? True, there is more hope of helping the angry child out of her form of selfishness than the conceited child out of hers; but on the other hand, the conceited child was not so terrible or dangerous as the wrathful one. The conceited one, however, was sometimes very angry, and then her anger was more spiteful than the other's; and, again, the wrathful one was often very conceited too. So that, on the whole, of two very unpleasant creatures, I would say that the king's daughter would have been the worse, had not the shepherd's been quite as bad.

But, as I have said, the wise woman had her eye upon her: she saw that something special must be done, else she would be one of those who kneel to their own shadows till feet grow on their knees; then go down on their hands till their hands grow into feet; then lay their faces on the ground till they grow into snouts; when at last they are a hideous sort of lizards, each of which believes himself the best, wisest, and loveliest being in the world, yea, the very centre of the universe. And so they run about forever looking for their own shadows, that they may worship them, and miserable because they cannot find them, being themselves too near the ground to have any shadows; and what becomes of them at last there is but one who knows.

The wise woman, therefore, one day walked up to the door of the shepherd's cottage, dressed like a poor woman, and asked for a drink of water. The shepherd's wife looked at her, liked her, and brought her a cup of milk. The wise woman took it, for she made it a rule to accept every kindness that was offered her.

Agnes was not by nature a greedy girl, as I have said; but self-conceit will go far to generate every other vice under the sun. Vanity, which is a form of self-conceit, has repeatedly shown itself as the deepest feeling in the heart of a horrible murderess.

That morning, at breakfast, her mother had stinted her in milk — just a little — that she might have enough to make some milk-porridge for their dinner. Agnes did not mind it at the time, but when she saw the milk now given to a beggar, as she called the wise woman — though, surely, one might ask a draught of water, and accept a draught of milk, without being a beggar in any such sense as Agnes's contemptuous use of the word implied — a cloud came upon her forehead, and a double vertical wrinkle settled over her nose. The wise woman saw it, for all her business was with Agnes though she little knew it, and, rising, went and offered the cup to the child, where she sat with her knitting in a corner. Agnes looked at it, did not want it, was inclined to refuse it from a beggar, but thinking it would show her consequence to assert her rights, took it and drank it up. For whoever is possessed by a devil, judges with the mind of that devil; and hence Agnes was guilty of such a meanness as many who are themselves capable of something just as bad will consider incredible.

The wise woman waited till she had finished it — then, looking into the empty cup, said:

"You might have given me back as much as you had no claim upon!"

Agnes turned away and made no answer — far less from shame than indignation.

The wise woman looked at the mother.

"You should not have offered it to her if you did not mean her to have it," said the mother, siding with the devil in her child against the wise woman and her child too. Some foolish people think they take another's part when they take the part he takes.

The wise woman said nothing, but fixed her eyes upon her, and soon the mother hid her face in her apron weeping. Then she turned again to Agnes, who had never looked round but sat with her back to both, and suddenly lapped her in the folds of her cloak. When the mother again lifted her eyes, she had vanished.

Never supposing she had carried away her child, but uncomfortable because of what she had said to the poor woman, the mother went to the door, and called after her as she toiled slowly up the hill. But she never turned her head; and the mother went back into her cottage.

The wise woman walked close past the shepherd and his dogs, and through the midst of his flock of sheep. The shepherd wondered where she could be going — right up the hill. There was something strange about her too, he thought; and he followed her with his eyes as she went up and up.

It was near sunset, and as the sun went down, a gray cloud settled on the top of the mountain, which his last rays turned into a rosy gold. Straight into this cloud the shepherd saw the woman hold her pace, and in it she vanished. He little imagined that his child was under her cloak.

He went home as usual in the evening, but Agnes had not come in. They were accustomed to such an absence now and then, and were not at first frightened; but when it grew dark and she did not appear, the husband set out with his dogs in one direction, and the wife in another, to seek their child. Morning came and they had not found her. Then the whole country-side arose to search for the missing Agnes; but day after day and night after night passed, and nothing was discovered of or concerning her, until at length all gave up the search in despair except the mother, although she was nearly convinced now that the poor woman had carried her off.

One day she had wandered some distance from her cottage, thinking she might come upon the remains of her daughter at the foot of some cliff, when she came suddenly, instead, upon a disconsolate-looking creature sitting on a stone by the side of a stream. Her hair hung in tangles from her head; her clothes were tattered, and through the rents her skin showed in many places; her cheeks were white, and worn thin with hunger; the hollows were dark under her eyes, and they stood out scared and wild. When she caught sight of the shepherdess, she jumped to her feet, and would have run away, but fell down in a faint.

At first sight the mother had taken her for her own child, but now she saw, with a pang of disappointment, that she had mistaken. Full of compassion, nevertheless, she said to herself:

"If she is not my Agnes, she is as much in need of help as if she were. If I cannot be good to my own, I will be as good as I can to some other woman's; and though I should scorn to be consoled for the loss of one by the presence of another, I yet may find some gladness in rescuing one child from the death which has taken the other."

Perhaps her words were not just like these, but her thoughts were. She took up the child, and carried her home. And this is how Rosamond came to occupy the place of the little girl whom she had envied in the picture.

"Straight into this cloud the shepherd saw the woman hold her pace"

"She came suddenly upon a disconsolate-looking creature"

CHAPTER VII

Notwithstanding the differences between the two girls, which were, indeed, so many that most people would have said they were not in the least alike, they were the same in this, that each cared more for her own fancies and desires than for any thing else in the world. But I will tell you another difference: the princess was like several children in one — such was the variety of her moods; and in one mood she had no recollection or care about any thing whatever belonging to a previous mood — not even if it had left her but a moment before, and had been so violent as to make her ready to put her hand in the fire to get what she wanted. Plainly she was the mere puppet of her moods, and more than that, any cunning nurse who knew her well enough could call or send away those moods almost as she pleased, like a showman pulling strings behind a show. Agnes, on the contrary, seldom changed her mood, but kept that of calm assured self-satisfaction. Father nor mother had ever by wise punishment helped her to gain a victory over herself, and do what she did not like or choose; and their folly in reasoning with one unreasonable had fixed her in her conceit. She would actually nod her head to herself in complacent pride that she had stood out against them. This, however, was not so difficult as to justify even the pride of having conquered, seeing she loved them so little, and paid so little attention to the arguments and persuasions they used. Neither, when she found herself wrapped in the dark folds of the wise woman's cloak, did she behave in the least like the princess, for she was not afraid. "She'll soon set me down," she said, too self-important to suppose that any one would dare do her an injury.

Whether it be a good thing or a bad not to be afraid depends on what the fearlessness is founded upon. Some have no fear, because they have no knowledge of the danger: there is nothing fine in that. Some are too stupid to be afraid: there is nothing fine in that. Some who are not easily frightened would yet turn their backs and run, the moment they were frightened: such never had more courage than fear. But the man who will do his work in spite of his fear is a man of true courage. The fearlessness of Agnes was only ignorance: she did not know what it was to be hurt: she had never read a single story of giant, or ogress, or wolf; and her mother had never carried out one of her threats of punishment. If the wise woman had but pinched her, she would have shown herself an abject little coward, trembling with fear at every change of motion so long as she carried her.

Nothing such, however, was in the wise woman's plan for the curing of her. On and on she carried her without a word. She knew that if she set her down she would never run after her like the princess, at least not before the evil thing was already upon her. On and on she went, never halting, never letting the light look in, or Agnes look out. She walked very fast, and got home to her cottage very soon after the princess had gone from it.

But she did not set Agnes down either in the cottage or in the great hall. She had other places, none of them alike. The place she had chosen for Agnes was a strange one — such a one as is to be found nowhere else in the wide world.

It was a great hollow sphere, made of a substance similar to that of the mirror which Rosamond had broken, but differently compounded. That substance no one could see by itself. It had neither door, nor window, nor any opening to break its perfect roundness.

The wise woman carried Agnes into a dark room, there undressed her, took from her hand her knitting-needles, and put her, naked as she was born, into the hollow sphere.

What sort of a place it was she could not tell. She could see nothing but a faint cold bluish light all about her. She could not feel that any thing supported her, and yet she did not sink. She stood for a while, perfectly calm, then sat down. Nothing bad could happen to *her* — she was so important! And, indeed, it was but this: she had cared only for Somebody, and now she was going to have only Somebody. Her own choice was going to be carried a good deal farther for her than she would have knowingly carried it for herself.

After sitting a while, she wished she had something to do, but nothing came. A little longer, and it grew wearisome. She would see whether she could not walk out of the strange luminous dusk that surrounded her.

Walk she found she could, well enough, but walk out she could not. On and on she went, keeping as much in a straight line as she might, but after walking until she was thoroughly tired, she found herself no nearer out of her prison than before. She had not, indeed, advanced a single step; for, in whatever direction she tried to go, the sphere turned round and round, answering her feet accordingly. Like a squirrel in his cage she but kept placing another spot of the cunningly suspended sphere under her feet, and she would have been still only at its lowest point after walking for ages.

At length she cried aloud; but there was no answer. It grew dreary and drearier — in her, that is: outside there was no change. Nothing was overhead, nothing under foot, nothing on either hand, but the same pale, faint, bluish glimmer. She wept at last, then grew very angry, and then sullen; but nobody heeded whether she cried or laughed. It was all the same to the cold unmoving twilight that rounded her. On and on went the dreary hours — or did they go at all? — "no change, no pause, no hope"; — on and on till she *felt* she was forgotten, and then she grew strangely still and fell asleep.

The moment she was asleep, the wise woman came, lifted her out, and laid her in her bosom; fed her with a wonderful milk, which she received without knowing it; nursed her all the night long, and, just ere she woke, laid her back in the blue sphere again.

When first she came to herself, she thought the horrors of the preceding day had been all a dream of the night. But they soon asserted themselves as facts, for here they were! — nothing to see but a cold blue light, and nothing to do but see it. Oh, how slowly the hours went by! She lost all notion of time. If she had been told that she had been there twenty years, she would have believed it — or twenty minutes — it would have been all the same: except for weariness, time was for her no more.

Another night came, and another still, during both of which the wise woman nursed and fed her. But she knew nothing of that, and the same one dreary day seemed ever brooding over her.

All at once, on the third day, she was aware that a naked child was seated beside her. But there was something about the child that made her shudder. She never looked at Agnes, but sat with her chin sunk on her chest, and her eyes staring at her own toes. She was the colour of pale earth, with a pinched nose, and a mere slit in her face for a mouth.

"How ugly she is!" thought Agnes. "What business has she beside me!"

But it was so lonely that she would have been glad to play with a serpent, and put out her hand to touch her. She touched nothing. The child, also, put out her hand — but in the direction away from Agnes. And that was well, for if she had touched Agnes it would have killed her. Then Agnes said, "Who are you?" And the little girl said, "Who are you?" "I am Agnes," said Agnes; and the little girl said, "I am Agnes." Then Agnes thought she was mocking her, and said, "You are ugly"; and the little girl said, "You are ugly."

Then Agnes lost her temper, and put out her hands to seize the little girl; but lo! the little girl was gone, and she found herself tugging at her own hair. She let go; and there was the little girl again! Agnes was furious now, and flew at her to bite her. But she found her teeth in her own arm, and the little girl was gone — only to return again; and each time she came back she was tenfold uglier than before. And now Agnes hated her with her whole heart.

The moment she hated her, it flashed upon her with a sickening disgust that the child was not another, but her Self, her Somebody, and that she was now shut up with her for ever and ever — no more for one moment ever to be alone. In her agony of despair, sleep descended, and she slept.

When she woke, there was the little girl, heedless, ugly, miserable, staring at her own toes. All at once, the creature began to smile, but with

❧   THE WISE WOMAN, OR THE LOST PRINCESS

"A naked child was seated beside her"

such an odious, self•satisfied expression, that Agnes felt ashamed of seeing her. Then she began to pat her own cheeks, to stroke her own body, and examine her finger-ends, nodding her head with satisfaction. Agnes felt that there could not be such another hateful, ape-like creature, and at the same time was perfectly aware she was only doing outside of her what she herself had been doing, as long as she could remember, inside of her.

She turned sick at herself, and would gladly have been put out of existence, but for three days the odious companionship went on. By the third day, Agnes was not merely sick but ashamed of the life she had hitherto led, was despicable in her own eyes, and astonished that she had never seen the truth concerning herself before.

The next morning she woke in the arms of the wise woman; the horror had vanished from her sight, and two heavenly eyes were gazing upon her. She wept and clung to her, and the more she clung, the more tenderly did the great strong arms close around her.

When she had lain thus for a while, the wise woman carried her into her cottage, and washed her in the little well; then dressed her in clean garments, and gave her bread and milk. When she had eaten it, she called her to her, and said very solemnly, —

"Agnes, you must not imagine you are cured. That you are ashamed of yourself now is no sign that the cause for such shame has ceased. In new circumstances, especially after you have done well for a while, you will be in danger of thinking just as much of yourself as before. So beware of yourself. I am going from home, and leave you in charge of the house. Do just as I tell you till my return."

She then gave her the same directions she had formerly given Rosamond — with this difference, that she told her to go into the picture-hall when she pleased, showing her the entrance, against which the clock no longer stood — and went away, closing the door behind her.

CHAPTER VIII

As soon as she was left alone, Agnes set to work tidying and dusting the cottage, made up the fire, watered the bed, and cleaned the inside of the windows: the wise woman herself always kept the outside of them clean. When she had done, she found her dinner — of the same sort she was used to at home, but better — in the hole of the wall. When she had eaten it, she went to look at the pictures.

By this time her old disposition had begun to rouse again. She had been doing her duty, and had in consequence begun again to think herself Somebody. However strange it may well seem, to do one's duty will make any one conceited who only does it sometimes. Those who do it always would as soon think of being conceited of eating their dinner as of doing their duty. What honest boy would pride himself on not picking pockets? A thief who was trying to reform would. To be conceited of doing one's duty is then a sign of how little one does it, and how little one sees what

THE WISE WOMAN, OR THE LOST PRINCESS

a contemptible thing it is not to do it. Could any but a low creature be conceived of not being contemptible? Until our duty becomes to us common as breathing, we are poor creatures.

So Agnes began to stroke herself once more, forgetting her late self-stroking companion, and never reflecting that she was now doing what she had then abhorred. And in this mood she went into the picture-gallery.

The first picture she saw represented a square in a great city, one side of which was occupied by a splendid marble palace, with great flights of broad steps leading up to the door. Between it and the square was a marble-paved court, with gates of brass, at which stood sentries in gorgeous uniforms, and to which was affixed the following proclamation in letters of gold, large enough for Agnes to read; —

> *"By the will of the King, from this time until further notice, every stray child found in the realm shall be brought without a moment's delay to the palace. Whoever shall be found having done otherwise shall straightway lose his head by the hand of the public executioner."*

Agnes's heart beat loud, and her face flushed.

"Can there be such a city in the world?" she said to herself. "If I only knew where it was, I should set out for it at once. *There* would be the place for a clever girl like me!"

Her eyes fell on the picture which had so enticed Rosamond. It was the very country where her father fed his flocks. Just round the shoulder of the hill was the cottage where her parents lived, where she was born and whence she had been carried by the beggar-woman.

"Ah!" she said, "they didn't know me there. They little thought what I could be, if I had the chance. If I were but in this good, kind, loving, generous king's palace, I should soon be such a great lady as they never saw! Then they would understand what a good little girl I had always been! And I shouldn't forget my poor parents like some I have read of. *I* would be generous. *I* should never be selfish and proud like girls in story-books!"

As she said this, she turned her back with disdain upon the picture of her home, and setting herself before the picture of the palace, stared at it with wide ambitious eyes, and a heart whose every beat was a throb of arrogant self-esteem.

The shepherd-child was now worse than ever the poor princess had

"The proclamation was in letters of gold large enough for Agnes to read"

been. For the wise woman had given her a terrible lesson, one of which the princess was not capable, and she had known what it meant; yet here she was as bad as ever, therefore worse than before. The ugly creature whose presence had made her so miserable had indeed crept out of sight and mind too — but where was she? Nestling in her very heart, where

THE WISE WOMAN, OR THE LOST PRINCESS

most of all she had her company and least of all could see her. The wise woman had called her out, that Agnes might see what sort of creature she was herself; but now she was snug in her soul's bed again, and she did not even suspect she was there.

After gazing a while at the palace picture, during which her ambitious pride rose and rose, she turned yet again in condescending mood, and honored the home picture with one stare more.

"What a poor, miserable spot it is compared with this lordly palace!" she said.

But presently she spied something in it she had not seen before, and drew nearer. It was the form of a little girl, building a bridge of stones over one of the hill-brooks.

"Ah, there I am myself!" she said. "That is just how I used to do. — No," she resumed, "it is not me. That snub-nosed little fright could never be meant for me! It was the frock that made me think so. But it *is* a picture of the place. I declare, I can see the smoke of the cottage rising from behind the hill! What a dull, dirty, insignificant spot it is! And what a life to lead there!"

She turned once more to the city picture. And now a strange thing took place. In proportion as the other, to the eyes of her mind, receded into the background, this, to her present bodily eyes, appeared to come forward and assume reality. At last, after it had been in this way growing upon her for some time, she gave a cry of conviction, and said aloud, —

"I do believe it is real! That frame is only a trick of the woman to make me fancy it a picture lest I should go and make my fortune. She is a witch, the ugly old creature! It would serve her right to tell the king and have her punished for not taking me to the palace — one of his poor lost children he is so fond of! I should like to see her ugly old head cut off. Anyhow I will try my luck without asking her leave. How she has ill used me!"

But at that moment, she heard the voice of the wise woman calling, "Agnes!" and, smoothing her face, she tried to look as good as she could, and walked back into the cottage. There stood the wise woman, looking all round the place, and examining her work. She fixed her eyes upon Agnes in a way that confused her, and made her cast hers down, for she felt as if she were reading her thoughts. The wise woman, however, asked no questions, but began to talk about her work, approving of some of it, which filled her with arrogance, and showing how some of it might have been done better, which filled her with resentment. But the wise woman seemed to take no care of what she might be thinking, and went straight on with her lesson. By the time it was over, the power of reading thoughts would not have been necessary to a knowledge of what was in the mind of Agnes, for it had all come to the surface — that is, up into her face, which is the surface of the mind. Ere it had time to sink down again, the wise woman caught up the little mirror, and held it before her: Agnes saw her Somebody — the very embodiment of miserable conceit and ugly ill-temper. She gave such a scream of horror that the wise woman pitied her, and laying aside the mirror, took her upon her knees, and talked to her most kindly and solemnly; in particular about the necessity of destroying the ugly things that come out of the heart — so ugly that they make the very face over them ugly also.

And what was Agnes doing all the time the wise woman was talking to her? Would you believe it? — instead of thinking how to kill the ugly things in her heart, she was with all her might resolving to be more careful of her face, that is, to keep down the things in her heart so that they should not show in her face, she was resolving to be a hypocrite as well as a self-worshipper. Her heart was wormy, and the worms were eating very fast at it now.

Then the wise woman laid her gently down upon the heather-bed, and she fell fast asleep, and had an awful dream about her Somebody.

When she woke in the morning, instead of getting up to do the work of the house, she lay thinking — to evil purpose. In place of taking her dream as a warning, and thinking over what the wise woman had said the night before, she communed with herself in this fashion: —

"If I stay here longer, I shall be miserable. It is nothing better than slavery. The old witch shows me horrible things in the day to set me dreaming horrible things in the night. If I don't run away, that rightful blue prison and the disgusting girl will come back, and I shall go out of my mind. How I do wish I could find the way to the good king's palace! I shall go and look at the picture again — if it be a picture — as soon as I've got my clothes on. The work can wait. It's not my work. It's the old witch's; and she ought to do it herself."

She jumped out of bed, and hurried on her clothes. There was no wise woman to be seen; and she hastened into the hall. There was the picture, with the marble palace, and the proclamation shining in letters of gold upon its gates of brass. She stood before it, and gazed and gazed;

and all the time it kept growing upon her in some strange way, until at last she was fully persuaded that it was no picture, but a real city, square, and marble palace, seen through a framed opening in the wall. She ran up to the frame, stepped over it, felt the wind blow upon her cheek, heard the sound of a closing door behind her, and was free. *Free* was she, with that creature inside her?

The same moment a terrible storm of thunder and lightning, wind and rain, came on. The uproar was appalling. Agnes threw herself upon the ground, hid her face in her hands, and there lay until it was over. As soon as she felt the sun shining on her, she rose. There was the city far away on the horizon. Without once turning to take a farewell look of the place she was leaving, she set off, as fast as her feet would carry her, in the direction of the city. So eager was she, that again and again she fell, but only to get up, and run on faster than before.

CHAPTER IX

The shepherdess carried Rosamond home, gave her a warm bath in the tub in which she washed her linen, made her some bread-and-milk, and after she had eaten it, put her to bed in Agnes's crib, where she slept all the rest of that day and all the following night.

When at last she opened her eyes, it was to see around her a far poorer cottage than the one she had left — very bare and uncomfortable indeed, she might well have thought; but she had come through such troubles of late, in the way of hunger and weariness and cold and fear, that she was not altogether in her ordinary mood of fault-finding, and so was able to lie enjoying the thought that at length she was safe, and going to be fed and kept warm. The idea of doing any thing in return for shelter and food and clothes, did not, however, even cross her mind.

But the shepherdess was one of that plentiful number who can be wiser concerning other women's children than concerning their own. Such will often give you very tolerable hints as to how you ought to manage your children, and will find fault neatly enough with the system you are trying to carry out; but all their wisdom goes off in talking, and there is none left for doing what they have themselves said. There is one road talk

"Agnes threw herself upon the ground"

never finds, and that is the way into the talker's own hands and feet. And such never seem to know themselves — not even when they are reading about themselves in print. Still, not being specially blinded in any direction but their own, they can sometimes even act with a little sense towards children who are not theirs. They are affected with a sort of blindness like that which renders some people incapable of seeing, except sideways.

She came up to the bed, looked at the princess, and saw that she was better. But she did not like her much. There was no mark of a princess about her, and never had been since she began to run alone. True, hunger had brought down her fat cheeks, but it had not turned down her impudent nose, or driven the sullenness and greed from her mouth. Nothing but the wise woman could do that — and not even she, without the aid of the princess herself. So the shepherdess thought what a poor substitute she had got for her own lovely Agnes — who was in fact equally repulsive, only in a way to which she had got used; for the selfishness in her love had blinded her to the thin pinched nose and the mean, self-satisfied mouth. It was well for the princess, though, sad as it is to say, that the shepherdess did not take to her, for then she would most likely have only done her harm instead of good.

"Now, my girl," she said, "you must get up, and do something. We can't keep idle folk here."

"I'm not a folk," said Rosamond; "I'm a princess."

"A pretty princess — with a nose like that! And all in rags too! If you tell such stories, I shall soon let you know what I think of you."

Rosamond then understood that the mere calling herself a princess, without having any thing to show for it, was of no use. She obeyed and rose, for she was hungry; but she had to sweep the floor ere she had any thing to eat.

The shepherd came in to breakfast, and was kinder than his wife. He took her up in his arms and would have kissed her; but she took it as an insult from a man whose hands smelt of tar, and kicked and screamed with rage. The poor man, finding he had made a mistake, set her down at once. But to look at the two, one might well have judged it condescension rather than rudeness in such a man to kiss such a child. He was tall, and almost stately, with a thoughtful forehead, bright eyes, eagle nose, and gentle mouth; while the princess was such as I have described her.

Not content with being set down and let alone, she continued to storm and scold at the shepherd, crying she was a princess, and would like to know what right he had to touch her! But he only looked down upon her from the height of his tall person with a benignant smile, regarding her as a spoiled little ape whose mother had flattered her by calling her a princess.

"Turn her out of doors, the ungrateful hussy!" cried his wife. "With your bread and your milk inside her ugly body, this is what she gives you for it! Troth, I'm paid for carrying home such an ill-bred tramp in my arms! My own poor angel Agnes! As if that ill-tempered toad were one hair like her!"

These words drove the princess beside herself; for those who are most given to abuse can least endure it. With fists and feet and teeth, as was her wont, she rushed at the shepherdess, whose hand was already raised to deal her a sound box on the ear, when a better appointed minister of vengeance suddenly showed himself. Bounding in at the cottage-door came one of the sheep-dogs, who was called Prince, and whom I shall not refer to with a *which,* because he was a very superior animal indeed, even for a sheep-dog, which is the most intelligent of dogs: he flew at the princess, knocked her down, and commenced shaking her so violently as to tear her miserable clothes to pieces. Used, however, to mouthing little lambs, he took care not to hurt her much, though for her good he left her a blue nip or two by way of letting her imagine what biting might be. His master, knowing he would not injure her, thought it better not to call him off, and in half a minute he left her of his own accord, and, casting a glance of indignant rebuke behind him as he went, walked slowly to the hearth, where he laid himself down with his tail toward her. She rose, terrified almost to death, and would have crept again into Agnes's crib for refuge; but the shepherdess cried —

"Come, come, princess! I'll have no skulking to bed in the good daylight. Go and clean your master's Sunday boots there."

"I will not!" screamed the princess, and ran from the house.

"Prince!" cried the shepherdess, and up jumped the dog, and looked in her face, wagging his bushy tail.

"Fetch her back," she said, pointing to the door.

With two or three bounds Prince caught the princess, again threw her down, and taking her by her clothes dragged her back into the cottage, and dropped her at his mistress' feet, where she lay like a bundle of rags.

"Get up," said the shepherdess.

Rosamond got up as pale as death.

"Go and clean the boots."

"I don't know how."

"Go and try. There are the brushes, and yonder is the blacking-pot."

Instructing her how to black boots, it came into the thought of the shepherdess what a fine thing it would be if she could teach this miserable little wretch, so forsaken and ill-bred, to be a good, well-behaved, respectable child. She was hardly the woman to do it, but every thing well meant is a help, and she had the wisdom to beg her husband to place Prince under her orders for a while, and not take him to the hill as usual, that he might help her in getting the princess into order.

When the husband was gone, and his boots, with the aid of her own finishing touches, at last quite respectably brushed, the shepherdess told the princess that she might go and play for a while, only she must not go out of sight of the cottage-door.

The princess went right gladly, with the firm intention, however, of getting out of sight by slow degrees, and then at once taking to her heels. But no sooner was she over the threshold than the shepherdess said to the dog, "Watch her"; and out shot Prince.

The moment she saw him, Rosamond threw herself on her face, trembling from head to foot. But the dog had no quarrel with her, and of the violence against which he always felt bound to protest in dog fashion, there was no sign in the prostrate shape before him; so he poked his nose under her, turned her over, and began licking her face and hands. When she saw that he meant to be friendly, her love for animals, which had had no indulgence for a long time now, came wide awake, and in a little while they were romping and rushing about, the best friends in the world.

Having thus seen one enemy, as she thought, changed to a friend, she began to resume her former plan, and crept cunningly farther and farther. At length she came to a little hollow, and instantly rolled down into it. Finding then that she was out of sight of the cottage, she ran off at full speed.

But she had not gone more than a dozen paces, when she heard a growling rush behind her, and the next instant was on the ground, with the dog standing over her, showing his teeth, and flaming at her with his eyes. She threw her arms round his neck, and immediately he licked her face, and let her get up. But the moment she would have moved a step farther from the cottage, there he was in front of her, growling, and showing his teeth. She saw it was of no use, and went back with him.

Thus was the princess provided with a dog for a private tutor — just the right sort for her.

Presently the shepherdess appeared at the door and called her. She would have disregarded the summons, but Prince did his best to let her know that, until she could obey herself, she must obey him. So she went into the cottage, and there the shepherdess ordered her to peel the potatoes for dinner. She sulked and refused. Here Prince could do nothing to help his mistress, but she had not to go far to find another ally.

"Very well, Miss Princess!" she said, "we shall soon see how you like to go without when dinner-time comes."

Now the princess had very little foresight, and the idea of future hunger would have moved her little; but happily, from her game of romps with Prince, she had begun to be hungry already, and so the threat had force. She took the knife and began to peel the potatoes.

By slow degrees the princess improved a little. A few more outbreaks of passion, and a few more savage attacks from Prince, and she had learned to try to restrain herself when she felt the passion coming on; while a few dinnerless afternoons entirely opened her eyes to the necessity of working in order to eat. Prince was her first, and Hunger her second dog-counsellor.

But a still better thing was that she soon grew very fond of Prince. Towards the gaining of her affections, he had three advantages: first, his nature was inferior to hers; next, he was a beast; and last, she was afraid

"The dog standing over her"

of him; for so spoiled was she that she could more easily love what was below than what was above her, and a beast, than one of her own kind, and indeed could hardly have ever come to love any thing much that she had not first learned to fear, and the white teeth and flaming eyes of the angry Prince were more terrible to her than any thing had yet been, except those of the wolf, which she had now forgotten. Then again, he was such a delightful playfellow, that so long as she neither lost her temper, nor went against orders, she might do almost any thing she pleased with him. In fact, such was his influence upon her, that she who had scoffed at the wisest woman in the whole world, and derided the wishes of her own father and mother, came at length to regard this dog as a superior being, and to look up to him as well as love him. And this was best of all.

The improvement upon her, in the course of a month, was plain. She had quite ceased to go into passions, and had actually begun to take a little interest in her work and try to do it well.

Still, the change was mostly an outside one. I do not mean that she was pretending. Indeed she had never been given to pretense of any sort. But the change was not in *her,* only in her mood. A second change of circumstances would have soon brought a second change of behaviour;

❧   THE WISE WOMAN, OR THE LOST PRINCESS

and, so long as that was possible, she continued the same sort of person she had always been. But if she had not gained much, a trifle had been gained for her: a little quietness and order of mind, and hence a somewhat greater possibility of the first idea of right arising in it, whereupon she would begin to see what a wretched creature she was, and must continue until she herself was right.

Meantime the wise woman had been watching her when she least fancied it, and taking note of the change that was passing upon her. Out of the large eyes of a gentle sheep she had been watching her — a sheep that puzzled the shepherd; for every now and then she would appear in his flock, and he would catch sight of her two or three times in a day, sometimes for days together, yet he never saw her when he looked for her, and never when he counted the flock into the fold at night. He knew she was not one of his; but where could she come from, and where could she go to? For there was no other flock within many miles, and he never could get near enough to her to see whether or not she was marked. Nor was Prince of the least use to him for the unravelling of the mystery; for although, as often as he told him to fetch the strange sheep, he went bounding to her at once, it was only to lie down at her feet.

At length, however, the wise woman had made up her mind, and after that the strange sheep no longer troubled the shepherd.

As Rosamond improved, the shepherdess grew kinder. She gave her all Agnes's clothes, and began to treat her much more like a daughter. Hence she had a great deal of liberty after the little work required of her was over, and would often spend hours at a time with the shepherd, watching the sheep and the dogs, and learning a little from seeing how Prince, and the others as well, managed their charge — how they never touched the sheep that did as they were told and turned when they were bid, but jumped on a disobedient flock, and ran along their backs, biting, and barking, and half choking themselves with mouthfuls of their wool.

Then also she would play with the brooks and learn their songs, and build bridges over them. And sometimes she would be seized with such delight of heart that she would spread out her arms to the wind, and go rushing up the hill till her breath left her, when she would tumble down in the heather, and lie there till it came back again.

A noticeable change had by this time passed also on her countenance. Her coarse, shapeless mouth had begun to show a glimmer of lines and curves about it, and the fat had not returned with the roses to her cheeks, so that her eyes looked larger than before; while, more noteworthy still, the bridge of her nose had grown higher, so that it was less of the impudent, insignificant thing inherited from a certain great-great-great-grandmother, who had little else to leave her. For a long time, it had fitted her very well, for it was just like her; but now there was ground for alteration, and already the granny who gave it her would not have recognized it. It was growing a little like Prince's; and Prince's was a long, perceptive, sagacious nose, — one that was seldom mistaken.

One day about noon, while the sheep were mostly lying down, and the shepherd, having left them to the care of the dogs, was himself stretched under the shade of a rock a little way apart, and the princess sat knitting, with Prince at her feet, lying in wait for a snap at a great fly, for even he had his follies — Rosamond saw a poor woman come toiling up the hill, but took little notice of her until she was passing, a few yards off, when she heard her utter the dog's name in a low voice.

Immediately on the summons, Prince started up and followed her — with hanging head, but gently-wagging tail. At first the princess thought he was merely taking observations, and consulting with his nose whether she was respectable or not, but she soon saw that he was following her in meek submission. Then she sprung to her feet and cried, "Prince, Prince!" But Prince only turned his head and gave her an odd look, as if he were trying to smile, and could not. Then the princess grew angry, and ran after him, shouting, "Prince, come here directly." Again Prince turned his head, but this time to growl and show his teeth.

The princess flew into one of her forgotten rages, and picking up a stone, flung it at the woman. Prince turned and darted at her, with fury in his eyes, and his white teeth gleaming. At the awful sight the princess turned also, and would have fled, but he was upon her in a moment, and threw her to the ground, and there she lay.

It was evening when she came to herself. A cool twilight wind, that somehow seemed to come all the way from the stars, was blowing upon her. The poor woman and Prince, the shepherd and his sheep, were all gone, and she was left alone with the wind upon the heather.

She felt sad, weak, and, perhaps, for the first time in her life, a little ashamed. The violence of which she had been guilty had vanished from her spirit, and now lay in her memory with the calm morning behind it, while in front the quiet dusky night was now closing in the loud shame betwixt a double peace. Between the two her passion looked ugly. It pained her to remember. She felt it was hateful, and *hers*.

But, alas, Prince was gone! That horrid woman had taken him away! The fury rose again in her heart, and raged — until it came to her mind how her dear Prince would have flown at her throat if he had seen her in such a passion. The memory calmed her, and she rose and went home. There, perhaps, she would find Prince, for surely he could never have been such a silly dog as to go away altogether with a strange woman!

She opened the door and went in. Dogs were asleep all about the cottage, it seemed to her, but nowhere was Prince. She crept away to her little bed, and cried herself asleep.

In the morning the shepherd and shepherdess were indeed glad to find she had come home, for they thought she had run away.

"Where is Prince?" she cried, the moment she waked.

"His mistress has taken him," answered the shepherd.

"Was that woman his mistress?"

"I fancy so. He followed her as if he had known her all his life. I am very sorry to lose him, though."

The poor woman had gone close past the rock where the shepherd lay. He saw her coming, and thought of the strange sheep which had been feeding beside him when he lay down. "Who can she be?" he said to himself; but when he noted how Prince followed her, without even looking up at him as he passed, he remembered how Prince had come to him. And this was how: as he lay in bed one fierce winter morning, just about to rise, he heard the voice of a woman call to him through the storm, "Shepherd, I have brought you a dog. Be good to him. I will come again and fetch him away." He dressed as quickly as he could, and went to the door. It was half snowed up, but on the top of the white mound before it stood Prince. And now he had gone as mysteriously as he had come, and he felt sad.

Rosamond was very sorry too, and hence when she saw the looks of the shepherd and shepherdess, she was able to understand them. And she tried for a while to behave better to them because of their sorrow. So the loss of the dog brought them all nearer to each other.

CHAPTER X

After the thunder-storm. Agnes did not meet with a single obstruction or misadventure. Everybody was strangely polite, gave her whatever she desired, and answered her questions, but asked none in return, and looked all the time as if her departure would be a relief. They were afraid, in fact, from her appearance, lest she should tell them that she was lost, when they would be bound, on pain of public execution, to take her to the palace.

But no sooner had she entered the city than she saw it would hardly do to present herself as a lost child at the palace-gates; for how were they to know that she was not an imposter, especially since she really was one, having run away from the wise woman? So she wandered about looking at every thing until she was tired, and bewildered by the noise and confusion all around her. The wearier she got, the more was she pushed in every direction. Having been used to a whole hill to wander upon, she was very awkward in the crowded streets, and often on the point of being run over by the horses, which seemed to her to be going every way like a frightened flock. She spoke to several persons, but no one stopped to answer her; and at length, her courage giving way, she felt lost indeed, and began to cry. A soldier saw her, and asked what was the matter.

"I've nowhere to go to," she sobbed.

"Where's your mother?" asked the soldier.

"I don't know," answered Agnes. "I was carried off by an old woman, who then went away and left me. I don't know where she is, or where I am myself."

"Come," said the soldier, "this is a case for his Majesty."

So saying, he took her by the hand, led her to the palace, and begged an audience of the king and queen. The porter glanced at Agnes, immediately admitted them, and showed them into a great splendid room, where the king and queen sat every day to review lost children, in the hope of one day thus finding their Rosamond. But they were by this time beginning to get tired of it. The moment they cast their eyes upon Agnes, the queen threw back her head, threw up her hands, and cried, "What a miserable, conceited, white-faced ape!" and the king turned upon the soldier in wrath, and cried, forgetting his own decree, "What do you mean by bringing such a dirty, vulgar-looking, pert creature into my palace? The dullest soldier in my army could never for a moment imagine a child like *that*, one hair's-breadth like the lovely angel we lost!"

THE WISE WOMAN, OR THE LOST PRINCESS

"*A soldier asked her what was the matter*"

"I humbly beg your Majesty's pardon," said the soldier, "but what was I to do? There stands your Majesty's proclamation in gold letters on the brazen gates of the palace."

"I shall have it taken down," said the king. "Remove the child."

"Please, your Majesty, what am I to do with her?"

"Take her home with you."

"I have six already, sire, and do not want her."

"Then drop her where you picked her up."

"If I do, sire, some one else will find her and bring her back to your Majesties."

"That will never do," said the king. "I cannot bear to look at her."

"For all her ugliness," said the queen, "she is plainly lost, and so is our Rosamond."

"It may be only a pretence, to get into the palace," said the king.

"Take her to the head scullion, soldier," said the queen, "and tell her to make her useful. If she should find out she has been pretending to be lost, she must let me know."

The soldier was so anxious to get rid of her, that he caught her up in his arms, hurried her from the room, found his way to the scullery, and gave her, trembling with fear, in charge to the head maid, with the queen's message.

As it was evident that the queen had no favor for her, the servants did as they pleased with her, and often treated her harshly. Not one amongst them liked her, nor was it any wonder, seeing that, with every step she took from the wise woman's house, she had grown more contemptible, for she had grown more conceited. Every civil answer given her, she attributed to the impression she made, not to the desire to get rid of her; and every kindness, to approbation of her looks and speech, instead of friendliness to a lonely child. Hence by this time she was twice as odious as before; for whoever has had such severe treatment as the wise woman gave her, and is not the better for it, always grows worse than before. They drove her about, boxed her ears on the smallest provocation, laid every thing to her charge, called her all manner of contemptuous names, jeered and scoffed at her awkwardnesses, and made her life so miserable that she was in a fair way to forget every thing she had learned, and know nothing but how to clean saucepans and kettles.

They would not have been so hard upon her, however, but for her irritating behaviour. She dared not refuse to do as she was told, but she obeyed now with a pursed-up mouth, and now with a contemptuous smile. The only thing that sustained her was her constant contriving how to get out of the painful position in which she found herself. There is but one true way, however, of getting out of any position we may be in, and that is, to do the work of it so well that we grow fit for a better: I need not say this was not the plan upon which Agnes was cunning enough to fix.

She had soon learned from the talk around her the reason of the proclamation which had brought her hither.

"Was the lost princess so very beautiful?" she said one day to the youngest of her fellow-servants.

"Beautiful!" screamed the maid; "she was just the ugliest little toad you ever set eyes upon."

"What was she like?" asked Agnes.

"She was about your size, and quite as ugly, only not in the same way; for she had red cheeks, and a cocked little nose, and the biggest, ugliest mouth you ever saw."

Agnes fell a-thinking.

"Is there a picture of her anywhere in the palace?" she asked

"How should I know? You can ask a housemaid."

Agnes soon learned that there was one, and contrived to get a peep of it. Then she was certain of what she had suspected from the description of her, namely, that she was the same she had seen in the picture at the wise woman's house. The conclusion followed, that the lost princess must be staying with her father and mother, for assuredly in the picture she wore one of her frocks.

She went to the head scullion, and with a humble manner, but proud heart, begged her to procure for her the favor of a word with the queen.

"A likely thing indeed!" was the answer, accompanied by a resounding box on the ear.

She tried the head cook next, but with no better success, and so was driven to her meditations again, the result of which was that she began to drop hints that she knew something about the princess. This came at length to the queen's ears, and she sent for her.

Absorbed in her own selfish ambitions, Agnes never thought of the risk to which she was about to expose her parents, but told the queen that in her wanderings she had caught sight of just such a lovely creature as she described the princess, only dressed like a peasant — saying, that, if the king would permit her to go and look for her, she had little doubt of bringing her back safe and sound within a few weeks.

But although she spoke the truth, she had such a look of cunning on her pinched face, that the queen could not possibly trust her, but believed that she made the proposal merely to get away, and have money given her for her journey. Still there was a chance, and she would not say any thing until she had consulted the king.

Then they had Agnes up before the lord chancellor, who, after much questioning of her, arrived at last, he thought, at some notion of the part of the country described by her — that was, if she spoke the truth, which, from her looks and behaviour, he also considered entirely doubtful. Thereupon she was ordered back to the kitchen, and a band of soldiers, under a clever lawyer, sent out to search every foot of the supposed region. They were commanded not to return until they brought with them, bound hand and foot, such a shepherd pair as that of which they received a full description.

And now Agnes was worse off than before. For to her other miseries was added the fear of what would befall her when it was discovered that the persons of whom they were in quest, and whom she was certain they must find, were her own father and mother.

By this time the king and queen were so tired of seeing lost children, genuine or pretended — for they cared for no child any longer than there seemed a chance of its turning out their child — that with this new hope, which, however poor and vague at first, soon began to grow upon such imaginations as they had they commanded the proclamation to be taken down from the palace gates, and directed the various sentries to admit no child whatever, lost or found, be the reason or pretense what it might, until further orders.

"I'm sick of children!" said the king to his secretary, as he finished dictating the direction.

CHAPTER XI

After Prince was gone, the princess, by degrees, fell back into some of her bad old ways, from which only the presence of the dog, not her own betterment, had kept her. She never grew nearly so selfish again, but she

THE WISE WOMAN, OR THE LOST PRINCESS

"Agnes before the lord chancellor"

began to let her angry old self lift up its head once more, until by and by she grew so bad that the shepherdess declared she should not stop in the house a day longer, for she was quite unendurable.

"It is all very well for you, husband," she said, "for you haven't her all day about you, and only see the best of her. But if you had her in work instead of play hours, you would like her no better than I do. And then it's not her ugly passions only, but when she's in one of her tantrums, it's impossible to get any work out of her. At such times she's just as obstinate as — as — as" —

She was going to say "as Agnes," but the feelings of a mother overcame her, and she could not utter the words.

"In fact," she said instead, "she makes my life miserable."

The shepherd felt he had no right to tell his wife she must submit to have her life made miserable, and therefore, although he was really much attached to Rosamond, he would not interfere; and the shepherdess told her she must look out for another place.

The princess was, however, this much better than before, even in respect of her passions, that they were not quite so bad, and after one was over, she was really ashamed of it. But not once, ever since the departure of Prince, had she tried to check the rush of the evil temper when it came upon her. She hated it when she was out of it, and that was something; but while she was in it, she went full swing with it wherever the prince of the power of it pleased to carry her. Nor was this all: although she might by this time have known well enough that as soon as she was out of it she was certain to be ashamed of it, she would yet justify it to herself with twenty different arguments that looked very poor indeed afterwards, if then she had ever remembered them.

She was not sorry to leave the shepherd's cottage, for she felt certain of soon finding her way back to her father and mother; and she would, indeed, have set out long before, but that her foot had somehow got hurt when Prince gave her his last admonition, and she had never since been able for long walks, which she sometimes blamed as the cause of her temper growing worse. But if people are good-tempered only when they are comfortable, what thanks have they? — Her foot was now much better; and as soon as the shepherdess had thus spoken, she resolved to set out at once, and work or beg her way home. At the moment she was quite unmindful of what she owed the good people, and, indeed, was as yet incapable of understanding a tenth part of her obligation to them. So she bade them good-by without a tear, and limped her way down the hill, leaving the shepherdess weeping, and the shepherd looking very grave.

When she reached the valley she followed the course of the stream, knowing only that it would lead her away from the hill where the sheep fed, into richer lands where were farms and cattle. Rounding one of the roots of the hill she saw before her a poor woman walking slowly along the road with a burden of heather upon her back, and presently passed her, but had gone only a few paces farther when she heard her calling after her in a kind old voice —

"Your shoe-tie is loose, my child."

But Rosamond was growing tired, for her foot had become painful, and so she was cross, and neither returned answer, nor paid heed to the warning. For when we are cross, all our other faults grow busy, and poke up their ugly heads like maggots, and the princess's old dislike to doing any thing that came to her with the least air of advice about it returned in full force.

"My child," said the woman again, "if you don't fasten your shoe-tie, it will make you fall."

⁂ THE WISE WOMAN, OR THE LOST PRINCESS

"Mind your own business," said Rosamond, without even turning her head, and had not gone more than three steps when she fell flat on her face on the path. She tried to get up, but the effort forced from her a scream, for she had sprained the ankle of the foot that was already lame.

The old woman was by her side instantly.

"Where are you hurt, child?" she asked, throwing down her burden and kneeling beside her.

"Go away," screamed Rosamond. "*You* made me fall, you bad woman!"

The woman made no reply, but began to feel her joints, and soon discovered the sprain. Then, in spite of Rosamond's abuse, and the violent pushes and even kicks she gave her, she took the hurt ankle in her hands, and stroked and pressed it, gently kneading it, as it were, with her thumbs, as if coaxing every particle of muscles into its right place. Nor had she done so long before Rosamond lay still. At length she ceased, and said: —

"Now, my child, you may get up."

"I can't get up, and I'm not your child," cried Rosamond. "Go away."

Without another word the woman left her, took up her burden, and continued her journey.

In a little while Rosamond tried to get up, and not only succeeded, but found she could walk, and, indeed, presently discovered that her ankle and foot also were now perfectly well.

"I wasn't much hurt after all," she said to herself, nor sent a single grateful thought after the poor woman, whom she speedily passed once more upon the road without even a greeting.

Late in the afternoon she came to a spot where the path divided into two, and was taking the one she liked the looks of better, when she started at the sound of the poor woman's voice, whom she thought she had left far behind, again calling her. She looked round, and there she was, toiling under her load of heather as before.

"You are taking the wrong turn, child," she cried.

"How can you tell that?" said Rosamond. "You know nothing about where I want to go."

"I know that road will take you where you don't want to go," said the woman.

"I shall know when I get there, then," returned Rosamond, "and no thanks to you."

She set off running. The woman took the other path, and was soon out of sight.

By and by, Rosamond found herself in the midst of a peat-moss — a flat, lonely, dismal, black country. She thought, however, that the road would soon lead her across to the other side of it among the farms, and went on without anxiety. But the stream, which had hitherto been her guide, had now vanished; and when it began to grow dark, Rosamond found that she could no longer distinguish the track. She turned,therefore, but only to find that the same darkness covered it behind as well as before. Still she made the attempt to go back by keeping as direct a line as she could, for the path was straight as an arrow. But she could not see enough even to start her in a line, and she had not gone far before she found herself hemmed in, apparently on every side, by ditches and pools of black, dismal, slimy water. And now it was so dark that she could see nothing more than the gleam of a bit of clear sky now and then in the water. Again and again she stepped knee-deep in black mud, and once tumbled down in the shallow edge of a terrible pool; after which she gave up the attempt to escape the meshes of the watery net, stood still, and began to cry bitterly, despairingly. She saw now that her unreasonable anger had made her foolish as well as rude, and felt that she was justly punished for her wickedness to the poor woman who had been so friendly to her. What would Prince think of her, if he knew? She cast herself on the ground, hungry, and cold, and weary.

Presently, she thought she saw long creatures come heaving out of the black pools. A toad jumped upon her, and she shrieked, and sprang to her feet, and would have run away headlong, when she spied in the distance a faint glimmer. She thought it was a Will-o'-the-wisp. What could he be after? Was he looking for her? She dared not run, lest he should see and pounce upon her. The light came nearer, and grew brighter and larger. Plainly, the little fiend was looking for her — he would torment her. After many twistings and turnings among the pools, it came straight towards her, and she would have shrieked, but that terror made her dumb.

It came nearer and nearer, and lo! it was borne by a dark figure, with a burden on its back: it was the poor woman, and no demon, that was looking for her! She gave a scream of joy, fell down weeping at her feet, and clasped her knees. Then the poor woman threw away her burden, laid down her lantern, took the princess up in her arms, folded her cloak around her, and having taken up her lantern again, carried her slowly and

THE WISE WOMAN, OR THE LOST PRINCESS

"She fell down weeping at her feet"

carefully through the midst of the black pools, winding hither and thither.
All night long she carried her thus, slowly and wearily, until at length the
darkness grew a little thinner, an uncertain hint of light came from the
east, and the poor woman, stopping on the brow of a little hill, opened
her cloak, and set the princess down.

"I can carry you no farther," she said. "Sit there on the grass till the
light comes. I will stand here by you."

Rosamond had been asleep. Now she rubbed her eyes and looked,
but it was too dark to see any thing more than that there was a sky over
her head. Slowly the light grew, until she could see the form of the poor
woman standing in front of her; and as it went on growing, she began to
think she had seen her somewhere before, till all at once she thought of
the wise woman, and saw it must be she. Then she was so ashamed that
she bent down her head, and could look at her no longer. But the poor
woman spoke, and the voice was that of the wise woman, and every word
went deep into the heart of the princess.

"Rosamond," she said, "all this time, ever since I carried you from your father's palace, I have been doing what I could to make you a lovely creature: ask yourself how far I have succeeded."

All her past story, since she found herself first under the wise woman's cloak, arose, and glided past the inner eyes of the princess, and she saw, and in a measure understood, it all. But she sat with her eyes on the ground, and made no sign.

Then said the wise woman: —

"Below there is the forest which surrounds my house. I am going home. If you please to come there to me, I will help you, in a way I could not do now, to be good and lovely. I will wait you there all day, but if you start at once, you may be there long before noon. I shall have your breakfast waiting for you. One thing more: the beasts have not yet all gone home to their holes; but I give you my word, not one will touch you so long as you keep coming nearer to my house."

She ceased. Rosamond sat waiting to hear something more; but nothing came. She looked up; she was alone.

Alone once more! Always being left alone, because she would not yield to what was right! Oh, how safe she had felt under the wise woman's cloak! She had indeed been good to her, and she had in return behaved like one of the hyenas of the awful wood! What a wonderful house it was she lived in! And again all her own story came up into her brain from her repentant heart.

"Why didn't she take me with her?" she said. "I would have gone gladly." And she wept. But her own conscience told her that, in the very middle of her shame and desire to be good, she had returned no answer to the words of the wise woman; she had sat like a tree-stump, and done nothing. She tried to say there was nothing to be done; but she knew at once that she could have told the wise woman she had been very wicked, and asked her to take her with her. Now there was nothing to be done.

"Nothing to be done!" said her conscience. "Cannot you rise, and walk down the hill, and through the wood?"

"But the wild beasts!"

"There it is! You don't believe the wise woman yet! Did she not tell you the beasts would not touch you?"

"But they are so horrid!"

"Yes, they are; but it would be far better to be eaten up alive by them than live on — such a worthless creature as you are. Why, you're not fit to be thought about by any but bad ugly creatures."

This was how herself talked to her.

CHAPTER XII

All at once she jumped to her feet, and ran at full speed down the hill and into the wood. She heard howlings and yellings on all sides of her, but she ran straight on, as near as she could judge. Her spirits rose as she ran. Suddenly she saw before her, in the dusk of the thick wood, a group of some dozen wolves and hyenas, standing all together right in her way, with their green eyes fixed upon her staring. She faltered one step, then bethought her of what the wise woman had promised, and keeping straight on, dashed right into the middle of them. They fled howling, as if she had struck them with fire. She was no more afraid after that, and ere the sun was up she was out of the wood and upon the heath, which no bad thing could step upon and live. With the first peep of the sun above the horizon, she saw the little cottage before her, and ran as fast as she could run towards it. When she came near it, she saw that the door was open, and ran straight into the outstretched arms of the wise woman.

The wise woman kissed her and stroked her hair, set her down by the fire, and gave her a bowl of bread and milk.

When she had eaten it she drew her before her where she sat, and spoke to her thus: —

"Rosamond, if you would be a blessed creature instead of a mere wretch, you must submit to be tried."

"Is that something terrible?" asked the princess, turning white.

"No, my child; but it is something very difficult to come well out of. Nobody who has not been tried knows how difficult it is; but whoever has come well out of it, and those who do not overcome never do come out of it, always looks back with horror, not on what she has come through, but on the very idea of the possibility of having failed, and being still the same miserable creature as before."

"You will tell me what it is before it begins?" said the princess.

"I will not tell you exactly. But I will tell you some things to help

"She dashed right into the middle of them"

you. One great danger is that perhaps you will think you are in it before it has really begun, and say to yourself, 'Oh! this is really nothing to me. It may be a trial to some, but for me I am sure it is not worth mentioning.' And then, before you know, it will be upon you, and you will fail utterly and shamefully."

"I will be very, very careful," said the princess. "Only don't let me be frightened."

"You shall not be frightened, except it be your own doing. You are already a brave girl, and there is no occasion to try you more that way. I saw how you rushed into the middle of the ugly creatures; and as they ran from you, so will all kinds of evil things, as long as you keep them outside of you, and do not open the cottage of your heart to let them in. I will tell you something more about what you will have to go through.

"Nobody can be a real princess — do not imagine you have yet been anything more than a mock one— until she is a princess over herself, that is, until, when she finds herself unwilling to do the thing that is right, she makes herself do it. So long as any mood she is in makes her do the thing she will be sorry for when that mood is over, she is a slave, and no princess. A princess is able to do what is right even should she unhappily be in a mood that would make another unable to do it. For instance, if you should be cross and angry, you are not a whit the less bound to be just, yes, kind even — a thing most difficult in such a mood — though ease itself in a good mood, loving and sweet. Whoever does what she is bound to do, be she the dirtiest little girl in the street, is a princess, worshipful, honorable. Nay, more; her might goes farther than she could send it, for if she act so, the evil mood will wither and die, and leave her loving and clean. — Do you understand me, dear Rosamond?"

As she spoke, the wise woman laid her hand on her head and looked — oh, so lovingly! — into her eyes.

"I am not sure," said the princess, humbly.

"Perhaps you will understand me better if I say it just comes to this, that you must *not do* what is wrong, however much you are inclined to do it, and you must *do* what is right, however much you are disinclined to do it."

"I understand that," said the princess.

"I am going, then, to put you in one of the mood-chambers of which I have many in the house. Its mood will come upon you, and you will have to deal with it."

She rose and took her by the hand. The princess trembled a little, but never thought of resisting.

The wise woman led her into the great hall with the pictures, and through a door at the farther end, opening upon another large hall, which was circular, and had doors close to each other all round it. Of these she opened one, pushed the princess gently in, and closed it behind her.

The princess found herself in her old nursery. Her little white rabbit came to meet her in a lumping canter as if his back were going to tumble over his head. Her nurse, in her rocking-chair by the chimney corner, sat just as she had used. The fire burned brightly, and on the table were many of her wonderful toys, on which, however, she now looked with some contempt. Her nurse did not seem at all surprised to see her, any more than if the princess had but just gone from the room and returned again.

"Oh! how different I am from what I used to be!" thought the princess to herself, looking from her toys to her nurse. "The wise woman has done me so much good already! I will go and see mamma at once, and tell her I am very glad to be at home again, and very sorry I was so naughty."

She went towards the door.

"Your queen-mamma, princess, cannot see you now," said her nurse.

"I have yet to learn that it is my part to take orders from a servant," said the princess with temper and dignity.

"I beg your pardon, princess," returned her nurse, politely; "but it is my duty to tell you that your queen-mamma is at this moment engaged. She is alone with her most intimate friend, the Princess of the Frozen Regions."

"I shall see for myself," returned the princess, bridling, and walked to the door.

Now little bunny, leap-frogging near the door, happened that moment to get about her feet, just as she was going to open it, so that she tripped and fell against it, striking her forehead a good blow. She caught up the rabbit in a rage, and, crying, "It is all your fault, you ugly old wretch!" threw it with violence in her nurse's face.

Her nurse caught the rabbit, and held it to her face, as if seeking to soothe its fright. But the rabbit looked very limp and odd, and, to her amazement, Rosamond presently saw that the thing was no rabbit, but a pocket-handkerchief. The next moment she removed it from her face, and Rosamond beheld — not her nurse, but the wise woman — standing on her own hearth, while she herself stood by the door leading from the cottage into the hall.

"First trial a failure," said the wise woman quietly.

Overcome with shame, Rosamond ran to her, fell down on her knees, and hid her face in her dress.

"Need I say any thing?" said the wise woman, stroking her hair.

"No, no," cried the princess. "I am horrid."

"You know now the kind of thing you have to meet: are you ready to try again?"

"*May* I try again?" cried the princess, jumping up. "I'm ready. I do not think I shall fail this time."

"The trial will be harder."

Rosamond drew in her breath, and set her teeth. The wise woman looked at her pitifully, but took her by the hand, led her to the round hall, opened the same door, and closed it after her.

The princess expected to find herself again in the nursery, but in the wise woman's house no one ever has the same trial twice. She was in a beautiful garden, full of blossoming trees and the loveliest roses and lilies.

❧ THE WISE WOMAN, OR THE LOST PRINCESS

A lake was in the middle of it, with a tiny boat. So delightful was it that Rosamond forgot all about how or why she had come there, and lost herself in the joy of the flowers and the trees and the water. Presently came the shout of a child, merry and glad, and from a clump of tulip trees rushed a lovely little boy, with his arms stretched out to her. She was charmed at the sight, ran to meet him, caught him up in her arms, kissed him, and could hardly let him go again. But the moment she set him down he ran from her towards the lake, looking back as he ran, and crying "Come, come."

She followed. He made straight for the boat, clambered into it, and held out his hand to help her in. Then he caught up the little boat-hook, and pushed away from the shore: there was a great white flower floating a few yards off, and that was the little fellow's goal. But, alas! no sooner had Rosamond caught sight of it, huge and glowing as a harvest moon, than she felt a great desire to have it herself. The boy, however, was in the bows of the boat, and caught it first. It had a long stem, reaching down to the bottom of the water, and for a moment he tugged at it in vain, but at last it gave way so suddenly, that he tumbled back with the flower into the bottom of the boat. Then Rosamond, almost wild at the danger it was in as he struggled to rise, hurried to save it, but somehow between them it came in pieces, and all its petals of fretted silver were scattered about the boat. When the boy got up, and saw the ruin his companion had occasioned, he burst into tears, and having the long stalk of the flower still in his hand, struck her with it across the face. It did not hurt her much, for he was a very little fellow, but it was wet and slimy. She tumbled rather than rushed at him, seized him in her arms, tore him from his frightened grasp, and flung him into the water. His head struck on the boat as he fell, and he sank at once to the bottom, where he lay looking up at her with white face and open eyes.

The moment she saw the consequences of her deed she was filled with horrible dismay. She tried hard to reach down to him through the water, but it was far deeper than it looked, and she could not. Neither could she get her eyes to leave the white face: its eyes fascinated and fixed hers; and there she lay leaning over the boat and staring at the death she had made. But a voice crying, "Ally! Ally!" shot to her heart, and springing to her feet she saw a lovely lady come running down the grass to the brink of the water with her hair flying about her head.

"Where is my Ally?" she shrieked.

But Rosamond could not answer, and only stared at the lady, as she had before stared at her drowned boy.

Then the lady caught sight of the dead thing at the bottom of the water, and rushed in, and, plunging down, struggled and groped until she reached it. Then she rose and stood up with the dead body of her little son in her arms, his head hanging back, and the water streaming from him.

"See what you have made of him, Rosamond!" she said, holding the body out to her; "and this is your second trial, and also a failure."

The dead child melted away from her arms, and there she stood, the wise woman, on her own hearth, while Rosamond found herself beside the little well on the floor of the cottage, with one arm wet up to the shoulder. She threw herself on the heather-bed and wept from relief and vexation both.

The wise woman walked out of the cottage, shut the door, and left her alone. Rosamond was sobbing, so that she did not hear her go. When at length she looked up, and saw that the wise woman was gone, her misery returned afresh and tenfold, and she wept and wailed. The hours passed, the shadows of evening began to fall, and the wise woman entered.

CHAPTER XIII

She went straight to the bed, and taking Rosamond in her arms, sat down with her by the fire.

"My poor child!" she said. "Two terrible failures! And the more the harder! They get stronger and stronger. What is to be done?"

"Couldn't you help me?" said Rosamond piteously.

"Perhaps I could, now you ask me," answered the wise woman. "When you are ready to try again, we shall see."

"I am very tired of myself," said the princess. "But I can't rest till I try again."

"That is the only way to get rid of your weary, shadowy self, and find your strong, true self. Come, my child; I will help you all I can, for now I *can* help you."

Yet again she led her to the same door, and seemed to the princess

❧   THE WISE WOMAN, OR THE LOST PRINCESS

"See what you have made of him, Rosamond"

to send her yet again alone into the room. She was in a forest, a place half wild, half tended. The trees were grand, and full of the loveliest birds, of all glowing, gleaming and radiant colours, which, unlike the brilliant birds we know in our world, sang deliciously, every one according to his colour. The trees were not at all crowded, but their leaves were so thick, and their boughs spread so far, that it was only here and there a sunbeam could get straight through. All the gentle creatures of a forest were there, but no creatures that killed, not even a weasel to kill the rabbits, or a beetle to eat the snails out of their striped shells. As to the butterflies, words would but wrong them if they tried to tell how gorgeous they were. The princess's delight was so great that she neither laughed nor ran, but walked about with a solemn countenance and stately step.

"But where are the flowers?" she said to herself at length.

They were nowhere. Neither on the high trees, nor on the few shrubs that grew here and there amongst them, were there any blossoms; and in the grass that grew everywhere there was not a single flower to be seen.

"Ah, well!" said Rosamond again to herself; "where all the birds and butterflies are living flowers, we can do without the other sort."

Still she could not help feeling that flowers were wanted to make the beauty of the forest complete.

Suddenly she came out on a little open glade; and there, on the root of a great oak, sat the loveliest little girl, with her lap full of flowers of all colours, but of such kinds as Rosamond had never before seen. She was playing with them — burying her hands in them, tumbling them about, and every now and then picking one from the rest, and throwing it away. All the time she never smiled, except with her eyes, which were as full as they could hold of the laughter of the spirit — a laughter which in this world is never heard, only sets the eyes alight with a liquid shining. Rosamond drew nearer, for the wonderful creature would have drawn a tiger to her side, and tamed him on the way. A few yards from her, she came upon one of her cast-away flowers and stooped to pick it up, as well she might where none grew save in her own longing. But to her amazement she found, instead of a flower thrown away to wither, one fast rooted and quite at home. She left it, and went to another; but it also was fast in the soil, and growing comfortably in the warm grass. What could it mean? One after another she tried, until at length she was satisfied that it was the same with every flower the little girl threw from her lap.

She watched then until she saw her throw one, and instantly bounded to the spot. But the flower had been quicker than she: there it grew, fast fixed in the earth, and, she thought, looked at her roguishly. Something evil moved in her, and she plucked it.

"Don't! don't!" cried the child. "My flowers cannot live in your hands."

Rosamond looked at the flower. It was withered already. She threw

❧   THE WISE WOMAN, OR THE LOST PRINCESS

"With her lap full of flowers"

it from her, offended. The child rose, with difficulty keeping her lapful together, picked it up, carried it back, sat down again, spoke to it, kissed it, sang to it — oh! such a sweet, childish little song! — the princess never could recall a word of it — and threw it away. Up rose its little head, and there it was, busy growing again!

Rosamond's bad temper soon gave way: the beauty and sweetness of the child had overcome it; and anxious to make friends with her, she drew near, and said:

"Won't you give me a little flower, please, you beautiful child?"

"There they are; they are all for you," answered the child, pointing with her outstretched arm and forefinger all round.

THE WISE WOMAN, OR THE LOST PRINCESS

"But you told me, a minute ago, not to touch them."

"Yes, indeed, I did."

"They can't be mine, if I'm not to touch them."

"If, to call them yours, you must kill them, then they are not yours, and never, never can be yours. They are nobody's when they are dead."

"But you don't kill them."

"I don't pull them; I throw them away. I live them."

"How is it that you make them grow?"

"I say, 'You darling!' and throw it away and there it is."

"Where do you get them?"

"In my lap."

"I wish you would let me throw one away."

"Have you got any in your lap? Let me see."

"No; I have none."

"Then you can't throw one away, if you haven't got one."

"You are mocking me!" cried the princess.

"I am not mocking you," said the child, looking her full in the face, with reproach in her large blue eyes.

"Oh, that's where the flowers come from!" said the princess to herself, the moment she saw them, hardly knowing what she meant.

Then the child rose as if hurt, and quickly threw away all the flowers she had in her lap, but one by one, and without any sign of anger. When they were all gone, she stood a moment, and then, in a kind of chanting cry, called, two or three times, "Peggy! Peggy! Peggy!"

A low, glad cry, like the whinny of a horse, answered, and, presently, out of the wood on the opposite side of the glade, came gently trotting the loveliest little snow-white pony, with great shining blue wings, half-lifted from his shoulders. Straight towards the little girl, neither hurrying nor lingering, he trotted with light elastic tread.

Rosamond's love for animals broke into a perfect passion of delight at the vision. She rushed to meet the pony with such haste, that, although clearly the best trained animal under the sun, he started back, plunged, reared, and struck out with his fore-feet ere he had time to observe what sort of a creature it was that had so startled him. When he perceived it was a little girl, he dropped instantly upon all fours, and content with avoiding her, resumed his quiet trot in the direction of his mistress. Rosamond stood gazing after him in miserable disappointment.

When he reached the child, he laid his head on her shoulder, and she put her arm up round his neck; and after she had talked to him a little, he turned and came trotting back to the princess.

Almost beside herself with joy, she began caressing him in the rough way which, notwithstanding her love for them, she was in the habit of using with animals; and she was not gentle enough, in herself even, to see that he did not like it, and was only putting up with it for the sake of his mistress. But when, that she might jump upon his back, she laid hold of one of his wings, and ruffled some of the blue feathers, he wheeled suddenly about, gave his long tail a sharp whisk which threw her flat on the grass, and trotting back to his mistress, bent down his head before her as if asking excuse for ridding himself of the unbearable.

The princess was furious. She had forgotten all her past life up to the time when she first saw the child: her beauty had made her forget, and yet she was now on the very borders of hating her. What she might have done, or rather tried to do, had not Peggy's tail struck her down with such force that for a moment she could not rise, I cannot tell.

But while she lay half-stunned, her eyes fell on a little flower just under them. It stared up in her face like the living thing it was, and she could not take her eyes off its face. It was like a primrose trying to express doubt instead of confidence. It seemed to put her half in mind of something, and she felt as if shame were coming. She put out her hand to pluck it; but the moment her fingers touched it, the flower withered up, and hung as dead on its stalks as if a flame of fire had passed over it.

Then a shudder thrilled through the heart of the princess, and she thought with herself, saying — "What sort of a creature am I that the flowers wither when I touch them, and the ponies despise me with their tails? What a wretched, coarse, ill-bred creature I must be! There is that lovely child giving life instead of death to the flowers, and a moment ago I was hating her! I am made horrid, and I shall be horrid, and I hate myself, and yet I can't help being myself!"

She heard the sound of galloping feet, and there was the pony, with the child seated betwixt his wings, coming straight on at full speed for where she lay.

"I don't care," she said. "They may trample me under their feet if they like. I am tired and sick of myself — a creature at whose touch the flowers wither!"

On came the winged pony. But while yet some distance off, he gave a great bound, spread out his living sails of blue, rose yards and yards above her in the air, and alighted as gently as a bird, just a few feet on the other side of her. The child slipped down and came and kneeled over her.

"Did my pony hurt you?" she said. "I am so sorry!"

"Yes, he hurt me," answered the princess, "but not more than I deserved, for I took liberties with him, and he did not like it."

"Oh, you dear!" said the little girl. "I love you for talking so of my Peggy. He is a good pony, though a little playful sometimes. Would you like a ride upon him?"

"You darling beauty!" cried Rosamond, sobbing. "I do love you so, you are so good. How did you become so sweet?"

"Would you like to ride my pony?" repeated the child, with a heavenly smile in her eyes.

"No, no; he is fit only for you. My clumsy body would hurt him," said Rosamond.

"You don't mind me having such a pony?" said the child.

"What! mind it?" cried Rosamond, almost indignantly. Then remembering certain thoughts that had but a few moments before passed through her mind, she looked on the ground and was silent.

"You don't mind it, then?" repeated the child.

"I am very glad there is such a you and such a pony, and that such a you has got such a pony," said Rosamond, still looking on the ground. "But I do wish the flowers would not die when I touch them. I was cross to see you make them grow, but now I should be content if only I did not make them wither."

As she spoke, she stroked the little girl's bare feet, which were by her, half buried in the soft moss, and as she ended she laid her cheek on them and kissed them.

"Dear princess!" said the little girl, "the flowers will not always wither at your touch. Try now — only do not pluck it. Flowers ought never to be plucked except to give away. Touch it gently."

A silvery flower, something like a snowdrop, grew just within her reach. Timidly she stretched out her hand and touched it. The flower trembled, but neither shrank nor withered.

"Touch it again," said the child.

It changed colour a little, and Rosamond fancied it grew larger.

"Touch it again," said the child.

It opened and grew until it was as large as a narcissus, and changed and deepened in colour till it was a red glowing gold.

Rosamond gazed motionless. When the transfiguration of the flower was perfected, she sprang to her feet with clasped hands, but for very ecstasy of joy stood speechless, gazing at the child.

"Did you never see me before, Rosamond?" she asked.

"No, never," answered the princess. "I never saw any thing half so lovely."

"Look at me," said the child.

And as Rosamond looked, the child began, like the flower, to grow larger. Quickly through every gradation of growth she passed, until she stood before her a woman perfectly beautiful, neither old nor young; for hers was the old age of everlasting youth.

Rosamond was utterly enchanted, and stood gazing without word or movement until she could endure no more delight. Then her mind collapsed to the thought — had the pony grown too? She glanced round. There was no pony, no grass, no flowers, no bright-birded forest — but the cottage of the wise woman — and before her, on the hearth of it, the goddess-child, the only thing unchanged.

She gasped with astonishment.

"You must set out for your father's palace immediately," said the lady.

"But where is the wise woman?" asked Rosamond, looking all about.

"Here," said the lady.

And Rosamond, looking again, saw the wise woman, folded as usual in her long dark cloak.

"And it was you all the time?" she cried in delight, and kneeled before her, burying her face in her garments.

"It always is me, all the time," said the wise woman, smiling.

"But which is the real you?" asked Rosamond; "this or that?"

"Or a thousand others?" returned the wise woman. "But the one you have just seen is the likest to the real me that you are able to see just yet — but — . And that me you could not have seen a little while ago. — But, my darling child," she went on, lifting her up and clasping her to her bosom, "you must not think, because you have seen me once, that therefore you are capable of seeing me at all times. No; there are many things in you yet that must be changed before that can be. Now, however, you will seek me. Every time you feel you want me, that is a sign I am wanting you. There are yet many rooms in my house you may have to go through; but when you need no more of them, then you will be able to throw flowers like the little girl you saw in the forest."

The princess gave a sigh.

"Do not think, "the wise woman went on, "that the things you have seen in my house are mere empty shows. You do not know, you cannot yet think, how living and true they are. — Now you must go."

She led her once more into the great hall, and there showed her the picture of her father's capital, and his palace with the brazen gates.

"There is your home," she said. "Go to it."

The princess understood, and a flush of shame rose to her forehead. She turned to the wise woman and said:

"Will you forgive *all* my naughtiness, and *all* the trouble I have given you?"

"If I had not forgiven you, I would never have taken the trouble to punish you. If I had not loved you, do you think I would have carried you away in my cloak?"

"How could you love such an ugly, ill-tempered, rude, hateful little wretch?"

"I saw, through it all, what you were going to be," said the wise woman, kissing her. "But remember you have yet only *begun* to be what I saw."

"I will try to remember," said the princess, holding her cloak, and looking up in her face.

"Go, then," said the wise woman.

Rosamond turned away on the instant, ran to the picture, stepped over the frame of it, heard a door close gently, gave one glance back, saw behind her the loveliest palace-front of alabaster, gleaming in the pale-yellow light of an early summer-morning, looked again to the eastward, saw the faint outline of her father's city against the sky, and ran off to reach it.

It looked much further off now than when it seemed a picture, but the sun was not yet up, and she had the whole of a summer day before her.

CHAPTER XIV

The soldiers sent out by the king, had no great difficulty in finding Agnes's father and mother, of whom they demanded if they knew any thing of such a young princess as they described. The honest pair told them the truth in every point — that, having lost their own child and found another, they had taken her home, and treated her as their own; that she had indeed called herself a princess, but they had not believed her, because she did not look like one; that, even if they had, they did not know how they could have done differently, seeing they were poor people, who could not afford to keep any idle person about the place; that they had done their best to teach her good ways, and had not parted with her until her bad temper rendered it impossible to put up with her any longer; that, as to the king's proclamation, they heard little of the world's news on their lonely hill, and it had never reached them; that if it had, they did not know how either of them could have gone such a distance from home, and left their sheep or their cottage, one or the other, uncared for.

"You must learn, then, how both of you can go, and your sheep must take care of your cottage," said the lawyer, and commanded the soldiers to bind them hand and foot.

Heedless of their entreaties to be spared such an indignity, the soldiers obeyed, bore them to a cart, and set out for the king's palace, leaving the cottage door open, the fire burning, the pot of potatoes boiling upon it, the sheep scattered over the hill, and the dogs not knowing what to do.

Hardly were they gone, however, before the wise woman walked up, with Prince behind her, peeped into the cottage, locked the door, put the key in her pocket, and then walked away up the hill. In a few minutes there arose a great battle between Prince and the dog which filled his former place — a well-meaning but dull fellow, who could fight better than feed. Prince was not long in showing him that he was meant for his master, and then, by his efforts, and directions to the other dogs, the sheep were soon gathered again, and out of danger from foxes and bad dogs. As soon as this was done, the wise woman left them in charge of Prince, while she went to the next farm to arrange for the folding of the sheep and the feeding of the dogs.

When the soldiers reached the palace, they were ordered to carry their prisoners at once into the presence of the king and queen, in the throne room. Their two thrones stood upon a high dais at one end, and on the floor at the foot of the dais, the soldiers laid their helpless prisoners. The queen commanded that they should be unbound, and ordered them to stand up. They obeyed with the dignity of insulted innocence, and their bearing offended their foolish majesties.

Meantime the princess, after a long day's journey, arrived at the palace, and walked up to the sentry at the gate.

"The wise woman locked the door"

"Stand back," said the sentry.

"I wish to go in, if you please," said the princess gently.

"Ha! ha! ha!" laughed the sentry, for he was one of those dull people who form their judgment from a person's clothes, without even looking in his eyes; and as the princess happened to be in rags, her request was amusing, and the booby thought himself quite clever for laughing at her so thoroughly.

"I am the princess," Rosamond said quietly.

"*What* princess?" bellowed the man.

"The princess Rosamond. Is there another?" she answered and asked.

But the man was so tickled at the wondrous idea of a princess in rags, that he scarcely heard what she said for laughing. As soon as he recovered a little, he proceeded to chuck the princess under the chin, saying —

"You're a pretty girl, my dear, though you ain't no princess."

Rosamond drew back with dignity.

"You have spoken three untruths at once," she said. "I am *not* pretty, and I *am* a princess, and if I were dear to you, as I ought to be, you would not laugh at me because I am badly dressed, but stand aside, and let me go to my father and mother."

The tone of her speech, and the rebuke she gave him, made the man look at her; and looking at her, he began to tremble inside his foolish body, and wonder whether he might not have made a mistake. He raised his hand in salute, and said —

"I beg your pardon, miss, but I have express orders to admit no child whatever within the palace gates. They tell me his majesty the king says he is sick of children."

"He may well be sick of me!" thought the princess; "but it can't mean that he does not want me home again. — I don't think you can very well call me a child," she said, looking the sentry full in the face.

"You ain't very big, miss," answered the soldier, "but so be you say you ain't a child, I'll take the risk. The king can only kill me, and a man must die once."

He opened the gate, stepped aside, and allowed her to pass. Had she lost her temper, as every one but the wise woman would have expected of her, he certainly would not have done so.

She ran into the palace, the door of which had been left open by the porter when he followed the soldiers and prisoners to the throne-room, and bounded up the stairs to look for her father and mother. As she passed the door of the throne-room she heard an unusual noise in it, and running to the king's private entrance, over which hung a heavy curtain, she peeped past the edge of it, and saw, to her amazement, the shepherd and shepherdess standing like culprits before the king and queen, and the same moment heard the king say —

"Peasants, where is the princess Rosamond?"

"Truly, sire, we do not know," answered the shepherd.

"You ought to know," said the king.

"Sire, we could keep her no longer."

"You confess, then," said the king, suppressing the outbreak of the wrath that boiled up in him, "that you turned her out of your house."

For the king had been informed by a swift messenger of all that had passed long before the arrival of the prisoners.

"We did, sire; but not only could we keep her no longer, but we knew not that she was the princess."

"You ought to have known, the moment you cast your eyes upon her," said the king. "Any one who does not know a princess the moment he sees her, ought to have his eyes put out."

"Indeed he ought," said the queen.

To this they returned no answer, for they had none ready.

"Why did you not bring her at once to the palace," pursued the king, "whether you knew her to be a princess or not? My proclamation left nothing to your judgment. It said *every child.*"

"We heard nothing of the proclamation, sire."

"You ought to have heard," said the king. "It is enough that I make proclamations; it is for you to read them. Are they not written in letters of gold upon the brazen gates of this palace?"

"A poor shepherd, your majesty — how often must he leave his flock, and go hundreds of miles to look whether there may not be something in letters of gold upon the brazen gates? We did not know that your majesty had made a proclamation, or even that the princess was lost."

"You ought to have known," said the king.

The shepherd held his peace.

"But," said the queen, taking up the word, "all that is as nothing, when I think how you misused the darling."

The only ground the queen had for saying thus, was what Agnes had told her as to how the princess was dressed; and her condition seemed

❧ THE WISE WOMAN, OR THE LOST PRINCESS

to the queen so miserable, that she had imagined all sorts of oppression and cruelty.

But this was more than the shepherdess, who had not yet spoken, could bear.

"She would have been dead, and *not* buried, long ago, madam, if I had not carried her home in my two arms."

"Why does she say her *two* arms?" said the king to himself. "Has she more than two? Is there treason in that?"

"You dressed her in cast-off clothes," said the queen.

"I dressed her in my own sweet child's Sunday clothes. And this is what I get for it!" cried the shepherdess, bursting into tears.

"And what did you do with the clothes you took off her? Sell them?"

"Put them in the fire, madam. They were not fit for the poorest child in the mountains. They were so ragged that you could see her skin through them in twenty different places."

"You cruel woman, to torture a mother's feelings so!" cried the queen, and in her turn burst into tears.

"And I'm sure," sobbed the shepherdess, "I took every pains to teach her what it was right for her to know. I taught her to tidy the house, and" —

"Tidy the house?" moaned the queen. "My poor wretched offspring!"

"And peel potatoes, and" —

"Peel the potatoes!" cried the queen. "Oh, horror!"

"And black her master's boots," said the shepherdess.

"Black her master's boots!" shrieked the queen. "Oh, my white-handed princess! Oh, my ruined baby!"

"What I want to know," said the king, paying no heed to this maternal duel, but patting the top of his sceptre as if it had been the hilt of a sword which he was about to draw, "is, where the princess is now."

The shepherd made no answer, for he had nothing to say more than he had said already.

"You have murdered her!" shouted the king. "You shall be tortured till you confess the truth; and then you shall be tortured to death, for you are the most abominable wretches in the whole wide world."

"Who accuses me of crime?" cried the shepherd, indignant.

"I accuse you," said the king; "but you shall see, face to face, the chief witness to your villainy. Officer, bring the girl."

Silence filled the hall while they waited. The king's face was swollen with anger. The queen hid hers behind her handkerchief. The shepherd and shepherdess bent their eyes on the ground, wondering. It was with difficulty Rosamond could keep her place, but so wise had she already become that she saw it would be far better to let every thing come out before she interfered.

At length the door opened, and in came the officer, followed by Agnes, looking white as death and mean as sin.

The shepherdess gave a shriek, and darted towards her with arms spread wide; the shepherd followed, but not so eagerly.

"My child! my lost darling! my Agnes!" cried the shepherdess.

"Hold them asunder," shouted the king. "Here is more villainy! What! have I a scullery-maid in my house born of such parents? The parents of such a child must be capable of any thing. Take all three of them to the rack. Stretch them till their joints are torn asunder, and give them no water. Away with them!"

The soldiers approached to lay hands on them. But, behold! a girl all in rags, with such a radiant countenance that it was right lovely to see, darted between, and careless of the royal presence, flung herself upon the shepherdess, crying, —

"Do not touch her. She is my good, kind mistress."

But the shepherdess could hear or see no one but her Agnes, and pushed her away. Then the princess turned, with the tears in her eyes, to the shepherd, and threw her arms about his neck and pulled down his head and kissed him. And the tall shepherd lifted her to his bosom and kept her there, but his eyes were fixed on his Agnes.

"What is the meaning of this?" cried the king, starting up from his throne. "How did that ragged girl get in here? Take her away with the rest. She is one of them, too."

But the princess made the shepherd set her down, and before any one could interfere she had run up the steps of the dais and then the steps of the king's throne like a squirrel, flung herself upon the king, and begun to smother him with kisses.

All stood astonished, except the three peasants, who did not even see what took place. The shepherdess kept calling to her Agnes, but she was so ashamed that she did not dare even lift her eyes to meet her mother's, and the shepherd kept gazing on her in silence. As for the king, he was so breathless and aghast with astonishment, that he was too feeble to fling the ragged child from him, as he tried to do. But she left him, and running down the steps of the one throne and up those of the other, began kissing the queen next. But the queen cried out, —

"Get away, you great rude child! — Will nobody take her to the rack?"

Then the princess, hardly knowing what she did for joy that she had come in time, ran down the steps of the throne and the dais, and placing herself between the shepherd and shepherdess, took a hand of each, and stood looking at the king and queen.

Their faces began to change. At last they began to know her. But she was so altered — so lovelily altered, that it was no wonder they should not have known her at the first glance; but it was the fault of the pride and anger and injustice with which their hearts were filled, that they did not know her at the second.

The king gazed and the queen gazed, both half risen from their thrones, and looking as if about to tumble down upon her, if only they could be right sure that the ragged girl was their own child. A mistake would be such a dreadful thing!

"My darling!" at last shrieked the mother, a little doubtfully.

"My pet of pets?" cried the father, with an interrogative twist of tone.

Another moment, and they were half-way down the steps of the dais.

"Stop!" said a voice of command from somewhere in the hall, and, king and queen as they were, they stopped at once half-way, then drew themselves up, stared, and began to grow angry again, but durst not go farther.

The wise woman was coming slowly up through the crowd that filled the hall. Every one made way for her. She came straight on until she stood in front of the king and queen.

"Miserable man and woman!" she said, in words they alone could hear, "I took your daughter away when she was worthy of such parents; I bring her back, and they are unworthy of her. That you did not know her when she came to you is a small wonder, for you have been blind in souls all your lives: now be blind in body until your better eyes are unsealed."

She threw her cloak open. It fell to the ground, and the radiance that flashed from her robe of snowy whiteness, from her face of awful beauty, and from her eyes that shone like pools of sunlight, smote them blind.

Rosamond saw them give a great start, shudder, waver to and fro,

"The King and Queen punished"

then sit down on the steps of the dais; and she knew they were punished, but knew not how. She rushed up to them, and catching a hand of each said —

"Father, dear father! mother dear! I will ask the wise woman to forgive you."

"Oh, I am blind! I am blind!" they cried together. "Dark as night! Stone blind!"

Rosamond left them, sprang down the steps, and kneeling at her feet, cried, "Oh, my lovely wise woman! do let them see. Do open their eyes, dear, good, wise woman."

The wise woman bent down to her, and said, so that none else could hear,

"I will one day. Meanwhile you must be their servant, as I have been yours. Bring them to me, and I will make them welcome."

Rosamond rose, went up the steps again to her father and mother, where they sat like statues with closed eyes, half-way from the top of the dais where stood their empty thrones, seated herself between them, took a hand of each, and was still.

THE WISE WOMAN, OR THE LOST PRINCESS

All this time very few in the room saw the wise woman. The moment she threw off her cloak she vanished from the sight of almost all who were present. The woman who swept and dusted the hall and brushed the thrones, saw her, and the shepherd had a glimmering vision of her; but no one else that I know of caught a glimpse of her. The shepherdess did not see her. Nor did Agnes, but she felt the presence upon her like the heat of a furnace seven times heated.

As soon as Rosamond had taken her place between her father and mother, the wise woman lifted her cloak from the floor, and threw it again around her. Then everybody saw her, and Agnes felt as if a soft dewy cloud had come between her and the torrid rays of a vertical sun. The wise woman turned to the shepherd and shepherdess.

"For you," she said, "you are sufficiently punished by the work of your own hands. Instead of making your daughter obey you, you left her to be a slave to herself; you coaxed when you ought to have compelled; you praised when you ought to have been silent; you fondled when you ought to have punished; you threatened when you ought to have inflicted — and there she stands, the full-grown result of your foolishness! She is your crime and your punishment. Take her home with you, and live hour after hour with the pale-hearted disgrace you call your daughter. What she is, the worm at her heart has begun to teach her. When life is no longer endurable, come to me."

"Madam," said the shepherd, "may I not go with you now?"

"You shall," said the wise woman.

"Husband! husband!" cried the shepherdess, "how are we two to get home without you?"

"I will see to that," said the wise woman. "But little of home you will find it until you have come to me. The king carried you hither, and he shall carry you back. But your husband shall not go with you. He cannot now if he would."

The shepherdess looked and saw that the shepherd stood in a deep sleep. She went to him and sought to rouse him, but neither tongue nor hands were of the slightest avail.

The wise woman turned to Rosamond.

"My child," she said, "I shall never be far from you. Come to me when you will. Bring them to me."

Rosamond smiled and kissed her hand, but kept her place by her parents. They also were now in a deep sleep like the shepherd.

The wise woman took the shepherd by the hand, and led him away.

And that is all my double story. How double it is, if you care to know, you must find out. If you think it is not finished — I never knew a story that was. I could tell you a great deal more concerning them all, but I have already told more than is good for those who read but with their foreheads, and enough for those whom it has made look a little solemn, and sigh as they close the book.

Little Daylight

No house of any pretension to be called a palace is in the least worthy of the name, except it has a wood near it — very near it — and the nearer the better. Not all round it — I don't mean that, for a palace ought to be open to the sun and wind, and stand high and brave, with weathercocks glittering and flags flying; but on one side of every palace there must be a wood. And there was a very grand wood indeed beside the palace of the king who was going to be Daylight's father; such a grand wood, that nobody yet had ever got to the other end of it. Near the house it was kept very trim and nice, and it was free of brushwood for a long way in; but by degrees it got wild, and it grew wilder, and wilder, and wilder, until some said wild beasts at last did what they liked in it. The king and his courtiers often hunted, however, and this kept the wild beasts far away from the palace.

One glorious summer morning, when the wind and sun were out together, when the vanes were flashing and the flags frolicking against the blue sky, little Daylight made her appearance from somewhere — nobody could tell where — a beautiful baby, with such bright eyes that she might have come from the sun, only by and by she showed such lively ways that she might equally well have come out of the wind. There was great jubilation in the palace, for this was the first baby the queen had had, and there is as much happiness over a new baby in a palace as in a cottage.

But there is one disadvantage of living near a wood: you do not know quite who your neighbors may be. Everybody knew there were in it several fairies, living within a few miles of the palace, who always had

"A beautiful baby"

had something to do with each new baby that came; for fairies live so much longer than we, that they can have business with a good many generations of human mortals. The curious houses they lived in were well known, also, — one, a hollow oak; another, a birch-tree, though nobody could ever find how that fairy made a house of it; another, a hut of growing trees intertwined, and patched up with turf and moss. But there was another fairy who had lately come to the place, and nobody even knew she was a fairy except the other fairies. A wicked old thing she was, always concealing her power, and being as disagreeable as she could, in order to tempt people to give her offence, that she might have the pleasure of taking vengeance upon them. The people about thought she was a witch, and those who knew her by sight were careful to avoid offending her. She lived in a mud house, in a swampy part of the forest.

In all history we find that fairies give their remarkable gifts to prince or princess, or any child of sufficient importance in their eyes, always at the christening. Now this we can understand, because it is an ancient custom amongst human beings as well; and it is not hard to explain why wicked fairies should choose the same time to do unkind things; but it is difficult to understand how they should be able to do them, for you would fancy all wicked creatures would be powerless on such an occasion. But I never knew of any interference on the part of a wicked fairy that did not turn out a good thing in the end. What a good thing, for instance, it was that one princess should sleep for a hundred years! Was she not saved from all the plague of young men who were not worthy of her? And did she not come awake exactly at the right moment when the right prince kissed her? For my part, I cannot help wishing a good many girls would sleep till just the same fate overtook them. It would be happier for them, and more agreeable to their friends.

Of course all the known fairies were invited to the christening. But the king and queen never thought of inviting an old witch. For the power of the fairies they have by nature; whereas a witch gets her power by wickedness. The other fairies, however, knowing the danger thus run, provided as well as they could against accidents from her quarter. But they could neither render her powerless, nor could they arrange their gifts in reference to hers beforehand, for they could not tell what those might be.

Of course the old hag was there without being asked. Not to be asked was just what she wanted, that she might have a sort of a reason for doing what she wished to do. For somehow even the wickedest of creatures likes a pretext for doing the wrong thing.

Five fairies had one after the other given the child such gifts as each counted best, and the fifth had just stepped back to her place in the surrounding splendour of ladies and gentlemen, when, mumbling a laugh between her toothless gums, the wicked fairy hobbled out into the middle of the circle, and at the moment when the archbishop was handing the baby to the lady at the head of the nursery department of state affairs, addressed him thus, giving a bite or two to every word before she could part with it:

"Please your Grace, I'm very deaf: would your Grace mind repeating the princess's name?"

"With pleasure, my good woman," said the archbishop, stooping to shout in her ear: "the infant's name is little Daylight."

"And little daylight it shall be," cried the fairy, in the tone of a dry axle, "and little good shall any of her gifts do her. For I bestow upon her the gift of sleeping all day long, whether she will or not. Ha, ha! He, he! Hi, hi!"

Then out started the sixth fairy, who, of course, the others had arranged should come after the wicked one, in order to undo as much as she might.

"If she sleep all day," she said, mournfully, "she shall, at least, wake all night."

"A nice prospect for her mother and me!" thought the poor king; for they loved her far too much to give her up to nurses, especially at night, as most kings and queens do — and are sorry for it afterwards.

"You spoke before I had done," said the wicked fairy. "That's against the law. It gives me another chance."

"I beg your pardon," said the other fairies, all together.

"She did. I hadn't done laughing," said the crone. "I had only got to Hi, hi! and I had to go through Ho, ho! and Hu, hu! So I decree that if she wakes all night she shall wax and wane with its mistress the moon. And what that may mean I hope her royal parents will live to see. Ho, ho! Hu, hu!"

But out stepped another fairy, for they had been wise enough to keep two in reserve, because every fairy knew the trick of one.

"Until," said the seventh fairy, "a prince comes who shall kiss her without knowing it."

LITTLE DAYLIGHT

The wicked fairy made a horrid noise like an angry cat, and hobbled away. She could not pretend that she had not finished her speech this time, for she had laughed Ho, ho! and Hu, hu!

"I don't know what that means," said the poor king to the seventh fairy.

"Don't be afraid. The meaning will come with the thing itself," said she.

The assembly broke up, miserable enough — the queen, at least, prepared for a good many sleepless nights, and the lady at the head of the nursery department anything but comfortable in the prospect before her, for of course the queen could not do it all. As for the king, he made up his mind, with what courage he could summon, to meet the demands of the case, but wondered whether he could with any propriety require the First Lord of the Treasury to take a share in the burden laid upon him.

I will not attempt to describe what they had to go through for some time. But at last the household settled into a regular system — a very irregular one in some respects. For at certain seasons the palace rang all night with burst of laughter from little Daylight, whose heart the old fairy's curse could not reach; she was Daylight still, only a little in the wrong place, for she always dropped asleep at the first hint of dawn in the east. But her merriment was of short duration. When the moon was at the full, she was in glorious spirits, and as beautiful as it was possible for a child of her age to be. But as the moon waned, she faded, until at last she was wan and withered like the poorest, sickliest child you might come upon in the streets of a great city in the arms of a homeless mother. Then the night was quiet as the day, for the little creature lay in her gorgeous cradle night and day with hardly a motion, and indeed at last without even a moan, like one dead. At first they often thought she was dead, but at last they got used to it, and only consulted the almanac to find the moment when she would begin to revive, which, of course, was with the first appearance of the silver thread of the crescent moon. Then she would move her lips, and they would give her a little nourishment; and she would grow better and better and better, until for a few days she was splendidly well. When well, she was always merriest out in the moonlight; but even when near her worst, she seemed better when, in warm summer nights, they carried her cradle out into the light of the waning moon. Then in her sleep she would smile the faintest, most pitiful smile.

For a long time very few people ever saw her awake. As she grew older she became such a favourite, however, that about the palace there were always some who would contrive to keep awake at night, in order to be near her. But she soon began to take every chance of getting away from her nurses and enjoying her moonlight alone. And thus things went on until she was nearly seventeen years of age. Her father and mother had by that time got so used to the odd state of things that they had ceased to wonder at them. All their arrangements had reference to the state of the Princess Daylight, and it is amazing how things contrive to accommodate themselves. But how any prince was ever to find and deliver her, appeared inconceivable.

As she grew older she had grown more and more beautiful, with the sunniest hair and the loveliest eyes of heavenly blue, brilliant and profound as the sky of a June day. But so much more painful and sad was the change as her bad time came on. The more beautiful she was in the full moon, the more withered and worn did she become as the moon waned. At the time at which my story has now arrived, she looked, when the moon was small or gone, like an old woman exhausted with suffering. This was the more painful that her appearance was unnatural; for her hair and eyes did not change. Her wan face was both drawn and wrinkled, and had an eager hungry look. Her skinny hands moved as if wishing, but unable, to lay hold of something. Her shoulders were bent forward, her chest went in, and she stooped as if she were eighty years old. At last she had to be put to bed, and there await the flow of the tide of life. But she grew to dislike being seen, still more being touched by any hands, during this season. One lovely summer evening, when the moon lay all but gone upon the verge of the horizon, she vanished from her attendants, and it was only after searching for her a long time in great terror, that they found her fast asleep in the forest, at the foot of a silver birch, and carried her home.

A little way from the palace there was a great open glade, covered with the greenest and softest grass. Thus was her favourite haunt; for here the full moon shone free and glorious, while through a vista in the trees she could generally see more or less of the dying moon as it crossed the opening. Here she had a little rustic house built for her, and here she mostly resided. None of the court might go there without leave, and her own attendants had learned by this time not to be officious in waiting upon her, so that she was very much at liberty. Whether the good fairies had anything to do with it or not I cannot tell, but at last she got into the way of retreating further into the wood every night as the moon waned, so that sometimes they had great trouble in finding her; but as she was always very angry if she discovered they were watching her, they scarcely dared to do so. At length one night they thought they had lost her altogether. It was morning before they found her. Feeble as she was, she had wandered into a thicket a long way from the glade, and there she lay — fast asleep, of course.

Although the fame of her beauty and sweetness had gone abroad, yet as everybody knew she was under a bad spell, no king in the neighbourhood had any desire to have her for a daughter-in-law. There were serious objections to such a relation.

About this time in a neighbouring kingdom, in consequence of the wickedness of the nobles, an insurrection took place upon the death of the old king, the greater part of the nobility was massacred, and the young prince was compelled to flee for his life, disguised like a peasant. For some time, until he got out of the country, he suffered much from hunger and fatigue; but when he got into that ruled by the princess's father, and had no longer any fear of being recognized, he fared better, for the people were kind. He did not abandon his disguise, however. One tolerable reason was that he had no other clothes to put on, and another that he had very little money, and did not know where to get any more. There was no good in telling everybody he met that he was a prince, for he felt that a prince ought to be able to get on like other people, else his rank only made a fool of him. He had read of princes setting out upon adventure; and here he was out in similar case, only without having had a choice in the matter. He would go on, and see what would come of it.

For a day or two he had been walking through the palace-wood, and had had next to nothing to eat, when he came upon the strangest little house, inhabited by a very nice tidy motherly old woman. This was one of the good fairies. The moment she saw him she knew quite well who he was and what was going to come of it; but she was not at liberty to interfere with the orderly march of events. She received him with the kindness she would have shown to any other traveller, and gave him bread and milk, which he thought the most delicious food he had ever tasted, wondering that they did not have it for dinner at the palace sometimes. The old woman pressed him to stay all night. When he awoke he was amazed to find how well and strong he felt. She would not take any of the money he offered, but begged him, if he found occasion of continuing in the neighbourhood, to return and occupy the same quarters.

"Thank you much, good mother," answered the prince; "but there is little chance of that. The sooner I get out of this wood the better."

"I don't know that," said the fairy.

"What do you mean?" asked the prince.

"Why how *should* I know?" returned she.

"I can't tell," said the prince.

"Very well," said the fairy.

"How strangely you talk!" said the prince.

"Do I?" said the fairy.

"Yes, you do," said the prince.

"Very well," said the fairy.

The prince was not used to be spoken to in this fashion, so he felt a little angry and turned and walked away. But this did not offend the fairy. She stood at the door of her little house looking after him till the trees hid him quite. Then she said "At last!" and went in.

The prince wandered and wandered, and got nowhere. The sun sank and sank and went out of sight, and he seemed no nearer the end of the wood than ever. He sat down on a fallen tree, ate a bit of bread the old woman had given him, and waited for the moon; for, although he was not much of an astronomer, he knew the moon would rise some time, because she had risen the night before. Up she came, slow and slow, but of a good size, pretty nearly round indeed; whereupon, greatly refreshed with his piece of bread, he got up and went — he knew not whither.

After walking a considerable distance, he thought he was coming to the outside of the forest; but when he reached what he thought the last of it, he found himself only upon the edge of a great open space in it, covered with grass. The moon shone very bright, and he thought he had never seen a more lovely spot. Still it looked dreary because of its loneliness, for he could not see the house at the other side. He sat down weary again, and gazed into the glade. He had not seen so much room for several days.

All at once he espied something in the middle of the grass. What could it be? It moved; it came nearer. Was it a human creature, gliding across — a girl dressed in white, gleaming in the moonshine? She came nearer and nearer. He crept behind a tree and watched, wondering. It must be some strange being of the wood — a nymph whom the moonlight and the warm dusky air had enticed from her tree. But when she came close to where he stood, he no longer doubted she was human — for he had caught sight of her sunny hair, and her clear blue eyes, and the loveliest face and form that he had ever seen. All at once she began singing like a nightingale, and dancing to her own music, with her eyes ever turned towards the moon. She passed close to where he stood, dancing on by the edge of the trees and away in a great circle towards the other side, until he could see but a spot of white in the yellowish green of the moonlit grass. But when he feared it would vanish quite, the spot grew, and became a figure once more. She approached him again, singing and dancing and waving her arms over her head, until she had completed the circle. Just opposite his tree she stood, ceased her song, dropped her arms, and broke out into a long clear laugh, musical as a brook. Then, as if tired, she threw herself on the grass, and lay gazing at the moon. The prince was almost afraid to breathe lest he should startle her, and she should vanish from his sight. As to venturing near her, that never came into his head.

She had lain for a long hour or longer, when the prince began again to doubt concerning her. Perhaps she was but a vision of his own fancy. Or was she a spirit of the wood, after all? If so, he too would haunt the wood, glad to have lost kingdom and everything for the hope of being near. He would build him a hut in the forest, and there he would live for the pure chance of seeing her again. Upon nights like this at least she would come out and bask in the moonlight, and make his soul blessed. But while he thus dreamed she sprang to her feet, turned her face full to the moon, and began singing as if she would draw her down from the sky by the power of her entrancing voice. She looked more beautiful than ever. Again she began dancing to her own music, and danced away into the distance. Once more she returned in a similar manner; but although he was watching as eagerly as before, what with fatigue and what with gazing, he fell fast asleep before she came near him. When he awoke it was broad daylight, and the princess was nowhere.

He could not leave the place. What if she should come the next night! He would gladly endure a day's hunger to see her yet again: he would buckle his belt quite tight. He walked round the glade to see if he could discover any prints of her feet. But the grass was so short, and her steps had been so light, that she had not left a single trace behind her.

He walked half-way round the wood without seeing anything to account for her presence. Then he spied a lovely little house, with thatched roof and low eaves, surrounded by an exquisite garden, with doves and peacocks walking in it. Of course this must be where the gracious lady who loved the moonlight lived. Forgetting his appearance, he walked towards the door, determined to make inquiries, but as he passed a little pond full of gold and silver fishes, he caught sight of himself, and turned to find the door to the kitchen. There he knocked, and asked for a piece of bread. The good-natured cook brought him in, and gave him an excellent breakfast, which the prince found nothing the worse for being served in the kitchen. While he ate, he walked with his entertainer, and learned that this was the favourite retreat of the Princess Daylight. But he learned nothing more, both because he was afraid of seeming inquisitive, and because the cook did not choose to be heard talking about her mistress to a peasant lad who had begged for his breakfast.

As he rose to take his leave, it occurred to him that he might not be so far from the old woman's cottage as he had thought, and he asked the cook whether she knew anything of such a place, describing it as well as he could. She said she knew it well enough, adding with a smile —

"It's there you're going, is it?"

"Yes, if it's not far off."

"It's not more than three miles. But mind what you are about, you know."

"Why do you say that?"

"If you're after any mischief, she'll make you repent it."

"The best thing that could happen under the circumstances," remarked the prince.

"What do you mean by that?" asked the cook.

"Why, it stands to reason," answered the prince, "that if you wish to do anything wrong, the best thing for you is to be made to repent of it."

"I see," said the cook. "Well, I think you may venture. She's a good old soul."

"Which way does it lie from here?" asked the prince.

She gave him full instructions; and he left her with many thanks.

Being now refreshed, however, the prince did not go back to the cottage that day: he remained in the forest, amusing himself as best he could, but waiting anxiously for the night, in the hope that the princess would again appear. Nor was he disappointed, for, directly the moon rose, he spied a glimmering shape far across the glade. As it drew nearer, he saw it was she indeed — not dressed in white as before: in a pale blue like the sky, she looked lovelier still. He thought it was that the blue suited her yet better than the white; he did not know that she was really more beautiful because the moon was nearer the full. In fact the next night was full moon, and the princess would then be at the zenith of her loveliness.

The prince feared for some time that she was not coming near his hiding-place that night; but the circles in her dance ever widened as the moon rose, until at last they embraced the whole glade, and she came still closer to the trees where he was hiding than she had come the night before. He was entranced with her loveliness, for it was indeed a marvellous thing. All night long he watched her, but dared not go near her. He would have been ashamed of watching her too, had he not become almost incapable of thinking of anything but how beautiful she was. He watched the whole night long, and saw that as the moon went down she retreated in smaller and smaller circles, until at last he could see her no more.

Weary as he was, he set out for the old woman's cottage, where he arrived just in time for her breakfast, which she shared with him. He then went to bed, and slept for many hours. When he awoke, the sun was down, and he departed in great anxiety lest he should lose a glimpse of the lovely vision. But, whether it was by the machinations of the swamp-fairy, or merely that it is one thing to go and another to return by the same road, he lost his way. I shall not attempt to describe his misery when the moon rose, and he saw nothing but trees, trees, trees. She was high in the heavens before he reached the glade. Then indeed his troubles vanished, for there was the princess coming dancing towards him, in a dress that shone like gold, and with shoes that glimmered through the grass like fire-flies. She was of course still more beautiful than before. Like an embodied sunbeam she passed him, and danced away into the distance.

Before she returned in her circle, clouds had begun to gather about the moon. The wind rose, the trees moaned, and their lighter branches leaned all one way before it. The prince feared that the princess would go in, and he should see her no more that night. But she came dancing on more jubilant than ever, her golden dress and her sunny hair streaming out upon the blast, waving her arms towards the moon, and in the exuberance of her delight ordering the clouds away from off her face. The prince could hardly believe she was not a creature of the elements, after all.

By the time she had completed another circle, the clouds had gathered deep, and there were growlings of distant thunder. Just as she passed the tree where he stood, a flash of lightning blinded him for a moment, and when he saw again, to his horror, the princess lay on the ground. He darted to her, thinking she had been struck; but when she heard him coming, she was on her feet in a moment.

"What do you want?" she asked.

"I beg your pardon. I thought — the lightning — " said the prince, hesitating.

"There is nothing the matter," said the princess, waving him off rather haughtily.

The poor prince turned and walked towards the wood.

"Come back," said Daylight; "I like you. You do what you are told. Are you good?"

"Not so good as I should like to be," said the prince.

"Then go and grow better," said the princess.

Again the disappointed prince turned and went.

"Come back," said the princess.

He obeyed, and stood before her waiting.

"Can you tell me what the sun is like?" she asked.

"No," he answered. "But where's the good of asking what you know?"

"But I don't know," she rejoined.

"Why, everybody knows."

"That's the very thing: I'm not everybody. I've never seen the sun."

"Then you can't know what it's like till you do see it."

"I think you must be a prince," said the princess.

"Do I look like one?" said the prince.

"I can't quite say that."

"Then why do you think so?"

"Because you both do what you are told and speak the truth. — Is the sun so very bright?"

"As bright as the lightning."

"But it doesn't go out like that, does it?"

"Oh no. It shines like the moon, rises and sets like the moon, is much the same shape as the moon, only so bright that you can't look at it for a moment."

"But I *would* look at it," said the princess.

"But you couldn't," said the prince.

"But I could," said the princess.

"Why don't you, then?"

"Because I can't."

"Why can't you?"

"Because I can't wake. And I never shall wake until — "

Here she hid her face in her hands, turned away, and walked in the slowest, stateliest manner towards the house. The prince ventured to follow her at a little distance, but she turned and made a repellent gesture, which, like a true gentleman-prince, he obeyed at once. He waited a long time, but as she did not come near him again, and as the night had now cleared, he set off at last for the old woman's cottage.

It was long past midnight when he reached it, but, to his surprise, the old woman was paring potatoes at the door. Fairies are fond of doing odd things. Indeed, however they may dissemble, the night is always their day. And so it is with all who have fairy blood in them.

"Why, what are you doing there, this time of the night, mother?" said the prince; for that was the kind way in which any young man in his country would address a woman who was much older than himself.

"Getting your supper ready, my son," she answered.

"Oh! I don't want any supper," said the prince.

"Ah! you've seen Daylight," said she.

"I've seen a princess who never saw it," said the prince.

"Do you like her?" asked the fairy.

"Oh! don't I?" said the prince. "More than you would believe, mother."

"A fairy can believe anything that ever was or ever could be," said the old woman.

"Then you are a fairy?" asked the prince.

"Yes," said she.

"Then what do you do for things not to believe?" asked the prince.

"There's plenty of them — everything that never was nor ever could be."

"Plenty, I grant you," said the prince. "But do you believe there could be a princess who never saw the daylight? Do you believe that, now?"

This the prince said, not that he doubted the princess, but that he wanted the fairy to tell him more. She was too old a fairy, however, to be caught so easily.

"Of all people, fairies must not tell secrets. Besides, she's a princess."

"Well, I'll tell *you* a secret. I'm a prince."

"I know that."

"How do you know it?"

"By the curl of the third eyelash on your left eyelid."

"Which corner do you count from?"

"That's a secret."

"Another secret? Well, at least, if I am a prince, there can be no harm in telling me about a princess."

"It's just princes I can't tell."

"There ain't any more of them — are there?" said the prince.

"What! you don't think you're the only prince in the world, do you?"

"Oh, dear, no! not at all. But I know there's one too many just at present, except the princess — "

"Yes, yes, that's it," said the fairy.

"What's *it?*" asked the prince.

But he could get nothing more out of the fairy, and had to go to bed unanswered, which was something of a trial.

Now wicked fairies will not be bound by the laws which the good fairies obey, and this always seems to give the bad the advantage over the good, for they use means to gain their ends which the others will not. But it is all of no consequence, for what they do never succeeds; nay, in the end it brings about the very thing they are trying to prevent. So you see that somehow, for all their cleverness, wicked fairies are dreadfully stupid, for, although from the beginning of the world they have really helped instead of thwarting the good fairies, not one of them is a bit the wiser for it. She will try the bad thing just as they all did before her; and succeed no better of course.

The prince had so far stolen a march upon the swamp-fairy that she did not know he was in the neighbourhood until after he had seen the princess those three times. When she knew it, she consoled herself by thinking that the princess must be far too proud and too modest for any young man to venture even to speak to her before he had seen her six times at least. But there was even less danger than the wicked fairy thought; for, however much the princess might desire to be set free, she was dreadfully afraid of the wrong prince. Now, however, the fairy was going to do all she could.

She so contrived it by her deceitful spells, that the next night the prince could not by any endeavor find his way to the glade. It would take me too long to tell her tricks. They would be amusing to us, who know that they could not do any harm, but they were something other than amusing to the poor prince. He wandered about the forest till daylight, and then fell fast asleep. The same thing occurred for seven following days, during which neither could he find the good fairy's cottage. After the third quarter of the moon, however, the bad fairy thought she might be at ease about the affair for a fortnight at least, for there was no chance of the prince wishing to kiss the princess during that period. So the first day of the fourth quarter he did find the cottage, and the next day he found the glade. For nearly another week he haunted it. But the princess never came. I have little doubt she was on the farther edge of it some part of every night, but at this period she always wore black, and, there being little or no light, the prince never saw her. Nor would he have known her if he had seen her. How could he have taken the worn decrepit creature she was now, for the glorious Princess Daylight?

At last, one night when there was no moon at all, he ventured near the house. There he heard voices talking, although it was past midnight; for her women were in considerable uneasiness, because the one whose turn it was to watch her had fallen asleep, and had not seen which way she went, and this was a night when she would probably wander very far, describing a circle which did not touch the open glade at all, but stretched away from the back of the house, deep into that side of the forest — a part of which the prince knew nothing. When he understood from what they said that she had disappeared, and that she must have gone somewhere in the said direction, he plunged at once into the wood to see if he could find her. For hours he roamed with nothing to guide him but the vague notion of a circle which on one side bordered on the house, for so much had he picked up from the talk he had overheard.

It was getting towards the dawn, but as yet there was no streak of light in the sky, when he came to a great birch-tree, and sat down weary at the foot of it. While he sat — very miserable, you may be sure — full of fear for the princess, and wondering how her attendants could take it so quietly, he bethought himself that it would not be a bad plan to light a fire, which, if she were anywhere near, would attract her. This he managed with a tinder-box, which the good fairy had given him. It was just beginning to blaze up, when he heard a moan, which seemed to come from the other side of the tree. He sprung to his feet, but his heart throbbed so that he had to lean for a moment against the tree before he could move. When he got round, there lay a human form in a little dark heap on the earth. There was light enough from his fire to show that it was not the princess. He lifted it in his arms, hardly heavier than a child, and carried it to the flame. The countenance was that of an old woman, but it had a fearfully strange look. A black hood concealed her hair, and her eyes were closed. He laid her down as comfortably as he could, chafed her hands, put a little cordial from a bottle, also the gift of the fairy, into her mouth; took off his coat and wrapped it about her, and in short did the best he could. In a little while she opened her eyes and looked at him — so pitifully! The tears rose and flowed down her gray wrinkled cheeks, but she said never a word. She closed her eyes again, but the tears kept on flowing, and her whole appearance was so utterly pitiful that the prince was very near crying too. He begged her to tell him what was the matter, promising to do all he could to help her; but still she did not speak. He thought she was dying, and took her in his arms again to carry her to the princess's house, where he thought the good-natured cook might be able to do something for her. When he lifted her, the tears flowed yet faster, and she gave such a sad moan that it went to his very heart.

"Mother, mother!" he said — "Poor mother!" and kissed her on the withered lips.

She started; and what eyes they were that opened upon him! But he did not see them, for it was still very dark, and he had enough to do to make his way through the trees towards the house.

Just as he approached the door, feeling more tired than he could have imagined possible — she was such a little thin old thing — she began to move, and became so restless that, unable to carry her a moment longer, he thought to lay her on the grass. But she stood upright on her feet. Her hood had dropped, and her hair fell about her. The first gleam of the morning was caught on her face: that face was bright as the never-aging Dawn, and her eyes were lovely as the sky of darkest blue. The prince recoiled in over-mastering wonder. It was Daylight herself whom he had brought from the forest! He fell at her feet, nor dared look up until she laid her hand upon his head. He rose then.

"You kissed me when I was an old woman: there! I kiss you when I am a young princess," murmured Daylight. — "Is that the sun coming?"

The Gray Wolf

One evening-twilight in spring, a young English student, who had wandered northwards as far as the outlying fragments of Scotland called the Orkney and Shetland islands, found himself on a small island of the latter group, caught in a storm of wind and hail, which had come on suddenly. It was in vain to look about for any shelter; for not only did the storm entirely obscure the landscape, but there was nothing around him save a desert moss.

At length, however, as he walked on for mere walking's sake, he found himself on the verge of a cliff, and saw, over the brow of it, a few feet below him, a ledge of rock, where he might find some shelter from the blast, which blew from behind. Letting himself down by his hands, he alighted upon something that crunched beneath his tread, and found the bones of many small animals scattered about in front of a little cave in the rock, offering the refuge he sought. He went in, and sat upon a stone. The storm increased in violence, and as the darkness grew he became uneasy, for he did not relish the thought of spending the night in the cave. He had parted from his companions on the opposite side of the island, and it added to his uneasiness that they must be full of apprehension about him. At last there came a lull in the storm, and the same instant he heard a footfall, stealthy and light as that of a wild beast, upon the bones at the mouth of the cave. He started up in some fear, though the least thought might have satisfied him that there could be no very dangerous animals upon the island. Before he had time to think, however, the face of a woman appeared in the opening. Eagerly the wanderer spoke. She started at the sound of his voice. He could not see her well, because she was turned towards the darkness of the cave.

"Will you tell me how to find my way across the moor to Shielness?" he asked.

"You cannot find it to-night," she answered, in a sweet tone, and with a smile that bewitched him, revealing the whitest of teeth.

"What am I to do then?" he asked.

"My mother will give you shelter, but that is all she has to offer."

"And that is far more than I expected a minute ago," he replied. "I shall be most grateful."

She turned in silence and left the cave. The youth followed.

She was barefooted, and her pretty brown feet went catlike over the sharp stones, as she led the way down a rocky path to the shore. Her garments were scanty and torn, and her hair blew tangled in the wind. She seemed about five and twenty, lithe and small. Her long fingers kept clutching and pulling nervously at her skirts as she went. Her face was very gray in complexion, and very worn, but delicately formed, and smooth-skinned. Her thin nostrils were tremulous as eyelids, and her lips, whose curves were faultless, had no colour to give sign of indwelling blood. What her eyes were like he could not see, for she had never lifted the delicate films of her eyelids.

At the foot of the cliff they came upon a little hut leaning against it, and having for its inner apartment a natural hollow within it. Smoke was spreading over the face of the rock, and the grateful odour of food gave hope to the hungry student. His guide opened the door of the cottage; he followed her in, and saw a woman bending over a fire in the middle of the floor. On the fire lay a large fish broiling. The daughter spoke a few words, and the mother turned and welcomed the stranger. She had an old and very wrinkled, but honest face, and looked troubled. She dusted the only chair in the cottage, and placed it for him by the side of the fire, opposite the one window, whence he saw a little patch of yellow sand over which the spent waves spread themselves out listlessly. Under this window there was a bench, upon which the daughter threw herself in an unusual posture, resting her chin upon her hand. A moment after, the youth caught the first glimpse of her blue eyes. They were fixed upon him with a strange look of greed, amounting to craving, but as if aware that they belied or betrayed her, she dropped them instantly. The moment she veiled them, her face, notwithstanding its colourless complexion, was almost beautiful.

THE GRAY WOLF

When the fish was ready, the old woman wiped the deal table, steadied it upon the uneven floor, and covered it with a piece of fine table-linen. She then laid the fish on a wooden platter, and invited the guest to help himself. Seeing no other provision, he pulled from his pocket a hunting knife, and divided a portion from the fish, offering it to the mother first.

"Come, my lamb," said the old woman; and the daughter approached the table. But her nostrils and mouth quivered with disgust.

The next moment she turned and hurried from the hut.

"She doesn't like fish," said the old woman, "and I haven't anything else to give her."

"She does not seem in good health," he rejoined.

The woman answered only with a sigh, and they ate their fish with the help of a little rye-bread. As they finished their supper, the youth heard the sound as of the pattering of a dog's feet upon the sand close to the door; but ere he had time to look out of the window, the door opened and the young woman entered. She looked better, perhaps from having just washed her face. She drew a stool to the corner of the fire opposite him. But as she sat down, to his bewilderment, and even horror, the student spied a single drop of blood on her white skin within her torn dress. The woman brought out a jar of whisky, put a rusty old kettle on the fire, and took her place in front of it. As soon as the water boiled, she proceeded to make some toddy in a wooden bowl.

Meantime the youth could not take his eyes off the young woman, so that at length he found himself fascinated, or rather bewitched. She kept her eyes for the most part veiled with the loveliest eyelids fringed with darkest lashes, and he gazed entranced; for the red glow of the little oil-lamp covered all the strangeness of her complexion. But as soon as he met a stolen glance out of those eyes unveiled, his soul shuddered within him. Lovely face and craving eyes alternated fascination and repulsion.

The mother placed the bowl in his hands. He drank sparingly, and passed it to the girl. She lifted it to her lips, and as she tasted — only tasted it — looked at him. He thought the drink must have been drugged and have affected his brain. Her hair smoothed itself back, and drew her forehead backwards with it; while the lower part of her face projected towards the bowl, revealing, ere she sipped, her dazzling teeth in strange prominence. But the same moment the vision vanished; she returned the vessel to her mother, and rising, hurried out of the cottage.

Then the old woman pointed to a bed of heather in one corner with a murmured apology; and the student, wearied both with the fatigues of the day and the strangeness of the night, threw himself upon it, wrapped in his cloak. The moment he lay down, the storm began afresh, and the wind blew so keenly through the crannies of the hut, that it was only by drawing his cloak over his head that he could protect himself from its currents. Unable to sleep, he lay listening to the uproar, which grew in violence, till the spray was dashing against the window. At length the door opened, and the young woman came in, made up the fire, drew the bench before it, and lay down in the same strange posture, with her chin propped on her hand and elbow, and her face turned towards the youth. He moved a little; she dropped her head, and lay on her face, with her arms crossed beneath her forehead. The mother had disappeared.

Drowsiness crept over him. A movement of the bench roused him, and he fancied he saw some four-footed creature as tall as a large dog trot quietly out of the door. He was sure he felt a rush of cold wind. Gazing fixedly through the darkness, he thought he saw the eyes of the damsel encountering his, but a glow from the falling together of the remnants of the fire, revealed clearly enough that the bench was vacant. Wondering what could have made her go out in such a storm, he fell fast asleep.

In the middle of the night he felt a pain in his shoulder, came broad awake, and saw the gleaming eyes and grinning teeth of some animal close to his face. Its claws were in his shoulder, and its mouth in the act of seeking his throat. Before it had fixed its fangs, however, he had its throat in one hand, and sought his knife with the other. A terrible struggle followed; but regardless of the tearing claws, he found and opened his knife. He had made one futile stab, and was drawing it for a surer, when, with a spring of the whole body, and one wildly-contorted effort, the creature twisted its neck from his hold, and with something betwixt a scream and a howl, darted from him. Again he heard the door open; again the wind blew in upon him, and it continued blowing; a sheet of spray dashed across the floor, and over his face. He sprung from his couch and bounded to the door.

It was a wild night — dark, but for the flash of whiteness from the waves as they broke within a few yards of the cottage; the wind was raving, and the rain pouring down the air. A gruesome sound as of mingled weeping and howling came from somewhere in the dark. He turned again into the hut and closed the door, but could find no way of securing it.

The lamp was nearly out, and he could not be certain whether the form of the young woman was upon the bench or not. Overcoming a strong repugnance, he approached it, and put out his hands — there was nothing there. He sat down and waited for the daylight: he dared not sleep any more.

When the day dawned at length, he went out yet again, and looked around. The morning was dim and gusty and gray. The wind had fallen, but the waves were tossing wildly. He wandered up and down the little strand, longing for more light.

At length he heard a movement in the cottage. By and by the voice of the old woman called to him from the door.

"You're up early, sir. I doubt you didn't sleep well."

"Not very well," he answered. "But where is your daughter?"

"She's not awake yet," said the mother. "I'm afraid I have but a poor breakfast for you. But you'll take a dram and a bit of fish. It's all I've got."

Unwilling to hurt her, though hardly in good appetite, he sat down at the table. While they were eating, the daughter came in, but turned her face away and went to the further end of the hut. When she came forward after a minute or two, the youth saw that her hair was drenched, and her face whiter than before. She looked ill and faint, and when she raised her eyes, all their fierceness had vanished, and sadness had taken its place. Her neck was now covered with a cotton handkerchief. She was modestly attentive to him, and no longer shunned his gaze. He was gradually yielding to the temptation of braving another night in the hut, and seeing what would follow, when the old woman spoke.

"The weather will be broken all day, sir," she said. "You had better be going, or your friends will leave without you."

Ere he could answer, he saw such a beseeching glance on the face of the girl, that he hesitated, confused. Glancing at the mother, he saw the flash of wrath in her face. She rose and approached her daughter, with her hand lifted to strike her. The young woman stooped her head with a cry. He darted round the table to interpose between them. But the mother had caught hold of her; the handkerchief had fallen from her neck; and the youth saw five blue bruises on her lovely throat — the marks of the four fingers and the thumb of a left hand. With a cry of horror he darted from the house, but as he reached the door he turned. His hostess was lying motionless on the floor, and a huge gray wolf came bounding after him.

There was no weapon at hand; and if there had been, his inborn chivalry would never have allowed him to harm a woman even under the guise of a wolf. Instinctively, he set himself firm, leaning a little forward, with half outstretched arms, and hands curved ready to clutch again at the throat upon which he had left those pitiful marks. But the creature as she sprung eluded his grasp, and just as he expected to feel her fangs, he found a woman weeping on his bosom, with her arms around his neck. The next instant, the gray wolf broke from him, and bounded howling up the cliff. Recovering himself as he best might, the youth followed, for it was the only way to the moor above, across which he must now make his way to find his companions.

All at once he heard the sound of a crunching of bones — not as if a creature was eating them, but as if they were ground by the teeth of rage and disappointment; looking up, he saw close above him the mouth of the little cavern in which he had taken refuge the day before. Summoning all his resolution, he passed it slowly and softly. From within came the sounds of a mingled moaning and growling.

Having reached the top, he ran at full speed for some distance across the moor before venturing to look behind him. When at length he did so, he saw, against the sky, the girl standing on the edge of the cliff, wringing her hands. One solitary wail crossed the space between. She made no attempt to follow him, and he reached the opposite shore in safety.

The Cruel Painter

Among the young men assembled at the University of Prague, in the year 159–, was one Karl von Wolkenlicht. A somewhat careless student, he yet held a fair position in the estimation of both professors and men, because he could hardly look at a proposition without understanding it. Where such proposition, however, had to do with anything relating to the deeper insights of the nature, he was quite content that, for him, it should remain a proposition; which, however, he laid up in one of his mental cabinets, and was ready to reproduce at a moment's notice. This mental agility was more than matched by the corresponding corporeal excellence, and both aided in producing results in which his remarkable strength was equally apparent. In all games depending upon the combination of muscle and skill, he had scarce rivalry enough to keep him in practice. His strength, however, was embodied in such a softness of muscular outline, such a rare Greek-like style of beauty, and associated with such gentleness of manner and behaviour, that, partly from the truth of the resemblance, partly from the absurdity of the contrast, he was known throughout the university by the diminutive of the feminine form of his name, and was always called Lottchen.

"I say, Lottchen," said one of his fellow-students, called Ricter, across the table in a wine-cellar they were in the habit of frequenting, "do you know, Heinrich Höllenrachen here says that he saw this morning, with mortal eyes, whom do you think? — Lilith."

"Adam's first wife?" asked Lottchen, with an attempt at carelessness, while his face flushed like a maiden's.

"None of your chaff!" said Richter. "Your face is honester than your tongue, and confesses what you cannot deny, that you would give your chance of salvation — a small one to be sure, but all you've got — for one peep at Lilith. Wouldn't you now, Lottchen?"

"Go to the devil!" was all Lottchen's answer to his tormentor; but he turned to Heinrich, to whom the students had given the surname above mentioned, because of the enormous width of his jaws, and said with eagerness and envy, disguising them as well as he could, under the appearance of curiosity:

"You don't mean it, Heinrich? You've been taking the beggar in! Confess now."

"Not I. I saw her with my two eyes."

"Notwithstanding the different planes of their orbits," suggested Richter.

"Yes, notwithstanding the fact that I can get a parallax to any of the fixed stars in a moment, with only the breadth of my nose for the base," answered Heinrich, responding at once to the fun, and careless of the personal defect insinuated. "She was near enough for even me to see her perfectly."

"When? Where? How?" asked Lottchen.

"Two hours ago. In the churchyard of St. Stephen's. By a lucky chance. Any more little questions, my child?" answered Höllenrachen.

"What could have taken her there, who is seen nowhere?" said Richter.

"She was seated on a grave. After she left, I went to the place; but it was a new-made grave. There was no stone up. I asked the sexton about her. He said he supposed she was the daughter of the woman buried there last Thursday. I knew it was Lilith."

"Her mother dead?" said Lottchen, musingly. Then he thought with himself — "She will be going there again, then!" But he took care that this ghost-thought should wander unembodied. "But how did you know her, Heinrich? You never saw her before."

"How do you come to be over head and ears in love with hear, Lottchen, and you haven't seen her at all?" interposed Richter.

"Will you or will you not go to the devil?" rejoined Lottchen, with a comic *crescendo;* to which the other replied with a laugh.

"No one could miss knowing her," said Heinrich.

"Is she so very like, then?"

"It is always herself, her very self."

A fresh flask of wine, turning out to be not up to the mark, brought the current of conversation against itself; not much to the dissatisfaction of Lottchen, who had already resolved to be in the churchyard of St. Stephen's at sun-down the following day, in the hope that he too might be favoured with a vision of Lilith.

This resolution he carried out. Seated in a porch of the church, not knowing in what direction to look for the apparition he hoped to see, and desirous as well of not seeming to be on the watch for one, he was gazing at the fallen rose-leaves of the sunset, withering away upon the sky; when, glancing aside by an involuntary movement, he saw a woman seated upon a new-made grave, not many yards from where he sat, with her face buried in her hands, and apparently weeping bitterly. Karl was in the shadow of the porch, and could see her perfectly, without much danger of being discovered by her; so he sat and watched her. She raised her head for a moment, and the rose-flush of the west fell over it, shining on the tears with which it was wet, and giving the whole a bloom which did not belong to it, for it was always pale, and now pale as death. It was indeed the face of Lilith, the most celebrated beauty of Prague.

Again she buried her face in her hands; and Karl sat with a strange feeling of helplessness, which grew as he sat; and the longing to help her whom he could not help, drew his heart towards her with a trembling reverence which was quite new to him. She wept on. The western roses withered slowly away, and the clouds blended with the sky, and the stars gathered like drops of glory sinking through the vault of night, and the trees about the church yard grew black, and Lilith almost vanished in the wide darkness. At length she lifted her head, and seeing the night around her, gave a little broken cry of dismay. The minutes had swept over her head, not through her mind, and she did not know that the dark had come.

Hearing her cry, Karl rose and approached her. She heard his footsteps, and started to her feet. Karl spoke —

"Do not be frightened," he said. "Let me see you home. I will walk behind you."

"Who are you?" she rejoined.

"Karl Wolkenlicht."

"I have heard of you. Thank you. I can go home alone."

Yet, as if in a half-dreamy, half-unconscious mood, she accepted his offered hand to lead her through the graves, and allowed him to walk beside her, till, reaching the corner of a narrow street, she suddenly bade him good-night and vanished. He thought it better not to follow her, so he returned her good-night and went home.

How to see her again was his first thought the next day; as, in fact, how to see her at all had been his first thought for many days. She went nowhere that ever he heard of; she knew nobody that he knew; she was never seen at church, or at market; never seen in the street. Her home had a dreary, desolate aspect. It looked as if no one ever went out or in. It was like a place on which decay had fallen because there was no indwelling spirit. The mud of years was baked upon its door, and no faces looked out of its dusty windows.

How then could she be the most celebrated beauty of Prague? How, then, was it that Heinrich Höllenrachen knew her the moment he saw her? Above all, how was it that Karl Wolkenlicht had, in fact, fallen in love with her before ever he saw her? It was thus:

Her father was a painter. Belonging thus to the public, it had taken the liberty of re-naming him. Every one called him Teufelsbürst, or Devilsbrush. It was a name with which, to judge from the nature of his representations, he could hardly fail to be pleased. For, not as a nightmare-dream, which may alternate with the loveliest visions, but as his ordinary every-day work, he delighted to represent human suffering.

Not an aspect of human woe or torture, as expressed in countenance or limb, came before his willing imagination, but he bore it straightway to his easel. In the moments that precede sleep, when the black space before the eyes of the poet teems with lovely faces, or dawns into a spirit-landscape, face after face of suffering, in all varieties of expression, would crowd, as if compelled by the accompanying fiends, to present themselves, in awful levée, before the inner eye of the expectant master. Then he would rise, light his lamp, and, with rapid hand, make notes of his visions; recording with swift successive sweeps of his pencil, every individual face which had rejoiced his evil fancy. Then he would return to his couch, and well satisfied, fall asleep, to dream yet further embodiments of human ill.

What wrong could man or mankind have done him, to be thus fearfully pursued by the vengeance of the artist's hate?

Another characteristic of the faces and forms which he drew was, that they were all beautiful in the original idea. The lines of each face, however distorted by pain, would have been, in rest, absolutely beautiful; and the whole of the execution bore witness to the fact that upon this original beauty the painter had directed the artillery of anguish, to bring down the sky-soaring heights of its divinity to the level of a hated existence. To do this, he worked in perfect accordance with artistic law, falsifying no line of the original forms. It was the suffering, rather than his pencil, that wrought the change. The latter was the willing instrument to record what the imagination conceived with a cruelty composed enough to be correct.

To enhance the beauty he had thus distorted, and so to enhance yet further the suffering that produced the distortion, he would often represent attendant demons, whom he made as ugly as his imagination could compass; avoiding, however, all grotesqueness beyond what was sufficient to indicate that they were demons, and not men. Their ugliness rose from hate, envy, and all evil passions; amongst which he especially delighted to represent a gloating exultation over human distress. And often in the midst of his clouds of demon faces, would some one who knew him recognise the painter's own likeness, such as the mirror might have presented it to him when he was busiest over the incarnation of some exquisite torture.

But, apparently with the wish to avoid being supposed to choose such representations for their own sakes, he always found a story, often in the histories of the church, whose name he gave to the painting, and which he pretended to have inspired the pictorial conception. No one, however, who looked upon his suffering martyrs, could suppose for a moment that he honoured their martyrdom. They were but the vehicles for his hate of humanity. He was the torturer, and not Diocletian or Nero.

But, stranger yet to tell, there was no picture, whatever its subject, into which he did not introduce one form of placid and harmonious loveliness. In this, however, his fierceness was only more fully displayed. For in no case did this form manifest any relation either to the actors or the endurers in the picture. Hence its very loveliness became almost hateful to those who beheld it. Not a shade crossed the still sky of that brow, not a ripple disturbed the still sea of that cheek. She did not hate, she did not love the sufferers: the painter would not have her hate, for that would be to the injury of her loveliness; would not have her love, for he hated. Sometimes she floated above, as a still, unobservant angel, her gaze turned upward, dreaming along, careless as a white summer cloud, across the blue. If she looked down on the scene below, it was only that the beholder might see that she saw and did not care — that not a feather of her outspread pinions would quiver at the sight. Sometimes she would stand in the crowd, as if she had been copied there from another picture, and had nothing to do with this one, nor any right to be in it at all. Or when the red blood was trickling drop by drop from the crushed limb, she might be seen standing nearest, smiling over a primrose or the bloom on a peach. Some had said that she was the painter's wife; that she had been false to him; that he had killed her; and, finding that that was no sufficing revenge, thus half in love, and half in deepest hate, immortalized his vengeance. But it was now universally understood that it was his daughter, of whose loveliness extravagant reports went abroad; though all said, doubtless reading this from her father's pictures, that she was a beauty without a heart. Strange theories of something else supplying its place were rife among the anatomical students. With the girl in the pictures, the wild imagination of Lottchen, probably in part from her apparently absolute unattainableness and her undisputed heartlessness, had fallen in love, as far as the mere imagination can fall in love.

But again, how was he to see her? He haunted the house night after night. Those blue eyes never met his. No step responsive to his came from that door. It seemed to have been so long unopened that it had grown as fixed and hard as the stones that held its bolts in their passive clasp. He dared not watch in the day-time, and with all his watching at night, he never saw father or daughter or domestic cross the threshold. Little he thought that, from a shot-window near the door, a pair of blue eyes, like Lilith's, but paler and colder, were watching him, just as a spider watches the fly that is likely ere long to fall into his toils. And into those toils Karl soon fell. For her form darkened the page; her form stood on the threshold of sleep; and when, overcome with watching, he did enter its precincts, her form entered with him, and walked by his side. He must find her; or the world might go to the bottomless pit for him. But how?

Yes. He would be a painter. Teufelsbürst would receive him as a humble apprentice. He would grind his colours, and Teufelsbürst would teach him the mysteries of the science which is the handmaiden of art. Then he might see *her,* and that was all his ambition.

In the clear morning light of a day in autumn, when the leaves were beginning to fall seared from the hand of that Death which has his dance in the chapels of nature as well as in the cathedral aisles of men — he walked up and knocked at the dingy door. The spider painter opened it himself. He was a little man, meagre and pallid, with those faded blue eyes, a low nose in three distinct divisions, and thin, curveless, cruel lips. He wore no hair on his face; but long grey locks, long as a woman's, were scattered over his shoulders, and hung down on his breast. When Wolkenlicht had explained his errand, he smiled a smile in which hypocrisy could not hide the cunning, and, after many difficulties, consented to receive him as a pupil, on condition that he would become an inmate of his house. Wolkenlicht's heart bounded with delight, which he tried to hide: the second smile of Teufelsbürst might have shown him that he had ill succeeded. The fact that he was not a native of Prague, but, coming from a distant part of the country, was entirely his own master in the city, rendered this condition perfectly easy to fulfil; and that very afternoon, he entered the studio of Teufelsbürst as his scholar and servant.

It was a great room, filled with the appliances and results of art. Many pictures, festooned with cobwebs, were hung carelessly on the dirty walls. Others, half finished, leaned against them, on the floor. Several, in different stages of progress, stood upon easels. But all spoke the cruel bent of the artist's genius. In one corner a lay-figure was extended on a couch, covered with a pall of black velvet. Through its folds, the form beneath was easily discernible; and one hand and fore-arm protruded from beneath it, at right angles to the rest of the frame. Lottchen could not help shuddering when he saw it. Although he overcame the feeling in a moment, he felt a great repugnance to seating himself with his back towards it, as the arrangement of an easel, at which Teufelsbürst wished him to draw, rendered necessary. He contrived to edge himself round, so that when he lifted his eyes he should see the figure, and be sure that it could not rise without his being aware of it. But his master saw and understood his altered position; and under some pretence about the light, compelled him to resume the position in which he had placed him at first; after which he sat watching, over the top of his picture, the expression of his countenance as he tried to draw; reading in it the horrid fancy that the figure under the pall had risen, and was stealthily approaching to look over his shoulder. But Lottchen resisted the feeling, and, being already no contemptible draughtsman, was soon interested enough to forget it. And then, any moment, *she* might enter.

Now began a system of slow torture, for the chance of which the painter had been long on the watch — especially since he had first seen Karl lingering about the house. His opportunities of seeing physical suffering were nearly enough even for the diseased necessities of his art; but now he had one in his power, on whom, his own will fettering him, he could try any experiments he pleased for the production of a kind of suffering, in the observation of which he did not consider that he had yet had sufficient experience. He would hold the very heart of the youth in his hand, and wring it and torture it to his own content. And lest Karl should be strong enough to prevent those expressions of pain for which he lay on the watch, he would make use of further means, known to himself, and known to few besides.

All that day Karl saw nothing of Lilith; but he heard her voice once — and that was enough for one day. The next, she was sitting to her father the greater part of the day, and he could see her as often as he dared glance up from his drawing. She had looked at him when she entered, but had shown no sign of recognition; and all day long she took no further notice of him. He hoped, at first, that this came of the intelligence of love; but he soon began to doubt it. For he saw that, with the holy shadow of sorrow, all that distinguished the expression of her countenance from that which the painter so constantly reproduced, had vanished likewise. It was the very face of the unheeding angel whom, as often as he lifted his eyes higher than hers, he saw on the wall above her, playing on a psaltery in the smoke of the torment ascending for ever from burning Babylon. — The power of the painter had not merely wrought for the representation of the woman of his imagination: it had had scope as well in realizing her.

Karl soon began to see that communication, other than of the eyes, was all but hopeless; and to any attempt in that way she seemed altogether indisposed to respond. Nor, if she had wished it, would it have been safe; for as often as he glanced towards her, instead of hers, he met the blue eyes of the painter, gleaming upon him like winter-lightning. His tones, his gestures, his words, seemed kind: his glance and his smile refused to be disguised.

The first day he dined alone in the studio waited upon by an old woman; the next he was admitted to the family table, with Teufelsbürst and Lilith. The room offered a strange contrast to the study. As far as handicraft, directed by a sumptuous taste, could construct a house-para-dise, this was one. But it seemed rather a paradise of demons; for the walls were covered with Teufelsbürst's paintings. During the dinner Lilith's gaze scarcely met that of Wolkenlicht; and once or twice, when their eyes did meet, her glance was so perfectly unconcerned, that Karl wished he might look at her for ever without the fear of her looking at him again. She seemed like one whose love had rushed out glowing with seraphic fire, to be frozen to death in a more than wintry cold: she now walked lonely without her love. In the evenings, he was expected to continue his drawing by lamp-light; and at night he was conducted by Teufelsbürst to his chamber. Not once did he leave him there without locking and bolting the door on the outside. But he felt nothing except the coldness of Lilith.

Day after day she sat to her father, in every variety of costume that could best show the variety of her beauty. How much greater that beauty might be, if it ever blossomed into a beauty of soul, Wolkenlicht never imagined; for he soon loved her enough to attribute to her all the possibilities of her face as actual possessions of her being. To account for everything that seemed to contradict this perfection, his brain was prolific in inventions; till he was compelled at last to see that she was in the condition of a rose-bud, which on the point of blossoming, has been chilled into a changeless bud by the cold of an untimely frost. For one day, after the father and daughter had become a little more accustomed to his silent presence, a conversation began between them, which went on until he saw that Teufelsbürst believed in nothing except his art. How much of his feeling for that could be dignified by the name of belief, seeing its objects were such as they were, might have been questioned. It seemed to Wolkenlicht to amount only to this: that, amidst a thousand distastes, it was a pleasant thing to re-produce on the canvas the forms he beheld around him, modifying them to express the prevailing feelings of his own mind.

A more desolate communication between souls than that which then passed between father and daughter could hardly be imagined. The father spoke of humanity and all its experiences in a tone of the bitterest scorn. He despised men and himself amongst them; and rejoiced to think that the generations rose and vanished, brood after brood, as the crops of corn grew and disappeared. Lilith, who listened to it all unmoved, taking only an intellectual interest in the question, remarked that even the corn had more life than that; for, after its death, it rose again in the new crop. Whether she meant that the corn was therefore superior to man, forgetting that the superior can produce being without losing its own, or only advanced an objection to her father's argument, Wolkenlicht could not tell. But Teufelsbürst laughed like the sound of a saw, and said: "Follow out the analogy, my Lilith, and you will see that man is like the corn that springs again after it is buried; but unfortunately the only result we know of is a vampire."

Wolkenlicht looked up, and saw a shudder pass through the frame, and over the pale thin face of the painter. This he could not account for. But Teufelsbürst could have explained it, for there were strange whispers abroad, and they had reached his ear; and his philosophy was not quite enough for them. But the laugh with which Lilith met this frightful attempt at wit, grated dreadfully on Wolkenlicht's feeling. With her, too, however, a reaction seemed to follow. For, turning around a moment after, and looking at the picture on which her father was working, the tears rose in her eyes, and she said: "Oh! father, how like my mother you have made me this time!" "Child!" retorted the painter with a cold fierceness, "you have no mother. That which is gone out is gone out. Put no name in my hearing on that which is not. Where no substance is, how can there be a name?"

Lilith rose and left the room. Wolkenlicht now understood that Lilith was a frozen bud, and could not blossom into a rose. But pure love lives by faith. It loves the vaguely beheld and unrealized ideal. It dares believe that the loved is not all that she ever seemed. It is in virtue of this that love lives on. And it was in virtue of this, that Wolkenlicht loved Lilith yet more after he discovered what a grave of misery her unbelief was digging for her within her own soul. For her sake he would bear anything — bear even with calmness the torments of his own love; he would stay on, hoping and hoping. — The text, that we know not what a day may bring forth, is just as true of good things as of evil things; and out of Time's womb the facts must come.

But with the birth of this resolution to endure, his suffering abated; his face grew more calm; his love, no less earnest, was less imperious; and he did not look up so often from his work when Lilith was present. The master could see that his pupil was more at ease, and that he was making rapid progress in his art. This did not suit his designs, and he would betake himself to his further schemes.

For this purpose he proceeded first to simulate a friendship for Wolkenlicht, the manifestations of which he gradually increased, until, after a day or two, he asked him to drink wine with him in the evening. Karl readily agreed. The painter produced some of his best; but took care not to allow Lilith to taste it; for he had cunningly prepared and mingled with it a decoction of certain herbs and other ingredients, exercising specific actions upon the brain, and tending to the inordinate excitement of those portions of it which are principally under the rule of the imagination. By the reaction of the brain during the operation of these stimulants, the imagination is filled with suggestions and images. The nature of these is determined by the prevailing mood of the time. They are such as the imagination would produce of itself; but increased in number and intensity. Teufelsbürst, without philosophizing about it, called his preparation simply a love-philtre, a concoction well known by name, but the composition of which was the secret of only a few. Wolkenlicht had, of course, not the least suspicion of the treatment to which he was subjected.

Teufelsbürst was, however, doomed to fresh disappointment. Not that his potion failed in the anticipated effect; for now Karl's real sufferings began; but that such was the strength of Karl's will, and his fear of doing anything that might give a pretext for banishing him from the presence of Lilith, that he was able to conceal his feelings far too successfully for the satisfaction of Teufelsbürst's art. Yet he had to fetter himself with all the restraints that self-exhortation could load him with, to refrain from falling at the feet of Lilith and kissing the hem of her garment. For that, as the lowliest part of all that surrounded her, itself kissing the earth, seemed to come nearest within the reach of his ambition, and therefore to draw him the most.

No doubt the painter had experience and penetration enough to preceive that he was suffering intensely; but he wanted to see the suffering embodied in outward signs, bringing it within the region over which his pencil held sway. He kept on, therefore, trying one thing after another, and rousing the poor youth to agony; till to his other sufferings were added, at length, those of failing health; a fact which notified itself evidently enough even for Teufelsbürst, though its signs were not of the sort he chiefly desired. But Karl endured all bravely.

Meantime, for various reasons, he scarcely ever left the house.

I must now interrupt the course of my story to introduce another element.

A few years before the period of my tale, a certain shoemaker of the city had died under circumstances more than suggestive of suicide. He was buried, however, with such precautions, that six weeks elapsed before the rumour of the facts broke out; upon which rumour, not before, the most fearful reports began to be circulated, supported by what seemed to the people of Prague incontestable evidence. — A *spectrum* of the deceased appeared to multitudes of persons, playing horrible pranks, and occasioning indescribable consternation throughout the whole town. This went on till at last, about eight months after his burial, the magistrates caused his body to be dug up; when it was found in just the condition of the bodies of those who in the eastern countries of Europe are called *vampires*. They buried the corpse under the gallows; but neither the digging up nor the re-burying were of avail to banish the spectre. Again the spade and pick-axe were set to work, and the dead man, being found considerably improved in *condition* since his last interment, was, with various horrible indignities, burnt to ashes, "after which the *spectrum* was never seen more."

And a second epidemic of the same nature had broken out a little before the period to which I have brought my story.

About midnight, after a calm frosty day, for it was now winter, a terrible storm of wind and snow came on. The tempest howled frightfully about the house of the painter, and Wolkenlicht found some solace in listening to the uproar, for his troubled thoughts would not allow him to sleep. It raged on all the next three days, till about noon on the fourth day, when it suddenly fell, and all was calm. The following night, Wolkenlicht, lying awake, heard unaccountable noises in the next house, as of things thrown about, of kicking and fighting horses, and of opening and shutting gates. Flinging wide his lattice and looking out, the noise of howling dogs came to him from every quarter of the town. The moon was bright and the air was still. In a little while he heard the sounds of a horse going at full gallop round the house, so that it shook as if it would fall; and flashes of light shone into his room. How much of this may have been owing to the effect of the drugs on poor Lottchen's brain, I leave my readers to determine. But when the family met at breakfast in the morning, Teufelsbürst, who had been already out of doors, reported that he had found the marks of strange feet in the snow, all about the house and through the garden at the back; stating, as his belief, that the tracks must be continued over the roofs, for there was no passage otherwise. There was a wicked gleam in his eye as he spoke; and Lilith believed that he was only trying an experiment on Karl's nerves. He persisted that he had never seen any footprints of the sort before. Karl informed him of his experiences during the night; upon which Teufelsbürst looked a little graver still, and proceeded to tell them that the storm, whose snow was still covering the ground, had arisen the very moment that their next door neighbour died, and had ceased as suddenly the moment he was buried, though it had raged furiously all the time of the funeral, so that "it made men's bodies quake and their teeth chatter in their heads." Karl had heard that the man, whose name was John Kuntz, was dead and buried. He knew that he had been a very wealthy, and therefore most respectable, alderman of the town; that he had been very fond of horses; and that he had died in consequence of a kick received from one of his own, as he was looking at his hoof. But he had not heard that, just before he died, a black cat "opened the casement with her nails, ran to his bed, and violently scratched his face and the bolster, as if she endeavoured by force to remove him out of the place where he lay. But the cat afterwards was suddenly gone, and she was no sooner gone, but he breathed his last."

So said Teufelsbürst, as the reporter of the town-talk. Lilith looked very pale and terrified; and it was perhaps owing to this that the painter brought no more tales home with him. There were plenty to bring, but he heard them all and said nothing. The fact was that the philosopher himself could not resist the infection of the fear that was literally raging in the city; and perhaps the reports that he himself had sold himself to the devil, had sufficient response from his own evil conscience to add to the influence of the epidemic upon him. The whole place was infested with the presence of the dead Kuntz, till scarce a man or woman would dare to be alone. He strangled old men; insulted women; squeezed children to death; knocked out the brains of dogs against the ground; pulled up posts; turned milk into blood; nearly killed a worthy clergyman by breathing upon him the intolerable airs of the grave, cold and malignant and noisome; and, in short, filled the city with a perfect madness of fear, so that every report was believed without the smallest doubt or investigation.

Though Teufelsbürst brought home no more of the town-talk, the old servant was a faithful purveyor, and frequented the news-mart assiduously. Indeed she had some nightmare experiences of her own that she was proud to add to the stock of horrors which the city enjoyed with such a hearty community of goods. For those regions were not far removed from the very birth-place and home of the vampire. The belief in vampires is the quintessential concentration and embodiment of all the passion of fear in Hungary and the adjacent regions. Nor of all the other inventions of the human imagination, has there ever been one so perfect in crawling terror as this. Lilith and Karl were quite familiar with the popular ideas on the subject. It did not require to be explained to them, that a vampire was a body retaining a kind of animal life after the soul had departed. If any relation continued between it and the vanished ghost, it was only sufficient to make it restless in its grave. Possessed of vitality enough to keep it uncorrupted and pliant, its only instinct was a blind hunger for the sole food which could keep its awful life persistent — living human blood. Hence it, or if not it, a sort of semi-material exhalation of essence of it, retaining its form and material relations, crept from its tomb, and went roaming about till it found some one asleep, towards whom it had an attraction, founded on old affection. It sucked the blood of this unhappy being, transferring so much of its life to itself as a vampire could assimilate. Death was the certain consequence. If suspicion conjectured aright, and they opened the proper grave, the body of the vampire would be found perfectly fresh and plump, sometimes indeed of rather florid complexion; — with grown hair, eyes half open, and the stains of recent blood about its greedy leech-like lips. Nothing remained but to consume the corpse to ashes, upon which the vampire would show itself no more. But what added infinitely to the horror was the certainty that whoever died from the mouth of the vampire, wrinkled grandsire, or delicate maiden, must in turn rise from the grave, and go forth a vampire, to suck the blood of the dearest left behind. This was the generation of the vampire brood. Lilith trembled at the very name of the creature. Karl was too much in love to be afraid of anything. Yet the evident fear of the unbelieving painter took a hold of his imagination; and, under the influence of the potions of which he still partook unwittingly — when he was not thinking about Lilith, he was thinking about the vampire.

Meantime, the condition of things in the painter's household continued much the same for Wolkenlicht — work all day; no communication between the young people; the dinner and the wine; silent reading when work was done, with stolen glances many over the top of the book, glances that were never returned; the cold good night; the locking of the door; the wakeful night and the drowsy morning. But at length a change came, and sooner than any of the party had expected. For, whether it was that the impatience of Teufelsbürst had urged him to yet more dangerous experiments, or that the continuance of those he had been so long employing had overcome at length the vitality of Wolkenlicht — one afternoon, as he was sitting at his work, he suddenly dropped from his chair, and his master hurrying to him in some alarm, found him rigid and apparently lifeless. Lilith was not in the study when this took place. In justice to Teufelsbürst, it must be confessed that he employed all the skill he was master of, which for beneficent purposes was not very great, to restore the youth; but without avail. At last, hearing the footsteps of Lilith, he desisted in some consternation; and that she might escape being shocked by the sight of a dead body where she had been accustomed to see a living one, he removed the lay figure from the couch and laid Karl in its place, covering him with the black velvet pall. He was just in time. She started at seeing no one in Karl's place, and said:

"Where is your pupil, father?"

"Gone home," he answered, with a kind of convulsive grin.

She glanced round the room, caught sight of the lay figure where it had not been before, looked at the couch, and saw the pall yet heaved up from beneath, opened her eyes till the entire white sweep around the iris suggested a new expression of consternation to Teufelsbürst, though from a quarter whence he did not desire or look for it; and then, without a word, sat down to a drawing she had been busy upon the day before. But her father, glancing at her now, as Wolkenlicht had used to do, could not help seeing that she was frightfully pale. She showed no other sign of uneasiness. As soon as he released her, she withdrew, with one more glance, as she passed, at the couch and the figure blocked out in black upon it. She hastened to her chamber, shut and locked the door, sat down on the side of the couch, and fell, not a-weeping, but a-thinking. Was he dead? What did it matter? They would all be dead soon. Her mother was dead already. It was only that earth could not bear more children, except she devoured those to whom she had already given birth. But what if they had to come back in another form, and live another sad, hopeless, loveless life over again? — And so she went on questioning, and receiving no replies; while through all her thoughts passed and repassed the eyes of Wolkenlicht, which she had often felt to be upon her when she did not see them, wild with repressed longing, the light of their love shining through the veil of diffused tears, ever gathering and never overflowing. Then came the pale face, so worshipping, so distant in its self-withdrawn devotion, slowing dawning out of the vapours of her reverie. When it vanished, she tried to see it again. It would not come when she called it; but when her thoughts left knocking at the door of the lost and wandered away, out came the pale, troubled, silent face again, gathering itself up from some unknown nook in her world of phantasy, and, once more, when she tried to steady it by the fixedness of her own regard, fading back into the mist. So the phantasm of the dead drew near and wooed, as the living had never dared. — What if there were any good in loving? What if men and women did not die all out, but some dim shade of each, like that pale, mind-ghost of Wolkenlicht, floated through the eternal vapours of chaos? And what if they might sometimes cross each other's path, meet, know that they met, love on? Would not that revive the withered memory, fix the fleeting ghost, give a new habitation, a body even, to the poor, unhoused wanderers, frozen by the eternal frosts, no longer thinking beings, but thoughts wandering through the brain of the "Melancholy Mass"? Back with the thought came the face of the dead Karl, and the maiden threw herself on her bed in a flood of bitter tears. She could have loved him if he had only lived: she did love him, for he was dead. But even in the midst of the remorse that followed, — for had she not killed him? — life seemed a less hard and hopeless thing than before. For it is love itself and not its responses or results that is the soul of life and its pleasures.

Two hours passed ere she could again show herself to her father, from whom she seemed in some new way divided by the new feeling in which he did not, and could not share. But at last, lest he should seek her, and finding her, should suspect her thoughts, she descended and sought him. — For there is a maidenliness in sorrow, that wraps her garments close around her. — But he was not to be seen; the door of the study was locked. A shudder passed through her as she thought of what her father, who lost no opportunity of furthering his all but perfect acquaintance with the human form and structure, might be about with the figure which she knew lay dead beneath that velvet pall, but which had arisen to haunt the hollow caves and cells of her living brain. She rushed away, and up once more to her silent room, through the darkness which had now settled down in the house; threw herself again on her bed, and lay almost paralysed with horror and distress.

But Teufelsbürst was not about anything so frightful as she supposed, though something frightful enough. I have already implied that Wolkenlicht was, in form, as fine an embodiment of youthful manhood as any old Greek republic could have provided one of its sculptors with as a model for an Apollo. It is true, that to the eye of a Greek artist he would have not been more acceptable in consequence of the regimen he had been going through for the last few weeks; but the emaciation of Wolkenlicht's frame, and the consequent prominence of the muscles, indicating the pain he had gone through, were peculiarly attractive to Teufelsbürst. — He was busy preparing to take a cast of the body of his dead pupil, that it might aid to the perfection of his future labours.

He was deep in the artistic enjoyment of a form, at the same time so beautiful and strong, yet with the lines of suffering in every limb and feature, when his daughter's hand was laid on the latch. He started, flung the velvet drapery over the body, and went to the door. But Lilith had vanished. He returned to his labours. The operation took a long time, for he performed it very carefully. Towards midnight, he had finished encasing the body in a close-clinging shell of plaster, which, when broken off, and fitted together, would be the matrix to the form of the dead Wolkenlicht. Before leaving it to harden till the morning, he was just proceeding to strengthen it with an additional layer all over, when a flash of lightning, reflected in all its dazzle from the snow without, almost blinded him. A peal of long-drawn thunder followed; the wind rose; and just such a storm came on as had risen some time before at the death of Kuntz, whose spectre was still tormenting the city. The gnomes of terror, deep hidden in the caverns of Teufelsbürst's nature, broke out jubilant. With trembling hands he tried to cast the pall over the awful white chrysalis, — failed, and fled to his chamber. And there lay the studio naked to the eyes of the lightning, with its tortured forms throbbing out of the dark, and quivering, as with life, in the almost continuous palpitations of the light; while on the couch lay the motionless mass of whiteness, gleaming blue in the lightning, almost more terrible in its crude indications of the human form, than that which it enclosed. It lay there as if dropped from some tree of chaos, haggard with the snows of eternity — a huge mis-shapen nut, with a corpse for its kernel.

But the lightning would soon have revealed a more terrible sight still, had there been any eyes to behold it. At midnight, while a peal of thunder was just dying away in the distance, the crust of death flew asunder, rending in all directions; and, pale as his investiture, staring with ghastly eyes, the form of Karl started up sitting on the couch. Had he not been far beyond ordinary men in strength, he could not thus have rent his sepulchre. Indeed, had Teufelsbürst been able to finish his task by the additional layer of gypsum which he contemplated, he must have died the moment life revived; although, so long as the trance lasted, neither the exclusion from the air, nor the practical solidification of the walls of his chest, could do him any injury. He had lain unconscious throughout the operations of Teufelsbürst, but now the catalepsy had passed away, possibly under the influence of the electric condition of the atmosphere. Very likely the strength he now put forth was intensified by a convulsive reaction of all

THE CRUEL PAINTER ☙ 415

the powers of life, as is not infrequently the case in sudden awakenings from similar interruptions of vital activity. The coming to himself and the bursting of his case were simultaneous. He sat staring about him, with, of all his mental faculties, only his imagination awake, from which the thoughts that occupied it when he fell senseless had not yet faded. These thoughts had been compounded of feelings about Lilith, and speculations about the vampire that haunted the neighbourhood; and the fumes of the last drug of which he had partaken, still hovering in his brain, combined with these thoughts and fancies to generate the delusion that he had just broken from the embrace of his coffin, and risen, the last-born of the vampire-race. The sense of unavoidable obligation to fulfil his doom, was yet mingled with a faint flutter of joy, for he knew that he must go to Lilith. With a deep sigh, he rose, gathered up the pall of black velvet, flung it around him, stepped from the couch, and left the study to find her.

Meantime, Teufelsbürst had sufficiently recovered to remember that he had left the door of the studio unfastened, and that anyone entering would discover in what he had been engaged, which, in the case of his getting into any difficulty about the death of Karl, would tell powerfully against him. He was at the farther end of a long passage, leading from the house to the studio, on his way to make all secure, when Karl appeared at the door, and advanced towards him. The painter, seized with invincible terror, turned and fled. He reached his room, and fell senseless on the floor. The phantom held on its way, heedless.

Lilith, on gaining her room the second time, had thrown herself on her bed as before, and had wept herself into a troubled slumber. She lay dreaming — and dreadful dreams. Suddenly she awoke in one of those peals of thunder which tormented the high regions of the air, as a storm billows the surface of the ocean. She lay awake and listened. As it died away, she thought she heard, mingling with its last muffled murmurs, the sound of moaning. She turned her face towards the room in keen terror. But she saw nothing. Another light, long-drawn sigh reached her ear, and at the same moment a flash of lightning illumined the room. In the corner farthest from her bed, she spied a white face, nothing more. She was dumb and motionless with fear. Utter darkness followed, a darkness that seemed to enter into her very brain. Yet she felt that the face was slowly crossing the black gulf of the room, and drawing near to where she lay. The next flash revealed, as it bended over her, the ghastly face of Karl, down which flowed fresh tears. The rest of his form was lost in blackness. Lilith did not faint, but it was the very force of her fear that seemed to keep her alive. It became for the moment the atmosphere of her life. She lay trembling and staring at the spot in the darkness where she supposed the face of Karl still to be. But the next flash showed her the face far off, looking at her through the panes of her lattice-window.

For Lottchen, as soon as he saw Lilith, seemed to himself to go through a second stage of awaking. Her face made him doubt whether he could be a vampire after all; for instead of wanting to bite her arm and suck the blood, he all but fell down at her feet in a passion of speechless love. The next moment he became aware that his presence must be at least very undesirable to her; and in an instant he had reached her window, which he knew looked upon a lower roof that extended between two different parts of the house, and before the next flash came, he had stepped through the lattice and closed it behind him.

Believing his own room to be attainable from this quarter, he proceeded along the roof in the direction he judged best. The cold winter air by degrees restored him entirely to his right mind, and he soon comprehended the whole of the circumstances in which he found himself. Peeping through a window he was passing, to see whether it belonged to his room, he spied Teufelsbürst, who, at the very moment, was lifting his head from the faint into which he had fallen at the first sight of Lottchen. The moon was shining clear, and in its light the painter saw, to his horror, the pale face staring in at his window. He thought it had been there ever since he had fainted, and dropped again in a deeper swoon than before. Karl saw him fall, and the truth flashed upon him that the wicked artist took him for what he had believed himself to be when first he recovered from his trance — namely, the vampire of the former Karl Wolkenlicht. The moment he comprehended it, he resolved to keep up the delusion if possible. Meantime he was innocently preparing a new ingredient for the popular dish of horrors to be served at the ordinary of the city the next day. For the old servant's were not the only eyes that had seen him besides those of Teufelsbürst. What could be more like a vampire, dragging his pall after him, than this apparition of poor, half-frozen Lottchen, crawling across the roof? Karl remembered afterwards that he had heard the dogs howling awfully in every direction, as he crept along; but this was hardly necessary to make those who saw him conclude that it was the same phantasm of John Kuntz, which had been infesting the whole city, and especially the house next door to the painter's, which had been the dwelling of the respectable alderman who had degenerated into this most disreputable of moneyless vagabonds. What added to the consternation of all who heard of it, was the sickening conviction that the extreme measures which they had resorted to in order to free the city from the ghoul, beyond which nothing could be done, had been utterly unavailing, successful as they had proved in every other known case of the kind. For, urged as well by various horrid signs about his grave, which not even its close proximity to the altar could render a place of repose, they had opened it, had found in the body every peculiarity belonging to a vampire, had pulled it out with the greatest difficulty on account of a quite supernatural ponderosity; which rendered the horse which had killed him — a strong animal — all but unable to drag it along, and had at last, after cutting it in pieces, and expending on the fire two hundred and sixteen great billets, succeeded in conquering its incombustibleness, and reducing it to ashes. Such, at least, was the story which had reached the painter's household, and was believed by many; and if all this did not compel the perturbed corpse to rest, what more could be done?

When Karl had reached his room, and was dressing himself, the thought struck him that something might be made of the report of the extreme weight of the body of old Kuntz, to favour the continuance of the delusion of Teufelsbürst, although he hardly knew yet to what use he could turn this delusion. He was convinced that he would have made no progress however long he might have remained in his house; and that he would have more chance of favour with Lilith if he were to meet her in any other circumstances whatever, than those in which he invariably saw her — namely, surrounded by her father's influences, and watched by her father's cold blue eyes.

As soon as he was dressed, he crept down to the studio, which was now quiet enough, the storm being over, and the moon filling it with her steady shine. In the corner lay in all directions the fragments of the mould which his own body had formed and filled. The bag of plaster and the bucket of water which the painter had been using stood beside. Lottchen gathered all the pieces together, and then making his way to an out-house where he had seen various odds and ends of rubbish lying, chose from the heap as many pieces of old iron and other metal as he could find. To these he added a few large stones from the garden. When he had got all into the studio, he locked the door, and proceeded to fit together the parts of the mould, filling up the hollow as he went on with the heaviest things he could get into it, and solidifying the whole by pouring in plaster; till,

THE CRUEL PAINTER

having at length completed it, and obliterated, as much as possible, the marks of joining, he left it to harden, with the conviction that now it would make a considerable impression on Teufelsbürst's imagination, as well as on his muscular sense. He then left everything else as nearly undisturbed as he could; and, knowing all the ways of the house, was soon in the street, without leaving any signs of his exit.

Karl soon found himself before the house in which his friend Höllenrachen resided. Knowing his studious habits, he had hoped to see his light still burning, nor was he disappointed. He contrived to bring him to his window, and a moment after, the door was cautiously opened.

"Why, Lottchen, where do you come from?"

"From the grave, Heinrich, or next door to it."

"Come in, and tell me about it. We thought the old painter had made a model of you, and tortured you to death."

"Perhaps you were not far wrong. But get me a horn of ale, for even a vampire is thirsty, you know."

"A vampire!" exclaimed Heinrich, retreating a pace, and involuntarily putting himself upon his guard.

Karl laughed.

"My hand was warm, was it not, old fellow?" he said. "Vampires are cold, all but the blood."

"What a fool I am!" rejoined Heinrich. "But you know we have been hearing such horrors lately that a fellow may be excused for shuddering a little when a pale-faced apparition tells him at two o'clock in the morning that he is a vampire, and thirsty, too."

Karl told him the whole story; and the mental process of regarding it for the sake of telling it, revealed to him pretty clearly some of the treatment of which he had been unconscious at the time. Heinrich was quite sure that his suspicions were correct. And now the question was, what was to be done next.

"At all events," said Heinrich, "we must keep you out of the way for some time. I will represent to my landlady that you are in hiding from enemies, and her heart will rule her tongue. She can let you have a garret-room, I know; and I will do as well as I can to bear you company. We shall have time then to invent some plan of operation."

To this proposal Karl agreed with hearty thanks, and soon all was arranged. The only conclusion they could yet arrive at was, that somehow or other the old demon-painter must be tamed.

Meantime, how fared it with Lilith? She too had no doubt that she had seen the body-ghost of poor Karl, and that the vampire had, according to rule, paid her the first visit because he loved her best. This was horrible enough if the vampire were not really the person he represented; but if in any sense it were Karl himself, at least it gave some expectation of a more prolonged existence than her father had taught her to look for; and if love anything like her mother's still lasted, even along with the habits of a vampire, there was something to hope for in the future. And then, though he had visited her, he had not, as far as she was aware, deprived her of a drop of blood. She could not be certain that he had not bitten her, for she had been in such a strange condition of mind that she might not have felt it, but she believed that he had restrained the impulses of his vampire nature, and had left her, lest he should yet yield to them. She fell fast asleep; and, when morning came, there was not, as far as she could judge, one of those triangular leech-like perforations to be found upon her whole body. Will it be believed that the moment she was satisfied of this, she was seized by a terrible jealousy, lest Karl should have gone and bitten someone else? Most people will wonder that she should not have gone out of her senses at once; but there was all the difference between a visit from a real vampire and a visit from a man she had begun to love, even although she took him for a vampire. All the difference does *not* lie in a name. They were very different causes, and the effects must be very different.

When Teufelsbürst came down in the morning, he crept into the studio like a murderer. There lay the awful white block, seeming to his eyes just the same as he had left it. What was to be done with it? He dared not open it. Mould and model must go together. But whither? If inquiry should be made after Wolkenlicht, and this were discovered anywhere on his premises, would it not be enough to bring him at once to the gallows? Therefore it would be dangerous to bury it in the garden; or in the cellar.

"Besides," thought he, with a shudder, "that would be to fix the vampire as a guest for ever." — And the horrors of the past night rushed back upon his imagination with renewed intensity. What would it be to have the dead Karl crawling about his house for ever, now inside, now out, now sitting on the stairs, now staring in at the windows?

He would have dragged it to the bottom of his garden, past which the Moldau flowed, and plunged it into the stream, but then, should the spectre continue to prove troublesome, it would be almost impossible to reach the body so as to destroy it by fire; besides which, he could not do it without assistance, and the probability of discovery. If, however, the apparition should turn out to be no vampire, but only a respectable ghost, they might manage to endure its presence till it should be weary of haunting them.

He resolved at last to convey the body for the meantime into a concealed cellar in the house, seeing something must be done before his daughter came down. Proceeding to remove it, his consternation was greatly increased when he discovered how the body had grown in weight since he had thus disposed of it, leaving on his mind scarcely a hope that it could turn out not to be a vampire after all. He could scarcely stir it, and there was but one whom he could call to his assistance — the old woman who acted as his housekeeper and servant.

He went to her room, roused her, and told her the whole story. Devoted to her master for many years, and not quite so sensitive to fearful influences as when less experienced in horrors, she showed immediate readiness to render him assistance. Utterly unable, however, to lift the mass between them, they could only drag and push it along; and such a slow toil was it that there was no time to remove the traces of its track, before Lilith came down and saw a broad white line leading from the door of the studio down the cellar-stairs. She knew in a moment what it meant; but not a word was uttered about the matter, and the name of Karl Wolkenlicht seemed to be entirely forgotten.

But how could the affairs of a house go on all the same when every one of the household knew that a dead body lay in the cellar? — nay more, that, although it lay still and dead enough all day, it would come half alive at nightfall, and turning the whole house into a sepulchre by its presence, go creeping about like a cat all over it in the dark — perhaps with phosphorescent eyes? So it was not surprising that the painter abandoned his studio early, and that the three found themselves together in the gorgeous room formerly described, as soon as twilight began to fall.

Already Teufelsbürst had begun to experience a kind of shrinking from the horrid faces in his own pictures, and to feel disgusted at the abortions of his own mind. But all that he and the old woman now felt was an increasing fear as the night drew on, a kind of sickening and paralysing terror. The thing down there would not lie quiet — at least its phantom in the cellars of their imagination would not. As much as possible, however, they avoided alarming Lilith, who, knowing all they knew, was as silent as they. But her mind was in a strange state of excitement, partly from the presence of a new sense of love, the pleasure of which all the atmosphere of grief into which it grew could not totally quench. It comforted her somehow, as a child may comfort when his father is away.

Bedtime came, and no one made a move to go. Without a word spoken on the subject, the three remained together all night; the elders nodding and slumbering occasionally, and Lilith getting some share of repose on a couch. All night the shape of death might be somewhere about the house; but it did not disturb them. They heard no sound, saw no sight; and when the morning dawned, they separated, chilled and stupid, and for the time beyond fear, to seek repose in their private chambers. There they remained equally undisturbed.

But when the painter approached his easel a few hours after, looking more pale and haggard still than he was wont, from the fears of the night, a new bewilderment took possession of him. He had been busy with a fresh embodiment of his favourite subject, into which he had sketched the form of the student as the sufferer. He had represented poor Wolkenlicht as just beginning to recover from a trance, while a group of surgeons, unaware of the signs of returning life, were absorbed in a minute dissection of one of the limbs. At an open door he had painted Lilith passing, with her face buried in a bunch of sweet-peas. But when he came to the picture, he found, to his astonishment and terror, that the face of one of the group was now turned towards that of the victim, regarding his revival with demoniac satisfaction, and taking pains to prevent the others from discovering it. The face of this prince of torturers was that of Teufelsbürst himself. Lilith had altogether vanished, and in her place stood the dim vampire reiteration of the body that lay extended on the table, staring greedily at the assembled company. With trembling hands the painter removed the picture from the easel, and turned its face to the wall.

Of course this was the work of Lottchen. When he left the house, he took with him the key of a small private door, which was so seldom used that, while it remained closed, the key would not be missed, perhaps for many months. Watching the windows, he had chosen a safe time to enter, and had been hard at work all night on these alterations. Teufelsbürst attributed them to the vampire, and left the picture as he found it, not daring to put brush to it again.

The next night was passed much after the same fashion. But the fear had begun to die away a little in the hearts of the women, who did not know what had taken place in the study on the previous night. It burrowed, however, with gathered force in the vitals of Teufelsbürst. But this night likewise passed in peace; and before it was over, the old woman had taken to speculating in her own mind as to the best way of disposing of the body, seeing it was not at all likely to be troublesome. But when the painter entered his study in trepidation the next morning, he found that the form of the lovely Lilith was painted out of every picture in the room. This could not be concealed; and Lilith and the servant became aware that the studio was the portion of the house in haunting which the vampire left the rest in peace.

Karl recounted all the tricks he had played to his friend Heinrich, who begged to be allowed to bear him company the following night. To this Karl consented, thinking it would be considerably more agreeable to have a companion. So they took a couple of bottles of wine and some provisions with them, and before midnight found themselves snug in the study. They sat very quiet for some time, for they knew that if they were seen, two vampires would not be so terrible as one, and might occasion discovery. But at length Heinrich could bear it no longer.

"I say, Lottchen, let's go and look for your dead body. What has the old beggar done with it?"

"I think I know. Stop; let me peep out. All right! Come along."

With a lamp in his hand, he led the way to the cellars, and after searching about a little, they discovered it.

"It looks horrid enough," said Heinrich, "but I think a drop or two of wine would brighten it up a little."

So he took a bottle from his pocket, and after they had had a glass apiece, he dropped a third in blots all over the plaster. Being red wine, it had the effect Höllenrachen desired.

"When they visit it next, they will know that the vampire can find the food he prefers," said he.

In a corner close by the plaster, they found the clothes Karl had worn.

"Hillo!" said Heinrich, "we'll make something of this find."

So he carried them with him to the study. There he got hold of the lay-figure.

"What are you about, Heinrich?"

"Going to make a scarecrow to keep the ravens off old Teufel's pictures," answered Heinrich, as he went on dressing the lay-figure in

Karl's clothes. He next seated the creature at an easel with its back to the door, so that it should be the first thing the painter should see when he entered. Karl meant to remove this before he went, for it was too comical to fall in with the rest of his proceedings. But the two sat down to their supper, and by the time they had finished the wine, they thought they should like to go to bed. So they got up and went home, and Karl forgot the lay-figure, leaving it in busy motionlessness all night before the easel.

When Teufelsbürst saw it, he turned and fled with a cry that brought his daughter to his help. He rushed past her, able only to articulate:

"The vampire! The vampire! Painting!"

Far more courageous than he, because her conscience was more peaceful, Lilith passed on to the studio. She too recoiled a step or two when she saw the figure; but with the sight of the back of Karl, as she supposed it to be, came the longing to see the face that was on the other side. So she crept round and round by the wall, as far off as she could. The figure remained motionless. It was a strange kind of shock that she experienced when she saw the face, disgusting from its inanity. The absurdity next struck her; and with the absurdity flashed into her mind the conviction that this was not the doing of a vampire; for of all creatures under the moon, he could not be expected to be a humourist. A wild hope sprang up in her mind that Karl was not dead. Of this she soon resolved to make herself sure.

She closed the door of the studio; in the strength of her new hope, undressed the figure, put it in its place, concealed the garments — all the work of a few minutes; and then, finding her father just recovering from the worst of his fear, told him there was nothing in the studio but what ought to be there, and persuaded him to go and see. He not only saw no one, but found that no further liberties had been taken with his pictures. Reassured, he soon persuaded himself that the spectre in this case had been the offspring of his own terror-haunted brain. But he had no spirit for painting now. He wandered about the house, himself haunting it like a restless ghost.

When night came, Lilith retired to her own room. The waters of fear had begun to subside in the house; but the painter and his old attendant did not follow her example.

As soon, however, as the house was quite still, Lilith glided noiselessly down the stairs, went into the studio, where as yet there assuredly was no vampire, and concealed herself in a corner.

As it would not do for an earnest student like Heinrich to be away from his work very often, he had not asked to accompany Lottchen this time. And indeed Karl himself, a little anxious about the result of the scarecrow, greatly preferred going alone.

While she was waiting for what might happen, the conviction grew upon Lilith, as she reviewed all the past of the story, that these phenomena were the work of the real Karl, and of no vampire. In a few moments she was still more sure of this. Behind the screen where she had taken refuge, hung one of the pictures out of which her portrait had been painted the night before last. She had taken a lamp with her into the study, with the intention of extinguishing it the moment she heard any sign of approach; but as the vampire lingered, she began to occupy herself with examining the picture beside her. She had not looked at it long, before she wetted the tip of her forefinger, and began to rub away at the obliteration. Her suspicions were instantly confirmed: the substance employed was only a gummy wash over the paint. The delight she experienced at the discovery threw her into a mischievous humour.

"I will see," she said to herself, "whether I cannot match Karl Wolkenlicht at this game."

In a closet in the room hung a number of costumes, which Lilith had at different times worn for her father. Among them was a large white drapery, which she easily disposed as a shroud. With the help of some chalk, she soon made herself ghastly enough, and then placing her lamp on the floor behind the screen, and setting a chair over it, so that it should throw no light in any direction, she waited once more for the vampire. Nor had she much longer to wait. She soon heard a door move, the sound of which she hardly knew, and then the studio door opened. Her heart beat dreadfully, not with fear lest it should be a vampire after all, but with hope that it was Karl. To see him once more was too great joy. Would she not make up to him for all her coldness! But would he care for her now? Perhaps he had been quite cured of his longing for a hard heart like hers. She peeped. It was he sure enough, looking as handsome as ever. He was holding his light to look at her last work, and the expression of his face, even in regarding her handiwork, was enough to let her know that he loved her still. If she had not seen this, she dared not have shown herself from her hiding-place. Taking the lamp in her hand, she got upon the chair, and looked over the screen, letting the light shine from below upon her face. She then made a slight noise to attract Karl's attention. He looked up, evidently rather startled, and saw the face of Lilith in the air. He gave a stifled cry, threw himself on his knees, with his arms stretched towards her, and moaned —

"I have killed her! I have killed her!"

Lilith descended, and approached him noiselessly. He did not move. She came close to him and said:

"Are you Karl Wolkenlicht?"

His lips moved, but no sound came.

"If you are a vampire, and I am a ghost," she said — but a low happy laugh alone concluded the sentence.

Karl sprang to his feet. Lilith's laugh changed into a burst of sobbing and weeping, and in another moment the ghost was in the arms of the vampire.

Lilith had no idea how far her father had wronged Karl, and though, from thinking over the past, he had no doubt that the painter had drugged him, he did not wish to pain her by imparting this conviction. But Lilith was afraid of a reaction of rage and hatred in her father after the terror was removed; and Karl saw that he might thus be deprived of all further intercourse with Lilith, and all chance of softening the old man's heart towards him; while Lilith would not hear of forsaking him who had banished all the human race but herself. They managed at length to agree upon a plan of operation.

The first thing they did was to go to the cellar where the plaster mass lay, Karl carrying with him a great axe used for cleaving wood. Lilith shuddered when she saw it, stained as it was with the wine Heinrich had spilt over it, and almost believed herself the midnight companion of a vampire after all, visiting with him the terrible corpse in which he lived all day. But Karl soon reassured her; and a few good blows of the axe revealed a very different core to that which Teufelsbürst supposed to be in it. Karl broke it into pieces, and with Lilith's help, who insisted on carrying her share, the whole was soon at the bottom of the Moldau, and every trace of its ever having existed removed. Before morning, too, the form of Lilith had dawned anew in every picture. There was no time to restore to its former condition the one Karl had first altered; for in it the changes were all that they seemed; nor indeed was he capable of restoring it in the master's style; but they put it quite out of the way, and hoped that sufficient time might elapse before the painter thought of it again.

When they had done, and Lilith, for all his entreaties, would remain with him no longer, Karl took his former clothes with him, and having spent the rest of the night in his old room, dressed in them in the morning. When Teufelsbürst entered his studio next day, there sat Karl, as if nothing had happened, finishing the drawing on which he had been at work when the fit of insensibility came upon him. The painter started, stared, rubbed his eyes, thought it was another spectral illusion, but was on the point of yielding to his terror, when Karl rose, and approached him with a smile. The healthy, sunshiny countenance of Karl, let him be ghost or goblin, could not fail to produce somewhat of a tranquillizing effect on Teufelsbürst. He took his offered hand mechanically, his countenance utterly vacant with idiotic bewilderment. Karl said:

"I was not well, and thought it better to pay a visit to a friend for a few days; but I shall soon make up for lost time, for I am all right now."

He sat down at once, taking no notice of his master's behaviour, and went on with his drawing. Teufelsbürst stood staring at him for some minutes without moving, then suddenly turned and left the room. Karl heard him hurrying down the cellar stairs. In a few moments he came up again. Karl stole a glance at him. There he stood in the same spot, no doubt more full of bewilderment than ever; but it was not possible that his face should express more. At last he went to his easel, and sat down with a long-drawn sigh as if of relief. But though he sat at his easel, he painted none that day; and as often as Karl ventured a glance, he saw him still staring at him. The discovery that his pictures were restored to their former condition aided, no doubt, in leading him to the same conclusion as the other facts, whatever that conclusion might be — probably that he had been the sport of some evil power, and had been for the greater part of a week utterly bewitched. Lilith had taken care to instruct the old woman, with whom she was all-powerful; and as neither of them showed the smallest traces of the astonishment which seemed to be slowly vitrifying his own brain, he was at last perfectly satisfied that things had been going on all right everywhere but in his inner man; and in this conclusion he certainly was not far wrong in more senses than one. But when all was restored again to the old routine, it became evident that the peculiar direction of his art in which he had hitherto indulged had ceased to interest him. The shock had acted chiefly upon that part of his mental being which had been so absorbed. He would sit for hours without doing anything, apparently plunged in meditation. — Several weeks elapsed without any change, and both Lilith and Karl were getting dreadfully anxious about him. Karl paid him every attention; and the old man, for he now looked much older than before, submitted to receive his services as well as those of Lilith. At length, one morning, he said in a slow thoughtful tone:

"Karl Wolkenlicht, I should like to paint you."

"Certainly, sir," answered Karl, jumping up, "where would you like me to sit?"

So the ice of silence and inactivity was broken, and the painter drew and painted; and the spring of his art flowed once more; and he made a beautiful portrait of Karl — a portrait without evil or suffering. And as soon as he had finished Karl, he began once more to paint Lilith; and when he had painted her, he composed a picture for the very purpose of introducing them together; and in this picture there was neither ugliness nor torture, but human feeling and human hope instead. Then Karl knew that he might speak to him of Lilith; and he spoke, and was heard with a smile. But he did not dare to tell him the truth of the vampire story till one day that Teufelsbürst was lying on the floor of a room in Karl's ancestral castle, half smothered in grand-children; when the only answer it drew from the old man was a kind of shuddering laugh, and the words — "Don't speak of it, Karl, my boy!"

The History of
Photogen and Nycteris

A DAY AND NIGHT MÄHRCHEN

[The Day Boy and the Night Girl]

CHAPTER I

Watho

There was once a witch who desired to know everything. But the wiser a witch is, the harder she knocks her head against the wall when she comes to it. Her name was Watho, and she had a wolf in her mind. She cared for nothing in itself — only for knowing it. She was not naturally cruel, but the wolf had made her cruel.

She was tall and graceful, with white skin, red hair, and black eyes, which had a red fire in them. She was straight and strong, but now and then would fall bent together, shudder, and sit for a moment with her head turned over her shoulder, as if the wolf had got out of her mind on to her back.

CHAPTER II

Aurora

This witch got two ladies to visit her. One of them belonged to the court, and her husband had been sent on a far and difficult embassy. The other was a young widow whose husband had lately died, and who had since lost her sight. Watho lodged them in different parts of her castle, and they did not know of each other's existence.

The castle stood on the side of a hill sloping gently down into a narrow valley, in which was a river, with a pebbly channel and a continual song. The garden went down to the bank of the river, enclosed by high walls, which crossed the river and there stopped. Each wall had a double row of battlements, and between the rows was a narrow walk.

In the topmost story of the castle the Lady Aurora occupied a spacious apartment of several large rooms looking southward. The windows projected oriel-wise over the garden below, and there was a splendid view from them both up and down and across the river. The opposite side of the valley was steep, but not very high. Far away snowpeaks were visible. These rooms Aurora seldom left, but their airy spaces, the brilliant landscape and sky, the plentiful sunlight, the musical instruments, books, pictures, curiosities, with the company of Watho, who made herself charming, precluded all dullness. She had venison and feathered game to eat, milk and pale sunny sparkling wine to drink.

She had hair of the yellow gold, waved and rippled; her skin was fair, not white like Watho's, and her eyes were of the blue of the heavens when bluest; her features were delicate but strong, her mouth large and finely curved, and haunted with smiles.

CHAPTER III

Vesper

Behind the castle the hill rose abruptly; the north-eastern tower, indeed, was in contact with the rock, and communicated with the interior of it.

ꝗ

For in the rock was a series of chambers, known only to Watho and the one servant whom she trusted, called Falca. Some former owner had constructed these chambers after the tomb of an Egyptian king, and probably with the same design, for in the center of one of them stood what could only be a sarcophagus, but that and others were walled off. The sides and roofs of them were carved in low relief, and curiously painted. Here the witch lodged the blind lady, whose name was Vesper. Her eyes were black, with long black lashes; her skin had a look of darkened silver, but was of purest tint and grain; her hair was black and fine and straight-flowing; her features were exquisitely formed, and if less beautiful yet more lovely from sadness; she always looked as if she wanted to lie down and not rise again. She did not know she was lodged in a tomb, though now and then she wondered she never touched a window. There were many couches, covered with richest silk, and soft as her own cheek, for her to lie upon; and the carpets were so thick, she might have cast herself down anywhere — as befitted a tomb. The place was dry and warm, and cunningly pierced for air, so that it was always fresh, and lacked only sunlight. There the witch fed her upon milk, and wine dark as a carbuncle, and pomegranates, and purple grapes, and birds that dwell in marshy places; and she played to her mournful tunes, and caused wailful violins to attend her, and told her sad tales, thus holding her ever in an atmosphere of sweet sorrow.

CHAPTER IV

Photogen

Watho at length had her desire, for witches often get what they want: a splendid boy was born to the fair Aurora. Just as the sun rose, he opened his eyes. Watho carried him immediately to a distant part of the castle, and persuaded the mother that he never cried but once, dying the moment he was born. Overcome with grief, Aurora left the castle as soon as she was able, and Watho never invited her again.

And now the witch's care was, that the child should not know darkness. Persistently she trained him until at last he never slept during the day, and never woke during the night. She never let him see anything black, and even kept all dull colors out of his way. Never, if she could help it, would she let a shadow fall upon him, watching against shadows as if they had been live things that would hurt him. All day he basked in the full splendour of the sun, in the same large rooms his mother had occupied. Watho used him to the sun, until he could bear more of it than any dark-blooded African. In the hottest of every day, she stript him and laid him in it, that he might ripen like a peach; and the boy rejoiced in it, and would resist being dressed again. She brought all her knowledge to bear on making his muscles strong and elastic and swiftly responsive — that his soul, she said laughing, might sit in every fibre, be all in every part, and awake the moment of call. His hair was of the red gold, but his eyes grew darker as he grew, until they were as black as Vesper's. He was the merriest of creatures, always laughing, always loving, for a moment raging, then laughing afresh. Watho called him Photogen.

CHAPTER V

Nycteris

Five or six months after the birth of Photogen, the dark lady also gave birth to a baby: in the windowless tomb of a blind mother, in the dead of night, under the feeble rays of a lamp in an alabaster globe, a girl came into the darkness with a wail. And just as she was born for the first time, Vesper was born for the second, and passed into a world as unknown to her as this was to her child — who would have to be born yet again before she could see her mother.

Watho called her Nycteris, and she grew as like Vesper as possible — in all but one particular. She had the same dark skin, dark eyelashes and brows, dark hair, and gentle sad look; but she had just the eyes of Aurora, the mother of Photogen, and if they grew darker as she grew older, it was only a darker blue. Watho, with the help of Falca, took the greatest possible care of her — in every way consistent with her plans, that is, — the main point in which was that she should never see any light but what came from the lamp. Hence her optic nerves, and indeed her whole apparatus for seeing, grew both larger and more sensitive; her eyes, indeed, stopped short only of being too large. Under her dark hair and forehead and eyebrows, they looked like two breaks in a cloudy night-sky, through which peeped the heaven where the stars and no clouds live. She was a sadly dainty little creature. No one in the world except those two was aware of the being of the little bat. Watho trained her to sleep during the day, and wake during the night. She taught her music, in which she was herself proficient, and taught her scarcely anything else.

CHAPTER VI

How Photogen Grew

The hollow in which the castle of Watho lay, was a cleft in a plain rather than a valley among hills, for at the top of its steep sides, both north and south, was a table-land, large and wide. It was covered with rich grass and flowers, with here and there a wood, the outlying colony of a great forest. These grassy plains were the finest hunting grounds in the world. Great herds of small, but fierce cattle, with humps and shaggy manes, roved about them, also antelopes and gnus, and the tiny roedeer, while the woods were swarming with wild creatures. The tables of the castle were mainly supplied from them. The chief of Watho's huntsmen was a fine fellow, and when Photogen began to outgrow the training she could give him, she handed him over to Fargu. He with a will set about teaching him all he knew. He got him pony after pony, larger and larger as he grew, every one less manageable than that which had preceded it, and advanced him from pony to horse, and from horse to horse, until he was equal to anything in that kind which the country produced. In similar fashion he trained him to the use of bow and arrow, substituting every three months a stronger bow and longer arrows; and soon he became, even on horseback, a wonderful archer. He was but fourteen when he killed his first bull, causing jubilation among the huntsmen, and, indeed, through all the castle, for there too he was the favourite. Every day, almost as soon as the sun was up, he went out hunting, and would in general be out nearly the whole of the day. But Watho had laid upon Fargu just one commandment, namely, that Photogen should on no account, whatever the plea, be out until sundown, or so near it as to wake in him the desire of seeing what was going to happen; and this commandment Fargu was anxiously careful not to break; for, although he would not have trembled had a whole herd of bulls come down upon him, charging at full speed across the level, and not an arrow left in his quiver, he was more than afraid of his mistress. When she looked at him in a certain way, he felt, he said, as if his heart turned to ashes in his breast, and what ran in his veins was no longer blood, but milk and water. So that, ere long, as Photogen grew older, Fargu began to tremble, for he found it steadily growing harder to restrain him. So full of life was he, as Fargu said to his mistress, much to her content, that he was more like a live thunderbolt than a human being. He did not know what fear was, and that not because he did not know danger; for he had had a severe laceration from the razor-like tusk of a boar — whose spine, however, he had severed with one blow of his hunting-knife, before Fargu could reach him with defence. When he would spur his horse into the midst of a herd of bulls, carrying only his bow and his short sword, or shoot an arrow into a herd, and go after it as if to reclaim it for a runaway shaft, arriving in time to follow it with a spear-thrust before the wounded animal knew which way to charge, Fargu thought with terror how it would be when he came to know the temptation of the huddle-spot leopards, and the knife-clawed lynxes, with which the forest was haunted. For the boy had been so steeped in the sun, from childhood so saturated with his influence, that he looked upon every danger from a sovereign height of courage. When, therefore, he was approaching his sixteenth year, Fargu ventured to beg of Watho that she would lay her commands upon the youth himself, and release him from responsibility for him. One might as soon hold a tawny-maned lion as Photogen, he said. Watho called the youth, and in the presence of Fargu laid her command upon him never to be out when the rim of the sun should touch the horizon, accompanying the prohibition with hints of consequences, none the less awful that they were obscure. Photogen listened respectfully, but, knowing neither the taste of fear nor the temptation of the night, her words were but sounds to him.

CHAPTER VII

How Nycteris Grew

The little education she intended Nycteris to have, Watho gave her by word of mouth. Not meaning she should have light enough to read by, to leave other reasons unmentioned, she never put a book in her hands. Nycteris, however, saw so much better than Watho imagined, that the light she gave her was quite sufficient, and she managed to coax Falca into teaching her the letters, after which she taught herself to read, and Falca now and then brought her a child's book. But her chief pleasure was in her instrument. Her very fingers loved it, and would wander about over its keys like feeding sheep. She was not unhappy. She knew nothing of the world except the tomb in which she dwelt, and had some pleasure in everything she did. But she desired, nevertheless, something more or different. She did not know what it was, and the nearest she could come to expressing it to herself was — that she wanted more room. Watho and Falca would go from her beyond the shine of the lamp, and come again; therefore surely there must be more room somewhere. As often as she was left alone, she would fall to poring over the colored bas-reliefs on the walls. These were intended to represent various of the powers of Nature under allegorical similitudes, and as nothing can be made that does not belong to the general scheme, she could not fail at least to imagine a flicker of relationship between some of them, and thus a shadow of the reality of things found its way to her.

There was one thing, however, which moved and taught her more than all the rest — the lamp, namely, that hung from the ceiling, which she always saw alight, though she never saw the flame, only the slight condensation towards the center of the alabaster globe. And besides the operation of the light itself after its kind, the indefiniteness of the globe, and the softness of the light, giving her the feeling as if her eyes could go in and into its whiteness, were somehow also associated with the idea of space and room. She would sit for an hour together gazing up at the lamp, and her heart would swell as she gazed. She would wonder what had hurt her, when she found her face wet with tears, and then would wonder how she could have been hurt without knowing it. She never looked thus at the lamp except when she was alone.

CHAPTER VIII

The Lamp

Watho having given orders, took it for granted they were obeyed, and that Falca was all night long with Nycteris, whose day it was. But Falca could not get into the habit of sleeping through the day, and would often leave her alone half the night. Then it seemed to Nycteris that the white lamp was watching over her. As it was never permitted to go out — except while she was awake at least — Nycteris, except by shutting her eyes, knew less about darkness than she did about light. Also, the lamp being fixed high overhead, and in the centre of everything, she did not know much about shadows either. The few there were fell almost entirely on the floor, or kept like mice about the foot of the walls.

Once, when she was thus alone, there came the noise of a far-off rumbling: she had never before heard a sound of which she did not know the origin, and here therefore was a new sign of something beyond these chambers. Then came a trembling, then a shaking; the lamp dropped from the ceiling to the floor with a great crash, and she felt as if both her eyes were hard shut and both her hands over them. She concluded that it was the darkness that had made the rumbling and the shaking, and rushing into the room, had thrown down the lamp. She sat trembling. The noise and the shaking ceased, but the light did not return. The darkness had eaten it up!

Her lamp gone, the desire at once awoke to get out of her prison. She scarcely knew what *out* meant; out of one room into another, where there was not even a dividing door, only an open arch, was all she knew of the world. But suddenly she remembered that she had heard Falca speak of the lamp *going out:* this must be what she had meant? And if the lamp had gone out, where had it gone? Surely where Falca went, and like her it would come again. But she could not wait. The desire to go out grew irresistible. She must follow her beautiful lamp! She must find it! She must see what it was about!

Now there was a curtain covering a recess in the wall, where some of her toys and gymnastic things were kept; and from behind that curtain Watho and Falca always appeared, and behind it they vanished. How they came out of solid wall, she had not an idea, all up to the wall was open space, and all beyond it seemed wall; but clearly the first and only thing she could do, was to feel her way behind the curtain. It was so dark that a cat could not have caught the largest of mice. Nycteris could see better than any cat, but now her great eyes were not of the smallest use to her. As she went she trod upon a piece of the broken lamp. She had never worn shoes or stockings, and the fragment, though, being of soft alabaster, it did not cut, yet hurt her foot. She did not know what it was, but as it had not been there before the darkness came, she suspected that it had to do with the lamp. She kneeled therefore, and searched with her hands, and bringing two large pieces together, recognized the shape of the lamp. Therewith it flashed upon her that the lamp was dead, that this brokenness was the death of which she had read without understanding, that the darkness had killed the lamp. What then could Falca have meant when she spoke of the lamp *going out?* There was the lamp — dead, indeed, and so changed that she would never have taken it for a lamp but for the shape! No, it was not the lamp any more now it was dead, for all that made it a lamp was gone, namely, the bright shining of it. Then it must be the shine, the light, that had gone out! That must be what Falca meant — and it must be somewhere in the other place in the wall. She started afresh after it, and groped her way to the curtain.

Now she had never in her life tried to get out, and did not know how; but instinctively she began to move her hands about over one of the walls behind the curtain, half expecting them to go into it, as she supposed Watho and Falca did. But the wall repelled her with inexorable hardness, and she turned to the one opposite. In so doing, she set her foot upon an ivory die, and as it met sharply the same spot the broken alabaster had already hurt, she fell forward with her out-stretched hands against the wall. Something gave way, and she tumbled out of the cavern.

CHAPTER IX

Out

But alas! *out* was very much like *in,* for the same enemy, the darkness, was here also. The next moment, however, came a great gladness — a firefly, which had wandered in from the garden. She saw the tiny spark in the distance. With slow pulsing ebb and throb of light, it came pushing itself through the air, drawing nearer and nearer, with that motion which more resembles swimming than flying, and the light seemed the source of its own motion.

"My lamp! my lamp!" cried Nycteris. "It is the shiningness of my lamp, which the cruel darkness drove out. My good lamp has been waiting for me here all the time! It knew I would come after it, and waited to take me with it."

She followed the firefly, which, like herself, was seeking the way out. If it did not know the way, it was yet light; and, because all light is one, any light may serve to guide to more light. If she was mistaken in thinking it the spirit of her lamp, it was of the same spirit as her lamp — and had wings. The gold-green jet-boat, driven by light, went throbbing before her through a long narrow passage. Suddenly it rose higher, and the same moment Nycteris fell upon an ascending stair. She had never seen a stair before, and found going-up a curious sensation. Just as she reached what seemed the top, the firefly ceased to shine, and so disappeared. She was in utter darkness once more. But when we are following the light, even its extinction is a guide. If the firefly had gone on shining, Nycteris would have seen the stair turn, and would have gone up to Watho's bedroom; whereas now, feeling straight before her, she came to a latched door, which after a good deal of trying she managed to open — and stood in a maze of wondering perplexity, awe, and delight. What was it? Was it outside of her, or something taking place in her head? Before her was a very long and very narrow passage, broken up she could not tell how, and spreading out above and on all sides to an infinite height and breadth and distance — as if space itself were growing out of a trough. It was brighter than her rooms had ever been — brighter than if six alabaster lamps had been burning in them. There was a quantity of strange streaking and mottling about it, very different from the shapes on her walls. She was in a dream of pleasant perplexity, of delightful bewilderment. She could not tell whether she was upon her feet or drifting about like the firefly, driven by the pulses of an inward bliss. But she knew little as yet of her inheritance. Unconsciously she took one step forward from the threshold, and the girl who had been from her very birth a troglodyte,* stood in the ravishing glory of a southern night, lit by a perfect moon — not the moon of our northern clime, but a moon like silver glowing in a furnace — a moon

*A cave dweller

one could see to be a globe — not far off, a mere flat disc on the face of the blue, but hanging down halfway, and looking as if one could see all round it by a mere bending of the neck.

"It is my lamp!" she said, and stood dumb with parted lips. She looked and felt as if she had been standing there in silent ecstasy from the beginning.

"No, it is not my lamp," she said after a while; "it is the mother of all the lamps."

And with that she fell on her knees, and spread out her hands to the moon. She could not in the least have told what was in her mind, but the action was in reality just a begging of the moon to be what she was — that precise incredible splendor hung in the far-off roof, that very glory essential to the being of poor girls born and bred in caverns. It was a resurrection — nay, a birth itself, to Nycteris. What the vast blue sky, studded with tiny sparks like the heads of diamond nails, could be; what the moon, looking so absolutely content with light — why, she knew less about them than you and I! but the greatest of astronomers might envy the rapture of such a first impression at the age of sixteen. Immeasurably imperfect it was, but false the impression could not be, for she saw with eyes made for seeing, and saw indeed what many men are too wise to see.

As she knelt, something softly flapped her, embraced her, stroked her, fondled her. She rose to her feet, but saw nothing, did not know what it was. It was likest a woman's breath. For she knew nothing of the air even, had never breathed the still newborn freshness of the world. Her breath had come to her only through long passages and spirals in the rock. Still less did she know of the air alive with motion — of that thrice blessed thing, the wind of a summer night. It was like a spiritual wine, filling her whole being with an intoxication of purest joy. To breathe was a perfect existence. It seemed to her the light itself she drew into her lungs. Possessed by the power of the gorgeous night, she seemed at one and the same moment annihilated and glorified.

She was in the open passage or gallery that ran round the top of the garden walls, between the cleft battlements, but she did not once look down to see what lay beneath. Her soul was drawn to the vault above her, with its lamp and its endless room. At last she burst into tears, and her heart was relieved, as the night itself is relieved by its lightning and rain.

And now she grew thoughtful. She must hoard this splendour! What a little ignorance her gaolers had made of her! Life was a mighty bliss, and they had scraped hers to the bare bone! They must not know that she knew. She must hide her knowledge — hide it even from her own eyes, keeping it close in her bosom, content to know that she had it, even when she could not brood on its presence, feasting her eyes with its glory. She turned from the vision, therefore, with a sigh of utter bliss, and with soft quiet steps and groping hands, stole back into the darkness of the rock. What was darkness or the laziness of Time's feet to one who had seen what she had that night seen? She was lifted above all weariness — above all wrong.

When Falca entered, she uttered a cry of terror. But Nycteris called to her not to be afraid, and told her how there had come a rumbling and a shaking, and the lamp had fallen. Then Falca went and told her mistress, and within an hour a new globe hung in the place of the old one. Nycteris thought it did not look so bright and clear as the former, but she made no lamentation over the change; she was far too rich to heed it. For now, prisoner as she knew herself, her heart was full of glory and gladness; at times she had to hold herself from jumping up, and going dancing and singing about the room. When she slept, instead of dull dreams, she had splendid visions. There were times, it is true, when she became restless, and impatient to look upon her riches, but then she would reason with herself, saying, "What does it matter if I sit here for ages with my poor pale lamp, when out there a lamp is burning at which ten thousand little lamps are glowing with wonder?"

She never doubted she had looked upon the day and the sun, of which she had read; and always when she read of the day and the sun, she had the night and the moon in her mind; and when she read of the night and the moon, she thought only of the cave and the lamp that hung there.

CHAPTER X

The Great Lamp

It was some time before she had a second opportunity of going out, for Falca, since the fall of the lamp, had been a little more careful, and seldom left her for long. But one night, having a little headache, Nycteris lay down upon her bed, and was lying with her eyes closed, when she heard Falca come to

THE HISTORY OF PHOTOGEN AND NYCTERIS

her, and felt she was bending over her. Disinclined to talk, she did not open her eyes, and lay quite still. Satisfied that she was asleep, Falca left her, moving so softly that her very caution made Nycteris open her eyes and look after her — just in time to see her vanish — through a picture, as it seemed, that hung on the wall a long way from the usual place of issue. She jumped up, her headache forgotten, and ran in the opposite direction; got out, groped her way to the stair, climbed, and reached the top of the wall. — Alas! the great room was not so light as the little one she had left. Why? — Sorrow of sorrows! the great lamp was gone! Had its globe fallen? and its lovely light gone out upon great wings, a resplendent firefly, oaring itself through a yet grander and lovelier room? She looked down to see if it lay anywhere broken to pieces on the carpet below; but she could not even see the carpet. But surely nothing very dreadful could have happened — no rumbling or shaking, for there were all the little lamps shining brighter than before, not one of them looking as if any unusual matter had befallen. What if each of those little lamps was growing into a big lamp, and after being a big lamp for a while, had to go out and grow a bigger lamp still — out there, beyond this *out?* — Ah! here was the living thing that would not be seen, come to her again — bigger to-night! with such loving kisses, and such liquid strokings of her cheeks and forehead, gently tossing her hair, and delicately toying with it! But it ceased, and all was still. Had it gone out? What would happen next? Perhaps the little lamps had not to grow great lamps, but to fall one by one and go out first? — With that, came from below a sweet scent, then another, and another. Ah, how delicious! Perhaps they were all coming to her only on their way out after the great lamp! — Then came the music of the river, which she had been too absorbed in the sky to note the first time. What was it? Alas! alas! another sweet living thing on its way out. They were all marching slowly out in long lovely file, one after the other, each taking its leave of her as it passed! It must be so: here were more and more sweet sounds, following and fading! The whole of the *Out* was going out again; it was all going after the great lovely lamp! She would be left the only creature in the solitary day! Was there nobody to hang up a new lamp for the old one, and keep the creatures from going? — She crept back to her rock very sad. She tried to comfort herself by saying that anyhow there would be room out there; but as she said it she shuddered at the thought of *empty* room.

When next she succeeded in getting out, a half-moon hung in the east: a new lamp had come, she thought, and all would be well.

It would be endless to describe the phases of feeling through which

Nycteris passed, more numerous and delicate than those of a thousand changing moons. A fresh bliss bloomed in her soul with every varying aspect of infinite nature. Ere long she began to suspect that the new moon was the old moon, gone out and come in again like herself; also that, unlike herself, it wasted and grew again; that it was indeed a live thing, subject like herself to caverns, and keepers, and solitudes, escaping and shining when it could. Was it a prison like hers it was shut in? and did it grow dark when the lamp left it? Where could be the way into it? — With that first she began to look below, as well as above and around her; and then first noted the tops of the trees between her and the floor. There were palms with their red-fingered hands full of fruit; eucalyptus trees crowded with little boxes of powder-puffs; oleanders with their half-caste roses; and orange trees with their clouds of young silver stars, and their aged balls of gold. Her eyes could see colours invisible to ours in the moonlight, and all these she could distinguish well, though at first she took them for the shapes and colours of the carpet of the great room. She longed to get down among them, now she saw they were real creatures, but she did not know how. She went along the whole length of the wall to the end that crossed the river, but found no way of going down. Above the river she stopped to gaze with awe upon the rushing water. She knew nothing of water but from what she drank and what she bathed in; and, as the moon shone on the dark, swift stream, singing lustily as it flowed, she did not doubt the river was alive, a swift rushing serpent of life, going — out? — whither? And then she wondered if what was brought into her rooms had been killed that she might drink it, and have her bath in it.

Once when she stepped out upon the wall, it was into the midst of a fierce wind. The trees were all roaring. Great clouds were rushing along the skies, and tumbling over the little lamps: the great lamp had not come yet. All was in tumult. The wind seized her garments and hair, and shook them as if it would tear them from her. What could she have done to make the gentle creature so angry? Or was this another creature altogether — of the same kind, but hugely bigger, and of a very different temper and behaviour? But the whole place was angry! Or was it that the creatures dwelling in it, the wind, and the trees, and the clouds, and the river, had all quarreled, each with all the rest? Would the whole come to confusion and disorder? But, as she gazed wondering and disquieted, the moon, larger than ever she had seen her, came lifting herself above the horizon to look, broad and red as if she, too, were swollen with anger that she had been roused from her rest by their noise, and compelled to hurry up to see what her children were about, thus rioting in her absence, lest they should rack the whole frame of things. And as she rose, the loud wind grew quieter and scolded less fiercely, the trees grew stiller and moaned with a lower complaint, and the clouds hunted and hurled themselves less wildly across the sky. And as if she were pleased that her children obeyed her very presence, the moon grew smaller as she ascended the heavenly stair; her puffed cheeks sank, her complexion grew clearer, and a sweet smile spread over her countenance, as peacefully she rose and rose. But there was treason and rebellion in her court; for, ere she reached the top of her great stairs, the clouds had assembled, forgetting their late wars, and very still they were as they laid their heads together and conspired. Then combining, and lying silently in wait until she came near, they threw themselves upon her, and swallowed her up. Down from the roof came spots of wet, faster and faster, and they wetted the cheeks of Nycteris; and what could they be but the tears of the moon, crying because her children were smothering her? Nycteris wept too, and not knowing what to think, stole back in dismay to her room.

The next time, she came out in fear and trembling. There was the moon still! away in the west — poor, indeed, and old, and looking dreadfully worn, as if all the wild beasts in the sky had been gnawing at her — but there she was, alive still, and able to shine!

CHAPTER XI

The Sunset

Knowing nothing of darkness, or stars, or moon, Photogen spent his days in hunting. On a great white horse he swept over the grassy plains, glorying in the sun, fighting the wind, and killing the buffaloes.

One morning, when he happened to be on the ground a little earlier than usual, and before his attendants, he caught sight of an animal unknown to him, stealing from a hollow into which the sunrays had not yet reached. Like a swift shadow it sped over the grass, slinking southward to the forest. He gave chase, noted the body of a buffalo it had half eaten, and pursued it the harder. But with great leaps and bounds the creature shot farther and farther ahead of him, and vanished. Turning therefore defeated, he met Fargu, who had been following him as fast as his horse could carry him.

"What animal was that, Fargu?" he asked. "How he did run!"

Fargu answered he might be a leopard, but he rather thought from his pace and look that he was a young lion.

"What a coward he must be!" said Photogen.

"Don't be too sure of that," rejoined Fargu. "He is one of the creatures the sun makes uncomfortable. As soon as the sun is down, he will be brave enough."

He had scarcely said it, when he repented; nor did he regret it the less when he found that Photogen made no reply. But alas! said was said.

"Then," said Photogen to himself, "that contemptible beast is one of the terrors of sundown, of which Madam Watho spoke!"

He hunted all day, but not with his usual spirit. He did not ride so hard, and did not kill one buffalo. Fargu to his dismay observed also that he took every pretext for moving farther south, nearer to the forest. But all at once, the sun now sinking in the west, he seemed to change his mind, for he turned his horse's head, and rode home so fast that the rest could not keep him in sight. When they arrived, they found his horse in the stable, and concluded that he had gone into the castle. But he had in truth set out again by the back of it. Crossing the river a good way up the valley, he reascended to the ground they had left, and just before sunset reached the skirts of the forest.

The level orb shone straight in between the bare stems, and saying to himself he could not fail to find the beast, he rushed into the wood. But even as he entered, he turned, and looked to the west. The rim of the red was touching the horizon, all jagged with broken hills. "Now," said Photogen, "we shall see"; but he said it in the face of a darkness he had not proved. The moment the sun began to sink among the spikes and saw-edges, with a kind of sudden flap at his heart a fear inexplicable laid hold of the youth; and as he had never felt anything of the kind before, the very fear itself terrified him. As the sun sank, it rose like the shadow of the world, and grew deeper and darker. He could not even think what it might be, so utterly did it enfeeble him. When the last flaming scimitar-edge of the sun went out like a lamp, his horror seemed to blossom into very madness. Like the closing lids of an eye — for there was no

THE HISTORY OF PHOTOGEN AND NYCTERIS

twilight, and this night no moon — the terror and the darkness rushed together, and he knew them for one. He was no longer the man he had known, or rather thought himself. The courage he had had was in no sense his own — he had only had courage, not been courageous; it had left him, and he could scarcely stand — certainly not stand straight, for not one of his joints could he make stiff or keep from trembling. He was but a spark of the sun, in himself nothing.

The beast was behind him — stealing upon him! He turned. All was dark in the wood, but to his fancy the darkness here and there broke into pairs of green eyes, and he had not the power even to raise his bow-hand from his side. In the strength of despair he strove to rouse courage enough — not to fight — that he did not even desire — but to run. Courage to flee home was all he could ever imagine, and it would not come. But what he had not, was ignominiously given him. A cry in the wood, half a screech, half a growl, sent him running like a boar-wounded cur. It was not even himself that ran, it was the fear that had come alive in his legs: he did not know that they moved. But as he ran he grew able to run — gained courage at least to be a coward. The stars gave a little light. Over the grass he sped, and nothing followed him. "How fallen, how changed," from the youth who had climbed the hill as the sun went down! A mere contempt to himself, the self that contemned was a coward with the self it contemned! There lay the shapeless black of a buffalo, humped upon the grass: he made a wide circuit, and swept on like a shadow driven in the wind. For the wind had arisen, and added to his terror: it blew from behind him. He reached the brow of the valley, and shot down the steep descent like a falling star. Instantly the whole upper country behind him arose and pursued him! The wind came howling after him, filled with screams, shrieks, yells, roars, laughter, and chattering, as if all the animals of the forest were careering with it. In his ears was a trampling rush, the thunder of the hoofs of the cattle, in career from every quarter of the wide plains to the brow of the hill above him! He fled straight for the castle, scarcely with breath enough to pant.

As he reached the bottom of the valley, the moon peered up over its edge. He had never seen the moon before — except in the daytime, when he had taken her for a thin bright cloud. She was a fresh terror to him — so ghostly! so ghastly! so gruesome! — so knowing as she looked over the top of her garden-wall upon the world outside! That was the night itself! the darkness alive — and after him! the horror of horrors coming down the sky to curdle his blood, and turn his brain to a cinder! He gave a sob, and made straight for the river, where it ran between the two walls, at the bottom of the garden. He plunged in, struggled through, clambered up the bank, and fell senseless on the grass.

CHAPTER XII

The Garden

Although Nycteris took care not to stay out long at a time, and used every precaution, she could hardly have escaped discovery so long, had it not been that the strange attacks to which Watho was subject had been more frequent of late, and had at last settled into an illness which kept her to her bed. But whether from an excess of caution or from suspicion, Falca, having now to be much with her mistress both day and night, took it at length into her head to fasten the door as often as she went by her usual place of exit; so that one night, when Nycteris pushed, she found, to her surprise and dismay, that the wall pushed her again, and would not let her through; nor with all her searching could she discover wherein lay the cause of the change. Then first she felt the pressure of her prison-walls, and turning, half in despair, groped her way to the picture where she had once seen Falca disappear. There she soon found the spot by pressing upon which the wall yielded. It let her through into a sort of cellar, where was a glimmer of light from a sky whose blue was paled by the moon. From the cellar she got into a long passage, into which the moon was shining, and came to a door. She managed to open it, and, to her great joy, found herself in *the other place*, not on the top of the wall, however, but in the garden she had longed to enter. Noiseless as a fluffy moth she flitted away into the covert of the trees and shrubs, her bare feet welcomed by the softest of carpets, which, by the very touch, her feet knew to be alive, whence it came that it was so sweet and friendly to them. A soft little wind was out among the trees, running now here, now there, like a child that had got its will. She went dancing over the grass, looking behind her at her shadow, as she went. At first she had taken it for a little black creature that made game of her, but when she perceived that it was only

❧ THE HISTORY OF PHOTOGEN AND NYCTERIS

where she kept the moon away, and that every tree, however great and grand a creature, had also one of these strange attendants, she soon learned not to mind it, and by and by it became the source of as much amusement to her, as to any kitten its tail. It was long before she was quite at home with the trees, however. At one time they seemed to disapprove of her; at another not even to know she was there, and to be altogether taken up with their own business. Suddenly, as she went from one to another of them, looking up with awe at the murmuring mystery of their branches and leaves, she spied one a little way off, which was very different from all the rest. It was white, and dark, and sparkling, and spread like a palm — a small slender palm, without much head; and it grew very fast, and sang as it grew. But it never grew any bigger, for just as fast as she could see it growing, it kept falling to pieces. When she got close to it, she discovered that it was a water-tree — made of just such water as she washed with — only it was alive, of course, like the river — a different sort of water from that, doubtless, seeing the one crept swiftly along the floor, and the other shot straight up, and fell, and swallowed itself, and rose again. She put her feet into the marble basin, which was the flower-pot in which it grew. It was full of real water, living and cool — so nice, for the night was hot!

But the flowers! ah, the flowers! she was friends with them from the very first. What wonderful creatures they were! — and so kind and beautiful — always sending out such colours and such scents — red scent, and white scent, and yellow scent — for the other creatures! The one that was invisible and everywhere, took such a quantity of their scents, and carried it away! yet they did not seem to mind. It was their talk, to show they were alive, and not painted like those on the walls of her rooms, and on the carpets.

She wandered along down the garden, until she reached the river. Unable then to get any further — for she was a little afraid, and justly, of the swift watery serpent — she dropped on the grassy bank, dipped her feet in the water, and felt it running and pushing against them. For a long time she sat thus, and her bliss seemed complete, as she gazed at the river, and watched the broken picture of the great lamp overhead, moving up one side of the roof, to go down the other.

CHAPTER XIII

Something Quite New

A beautiful moth brushed across the great blue eyes of Nycteris. She sprang to her feet to follow it — not in the spirit of the hunter, but of the lover. Her heart — like every heart, if only its fallen sides were cleared away — was an inexhaustible fountain of love: she loved everything she saw. But as she followed the moth, she caught sight of something lying on the bank of the river, and not yet having learned to be afraid of anything, ran straight to see what it was. Reaching it, she stood amazed. Another girl like herself! But what a strange-looking girl! — so curiously dressed too! — and not able to move! Was she dead? Filled suddenly with pity, she sat down, lifted Photogen's head, laid it on her lap, and began stroking his face. Her warm hands brought him to himself. He opened his black eyes, out of which had gone all the fire, and looked up with a strange sound of fear, half moan, half gasp. But when he saw her face, he drew a deep breath, and lay motionless — gazing at her: those blue marvels above him, like a better sky, seemed to side with courage and assuage his terror. At length, in a trembling, awed voice, and a half whisper, he said, "Who are you?"

"I am Nycteris," she answered.

"You are a creature of the darkness, and love the night," he said, his fear beginning to move again.

"I may be a creature of the darkness," she replied. "I hardly know what you mean. But I do not love the night. I love the day — with all my heart; and I sleep all the night long."

"How can that be?" said Photogen, rising on his elbow, but dropping his head on her lap again the moment he saw the moon; " — how can it be," he repeated, "when I see your eyes there — wide awake?"

She only smiled and stroked him, for she did not understand him, and thought he did not know what he was saying.

"Was it a dream then?" resumed Photogen, rubbing his eyes. But with that his memory came clear, and he shuddered, and cried, "Oh horrible! horrible! to be turned all at once into a coward! a shameful, contemptible, disgraceful coward! I am ashamed — ashamed — and *so* frightened! It is all so frightful!"

"What is so frightful?" asked Nycteris, with a smile like that of a mother to her child waked from a bad dream.

"All, all," he answered; "all this darkness and the roaring."

"My dear," said Nycteris, "there is no roaring. How sensitive you must be! What you hear is only the walking of the water, and the running about of the sweetest of all the creatures. She is invisible, and I call her Everywhere, for she goes through all the other creatures and comforts them. Now she is amusing herself, and them too, with shaking them and kissing them, and blowing in their faces. Listen: do you call that roaring? You should hear her when she is rather angry, though! I don't know why, but she is sometimes, and then she does roar a little."

"It is so horribly dark!" said Photogen, who, listening while she spoke, had satisfied himself that there was no roaring.

"Dark!" she echoed. "You should be in my room when an earthquake has killed my lamp. I do not understand. How *can* you call this dark? Let me see: yes, you have eyes, and big ones, bigger than Madam Watho's or Falca's — not so big as mine, I fancy — only I never saw mine. But then — oh yes! — I know now what is the matter! You can't see with them because they are so black. Darkness can't see, of course. Never mind: I will be your eyes, and teach you to see. Look here — at these lovely white things in the grass, and with red sharp points all folded together into one. Oh, I love them so! I could sit looking at them all day, the darlings!"

Photogen looked close at the flowers, and thought he had seen something like them before, but could not make them out. As Nycteris had never seen an open daisy, so had he never seen a closed one.

Thus instinctively Nycteris tried to turn him away from his fear; and the beautiful creature's strange, lovely talk helped not a little to make him forget it.

"You call it dark!" she said again, as if she could not get rid of the absurdity of the idea; "why, I could count every blade of the green hair — I suppose it is what the books call grass — within two yards of me! And just look at the great lamp! It is brighter than usual to-day, and I can't think why you should be frightened, or call it dark!"

As she spoke, she went on stroking his cheeks and hair, and trying to comfort him. But oh how miserable he was! and how plainly he looked it! He was on the point of saying that her great lamp was dreadful to him, looking like a witch, walking in the sleep of death; but he was not so ignorant as Nycteris, and knew even in the moonlight that she was a woman, though he had never seen one so young or so lovely before; and while she comforted his fear, her presence made him the more ashamed of it. Besides, not knowing her nature, he might annoy her, and make her leave him to his misery. He lay still therefore, hardly daring to move: all the little life he had seemed to come from her, and if he were to move, she might move; and if she were to leave him, he must weep like a child.

"How did you come here?" asked Nycteris, taking his face between her hands.

"Down the hill," he answered.

"Where do you sleep?" she asked.

He signed in the direction of the house. She gave a little laugh of delight.

"When you have learned not to be frightened, you will always be wanting to come out with me," she said.

She thought with herself she would ask her presently, when she had come to herself a little, how she had made her escape, for she must, of course, like herself have got out of a cave, in which Watho and Falca had been keeping her.

"Look at the lovely colours," she went on, pointing to a rose-bush, on which Photogen could not see a single flower. "They are far more beautiful — are they not? — than any of the colours upon your walls. And then they are alive, and smell so sweet!"

He wished she would not make him keep opening his eyes to look at things he could not see; and every other moment would start and grasp tight hold of her, as some fresh pang of terror shot into him.

"Come, come, dear!" said Nycteris; "you must not go on this way. You must be a brave girl, and — — "

"A girl!" shouted Photogen, and started to his feet in wrath. "If you were a man, I should kill you."

"A man?" repeated Nycteris: "what is that? How could I be that? We are both girls — are we not?"

"No, I am not a girl," he answered; " — although," he added, changing his tone, and casting himself on the ground at her feet, "I have given you too good reason to call me one."

"Oh, I see!" returned Nycteris. "No, of course! you can't be a girl: girls are not afraid — without reason. I understand now: it is because you are not a girl that you are so frightened."

Photogen twisted and writhed upon the grass.

"No, it is not," he said sulkily; "it is this horrible darkness that creeps into me, goes all through me, into the very marrow of my bones — that is what makes me behave like a girl. If only the sun would rise!"

"The sun! what is it?" cried Nycteris, now in her turn conceiving a vague fear.

Then Photogen broke into a rhapsody, in which he vainly sought to forget his.

"It is the soul, the life, the heart, the glory of the universe," he said. "The worlds dance like motes in his beams. The heart of man is strong and brave in his light, and when it departs his courage grows from him — goes with the sun, and he becomes such as you see me now."

"Then that is not the sun?" said Nycteris, thoughtfully, pointing up to the moon.

"That!" cried Photogen, with utter scorn; "I know nothing about *that*, except that it is ugly and horrible. At best it can be only the ghost of a dead sun. Yes, that is it! That is what makes it look so frightful."

"No," said Nycteris, after a long, thoughtful pause; "you must be wrong there. I think the sun is the ghost of a dead moon, and that is how he is so much more splendid, as you say. — Is there, then, another big room, where the sun lives in the roof?"

"I do not know what you mean," replied Photogen. "But you mean to be kind, I know, though you should not call a poor fellow in the dark a girl. If you will let me lie here, with my head in your lap, I should like to sleep. Will you watch me, and take care of me?"

"Yes, that I will," answered Nycteris, forgetting all her own danger. So Photogen fell asleep.

CHAPTER XIV

The Sun

There Nycteris sat, and there the youth lay, all night long, in the heart of the great cone-shadow of the earth, like two Pharaohs in one pyramid. Photogen slept, and slept; and Nycteris sat motionless lest she should wake him, and so betray him to his fear.

The moon rode high in the blue eternity; it was a very triumph of glorious night; the river ran babble-murmuring in deep, soft syllables; the fountain kept rushing moonward, and blossoming momently to a great silvery flower, whose petals were for ever falling like snow, but with a continuous musical clash, into the bed of its exhaustion beneath; the wind woke, took a run among the trees, went to sleep, and woke again; the daisies slept on their feet at hers, but she did not know they slept; the roses might well seem awake, for their scent filled the air, but in truth they slept also, and the odour was that of their dreams; the oranges hung like gold lamps in the trees, and their silvery flowers were the souls of their yet unembodied children; the scent of the acacia blooms filled the air like the very odour of the moon herself.

At last, unused to the living air, and weary with sitting so still and so long, Nycteris grew drowsy. The air began to grow cool. It was getting near the time when she too was accustomed to sleep. She closed her eyes just a moment, and nodded — opened them suddenly wide, for she had promised to watch.

In that moment a change had come. The moon had got round, and was fronting her from the west, and she saw that her face was altered, that she had grown pale, as if she too were wan with fear, and from her lofty place espied a coming terror. The light seemed to be dissolving out of her; she was dying — she was going out! And yet everything around looked strangely clear — clearer than ever she had seen anything before: how could the lamp be shedding more light when she herself had less? Ah, that was just it! See how faint she looked! It was because the light was forsaking her, and spreading itself over the room, that she grew so thin and pale! She was giving up everything! She was melting away from the roof like a bit of sugar in water.

Nycteris was fast growing afraid, and sought refuge with the face upon her lap. How beautiful the creature was! — what to call it she could not think, for it had been angry when she called it what Watho called her. And, wonder upon wonder! now, even in the cold change that was passing upon the great room, the color as of a red rose was rising in the wan cheek. What beautiful yellow hair it was that spread over her lap! What great huge breaths the creature took! And what were those curious things it carried? She had seen them on her walls, she was sure.

Thus she talked to herself while the lamp grew paler and paler, and everything kept growing yet clearer. What could it mean? The lamp was dying — going out into the other place of which the creature in her lap

❦   THE HISTORY OF PHOTOGEN AND NYCTERIS

had spoken, to be a sun! But why were the things growing clearer before it was yet a sun? That was the point. Was it her growing into a sun that did it? Yes! yes! it was coming death! She knew it, for it was coming upon her also! She felt it coming! What was she about to grow into! Something beautiful, like the creature in her lap? It might be! Anyhow, it must be death; for all her strength was going out of her, while all around her was growing so light she could not bear it! She must be blind soon! Would she be blind or dead first?

For the sun was rushing up behind her. Photogen woke, lifted his head from her lap, and sprang to his feet. His face was one radiant smile. His heart was full of daring — that of the hunter who will creep into the tiger's den. Nycteris gave a cry, covered her face with her hands, and pressed her eyelids close. Then blindly she stretched out her arms to Photogen, crying, "Oh, I am *so* frightened! What is this? It must be death! I don't wish to die yet. I love this room and the old lamp. I do not want the other place! This is terrible. I want to hide. I want to get into the sweet, soft, dark hands of all the other creatures. Ah me! ah me!"

"What is the matter with you, girl?" said Photogen, with the arrogance of all male creatures until they have been taught by the other kind. He stood looking down upon her over his bow, of which he was examining the string. "There is no fear of anything now, child. It is day. The sun is all but up. Look! he will be above the brow of yon hill in one moment more! Good-bye. Thank you for my night's lodging. I'm off. Don't be a goose. If ever I can do anything for you — and all that, you know!"

"Don't leave me: oh, don't leave me!" cried Nycteris. "I am dying! I am dying! I cannot move. The light sucks all the strength out of me. And oh, I am *so* frightened!"

But already Photogen had splashed through the river, holding high his bow that it might not get wet. He rushed across the level, and strained up the opposing hill. Hearing no answer, Nycteris removed her hands. Photogen had reached the top, and the same moment the sunrays alighted upon him: the glory of the king of day crowded blazing upon the golden-haired youth. Radiant as Apollo, he stood in mighty strength, a flashing shape in the midst of flame. He fitted a glowing arrow to a gleaming bow. The arrow parted with a keen musical twang of the bowstring, and Photogen, darting after it, vanished with a shout. Up shot Apollo himself, and from his quiver scattered astonishment and exultation. But the brain of poor Nycteris was pierced through and through. She fell down in utter darkness. All around her was a flaming furnace. In despair and feebleness and agony, she crept back, feeling her way with doubt and difficulty and enforced persistence to her cell. When at last the friendly darkness of her chamber folded her about with its cooling and consoling arms, she threw herself on her bed and fell fast asleep. And there she slept on, one alive in a tomb, while Photogen, above in the sun-glory, pursued the buffaloes on the lofty plain, thinking not once of her where she lay dark and forsaken, whose presence had been his refuge, her eyes and her hands his guardians through the night. He was in his glory and his pride; and the darkness and its disgrace had vanished for a time.

CHAPTER XV

The Coward Hero

But no sooner had the sun reached the noonstead, than Photogen began to remember the past night in the shadow of that which was at hand, and to remember it with shame. He had proved himself — and not to himself only, but to a girl as well — a coward! — one bold in the daylight, while there was nothing to fear, but trembling like any slave when the night arrived. There was, there must be, something unfair in it! A spell had been cast upon him! He had eaten, he had drunk something that did not agree with courage! In any case he had been taken unprepared! How was he to know what the going down of the sun would be like? It was no wonder he should have been surprised into terror, seeing it was what it was — in its very nature so terrible! Also, one could not see where danger might be coming from! You might be torn in pieces, carried off, or swallowed up, without even seeing where to strike a blow! Every possible excuse he caught at, eager as a self-lover to lighten his self-contempt. That day he astonished the huntsmen — terrified them with his reckless daring — all to prove to himself he was no coward. But nothing eased his shame. One thing only had hope in it — the resolve to encounter the dark in solemn earnest, now that he knew something of what it was. It was nobler to meet a recognized danger than to rush contemptuously into what seemed nothing — nobler still to encounter a nameless horror. He could conquer fear and wipe out

♪ THE HISTORY OF PHOTOGEN AND NYCTERIS

disgrace together. For a marksman and swordsman like him, he said, one with his strength and courage, there was but danger. Defeat there was not. He knew the darkness now, and when it came he would meet it as fearless and cool as now he felt himself. And again he said, "We shall see!"

He stood under the boughs of a great beech as the sun was going down, far away over the jagged hills: before it was half down, he was trembling like one of the leaves behind him in the first sigh of the night-wind. The moment the last of the glowing disc vanished, he bounded away in terror to gain the valley, and his fear grew as he ran. Down the side of the hill, an abject creature, he went bounding and rolling and running; fell rather than plunged into the river, and came to himself, as before, lying on the grassy bank in the garden.

But when he opened his eyes, there were no girl-eyes looking down into his; there were only the stars in the waste of the sunless Night — the awful all-enemy he had again dared, but could not encounter. Perhaps the girl was not yet come out of the water! He would try to sleep, for he dared not move, and perhaps when he woke he would find his head on her lap, and the beautiful dark face, with its deep blue eyes, bending over him. But when he woke he found his head on the grass, and although he sprang up with all his courage, such as it was, restored, he did not set out for the chase with such an *elan* as the day before; and, despite the sun-glory in his heart and veins, his hunting was this day less eager; he ate little, and from the first was thoughtful even to sadness. A second time he was defeated and disgraced! Was his courage nothing more than the play of the sunlight on his brain? Was he a mere ball tossed between the light and the dark? Then what a poor contemptible creature he was! But a third chance lay before him. If he failed the third time, he dared not foreshadow what he must then think of himself! It was bad enough now — but then!

Alas! it went no better. The moment the sun was down, he fled as if from a legion of devils.

Seven times in all, he tried to face the coming night in the strength of the past day, and seven times he failed — failed with such increase of failure, with such a growing sense of ignominy, overwhelming at length all the sunny hours and joining night to night, that, what with misery, self-accusation, and loss of confidence, his daylight courage too began to fade, and at length, from exhaustion, from getting wet, and then lying out of doors all night, and night after night, — worst of all, from the con-suming of the deathly fear, and the shame of shame, his sleep forsook him, and on the seventh morning, instead of going to the hunt, he crawled into the castle, and went to bed. The grand health, over which the witch had taken such pains, had yielded, and in an hour or two he was moaning and crying out in delirium.

CHAPTER XVI

An Evil Nurse

Watho was herself ill, as I have said, and was the worse tempered; and, besides, it is a peculiarity of witches, that what works in others to sympathy, works in them to repulsion. Also, Watho had a poor, helpless, rudimentary spleen of a conscience left, just enough to make her uncomfortable, and therefore more wicked. So, when she heard that Photogen was ill, she was angry. Ill, indeed! after all she had done to saturate him with the life of the system, with the solar might itself! He was a wretched failure, the boy! And because he was *her* failure, she was annoyed with him, began to dislike him, grew to hate him. She looked on him as a painter might upon a picture, or a poet upon a poem, which he had only succeeded in getting into an irrecoverable mess. In the hearts of witches, love and hate lie close together, and often tumble over each other. And whether it was that her failure with Photogen foiled also her plans in regard to Nycteris, or that her illness made her yet more of a devil's wife, certainly Watho now got sick of the girl too, and hated to know her about the castle.

She was not too ill, however, to go to poor Photogen's room and torment him. She told him she hated him like a serpent, and hissed like one as she said it, looking very sharp in the nose and chin, and flat in the forehead. Photogen thought she meant to kill him, and hardly ventured to take anything brought him. She ordered every ray of light to be shut out of his room; but by means of this he got a little used to the darkness. She would take one of his arrows, and now tickle him with the feather end of it, now prick him with the point till the blood ran down. What she meant finally I cannot tell, but she brought Photogen speedily to the determination of making his escape from the castle: what he should do then he would think afterwards. Who could tell but he might find his

❧ THE HISTORY OF PHOTOGEN AND NYCTERIS

mother somewhere beyond the forest! If it were not for the broad patches of darkness that divided day from day, he would fear nothing!

But now, as he lay helpless in the dark, ever and anon would come dawning through it the face of the lovely creature who on that first awful night nursed him so sweetly: was he never to see her again? If she was, as he had concluded, the nymph of the river, why had she not re-appeared? She might have taught him not to fear the night, for plainly she had no fear of it herself! But then, when the day came, she did seem frightened: — why was that, seeing there was nothing to be afraid of then? Perhaps one so much at home in the darkness, was correspondingly afraid of the light! Then his selfish joy at the rising of the sun, blinding him to her condition, had made him behave to her, in ill return for her kindness, as cruelly as Watho behaved to him! How sweet and dear and lovely she was! If there were wild beasts that came out only at night, and were afraid of the light, why should there not be girls too, made the same way — who could not endure the light, as he could not bear the darkness? If only he could find her again! Ah, how differently he would behave to her! But alas! perhaps the sun had killed her — melted her — burned her up! — dried her up — that was it, if she was the nymph of the river!

CHAPTER XVII

Watho's Wolf

From that dreadful morning Nycteris had never got to be herself again. The sudden light had been almost death to her; and now she lay in the dark with the memory of a terrific sharpness — a something she dared scarcely recall, lest the very thought of it should sting her beyond endurance. But this was as nothing to the pain which the recollection of the rudeness of the shining creature whom she had nursed through his fear caused her; for, the moment his suffering passed over to her, and he was free, the first use he made of his returning strength had been to scorn her! She wondered and wondered; it was all beyond her comprehension.

Before long, Watho was plotting evil against her. The witch was like a sick child weary of his toy: she would pull her to pieces, and see how she liked it. She would set her in the sun, and see her die, like a jelly from the salt ocean cast out on a hot rock. It would be a sight to soothe her wolf-pain. One day, therefore, a little before noon, while Nycteris was in her deepest sleep she had a darkened litter brought to the door, and in that she made two of her men carry her to the plain above. There they took her out, laid her on the grass, and left her.

Watho watched it all from the top of her high tower, through her telescope; and scarcely was Nycteris left, when she saw her sit up, and the same moment cast herself down again with her face to the ground.

"She'll have a sunstroke," said Watho, "and that'll be the end of her."

Presently, tormented by a fly, a huge-humped buffalo, with great shaggy mane, came galloping along, straight for where she lay. At sight of the thing on the grass, he started, swerved yards aside, stopped dead, and then came slowly up, looking malicious. Nycteris lay quite still, and never even saw the animal.

"Now she'll be trodden to death!" said Watho. "That's the way those creatures do."

When the buffalo reached her, he sniffed at her all over, and went away; then came back, and sniffed again; then all at once went off as if a demon had him by the tail.

Next came a gnu, a more dangerous animal still, and did much the same; then a gaunt wild boar. But no creature hurt her, and Watho was angry with the whole creation.

At length, in the shade of her hair, the blue eyes of Nycteris began to come to themselves a little, and the first thing they saw was a comfort. I have told already how she knew the night-daisies, each a sharp-pointed little cone with a red tip; and once she had parted the rays of one of them, with trembling fingers, for she was afraid she was dreadfully rude, and perhaps was hurting it; but she did want, she said to herself, to see what secret it carried so carefully hidden; and she found its golden heart. But now, right under her eyes, inside the veil of her hair, in the sweet twilight of whose blackness she could see it perfectly, stood a daisy with its red tip opened wide into a carmine ring, displaying its heart of gold on a platter of silver. She did not at first recognize it as one of those cones come awake, but a moment's notice revealed what it was. Who then could have been so cruel to the lovely little creature, as to force it open like that, and spread it heart-bare to the terrible death-lamp? Whoever it was, it must be the same that had thrown her out there to be burned to death in its fire! But she had her hair, and could hang her head, and make a small sweet night of her own about her! She tried to bend the daisy down and away from the sun, and to make its petals hang about it like her hair, but she could not. Alas! it was burned and dead already! She did not know that it could not yield to her gentle force because it was drinking life, with all the eagerness of life, from what she called the death-lamp. Oh, how the lamp burned her!

But she went on thinking — she did not know how; and by and by began to reflect that, as there was no roof to the room except that in which the great fire went rolling about, the little Red-tip must have seen the lamp a thousand times, and must know it quite well! and it had not killed it! Nay, thinking about it farther, she began to ask the question whether this, in which she now saw it, might not be its more perfect condition. For not only now did the whole seem perfect, as indeed it did before, but every part showed its own individual perfection as well, which perfection made it capable of combining with the rest into the higher perfection of a whole. The flower was a lamp itself! The golden heart was the light, and the silver border was the alabaster globe, skillfully broken, and spread wide to let out the glory. Yes; the radiant shape was plainly its perfection! If, then, it was the lamp which had opened it into that shape, the lamp could not be unfriendly to it, but must be of its own kind, seeing it made it perfect! And again, when she thought of it, there was clearly no little resemblance between them. What if the flower then was the little great-grandchild of the lamp, and he was loving it all the time? And what if the lamp did not mean to hurt her, only could not help it? The red tips looked as if the flower had some time or other been hurt: what if the lamp was making the best it could of her — opening her out somehow like the flower? She would bear it patiently, and see. But how coarse the colour of the grass was! Perhaps, however, her eyes not being made for the bright lamp, she did not see them as they were! Then she remembered how different were the eyes of the creature that was not a girl and was afraid of the darkness! Ah, if the darkness would only come again, all arms, friendly and soft everywhere about her! She would wait and wait, and bear, and be patient.

She lay so still that Watho did not doubt she had fainted. She was pretty sure she would be dead before the night came to revive her.

CHAPTER XVIII

Refuge

Fixing her telescope on the motionless form, that she might see it at once when the morning came, Watho went down from the tower to Photogen's room. He was much better by this time, and before she left him, he had resolved to leave the castle that very night. The darkness was terrible indeed, but Watho was worse than even the darkness, and he could not escape in the day. As soon, therefore, as the house seemed still, he tightened his belt, hung to it his hunting-knife, put a flask of wine and some bread in his pocket, and took his bow and arrows. He got from the house, and made his way at once up to the plain. But what with his illness, the terrors of the night, and his dread of the wild beasts, when he got to the level he could not walk a step further, and sat down, thinking it better to die than to live. In spite of his fears, however, sleep contrived to overcome him, and he fell at full length on the soft grass.

He had not slept long when he woke with such a strange sense of comfort and security, that he thought the dawn at last must have arrived. But it was dark night about him. And the sky — no, it was not the sky, but the blue eyes of his naiad looking down upon him! Once more he lay with his head in her lap, and all was well, for plainly the girl feared the darkness as little as he the day.

"Thank you," he said. "You are like live armour to my heart; you keep the fear off me. I have been very ill since then. Did you come up out of the river when you saw me cross?"

"I don't live in the water," she answered. "I live under the pale lamp, and I die under the bright one."

"Ah, yes! I understand now," he returned. "I would not have behaved as I did last time if I had understood; but I thought you were mocking me; and I am so made that I cannot help being frightened at the darkness. I beg your pardon for leaving you as I did, for, as I say, I did not understand. Now I believe you were really frightened. Were you not?"

"I was, indeed," answered Nycteris, "and shall be again. But why you should be, I cannot in the least understand. You must know how gentle and sweet the darkness is, how kind and friendly, how soft and velvety! It holds you to its bosom and loves you. A little while ago, I lay faint and dying under your hot lamp. — What is it you call it?"

   THE HISTORY OF PHOTOGEN AND NYCTERIS

"The sun," murmured Photogen: "how I wish he would make haste!"

"Ah! do not wish that. Do not, for my sake, hurry him. I can take care of you from the darkness, but I have no one to take care of me from the light. — As I was telling you, I lay dying in the sun. All at once I drew a deep breath. A cool wind came and ran over my face. I looked up. The torture was gone, for the death-lamp itself was gone. I hope he does not die and grow brighter yet. My terrible headache was all gone, and my sight was come back. I felt as if I were new made. But I did not get up at once, for I was tired still. The grass grew cool about me, and turned soft in colour. Something wet came upon it, and it was now so pleasant to my feet, that I rose and ran about. And when I had been running about a long time, all at once I found you lying, just as I had been lying a little while before. So I sat down beside you to take care of you, till your life — and my death — should come again."

"How good you are, you beautiful creature! — Why, you forgave me before ever I asked you!" cried Photogen.

Thus they fell a talking, and he told her what he knew of his history, and she told him what she knew of hers, and they agreed they must get away from Watho as far as ever they could.

"And we must set out at once," said Nycteris.

"The moment the morning comes," returned Photogen.

"We must not wait for the morning," said Nycteris, "for then I shall not be able to move, and what would you do the next night? Besides, Watho sees best in the daytime. Indeed, you must come now, Photogen. — You must."

"I can not; I dare not," said Photogen. "I cannot move. If I but lift my head from your lap, the very sickness of terror seizes me."

"I shall be with you," said Nycteris soothingly. "I will take care of you till your dreadful sun comes, and then you may leave me, and go away as fast as you can. Only please put me in a dark place first, if there is one to be found."

"I will never leave you again, Nycteris," cried Photogen. "Only wait till the sun comes, and brings me back my strength, and we will go away together, and never, never part any more."

"No, no," persisted Nycteris; "we must go now. And you must learn to be strong in the dark as well as in the day, else you will always be only half brave. I have begun already — not to fight your sun, but to try to get at peace with him, and understand what he really is, and what he means with me — whether to hurt me or to make the best of me. You must do the same with my darkness."

"But you don't know what mad animals there are away there towards the south," said Photogen. "They have huge green eyes, and they would eat you up like a bit of celery, you beautiful creature!"

"Come, come! you must," said Nycteris, "or I shall have to pretend to leave you, to make you come. I have seen the green eyes you speak of, and I will take care of you from them."

"You! How can you do that? If it were day now, I could take care of you from the worst of them. But as it is, I can't even see them for this abominable darkness. I could not see your lovely eyes but for the light that is in them; that lets me see straight into heaven through them. They are windows into the very heaven beyond the sky. I believe they are the very place where the stars are made."

"You come then, or I shall shut them," said Nycteris, "and you shan't see them any more till you are good. Come. If you can't see the wild beasts, I can."

"You can! and you ask me to come!" cried Photogen.

"Yes," answered Nycteris. "And more than that, I see them long before they can see me, so that I am able to take care of you."

"But how?" persisted Photogen. "You can't shoot with bow and arrow, or stab with a hunting-knife."

"No, but I can keep out of the way of them all. Why, just when I found you, I was having a game with two or three of them at once. I see, and scent them too, long before they are near me — long before they can see or scent me."

"You don't see or scent any now, do you?" said Photogen, uneasily, rising on his elbow.

"No — none at present. I will look," replied Nycteris, and sprang to her feet.

"Oh, oh! do not leave me — not for a moment," cried Photogen, straining his eyes to keep her face in sight through the darkness.

"Be quiet, or they will hear you," she returned. "The wind is from the south, and they cannot scent us. I have found out all about that. Ever since the dear dark came, I have been amusing myself with them, getting every now and then just into the edge of the wind, and letting one have a sniff of me."

"Oh, horrible!" cried Photogen. "I hope you will not insist on doing so any more. What was the consequence?"

"Always, the very instant, he turned with flashing eyes, and bounded towards me — only he could not see me, you must remember. But my eyes being so much better than his, I could see him perfectly well, and would run away round him until I scented him, and then I knew he could not find me anyhow. If the wind were to turn, and run the other way now, there might be a whole army of them down upon us, leaving no room to keep out of their way. You had better come."

She took him by the hand. He yielded and rose, and she led him away. But his steps were feeble, and as the night went on, he seemed more and more ready to sink.

"Oh dear! I am so tired! and so frightened!" he would say.

"Lean on me," Nycteris would return, putting her arm round him, or patting his cheek. "Take a few steps more. Every step away from the castle is clear gain. Lean harder on me. I am quite strong and well now."

So they went on. The piercing night-eyes of Nycteris descried not a few pairs of green ones gleaming like holes in the darkness, and many a round she made to keep far out of their way; but she never said to Photogen she saw them. Carefully she kept him off the uneven places, and on the softest and smoothest of the grass, talking to him gently all the way as they went — of the lovely flowers and the stars — how comfortable the flowers looked, down in their green beds, and how happy the stars up in their blue beds!

When the morning began to come, he began to grow better, but was dreadfully tired with walking instead of sleeping, especially after being so long ill. Nycteris too, what with supporting him, what with growing fear of the light which was beginning to ooze out of the east, was very tired. At length, both equally exhausted, neither was able to help the other. As if by consent they stopped. Embracing each the other, they stood in the midst of the wide, grassy land, neither of them able to move a step, each supported only by the leaning weakness of the other, each ready to fall if the other should move. But while the one grew weaker still, the other had begun to grow stronger. When the tide of the night began to ebb, the tide of the day began to flow; and now the sun was rushing to the horizon, borne upon its foaming billows. And ever as he came, Photogen revived. At last the sun shot up into the air, like a bird from the hand of the Father of Lights. Nycteris gave a cry of pain, and hid her face in her hands.

"Oh me!" she sighed; "I am *so* frightened! The terrible light stings so!"

But the same instant, through her blindness, she heard Photogen give a low, exultant laugh, and the next felt herself caught up: she who all night long had tended and protected him like a child, was now in his arms, borne along like a baby, with her head lying on his shoulder. But she was the greater, for, suffering more, she feared nothing.

CHAPTER XIX

The Werewolf

At the very moment when Photogen caught up Nycteris, the telescope of Watho was angrily sweeping the table-land. She swung it from her in rage, and running to her room, shut herself up. There she anointed herself from top to toe with a certain ointment; shook down her long, red hair, and tied it round her waist; then began to dance, whirling round and round faster and faster, growing angrier and angrier, until she was foaming at the mouth with fury. When Falca went looking for her, she could not find her anywhere.

As the sun rose, the wind slowly changed and went round, until it blew straight from the north. Photogen and Nycteris were drawing near the edge of the forest, Photogen still carrying Nycteris, when she moved a little on his shoulder uneasily, and murmured in his ear,

"I smell a wild beast — that way, the way the wind is coming."

Photogen turned, looked back towards the castle, and saw a dark speck on the plain. As he looked, it grew larger: it was coming across the grass with the speed of the wind. It came nearer and nearer. It looked long and low, but that might be because it was running at a great stretch. He set Nycteris down under a tree, in the black shadow of its bole, strung his bow, and picked out his heaviest, longest, sharpest arrow. Just as he set the notch on the string, he saw that the creature was a tremendous wolf, rushing straight at him. He loosened his knife in its sheath, drew another arrow half-way from the quiver, lest the first should fail, and took his aim — at a good distance, to leave time for a second chance. He shot. The arrow rose, flew straight, descended, struck the beast, and started again into the air, doubled like a letter V. Quickly Photogen snatched the other,

THE HISTORY OF PHOTOGEN AND NYCTERIS

shot, cast his bow from him, and drew his knife. But the arrow was in the brute's chest, up to the feather; it tumbled heels over head with a great thud of its back on the earth, gave a groan, made a struggle or two, and lay stretched out motionless.

"I've killed it, Nycteris," cried Photogen. "It is a great red wolf."

"Oh, thank you!" answered Nycteris feebly from behind the tree. "I was sure you would. I was not a bit afraid."

Photogen went up to the wolf. It *was* a monster! But he was vexed that his first arrow had behaved so badly, and was the less willing to lose the one that had done him such good service: with a long and a strong pull, he drew it from the brute's chest. Could he believe his eyes? There lay — no wolf, but Watho, with her hair tied round her waist! The foolish witch had made herself invulnerable, as she supposed, but had forgotten that, to torment Photogen therewith, she had handled one of his arrows. He ran back to Nycteris and told her.

She shuddered and wept, and would not look.

CHAPTER XX

All Is Well

There was now no occasion to fly a step farther. Neither of them feared any one but Watho. They left her there, and went back. A great cloud came over the sun, and rain began to fall heavily, and Nycteris was much refreshed, grew able to see a little, and with Photogen's help walked gently over the cool wet grass.

They had not gone far before they met Fargu and the other huntsmen. Photogen told them he had killed a great red wolf, and it was Madam Watho. The huntsmen looked grave, but gladness shone through.

"Then," said Fargu, "I will go and bury my mistress."

But when they reached the place, they found she was already buried — in the maws of sundry birds and beasts which had made their breakfast of her.

Then Fargu, overtaking them, would, very wisely, have Photogen go to the king, and tell him the whole story. But Photogen, yet wiser than

Fargu, would not set out until he had married Nycteris; "for then," he said, "the king himself can't part us: and if ever two people couldn't do the one without the other, those two are Nycteris and I. She has got to teach me to be a brave man in the dark, and I have got to look after her until she can bear the heat of the sun, and he helps her to see, instead of blinding her."

They were married that very day. And the next day they went together to the king, and told him the whole story. But whom should they find at the court but the father and mother of Photogen, both in high favor with the king and queen. Aurora nearly died for joy, and told them all how Watho had lied, and made her believe her child was dead.

No one knew anything of the father or mother of Nycteris; but when Aurora saw in the lovely girl her own azure eyes shining through night and its clouds, it made her think strange things, and wonder how even the wicked themselves may be a link to join together the good. Through Watho, the mothers, who had never seen each other, had changed eyes in their children.

The king gave them the castle and lands of Watho, and there they lived and taught each other for many years that were not long. But hardly had one of them passed, before Nycteris had come to love the day best, because it was the clothing and crown of Photogen, and she saw that the day was greater than the night, and the sun more lordly than the moon; and Photogen had come to love the night best, because it was the mother and home of Nycteris.

"But who knows," Nycteris would say to Photogen, "that, when we go out, we shall not go into a day as much greater than your day as your day is greater than my night?"

The Giant's Heart

There was once a giant who lived on the borders of Giantland where it touched on the country of common people.

Everything in Giantland was so big that the common people saw only a mass of awful mountains and clouds; and no living man had ever come from it, as far as anybody knew, to tell what he had seen in it.

Somewhere near the borders, on the other side, by the edge of a great forest, lived a labourer with his wife and a great many children. One day Tricksey-Wee, as they called her, teased her brother Buffy-Bob, till he could not bear it any longer, and gave her a box on the ear. Tricksey-Wee cried; and Buffy-Bob was so sorry and so ashamed of himself that he cried too, and ran off into the wood. He was so long gone that Tricksey-Wee began to be frightened, for she was very fond of her brother; and she was so distressed that she had first teased him and then cried, that at last she ran into the wood to look for him, though there was more chance of losing herself than of finding him. And, indeed, so it seemed likely to turn out; for, running on without looking, she at length found herself in a valley she knew nothing about. And no wonder; for what she thought was a valley with round, rocky sides, was no other than the space between two of the roots of a great tree that grew on the borders of Giantland. She climbed over the side of it, and went towards what she took for a black, round-topped mountain, far away; but which she soon discovered to be close to her, and to be a hollow place so great that she could not tell what it was hollowed out of. Staring at it, she found that it was a doorway; and going nearer and staring harder, she saw the door, far in, with a knocker of iron upon it, a great many yards above her head, and as large as the anchor of a big ship. Now nobody had ever been unkind to Tricksey-Wee, and therefore she was not afraid of anybody. For Buffy-Bob's box on the ear she did not think worth considering. So spying a little hole at the bottom of the door which had been nibbled by some giant mouse, she crept through it, and found herself in an enormous hall. She could not have seen the other end of it at all, except for the great fire that was burning there, diminished to a spark in the distance. Towards this fire she ran as fast as she could, and was not far from it when something fell before her with a great clatter, over which she tumbled, and went rolling on the floor. She was not much hurt, however, and got up in a moment. Then she saw that what she had fallen over was not unlike a great iron bucket. When she examined it more closely, she discovered that it was a thimble; and looking up to see who had dropped it, beheld a huge face, with spectacles as big as the round windows in a church, bending over her, and looking everywhere for the thimble. Tricksey-Wee immediately laid hold of it in both her arms, and lifted it about an inch nearer to the nose of the peering giantess. This movement made the old lady see where it was, and, her finger popping into it, it vanished from the eyes of Tricksey-Wee, buried in the folds of a white stocking like a cloud in the sky, which Mrs. Giant was busy darning. For it was Saturday night, and her husband would wear nothing but white stockings on Sunday. To be sure, he did eat little children, but only *very* little ones; and if ever it crossed his mind that it was wrong to do so, he always said to himself that he wore whiter stockings on Sunday than any other giant in all Giantland.

At the same instant Tricksey-Wee heard a sound like the wind in a tree full of leaves, and could not think what it could be; till, looking up, she found that it was the giantess whispering to her; and when she tried very hard she could hear what she said well enough.

"Run away, dear little girl," she said, "as fast as you can; for my husband will be home in a few minutes."

"But I've never been naughty to your husband," said Tricksey-Wee, looking up in the giantess's face.

"That doesn't matter. You had better go. He is fond of little children, particularly little girls."

"Oh, then he won't hurt me."

"I am not sure of that. He is so fond of them that he eats them up;

　　　　　　　　　　　　　　　　THE GIANT'S HEART

"Tricksey-Wee with the giantess's thimble"

and I am afraid he couldn't help hurting you a little. He's a very good man, though."

"Oh! then — " began Tricksey-Wee, feeling rather frightened; but before she could finish her sentence she heard the sound of footsteps very far apart and very heavy. The next moment, who should come running towards her, full speed, and as pale as death, but Buffy-Bob. She held out her arms. and he ran into them. But when she tried to kiss him, she only kissed the back of his head; for his white face and round eyes were turned to the door.

"Run, children; run and hide," said the giantess.

"Come, Buffy," said Tricksey; "yonder's a great brake; we'll hide in it."

The brake was a big broom; and they had just got into the bristles of it when they heard the door open with a sound of thunder, and in stalked the giant. You would have thought you saw the whole earth through the door when he opened it, so wide was it; and when he closed it, it was like nightfall.

"Where is that little boy?" he cried, with a voice like the bellowing of a cannon. "He looked a very nice boy indeed. I am almost sure he crept through the mousehole at the bottom of the door. Where is he, my dear?"

"I don't know," answered the giantess.

"But you know it is wicked to tell lies; don't you, my dear?" retorted the giant.

"Now, you ridiculous old Thunderthump!" said his wife, with a smile as broad as the sea in the sun, "how can I mend your white stockings and look after little boys? You have got plenty to last you over Sunday, I am sure. Just look what good little boys they are!"

Tricksey-Wee and Buffy-Bob peered through the bristles, and discovered a row of little boys, about a dozen, with very fat faces and goggle eyes, sitting before the fire, and looking stupidly into it. Thunderthump intended the most of these for pickling, and was feeding them well before salting them. Now and then, however, he could not keep his teeth off them, and would eat one by the bye, without salt.

He strode up to the wretched children. Now what made them very wretched indeed was, that they knew if they could only keep from eating, and grow thin, the giant would dislike them, and turn them out to find their way home; but notwithstanding this, so greedy were they, that they ate as much as ever they could hold. The giantess, who fed them, comforted

"Giant Thunderthump"

herself with thinking that they were not real boys and girls, but only little pigs pretending to be boys and girls.

"Now tell me the truth," cried the giant, bending his face down over them. They shook with terror, and every one hoped it was somebody else the giant liked best. "Where is the little boy that ran into the hall just now? Whoever tells me a lie shall be instantly boiled."

"He's in the broom," cried one dough-faced boy. "He's in there, and a little girl with him."

"The naughty children," cried the giant, "to hide from *me!*" And he made a stride towards the broom.

"Catch hold of the bristles, Bobby. Get right into a tuft, and hold on," cried Tricksey-Wee, just in time.

The giant caught up the broom, and seeing nothing under it, set it down again with a force that threw them both on the floor. He then made two strides to the boys, caught the dough-faced one by the neck, took the lid off a great pot that was boiling on the fire, popped him in as if he had been a trussed chicken, put the lid on again, and saying, "There, boys! See what comes of lying!" asked no more questions; for, as he always kept his word, he was afraid he might have to do the same to them all: and he did not like boiled boys. He liked to eat them crisp, as radishes, whether forked or not, ought to be eaten. He then sat down, and asked his wife if his supper was ready. She looked into the pot, and throwing the boy out with the ladle, as if he had been a black beetle that had tumbled in and had had the worst of it, answered that she thought it was. Whereupon he rose to help her; and taking the pot from the fire, poured the whole contents, bubbling and splashing, into a dish like a vat. Then they sat down to supper. The children in the broom could not see what they had; but it seemed to agree with them; for the giant talked like thunder, and the giantess answered like the sea, and they grew chattier and chattier. At length the giant said, —

"I don't feel quite comfortable about that heart of mine." And as he spoke, instead of laying his hand on his bosom, he waved it away towards the corner where the children were peeping from the broom bristles, like frightened little mice.

"Well, you know, my darling Thunderthump," answered his wife, "I always thought it ought to be nearer home. But you know best, of course."

"Ha! ha! You don't know where it is, wife. I moved it a month ago."

"What a man you are, Thunderthump! You trust any creature alive rather than your own wife."

Here the giantess gave a sob which sounded exactly like a wave going flop into the mouth of a cave up to the roof.

"Where have you got it now?" she resumed, checking her emotion.

"Well, Doodlem, I don't mind telling *you*," answered the giant soothingly. "The great she-eagle has got it for a nest egg. She sits on it night and day, and thinks she will bring the greatest eagle out of it that ever sharpened his beak on the rocks of Mount Skycrack. I can warrant no one else will touch it while she has got it. But she is rather capricious, and I confess I am not easy about it; for the least scratch of one of her claws would do for me at once. And she *has* claws."

I refer any one who doubts this part of my story to certain chronicles of Giantland preserved among the Celtic nations. It was quite a common thing for a giant to put his heart out to nurse, because he did not like the trouble and responsibility of doing it himself; although I must confess it was a dangerous sort of plan to take, especially with such a delicate viscus as the heart.

All this time Buffy-Bob and Tricksey-Wee were listening with long ears.

"Oh!" thought Tricksey-Wee, "If I could but find the giant's cruel heart, wouldn't I give it a squeeze!"

The giant and giantess went on talking for a long time. The giantess kept advising the giant to hide his heart somewhere in the house; but he seemed afraid of the advantage it would give her over him.

"You could hide it at the bottom of the flour-barrel," said she.

"That would make me feel chokey," answered he.

"Well, in the coal-cellar. Or in the dust-hole — that's the place! No one would think of looking for your heart in the dust-hole."

"Worse and worse!" cried the giant.

"Well, the water-butt," suggested she.

"No, no; it would grow spongy there," said he.

"Well, what *will* you do with it?"

"I will leave it a month longer where it is, and then I will give it to the Queen of the Kangaroos, and she will carry it in her pouch for me. It is best to change its place, you know, lest my enemies should scent it out. But, dear Doodlem, it's a fretting care to have a heart of one's own to look after. The responsibility is too much for me. If it were not for a bite of a radish now and then, I never could bear it."

Here the giant looked lovingly towards the row of little boys by the fire, all of whom were nodding, or asleep on the floor.

"Why don't you trust it to me, dear Thunderthump?" said his wife. "I would take the best possible care of it."

"I don't doubt it, my love. But the responsibility would be too much for *you*. You would no longer be my darling, light-hearted, airy, laughing Doodlem. It would transform you into a heavy, oppressed woman, weary of life — as I am."

The giant closed his eyes and pretended to go to sleep. His wife got his stockings, and went on with her darning. Soon the giant's pretence became reality, and the giantess began to nod over her work.

"Now, Buffy," whispered Tricksey-Wee, "now's our time. I think it's moonlight, and we had better be off. There's a door with a hole for the cat just behind us."

"All right," said Bob; "I'm ready."

So they got out of the broom-brake and crept to the door. But to their great disappointment, when they got through it, they found themselves in a sort of shed. It was full of tubs and things, and, though it was built of wood only, they could not find a crack.

"Let us try this hole," said Tricksey; for the giant and giantess were sleeping behind them, and they dared not go back.

"All right," said Bob.

He seldom said anything else than *All right.*

Now this hole was in a mound that came in through the wall of the shed, and went along the floor for some distance. They crawled into it, and found it very dark. But groping their way along, they soon came to a small crack, through which they saw grass, pale in the moonshine. As they crept on, they found the hole began to get wider and lead upwards.

"What is that noise of rushing?" said Buffy-Bob.

"I can't tell," replied Tricksey; "for, you see, I don't know what we are in."

The fact was, they were creeping along a channel in the heart of a giant tree; and the noise they heard was the noise of the sap rushing along in its wooden pipes. When they laid their ears to the wall, they heard it gurgling along with a pleasant noise.

"It sounds kind and good," said Tricksey. "It is water running. Now

❧   THE GIANT'S HEART

it must be running from somewhere to somewhere. I think we had better go on, and we shall come somewhere."

It was now rather difficult to go on, for they had to climb as if they were climbing a hill; and now the passage was wide. Nearly worn out, they saw light overhead at last, and creeping through a crack into the open air, found themselves on the fork of a huge tree. A great, broad, uneven space lay around them, out of which spread boughs in every direction, the smallest of them as big as the biggest tree in the country of common people. Overhead were leaves enough to supply all the trees they had ever seen. Not much moonlight could come through, but the leaves would glimmer white in the wind at times. The tree was full of giant birds. Every now and then, one would sweep through, with a great noise. But, except for an occasional chirp, sounding like a shrill pipe in a great organ, they made no noise. All at once an owl began to hoot. He thought he was singing. As soon as he began, other birds replied, making rare game of him. To their astonishment, the children found they could understand every word they sang. And what they sang was something like this: —

> "I will sing a song.
>   I'm the owl."
> "Sing a song, you sing-song
>   Ugly fowl!
> What will you sing about,
> Night in and Day out?"
>
> "Sing about the night;
>   I'm the owl."
> "You could not see for the light,
>   Stupid fowl!
> "Oh! the moon! and the dew!
> And the shadows! — tu-whoo!"

The owl spread out his silent, soft, sly wings, and lighting between Tricksey-Wee and Buffy-Bob, nearly smothered them closing up one under each wing. It was like being buried in a down bed. But the owl did not like anything between his sides and his wings, so he opened his wings again, and the children made haste to get out. Tricksey-Wee immediately

"Buffy-Bob, Tricksey-Wee, and the giant owl"

went in front of the bird, and looking up into his huge face, which was as round as the eyes of the giantess's spectacles, and much bigger, dropped a pretty courtesy, and said, —

"Please, Mr. Owl, I want to whisper to you."

"Very well, small child," answered the owl looking important, and stooping his ear towards her. "What is it?"

"Please tell me where the eagle lives that sits on the giant's heart."

"Oh, you naughty child! That's a secret. For shame!"

And with a great hiss that terrified them, the owl flew into the tree. All birds are fond of secrets; but not many of them can keep them so well as the owl.

So the children went on because they did not know what else to do. They found the way very rough and difficult, the tree was so full of humps and hollows. Now and then they plashed into a pool of rain; now and then they came upon twigs growing out of the trunk where they had no business, and they were as large as full-grown poplars. Sometimes they came upon great cushions of soft moss, and on one of them they lay down and rested. But they had not lain long before they spied a large nightingale sitting on a branch, with its bright eyes looking up at the moon. In a moment more he began to sing, and the birds about him began to reply, but in a very different tone from that in which they had replied to the owl. Oh, the birds did call the nightingale such pretty names! The nightingale sang, and the birds replied like this:

> "I will sing a song.
>   I'm the nightingale."
> "Sing a song, long, long,
>   Little Neverfail!
> What will you sing about,
> Light in or light out?"
>
> "Sing about the light
>   Gone away;
> Down, away, and out of sight —
>   Poor lost day!
> Mourning for the day dead,
> O'er his dim bed."

The nightingale sang so sweetly, that the children would have fallen asleep but for fear of losing any of the song. When the nightingale stopped, they got up and wandered on. They did not know where they were going, but they thought it best to keep going on, because then they might come upon something or other. They were very sorry they had forgotten to ask the nightingale about the eagle's nest, but his music had put everything else out of their heads. They resolved, however, not to forget the next time they had a chance. So they went on and on, till they were both tired, and Tricksey-Wee said at last, trying to laugh, —

"I declare my legs feel just like a Dutch doll's."

"Then here's the place to go to bed in," said Buffy-Bob.

They stood at the edge of a last year's nest, and looked down with delight into the round, mossy cave. Then they crept gently in, and, lying down in each other's arms, found it so deep, and warm, and comfortable, and soft, that they were soon fast asleep.

Now close beside them, in a hollow, was another nest, in which lay a lark and his wife; and the children were awakened, very early in the morning, by a dispute between Mr. and Mrs. Lark.

"Let me up," said the lark.

"It is not time," said the lark's wife.

"It is," said the lark, rather rudely. "The darkness is quite thin. I can almost see my own beak."

"Nonsense!" said the lark's wife. "You know you came home yesterday morning quite worn out — you had to fly so very high before you saw him. I am sure he would not mind if you took it a little easier. Do be quiet and go to sleep again."

"That's not it at all," said the lark. "He doesn't want me. I want him. Let me up, I say."

He began to sing; and Tricksey-Wee and Buffy-Bob, having now learned the way, answered him: —

> "I will sing a song.
>   I'm the Lark."
> "Sing, sing, Throat-strong,
>   Little Kill-the-dark.
> What will you sing about,
> Now the night is out?"

THE GIANT'S HEART

"I can only call;
I can't think.
Let me up — that's all.
Let me drink!
Thirsting all the long night
For a drink of light."

By this time the lark was standing on the edge of his nest and looking at the children.

"Poor little things! You can't fly," said the lark.

"No; but we can look up," said Tricksey.

"Ah, you don't know what it is to see the very first of the sun."

"But we know what it is to wait till he comes. He's no worse for your seeing him first, is he?"

"Oh no, certainly not," answered the lark, with condescension; and then, bursting into his *Jubilate,* he sprang aloft, clapping his wings like a clock running down.

"Tell us where — " began Buffy-Bob.

But the lark was out of sight. His song was all that was left of him. That was everywhere, and he was nowhere.

"Selfish bird!" said Buffy. "It's all very well for larks to go hunting the sun, but they have no business to despise their neighbors, for all that."

"Can I be of any use to you?" said a sweet bird-voice out of the nest.

This was the lark's wife, who stayed at home with the young larks while her husband went to church.

"Oh! thank you. If you please," answered Tricksey-Wee.

And up popped a pretty brown head; and then up came a brown feathery body; and last of all came the slender legs on to the edge of the nest. There she turned, and, looking down into the nest, from which came a whole litany of chirpings for breakfast, said, "Lie still, little ones." Then she turned to the children.

"My husband is King of the Larks," she said.

Buffy-Bob took off his cap, and Tricksey-Wee courtesied very low.

"Oh, it's not me," said the bird, looking very shy. "I am only his wife. It's my husband."

And she looked up after him into the sky, whence his song was still falling like a shower of musical hailstones. Perhaps *she* could see him.

THE GIANT'S HEART   ❧   479

"He's a splendid bird," said Buffy-Bob; "only you know he *will* get up a little too early."

"Oh, no! he doesn't. It's only his way, you know. But tell me what I can do for you."

"Tell us, please, Lady Lark, where the she-eagle lives that sits on Giant Thunderthump's heart."

"Oh! that is a secret."

"Did you promise not to tell?"

No; but larks ought to be discreet. They see more than other birds."

"But you don't fly up high like your husband, do you?"

"Not often. But it's no matter. I come to know things for all that."

"Do tell me, and I will sing you a song," said Tricksey-Wee.

"Can you sing too? — You have got no wings!"

"Yes. And I will sing you a song I learned the other day about a lark and his wife."

"Please do," said the lark's wife. "Be quiet, children, and listen."

Tricksey-Wee was very glad she happened to know a song which would please the lark's wife, at least, whatever the lark himself might have thought of it, if he had heard it. So she sang: —

" 'Good-morrow, my lord!' in the sky alone,
Sang the lark, as the sun ascended his throne.
'Shine on me, my lord; I only am come,
Of all your servants, to welcome you home.
I have flown a whole hour, right up, I swear,
To catch the first shine of your golden hair!'

" 'Must I thank you, then,' said the king, 'Sir Lark,
For flying so high, and hating the dark?
You ask a full cup for half a thirst:
Half is love of me, and half love to be first.
There's many a bird that makes no haste,
But waits till I come. That's as much to my taste.'

"And the king hid his head in a turban of cloud;
And the lark stopped singing, quite vexed and cowed.
But he flew up higher, and thought, 'Anon,
The wrath of the king will be over and gone;

And his crown, shining out of its cloudy fold,
Will change my brown feathers to a glory of gold.'

"So he flew, with the strength of a lark he flew.
But as he rose the cloud rose too;
And not a gleam of the golden hair
Came through the depth of the misty air;
Till, weary with flying, with sighing sore,
The strong sun-seeker could do no more.

"His wings had had no chrism of gold,
And his feathers felt withered and worn and old;
So he quivered and sank, and dropped like a stone.
And there on his nest, where he left her, alone,
Sat his little wife on her little eggs,
Keeping them warm with wings and legs.

"Did I say alone? Ah, no such thing!
Full in her face was shining the king.
'Welcome, Sir Lark! You look tired,' said he.
'*Up* is not always the best way to me.
While you have been singing so high and away,
I've been shining to your little wife all day.'

"He had set his crown all about the nest,
And out of the midst shone her little brown breast;
And so glorious was she in russet gold,
That for wonder and awe Sir Lark grew cold.
He popped his head under her wing, and lay
As still as a stone, till the king was away."

As soon as Tricksey-Wee had finished her song, the lark's wife began
a low, sweet, modest little song of her own; and after she had piped away
for two or three minutes, she said, —
"You dear children, what can I do for you?"
"Tell us where the she-eagle lives, please," said Tricksey-Wee.
"Well, I don't think there can be much harm in telling such wise, good
children," said Lady Lark; "I am sure you don't want to do any mischief."

"Oh, no; quite the contrary," said Buffy-Bob.

"Then I'll tell you. She lives on the very topmost peak of Mount Skycrack; and the only way to get up is to climb on the spiders' webs that cover it from top to bottom."

"That's rather serious," said Tricksey-Wee.

"But you don't want to go up, you foolish little thing! You can't go. And what do you want to go up for?"

"That is a secret," said Tricksey-Wee.

"Well, it's no business of mine," rejoined Lady Lark, a little offended, and quite vexed that she had told them. So she flew away to find some breakfast for her little ones, who by this time were chirping very impatiently. The children looked at each other, joined hands, and walked off.

In a minute more the sun was up, and they soon reached the outside of the tree. The bark was so knobby and rough, and full of twigs, that they managed to get down, though not without great difficulty. Then, far away to the north they saw a huge peak, like the spire of a church, going right up into the sky. They thought this must be Mount Skycrack, and turned their faces towards it. As they went on, they saw a giant or two, now and then, striding about the fields or through the woods, but they kept out of their way. Nor were they in much danger; for it was only one or two of the border giants that were so very fond of children.

At last they came to the foot of Mount Skycrack. It stood in a plain alone, and shot right up, I don't know how many thousand feet, into the air, a long, narrow, spearlike mountain. The whole face of it, from top to bottom, was covered with a network of spiders' webs, the threads of various sizes, from that of silk to that of whipcord. The webs shook, and quivered, and waved in the sun, glittering like silver. All about ran huge greedy spiders, catching huge silly flies, and devouring them.

Here they sat down to consider what could be done. The spiders did not heed them, but ate away at the flies. — Now at the foot of the mountain, and all round it, was a ring of water, not very broad, but very deep. As they sat watching them, one of the spiders, whose web was woven across this water, somehow or other lost his hold, and fell in on his back. Tricksey-Wee and Buffy-Bob ran to his assistance, and laying hold each of one of his legs, succeeded, with the help of the other legs, which struggled spiderfully, in getting him out upon dry land. As soon as he had shaken himself, and dried himself a little, the spider turned to the children, saying, —

"And now, what can I do for you?"

"Tell us, please," said they, "how we can get up the mountain to the she-eagle's nest."

"Nothing is easier," answered the spider. "Just run up there, and tell them all I sent you, and nobody will mind you."

"But we haven't got claws like you, Mr. Spider," said Buffy.

"Ah! no more you have, poor unprovided creatures! Still, I think we can manage it. Come home with me."

"You won't eat us, will you?" said Buffy.

"My dear child," answered the spider, in a tone of injured dignity, "I eat nothing but what is mischievous or useless. You have helped me, and now I will help you."

The children rose at once, and climbing as well as they could, reached the spider's nest in the centre of the web. Nor did they find it very difficult; for whenever too great a gap came, the spider spinning a strong cord stretched it just where they would have chosen to put their feet next. He left them in his nest, after bringing them two enormous honey-bags, taken from bees that he had caught; but presently about six of the wisest of the spiders came back with him. It was rather horrible to look up and see them all round the mouth of the nest, looking down on them in contemplation, as if wondering whether they would be nice eating. At length one of them said, — "Tell us truly what you want with the eagle, and we will try to help you."

Then Tricksey-Wee told them that there was a giant on the borders who treated little children no better than radishes, and that they had narrowly escaped being eaten by him; that they had found out that the great she-eagle of Mount Skycrack was at present sitting on his heart; and that, if they could only get hold of the heart, they would soon teach the giant better behaviour.

"But," said their host, "if you get at the heart of the giant, you will find it as large as one of your elephants. What can you do with it?"

"The least scratch will kill it," replied Buffy-Bob.

"Ah! but you might do better than that," said the spider. — "Now we have resolved to help you. Here is a little bag of spider-juice. The giants cannot bear spiders, and this juice is dreadful poison to them. We are all ready to go up with you, and drive the eagle away. Then you must put the heart into this other bag, and bring it down with you; for then the giant will be in your power."

"But how can we do that?" said Buffy. "The bag is not much bigger than a pudding-bag."

"But it is as large as you will be able to carry."

"Yes; but what are we to do with the heart?"

"Put it into the bag, to be sure. Only, first you must squeeze out a drop of the other bag upon it. You will see what will happen."

"Very well; we will do as you tell us," said Tricksey-Wee. "And now, if you please, how shall we go?"

"Oh, that's our business," said the first spider. "You come with me, and my grandfather will take your brother. Get up."

So Tricksey-Wee mounted on the narrow part of the spider's back, and held fast. And Buffy-Bob got on the grandfather's back. And up they scrambled, over one web after another, up and up — so fast! And every spider followed; so that, when Tricksey-Wee looked back, she saw a whole army of spiders scrambling after them.

"What can we want with so many?" she thought; but she said nothing.

The moon was now up, and it was a splendid sight below and around them. All Giantland was spread out under them, with its great hills, lakes, trees, and animals. And all above them was the clear heaven, and Mount Skycrack rising into it, with its endless ladders of spiderwebs, glittering like cords made of moonbeams. And up the moonbeams went, crawling and scrambling and racing, a huge army of spiders.

At length they reached all but the very summit, where they stopped. Tricksey-Wee and Buffy-Bob could see above them a great globe of feathers, that finished off the mountain like an ornamental knob.

"But how shall we drive her off?" said Buffy.

"We'll soon manage that," answered the grandfather-spider. "Come on you, down there."

Up rushed the whole army, past the children, over the edge of the nest, on to the she-eagle, and buried themselves in her feathers. In a moment she became very restless, and went pecking about with her beak. All at once she spread out her wings, with a sound like a whirlwind, and flew off to bathe in the sea; and then the spiders began to drop from her in all directions on their gossamer wings. The children had to hold fast to keep the wind of the eaglets flight from blowing them off. As soon as it was over, they looked into the nest, and there lay the giant's heart — an awful and ugly thing.

"Make haste, child!" said Tricksey's spider.

So Tricksey took her bag, and squeezed a drop out of it upon the heart. She thought she heard the giant give a far-off roar of pain, and she nearly fell from her seat with terror. The heart instantly began to shrink. It shrank and shrivelled till it was nearly gone; and Buffy-Bob caught it up and put it into his bag. Then the two spiders turned and went down again as fast as they could. Before they got to the bottom, they heard the shrieks of the she-eagle over the loss of her egg; but the spiders told them not to be alarmed, for her eyes were too big to see them. — By the time they reached the foot of the mountain, all the spiders had got home, and were busy again catching flies, as if nothing had happened.

After renewed thanks to their friends, the children set off, carrying the giant's heart with them.

"If you should find it at all troublesome, just give it a little more spider-juice directly," said the grandfather, as they took their leave.

Now the giant had given an awful roar of pain the moment they anointed his heart, and had fallen down in a fit, in which he lay so long that all the boys might have escaped if they had not been so fat. One did, and got home in safety. For days the giant was unable to speak. The first words he uttered were, —

"Oh, my heart! my heart!"

"Your heart is safe enough, dear Thunderthump," said his wife. "Really, a man of your size ought not to be so nervous and apprehensive. I am ashamed of you."

"You have no heart, Doodlem," answered he. "I assure you that at this moment mine is in the greatest danger. It has fallen into the hands of foes, though who they are I cannot tell."

Here he fainted again; for Tricksey-Wee, finding the heart beginning to swell a little, had given it the least touch of spider-juice.

Again he recovered, and said, —

"Dear Doodlem, my heart is coming back to me. It is coming nearer and nearer."

After lying silent for hours, he exclaimed, —

"It is in the house, I know!"

And he jumped up and walked about, looking in every corner.

As he rose, Tricksey-Wee and Buffy-Bob came out of the hole in the tree-root, and through the cat-hole in the door, and walked boldly towards the giant. Both kept their eyes busy watching him. Led by the love of his own heart, the giant soon spied them, and staggered furiously towards them.

"I will eat you, you vermin!" he cried. "Here with my heart!"

Tricksey gave the heart a sharp pinch. Down fell the giant on his knees, blubbering, and crying, and begging for his heart.

"You shall have it, if you behave yourself properly," said Tricksey.

"How shall I behave myself properly?" asked he, whimpering.

"Take all those boys and girls, and carry them home at once."

"I'm not able; I'm too ill. I should fall down."

"Take them up directly."

"I can't, till you give me my heart."

"Very well!" said Tricksey; and she gave the heart another pinch.

The giant jumped to his feet, and catching up all the children, thrust some into his waistcoat-pockets, some into his breast-pocket, put two or three into his hat, and took a bundle of them under each arm. Then he staggered to the door.

All this time poor Doodlem was sitting in her arm-chair, crying, and mending a white stocking.

The giant led the way to the borders. He could not go fast but that Buffy and Tricksey managed to keep up with him. When they reached the borders, they thought it would be safer to let the children find their own way home. So they told him to set them down. He obeyed.

"Have you put them all down, Mr. Thunderthump?" asked Tricksey-Wee.

"Yes," said the giant.

"That's a lie!" squeaked a little voice; and out came a head from his waistcoat pocket.

Tricksey-Wee pinched the heart till the giant roared with pain.

"You're not a gentleman. You tell stories," she said.

"He was the thinnest of the lot," said Thunderthump, crying.

"Are you all there now, children?" asked Tricksey.

"Yes, ma'am," returned they, after counting themselves very carefully, and with some difficulty; for they were all stupid children.

"Now," said Tricksey-Wee to the giant, "will you promise to carry off no more children, and never to eat a child again all your life?"

"Yes, yes! I promise," answered Thunderthump, sobbing.

"The Giant on his knees"

"And you will never cross the borders of Giantland?"

"Never."

"And you shall never again wear white stockings on a Sunday, all your life long. — Do you promise?"

The giant hesitated at this, and began to expostulate; but Tricksey-Wee, believing it would be good for his morals, insisted; and the giant promised.

Then she required of him, that, when she gave him back his heart, he should give it to his wife to take care of for him for ever after. The poor giant fell on his knees, and began again to beg. But Tricksey-Wee giving the heart a slight pinch, he bawled out, —

"Yes, yes! Doodlem shall have it, I swear. Only she must not put it in the flour barrel, or in the dust-hole."

"Certainly not. Make your own bargain with her. — And you promise not to interfere with my brother and me, or to take any revenge for what we have done?"

"Yes, yes, my dear children; I promise everything. Do, pray make haste and give me back my poor heart."

"Wait there, then, till I bring it to you."

"Yes, yes. Only make haste, for I feel very faint."

Tricksey-Wee began to undo the mouth of the bag. But Buffy-Bob, who had got very knowing on his travels, took out his knife with the pretence of cutting the string; but, in reality, to be prepared for any emergency.

No sooner was the heart out of the bag, than it expanded to the size of a bullock; and the giant, with a yell of rage and vengeance, rushed on the two children, who had stepped sideways from the terrible heart. But Buffy-Bob was too quick for Thunderthump. He sprang to the heart, and buried his knife in it, up to the hilt. A fountain of blood spouted from it; and with a dreadful groan the giant fell dead at the feet of little Tricksey-Wee, who could not help being sorry for him after all.

Papa's Story

[A Scot's Christmas Story]

"O tell us a story, papa," said a wise-faced little girl, one winter night, as she intermitted for a moment her usual occupation of the hour before bed-time — that, namely, of sucking her thumb, earnestly and studiously followed, as if the fate of the world lay on the faithfulness of the process; "Do tell us a story, papa."

"Yes, do, papa," chimed in several more children. "It is *such* a long time since you told us a story."

"I don't think papa ever told us a story," said one of the youngest.

"Oh, Dolly!" exclaimed half a dozen. But her next elder sister took up the speech.

"Yes, I dare say. But you were only born last year, and papa has been away for months and months."

Now, Dolly was five, and her papa had been away for three weeks.

"Well," interposed their papa, "I will try. What shall it be about?"

"Oh! about Scotland," cried the eldest.

"Why do you want a story about Scotland?"

"Because you will like it best yourself, papa."

"I don't want one about Scotland. I'm not a Scotchman, though papa is," cried Dolly, "I'm an Englishman."

"I like Scotch stories," said the sucker of thumbs; "only I can't understand the curious words. They sound so rough, I never can understand them."

"Well, my darlings, I will tell you one about Scotland, and there shan't be a Scotch word in it. If one single one comes out of my mouth you may punish me anyway you please."

"Oh, that's jolly! How shall we punish papa if he says one Scotch word?"

"Pull his beard!" said Dolly.

"No, that would be rude!" cried three or four.

Whereupon Dolly's face changed, and she took to her thumb, like Katy.

"Make him pay a fine."

"That's no use, papa's so rich!"

Whereas the chief difficulty papa had in telling the story was the thought of the butcher's bill popping in through twenty different keyholes.

"Make him pay a kiss to each of us for every word!"

"No, that would stop the story!"

"Kiss him to death when it's done!"

"Yes! — yes! — yes — kiss him to death when it's done!"

So it was agreed; and papa began.

"You know, my darlings, there are a great many hills in Scotland, which are green with grass to the very top, and the sheep feed all over them?"

"Oh, yes! I know! Like Hampstead-hill."

"No. Like that place in the City — Ludgate-hill."

"No, my dears; not like either of those. Just come to the window, and I will try to show you. You see that star shining so brightly away there?"

"Yes. But that is not a hill, papa; it's a star!"

"Yes, it's a star. But suppose you could not see that star for a great heap of rock and earth and stone rising up between you and the star, covered with grass, and with streams of water running down its sides in every direction, that heap would be a hill. And in some parts of Scotland there are a great many of these hills crowded together, only divided from each other by deep places called valleys. They all grow out of one root — that is the earth. The tops of these hills are high up and lonely in the air, with the stars above them, and often the clouds round about them like torn garments."

"What's *garments*, Kitty?"

"Frocks, Dolly."

"What tears them, then?"

"The wind tears them; and goes roaring and raving about the hills; and makes such a noise against the steep rocks, running into the holes in them and out again, that those hills are sometimes very awful places. But in the sunshine, although they do look lonely, they are so bright and beautiful, that all the boys and girls fancy the way to heaven lies up those hills."

"And doesn't it?"

"No."

"Where is it, then?"

"Ah! that's just what you come here to find out. But you must let me go on with my story now. In the winter, on the other hand, they are such wild howling places, with the hard hailstones beating upon them, and the soft, smothering snowflakes heaping up dreadful wastes of whiteness upon them, that if ever there was a child out on them he would die with fear, if he did not die with cold. But there are only sheep there, and they don't stay very high up the hills when the winter once begins to come over the mountains."

"What's mountains?"

"Mountains are higher hills yet."

"Higher yet! They can't be higher yet."

"Oh! yes, they are; and there are higher and higher yet, till you could hardly believe it, even when you saw them.

"Well, as the winter comes over the tops of the hills the sheep come down their sides, because it is warmer the lower down you come; and even a foot thick of wool on their backs and sides could not keep out the terrible cold up there.

"But the sheep are not very knowing creatures, so they are something better instead. They are wise — that is, they are obedient — creatures, obedience being the very best wisdom. For, because they are not very knowing, they have a man to take care of them, who knows where to take them, especially when a storm comes on. Not that the sheep are so very silly as not to know where to go to get out of the wind, but they don't and can't think that some ways of getting out of danger are still more dangerous still. They would lie down in a quiet place, and lie there till the snow settled down over them and smothered them. They would not feel it cold, their wool is so thick. Or they would tumble down steep places and be killed, or buried in the snow, or carried away by the stream at the bottom. So, though they know a little, they don't know enough, and need a shepherd to take care of them.

"Now the shepherd, though he is wise, is not quite clever enough for all that is wanted of him up in those strange, terrible hills; and he needs another to help him. Now, who do you think helps the shepherd? Ah! you know, Maggy; but you mustn't tell. I will tell. It is a curious creature with four legs — the shepherd has only two, you know; — and he is covered all over with long hair of three different colours mixed — black, and brown, and white; and he has a long nose and a longer tongue, which he knows how to hold. This tongue it is a great comfort to him sometimes to hang out of his mouth as far as ever it will hang. And he has a still longer tail, which is a greater comfort to him yet. I don't know what ever he would do without his tail; for, when his master speaks kindly to him, he is so full of delight, that I think he would die if he hadn't his tail to wag. He lets his gladness off by wagging his tail, so that it shan't burst his dear, honest, good dog-heart. Ah! there, I've told you. He's a dog, you see; and the very wisest and cleverest of all dogs. He could be taught anything. Only he is such a gentleman, though dressed very plainly, as a great many gentlemen are, that it would be a shame to teach him some of the things they teach common-place rich dogs.

"Well, the shepherd tells the dog what he wants done, and off the dog runs to do it; for he can run three times as fast as the shepherd, and can get up and down places much better. I am not sure that he can see better than the shepherd, but I know he can smell better. So that he is just four legs and a long nose to the shepherd, besides the love he gives him, which would comfort any good man, even if it were offered him by a hedgehog or a hen. And for his understanding, if I were to tell Willie how much I believe he understands — if I weren't his papa, that is — Willie, there, who has such a high opinion of his own judgment, and shakes his head so knowingly when he hears anything for the first time, as if it were a shame for anything to come into existence without letting him know first — Willie, I say, would consider me silly for believing it, or, what would be a great deal worse, would think that I didn't really believe it, though I said it.

"One evening, in the beginning of April, the weakly sun of the season had gone down with a pale face behind the shoulder of a hill in the background of my story. If you had been there and had climbed up that hill, you would have seen him a great while longer, provided he had not, in the mean time, set behind a mountain of cloud, which, at this season of the year, he was very ready to do, and which, I suspect, he actually did this very evening about which I am telling you. And because he was gone down, the peat-fires upon the hearths of the cottages all began to glow more brightly, as if they were glad he was gone at last and had left them their work to do — or, rather, as if they wanted to do all they could to make up for his absence. And on one hearth in particular the peat-fire glowed very brightly. There was a pot hanging over it, with supper in it; and there was a little girl sitting by it, with a sweet, thoughtful face. Her hair was done up in a silken net, for it was the custom with Scotch girls — they wore no bonnet — to have their hair so arranged, many years before it became a fashion in London. She had a bunch of feathers, not in her hair, but fastened to her side by her apron-string, in the quill-ends of which was stuck the end of one of her knitting-needles, while the other was loose in her hand. But both were fast and busy in the loops of a blue-ribbed stocking, which she was knitting for her father.

"He was out on the hills. He had that morning taken his sheep higher up than before, and Nelly knew this; but it could not be long now till she would hear his footsteps, and measure the long stride between which brought him and happiness home together."

"But hadn't she any mother?"

"Oh! yes, she had. If you had been in the cottage that night you would have heard a cough every now and then, and would have found that Nelly's mother was lying in a bed in the room — not a bed with curtains, but a bed with doors like a press. This does not seem a nice way of having a bed; but we should all be glad of the wooden curtains about us at night if we lived in such a cottage, on the side of a hill along which the wind swept like a wild river, only ten times faster than any river would run even down the hillside. Through the cottage it would be spouting, and streaming, and eddying, and fighting, all night long; and a poor woman with a cough, or a man who has been out in the cold all day, is very glad of such a place to lie in, and leave the rest of the house to the wind and the fairies.

"Nelly's mother was ill, and there was little hope of her getting well again. What she could have done without Nelly, I can't think. It was so much easier to be ill with Nelly sitting there. For she was a good Nelly.

"After a while Nelly rose and put some peats on the fire, and hung the pot a link or two higher on the chain; for she was a wise creature, though she was only twelve, and could cook very well, because she took trouble, and thought about it. Then she sat down to her knitting again, which was a very frugal amusement.

" 'I wonder what's keeping your father, Nelly,' said her mother from the bed.

" 'I don't know, mother. It's not very late yet. He'll be home by and by. You know he was going over the shoulder of the hill to-day.'

"Now that was the same shoulder of the hill that the sun went down behind. And at the moment the sun was going down behind it, Nelly's father was standing on the top of it, and Nelly was looking up to the very place where he stood, and yet she did not see him. He was not too far off to be seen, but the sun was in her eyes, and the light of the sun hid him from her. He was then coming across with the sheep, to leave them for the night in a sheltered place — within a circle of stones that would keep the wind off them; and he ought, by rights, to have been home at least half an hour ago. — At length Nelly heard the distant sound of a heavy shoe upon the point of a great rock that grew up from the depths of the earth and just came through the surface in the path leading across the furze and brake to their cottage. She always watched for that sound — the sound of her father's shoe, studded thick with broad-headed nails, upon the top of that rock. She started up; but instead of rushing out to meet him, went to the fire and lowered the pot. Then taking up a wooden bowl, half full of oatmeal neatly pressed down into it, with a little salt on the top, she proceeded to make a certain dish for her father's supper, of which strong Scotchmen are very fond. By the time her father reached the door, it was ready, and set down with a plate over it to keep it hot, though it had a great deal more need, I think, to be let cool a little.

"When he entered, he looked troubled. He was a tall man, dressed in rough grey cloth, with a broad, round, blue bonnet, as they call it. His face looked as if it had been weather-beaten into peace."

"Beaten into pieces, papa! How dreadful!"

"Be quiet, Dolly; that's not what papa means."

"I want to know, then."

"Well, Dolly, I think it would take twenty years at least to make it plain to you, so I had better go on with my story, especially as you will come to understand it one day without my explaining it. The shepherd's face, I say, was weather-beaten and quiet, with large, grand features, in which the docility of his dogs and the gentleness of his sheep were mingled with the strength and wisdom of a man who had to care for both dogs and sheep.

" 'Well, Nelly,' he said, laying his hand on her forehead as she looked up into his face, 'how's your mother?'

"And without waiting for an answer he went to the bed, where the pale face of his wife lay upon the pillow. She held out her thin, white hand to him, and he took it so gently in his strong, brown hand. But, before he had spoken, she saw the trouble on his face, and said,

" 'What has made you so late to-night, John?'

" 'I was nearly at the fold,' said the shepherd, 'before I saw that one of the lambs was missing. So, after I got them all in, I went back with the dogs to look for him.'

" 'Where's Jumper, then?' asked Nelly, who had been patting the neck and stroking the ears of the one dog which had followed at the shepherd's heels, and was now lying before the fire, enjoying the warmth none the less that he had braved the cold all day without minding it a bit.

" 'When we couldn't see anything of the lamb,' replied her father, 'I told Jumper to go after him and bring him to the house; and Blackfoot and I came home together. I doubt he'll have a job of it, poor dog! for it's going to be a rough night; but if dog can bring him, he will.'

"As the shepherd stopped speaking, he seated himself by the fire and drew the wooden bowl towards him. Then he lifted his blue bonnet from his head, and said grace, half aloud, half murmured to himself. Then he put his bonnet on his head again, for his head was rather bald, and, as I told you, the cottage was a draughty place. And just as he put it on, a blast of wind struck the cottage and roared in the wide chimney. The next moment the rain dashed against the little window of four panes, and fell hissing into the peat-fire.

" 'There it comes,' said the shepherd.

" 'Poor Jumper!' said Nelly.

" 'And poor little lamb!' said the shepherd.

" 'It's the lamb's own fault,' said Nelly; 'he shouldn't have run away.'

" 'Ah! yes,' returned her father; 'but then the lamb didn't know what he was about exactly.'

"When the shepherd had finished his supper, he rose and went out to see whether Jumper and the lamb were coming; but the dark night would have made the blackest dog and the whitest lamb both of one colour, and he soon came in again. Then he took the Bible and read a chapter to his wife and daughter, which did them all good, even though Nelly did not understand very much of it. And then he prayed a prayer, and was very near praying for Jumper and the lamb, only he could not quite. And there he was wrong. He should have prayed about whatever troubled him or could be done good to. But he was such a good man that I am almost ashamed of saying he was wrong.

"And just as he came to the *Amen* in his prayer, there came a whine to the door. And he rose from his knees and went and opened the door. And there was the lamb with Jumper behind him. And Jumper looked dreadfully wet, and draggled, and tired, and the curls had all come out of his long hair. And yet he seemed as happy as dog could be, and looked up in the face of the shepherd triumphantly, as much as to say, 'Here he is, Master!' And the lamb looked scarcely anything the worse; for his thick, oily wool had kept away the wet; and he hadn't been running about everywhere looking for Jumper as Jumper had been for him.

"And Jumper, after Nelly had given him his supper, lay down by the fire beside the other dog, which made room for him to go next to the glowing peats; and the lamb, which had been eating all day and didn't want any supper, lay down beside him. And then Nelly bade her father and mother and the dogs good-night, and went away to bed likewise, thinking the wind might blow as it pleased now, for sheep and dogs, and father and all, were safe for the whole of the dark, windy hours between that and the morning. It is so nice to know that there is a long *nothing to do;* — but only after everything is done.

"But there are other winds in the world besides those which shake the fleeces of sheep and the beards of men, or blow ships to the bottom of the sea, or scatter the walls of cottages abroad over the hillsides. There are winds that blow up huge storms inside the hearts of men and women, and blow till the great clouds full of tears go up, and rain down from the eyes to quiet them.

"What can papa mean?"

"Never you mind, Dolly. You'll know soon enough. I'm fourteen, and I know what papa means."

"Nelly lay down in her warm bed, feeling as safe and snug as ever child felt in a large, rich house in a great city. For there was the wind howling outside to make it all the quieter inside; and there was the great, bare, cold hill before the window, which, although she could not see it, and only knew that it was there, made the bed in which she lay so close, and woolly, and warm. Now this bed was separated from her father and mother's only by a thin partition, and she heard them talking. And they had not talked long before that other cold wind that was blowing through

"And there was the lamb with Jumper behind him"

their hearts blew into hers too. And I will tell you what they said to each other that made the cold wind blow into her heart.

" 'It wasn't the loss of the lamb, John, that made you look so troubled when you came home to night,' said her mother.

" 'No, it wasn't, Jane, I must confess,' returned her father.

" 'You've heard something about Willie.'

" 'I can't deny it.'

" 'What is it?'

" 'I'll tell you in the morning.'

" 'I shan't sleep a wink for thinking whatever it can be, John. You had better tell me now. If the Lord would only bring that stray lamb back to his fold, I should die happy — sorry as I should be to leave Nelly and you, my own John.'

" 'Don't talk about dying, Annie. It breaks my heart.'

" 'We won't talk about it, then. But what's this about Willie? And how came you to hear it?'

" 'I was close to the hill-road, when I saw James Jamieson, the carrier, coming up the hill with his cart. I ran and met him.'

" 'And he told you? What did he tell you?'

" 'Nothing very particular. He only hinted that he had heard, from Wauchope the merchant, that a certain honest man's son — he meant me, Annie — was going the wrong road. And I said to James Jamieson — What road could the man mean? And James said to me — He meant the broad road, of course. And I sat down on a stone, and I heard no more; at least, I could not make sense of what James went on to say; and when I lifted my head, James and his cart were just out of sight over the top of the hill. I daresay that was how I lost the lamb.'

"A deep silence followed, and Nelly understood that her mother could not speak. At length a sob and a low weeping came through the boards to her keen mountain ear. But not another word was spoken; and, although Nelly's heart was sad, she soon fell fast asleep.

"Now, Willie had gone to college, and had been a very good boy for the first winter. They go to college only in winter in Scotland. And he had come home in the end of March and had helped his father to work their little farm, doing his duty well to the sheep and to everything and everybody; for learning had not made him the least unfit for work. Indeed, work that learning does really make a man unfit for, cannot be fit work for that man — perhaps is not fit work for anybody. When winter came,

PAPA'S STORY

he had gone back to Edinburgh, and he ought to have been home a week ago, and he had not come. He had written to say that he had to finish some lessons he had begun to give, and could not be home till the end of the month. Now this was so far true that it was not a lie. But there was more in it: he did not want to go home to the lonely hillside — so lonely, that there were only a father and a mother and a sister there. He had made acquaintance with some students who were fonder of drinking whisky than of getting up in the morning to write abstracts, and he didn't want to leave them.

"Nelly was, as I have said, too young to keep awake because she was troubled; and so, before half an hour was over, was fast asleep and dreaming. And the wind outside, tearing at the thatch of the cottage, mingled with her dream.

"I will tell you what her dream was. — She thought they were out in the dark and the storm, she and her father. But she was no longer Nelly; she was Jumper. And her father said to her, 'Jumper, go after the black lamb and bring him home.' And away she galloped over the stones, and through the furze, and across the streams, and up the rocks, and jumped the stone fences, and swam the pools of water, to find the little black lamb. And all the time, somehow or other, the little black lamb was her brother Willie. And nothing could turn the dog Jumper, though the wind blew as if it would blow him off all his four legs, and off the hill, as one blows a fly off a book. And the hail beat in Jumper's face, as if it would put out his eyes or knock holes in his forehead, and yet Jumper went on."

"But it wasn't Jumper; it was Nelly, you know."

"I know that, but I am talking about the dog Jumper, that Nelly thought she was. He went on and on, and over the top of the cold wet hill, and was beginning to grow hopeless about finding the black lamb, when, just a little way down the other side, he came upon him behind a rock. He was standing in a miry pool, all wet with rain. Jumper would never have found him, the night was so dark and the lamb was so black, but that he gave a bleat; whereupon Jumper tried to say Willie, but could not, and only gave a gobbling kind of bark. So he jumped upon the lamb, and taking a mouthful of his wool, gave him a shake that made him pull his feet out of the mire, and then drove him off before him, trotting all the way home. When they came into the cottage, the black lamb ran up to Nelly's mother, and jumped into her bed, and Jumper jumped in after him; and then Nelly was Nelly and Willie was Willie, as they used to be, when Nelly would creep into Willie's bed in the morning and kiss him awake. Then Nelly woke, and was sorry that it was a dream. For Willie was still away, far off on the broad road, and how ever was he to be got home? Poor black lamb!

"She soon made up her mind. Only how to carry out her mind was the difficulty. All day long she thought about it. And she wrote a letter to her father, telling him what she was going to do; and when she went to her room the next night, she laid the letter on her bed, and, putting on her Sunday bonnet and cloak, waited till they should be asleep.

"The shepherd had gone to bed very sad. He, too, had been writing a letter. It had taken him all the evening to write, and Nelly had watched his face while he wrote it, and seen how the muscles of it worked with sorrow and pain as he slowly put word after word down on the paper. When he had finished it, and folded it up, and put a wafer on it, and addressed it, he left it on the table, and, as I said, went to bed, where he soon fell asleep; for even sorrow does not often keep people awake that have worked hard through the day in the open air. And Nelly was watching.

"When she thought he was asleep, she took a pair of stockings out of a chest and put them in her pocket. Then, taking her Sunday shoes in her hand, she stepped gently from her room to the cottage door, which she opened easily, for it was never locked. She then found that it was pitch dark; but she could keep the path well enough, for her bare feet told her at once when she was going off it. It is a great blessing to have bare feet. People with bare feet can always keep the path better, and keep their garments cleaner, too. Only they must be careful to wash them at night.

"So, dark as it was, she soon reached the road. There was no wind that night, and the clouds hid the stars. She would turn in the direction of Edinburgh, and let the carrier overtake her. For she felt rather guilty, and was anxious to get on.

"After she had walked a good while, she began to wonder that the carrier had not come up with her. The fact was that the carrier never left till the early morning. She was not a bit afraid, though, reasoning that, as she was walking in the same direction, it would take him so much the longer to get up with her.

"At length, after walking a long way — longer far than she thought, for she walked a great part of it half asleep — she began to feel a little tired, and sat down upon a stone by the roadside. There was a stone behind her, too. She could just see its grey face. She leaned her back against it, and fell fast asleep.

"When she woke she could not think where she was, or how she had got there. It was a dark, drizzly morning, and her feet were cold. But she was quite dry. For the rock against which she fell asleep in the night projected so far over her head that it had kept all the rain off her. She could not have chosen a better place, if she had been able to choose. But the sight around her was very dreary. In front lay a swampy ground, creeping away, dismal and wretched, to the horizon, where a long, low hill closed it. Behind her rose a mountain, bare and rocky, on which neither sheep nor shepherd was to be seen. Her home seemed to have vanished in the night, and left her either in a dream or in another world. And as she came to herself, the fear grew upon her that either she had missed the way in the dark or the carrier had gone past while she slept, either of which was dreadful to contemplate. She began to feel hungry, too, and she had not had the foresight to bring even a piece of oatcake with her.

"It was only dusky dawn yet. There was plenty of time. She would sit down again for a little while; for the rock had a homely look to her. It had been her refuge all night, and she was not willing to leave it. So she leaned her arms on her knees, and gazed out upon the dreary, grey, misty flat before her.

"Then she rose, and, turning her back on the waste, kneeled down, and prayed God that, as he taught Jumper to find lambs, he would teach her to find her brother. And thus she fell fast asleep again.

"When she woke once more and turned towards the road, whom should she see standing there but the carrier, staring at her. And his big, strong horses stood in the road too, with their carts behind them. They were not in the least surprised. She could not help crying, just a little, for joy.

"'Why, Nelly, what on earth are you doing here?' said the carrier.

"'Waiting for you,' answered Nelly.

"'Where are you going, child?'

"'To Edinburgh.'

"'What on earth are you going to do in Edinburgh?'

"'I am going to my brother Willie, at the college.'

"'But the college is over now.'

"'I know that,' said Nelly.

"'What's his address, then?' the carrier went on.

"'I don't know,' answered Nelly.

"'It's a lucky thing that I know, then. But you have no business to leave home this way.'

"'Oh! yes, I have.'

"'I am sure your father did not know of it, for when he gave me a letter this morning to take to Willie he did not say a word about you.'

"'He thought I was asleep in my bed,' returned Nelly, trying to smile. But the thought that the carrier had actually seen her father since she left home, was too much for her, and she cried.

"'I can't go back with you now,' said the carrier, 'so you must go on with me.'

"'That's just what I want,' said Nelly.

"So the carrier made her put on her shoes and stockings, for he was a kind man and had children of his own. Then he pulled out some of the straw that packed his cart, and made her a little bed on the tarpaulin that covered it, just where there was a soft bundle beneath. Then he lifted her up on it and covered her over with a few empty sacks. There Nelly was so happy, and warm, and comfortable, that, for the third time, she fell asleep.

"When she woke he gave her some bread and cheese for her breakfast, and some water out of a brook that crossed the road, and then Nelly began to look about her. The rain had ceased and the sun was shining, and the country looked very pleasant; but Nelly thought it a strange country. She could see so much farther! And corn was growing everywhere, and there was not a sheep to be seen, and there were many cows feeding in the fields.

"'Are we near Edinburgh?' she asked.

"'Oh, no!' answered the carrier; 'we are a long way from Edinburgh yet.'

"And so they journeyed on. The day was flecked all over with sunshine and rain; and when the rain's turn came, Nelly would creep under a corner of the tarpaulin till it was over. They slept part of the night at a small town they passed through.

"Nelly thought it a very long way to Edinburgh, though the carrier was kind to her, and gave her of everything that he had himself, except the whisky, which he did not think good for her.

"At length she spied, far away, a great hill, that looked like a couching lion.

"'Do you see that hill?' said the carrier.

"'I am just looking at it,' answered Nelly.

"'Edinburgh lies at the foot of that hill.'

"'Oh!' said Nelly; and scarcely took her eyes off it till it went out of sight again.

"Reaching the brow of an eminence, they saw Arthur's Seat (as the carrier said the hill was called) once more, and below it a great jagged ridge of what Nelly took to be broken rocks. But the carrier told her that was the Old Town of Edinburgh. Those fierce-looking splinters on the edge of the mass were the roofs, gables, and chimneys of the great houses once inhabited by the nobility of Scotland. But when you come near the houses you find them shabby-looking; for they are full of poor people, who cannot keep them clean and nice.

"But, certainly, my children, if you will excuse your Scotch papa for praising his own country's capital, I don't believe there ever was a city that looked so grand from the distance as that Old Town of Edinburgh. And when you get into the streets you can fancy yourself hundreds of years back in the story of Scotland. Seen thus through the perspective of time or distance, it is a great marvel to everyone with any imagination at all; and it was nothing less to little Nelly, even when she got into the middle of it. But her heart was so full of its dog-duties towards her black lamb of a brother that the toyshops and the sugarplum-shops could not draw it towards their mines of wonder and wealth.

"At length the cart stopped at a public-house in the Grassmarket — a wide, open place, with strange old houses all round it, and a huge rock, with a castle on its top, towering over it. There Nelly got down.

"'I can't go with you till I've unloaded my cart,' said the carrier.

"'I don't want you to go with me, please,' said Nelly. 'I think Willie would rather not. Please give me father's letter.'

"So the carrier gave her the letter, and got a little boy of the landlady's to show her the way up to the West-bow — a street of tall houses, so narrow that you might have shaken hands across it from window to window. But those houses are all pulled down now, I am sorry to say, and the street Nelly went up has vanished. From the West-bow they went up a stair into the High-street, and thence into a narrow court, and then up a winding stair, and so came to the floor where Willie's lodging was. There the little boy left Nelly.

"Nelly knocked two or three times before anybody came; and when at last a woman opened the door, what do you think the woman did the moment she inquired of Willie? — She shut the door in her face with a fierce scolding word. For Willie had vexed her that morning, and she thoughtlessly took her revenge upon Nelly without even asking her a question. Then, indeed, for a moment, Nelly's courage gave way. All at once she felt dreadfully tired, and sat down upon the stair and cried. And the landlady was so angry with Willie that she forgot all about the little girl that wanted to see him.

"So for a whole hour Nelly sat upon the stair, moving only to let people pass. She felt dreadfully miserable, but had not the courage to knock again, for fear of having the door shut in her face yet more hopelessly. At last a woman came up and knocked at the door. Nelly rose trembling and stood behind her. The door opened; the woman was welcomed; she entered. The door was again closing when Nelly cried out in agony,

"'Please, ma'am, I want to see my brother Willie!' and burst into sobs.

"The landlady, her wrath having by this time assuaged, was vexed with herself and ashamed that she had not let the child in.

"'Bless me!' she cried, 'have you been there all this time? Why didn't you tell me you were Willie's sister? Come in. You won't find him in, though. It's not much of his company we get, I can tell you.'

"'I don't want to come in, then,' sobbed Nelly, 'Please to tell me where he is, ma'am.'

"'How should I know where he is? At no good, I warrant. But you had better come in and wait, for it's your only chance of seeing him before to-morrow morning.'

"With a sore heart Nelly went in and sat down by the kitchen fire. And the landlady and her visitor sat and talked together, every now and then casting a look at Nelly, who kept her eyes on the ground, waiting with all her soul till Willie should come. Every time the landlady looked, she looked sooner the next time; and every time she looked, Nelly's sad face went deeper into her heart; so that, before she knew what was going on in herself, she quite loved the child; for she was a kind-hearted woman, though she was sometimes cross.

In a few minutes she went up to Nelly and took her bonnet off. Nelly submitted without a word. Then she made her a cup of tea; and while Nelly was taking it she asked her a great many questions. Nelly answered them all; and the landlady stared with amazement at the child's courage and resolution, and thought with herself,

"Nelly sat down upon the stair and cried"

"'Well, if anything can get Willie out of his bad ways, this little darling will do it.'

"Then she made her go to Willie's bed, promising to let her know the moment he came home.

"Nelly slept and slept till it was night. When she woke it was dark, but a light was shining through beneath the door. So she rose and put on her frock and shoes and stockings, and went to the kitchen.

"'You see he's not come yet, Nelly,' said the landlady.

"'Where can he be?' returned Nelly, sadly.

"'Oh! he'll be drinking with some of his companions in the public-house, I suppose.'

"'Where is the public-house?'

"'There are hundreds of them, child.'

"'I know the place he generally goes to,' said a young tradesman who sat by the fire.

"He had a garret-room in the house, and knew Willie by sight. And he told the landlady in a low voice where it was.

"'Oh! do tell me, please sir,' cried Nelly. 'I want to get him home.'

"'You don't think he'll mind you, do you?'

"'Yes, I do,' returned Nelly confidently.

"'Well, I'll show you the way if you like; but you'll find it a rough place, I can tell you. You'll wish yourself out of it pretty soon, with or without Willie.'

"'I won't leave it without him,' said Nelly, tying on her bonnet.

"'Stop a bit,' said the landlady. 'You don't think I am going to let the child out with nobody but you to look after her?'

"'Come along, then, ma'am.'

"The landlady put on her bonnet, and out they all went into the street.

"What a wonder it *might* have been to Nelly! But she only knew that she was in the midst of great lights, and carts and carriages rumbling over the stones, and windows full of pretty things, and crowds of people jostling along the pavements. In all the show she wanted nothing but Willie.

"The young man led them down a long dark close through an archway, and then into a court off the close, and then up an outside stone stair to a low-browed door, at which he knocked.

"'I don't much like the look of this place,' said the landlady.

"'Oh! there's no danger, I dare say, if you keep quiet. They'll never hurt the child. Besides, her brother'll see to that.'

"Presently the door was opened, and the young man asked after Willie.

"'Is he in?' he said.

"'He may be, or he may not,' answered a fat, frowzy woman, in a dirty cotton dress. 'Who wants him?'

"'This little girl.'

"'Please ma'am, I'm his sister.'

"'We want no sisters here.'

"And she proceeded to close the door. I dare say the landlady remembered with shame that that was just what she had done that morning.

"'Come! come!' interposed the young tradesman, putting his foot between the door and the post; 'don't be foolish. Surely you won't go to keep a child like that from speaking to her own brother! Why, the Queen herself would let her in.'

"This softened the woman a little, and she hesitated, with the latch in her hand.

"'Mother wants him,' said Nelly. 'She's very ill. I heard her cry about Willie. Let me in.'

"She took hold of the woman's hand, who drew it away hastily, but stepped back, at the same time, and let her enter. She then resumed her place at the door.

"'Devil a one of *you* shall come in!' she said, as if justifying the child's admission by the exclusion of the others.

"'We don't want, mistress,' said the young man. 'But we'll just see that no harm comes to her.'

"'D'ye think I'm not enough for that,' said the woman, with scorn. 'Let me see who dares to touch her! But you may stay where you are, if you like. The air's free.'

"So saying, she closed the door, with a taunting laugh.

"The passage was dark in which Nelly found herself; but she saw a light at the further end, through a keyhole, and heard the sounds of loud talk and louder laughter. Before the woman had closed the outer door, she had reached this room; nor did the woman follow either to guide or prevent her.

"A pause came in the noise. She tapped at the door.

"'Come in!' cried someone. And she entered.

"Round a table were seated four youths, drinking. Of them one was Willie, with flushed face and flashing eyes. They all stared when the child stood before them, in her odd, old-fashioned bonnet, and her little shawl pinned at the throat. Willie stared as much as any of them.

"Nelly spoke first.

"'Willie! Willie!' she cried, and would have rushed to him, but the table was between.

"'What do you want here, Nelly? Who the deuce let you come here?' said Willie, not quite unkindly.

"'I want you, Willie. Come home with me. Oh! please come home with me.'

"'I can't, now, Nelly, you see,' he answered. Then, turning to his companions, 'How could the child have found her way here?' he said, looking ashamed as he spoke.

"'You're fetched. That's all,' said one of them, with a sneer. 'Mother's sent for you.'

"'Go along!' said another; 'and mind you don't catch it when you get home!'

"'Nobody will say a word to you, Willie,' interposed Nelly.

"'Be a good boy, and don't do it again!' said the third, raising his glass to his lips.

"Willie tried to laugh, but was evidently vexed.

"'What are you standing there for, Nelly?' he said, sharply. 'This is no place for you.'

"'Nor for you either, Willie,' returned Nelly, without moving.

"'We're all very naughty, aren't we, Nelly?' said the first.

"'Come and give me a kiss, and I'll forgive you,' said the second.

"'You shan't have your brother; so you may trudge home again without him,' said the third.

"And then they all burst out laughing, except Willie.

"'Do go away, Nelly,' he said, angrily.

"'Where am I to go to?' she asked.

"'Where you came from.'

"'That's home,' said Nelly; 'but I can't go home to-night, and I daren't go home without you. Mother would die. She's very ill, Willie. I heard her crying last night.'

"It seemed to Nelly at the moment that it was only last night she left home.

" 'I'll just take the little fool to my lodgings and come back directly,' said Willie, rather stricken at this mention of his mother.

" 'Oh! yes. Do as you're bid!' they cried, and burst out laughing again. For they despised Willie because he was only a shepherd's son, although they liked to have his company because he was clever. But Willie was angry now.

" 'I tell you what,' he said, 'I'll go when and where I like.'

"Two of them were silent now, because they were afraid of Willie; for he was big and strong. The third, however, trusting to the others, said, with a nasty sneer,

" 'Go with its little sister to its little mammy!'

"Now Willie could not get out, so small was the room and so large the table, except one or other of those next him rose to let him pass. Neither did. Willie therefore jumped on the table, kicked the tumbler of the one who had last spoken into the breast of his shirt, jumped down, took Nelly by the hand, and left the house.

" 'The rude boys!' said Nelly. 'I would never go near them again, if I was you, Willie.'

"But Willie said never a word, for he was not pleased with Nelly, or with himself, or with his *friends*.

"When they got into the house he said, abruptly, 'What's the matter with mother, Nelly?'

" 'I don't know, Willie; but I don't think she'll ever get better. I'm sure father doesn't think it either.'

"Willie was silent for a long time. Then he said,

" 'How did you come here, Nelly?'

"And Nelly told him the whole story.

" 'And now you'll come home with me, Willie.'

" 'It was very foolish of you, Nelly. To think you could bring me home if I didn't choose!'

" 'But you do choose, don't you, Willie?'

" 'You might as well have written,' he said.

"Then Nelly remembered her father's letter, which the carrier had given her. And Willie took it, and sat down, with his back to Nelly, and read it through. Then he burst out crying, and laid his head on his arms and went on crying. And Nelly got upon a bar of the chair — for he was down on the table — and leaned over him, and put her arms round his neck, and said, crying to herself all the time,

"Nelly comforts Willie"

" 'Nobody said a word to the black lamb when Jumper brought him home, Willie.'

"And Willie lifted his head, and put his arms round Nelly, and drew her face to his, and kissed her as he used to kiss her years ago.

"And I needn't tell you anything more about it."

"Oh! yes. Tell us how they got home."

"They went home with the carrier the next day."

"And wasn't his father glad to see Willie?"

"He didn't say much. He held out his hand with a half smile on his mouth, and a look in his eye like the moon before a storm."

"And his mother?"

"His mother held out her arms, and drew him down to her bosom, and stroked his hair, and prayed God to bless Willie, her boy."

"And Nelly — weren't they glad to see Nelly?"

"They made more of Willie than they did of Nelly."

"And wasn't Nelly sorry?"

"No, she never noticed it — she was so busy making much of Willie, too."

"But I hope they didn't scold Nelly for going to fetch Willie?"

"When she went to bed that night, her father kissed her and said,

" 'The blessin' o' an auld father be upo' ye, my wee bairn!'

"There's Scotch," now exclaimed the whole company.

And in one moment papa was on the floor, buried beneath a mass of children.

The chief thumbsucker, after kissing till she was stupid, recovered her wits by sucking her thumb diligently for a whole minute, after which she said, "If we had been wolves, it would have been dangerous, papa."

And then they all went to bed.

Port in a Storm

"Papa," said my sister Effie, one evening as we all sat about the drawing-room fire. One after another, as nothing followed, we turned our eyes upon her. There she sat, still silent, embroidering the corner of a cambric handkerchief, apparently unaware that she had spoken.

It was a very cold night in the beginning of winter. My father had come home early, and we had dined early that we might have a long evening together, for it was my father's and mother's wedding-day, and we always kept it as the homeliest of holidays. My father was seated in an easy-chair by the chimney corner, with a jug of Burgundy near him, and my mother sat by his side, now and then taking a sip out of his glass.

Effie was now nearly nineteen; the rest of us were younger. What she was thinking about we did not know then, though we could all guess now. Suddenly she looked up, and seeing all eyes fixed upon her, became either aware or suspicious, and blushed rosy red.

"You spoke to me, Effie. What was it, my dear?"

"O yes, papa. I wanted to ask you whether you wouldn't tell us, to-night, the story about how you — "

"Well, my love?"

" — About how you — "

"I am listening, my dear."

"I mean, about mamma and you."

"Yes, yes. About how I got your mamma for a mother to you. Yes. I paid a dozen of port for her."

We all and each exclaimed *Papa!* and my mother laughed.

"Tell us all about it," was the general cry.

"Well, I will," answered my father. "I must begin at the beginning, though."

And, filling his glass with Burgundy, he began.

"As far back as I can remember, I lived with my father in an old manor-house in the country. It did not belong to my father, but to an elder brother of his, who at that time was captain of a seventy-four. He loved the sea more than his life; and, as yet apparently, had loved his ship better than any woman. At least he was not married.

"My mother had been dead for some years, and my father was now in very delicate health. He had never been strong, and since my mother's death, I believe, though I was too young to notice it, he had pined away. I am not going to tell you anything about him just now, because it does not belong to my story. When I was about five years old, as nearly as I can judge, the doctors advised him to leave England. The house was put into the hands of an agent to let — at least, so I suppose; and he took me with him to Madeira, where he died. I was brought home by his servant, and by my uncle's directions, sent to a boarding-school; from there to Eton, and from there to Oxford.

"Before I had finished my studies, my uncle had been an admiral for some time. The year before I left Oxford, he married Lady Georgiana Thornbury, a widow lady, with one daughter. Thereupon he bade farewell to the sea, though I dare say he did not like the parting, and retired with his bride to the house where he was born — the same house I told you I was born in, which had been in the family for many generations, and which your cousin now lives in.

"It was late in the autumn when they arrived at Culverwood. They were no sooner settled than my uncle wrote to me, inviting me to spend Christmas-tide with them at the old place. And here you may see my story has arrived at its beginning.

"It was with strange feelings that I entered the house. It looked so old-fashioned, and stately, and grand, to eyes which had been accustomed to all the modern commonplaces! Yet the shadowy recollections which hung about it gave an air of homeliness to the place, which, along with the grandeur, occasioned a sense of rare delight. For what can be better than to feel that you are in stately company, and at the same time perfectly at home in it? I am grateful to this day for the lesson I had from the sense of which I have spoken — that of mingled awe and tenderness in the aspect of the old hall as I entered it for the first time after fifteen years, having left it a mere child.

"I was cordially received by my old uncle and my new aunt. But the moment Kate Thornbury entered I lost my heart, and have never found it again to this day. I get on wonderfully well without it, though, for I have got the loan of a far better one till I find my own, which, therefore, I hope I never shall."

My father glanced at my mother as he said this, and she returned his look in a way which I can now interpret as a quiet, satisfied confidence. But the tears came in Effie's eyes. She had trouble before long, poor girl! But it is not her story I have to tell. — My father went on:

"Your mother was prettier then than she is now, but not so beautiful; beautiful enough, though, to make me think there never had been or could again be anything so beautiful. She met me kindly, and I met her awkwardly."

"You made me feel that I had no business there," said my mother, speaking for the first time in the course of the story.

"See there, girls," said my father. "You are always so confident in first impressions, and instinctive judgment! I was awkward because, as I said, I fell in love with your mother the moment I saw her; and she thought I regarded her as an intruder into the old family precincts.

"I will not follow the story of the days. I was very happy, except when I felt too keenly how unworthy I was of Kate Thornbury; not that she meant to make me feel it, for she was never other than kind; but she was such that I could not help feeling it. I gathered courage, however, and before three days were over, I began to tell her all my slowly reviving memories of the place, with my childish adventures associated with this and that room or outhouse or spot in the grounds; for the longer I was in the place the more my old associations with it revived, till I was quite astonished to find how much of my history in connection with Culverwood had been thoroughly imprinted on my memory. She never showed, at least, that she was weary of my stories; which, however interesting to me, must have been tiresome to any one who did not sympathize with what I felt towards my old nest. From room to room we rambled, talking or silent; and nothing could have given me a better chance, I believe, with a heart like your mother's. I think it was not long before she began to like me, at least, and liking had every opportunity of growing into something stronger, if only she too did not come to the conclusion that I was unworthy of her.

"My uncle received me like the jolly old tar that he was — welcomed me to the old ship — hoped we should make many a voyage together — and that I would take the run of the craft — all but in one thing.

" 'You see, my boy,' he said, 'I married above my station, and I don't want my wife's friends to say that I laid alongside of her to get hold of her daughter's fortune. No, no, my boy; your old uncle has too much salt water in him to do a dog's trick like that. So you take care of yourself — that's all. She might turn the head of a wiser man than ever came out of our family.'

"I did not tell my uncle that his advice was already too late; for that, though it was not an hour since I had first seen her, my head was so far turned already, that the only way to get it right again, was to go on turning it in the same direction; though, no doubt, there was a danger of over-hauling the screw. The old gentleman never referred to the matter again, nor took any notice of our increasing intimacy; so that I sometimes doubt even now if he could have been in earnest in the very simple warning he gave me. Fortunately, Lady Georgiana liked me — at least I thought she did, and that gave me courage."

"That's all nonsense, my dear," said my mother. "Mamma was nearly as fond of you as I was; but you never wanted courage."

"I knew better than to show my cowardice, I dare say," returned my father. "But," he continued, "things grew worse and worse, till I was certain I should kill myself, or go straight out of my mind, if your mother would not have me. So it went on for a few days, and Christmas was at hand.

"The admiral had invited several old friends to come and spend the Christmas week with him. Now you must remember that, although you look on me as an old-fashioned fogie — — "

"Oh, papa!" we all interrupted; but he went on.

"Yet my old uncle was an older-fashioned fogie, and his friends were much the same as himself. Now, *I* am fond of a glass of port, though I dare not take it, and must content myself with Burgundy. Uncle Bob would have called Burgundy pig-wash. *He* could not do without his port, though he was a moderate enough man, as customs were. Fancy, then, his dismay when, on questioning his butler, an old coxen of his own, and after going down to inspect in person, he found that there was scarcely more than a dozen of port in the wine-cellar. He turned white with dismay, and, till he had brought the blood back to his countenance by swearing, he was something awful to behold in the dim light of the tallow candle old Jacob held in his tattooed fist. I will not repeat the words he used; fortunately, they are out of fashion amongst gentlemen, although ladies, I understand, are beginning to revive the custom, now old, and always ugly. Jacob reminded his honour that he would not have more put down till he had got a proper cellar built, for the one there was, he had said, was not fit to put anything but dead men in. Thereupon, after abusing Jacob for not reminding him of the necessities of the coming season, he turned to me, and began, certainly not to swear at his own father, but to expostulate sideways with the absent shade for not having provided a decent cellar before his departure from this world of dinners and wine, hinting that it was somewhat selfish, and very inconsiderate of the welfare of those who were to come after him. Having a little exhausted his indignation, he came up, and wrote the most peremptory order to his wine-merchant, in Liverpool, to let him have thirty dozen of port before Christmas Day, even if he had to send it by post-chaise. I took the letter to the post myself, for the old man would trust nobody but me, and indeed would have preferred taking it himself; but in winter he was always lame from the effects of a bruise he had received from a falling spar in the battle of Aboukir.

"That night I remember well. I lay in bed wondering whether I might venture to say a word, or even to give a hint to your mother that there was a word that pined to be said if it might. All at once I heard a whine of the wind in the old chimney. How well I knew that whine! For my kind aunt had taken the trouble to find out from me what room I had occupied as a boy, and by the third night I spent there, she had got it ready for me. I jumped out of bed, and found that the snow was falling fast and thick. I jumped into bed again, and began wondering what my uncle would do if the port did not arrive. And then I thought that, if the snow went on falling as it did, and if the wind rose any higher, it might turn out that the roads through the hilly part of Yorkshire in which Culverwood lay, might very well be blocked up.

> "The north wind doth blow,
> And we shall have snow,
> And what will my uncle do then, poor thing?
> He'll run for his port,
> But he will run short,
> And have too much water to drink, poor thing!

"With the influences of the chamber of my childhood crowding upon me, I kept repeating the travestied rhyme to myself, till I fell asleep.

"Now, boys and girls, if I were writing a novel, I should like to make you, somehow or other, put together the facts — that I was in the room I have mentioned; that I had been in the cellar with my uncle for the first time that evening; that I had seen my uncle's distress, and heard his reflections upon his father. I may add that I was not myself, even then, so indifferent to the merits of a good glass of port as to be unable to enter into my uncle's dismay, and that of his guests at last, if they should find that the snowstorm had actually closed up the sweet approaches of the expected port. If I was personally indifferent to the matter, I fear it is to be attributed to your mother, and not to myself."

"Nonsense!" interposed my mother once more. "I never knew such a man for making little of himself and much of other people. You never drank a glass too much port in your life."

"That's why I'm so fond of it, my dear," returned my father. "I declare you make me quite discontented with my pig-wash here.

"That night I had a dream.

"The next day the visitors began to arrive. Before the evening after, they had all come. There were five of them — three tars and two land-crabs, as they called each other when they got jolly, which, by-the-way, they would not have done long without me.

"My uncle's anxiety visibly increased. Each guest, as he came down to breakfast, received each morning a more constrained greeting. — I beg your pardon, ladies; I forgot to mention that my aunt had lady-visitors, of course. But the fact is, it is only the port-drinking visitors in whom my story is interested, always excepted your mother.

"These ladies my admiral uncle greeted with something even approaching to servility. I understood him well enough. He instinctively sought to make a party to protect him when the awful secret of his cellar should be found out. But for two preliminary days or so, his resources would serve; for he had plenty of excellent claret and Madeira — stuff I don't know much about — and both Jacob and himself condescended to manoeuvre a little.

"The wine did not arrive. But the morning of Christmas Eve did. I was sitting in my room, trying to write a song for Kate — that's your mother, my dears — "

"I know, papa," said Effie, as if she were very knowing to know that.

" — — when my uncle came into the room, looking like Sintram with Death and the Other One after him — that's nonsense you read to me the other day, isn't it, Effie?"

"Not nonsense, dear papa," remonstrated Effie; and I loved her for saying it, for surely *that* is not nonsense.

"I didn't mean it," said my father; and turning to my mother, added: "It must be your fault, my dear, that my children are so serious that they always take a joke for earnest. However, it was no joke with my uncle. If he didn't look like Sintram he looked like t'other one.

"'The roads are frozen — I mean snowed up,' he said. 'There's just one bottle of port left, and what Captain Calker will say — I dare say I know, but I'd rather not. Damn this weather! — God forgive me! — that's not right — but it *is* trying — ain't it, my boy?'

"'What will you give me for a dozen of port, uncle?' was all my answer:

"'Give you? I'll give you Culverwood, you rogue.'

"'Done,' I cried.

"'That is,' stammered my uncle, 'that is,' and he reddened like the funnel of one of his hated steamers, 'that is, you know, always provided, you know. It wouldn't be fair to Lady Georgiana, now, would it? I put it to yourself — if she took the trouble, you know. You understand me, my boy?'

"'That's of course, uncle,' I said.

"'Ah! I see you're a gentleman like your father, not to trip a man when he stumbles,' said my uncle. For such was the dear old man's sense of honour, that he was actually uncomfortable about the hasty promise he had made without first specifying the exception. The exception, you know, has Culverwood at the present hour, and right welcome he is.

"'Of course, uncle,' I said — 'between gentlemen, you know. Still, I want my joke out, too. What will you give me for a dozen of port to tide you over Christmas Day?'

"'Give you, my boy? I'll give you — '

"But here he checked himself, as one that had been burned already.

"'Bah!' he said, turning his back, and going towards the door; 'what's the use of joking about serious affairs like this?'

"And so he left the room. And I let him go. For I had heard that the road from Liverpool was impassable, the wind and snow having continued every day since that night of which I told you. Meantime, I had never been able to summon the courage to say one word to your mother — I beg her pardon, I mean Miss Thornbury.

"Christmas Day arrived. My uncle was awful to behold. His friends were evidently anxious about him. They thought he was ill. There was such a hesitation about him, like a shark with a bait, and such a flurry, like a whale in his last agonies. He had a horrible secret which he dared not tell, and which yet *would* come out of its grave at the appointed hour.

"Down in the kitchen the roast beef and turkey were meeting their deserts. Up in the store-room — for Lady Georgiana was not above house-keeping, any more than her daughter — the ladies of the house were doing their part; and I was oscillating between my uncle and his niece, making myself amazingly useful now to one and now to the other. The turkey and the beef were on the table, nay, they had been well eaten, before I felt that my moment was come. Outside, the wind was howling, and driving the snow with soft pats against the window-panes. Eager-eyed I watched General Fortescue, who despised sherry or Madeira even during dinner, and would no more touch champagne than he would *eau sucrée;* but drank port after fish or with cheese indiscriminately — with eager eyes I watched how the last bottle dwindled out its fading life in the clear decanter. Glass after glass was supplied to General Fortescue by the fearless cockswain, who, if he might have had his choice, would rather have boarded a Frenchman than waited for what was to follow. My uncle scarcely ate at all, and the only thing that stopped his face from growing longer with the removal of every dish was that nothing but death could have made it longer than it was already. It was my interest to let matters go as far as they might up to a certain point, beyond which it was not my interest to let them go, if I could help it. At the same time I was curious to know how my uncle would announce — confess the terrible fact that in his house, on Christmas Day, having invited his oldest friends to share with him the festivities of the season, there was not one bottle more of port to be had.

"I waited till the last moment — till I fancied the admiral was opening his mouth, like a fish in despair, to make his confession. He had not even dared to make a confidante of his wife in such an awful dilemma. Then I pretended to have dropped my table-napkin behind my chair, and rising to seek it, stole round behind my uncle, and whispered in his ear:

"'What will you give me for a dozen of port now, uncle?'

"'Bah!' he said, 'I'm at the gratings; don't torture me.'

" 'I'm in earnest, uncle.'

"He looked round at me with a sudden flash of bewildered hope in his eye. In the last agony he was capable of believing in a miracle. But he made me no reply. He only stared.

" 'Will you give me Kate? I want Kate,' I whispered.

" 'I will, my boy. That is, if she'll have you. That is, I mean to say, if you produce the true tawny.'

" 'Of course, uncle; honour bright — as port in a storm,' I answered, trembling in my shoes and everything else I had on, for I was not more than three parts confident in the result.

"The gentlemen beside Kate happening at the moment to be occupied, each with the lady on his other side, I went behind her, and whispered to her as I had whispered to my uncle, though not exactly in the same terms. Perhaps I had got a little courage from the champagne I had drunk; perhaps the presence of the company gave me a kind of mesmeric strength; perhaps the excitement of the whole venture kept me up; perhaps Kate herself gave me courage, like a goddess of old, in some way I did not understand. At all events I said to her:

" 'Kate,' — we had got so far even then — 'my uncle hasn't another bottle of port in his cellar. Consider what a state General Fortescue will be in soon. He'll be tipsy for want of it. Will you come and help me to find a bottle or two?'

"She rose at once, with a white-rose blush — so delicate I don't believe any one saw it but myself. But the shadow of a stray ringlet could not fall on her cheek without my seeing it.

"When we got into the hall, the wind was roaring loud, and the few lights were flickering and waving gustily with alternate light and shade across the old portraits which I had known so well as a child — for I used to think what each would say first, if he or she came down out of the frame and spoke to me.

"I stopped, and taking Kate's hand, I said —

" 'I daren't let you come farther, Kate, before I tell you another thing: my uncle has promised, if I find him a dozen of port — you must have seen what a state the poor man is in — to let me say something to you — I suppose he meant your mamma, but I prefer saying it to you, if you will let me. Will you come and help me to find the port?'

"She said nothing, but took up a candle that was on a table in the hall, and stood waiting. I ventured to look at her. Her face was now celestial rosy red, and I could not doubt that she had understood me. She looked so beautiful that I stood staring at her without moving. What the servants could have been about that not one of them crossed the hall, I can't think.

"At last Kate laughed and said — 'Well?' I started, and I dare say took my turn at blushing. At least I did not know what to say. I had forgotten all about the guests inside. 'Where's the port?' said Kate. I caught hold of her hand again and kissed it."

"You needn't be quite so minute in your account, my dear," said my mother, smiling.

"I will be more careful in future, my love," returned my father.

" 'What do you want me to do?' said Kate.

" 'Only to hold the candle for me,' I answered, restored to my seven senses at last; and, taking it from her, I led the way, and she followed, till we had passed through the kitchen and reached the cellar-stairs. These were steep and awkward, and she let me help her down."

"Now, Edward!" said my mother.

"Yes, yes, my love, I understand," returned my father.

"Up to this time your mother had asked no questions; but when we stood in a vast, low cellar, which we had made several turns to reach, and I gave her the candle, and took up a great crowbar which lay on the floor, she said at last —

" 'Edward, are you going to bury me alive? or what *are* you going to do?'

" 'I'm going to dig you out,' I said, for I was nearly beside myself with joy, as I struck the crowbar like a battering-ram into the wall. You can fancy, John, that I didn't work the worse that Kate was holding the candle for me.

"Very soon, though with great effort, I had dislodged a brick, and the next blow I gave into the hole sent back a dull echo. I was right!

"I worked now like a madman, and, in a very few minutes more, I had dislodged the whole of the brick-thick wall which filled up an archway of stone and curtained an ancient door in the lock of which the key now showed itself. It had been well greased, and I turned it without much difficulty.

"I took the candle from Kate, and led her into a spacious region of sawdust, cobweb, and wine-fungus.

" 'There, Kate!' I cried, in delight.

" 'But,' said Kate, 'will the wine be good?'

"'General Fortescue will answer you that,' I returned, exultantly. 'Now come, and hold the light again while I find the port-bin.'

"I soon found not one, but several well-filled port-bins. Which to choose I could not tell. I must chance that. Kate carried a bottle and the candle, and I carried two bottles very carefully. We put them down in the kitchen with orders they should not be touched. We had soon carried the dozen to the hall-table by the dining-room door.

"When at length, with Jacob chuckling and rubbing his hands behind us, we entered the dining-room, Kate and I, for Kate would not part with her share in the joyful business, loaded with a level bottle in each hand, which we carefully erected on the sideboard, I presume, from the stare of the company, that we presented a rather remarkable appearance — Kate in her white muslin and I in my best clothes, covered with brick-dust, and cobwebs, and lime. But we could not be half so amusing to them as they were to us. There they sat with the dessert before them but no wine-decanters forthcoming. How long they had sat thus, I have no idea. If you think your mamma has, you may ask her. Captain Calker and General Fortescue looked positively white about the gills. My uncle, clinging to the last hope, despairingly, had sat still and said nothing, and the guests could not understand the awful delay. Even Lady Georgiana had begun to fear a mutiny in the kitchen, or something equally awful. But to see the flash that passed across my uncle's face, when he saw us appear with *ported arms!* He immediately began to pretend that nothing had been the matter.

"'What the deuce has kept you, Ned, my boy?' he said. 'Fair Hebe,' he went on, 'I beg your pardon. Jacob, you can go on decanting. It was very careless of you to forget it. Meantime, Hebe, bring that bottle to General Jupiter, there. He's got a corkscrew in the tail of his robe, or I'm mistaken.'

"Out came General Fortescue's corkscrew. I was trembling once more with anxiety. The cork gave the genuine plop; the bottle was lowered; glug, glug, glug, came from its beneficent throat, and out flowed something tawny as a lion's mane. The general lifted it lazily to his lips, saluting his nose on the way.

"'Fifteen! by Gyeove!' he cried. 'Well, Admiral, this *was* worth waiting for! Take care how you decant that, Jacob — on peril of your life.'

"My uncle was triumphant. He winked hard at me not to tell. Kate and I retired, she to change her dress, I to get mine well brushed, and my hands washed. By the time I returned to the dining-room, no one had any questions to ask. For Kate, the ladies had gone to the drawing-room before she was ready, and I believe she had some difficulty in keeping my uncle's counsel. But she did. — Need I say that was the happiest Christmas I ever spent?"

"But how did you find the cellar, papa?" asked Effie.

"Where are your brains, Effie? Don't you remember I told you that I had a dream?"

"Yes. But you don't mean to say the existence of that wine-cellar was revealed to you in a dream?"

"But I do, indeed. I had seen the wine-cellar built up just before we left for Madeira. It was my father's plan for securing the wine when the house was let. And very well it turned out for the wine, and me too. I had forgotten all about it. Everything had conspired to bring it to my memory, but had just failed of success. I had fallen asleep under all the influences I told you of — influences from the region of my childhood. They operated still when I was asleep, and, all other distracting influences being removed, at length roused in my sleeping brain the memory of what I had seen. In the morning I remembered not my dream only, but the event of which my dream was a reproduction. Still, I was under considerable doubt about the place, and in this I followed the dream only, as near as I could judge.

"The admiral kept his word, and interposed no difficulties between Kate and me. Not that, to tell the truth, I was ever very anxious about that rock ahead; but it was very possible that his fastidious honour or pride might have occasioned a considerable interference with our happiness for a time. As it turned out, he could not leave me Culverwood, and I regretted the fact as little as he did himself. His gratitude to me was, however, excessive, assuming occasionally ludicrous outbursts of thankfulness. I do not believe he could have been more grateful if I had saved his ship and its whole crew. For his hospitality was at stake. Kind old man!"

Here ended my father's story, with a light sigh, a gaze into the bright coals, a kiss of my mother's hand which he held in his, and another glass of Burgundy.

Uncle Cornelius, His Story

It was a dull evening in November. A drizzling mist had been falling all day about the old farm. Harry Heywood and his two sisters sat in the house-place, expecting a visit from their uncle, Cornelius Heywood. This uncle lived alone, occupying the first floor above a chemist's shop in the town, and had just enough of money over to buy books that nobody seemed ever to have heard of but himself; for he was a student in all those regions of speculation in which anything to be called knowledge is impossible.

"What a dreary night!" said Kate, "I wish uncle would come and tell us a story."

"A cheerful wish," said Harry. "Uncle Cornie is a lively companion, — isn't he? He can't even blunder through a Joe Miller without tacking a moral to it, and then try to persuade you that the joke of it depends on the moral."

"Here he comes!" said Kate, as three distinct blows with the knob of his walking-stick announced the arrival of Uncle Cornelius. She ran to the door to open it.

The air had been very still all day, but as he entered he seemed to have brought the wind with him, for the first moan of it pressed against rather than shook the casement of the low-ceiled room.

Uncle Cornelius was very tall, and very thin, and very pale, with large gray eyes that looked greatly larger because he wore spectacles of the most delicate hair-steel, with the largest pebble eyes that ever were seen. He gave them a kindly greeting, but too much in earnest even in shaking hands to smile over it. He sat down in the armchair by the chimney corner.

I have been particular in my description of him, in order that my reader may give due weight to his words. I am such a believer in words, that I believe everything depends on who says them. Uncle Cornelius Heywood's story, told word for word by Uncle Timothy Warren, would not have been the same story at all. Not one of the listeners would have believed a syllable of it from the lips of round-bodied, red-faced, small-eyed, little Uncle Tim; whereas from Uncle Cornie, — disbelieve one of his stories if you could!

One word more concerning him. His interest in everything conjectured or believed relative to the awful borderland of this world and the next, was only equalled by his disgust at the vulgar, unimaginative forms which curiosity about such subjects has assumed in the present day. With a yearning after the unseen like that of a child for the lifting of the curtain of a theatre, he declared that, rather than accept such a spirit-world as the would-be seers of the nineteenth century thought or pretended to reveal, — the prophets of a pauperized, workhouse immortality, invented by a poverty-stricken soul, and a sense so greedy that it would gorge on carrion, — he would rejoice to believe that a man had just as much of a soul as the cabbage of Iamblichus, namely, an aerial double of his body.

"I'm so glad you're come, uncle!" said Kate. "Why wouldn't you come to dinner? We have been so gloomy!"

"Well, Katey, you know I don't admire eating. I never could bear to see a cow tearing up the grass with her long tongue." As he spoke he looked very much like a cow. He had a way of opening his jaws while he kept his lips closely pressed together, that made his cheeks fall in, and his face look awfully long and dismal. "I consider eating," he went on, "such an animal exercise that it ought always to be performed in private. You never saw me dine, Kate."

"Never, uncle; but I have seen you drink; — nothing but water, I must confess."

"Yes, that is another affair. According to one eye-witness, that is no more than the disembodied can do. I must confess, however, that, although well attested, the story is to me scarcely credible. Fancy a glass of Bavarian beer lifted into the air without a visible hand, turned upside down, and set empty on the table! — and no splash on the floor or anywhere else!"

A solitary gleam of humour shone through the great eyes of the spectacles as he spoke.

"Oh, uncle! how can you believe such nonsense!" said Janet.

"I did not say I believed it, — did I? But why not? The story has at least a touch of imagination in it."

"That is a strange reason for believing a thing, uncle," said Harry.

"You might have a worse, Harry. I grant it is not sufficient; but it is better than that commonplace aspect which is the ground of most faith. I believe I did say that the story puzzled me."

"But how can you give it any quarter at all, uncle?"

"It does me no harm. There it is, — between the boards of an old German book. There let it remain."

"Well, you will never persuade me to believe such things," said Janet.

"Wait till I ask you, Janet," returned her uncle, gravely. "I have not the slightest desire to convince you. How did we get into this unprofitable current of talk? We will change it at once. How are consols, Harry?"

"Oh, uncle!" said Kate, "we were longing for a story, and just as I thought you were coming to one, off you go to consols!"

"I thought a ghost story at least was coming," said Janet.

"You did your best to stop it, Janet," said Harry.

Janet began an angry retort, but Cornelius interrupted her. "You never heard me tell a ghost story, Janet."

"You have just told one about a drinking ghost, uncle," said Janet, — in such a tone that Cornelius replied:

"Well, take that for your story, and let us talk of something else."

Janet apparently saw that she had been rude, and said as sweetly as she might, — "Ah! but you didn't make that one, uncle. You got it out of a German book."

"Make it! — Make a ghost story!" repeated Cornelius. "No; that I never did."

"Such things are not to be trifled with, are they?" said Janet.

"I at least have no inclination to trifle with them."

"But, really and truly, uncle," persisted Janet, "you don't believe in such things?"

"Why should I either believe or disbelieve in them? They are not essential to salvation, I presume."

"You must do the one or the other, I suppose."

"I beg your pardon. You suppose wrong. It would take twice the proof I have ever had to make me believe in them; and exactly your prejudice, and allow me to say ignorance, to make me disbelieve in them.

Neither is within my reach. I postpone judgment. But you, young people, of course, are wiser, and know all about the question."

"Oh, uncle! I'm so sorry!" said Kate. "I'm sure I did not mean to vex you."

"Not at all, not at all, my dear. — It wasn't you."

"Do you know," Kate went on, anxious to prevent anything unpleasant, for there was something very black perched on Janet's forehead, — "I have taken to reading about that kind of thing."

"I beg you will give it up at once. You will bewilder your brains till you are ready to believe anything, if only it be absurd enough. Nay, you may come to find the element of vulgarity essential to belief. I should be sorry to the heart to believe concerning a horse or dog what they tell you now-a-days about Shakespeare and Burns. What have you been reading, my girl?"

"Don't be alarmed, uncle. Only some Highland legends, which are too absurd either for my belief or for your theories."

"I don't know that, Kate."

"Why, what could you do with such shapeless creatures as haunt their fords and pools for instance? They are featureless as the faces of the mountains."

"And so much the more terrible."

"But that does not make it easier to believe in them," said Harry.

"I only said," returned his uncle, "that their shapelessness adds to their horror."

"But you allowed, — almost, at least, uncle," said Kate, "that you could find a place in your theories even for those shapeless creatures."

Cornelius sat silent for a moment; then, having first doubled the length of his face, and restored it to its natural condition, said thoughtfully, — I suspect, Katey, if you were to come upon an ichthyosaurus or a pterodactyl asleep in the shrubbery, you would hardly expect your report of it to be believed all at once either by Harry or Janet."

"I suppose not, uncle. But I can't see what — — "

"Of course such a thing could not happen here and now. But there was a time when and a place where such a thing may have happened. Indeed, in my time, a traveller or two have got pretty soundly disbelieved for reporting what they saw, — the last of an expiring race, which had strayed over the natural verge of its history, coming to life in some neglected swamp, itself a remnant of the slime of Chaos."

"I never heard you talk like that before, uncle," said Harry. "If you go on like that, you'll land me in a swamp, I'm afraid."

"I wasn't talking to you at all, Harry. Kate challenged me to find a place for kelpies, and such like, in the theories she does me the honour of supposing I cultivate."

"Then you think, uncle, that all these stories are only legends which, if you could follow them up, would lead you back to some one of the awful monsters that have since quite disappeared from the earth."

"It is possible those stories may be such legends; but that was not what I intended to lead you to. I gave you that only as something like what I am going to say now. What if, — mind, I only suggest it, — what if the direful creatures, whose report lingers in these tales, should have an origin far older still? What if they were the remnants of a vanishing period of the earth's history long antecedent to the birth of mastodon and iguanodon; a stage, namely, when the world, as we call it, had not yet become quite visible, was not yet so far finished as to part from the invisible world that was its mother, and which, on its part, had not then become quite invisible, — was only almost such; and when, as a credible consequence, strange shapes of those now invisible regions, Gorgons and Chimaeras dire, might be expected to gloom out occasionally from the awful Fauna of an ever-generating world upon that one which was being born of it. Hence, the life-periods of a world being long and slow, some of these huge, unformed bulks of half-created matter might, somehow, like the megatherium of later times, — a baby creation to them, — roll at age-long intervals, clothed in a mighty terror of shapelessness, into the half-recognition of human beings, whose consternation at the uncertain vision were barrier enough to prevent all further knowledge of its substance."

"I begin to have some notion of your meaning, uncle," said Kate.

"But then," said Janet, "all that must be over by this time. That world has been invisible now for many years."

"Ever since you were born, I suppose, Janet. The changes of a world are not to be measured by the changes of its generations."

"Oh, but, uncle, there can't be any such things. You know that as well as I do."

"Yes, just as well, and no better."

"There can't be any ghosts now. Nobody believes such things."

"Oh, as to ghosts, that is quite another thing. I did not know you were talking with reference to them. It is no wonder if one can get nothing sensible out of you, Janet, when your discrimination is no greater than to lump everything marvellous, kelpies, ghosts, vampires, doubles, witches, fairies, nightmares, and I don't know what all, under the one head of ghosts; and we hadn't been saying a word about them. If one were to disprove to you the existence of the afreets of Eastern tales, you would consider the whole argument concerning the reappearance of the departed upset. I congratulate you on your powers of analysis and induction, Miss Janet. But it matters very little whether we believe in ghosts, as you say, or not, provided we believe that we are ghosts, — that within this body, which so many people are ready to consider their own very selves, there lies a ghostly embryo, at least, which has an inner side to it God only can see, which says I concerning itself, and which will soon have to know whether or not it can appear to those whom it has left behind, and thus solve the question of ghosts for itself, at least."

"Then you do believe in ghosts, uncle?" said Janet, in a tone that certainly was not respectful.

"Surely I said nothing of the sort, Janet. The man most convinced that he had himself had such an interview as you hint at, would find, — ought to find it impossible to convince any one else of it."

"You are quite out of my depth, uncle," said Harry. "Surely any honest man ought to be believed?"

"Honesty is not all, by any means, that is necessary to being believed. It is impossible to convey a conviction of anything. All you can do is to convey a conviction that you are convinced. Of course, what satisfied you might satisfy another; but, till you can present him with the sources of your conviction, you cannot present him with the conviction, — and perhaps not even then."

"You can tell him all about it, can't you?"

"Is telling a man about a ghost, affording him the source of your conviction? Is it the same as a ghost appearing to him? Really, Harry! — You cannot even convey the impression a dream has made upon you."

"But isn't that just because it is only a dream?"

"Not at all. The impression may be deeper and clearer on your mind than any fact of the next morning will make. You will forget the next day altogether, but the impression of the dream will remain through all the following whirl and storm of what you call facts. Now a conviction may be likened to a deep impression on the judgment or the reason, or both. No one can feel it but the person who is convinced. It cannot be conveyed."

"I fancy that is just what those who believe in spirit-rapping would say."

"There are the true and false of convictions, as of everything else. I mean that a man may take that for a conviction in his own mind which is not a conviction, but only resembles one. But those to whom you refer profess to appeal to facts. It is on the ground of those facts, and with the more earnestness the more reason they can give for receiving them as facts, that I refuse all their deductions with abhorrence. I mean that, if what they say is true, the thinker must reject with contempt the claim to anything like revelation therein."

"Then you do not believe in ghosts, after all?" said Kate, in a tone of surprise.

"I did not say so, my dear. Will you be reasonable, or will you not?"

"Dear uncle, do tell us what you really think."

"I have been telling you what I think ever since I came, Katey; and you won't take in a word I say."

"I have been taking in every word, uncle, and trying hard to understand it as well. — Did you ever see a ghost, uncle?"

Cornelius Heywood was silent. He shut his lips and opened his jaws till his cheeks almost met in the vacuum. A strange expression crossed the strange countenance, and the great eyes of his spectacles looked as if, at the very moment, they were seeing something no other spectacles could see. Then his jaws closed with a snap, his countenance brightened, a flash of humour came through the goggle eyes of pebble, and, at length, he actually smiled as he said — "Really, Katey, you must take me for a simpleton!"

"How, uncle?"

"To think, if I had ever seen a ghost, I would confess the fact before a set of creatures like you, — all spinning your webs like so many spiders to catch and devour old Daddy Longlegs."

By this time Harry had grown quite grave. "Indeed, I am very sorry, uncle," he said, "if I have deserved such a rebuke."

"No, no, my boy," said Cornelius; "I did not mean it more than half. If I had meant it, I would not have said it. If you really would like — — ?" Here he paused.

"Indeed we should, uncle," said Kate, earnestly. "You should have heard what we were saying just before you came in."

"All you were saying, Katey?"

"Yes," answered Kate, thoughtfully. "The worst we said was that you could not tell a story without — — well, we did say tacking a moral to it."

"Well, well! I mustn't push it. A man has no right to know what people say about him. It unfits him for occupying his real position amongst them. He, least of all, has anything to do with it. If his friends won't defend him, he can't defend himself. Besides, what people say is so often untrue! — I don't mean to others, but to themselves. Their hearts are more honest than their mouths. But Janet doesn't want a strange story, I am sure."

Janet certainly was not one to have chosen for a listener to such a tale. Her eyes were so small that no satisfaction could possibly come of it. "Oh! I don't mind, uncle," she said, with half-affected indifference, as she searched in her box for silk to mend her gloves.

"You are not very encouraging, I must say," returned her uncle, making another cow-face.

"I will go away, if you like," said Janet, pretending to rise.

"No, never mind," said her uncle hastily. "If you don't want me to tell it, I want you to hear it; and, before I have done, that may have come to the same thing perhaps."

"Then you really are going to tell us a ghost-story!" said Kate, drawing her chair nearer to her uncle's; and then, finding this did not satisfy her sense of propinquity to the source of the expected pleasure, drawing a stool from the corner, and seating herself almost on the hearth-rug at his knee.

"I did not say so," returned Cornelius, once more. "I said I would tell you a strange story. You may call it a ghost-story if you like; I do not pretend to determine what it is. I confess it will look like one though."

After so many delays, Uncle Cornelius now plunged almost hurriedly into his narration.

"In the year 1820," he said, "in the month of August, I fell in love." Here the girls glanced at each other. The idea of Uncle Cornie in love, and in the very same century in which they were now listening to the confession, was too astonishing to pass without ocular remark; but, if he observed it, he took no notice of it; he did not even pause. "In the month of September, I was refused. Consequently, in the month of October, I was ready to fall in love again. Take particular care of yourself, Harry, for a whole month, at least, after your first disappointment; for you will never be more likely to do a foolish thing. Please yourself after the second. If you are silly then, you may take what you get, for you will deserve it, — except it be good fortune."

"Did you do a foolish thing then, uncle?" asked Harry, demurely.

"I did, as you will see; for I fell in love again."

"I don't see anything so foolish in that."

"I have repented it since, though. Don't interrupt me again, please. In the middle of October, then, in the year 1820, in the evening, I was walking across Russell Square, on my way home from the British Museum, where I had been reading all day. You see I have a full intention of being precise, Janet."

"I'm sure I don't know why you make the remark to me, uncle," said Janet, with an involuntary toss of her head. Her uncle only went on with his narrative.

"I begin at the very beginning of my story," he said; "for I want to be particular as to everything that can appear to have had anything to do with what came afterwards. I had been reading, I say, all the morning in the British Museum; and, as I walked, I took off my spectacles to ease my eyes. I need not tell you that I am short-sighted now, for that you know well enough. But I must tell you that I was short-sighted then, and helpless enough without my spectacles, although I was not quite so much so as I am now; — for I find it all nonsense about short-sighted eyes improving with age. Well, I was walking along the south side of Russell Square, with my spectacles in my hand, and feeling a little bewildered in consequence, — for it was quite the dusk of the evening, and short-sighted people require more light than others. I was feeling, in fact, almost blind. I had got more than half-way to the other side, when, from the crossing that cuts off the corner in the direction of Montagu Place, just as I was about to turn towards it, an old lady stepped upon the kerbstone of the pavement, looked at me for a moment, and passed, — an occurrence not very remarkable, certainly. But the lady was remarkable, and so was her dress. I am not good at observing, and I am still worse at describing dress; therefore, I can only say that hers reminded me of an old picture, — that is, I had never seen anything like it, except in old pictures. She had no bonnet, and looked as if she had walked straight out of an ancient drawing-room in her evening attire. Of her face I shall say nothing now. The next instant I met a man on the crossing, who stopped and addressed me. So short-sighted was I that, although I recognized his voice as one I ought to know, I could not identify him until I had put on my spectacles, which I did instinctively in the act of returning his greeting. At the same moment I glanced over my shoulder after the old lady. She was nowhere to be seen.

" 'What are you looking at?' asked James Hetheridge.

" 'I was looking after that old lady,' I answered, 'but I can't see her.'

" 'What old lady?' said Hetheridge with just a touch of impatience.

" 'You must have seen her,' I returned. 'You were not more than three yards behind her.'

" 'Where is she then?'

" 'She must have gone down one of the areas, I think. But she looked a lady, though an old-fashioned one.'

" 'Have you been dining?' asked James in a tone of doubtful inquiry.

" 'No,' I replied, not suspecting the insinuation; 'I have only just come from the Museum.'

" 'Then I advise you to call on your medical man before you go home.'

" 'Medical man!' I returned; 'I have no medical man. What do you mean? I never was better in my life.'

" 'I mean that there was no old lady. It was an illusion, and that indicates something wrong. Besides, you did not know me when I spoke to you.'

" 'That is nothing,' I returned. 'I had just taken off my spectacles, and without them I shouldn't know my own father.'

" 'How was it you saw the old lady, then?'

"The affair was growing serious under my friend's cross-questioning. I did not at all like the idea of his supposing me subject to hallucinations. So I answered, with a laugh, 'Ah! to be sure, that explains it. I am so blind without my spectacles, that I shouldn't know an old lady from a big dog.'

" 'There was no big dog,' said Hetheridge, shaking his head, as the fact for the first time dawned upon me that, although I had seen the old lady clear enough to make a sketch of her, even to the features of her careworn, eager old face, I had not been able to recognize the well-known countenance of James Hetheridge.

" 'That's what comes of reading till the optic nerve is weakened,' he went on, 'You will cause yourself serious injury if you do not pull up in time. I'll tell you what; I'm going home next week, — will you go with me?'

❧

"'You are very kind,' I answered, not altogether rejecting the proposal, for I felt that a little change to the country would be pleasant, and I was quite my own master. For I had unfortunately means equal to my wants, and had no occasion to follow any profession, — not a very desirable thing for a young man, I can tell you, Master Harry. I need not keep you over the commonplaces of pressing and yielding. It is enough to say that he pressed and that I yielded. The day was fixed for our departure together; but something or other, I forget what, occurred, to make him advance the date, and it was resolved that I should follow later in the month.

"It was a drizzly afternoon in the beginning of the last week of October when I left the town of Bradford in a post-chaise to drive to Lewton Grange, the property of my friend's father. I had hardly left the town, and the twilight had only begun to deepen, when, glancing from one of the windows of the chaise, I fancied I saw, between me and the hedge, the dim figure of a horse keeping pace with us. I thought, in the first interval of unreason, that it was a shadow of my own horse, but reminded myself the next moment that there could be no shadow where there was no light. When I looked again, I was at the first glance convinced that my eyes had deceived me. At the second, I believed once more that a shadowy something, with the movements of a horse in harness, was keeping pace with us. I turned away again with some discomfort, and not till we had reached an open moorland road, whence a little waterly light was visible on the horizon, could I summon up courage enough to look out once more. Certainly then there was nothing to be seen, and I persuaded myself that it had been all a fancy, and lighted a cigar. With my feet on the cushions before me, I had soon lifted myself on the clouds of tobacco far above all the terrors of the night, and believed them banished for ever. But, my cigar coming to an end just as we turned into the avenue that led up to the Grange, I found myself once more glancing nervously out of the window. The moment the trees were about me, there was, if not a shadowy horse out there by the side of the chaise, yet certainly more than half that conviction in here in my consciousness. When I saw my friend, however, standing on the doorstep, dark against the glow of the hall-fire, I forgot all about it; and I need not add that I did not make it a subject of conversation when I entered, for I was well aware that it was essential to a man's reputation that his senses should be accurate, though his heart might without prejudice swarm with shadows, and his judgment be a very stable of hobbies.

"I was kindly received. Mrs. Hetheridge had been dead for some years, and Laetitia, the eldest of the family, was at the head of the household. She had two sisters, little more than girls. The father was a burly, yet gentlemanlike Yorkshire squire, who ate well, drank well, looked radiant, and hunted twice a week. In this pastime his son joined him when in the humour, which happened scarcely so often. I, who had never crossed a horse in my life, took his apology for not being able to mount me very coolly, assuring him that I would rather loiter about with a book than be in at the death of the best-hunted fox in Yorkshire.

"I very soon found myself at home with the Hetheridges; and very soon again I began to find myself not so much at home; for Miss Hetheridge, — Laetitia as I soon ventured to call her, — was fascinating. I have told you, Katey, that there was an empty place in my heart. Look to the door then, Katey. That was what made me so ready to fall in love with Laetitia. Her figure was graceful, and I think, even now, her face would have been beautiful but for a certain contraction of the skin over the nostrils, suggesting an invisible thumb and forefinger pinching them, which repelled me, although I did not then know what it indicated. I had not been with her one evening before the impression it made on me had vanished, and that so entirely that I could hardly recall the perception of the peculiarity which had occasioned it. Her observation was remarkably keen, and her judgment generally correct. She had great confidence in it herself; nor was she devoid of sympathy with some of the forms of human imagination, only they never seemed to possess for her any relation to practical life. That was to be ordered by the judgment alone. I do not mean she ever said so. I am only giving the conclusions I came to afterwards. It is not necessary that you should have any more thorough acquaintance with her mental character. One point in her moral nature, of especial consequence to my narrative, will show itself by and by.

"I did all I could to make myself agreeable to her, and the more I succeeded the more delightful she became in my eyes. We walked in the garden and grounds together; we read, or rather I read and she listened; — read poetry, Katey — sometimes till we could not read any more for certain haziness and huskinesses which look now, I am afraid, considerably more absurd than they really were, or even ought to look. In short, I considered myself thoroughly in love with her."

"And wasn't she in love with you, uncle?"

"Don't interrupt me, child. I don't know. Honestly, I don't know. I hoped so then. I hope the contrary now. She liked me, I am sure. That is not much to say. Liking is very pleasant and very cheap. Love is as rare as a star."

"I thought the stars were anything but rare, uncle."

"That's because you never went out to find one for yourself, Katey. They would prove a few miles apart then."

"But it would be big enough when I did find it."

"Right, my dear. That is the way with love. — Laetitia was a good housekeeper. Everything was punctual as clockwork. I use the word advisedly. If her father, who was punctual to one date, — the dinner-hour, — made any remark to the contrary as he took up the carving-knife, Laetitia would instantly send one of her sisters to question the old clock in the hall, and report the time to half a minute. It was sure to be found that, if there was a mistake, the mistake was in the clock. But although it was certainly a virtue to have her household in such perfect order, it was not a virtue to be impatient with every infringement of its rules on the part of others. She was very severe, for instance, upon her two younger sisters if, the moment after the second bell had rung, they were not seated at the dinner-table, washed and aproned. Order was a very idol with her. Hence the house was too tidy for any sense of comfort. If you left an open book on the table, you would, on returning to the room a moment after, find it put aside. What the furniture of the drawing-room was like, I never saw; for not even on Christmas Day, which was the last day I spent there, was it uncovered. Everything in it was kept in bibs and pinafores. Even the carpet was covered with a cold and slippery sheet of brown holland. Mr. Hetheridge never entered that room, and therein was wise. James remonstrated once. She answered him quite kindly, even playfully, but no change followed. What was worse, she made very wretched tea. Her father never took tea; neither did James. I was rather fond of it, but I soon gave it up. Everything her father partook of was first-rate. Everything else was somewhat poverty-stricken. My pleasure in Laetitia's society prevented me from making practical deductions from such trifles."

"I shouldn't have thought you knew anything about eating, uncle," said Janet.

"The less a man eats, the more he likes to have it good, Janet. In short, — there can be no harm in saying it now, — Laetitia was so far from being like the name of her baptism, — and most names are so good that they are worth thinking about; no children are named after bad ideas,

— Laetitia was so far unlike hers as to be stingy, — an abominable fault. But, I repeat, the notion of such a fact was far from me then. And now for my story.

"The first of November was a lovely day, quite one of the 'halcyon days' of 'St. Martin's summer.' I was sitting in a little arbour I had just discovered, with a book in my hand, — not reading, however, but day-dreaming, — when, lifting my eyes from the ground, I was startled to see, through a thin shrub in front of the arbour, what seemed the form of an old lady seated, apparently reading from a book on her knee. The sight instantly recalled the old lady of Russell Square. I started to my feet, and then, clear of the intervening bush, saw only a great stone such as abounded on the moors in the neighbourhood, with a lump of quartz set on the top of it. Some childish taste had put it there for an ornament. Smiling at my own folly, I sat down again, and reopened my book. After reading for a while, I glanced up again, and once more started to my feet, overcome by the fancy that there verily sat the old lady reading. You will say it indicated an excited condition of the brain. Possibly; but I was, as far as I can recall, quite collected and reasonable. I was almost vexed this second time, and sat down once more to my book. Still, every time I looked up, I was startled afresh. I doubt, however, if the trifle is worth mentioning, or has any significance even in relation to what followed.

"After dinner I strolled out by myself, leaving father and son over their claret. I did not drink wine; and from the lawn I could see the windows of the library, whither Laetitia commonly retired from the din-ner-table. It was a very lovely soft night. There was no moon, but the stars looked wider awake than usual. Dew was falling, but the grass was not yet wet, and I wandered about on it for half an hour. The stillness was somehow strange. It had a wonderful feeling in it as if something were expected, — as if the quietness were the mould in which some event or other was about to be cast.

"Even then I was a reader of certain sorts of recondite lore. Suddenly I remembered that this was the eve of All Souls. This was the night on which the dead came out of their graves to visit their old homes. 'Poor dead!' I thought with myself; 'have you any place to call a home now? If you have, surely you will not wander back here, where all that you called home has either vanished or given itself to others, to be their home now and yours no more! What an awful doom the old fancy has allotted you! To dwell in your graves all the year, and creep out, this one night, to enter

at the midnight door, left open for welcome! A poor welcome truly! —
just an open door, a clean-swept floor, and a fire to warm your rain-sodden
limbs! The household asleep, and the house-place swarming with the
ghosts of ancient times, — the miser, the spendthrift, the profligate, the
coquette, — for the good ghosts sleep, and are troubled with no waking
like yours! Not one man, sleepless like yourselves, to question you, and be
answered after the fashion of the old nursery rhyme: —

> "'What makes your eyes so holed?'
> 'I've lain so long among the mould.'
> 'What makes your feet so broad?'
> 'I've walked more than ever I rode!'

"'Yet who can tell?' I went on to myself. 'It may be your hell to
return thus. It may be that only on this one night of all the year you can
show yourselves to him who can see you, but that the place where you
were wicked is the Hades to which you are doomed for ages.' I thought
and thought till I began to feel the air alive about me, and was enveloped
in the vapours that dim the eyes of those who strain them for one peep
through the dull mica windows that will not open on the world of ghosts.
At length I cast my fancies away, and fled from them to the library, where
the bodily presence of Laetitia made the world of ghosts appear shadowy
indeed.

"'What a reality there is about a bodily presence!' I said to myself,
as I took my chamber-candle in my hand. 'But what is there more real in
a body?' I said again, as I crossed the hall. 'Surely nothing,' I went on, as
I ascended the broad staircase to my room. 'The body must vanish. If
there be a spirit, that will remain. A body can but vanish. A ghost can
appear.'

"I woke in the morning with a sense of such discomfort as made me
spring out of bed at once. My foot lighted upon my spectacles. How they
came to be on the floor I could not tell, for I never took them off when
I went to bed. When I lifted them I found they were in two pieces; the
bridge was broken. This was awkward. I was so utterly helpless without
them! Indeed, before I could lay my hand on my hair-brush I had to peer
through one eye of the parted pair. When I looked at my watch after I
was dressed, I found I had risen an hour earlier than usual. I groped my
way down-stairs to spend the hour before breakfast in the library.

"No sooner was I seated with a book than I heard the voice of Laetitia scolding the butler, in no very gentle tones, for leaving the garden-door open all night. The moment I heard this, the strange occurrences I am about to relate began to dawn upon my memory. The door had been open the night long between All Saints and All Souls. In the middle of that night I awoke suddenly. I knew it was not the morning by the sensations I had, for the night feels altogether different from the morning. It was quite dark. My heart was beating violently, and I either hardly could or hardly dared breathe. A nameless terror was upon me, and my sense of hearing was, apparently by the force of its expectation, unnaturally roused and keen. There it was, — a slight noise in the room! — slight, but clear, and with an unknown significance about it! It was awful to think it would come again. I do believe it was only one of those creaks in the timbers which announce the torpid, age-long, sinking flow of every house back to the dust, — a motion to which the flow of the glacier is as a torrent, but which is no less inevitable and sure. Day and night it ceases not; but only in the night, when house and heart are still, do we hear it. No wonder it should sound fearful! for are we not the immortal dwellers in ever-crumbling clay? The clay is so near us, and yet not of us, that its every movement starts a fresh dismay. For what will its final ruin disclose? When it falls from about us, where shall we find that we have existed all the time?

"My skin tingled with the bursting of the moisture from its pores. Something was in the room beside me. A confused, indescribable sense of utter loneliness, and yet awful presence, was upon me, mingled with a dreary, hopeless desolation, as of burnt-out love and aimless life. All at once I found myself sitting up. The terror that a cold hand might be laid upon me, or a cold breath blow on me, or a corpse-like face bend down through the darkness over me, had broken my bonds! — I would meet half-way whatever might be approaching. The moment that my will burst into action the terror began to ebb.

"The room in which I slept was a large one, perfectly dreary with tidiness. I did not know till afterwards that it was Laetitia's room, which she had given up to me rather than prepare another. The furniture, all but one article, was modern and commonplace. I could not help remarking to myself afterwards how utterly void the room was of the nameless charm of feminine occupancy. I had seen nothing to wake a suspicion of its being a lady's room. The article I have excepted was an ancient bureau, elaborate and ornate, which stood on one side of the large bow window. The very morning before,

UNCLE CORNELIUS, HIS STORY

I had seen a bunch of keys hanging from the upper part of it, and had peeped in. Finding, however, that the pigeon-holes were full of papers, I closed it at once. I should have been glad to use it, but clearly it was not for me. At that bureau the figure of a woman was now seated in the posture of one writing. A strange dim light was around her, but whence it proceeded I never thought of inquiring. As if I, too, had stepped over the bourne, and was a ghost myself, all fear was now gone. I got out of bed, and softly crossed the room to where she was seated. 'If she should be beautiful!' I thought, — for I had often dreamed of a beautiful ghost that made love to me. The figure did not move. She was looking at a faded brown paper. 'Some old love-letter,' I thought, and stepped nearer. So cool was I now, that I actually peeped over her shoulder. With mingled surprise and dismay I found that the dim page over which she bent was that of an old account-book. Ancient household records, in rusty ink, held up to the glimpses of the waning moon, which shone through the parting in the curtains, their entries of shillings and pence! — Of pounds there was not one. No doubt pounds and farthings are much the same in the world of thought — the true spirit-world; but in the ghost-world this eagerness over shillings and pence must mean something awful! To think that coins which had since been worn smooth in other pockets and purses, which had gone back to the Mint, and been melted down, to come out again and yet again with the heads of new kings and queens, — that dinners, eaten by men and women and children whose bodies had since been eaten by the worms, — that polish for the floors, inches of whose thickness had since been worn away, — that the hundred nameless trifles of a life utterly vanished, should be perplexing, annoying, and, worst of all, interesting the soul of a ghost who had been in Hades for centuries! The writing was very old-fashioned, and the words were contracted. I could read nothing but the moneys and one single entry, — 'Corinths, Vs.'

"Currants for a Christmas pudding, most likely! — Ah, poor lady! the pudding and not the Christmas was her care; not the delight of the children over it, but the beggarly pence which it cost. And she cannot get it out of her head, although her brain was 'powdered all as thin as flour' ages ago in the mortar of Death. 'Alas, poor ghost!' It needs no treasured hoard left behind, no floor stained with the blood of the murdered child, no wickedly hidden parchment of landed rights! — An old account-book is enough for the hell of the house-keeping gentlewoman!

"She never lifted her face, or seemed to know that I stood behind her. I left her, and went into the bow window, where I could see her face.

I was right. It was the same old lady I had met in Russell Square, walking in front of James Hetheridge. Her withered lips went moving as if they would have uttered words had the breath been commissioned thither; her brow was contracted over her thin nose; and once and again her shining forefinger went up to her temple as if she were pondering some deep problem of humanity. How long I stood gazing at her I do not know, but at last I withdrew to my bed, and left her struggling to solve that which she could never solve thus. It was the symbolic problem of her own life, and she had failed to read it. I remember nothing more. She may be sitting there still, solving at the insolvable.

"I should have felt no inclination, with the broad sun of the squire's face, the keen eyes of James, and the beauty of Laetitia before me at the breakfast-table, to say a word about what I had seen, even if I had not been afraid of the doubt concerning my sanity which the story would certainly awaken. What with the memories of the night and the want of my spectacles, I passed a very dreary day, dreading the return of the night, for, cool as I had been in her presence, I could not regard the possible reappearance of the ghost with equanimity. But when the night did come, I slept soundly till the morning.

"The next day, not being able to read with comfort, I went wandering about the place, and at length began to fit the outside and inside of the house together. It was a large and rambling edifice, parts of it very old, parts comparatively modern. I first found my own window, which looked out of the back. Below this window, on one side, there was a door. I wondered whither it led, but found it locked. At the moment James approached from the stables. 'Where does this door lead?' I asked him. 'I will get the key,' he answered. 'It is rather a queer old place. We used to like it when we were children.' 'There's a stair, you see,' he said, as he threw the door open. 'It leads up over the kitchen.' I followed him up the stair. 'There's a door into your room,' he said, but it's always locked now. — And here's Grannie's room, as they call it, though why, I have not the least idea,' he added, as he pushed open the door of an old-fashioned parlour, smelling very musty. A few old books lay on a side-table. A china bowl stood beside them, with some shrivelled, scentless rose-leaves in the bottom of it. The cloth that covered the table was riddled by moths, and the spider-legged chairs were covered with dust.

"A conviction seized me that the old bureau must have belonged to this room, and I soon found the place where I judged it must have stood.

But the same moment I caught sight of a portrait on the wall above the spot I have fixed upon. 'By Jove!' I cried, involuntarily, 'that's the very old lady I met in Russell Square!"

" 'Nonsense!' said James. 'Old-fashioned ladies are like babies, — they all look the same. That's a very old portrait.'

" 'So I see,' I answered, 'It is like a Zucchero.'

" 'I don't know whose it is,' he answered hurriedly, and I thought he looked a little queer.

" 'Is she one of the family?' I asked.

" 'They say so; but who or what she was, I don't know. You must ask Letty,' he answered.

" 'The more I look at it,' I said, 'the more I am convinced it is the same old lady.'

" 'Well,' he returned with a laugh, 'my old nurse used to say she was rather restless. But it's all nonsense.'

" 'That bureau in my room looks about the same date as this furniture,' I remarked.

" 'It used to stand just there,' he answered, pointing to the space under the picture. 'Well I remember with what awe we used to regard it; for they said the old lady kept her accounts at it still. We never dared touch the bundles of yellow papers in the pigeon-holes. I remember thinking Letty a very heroine once when she touched one of them with the tip of her forefinger. She had got yet more courageous by the time she had it moved into her own room.'

" 'Then that is your sister's room I am occupying?' I said.

" 'Yes.'

" 'I am ashamed of keeping her out of it.'

" 'Oh! She'll do well enough.'

" 'If I were she, though,' I added, 'I would send that bureau back to its own place.'

" 'What do you mean, Heywood? Do you believe every old wife's tale that ever was told?'

" 'She may get a fright some day, — that's all!' I replied.

"He smiled with such an evident mixture of pity and contempt that for the moment I almost disliked him; and feeling certain that Laetitia would receive any such hint in a somewhat similar manner, I did not feel inclined to offer her any advice with regard to the bureau.

"Little occurred during the rest of my visit worthy of remark. Somehow or other I did not make much progress with Laetitia. I believe I had begun to see into her character a little, and therefore did not get deeper in love as the days went on. I know I became less absorbed in her society, although I was still anxious to make myself agreeable to her, — or perhaps, more properly, to give her a favourable impression of me. I do not know whether she perceived any difference in my behaviour, but I remember that I began again to remark the pinched look of her nose, and to be a little annoyed with her for always putting aside my book. At the same time, I daresay I was provoking, for I never was given to tidiness myself.

"At length Christmas Day arrived. After breakfast, the squire, James, and the two girls arranged to walk to church. Laetitia was not in the room at the moment. I excused myself on the ground of a headache, for I had had a bad night. When they left, I went up to my room, threw myself on the bed, and was soon fast asleep.

"How long I slept I do not know, but I woke again with that indescribable yet well-known sense of not being alone. The feeling was scarcely less terrible in the daylight than it had been in the darkness. With the same sudden effort as before, I sat up in the bed. There was the figure at the open bureau, in precisely the same position as on the former occasion. But I could not see it so distinctly. I rose as gently as I could and approached it, after the first physical terror. I am not a coward. Just as I got near enough to see the account book open on the folding cover of the bureau, she started up, and turning, revealed the face of Laetitia. She blushed crimson.

"'I beg your pardon, Mr. Heywood,' she said, in great confusion; 'I thought you had gone to church with the rest.'

"'I had lain down with a headache, and gone to sleep,' I replied. 'But, — forgive me, Miss Hetheridge,' I added, for my mind was full of the dreadful coincidence, — 'don't you think you would have been better at church than balancing your accounts on Christmas Day?'

"'The better day the better deed,' she said, with a somewhat offended air, and turned to walk from the room.

"'Excuse me, Laetitia,' I resumed, very seriously, 'but I want to tell you something.'

"She looked conscious. It never crossed me, that perhaps she fancied I was going to make a confession. Far other things were then in my mind. For I thought how awful it was, if she too, like the ancestral ghost, should have to do an age-long penance of haunting that bureau and those horrid

❧ UNCLE CORNELIUS, HIS STORY

figures, and I had suddenly resolved to tell her the whole story. She listened with varying complexion and face half turned aside. When I had ended, which I fear I did with something of a personal appeal, she lifted her head and looked me in the face, with just a slight curl on her thin lip, and answered me. 'If I had wanted a sermon, Mr. Heywood, I should have gone to church for it. As for the ghost, I am sorry for you.' So saying, she walked out of the room.

"The rest of the day I did not find very merry. I pleaded my headache as an excuse for going to bed early. How I hated the room now! Next morning, immediately after breakfast, I took my leave of Lewton Grange."

"And lost a good wife, perhaps, for the sake of a ghost, uncle!" said Janet.

"If I lost a wife at all, it was a stingy one. I should have been ashamed of her all my life long."

"Better than a spendthrift," said Janet.

"How do you know that?" returned her uncle. "All the difference I see is, that the extravagant ruins the rich, and the stingy robs the poor."

"But perhaps she repented, uncle," said Kate.

"I don't think she did, Katey. Look here."

"Uncle Cornelius drew from the breast-pocket of his coat a black-edged letter.

"I have kept up my friendship with her brother," he said. "All he knows about the matter is, that either we had a quarrel, or she refused me; — he is not sure which. I must say for Laetitia, that she was no tattler. Well, here's a letter I had from James this very morning. I will read it to you.

"'My dear Heywood, — We have had a terrible shock this morning. Letty did not come down to breakfast, and Lizzie went to see if she was ill. We heard her scream, and, rushing up, there was poor Letty, sitting at the old bureau, quite dead. She had fallen forward on the desk, and her housekeeping-book was crumpled up under her. She had been so all night long, we suppose, for she was not undressed, and was quite cold. The doctors say it was disease of the heart.'

"There!" said Uncle Cornie, folding up the letter.

"Do you think the ghost had anything to do with it, uncle?" asked Kate, almost under her breath.

"How should I know, my dear? Possibly."

"It's very sad," said Janet; "but I don't see the good of it all. If the ghost had come to tell that she had hidden away money in some secret place in the old bureau, one would see why she had been permitted to come back. But what was the good of those accounts after they were over and done with? I don't believe in the ghost."

"Ah, Janet, Janet! but those wretched accounts were not over and done with, you see. That is the misery of it."

Uncle Cornelius rose without another word, bade them good-night, and walked out into the wind.

Birth, Dreaming, Death

[The Schoolmaster's Story]

"In a little room, scantily furnished, lighted, not from the window, for it was dark without, and the shutters were closed, but from the peaked flame of a small, clear-burning lamp, sat a young man, with his back to the lamp and his face to the fire. No book or paper on the table indicated labour just forsaken; nor could one tell from his eyes, in which the light had all retreated inwards, whether his consciousness was absorbed in thought, or reverie only. The window curtains, which scarcely concealed the shutters, were of coarse texture, but of brilliant scarlet, — for he loved bright colours; and the faint reflection they threw on his pale, thin face, made it look more delicate than it would have seemed in pure daylight. Two or three bookshelves, suspended by cords from a nail in the wall, contained a collection of books, poverty-stricken as to numbers, with but few to fill up the chronological gap between the Greek New Testament and stray volumes of the poets of the present century. But his love for the souls of his individual books was the stronger that there was no possibility of its degenerating into avarice for the bodies or outsides whose aggregate constitutes the piece of house-furniture called a library.

"Some years before, the young man (my story is so short, and calls in so few personages, that I need not give him a name) had aspired, under the influence of religious and sympathetic feeling, to be a clergyman; but Providence, either in the form of poverty, or of theological difficulty, had prevented his prosecuting his studies to that end. And now he was only a village schoolmaster, nor likely to advance further. I have said *only* a village schoolmaster; but is it not better to be a teacher *of* babes than a preacher *to* men, at any time; not to speak of those troublous times of transition, wherein a difference of degree must so often assume the appearance of a difference of kind? That man is more happy — I will not say more blessed — who, loving boys and girls, is loved and revered by them, than he who, ministering unto men and women, is compelled to pour his words into the filter of religious suspicion, whence the water is allowed to pass away unheeded, and only the residuum is retained for the analysis of ignorant party-spirit.

"He had married a simple village girl, in whose eyes he was nobler than the noblest — to whom he was the mirror, in which the real forms of all things around were reflected. Who dares pity my poor village school-master? I fling his pity away. Had he not found in her love the verdict of God, that he was worth loving? Did he not in her possess the eternal and the unchangeable? Were not her eyes openings through which he looked into the great depths that could not be measured or represented? She was his public, his society, his critic. He found in her the heaven of his rest. God gave unto him immortality, and he was glad. For his ambition, it had died of its own mortality. He read the words of Jesus, and the words of great prophets whom he has sent; and learned that the wind-tossed anemone is a word of God as real and true as the unbending oak beneath which it grows — that reality is an absolute existence precluding degrees. If his mind was, as his room, scantily furnished, it was yet lofty; if his light was small, it was brilliant. God lived, and he lived. Perhaps the highest moral height which a man can reach, and at the same time the most difficult of attainment, is the willingness to be *nothing* relatively, so that he attain that positive excellence which the original conditions of his being render not merely possible, but imperative. It is nothing to a man to be greater or less than another; to be esteemed or otherwise by the public or private world in which he moves. Does he, or does he not, behold and love and live the unchangeable, the essential, the divine? This he can only do according as God has made him. He can behold and understand God in the least degree, as well as in the greatest, only by the godlike within him; and he that loves thus the good and great has no room, no thought, no necessity for comparison and difference. The truth satisfies him. He lives in its absoluteness. God makes the glow-worm as well as the star; the light in both is divine. If mine be an earth-star to gladden the wayside, I must cultivate humbly and rejoicingly its green earth-glow and not seek to blanch it to the whiteness of the stars that lie in the fields of blue. For to deny God in my own being is to cease to behold him in any. God and man can meet only by the man's becoming that which God meant him to be. Then he enters into the house of life, which is greater than the house of fame. It is better to be a child in a green field than a knight of many orders in a state ceremonial.

"All night long he had sat there, and morning was drawing nigh. He had not heard the busy wind all night, heaping up snow against the house, which will make him start at the ghostly face of the world when at length he opens the shutters, and it stares upon him so white. For up in a little room above, white-curtained, like the great earth without, there has been a storm, too, half the night-moanings and prayers — and some forbidden tears; but now, at length, it is over; and through the portals of two mouths instead of one, flows and ebbs the tide of the great air-sea which feeds the life of man. With the sorrow of the mother, the new life is purchased for the child; our very being is redeemed from nothingness with the pains of a death of which we know nothing.

"An hour has gone by since the watcher below has been delivered from the fear and doubt that held him. He has seen the mother and the child — the first she has given to life and him, and has returned to his lonely room, quiet and glad.

"But not long did he sit thus before thoughts of doubt awoke in his mind. He remembered his scanty income, and the somewhat feeble health of his wife. One or two small debts he had contracted seemed absolutely to press on his bosom; and the newborn child — 'oh! how doubly welcome,' he thought, 'if I were but half as rich again as I am!' — brought with it, as its own love, so its own care. The dogs of need, that so often hunt us up to heaven, seemed hard upon his heels; and he prayed to God with fervour; and as he prayed he fell asleep in his chair, and as he slept he dreamed. The fire and the lamp burned on as before, but threw no rays into his soul; yet now, for the first time, he seemed to become aware of the storm without; for his dream was as follows: —

"He lay in his bed, and listened to the howling of the wintry wind. He trembled at the thought of the pitiless cold, and turned to sleep again, when he thought he heard a feeble knocking at the door. He rose in haste, and went down with a light. As he opened the door, the wind, entering with a gust of frosty particles, blew out his candle; but he found it unnecessary, for the grey dawn had come. Looking out, he saw nothing at first; but a second look, turned downwards, showed him a little half-frozen child, who looked quietly, but beseechingly, in his face. His hair was filled with drifted snow, and his little hands and cheeks were blue with cold. The heart of the schoolmaster swelled to bursting with the spring-flood of love and pity that rose up within it. He lifted the child to his bosom, and carried him into the house, where, in the dream's incongruity, he found a fire blazing in the room in which he now slept. The child said never a word. He set him by the fire, and made haste to get hot water, and put him in a warm bath. He never doubted that this was a stray orphan who had wandered to him for protection, and he felt that he could not part with him again; even though the train of his previous troubles and doubts once more passed through the mind of the dreamer, and there seemed no answer to his perplexities for the lack of that cheap thing, gold — yea, silver. But when he had undressed and bathed the little orphan, and having dried him on his knees, set him down to reach something warm to wrap him in, the boy suddenly looked up in his face, as if revived, and said with a heavenly smile, 'I am the child Jesus.' 'The child Jesus!' said the dreamer, astonished. 'Thou art like any other child.' 'No, do not say so,' returned the boy; 'but say, *Any other child is like me.*' And the child and the dream slowly faded away; and he awoke with these words sounding in his heart — 'Whosoever shall receive one of such children in my name, receiveth me; and whosoever shall receive me, receiveth not me, but him that sent me.' It was the voice of God saying to him: 'Thou wouldst receive the child whom I sent thee out of the cold, stormy night; receive the new child out of the cold waste into the warm human house, as the door by which it can enter God's house, its home. If better could be done for it, or for thee, would I have sent it hither? Through thy love, my little one must learn my love and be blessed. And thou shalt not keep it without thy reward. For thy necessities in thy little house, is there not yet room? in thy barrel, it there not yet meal? and thy purse is not empty quite. Thou canst not eat more than a mouthful at once. I have made thee so. Is it any trouble to me to take care of thee? Only I prefer to feed thee from my own hand, and not from thy store.' And the schoolmaster sprang up in joy, ran upstairs, kissed his wife, and clasped the baby in his arms in the name of the child Jesus. And in that embrace, he knew that he received God to his heart. Soon, with a tender, beaming face, he was wading through the snow to the school-house, where he spent a happy day amidst the rosy faces and bright eyes of his boys and girls. These, likewise, he loved the more dearly and joyfully for that dream, and those words in his heart; so that, amidst their true child faces, (all going well with them, as not unfrequently happened in his schoolroom), he felt as if all the elements of Paradise were gathered around him, and knew that he was God's child, doing God's work.

"But while that dream was passing through the soul of the husband, another visited the wife, as she lay in the faintness and trembling joy of the new motherhood. For although she that has been mother before, is not the less a new mother to the new child, her former relation not covering with its wings the fresh bird in the nest of her bosom, yet there must be a peculiar delight in the thoughts and feelings that come with the first-born. — As she lay half in a sleep, half in a faint, with the vapours of a gentle delirium floating through her brain, without losing the sense of existence she lost the consciousness of its form, and thought she lay, not a young mother in her bed, but a nosegay of wild flowers in a basket, crushed, flattened and half-withered. With her in the basket lay other bunches of flowers, whose odours, some rare as well as rich, revealed to her the sad contrast in which she was placed. Beside her lay a cluster of delicately curved, faintly tinged, tea-scented roses; while she was only blue hyacinth bells, pale primroses, amethyst anemones, closed blood-coloured daisies, purple violets, and one sweet-scented, pure white orchis. The basket lay on the counter of a well-known little shop in the village, waiting for purchasers. By and by her own husband entered the shop, and approached the basket to choose a nosegay. 'Ah!' thought she, 'will he choose me? How dreadful if he should not, and I should be left lying here, while he takes another! But how should he choose me? They are all so beautiful; and even my scent is nearly gone. And he cannot know that it is I lying here. Alas! alas!' But as she thought thus, she felt his hand clasp her, heard the ransom-money fall, and felt that she was pressed to his face and lips, as he passed from the shop. He *had* chosen her; he *had* known her. She opened her eyes: her husband's kiss had awakened her. She did not speak, but looked up thankfully in his eyes, as if he had, in fact, like one of the old knights, delivered her from the transformation of some evil magic, by the counter-enchantment of a kiss, and restored her from a half-withered nosegay to be a woman, a wife, a mother. The dream comforted her much, for she had often feared that she, the simple, so-called uneducated girl, could not be enough for the great schoolmaster. But soon her thoughts flowed into another channel; the tears rose in her dark eyes, shining clear from beneath a stream that was not of sorrow; and it was only weakness that kept her from uttering audible words like these: — 'Father in heaven, shall I trust my husband's love, and doubt thine? Wilt thou meet less richly the fearing hope of thy child's heart, than he in my dream met the longing of his wife's? He was perfected in my eyes by the love he bore me — shall I find thee less complete? Here I lie on thy world, faint, and crushed, and withered; and my soul often seems as if it had lost all the odours that should float up in the sweet-smelling savour of thankfulness and love to thee. But thou hast only to take me, only to choose me, only to clasp me to thy bosom, and I shall be a beautiful singing angel, singing to God, and comforting my husband while I sing. Father, take me, possess me, fill me!'

"So she lay patiently waiting for the summer-time of restored strength that drew slowly nigh. With her husband and her child near her, in her soul, and God everywhere, there was for her no death, and no hurt. When she said to herself, 'How rich I am!' it was with the riches that pass not away — the riches of the Son of man; for in her treasures, the human and the divine were blended — were one.

"But there was a hard trial in store for them. They had learned to receive what the Father sent: they had now to learn that what he gave he gave eternally, after his own being — his own glory. For ere the mother awoke from her first sleep, the baby, like a frolicsome child-angel, that but tapped at his mother's window and fled, — the baby died; died while the mother slept away the pangs of its birth; died while the father was teaching other babes out of the joy of his new fatherhood.

"When the mother woke, she lay still in her joy — the joy of a doubled life; and knew not that death had been there, and had left behind only the little human coffin.

"'Nurse, bring me the baby,' she said at last. 'I want to see it.'

"But the nurse pretended not to hear.

"'I want to nurse it. Bring it.'

"She had not yet learned to say *him;* for it was her first baby.

"But the nurse went out of the room, and remained some minutes away. When she returned, the mother spoke more absolutely, and the nurse was compelled to reply — at last.

"'Nurse, do bring me the baby; I am quite able to nurse it now.'

"'Not yet, if you please, ma'am. Really you must rest a while first. Do try to go to sleep.'

"The nurse spoke steadily, and looked her, too, straight in the face;

and there was a constraint in her voice, a determination to be calm, that at once roused the suspicion of the mother; for though her first-born was dead, and she had given birth to what was now, as far as the eye could reach, the waxen image of a son, a child had come from God, and had departed to him again; and she was his mother.

"And the fear fell upon her heart that it might be as it was; and, looking at her attendant with a face blanched yet more with fear than with suffering, she said,

"'Nurse, is the baby — — ?'

"She could not say dead; for to utter the word would be at once to make it possible that the only fruit of her labour had been pain and sorrow.

"But the nurse saw that further concealment was impossible; and, without another word, went and fetched the husband, who, with face pale as the mother's, brought the baby, dressed in its white clothes, and laid it by its mother's side, where it lay too still.

"'Oh, ma'am, do not take on so,' said the nurse, as she saw the face of the mother grow like the face of the child, as if she were about to rush after him into the dark.

"But she was not 'taking on' at all. She only felt that pain at her heart, which is the farewell kiss of a long-cherished joy. Though cast out of paradise into a world that looked very dull and weary, yet, used to suffering, and always claiming from God the consolation it needed, and satisfied with that, she was able, presently, to look up in her husband's face, and try to reassure him of her well-being by a dreary smile.

"'Leave the baby,' she said; and they left it where it was. Long and earnestly she gazed on the perfect tiny features of the little alabaster countenance, and tried to feel that this was the child she had been so long waiting for. As she looked, she fancied she heard it breathe, and she thought — 'What if it should be only asleep!' but, alas! the eyes would not open, and when she drew it close to her, she shivered to feel it so cold. At length, as her eyes wandered over and over the little face, a look of her husband dawned unexpectedly upon it; and, as if the wife's heart awoke the mother's, she cried out, 'Baby! baby!' and burst into tears, during which weeping she fell asleep.

"When she awoke, she found the babe had been removed while she slept. But the unsatisfied heart of the mother longed to look again on the form of the child; and again, though with remonstrance from the nurse, it was laid beside her. All day and all night long, it remained by her side, like a little frozen thing that had wandered from its home, and now lay dead by the door.

"Next morning the nurse protested that she must part with it, for it made her fret; but she knew it quieted her, and she would rather keep her little lifeless babe. At length the nurse appealed to the father; and the mother feared he would think it necessary to remove it; but to her joy and gratitude he said, 'No, no; let her keep it as long as she likes.' And she loved her husband the more for that; for he understood her.

"Then she had the cradle brought near the bed, all ready as it was for a live child that had open eyes, and therefore needed sleep — needed the lids of the brain to close, when it was filled full of the strange colours and forms of the new world. But this one needed no cradle, for it slept on. It needed, instead of the little curtains to darken it to sleep, a great sunlight to wake it up from the darkness, and the ever-satisfied rest. Yet she laid it in the cradle, which she had set near her, where she could see it, with the little hand and arm laid out on the white coverlet. If she could only keep it so! Could not something be done, if not to awake it, yet to turn it to stone, and let it remain so for ever? No; the body must go back to its mother, the earth, and the *form*, which is immortal, being the thought of God, must go back to its Father — the Maker. And as it lay in the white cradle, a white coffin was being made for it. And the mother thought: 'I wonder which trees are growing coffins for my husband and me.'

"But ere the child, that had the prayer of Job in his grief, and had died from its mother's womb, was carried away to be buried, the mother prayed over it this prayer: — 'O God, if thou wilt not let me be a mother, I have one refuge: I will go back and be a child: I will be thy child more than ever. My mother-heart will find relief in childhood towards its Father. For is it not the same nature that makes the true mother and the true child? Is it not the same thought blossoming upward and blossoming downward? So there is God the Father and God the Son. Thou wilt keep my little son for me. He has gone home to be nursed for me. And when I grow well, I will be more simple, and truthful, and joyful in thy sight. And now thou art taking away my child, my plaything, from me. But I think how pleased I should be, if I had a daughter, and she loved me so well that she only smiled when I took her plaything from her. Oh! I will not disappoint thee — thou shalt have thy joy. Here I am, do with me what thou wilt; I will only smile.'

"And how fared the heart of the father? At first, in the bitterness of his grief, he called the loss of his child a punishment for his doubt and unbelief; and the feeling of punishment made the stroke more keen, and the heart less willing to endure it. But better thoughts woke within him ere long.

"The old woman who swept out his schoolroom, came in the evening to inquire after the mistress, and to offer her condolences on the loss of the baby. She came likewise to tell the news, that a certain old man of little respectability had departed at last, unregretted by a single soul in the village but herself, who had been his nurse through the last tedious illness.

"The schoolmaster thought with himself:

"'Can that soiled and withered leaf of a man, and my little snow-flake of a baby, have gone the same road? Will they meet by the way? Can they talk about the same thing — anything? They must part on the borders of the shining land, and they could hardly speak by the way.'

"'He will live four-and-twenty hours, nurse,' the doctor had said.

"'No, doctor; he will die to-night,' the nurse had replied; during which whispered dialogue, the patient had lain breathing quietly, for the last of suffering was nearly over.

"He was at the close of an ill-spent life, not so much selfishly towards others as indulgently towards himself. He had failed of true joy by trying often and perseveringly to create a false one; and now, about to knock at the gate of the other world, he bore with him no burden of the good things of this; and one might be tempted to say of him, that it were better he had not been born. The great majestic mystery lay before him — but when would he see its majesty?

"He was dying thus, because he had tried to live as Nature said he should not live; and he had taken his own wages — for the law of the Maker is the necessity of his creature. His own children had forsaken him, for they were not perfect as their Father in heaven, who maketh his sun to shine on the evil and on the good. Instead of doubling their care as his need doubled, they had thought of the disgrace he brought on them, and not of the duty they owed him; and now, left to die alone for them, he was waited on by this hired nurse, who, familiar with death-beds, knew better than the doctor, knew that he could live only a few hours.

"Stooping to his ear, she had told him, as gently as she could, — for she thought she ought not to conceal it — that he must die that night. He had lain silent for a few moments; then had called her, and, with broken and failing voice, had said, 'Nurse, you are the only friend I have;

give me one kiss before I die.' And the woman-heart had answered the prayer.

"'And,' said the old woman, 'he put his arms round my neck, and gave me a long kiss, such a long kiss! and then he turned his face away, and never spoke again.'

"So, with the last unction of a woman's kiss, with this baptism for the dead, he had departed.

"'Poor old man! he had not quite destroyed his heart yet,' thought the schoolmaster. 'Surely it was the child-nature that woke in him at the last, when the only thing left for his soul to desire, the only thing he could think of as a preparation for the dread something, was a kiss. Strange conjunction, yet simple and natural! Eternity — a kiss. Kiss me; for I am going to the Unknown! — Poor old man!' the schoolmaster went on in his thoughts, 'I hope my baby has met him, and put his tiny hand in the poor old shaking hand, and so led him across the borders into the shining land, and up to where Jesus sits, and said to the Lord: "Lord, forgive this old man, for he knew not what he did." And I trust the Lord has forgiven him.'

"And then the bereaved father fell on his knees, and cried out:

"'Lord, thou hast not punished me. Thou wouldst not punish for a passing thought of troubled unbelief, with which I strove. Lord, take my child and his mother and me, and do what thou wilt with us. I know thou givest not, to take again.'

"And ere the schoolmaster could call his protestantism to his aid, he had ended his prayer with the cry:

"'And O God! have mercy upon the poor old man, and lay not his sins to his charge.'

"For, though a woman's kiss may comfort a man to eternity, it is not all he needs. And the thought of his lost child had made the soul of the father compassionate."

He ceased, and we sat silent.

Sources

"The Fantastic Imagination" was originally printed as the Preface to the 1893 American edition of *The Light Princess and Other Fairy Tales,* and was reprinted in *A Dish of Orts* (1893).

"The Gifts of the Child Christ" and "The Butcher's Bills" were first published in *The Gifts of the Child Christ, and Other Tales* (1882).

"Stephen Archer" was first published in *Stephen Archer and Other Tales* (1908).

"The Broken Swords" was first published in *Monthly Christian Spectator* (1854).

"The Wow O' Rivven" ("The Bell") first appeared as "The Bell" in *Good Works* (1864) and was reprinted in *Adela Cathcart* (1864).

"The Light Princess," "The Shadows," "The Castle: A Parable," "The Cruel Painter," and "Birth, Dreaming, Death" ("The Schoolmaster's Story") were first published in *Adela Cathcart* (1864).

"The Carasoyn" ("The Fairy Fleet") appeared in two forms: the first part appeared as "The Fairy Fleet" in *Argosy* (1866); the expanded form appeared as "The Carasoyn" in *Works* (1871).

"Cross Purposes" and "The Golden Key" were first published in *Dealings with Fairies* (1867).

"The Wise Woman, or the Lost Princess: A Double Story" was serialized under the title "A Double Story" in *Good Things* (1874); it was also published as "Princess Rosamond" and "The Lost Princess" (1895).

"Little Daylight," "The Gray Wolf," and "Uncle Cornelius, His Story" were first published in *Works of Fancy and Imagination* (1871).

"The History of Photogen and Nycteris" ("The Day Boy and the Night Girl") was first published in *Graphic,* Christmas number (1879).

"The Giant's Heart" was first published in *Illustrated London News,* Christmas number (1863) entitled "Tell Us a Story."

"Papa's Story" ("A Scot's Christmas Story") was first published in *Illustrated London News* (1865).

"Port in a Storm" was first published in *Argosy* (1866).

Sources of Illustrations

"The Fantastic Imagination":
> *Undine* by De La Motte Fouqué, adapted from the German by W. L. Courtney, illustrated by Arthur Rackham (London: William Heinemann; New York: Doubleday, Page & Co., 1909).

"Stephen Archer" and "The Butcher's Bills":
> *Stephen Archer and Other Tales* by George MacDonald, illustrated by Cyrus Cuneo and G. H. Evison (London: Edwin Dalton, 1908).

"The Wow O' Rivven":
> *Good Words for 1864,* edited by Norman Macleod, D.D. (London: Publishing Office, n.d. [1865?]).

"The Light Princess," "The Shadows," and "Cross Purposes":
> *Dealings with the Fairies* by George MacDonald, illustrated by Arthur Hughes (London: Alexander Strahan, Publisher, 1867).

"The Golden Key":
> *Dealings with the Fairies* by George MacDonald, illustrated by Arthur Hughes (London: Alexander Strahan, Publisher, 1867).
> *The Light Princess and Other Fairy Stories* by George MacDonald (London: Blackie & Son, Ltd, n.d.).

"The Wise Woman, or the Lost Princess":
> *The Lost Princess or the Wise Woman* by George MacDonald, illustrated by A. G. Walker (London: Wells Gardner, Darton, & Co., 1895).

"Little Daylight":
> *Works of Fancy and Imagination* by George MacDonald (London: Alexander Strahan, Publisher, 1871).

"The Giant's Heart":
> *Dealings with the Fairies* by George MacDonald, illustrated by Arthur Hughes (London: Alexander Strahan, Publisher, 1867).
> *The Illustrated London News* (1863).

"Papa's Story":
> *The Illustrated London News* (1865).